A Reed in the Wind

Joanna Plantagenet, Queen of Sicily

BY

RACHEL BARD

Literary Network Press

Literary Network Press
23817 97th Avenue Southwest
Vashon, Washington 98070
USA

ALSO BY RACHEL BARD

Queen Without a Country, a historical novel

Isabella: Queen Without a Conscience, a historical novel

Navarra: the Durble Kingdom, a history

Newswriting Guide: A Handbook for Student Reporters

Editing Guide: A Handbook for Writers and Editors

Best Places of the Olympic Peninsula

Country Inns of the Pacific Northwest

Zucchini and All That Squash

CONTENTS

HISTORICAL PROLOGUE

In her own day, Joanna would not have been known as Joanna Plantagenet.

The term Plantagenet had originated as the nickname of Geoffrey of Anjou (1113-1151), Joanna's grandfather. The story goes that he often wore a sprig of broom (*genet*) in his hat when he went into battle, so his troops could keep him in sight. Not until the Wars of the Roses did English monarchs begin to use Plantagenet as a surname. In the 1460s, it was adopted by Richard, Duke of York and father of King Edward IV, to substantiate the Yorkist line's claim to the throne as superior to that of the Lancastrians.

In the next century Shakespeare popularized the term. Since then it has been widely recognized by historians, writers and readers and has become the accepted appellation for royal descendants of Geoffrey of Anjou.

Joanna was born into a world where England and France were enmeshed in a struggle to conquer or reconquer French territories claimed by both. The struggle had its roots in William of Normandy's conquest of England in 1066. By 1165 when Joanna was born, the adversaries—King Henry II of England and King Philip II of France— were still at it. Joanna, third daughter of Henry and his queen, Eleanor of Aquitaine, was, as customary with princesses, destined to further England's cause through a politically advantageous marriage. Henry and Eleanor recognized that an alliance with Sicily would be highly desirable, for in the twelfth century Sicily was a major power in Europe, controlling much of Italy as well as the home island.

This explains why, when we first meet Joanna at age eleven, the Sicilian ambassadors are hiding behind the screen in Winchester Palace.

1

The two Sicilians had been concealed by a screen in the great hall of King Henry's palace at Winchester for a quarter of an hour and nothing had happened.

"This is getting ridiculous, Florian," sniffed the younger ambassador, fidgeting. He yanked down the cuffs of his velvet tunic and wrapped his woolen scarf more snugly about his neck. "I do not care for this waiting about in the cold at the pleasure of an eleven-year-old girl. Even if she is the daughter of Henry the Second of England. And what a poor excuse for a king's great hall this is. It's more like a great barn. Bare floors, bare walls with the damp running down them. And cold as a witch's tit. Why couldn't they have laid a fire?"

"I don't care for it either, Arnolfo," said Count Florian of Camerota. As the seasoned justiciar of King William of Sicily, he'd served as his master's chief minister almost as long as Arnolfo had been alive. He considered his junior colleague to be still a neophyte when it came to diplomacy, in spite of the fact that he was soon to become a bishop. "But King William has sent us to represent him in his marriage negotiations, and what we observe will be useful when we meet with King Henry later in London. If Joanna is as well-favored as we have been told, well and good. But if she seems lacking in any respect, we can strike a harder bargain."

Arnolfo sniggered. "Rather like buying a horse, eh? First you watch him run and look at his teeth, then you make your offer, then you haggle."

Count Florian pursed his lips and frowned. But before he could say anything, they heard voices and quickly applied their eyes to the cracks in the screen.

Three women entered, followed by a girl who stopped at the doorway. Queen Eleanor, leader of the little procession, walked purposefully to the center of the hall and looked around, frowning.

"Why is there no fire here, Lady Elspeth? It is only Pentecost, it is not midsummer. More of Henry's niggardliness, I suppose. Please see to it."

The lady-in-waiting scurried out to summon a servant.

Eleanor, queen of England and duchess of Aquitaine, looked most striking when annoyed. She stood straight as a statue, hands clasped at her waist, glaring about the room. Her sapphire-blue gown was the color of her eyes. A jeweled circlet held the flowing white wimple that did not quite hide her brown-gold hair. If there were any tinges of gray they didn't show. If any wrinkles had tried to mar cheek or brow, they had been bidden to disappear. At fifty-four Eleanor still presented to the world an imperious and beautiful face.

She knew the Sicilians were there; it had all been planned. They had explained to her that their master had ordered them to observe the princess when she didn't know she was being observed so they could give him a candid, objective report. But not by the slightest glance or turn of the head did Eleanor betray the knowledge.

The women paced down the room to stand where a streamer of sun poured in through a window that pierced the thick stone wall. Motes of dust danced in the golden shaft. A servant scuttled in and hastily laid a fire in the enormous hearth. Another stood by, straining under the weight of a huge log, ready to throw it on.

Joanna still stood in the shadows at the doorway. But the ambassadors were dazzled by Eleanor.

"Amazing," whispered Florian. "After two husbands and how many children—eight?—how can this woman show so few signs of aging?"

"Perhaps she has been preserved by freezing in this horrid English climate."

For a time no one moved. A faint heat was beginning to be felt from the hearth.

"But I'll wager there's fire under that ice," murmured Arnolfo, still watching Eleanor. "As King Henry must know all too well or he wouldn't have shut her up here at Winchester. Poor lady, practically a prisoner in her own palace."

"That's not our business, Arnolfo. From what I hear he had good reasons. They say she's been encouraging her sons to take arms against their own father."

They cut short their gossip as Joanna moved to stand before the fire. Her back was to the men in the corner. She dangled a wooden doll by one leg. Her slight body seemed lost in a full-skirted gray gown. Two neatly shod feet peeped out below the hem. She wore no cap or headdress, and a tangle of long, curling brown locks fell to her thin shoulders.

"A scrawny little pullet," whispered Arnolfo.

One of the ladies came to stand beside her and held out her hands to warm them.

"Why Princess Joanna," she teased, "why ever are you carrying that sorry-looking doll? Surely you're too old to play with dolls."

The girl turned and looked up. Her narrow, sober face brightened when she smiled—a smile so disarming that the hardened ambassadors peering through their peepholes couldn't keep the corners of their lips from turning up in empathy. Suddenly she was enchanting. Her voice was high and childish but her diction was precise.

"Of course I'm not *playing* with it, Lady Marian. I'm *rescuing* it. My brother John found it in a chest and was going to give it to his hound as a toy. I told him it was my doll once and still is and he couldn't do such a cruel thing. So he threw it at me. I'm carrying it about so he won't take it back."

Lady Marian bent and hugged her. "Quite right, too. We mustn't encourage bad behavior." She cast a sidelong glance at Lady Elspeth that said, as plainly as words, "That John!"

If Queen Eleanor heard any of this she gave no sign. Just when the fire was burning briskly and making some headway against the cold and damp, she decided to leave.

She took Joanna's hand. "Come, daughter. It's time to find John so Brother William can hear the two of you say your lessons before supper. And who knows where the boy has got to."

Joanna looked up at her mother. Again that smile, but now with a touch of mischief.

"I know where, mother. He went to the kitchen. He always wants to see what's for supper."

Eleanor said only "Humph!" and led the girl out, walking slowly past the corner where the screen stood. Her ladies followed, casting wistful glances at the hearth.

As soon as the hall was empty the two Sicilians emerged to stand by the fire, stamping their feet and rubbing their hands to restore circulation.

"She seems sufficiently attractive," said Florian.

"She does," agreed Arnolfo. "One might even say beautiful."

"In fact, one *will* say beautiful." The justiciar slapped his companion on the back and grinned.

"And when we report to our king we mustn't fail to remark on her breeding, her tender heart, her lively spirit and her respect for her elders."

"Indeed, Arnolfo. But be careful—we mustn't say any of that when we meet King Henry. We'll tell him we judge the girl to be very young, not too well-formed, and sullen. But we'll say that with a suitably large dowry from Henry, King William of Sicily may be persuaded to accept her as his queen."

2

It was suppertime in Queen Eleanor's private dining hall at Winchester Palace. The candles were lit and the fire on the hearth was burning merrily. Eleanor looked at it with approval and loosened her shawl. Servants had just ladled steaming servings of beef and barley soup into the silver bowls of the six people gathered at the table. These were, besides the queen and her children Joanna and John, two of her ladies-in-waiting and Brother Jean-Pierre, the monk who tutored the royal offspring.

"Who were those two strange men behind the screen in the great hall today, mother?" Joanna asked.

Eleanor's spoon halted in midair between broth and mouth. She replaced the spoon in her bowl. Once she was satisfied that not a drop had fallen on the linen tablecloth, she gave her full attention to her daughter.

"I might have guessed you wouldn't be taken in. How did you know they were there? And why do you say they were strange?"

"For one thing, mother, that screen is usually up at the other end of the hall, near the door to the kitchen. So of course I wondered why it had been moved. Then I saw four feet below the screen. And they were wearing such funny shoes, nothing like what we see in England. They were gold and red with pointed toes and tassels. And they kept lifting them up and putting them down. I suppose they were getting numb with the cold."

Eleanor laughed, but before she could answer, John broke in. He'd been diligently dipping chunks of bread in his soup and stuffing them into his mouth. Still chewing, he blurted, "If I'd been there I would have gone over and stamped on their fancy shoes. That would have made them really dance!" Youngest of Eleanor and Henry's children, nine-year-old John had to get attention any way he could.

Eleanor frowned. "I hope you would not have done any such thing, John. Those men were the ambassadors of King William of Sicily. They are our guests and deserve our courtesy."

Lady Marian nodded approvingly. Lady Elspeth glared at the offending child. Brother Jean-Pierre cleared his throat as though he were about to make a major pronouncement, but said only, "Indeed." He was eager to finish his soup before the bowl was taken away.

Joanna persevered. "But why were they hiding behind the screen, mother?"

Eleanor took a few more sips of soup, then signaled the servant to remove the bowls.

"It will soon be no secret so I might as well tell all of you all now. King William has asked for Joanna's hand in marriage. He sent Count Florian and Count Arnolfo to begin the negotiations. But first, they were to observe Joanna when she was unaware of their presence, so they could judge her natural appearance and deportment."

The two ladies-in-waiting began whispering excitedly to each other. Brother Jean-Pierre beamed, proud that one of his pupils had such illustrious prospects. John glowered. What chance did he, as youngest son, have of making such a brilliant marriage?

Only Joanna appeared unmoved. But Eleanor, studying her serious face, knew that she was absorbing the news, taking her time to decide what she thought. That was her way: slow to arrive at a conviction, then steadfast, stubborn even, in adhering to it. Eleanor, with domineering King Henry for a husband and four headstrong sons, often wondered at this withdrawn child, so unlike the rest of the family. But there was a strong bond between mother and daughter. Eleanor found Joanna's undemanding presence a rest after contentious encounters with Henry.

To Joanna, who had spent all her eleven years with Eleanor either in England or in Eleanor's ancestral lands in France, her mother was the most beautiful, interesting person in the world and the one she most wanted to please.

Though Joanna's face was unreadable, there was a trace of anxiety in her voice when she asked, "Do you know what they thought of me, mother?"

"No, I haven't spoken to them since. But tomorrow at the state dinner they'll be able to judge you in quite a different setting. And to be sure"—she paused and looked at John—"to judge the rest of the family as well. Marriages like this are as much between families and kingdoms as between two individuals. That's the whole point."

"Does King William have a family?" Joanna asked.

"His mother, Queen Margaret, is still very much alive, I hear. She was regent until William came of age. And there's a younger brother, but I don't know anything about him. You may ask the ambassadors tomorrow. Very likely they'd consider your curiosity an encouraging sign of interest in your new role."

While the diners began attacking the platters of pickled fish that had been brought in, Joanna began making mental lists of what she'd ask the Sicilians.

She hadn't been greatly surprised at the news of her forthcoming betrothal. She'd been told all her life that in due course her parents would arrange an advantageous marriage for her. She was aware that they'd managed very well for her sisters. Matilda had gone off to marry Henry the Lion, nephew of the German emperor, before Joanna was born. And her sister Eleanor, at nine, had been sent to marry the king of Castile. Joanna had been only five at the time but she remembered her sister's unhappiness at being exiled to a strange stern land where she knew no one, much less her future husband.

I'm luckier, thought Joanna. I'm going to Sicily—that sunny, golden kingdom in the sea, far to the south of damp, chilly England. But what will King William be like? Old and ugly? What if he resembles mean-spirited John, rather than Richard, Joanna's beloved older brother? And would her mother be allowed to go with her? Joanna knew all about her father's decree that Eleanor must not leave Winchester without his permission. Surely he'd make an exception in this case.

Mulling over these matters, she methodically made her way through the slices of fish on her plate. They were swimming in a vinegary, spicy sauce, and she was rather glad of that. She suspected the fish had gone off a bit. She wondered if the fish would be fresher in Sicily. Probably; it was an island, after all.

Ladies Elspeth and Marian had hoped for a more enthusiastic reaction.

"Isn't this exciting, Princess Joanna? Just think, you'll be Queen of Sicily!" said Lady Marian. As the one most responsible for Joanna's daily upbringing, she was already hoping that she'd be delegated to go with the princess to her new home.

"Now, let's not get ahead of ourselves," Eleanor said. "I must remind you that the ambassadors have yet to discuss this with King Henry. A great deal will depend on the impression Joanna makes on them tomorrow. If it isn't favorable, King Henry may not be able to get their agreement to the amount of money and treasure that will change hands. Or indeed, the whole proposal may collapse. I suggest that we all leave the subject for now."

Silence ensued, broken only by the snaps and crackles from the fireplace and by John's muted invitations to his hound, waiting in the corner, to come lick the plate John had placed on the floor. Eleanor pretended not to notice.

The next morning Joanna accompanied her mother to the castle kitchens.

"If you become mistress of your own castle, or castello, or whatever they call it in Sicily, you must always watch over the cooks. Otherwise they may get careless and serve any old thing. And you can't always leave it to others to do the supervising. There's nothing like having the queen drop into the kitchen unannounced to keep them on their toes. Today, it's particularly important that we offer a suitable repast to the ambassadors. I'm sure their palates are much more refined than those of our usual guests."

Joanna nodded and filed the advice away. It was flattering to be addressed almost as an equal by her mother.

She regarded the large dark lump that was just going into the oven. "Do you think they will like suet pudding?" she asked doubtfully.

"Probably not, if they have any taste at all. But it will fill the bellies of our own people, while we ply the Sicilians with larks and figs and honey." She looked around. "All seems to be going as well as can be expected." She turned to leave.

Joanna wasn't so sure. The steamy, noisy kitchen seemed like pandemonium to her. The chief cook was shouting to the boy who was supposed to bring the geese. But the lad was dawdling and gossiping in a corner and couldn't hear because the scullery girl was making such a racket as she banged the pots and pans about.

"Gooseboy! Where are my geese?" bellowed the cook. "The stuffing's all ready, and if we don't get them in the oven this minute we'll be serving raw bloody fowl today." The startled boy ran across the room, dragging two large plucked geese behind him. He got a cuff on the ear for his trouble.

Taking her daughter's hand, Eleanor walked out and across the gardens to her private apartments. "We must begin preparing you for the banquet. And here come Lady Elspeth and Lady Marian. They'll help dress you." She plucked a sprig of lavender from a bush by the path. "Tuck this in your bodice when you go into the great hall this afternoon. I've always found a whiff of lavender very soothing to the nerves."

In the queen's bedroom, the high canopied bed, the chairs and chests were draped with garments. The two ladies fussed and discussed, while Joanna stood patiently. Lady Elspeth combed out her tangled hair so it fell in well-disciplined ringlets, a process which was interrupted by the occasional squeak of protest from the girl. Eleanor supervised while Lady Marian arrayed her in petticoats and underskirts. "I will look fat!" wailed Joanna as layer after layer was added.

"Well, we can't make you taller, so we will just have to add substance to your figure wherever we can," said Lady Marian.

They finished with a green silk gown, over which they added a sleeveless robe of the same silk. As final touch the queen placed a delicate diadem, set with diamonds, on her daughter's head.

She stood back to admire the result. "Yes, just as I intended. The color is exactly right to set off your brown hair." She brought her precious mirror that nobody else was allowed to touch. "Now see what you think of yourself, pretty Princess Joanna."

"Yes, I do look like a princess, don't I? At least from the neck up. Thank you, mother! Though the rest of me feels like a stuffed tub. I hope I don't waddle into the hall and tip over."

"I'm sure you won't. And most of the time you'll be sitting down and the ambassadors will be concentrating on your face. Now don't forget to smile as much as you can."

"I'll try." Basking in Eleanor's approval, she forgot all her misgivings, glad only to have pleased her mother. If she pleased the Sicilians as well, that would be all right too.

As for Eleanor, she thanked the Lord God of Hosts, the Virgin Mary and all the saints in heaven for this dutiful, calm and collected daughter.

3

King Henry arrived from London the morning after the state dinner and went at once to his audience chamber. Three courtiers and an armed knight took their places behind him, but took no part in the proceedings. Their purpose was to keep the king of England from appearing outnumbered by the emissaries from King William.

Henry surveyed his visitors, seated in a semicircle before him. Count Florian and Bishop-elect Arnulfo had been joined by Archbishop Rothrud of Rouen and a newly anointed bishop from Sicily. The churchmen were dazzling in their white satin cassocks, ermine-trimmed copes and massive gold or silver crosses and chains. The two ambassadors were almost as resplendent: their capes furred, their purple tunics cinched with jeweled belts, and Arnulfo with peacock feathers springing jauntily from his velvet cap.

They all far outshone Henry, who was still wearing his traveling garb—a short foxfur cape over a leather tunic, brown woolen hose and riding boots. The only sign of royalty was the golden crown on his close-cropped brown hair. And, perhaps, the outthrust jutting chin and the piercing eyes that missed nothing.

The king's secretary, seated at Henry's left, tidied the parchments on the table and handed Henry two sheets of vellum, covered with neat, sharply etched rows of writing, every paragraph beginning with a flowing capital letter.

Henry glanced at it, and spoke for the first time.

"I greet you, my lord Archbishop and gentlemen, and apologize for not being here to welcome you to Winchester. The pressure of affairs kept me in London. I thank you, as well, for bringing this marriage agreement. If it accords with my previous discussions with King William I see no reason why we cannot agree on the terms and sign it today." He began studying the pages.

After a few minutes of silence, when King Henry appeared to be reaching the end, the archbishop spoke. As cousin of King William of Sicily, he took precedence over the others. In an unhurried, mellifluous tone he doled out well-turned phrases like sugarplums.

"I hope and trust we may agree, your majesty. When King William adds his signature to yours and ours, the marriage settlement will be official, to the mutual benefit of both our great countries.
I see this as the beginning of a long, fruitful and harmonious friendship between the king of Sicily and your august majesty. I am confident that King William will

be giving thanks to God that, after so many delays and setbacks, this matter has reached such a happy conclusion."

Henry had been leaning back and listening, his square-jawed, broad-browed face implacable. At the reference to delays and setbacks he sat up and glared. The Plantagenet temper almost took over, but he managed to reply without shouting.

"May I remind you, Archbishop, that there would not have been so many delays and setbacks if King William had not broken off our negotiations six years ago when this engagement was first discussed."

"True, your majesty. But he had good reason, as I am sure you recall." The sugarplums were taking on some acidity.

Henry clenched his teeth and stared at the archbishop with contempt. His mind lurched back to 1170 and that wretched Becket affair. Some of his hotheaded nobles, thinking mistakenly they were acting in accord with their king's wishes, had murdered the archbishop of Canterbury in his own cathedral. Henry had become the pariah of Europe, scorned and avoided by all his fellow monarchs, including William of Sicily. The monstrous unfairness of that disgrace still rankled.

"I do recall. How could I forget?" His voice rose in his agitation. "But blameless as I was, didn't I nevertheless do public penance in Avranches? Didn't I permit the monks to flog me at Canterbury? Yet your king, or more likely his mother the regent, all at once decided we English were an unsuitable family to marry into." He finished in a roar and banged his fist on the table. The inkwell bounced, spilling a few black drops on the papers. The alarmed secretary jumped up and blotted them with the hem of his tunic.

Silence from the Sicilians. The archbishop pursed his lips in disapproval, the others looked worried. This was supposed to be a formality, a chance for both parties to congratulate each other on their wisdom and to vow eternal friendship.

Count Florian broke the silence. "Your majesty, we understand and sympathize with your unhappy memories. But is this not the time to let bygones be bygones? Whatever differences existed between our two kingdoms in the past will be totally obliterated when King William and Princess Joanna are married."

"*If* they are married." Henry was struggling to control himself. He took a gulp from his wine goblet and sat for a minute, tightlipped, holding in the angry words. "Even if I agree to 'let bygones be bygones,' there is another even more disturbing matter. I see nothing in this agreement," he held up the pages, "about King William's recognition of Queen Eleanor and myself. In addition to the dowry for the princess, it is customary to make significant gifts to the bride's parents. I believe in your country you refer to this as the Golden Treasury. Though King William and I have not discussed this, I have assumed that he intended to honor this obligation. But apparently not." He watched them, waiting for an answer.

None came. They looked at each other in dismay. Nobody had been told that this matter might come up, or instructed what to say if it did.

Henry rose, and the others hastily followed suit.

"My lord Archbishop and gentlemen," said the king, "either none of you is

aware of this custom, or you have chosen to ignore it. Or perhaps it is your king
who ignores it. In any case, it shows a serious lack of respect on the part of Sicily
for its ally, England. First you accuse me of murder, then you withhold the customary gifts to Joanna's parents."

His choler had returned. His face turned fiery red. "I will not suffer this insult
to England. I've had enough of these discussions. I consider them closed."

He stamped out of the hall. His two courtiers and the knight followed as
unobtrusively as they could. The secretary gathered his papers, looking pale and
shaken. The Sicilians straggled out, exchanging recriminations, their resplendent
robes swishing, their jeweled rings glittering.

None of them noticed Joanna, standing in a shadowy niche in the corridor.

She hadn't meant to eavesdrop. But as she walked along the corridor on the
way to her Latin lesson, she heard Henry's raised voice and his words, "*If* they are
married." Curiosity and alarm took over and she slipped into the niche, where she
listened to the stormy conclusion of the conference.

She was stunned. Her father had cancelled the marriage negotiations. Only
now did she realize how much she'd been anticipating the whole adventure—the
sea voyage, the arrival in an exotic country and the marriage to a handsome king.
(He was sure to be handsome!)

Utterly dejected, she went on to her lesson, where Brother Jean-Pierre wondered why his best pupil, normally so bright and responsive, looked at him blankly
and couldn't answer the simplest question.

"Well, my lord," said Eleanor, "now can you tell us about the marriage agreement? We have offered King William a generous dowry. What will he settle upon
our daughter in return?"

They were just finishing dinner that evening in the great hall at Winchester.
The dim, unembellished, drafty chamber where the Sicilians had spied on Joanna was transformed. It was now warmed by two well-established fires. Flaming
torches and candelabra cast a bright light over the twenty or so diners gathered in
the hall. The Sicilians were not among them; they had sent their regrets. One of
Eleanor's precious Persian carpets had been laid on the dais where the royal family
dined. Servers bustled about, bearing platters and replenishing wine goblets. The
lords and ladies of the court, seated at long tables below, chattered and laughed.
But at the head table where Eleanor, Henry, Archbishop Richard of Winchester,
Joanna and John were seated, there was little levity.

Joanna had been hoping desperately that she'd misheard Henry's outburst. His
answer to Eleanor's question didn't completely quash that possibility. He was looking at his wife attentively as though she were one of his clerks who had brought up
a debatable point.

"What will William settle on our daughter? Yes. I knew that the financial
matters would be topmost in your mind. In brief, my lady, King William offered all
the revenues of the County of San Angelo. I understand this is one of Sicily's most
prosperous regions, with vineyards and olive groves yielding dependable amounts.

She would also receive revenues from the cities of Liponti and Vestia, as well as several lesser towns and castles. Does that answer your question? I considered it a satisfactory settlement."

"So it would seem," agreed Eleanor. "Our daughter is well provided for. What about the bride's parents? Usually in these arrangements they are not forgotten."

Henry deliberately dipped a chunk of bread in the gravy on his plate, chewed it and swallowed it, washed it down with wine, and wiped his mouth on his sleeve. Eleanor shuddered and looked pointedly at the linen cloth beside his plate. Napkins were an innovation she had brought from France but they had not been universally or gratefully received.

Archbishop Richard intervened.

"I have been wondering the same thing. When I read the Sicilian proposal for the marriage agreement, I saw nothing about additional gifts for the king and queen. I hope they have not been overlooked, because" (bowing slightly to each of them in turn) "you have always been so generous in sharing your worldly goods with the church."

"I'm sorry to tell you they have been overlooked." Henry's voice was deceptively calm. "And as a result of this and other signs of disrespect, I broke off the negotiations."

The shocked silence was broken by yelps from John's vicinity. A hound was crouched at his feet and he had been offering it bones, then snatching them away.

"John!" his mother said. "If you are quite finished, will you be so good as to take your leave, and take your noisy dog with you?" The boy rose, tossed his shock of black hair out of his eyes and slouched out. The melancholy hound, used to being deceived but ever hopeful, padded after him.

Eleanor beckoned to Joanna, who jumped up and went to stand beside her mother. Things were moving too fast for her to comprehend.

Eleanor, icily polite, put an arm around Joanna and addressed her husband.

"Couldn't you have been less precipitate and left yourself open to more negotiations? After our daughter made such a good impression on the ambassadors, and just when things were going so well, why throw away this alliance that would mean so much to England? What can be gained by this rash action?"

Henry had been listening, not grim-faced but calmly, indulgently. At her last words he smiled—a wicked, self-congratulatory smile.

"I could not agree more. It would be a pity to break things off now. So after I gave the Sicilians time to worry about my rejection, but not enough time to send a messenger to King William, I sent word to them that I'd been reconsidering the matter and invited them to meet again tomorrow morning."

"At which time you'll take up the matter of the gifts to the bride's parents?"

"I shall. And you asked what could be gained by what you call my rash action? I think I can assure you, my lady, that England will come out of this with much better terms than before. The Sicilians want the marriage even more than we do. William must have an heir and needs an ally. I predict that when the ambassadors return and report to him how King Henry said no but then said maybe, William will be so grateful that he'll load even more gold and jewels onto the ships heading our way."

Eleanor smiled without warmth and rose. "My lord, you have again proved yourself a master at maneuvering. Let us hope that matters turn out as you expect." She raised her gown with one hand to keep the hem off the rushstrewn floor, took Joanna's arm with the other, and took her stately way out of the room.

At this signal the other diners at the lower tables, who had been pretending not to listen to the royal confrontation, also rose and filed out.

Eleanor was silent during the short walk to her apartment. At Joanna's door, she bent and kissed her daughter.

"Don't look so woebegone. I've seen your father work his way out of worse situations than this. Let's assume he'll do it again. And meantime, we'd best start making preparations for the journey. You'll need a whole new wardrobe, for one thing. Good night, my dear."

Lady Marian was waiting to help Joanna prepare for bed. It was late and the girl was very sleepy. Standing in her white shift in front of the fire and waiting for her nightdress to be slipped over her head, she thought about all that had happened in the last few days. She had become engaged to a king. The engagement had been broken off. Now, apparently, it was on again.

Or was it? She wished she could be as optimistic as her mother. But her father's words were still echoing in her ears. "These negotiations are closed."

It was more drama than she had experienced in all her eleven, nearly twelve, years.

4

The Sicilian ambassadors, having been mollified, went home two days later, vowing to urge King William to see to the Golden Treasury for Henry and Eleanor.

Shortly thereafter, early in June 1176, two men sat side by side at a small, document-laden table in the episcopal palace in Winchester, discussing weighty matters. One was Archbishop Richard of Winchester, self-contained, dignified, his portly figure tightly and tidily encased in his scarlet cassock.

The other, Hamelin Plantagenet, earl of Surrey, was long and loosejointed, with scarves and sleeves flying, as though he had put himself together in a great hurry with very little help from his creator or his valet. Earl Hamelin was the bastard son of King Henry's father and, as a quasi-royal, had always lurked on the outskirts of power. Now he was to be Joanna's official escort to Sicily, and he was enjoying his new importance.

"The eyes of Europe will be upon us," he said.

"Indeed. This is a momentous event. It is not every day that a daughter of the king of England marries the king of Sicily. We must spare no expense."

This was so indisputable that the earl did not reply.

"And since the princess is so very young, you will need to prepare her for her new role. What do you know of Sicily and its king?"

Hamelin beamed, glad to be asked. He had been making discreet inquiries of anyone who had been to Sicily or knew someone who had been there and had laid up what he considered quite a store of useful information.

"First of all, it is an island. That makes getting there difficult, but on the other hand makes it hard to invade. Nevertheless, our Norman ancestors managed it some time ago and have been running things ever since. I believe there is a volcano on the eastern coast that tends to erupt every once in a while. I suppose that's why the kings have always built their palaces in the west. Sicily receives a great deal more sunshine than we do and produces some very decent wines, though not as good as the French of course."

The archbishop stopped drumming his fingers on the table and interrupted. "So much for Sicily. What do you know of King William?"

"Oh, I know he's called William the Good, but I expect that may be simply because he doesn't raise as many hackles as his mother did when she was regent or his father did when he was king. And he's quite a pious person, they say, because he's building a very expensive cathedral at Monreale, somewhere over there near Palermo." As he spoke he flung an arm in the general direction of western Sicily and his cuff swept a pile of papers off the table. Unabashed—such contretemps were a commonplace in his feckless life—he bent to pick them up.

Perpendicular again, he said, "I only wish that you could accompany us, Archbishop, on this historic journey."

Archbishop Richard placed the fingertips of his plump hands together, looked toward the ceiling and said with a sigh, "That would be my wish too, Hamelin. But the king has most particularly told me my presence is essential in Winchester during the next few months. I am overseeing his new chapel dedicated to the late Archbishop Thomas à Becket. He has vowed to complete it by the end of this year, as the final act of his penance. Naturally I am glad to be of whatever service I can in this godly endeavor."

"Naturally. Just as I am glad to lend my assistance to the safe transport of his daughter to her new home."

These civilities out of the way, they attacked their lists and schedules. Presently, the archbishop leaned back and rested his folded his hands on the half-dome of his stomach.

"If all goes as we see it now, Hamelin, there will be a party of sixty. The princess's household alone comes to thirty. So do you agree, we will need at least seven vessels to transport the people and baggage from Greenwich to Honfleur in Normandy?"

Hamelin had tried unsuccessfully to keep up with the higher mathematics of this discussion.

"Absolutely," he said sagely.

"And one more for the soldiers' horses? And another for the provisions? And speaking of provisions…" And so on.

Somehow by the middle of August everything was nearly in place. Joanna was glad to see the approaching end of trying on of gowns, the sewing and packing. Then there were three new ladies who would, with Lady Marian, become her personal entourage. At her mother's bidding, she did her best to get to know them.

"There is nothing like a devoted lady at your side, Joanna," said Eleanor. "If she doesn't feel you like and trust her, she can become an enemy. But if she's loyal, she can be your eyes and ears in case of palace intrigues."

Joanna didn't want to even think about palace intrigues in the fair and pleasant Sicily she was dreaming of. But she filed this advice away in her orderly brain.

And the lessons! As soon as the marriage arrangements were definite, Eleanor had asked Brother Jean-Pierre to intensify Joanna's instruction in Latin and especially Norman French, widely spoken by the Norman rulers of Sicily. Though it was Joanna's native tongue, during her time in England some Anglo-Saxon impurities had crept into her speech.

Eleanor spoke earnestly to her daughter about her education. "This is important, Joanna. You mustn't fall behind during the journey. Brother Jean-Pierre will accompany you and will continue to prepare you to make a proper impression on King William. It's said the king not only knows French and Latin, but also reads and speaks Arabic."

"Oh dear, surely I'm not going to have to learn Arabic too!"

"Actually, it wouldn't be a bad idea. There are still many Saracens in Sicily; after all, it's only forty or fifty years since the Normans conquered the island. But I doubt very much if Brother Jean-Pierre is acquainted with the language."

Joanna threw herself energetically into the daily lessons. Beyond wishing to please her mother, she had the new incentive of wishing to please her future husband. Buried deep in her sober nature was a girl who dreamed romantic dreams of the handsome, accomplished young king who was waiting for her in Sicily.

Finally the time came to depart. August 26, 1176, was a perfect summer day with puffy white clouds scudding across the blue English sky like ducks paddling across a pond. The long, colorful procession passed through the ancient stone arch of Winchester's Westgate and wound its way down the hill. First came the herald bearing the banner with the royal coat of arms—three golden lions on a field of scarlet. Next, the trumpeter, blaring his warning to any stray peasants or sheepherders to keep out of the way of the royal procession. Then came the advance guard of a dozen knights, followed by Earl Hamelin in proud isolation. He jounced around in his saddle and his purple cloak flew behind him like a luffing sail. Then the senior members of the princess's household, including Brother Jean-Pierre, the physician, and Lady Gertrude, the elderly duenna whose task was to see that Joanna's ladies were attentive to their duties and didn't enjoy themselves too much. Then six more knights and the royal personage herself with Lady Marian at her side. She was followed by her brightly clad women, chattering and wondering what Sicily would be like.

Joanna, though the smallest and youngest in the party, was unmistakably the center of it all. Her horse's mane was interwoven with tasseled golden cords. He was caparisoned in gilt-edged scarlet and trotted proudly along, as though aware of his importance. Joanna, sitting stiffly upright in her saddle, wore a sweeping flame-red cloak that fell almost to the ground. Her shoulder-length brown hair was crowned with a golden tiara. Queen Eleanor had decreed that the time had come for her to dress as befitted her station.

She turned for a last glimpse of the city walls and Westgate, where her parents had wished her Godspeed, but the long train of servants and wagons behind her hid it from view. "Will I ever see Winchester again?" she wondered. But she was almost twelve, and old enough to look forward to adventure, not backward at her known world.

She caught the eye of Lady Marian, who was frowning with worry. Did her charge need comforting? This was such a tremendous disruption for her. Furthermore, the clouds had coalesced into gray, moisture-laden banks and she was sure she'd felt a raindrop.

Joanna called out, "Lady Marian! Cheer up! Before we know it we'll be in Sicily, where the sun always shines!"

5

Well, thank goodness that's over," said Joanna. She stood on the pier, swaying a little and stamping her feet to get used to solid ground again. To everybody's relief, the party had arrived at Honfleur on the northern Norman coast at midday. Alan Broadshares, Joanna's squire, guided her tottering steps to where the horses were already saddled. As he helped her onto her horse, he grinned up at her and said, "Ay, my lady, it was rather a rough crossing, but God's truth, I've seen many worse."

Alan, a battle-scarred veteran of King Henry's wars, had been retired from active service at forty and delegated as Joanna's personal attendant. At first he'd grumbled to his mates, "What am I then, a nursery maid?" But now, ten days into the journey, he'd changed his mind. "I will say I've never seen a young lass with so much pluck and curiosity," he said to the captain during the Channel crossing. Joanna spent hours on deck, reveling in the swift passage of the galley over the waves and asking Alan, or any seaman who was near, to show her where they were on the map that Brother Jean-Pierre had drawn for her. But more than once she'd gotten so queasy that she had to go below and lie down. Only then would Lady Marian allow herself to do the same.

The three new ladies, Adelaide, Beatrice and Charmaine, had suffered much more, or claimed so. Beatrice, slender and delicate, the black-haired and blue-eyed beauty of the trio, tried once to navigate the wildly pitching deck but came below in two minutes. "I would have been blown off my feet and into the sea if the captain hadn't seen me and hurried forward to help me. It was most unnerving. I do not feel at all well." And she took to her bed, not to rise until the end of the voyage.

Charmaine lay down in their stuffy little cabin the minute she was aboard and also stayed supine for the duration.

As for Adelaide, who at twenty-four was the oldest and who capitalized on that by claiming to be the wisest and most experienced, "I've often sailed before and never, never got seasick," she'd boasted after they embarked. But she managed to stay topside for only a quarter of an hour after Beatrice gave up and went below. When Adelaide saw that despite her squeals of terror and clutching for the nearest rail the captain ignored her, she joined the others.

Safely ashore at Honfleur, Joanna rode into a grubby town, devoted largely to fishermen and their strong-smelling wares and their nets spread to dry on every available surface. The unprepossessing wooden structures that lined the street along the river seemed to be mostly taverns or disreputable lodging houses.

Earl Hamelin appeared at her side.

"Isn't this a snug little port, Princess Joanna? Honfleur has an excellent anchorage and it's protected from the ocean storms, being located as it is well up the Seine River from the sea." She'd noticed him quizzing the captain of the galley at some length, pointing toward the French shore as they approached. She was gratified that her flighty uncle was making a creditable effort to inform himself on their travels. "But we won't stop here. We'll want to push on to the abbey at Jobie. Archbishop Richard has sent word to the abbot there to expect us."

"Good," said Lady Marian, who had joined them. "Let us be on the road as soon as possible. I cannot abide this vile odor another minute."

"Perhaps we should wait until all the galleys are unloaded and everybody is ready to ride," said Joanna. "My brother Richard told me that an army commander should never let the vanguard get out of sight of the main body, and we're practically an army."

Earl Hamelin had an answer for that. "I'll just go and tell the captain of the knights where we're going, and the rest can follow us. It isn't far, I believe."

So off they rode into the sunny September afternoon, with Earl Hamelin leading the way. That gangly, long-limbed gentleman, with legs and arms bent sharply at knee and elbow, leaning forward over his horse's neck, head bobbing up and down, looked more like a cricket on horseback than the noble half-brother of the King of England. Behind him came four knights, then Joanna and her household. They rode their horses at a walk along a broad track, bordered by golden fields of wheat and hay almost ready for the scythe. These were shortly replaced by apple orchards where the rosy fruit hung heavy on the boughs. Joanna, lulled by the warmth and calm, gave her horse its head.

But when the sunlight gave way to deep shade, she looked around, dismayed. Gone were the bright fields, the purple asters nodding by the roadside. They'd entered a gloomy forest where the road was overhung and darkened by low-lying branches of oak and ash. She was alarmed when the track narrowed and they had to ride in single file. Before long they came to a tiny community of four houses and a stable. She could hear loud voices ahead. Brother Jean-Pierre trotted his horse toward the head of the column. She followed, as did Alan and Lady Marian.

Earl Hamelin was shouting at a poor-looking villager, who was staring up at him with open mouth, shaking his head.

"This dolt pretends he doesn't understand me," the earl said to Jean-Pierre, throwing up his hands in frustration. "I'm worn out with asking him how to get to Jobie. Maybe you can get some sense out of him."

Brother Jean-Pierre, who had spent many years in France dealing with the lowly as well as the highborn, dismounted so he could confront the confused man face-to-face. He spoke slowly, in a conversational tone, and before long the "dolt" had become a willing informant.

"He says we should have gone to the left, back there where the road forked."

"I thought our brave leader assured us he knew the way," Lady Marian muttered to Joanna. The girl nodded. Alan said "Humph!" and they all turned to begin the dreary retracing of their route.

Long after dark, following the flame of a torch held by one of the leading knights, they heard the drum of hoofbeats ahead, and soon came up with the main body of their party.

"They must have started at least two hours after we did," marveled Lady Charmaine. "I wish I'd waited and come with them. At least they knew where they were going. I've never been so weary. I do hope we're almost there."

"You speak for all of us," said Lady Marian. If Earl Hamelin heard, he didn't show it.

When they reached the abbey, the walls looked forbidding and ghostly in the dim light of the half-moon. But the abbey gate was opened the moment they approached. The monks must have been watching out for them. In short order Joanna and her people were shown to the refectory, while the rest of the party were disposed here and there in the houses around the large courtyard. Silent but smiling brown-clad monks led them to their tables and brought large bowls of lentil soup along with chunks of crusty bread and pitchers of good red wine. Joanna was so tired that she hardly knew what she was eating and was glad to be led to a small room that she shared with Lady Marian. The beds were hard and narrow and did little to relieve their stiffness after the long day's ride. But at least the ocean wasn't heaving them about.

The next morning, much refreshed, she and her ladies made their way to the refectory for breakfast, where they saw Earl Hamelin, Brother Jean-Pierre and the abbot conferring earnestly in a corner. They seemed to have come to an agreement, because all three were nodding their heads vigorously. The earl said, "Thank you, father. I will see that the appropriate persons are made aware of the aid you are giving us." He clapped the abbot on the back. The abbot flinched in surprise but managed a pained smile. The earl disengaged himself with some difficulty from his low bench and came over to where Joanna was savoring her bread dipped in warm milk with honey. He made a little bow and stood with arms akimbo, all confidence.

"Well, princess, good news. Father Bertrand has graciously agreed to delegate one of his monks to guide us from here to Poitiers. The man apparently was at one time an itinerant friar in these parts and knows the way well. This should help us avoid any more unfortunate occurrences like yesterday's."

It wasn't exactly an apology but Joanna recognized it as at least an acknowledgment that something had gone wrong.

"Thank you, uncle. How long do you think it will take us to reach Poitiers? We're supposed to meet my brother Richard there, you know."

The earl's lips curled downward and he threw his head back to cast his eyes skyward, as though seeking divine help to deal with this preposterous supposition.

"I'd be surprised if Richard were there. He's been very busy going after King

Henry's enemies down south, I hear. I doubt if we'll see him before we get to Saint-Gilles down on the coast."

He sincerely hoped he was right. With such a bright and blazing knight as Prince Richard in the party, who would notice a bastard uncle? He'd be totally eclipsed.

Joanna, on the other hand, could hardly contain her eagerness. As they wended their way south she prattled on about her brother until Lady Marian became weary of the subject. She had never met Richard and doubted that any man alive could be such a paragon.

"You will like Richard, I know," Joanna told her. "He is very tall and very handsome with gorgeous blond hair. I wish I had hair like that! And he's braver than any other knight anywhere."

"Well, if you are so fond of Richard, I hope he is equally fond of you?"

"Yes, he is," the girl said with a firmness that Lady Marian felt might be the self-delusion of a bedazzled younger sister. But Joanna was right. Of all Henry's and Eleanor's children, only these two had come to genuinely care for each other. They'd been thrown together while young after Eleanor, tired of Henry's overbearing ways, left England and set up her own court in Poitiers. Despite the eight years' difference in their ages the brother and sister got on remarkably well. Richard, the budding knight and horseman, soaked up admiration and Joanna's was unstinting. Then, about the time that he became more interested in tournaments and hunting than in showing off for the little sister who trotted in his wake, Eleanor and Joanna were ordered back to England. Richard stayed in France, having been deemed old enough to start fighting King Henry's continental wars.

"It's two years since I've seen him," Joanna said. "But I don't expect he'll have changed much."

After six days, they reached the last few leagues of the road that gradually climbed to the city walls of Poitiers. And there, riding down the road toward them was a tall yellow-haired man on a tall, coal-black horse, both of them decked out in red and gold. A squire followed bearing aloft the Plantagenet banner with its three fierce, rampant lions.

"Richard!" shrieked Joanna. She squirmed down out of her saddle before Alan could help her and ran toward her brother. Richard dismounted and stood with open arms. As she hurtled to him, he swept her up as though she were a doll and gave her a crushing hug. Richard was laughing and Joanna was almost crying with happiness.

"Aren't you the proper little princess!" he cried as he set her down. "Your gown is quite respectable, in fact elegant, and your hair—what have they done to your hair? Why isn't it flying about like an unruly puppy's? How can it have become so ruly?"

"Well, Richard, now that I've turned twelve and I'm about to be married, I was told I must pay more attention to my appearance. But you've changed too."

He was even handsomer than she remembered. He'd let his hair grow so that it fell to his shoulders, and he'd acquired a fine, curly red-gold beard. The rest of his face had caught up to his large nose, which used to distress the boy by its dominance. Now, the nose's noble proportions were balanced by the broad brow, the wide-set blue eyes, the generous mouth and the square Plantagenet jaw. He had the self-assurance of a man who is used to being admired.

"Now, little sister, you and your friends must all be very tired and eager to get to the palace." He looked around at the rest of the party. Indeed, the three ladies, Adelaide, Beatrice and Charmaine, were drooping in their saddles. But when they felt Richard's eyes on them, each one straightened up, let the hood of her cloak fall, smoothed her hair and tried to look less travel-weary. Even Lady Marian, though she would never permit herself to droop and was sitting quite erect, found herself assuming a more pleasant expression than usual and wished briefly that she were twenty years younger. Watching the brother and sister, she was pleased that Richard seemed to be everything Joanna had promised.

Earl Hamelin spurred his way through the group, oblivious of whose horse his steed jostled or whose ribs his elbows poked.

"Well, Sir Richard, we are honored that you are here to greet us, though I suppose you won't stay for long. I understand that the local lords around Angoulême have holed up in the city and are daring the English to try to take it. What fools!" In his scorn he tossed his head and snorted like a horse. "But you'll soon show them, eh nephew?"

"As a matter of fact I've already showed them. It took us only six days to lift the siege of Angoulême, and those foolish lords are even now on their way to Winchester to submit to my father." He looked around at the knights, the ladies, the duenna and the tutor, and embraced the whole group in his wide, sunny smile. "So, since I am now fortunate enough to have time to accompany my sister to Saint-Gilles, perhaps I should learn who my companions will be. My good uncle, would you make the introductions?"

He would indeed and got most of the names right. Richard greeted everybody with a polite little nod of the head and appropriate greeting, but his eyes lit up and lingered longest on Lady Beatrice. She blushed at his gaze and lowered her eyes. "Becoming modesty," thought Lady Marian, who had observed the exchange of glances. "But calculated, I fear." Then she glanced at Lady Gertrude. The duenna's wise old eyes moved from Beatrice's face to Lady Marian's. The two women looked at each other a moment, thinking the same thing: "We'll have to watch that one."

If Joanna had seen any of this she gave no sign. Richard helped her up onto her horse and she rode proudly by his side up the hill to the palace, as full of chatter as any little sister reunited with her favorite brother.

6

After a few days in Poitiers, pleasant as the spacious old palace was, Richard was chafing to be off.

"If we're to meet King William's people in Saint-Gilles on time," he said to Joanna, "we're going to have to break camp." The brother and sister were sitting on a bench in the palace garden.

He eyed Adelaide, Beatrice and Charmaine, who were strolling in the garden, holding dainty parasols and twittering like ecstatic sparrows when they bent to take in the sweet scent of lavender. The duenna, old Lady Gertrude, had settled on a bench to doze in the sun.

"Your frivolous ladies will have to tear themselves away. It's high time we marched on."

Joanna didn't answer at once. She was remembering playing in this garden as a very young child, when Eleanor was in residence at Poitiers. She remembered warm lazy afternoons like this one. She looked up at the high stone walls that gave welcome shade on a hot summer's day. From three tall cypresses along the wall, sparrows and finches darted in and out, chirping loudly as though to drive away these interlopers in their private space.

"I suppose you're right," she said reluctantly. "Lady Marian was feeling quite unwell when we arrived, but she's better now. When do you think we should leave?"

Lady Marian and Earl Hamelin walked into the garden in time to hear these last words.

"Nonsense, Joanna," said the former with asperity. "I wasn't feeling unwell. No more tired from the journey than the rest of you." She flounced her skirts and sat on a bench.

"The sooner we leave, the better," said the earl. "That's my opinion, anyway." He sat at the other end of Lady Marian's bench and looked crossly at a sparrow that was bouncing up and down on a cypress twig near his head. He shook his fist at it. The bird flicked its tail and flew to the next tree.

The earl had been trying to think of ways to make himself indispensable so Richard wouldn't decide he was superfluous and send him home. So far he hadn't come up with anything except to second Richard's every order. On the other hand, he fretted, maybe it was better to be as inconspicuous as possible.

The former strategy seemed the right one now. Richard stood up quickly.

"That's settled, then. Uncle, get the word to the supply sergeant and the cart-
ers that we'll leave tomorrow morning. Lady Marian, tell the chateleine that we'll
want a fine meal this evening. Roast pig would go down very well. And I'll see that
the captain of the knights has his men ready." He strode off toward the palace.

"Now that's what I call a man of action," said Lady Marian admiringly.

"He's always been like that," said Joanna. "I've never been able to keep up with
him. But I do think he might say 'please' a little oftener."

"With a smile like his, who needs 'please'?"

Joanna noticed that Richard had paused to speak to her ladies. He must have
given them the news that they'd soon be leaving; their faces fell. But they cheered
up when he said a few more words and held out his arm for Lady Beatrice. She
accepted it and they made their way toward the palace, with Adelaide and Charmaine tripping along in the rear. The duenna woke and followed them.

Dinner a few hours later was as festive as Richard could have wished. All the
ladies, even Joanna, had dressed in their best, aware they wouldn't have another
chance for weeks or months. Richard and Joanna sat at the center of the head
table, on the dais of the great hall. Joanna was in emerald green, with a pearl-and-
emerald tiara crowning her brown hair, shiny from Lady Marian's brushing. She
looked more grownup than she felt. Richard wore his gold crown and his red tunic
and leggings with the aplomb of a king. Lady Marian on his right looked quite
drab in contrast, though she'd donned her finest gray silk gown. Earl Hamelin
on Joanna's left was almost blinding, in a purple tunic with long crimson sleeves
which more than once came dangerously close to immersion in his soup.

Not only was a roast pig presently borne in on a silver platter, but it was followed by four peacocks roasted to crackling crispness, with their brilliant tail feathers restored to them so they looked as though they'd been draped in rainbows.

"Remember, Joanna, when our mother held that grand state dinner for the
papal legate, and she ordered the fowl dressed like that? I thought it would be
amusing to see if the cooks could recreate her menu."

"No, I don't remember that, I must have been too young. But I do remember
how long those dinners lasted and how noisy they got."

"Yes, but, in spite of all the tootling of flutes and drumming of tabors and loud
talk, you usually managed to fall asleep before the pies and cakes came in."

She made a face at him. He grinned, and turned to say something to Lady
Marian. Earl Hamelin bent forward and waved his arm to get Richard's attention.
"Prince Richard, how long do you think we'll be on the road south?"

"If we didn't have the baggage train, we could be in Saint-Gilles in two weeks.
But I expect it will be a month or more before the whole household gets there. It
will be up to you, uncle, to keep them moving."

The earl leaned back, and though she was almost enveloped by the sweep of
his sleeve as he withdrew his arm, Joanna heard his sigh of relief. She'd been aware
of his anxiety about whether he was to stay with the party. On the whole, she was
glad to have him along. She'd gotten used to his foibles and knew he meant well.

"Some of those mule drivers are as lazy as their beasts," said Richard. "You'll have your hands full, uncle, urging them on."

"That, and making sure we don't take any wrong turns," said Lady Marian. The earl pretended he hadn't heard.

Joanna was feeling drowsy when the last tart had come and gone and when the servants were bringing in pitchers of sweetened wine and platters of figs and dried apples. She dragged herself to her feet, rubbing her eyes.

"Well, at least I stayed awake until the end of the feast this time," she said to Richard, "but now I'm going to bed. And if we're to leave early tomorrow, shouldn't you do the same?" Lady Marian rose too.

"Now you sound just like my mother," said Richard, but with good humor. He waved them off, turned to his right and beckoned to Lady Beatrice to move into Lady Marian's vacated chair. "But surely my three pretty maids aren't going to desert me."

"Oh no, it's early yet," said Adelaide. She was the least pretty of the three, with a rather long face and eyes just a bit too close together.

"I've finished my packing, so I can stay up as long as I like," said Charmaine, tossing her head so her blonde curls danced.

Beatrice said nothing, but slid into the chair next to Richard. Earl Hamelin took advantage of the shuffling of places to move down and sit between Adelaide and Charmaine.

Beatrice cast Richard a quick glance and a smile, then turned to whisper to Charmaine.

Charmaine nodded and said, "Prince Richard, we've heard that you are a very accomplished troubadour. Won't you give us a song? It would be such a pleasure to all of us here." She looked down at the ten or twelve knights and ladies at the tables below the dais. They appeared to be absorbed in their own conversations and goblets, but one bold knight who happened to have heard Charmaine called out, "Yea, Prince Richard, let's hear a verse or two!"

That was all it took. Richard gestured to his page to bring his viol, stood up, plucked the strings softly, and began. As Joanna walked from the brightness of the banquet chamber toward the dim hallway outside, she heard his clear, sweet tenor voice. "Oh hear my plea, my lady fair…" She turned and saw the light from the candelabra behind him making a halo around his golden hair. She saw him bow his head to address his song to Lady Beatrice at his side. She saw Beatrice place her hand on her bodice and, as though transfixed, look up at Richard with a half smile. Joanna blinked. She was too sleepy to try to figure it out.

Lady Marian, who had also turned for a last look, took Joanna's hand and led her out.

"Oh dear," she murmured.

7

After weeks of hard riding they finally arrived at Saint-Gilles. Richard had been stern about starting the days an hour after dawn and not calling a halt until dark. Earl Hamelin was just as assiduous in urging on the baggage train. He enjoyed his position of power, even if only over mules and muleteers.

But when they reached their goal there were no Sicilian ships waiting for them. The whole party halted on the broad esplanade along the shores of the Petit Rhône, the river that was the town's link to the Mediterranean.

The sun was just setting and in the gathering dusk everybody stared at the placid river in disbelief. All they saw were fishing boats coming in to anchor and workboats bringing field laborers home from the other side of the river.

Richard scowled. Joanna thought he looked just like her father when he was mightily displeased, lashing out at the nearest person.

"This was certainly the date we agreed on, wasn't it, uncle?" Richard snapped. "You must remember, Joanna. Didn't the king promise to have his ships here no later than mid-November? And here it is the nineteenth and no sign of them. I can't hang around waiting on some lazy sailors who could still be in Sicily, for all we know. I must get back to Aquitaine."

Alan Broadshares saw his young mistress flinching at Richard's harsh tone. An old soldier in England's service, he wasn't intimidated by Richard's mercurial temper. He knew it would subside as suddenly as it arose.

"Maybe those fellows over there can tell us something," he said, pointing down the quay. Four seamen had just come out of what looked like a tavern. They were laughing, bellowing and swigging in turn from a long-necked leather bottle. Alan dismounted and approached the group. The conversation got even louder, with much gesticulating and pointing toward the south, toward the boats in the river and toward the town behind them.

"They're sailors who are stuck here in Saint-Gilles because there's been a howling bad storm out at sea," Alan came back to report. "One of them rode up from Saintes-Maries this morning and he said he'd never seen such high waves. He said he didn't see any boats or galleys out in the thick of it, so he supposed any that had been caught by the storm had either gone down or had managed to find a protected cove to ride it out."

Richard's face got even darker with his displeasure.

"Sicilians are good sailors," said Brother Jean-Pierre. "I expect they knew enough to take shelter. Maybe they even made it to the mouth of the river and are on their way now."

"Sorry, but they aren't," said Alan. "The man said his road took him along the river all the way to Saint-Gilles, and he saw no galleys."

"So here we are, left to cool our heels and twiddle our thumbs," Richard grumped. "Well, let's make the best of it. Uncle, what do you know of the town? Where will we spend the night? There's an abbey, I believe?"

The earl struck his hand against his forehead and looked anguished. Though he'd been thoroughly briefed by Archbishop Richard about the lodgings they would find all the way from Winchester to Saint-Gilles, for the life of him he couldn't remember what he'd been told about Saint-Gilles.

Joanna came to his rescue.

"Yes, there is an abbey. Brother Jean-Pierre told me about it once. It was founded by Saint Gilles himself years and years ago. But I don't know if it has rooms for travelers. I hope it does so we can stay there and tomorrow I can see the saint's tomb."

"My liege," said Jean-Pierre, "Joanna is right, there is indeed an important abbey here. It has a hostelry because it's necessary to lodge the bands of pilgrims who come here to do honor to Saint Gilles."

During this colloquy the seamen had drawn closer to see who these fine visitors might be.

"And if you want a guide to the abbey, I'll gladly take you there," called one of them, a barrel-chested man with a bushy black beard and a wide, guileless grin.

"Thank you, my man," said Richard. In the last rays of the setting sun, everybody could see that his face had brightened and so had his mood.

Before they began the ascent into the city Richard gave instructions to his companions. "Since we are all weary from the journey, a day or so of rest here will be welcome. But don't wander too far. As soon as the Sicilian galleys appear at the anchorage, I'll see you aboard, and then take my leave." He turned to the hovering seaman. "Now then, friend, lead on."

The jolly sailor, doubtless sensing there would be generous payment for services rendered, invited his companions to help him guide the large party. One ran back to the tavern for torches to light the way up the twisting cobbled streets.

Tired and sleepy, Joanna rode behind her brother and Earl Hamelin. They were discussing plans for the next day.

"I'm afraid I shall have to pay a call on Count Raymond of Toulouse tomorrow, if he's in residence," Richard said. "Queen Eleanor is worried that he may intend to claim some of our lands in Aquitaine that lie along his borders. She was quite firm in telling me to advise him against such a rash move."

"Ah yes," said the earl. "So you too must be firm. Would you like me to come with you? Two of us might make more of an impression on the count."

Joanna tried to imagine the earl adding weight to any negotiations. She hoped

Richard would discourage him.

"No, thank you, uncle. You'd be more help to me if you would keep one eye on the harbor and the other on our flighty young ladies. Don't let them wander about unescorted and get into trouble. That old woman, Gertrude or Gawaine or whatever her name is, who's supposed to look after them is as likely to decide to take a nap as to do her duty. I can't imagine why my mother sent them along in the first place. They don't seem to be especially suitable companions for my sister, and they certainly don't do much in the way of waiting on her."

"I believe it was Archbishop Richard of Winchester who selected them, not Queen Eleanor. They're all highborn. He thought it would impress King William to see his bride-to-be accompanied by such beautiful and noble young ladies."

"Well, uncle, the archbishop must have a different idea of beauty than I do. Although that Beatrice is worth a second look. Such blue, blue eyes—have you noticed? And the way she flirts and flutters her eyelashes. To my way of thinking she's not quite as naïve and innocent as she lets on."

"To my way of thinking, Richard, she's not nearly as attractive as Lady Adelaide. Now there's a woman with character all over her face."

"Yes indeed. The character of a very wellbred horse." Richard let out a whoop of laughter so loud that it could be heard all along the train of travelers. The earl, pained, said nothing more.

When they entered the town square, a nearly full moon had just risen over the rooftops. Joanna looked up at the face of the abbey church that dominated the square. She saw three soaring arched entrances and a tall tower, shining like alabaster in the moonlight. All across the façade she could barely make out a profusion of carved figures. Some were tall and stately like saints; some were small and crowded together like sinners—with a few fearful beasts interspersed here and there. She looked for Brother Jean-Pierre to ask him what it all meant, but he was far behind her.

Their guide, who had disappeared into a side door of the church upon arrival, came out with several hooded monks.

"Now I've gotten you here safely, my liege, and these good brothers will see you all to your quarters in the hostelry." He and his companions stood there expectantly.

"Yes, you've done splendidly, and I thank you," Richard said. "Uncle, will you give these excellent men something to show our appreciation? I haven't a farthing on me."

The earl complied with a smothered groan. It wasn't the first time Prince Richard hadn't had a farthing on him.

Joanna cast a last longing look at the church and dismounted to follow the monk who had been assigned to guide the ladies of the party. As soon as they left the moonlit square they were in a maze of dark narrow streets, but after two turns their guide indicated their destination. It was a small house next to the main hostelry. Joanna and her women would stay here, while the rest of the party would be in the larger, more crowded lodgings next door.

The monk knocked, and a sleepy-looking woman opened the door, screwing up her wrinkled old face to peer and see who it was. "Fine time to be waking honest folk from their rest," she complained. The monk murmured something in her ear. She opened the door wide, gave a little bob of her head and managed a surly, "Welcome, Princess Joanna." She didn't sound very welcoming.

The other ladies were left to wait at the entrance. The old woman continued to mutter something about "Nobody ever tells me anything about who's coming, even when it's royalty," as she led Joanna and Lady Marian to their room. It seemed habitable enough. The wood floor looked as though it had been swept not too long ago. Long woolen curtains covered the windows. There were two narrow beds with thick brown coverlets. The old woman left but shortly clumped back in with a tray bearing a loaf of brown bread, a knife, a slab of cheese, a pitcher of wine and two mugs. She banged the tray on a table, poured the wine, and after looking at them as though daring them to ask for anything more, scuttled out the door.

"Well!" said Lady Marian. She untied her wimple and ran her fingers through her curly hair. "It's not exactly Westminster Palace, is it my dear? Still, let's make the best of it. May I help you to a portion of this fragrant crusty loaf, a slice of this mellow golden cheese and a glass of this excellent fruity local wine?"

Joanna fell in with her mood. "If you please, do so. And be so good as to serve my dinner in my private chamber, since I see no chair in the dining hall." She jumped up on her bed. "And do be quick, my good woman. The sooner I sup, the sooner I can sleep, and then it will be morning and we can go back to that beautiful church."

8

The next day there was still no sign of the Sicilian galleys. The morning had dawned chilly and windless. Fog had settled like a fall of soft cold goose-down to fill every cranny of the city's twisting streets. When at midmorning Joanna and Brother Jean-Pierre set out for the church square, a few tentative rays of sunlight were beginning to break through, but Lady Marian bundled the girl up warmly in a long brown cloak with a fur-lined hood. Walking along beside Jean-Pierre, in his brown habit and with his cowl raised, she looked like a little monk-in-training.

When they came out from the shadowy lanes into the broad square, they found it considerably warmer and very crowded. The sun, well above the rooftops by now, had dispersed the mists and beamed on tradesmen setting up their market stands, townspeople clustering around them hoping for an early bargain, and chattering pilgrims who had come to inspect the famous church. Joanna and Jean-Pierre pushed their way through the throng to stand at the foot of the church steps. Now in the bright daylight, Joanna could clearly make out what she had seen so dimly the night before. Faces, figures, beasts and flowers chased each other around the three great arched portals. She stared, open-mouthed, transfixed.

Jean-Pierre explained. "Here, Princess, we see the complete story of Christ's life, crucifixion and ascent into heaven. Over here at the beginning are Mary and Joseph, there are the ass and the sheep, and the Babe."

"I've never seen anything like this! Everything looks so real." She caught sight of the frieze over the left portal and tugged at her tutor's sleeve. "Oh, Jean-Pierre, who are those men running away and looking so frightened? Who's the fierce-looking man chasing them?"

"Well, he does look pretty fierce. But he had reason. That's Jesus sending the money-changers out of the temple."

After an hour of walking back and forth and going up the steps for closer looks, Joanna sighed. "What a lot of work it must have been for the sculptors, poor men. How long do you suppose it took?"

"Years and years, I'd think. And we could spend years here admiring it, Joanna, but we'd best go down now and see where the saint's entombed."

The monk who stood at the top of the stairway to the crypt gave Jean-Pierre a candle to light their way to the gloomy depths under the church. Following Jean-Pierre down the uneven stone steps, Joanna called, "Is there an effigy? Will we see what he really looked like?"

She had always been interested in the lives of the saints, especially the early martyrs who suffered grievous persecutions. Her favorites at the moment were Perpetua and Felicitas, who refused to renounce their faith. She'd been fascinated with the story of how they, along with several men who were equally steadfast in their devotion, had been sentenced to be torn apart by wild beasts before an amphitheater of spectators in Carthage. Sometimes, lying in bed before going to sleep, she thought of the two brave women and shivered, imagining their torment as the rapacious beasts howled and slavered. Later, Jean-Pierre told her that it was now reliably reported that though the men had been killed by rampaging lions and leopards, as an act of mercy the women had been charged by a cow. The creature had been goaded until she was enraged, but since she failed to do enough damage, Perpetua and Felicitas had been put to the sword. Joanna found much more drama in the earlier version.

She was almost disappointed that though Saint Gilles had undergone many privations, he was neither torn apart nor put to the sword, but lived to a ripe old age and died of natural causes. Still, he was an interesting saint. Brother Jean-Pierre had told her how he'd lived for years in a cave with a loyal bitch for his only companion. There he subsisted on wild herbs and milk from the dog's teats. The lame and the sick toiled to his retreat, and he'd cured them. He'd driven the evil spirits out of a man possessed by the Devil. He'd brought a prince on the point of death back to life and won the friendship of the king, who'd built this abbey for him.

"Yes, I believe there's an effigy," Jean-Pierre said, "but I can't promise it will show us what he really looked like. In my opinion, sculptors of effigies tend to make everybody look equally noble and handsome."

Joanna never had a chance to see the effigy. They stepped into the crypt, which was far larger than she'd expected, almost like a duplicate of the church above. She saw the saint's tomb far off at the dimly lit end of the vaulted nave. But before they could take a step toward it, a deafening clatter came from the staircase, where a crowd of pilgrims was rushing down to see the sights in the crypt. Joanna and Jean-Pierre were almost swept along with them, but he pulled her to the side and said testily, "We'll come back later when this rabble is gone. Such zeal is commendable, but I'm afraid they're less interested in prayer and reverence than in adding another name to their lists of saints' tombs and relics they've visited."

When they came up again into the brightness of the afternoon they saw Lady Marian and the duenna entering the square. Lady Marian had to slow her steps to match the pace of Lady Gertrude, who hobbled with the aid of a pair of canes. The long journey on horseback had not been easy on her joints.

Joanna ran through the crowd to meet them.

"If you're thinking of going down to see the tomb of Saint Gilles, this isn't a good time. It's too crowded."

"Where are your young charges, Lady Gertrude?" Jean-Pierre asked. "I hope you haven't left them unattended?"

"Earl Hamelin very kindly offered to show them about the city. He promised to take two knights along and to be watchful for any mischief-makers." The old lady's hooded eyes opened wide when she caught sight of the church. "Oh, I must see that from close up," she said. She began her uncertain progress across the square, where hurrying townsfolk swerved to avoid her swinging canes. Halfway across, she stopped so suddenly that a man behind her reeled. His heavy bag fell and burst open and onions began rolling every which way over the cobblestones. Men, women and children scrambled to retrieve them and thrust them into their own sacks and pockets; though a few returned them to their owner. Lady Gertrude, oblivious, was peering toward the foot of the church steps. She turned to call to the others and pointed. "See, there they are."

They looked where she was pointing and saw Earl Hamelin with his two knights and two of his young ladies, standing at the foot of the church steps. The earl was gesturing enthusiastically, urging his companions to look at the carvings.

"Uncle!" said Joanna when she reached the church. "What have you done with Lady Beatrice? Why isn't she with you?"

"Don't worry, Joanna. She's in good hands. Just as we were leaving the hostelry, Prince Richard came in. He couldn't find Count Raymond, so he came back to see if the galleys had arrived, which they haven't. So he decided to come with us to tour the city. But just then Lady Beatrice said she felt chilly, so he said he'd go back with her to fetch a cloak, then join us. I expect we'll see them any minute."

He took Lady Adelaide by the arm and helped her up the steps. Lady Charmaine trailed behind. The two knights sat on a step and waited patiently, listening with half an ear to the earl's lecture.

"Now my dears, you must let me explain it all. First, you see, there's Christ on the throne of heaven. And over here are Saint Peter and Saint John. Or is that Saint Paul? Well, no matter. And there are Cain and Abel—or possibly David and Goliath? And just beyond…"

Several pilgrims had attached themselves to the group, thinking this might be some official guide. One of them asked, "And who, good sir, are these men all in a row, following a man who looks like Jesus on a small horse?"

"Oh, that, I believe, is Jesus, after he told the money-changers to leave the temple, conducting them out."

Joanna, still at the foot of the steps, heard all this clearly. She looked anxiously at Jean-Pierre. "I thought you said that was Jesus leading the disciples into Jerusalem. Shouldn't we say something?"

"Never mind, they won't remember it anyway. And at least they're finding entertainment in the scriptures, and not in some tavern."

He was anxious to get up to the top of the city while the sun was still high and show Joanna what he'd heard was a glorious view. "All the way to the city of Avignon, they say. I hope you will come too, Lady Marian." She nodded. "And will you join us, Lady Gertrude?"

"No thank you, I've had enough sights for one day. I'll just go back to the hostelry and have a little lie-down."

"If you see Richard, will you tell him where we've gone?" Joanna asked her.

"I will, though who knows where he and that Beatrice have got themselves to." And off she tottered.

The remaining three set off up the winding road. Before long, they left the crowded city behind to come out on a meadow, beyond which a steep bluff plunged to the plain. A few benches had been placed there for visitors who were weary after the steep climb. They sat and stared. It was indeed a glorious view. Below them the Petit-Rhône wound like a silver-green ribbon through the greener land and fields and forests stretched off to the east. But strain their eyes as they might none could see anything that might be the walls of Avignon.

"I'm sorry," said Brother Jean-Pierre, as though it were his fault. "I'm afraid it's just too hazy today."

"Oh look!" cried Lady Marian, rising and shading her eyes with her hand as she looked downriver. "Can those be the Sicilian galleys?"

Six long, graceful vessels were tacking back and forth across the river, sails rigged to take advantage of every breath of wind. From their vantage point, the three could see the rowers' oars dipping into the water and rising to dip again, slowly, deliberately, with just enough force to keep the vessels underway when they came about. No need to hurry now. The end of their long voyage was in sight.

9

Early the next morning Joanna and Lady Marian were awakened by a muted but persistent knocking. Joanna opened one eye and saw that it was still dark. She heard Lady Marian groan as she stirred herself and muttered, "Now where can my robe have got to?" Joanna rolled over. Lady Marian would deal with whoever it was and then they could go back to sleep.

It was Alan, holding a candle that sent dark shadows flickering over his face. Respectful but firm, he said, "I am sorry to wake you so early, but Prince Richard sends word that the tide will be turning in an hour and a half and everybody must be on the galleys."

"Oh dear," said Lady Marian. "All right, we'll do our best. Thank you, Alan. And have you wakened the other ladies?"

"I have, and Lady Adelaide said to tell you that as soon as she can she'll be along to help you and the princess. Meantime this lass is here to assist."

Joanna raised her head off her pillow. In the light of the candle and of the banked fire she could see a short, stocky girl with rosy cheeks and a mass of red hair, standing behind Alan. She was looking down intently at the tray she was holding, keeping it level so nothing would spill or rattle.

"Her name is Mary. She's brought your breakfast."

Mary came in, Alan left and Joanna got out of bed. Lady Marian, brisk and businesslike, in short order showed Mary where to put the tray, told her to use the bellows on the fire, found Joanna's wool robe and wrapped her in it, and set two chairs at the table. While they ate their bread and cherry jam, at Lady Marian's instruction Mary began taking garments off hooks, folding them and placing them in chests or big wool bags.

"Very good, Mary," Lady Marian said approvingly. "You seem like a quick learner. Maybe we should see if you can go with us to Sicily."

The girl looked startled. "Oh, thank you, but I think I *am* going. Uncle Alan said he would arrange it with Earl Hamelin that I could be Princess Joanna's chambermaid. Uncle Alan said as far as he could tell the princess wasn't getting much help from those three…" She stopped suddenly, realizing she might be speaking out of turn. But Lady Marian only laughed.

Joanna looked up from her breakfast. "So Alan is your uncle? And you've been traveling along with us all this time? Why haven't I seen you?"

Before answering, Mary carefully folded a silk robe and placed it in a chest.

Now that there was more light Joanna saw that she was really quite pretty. She guessed that Mary was perhaps a year or so older than herself. Her red-brown curls framed a round face with a turned-up nose and blue eyes that widened when she spoke.

"Oh, you wouldn't have seen me because I've been way at the back with the cooks. Uncle Alan said if I worked hard as a kitchenmaid maybe something better would come along. And now it has, hasn't it?" Her grin was so merry that Joanna couldn't help returning it.

"Well!" said Lady Marian, taking a final sip of her barley water and setting her cup down decisively. "We shall see. I would certainly be glad of someone dependable to help with the princess's dressing and packing and unpacking and all that. Now, Mary, see if you can find a place to take this tray, then tell Alan that we'll be ready in fifteen minutes."

And so they were, in spite of Joanna's objections when Lady Marian told her she must wear one of the fine gowns that, except for one dinner in Poitiers, had stayed in their chests all the way from Winchester.

"While we were on the road so long, my dear, with very little time to brush and clean your clothes, of course we had to wear the same old gowns day after day. But King William will undoubtedly have delegated some of his courtiers to meet us, and it's important for you to make a good impression." She placed a finger on her chin and considered. "I think the blue wool, the one with the silver sash and silver embroidery around the hem." Joanna was persuaded. She did rather like that one. It made her feel more grown-up.

Mary, who had never tied a bow in a sash in her life, much less a silver one, earnestly attended to Lady Marian's directions and got it right on the second try.

"Very good, Mary. Now help me with the buttons on the princess's cloak, put on your own and we'll be off."

Lady Adelaide eventually strolled in to lend a hand only to meet Lady Marian shepherding her little party out the door, followed by two stout men puffing under the weight of chests and bags. At the street they found their horses saddled and the pack animals waiting.

When they reached the riverfront they saw that a dozen more vessels had joined the six galleys they'd seen the previous afternoon. Richard, his hair flying and his face as red as a brick, was striding about and shouting, urging haste. With an anxious eye on the tide that was just beginning to rise, he enlisted Alan and they almost pushed the confused company onto the ships. Many of the party had returned to England, but there were still about forty travelers to Sicily. Knights and squires, cooks and laundresses, servingmen and maids, all the household needed by a queen of Sicily and all their stores and baggage had to be squeezed into the boats. Scores of citizens of Saint-Gilles, who had never seen such a commotion on their river, had gathered to watch the show. The sun, still low in the east, lent brightness if not warmth to the scene. Several enterprising fellows, taking advantage of the festive mood, had brought flutes and drums to give an impromptu concert.

Joanna hardly had time to take all this in when Richard, out of breath but apparently satisfied that everybody and everything were going to fit, appeared at her side. He seized her arm and led her and Lady Marian to the largest vessel and helped them onto the short gangway and onto the deck. He looked around critically. "It's not the most graceful—far too fat in the middle for that. But these gentlemen say it's the most comfortable and seaworthy."

Only then did Joanna notice the two elegant strangers who had followed them onto the galley. No, not strangers. She recognized them first by their fancy shoes. They were the Sicilian ambassadors, Florian and Arnolfo, who had come to Winchester all those months ago to see if she'd make a suitable bride for King William. She held out her hand and smiled, as she'd seen her mother do. Count Florian bowed over it.

"We are pleased to see you again, Princess Joanna. And to see you looking so well." He caught Bishop-elect Arnolfo's eye. Both were amazed at how much she seemed to have matured and how at ease she was. This wasn't the little girl playing dress-up they'd observed at the banquet in Winchester. This was a princess who was perfectly aware she would soon be a queen.

"We bring King William's respectful greetings and his wishes for a speedy and comfortable voyage until he can welcome you to Sicily," said Arnolfo.

"Thank you, Count Florian and you, Bishop Arnolfo. I hope for the same."

Earl Hamelin appeared with Adelaide, Beatrice and Charmaine. Now that Richard would be leaving them, the earl would be in charge of the expedition. He looked flustered already. His long pale face was flushed, and he kept brushing straggling strands of his sparse brown hair off his perspiring forehead.

Richard frowned at this tardy arrival. "Where is Lady Gertrude, uncle? Why didn't she bring the ladies?"

"She declared this morning that she isn't well enough for the journey and intends to stay in Saint-Gilles," said the earl unhappily. "So there was nobody else but me to escort them to the boats."

"That may be just as well," said Richard. With one of his characteristic quick decisions, he decreed that from now on Lady Adelaide, as the oldest and most experienced, would assume responsibility for the morals and safety of the two younger women. She blushed with pride at the news. "And be sure, Lady Adelaide, that you and the others serve my sister well."

The earl, visibly relieved that he was not to be demoted from majordomo to lady tender, wiped his brow with a huge blue silk handkerchief that he extracted from the pocket of his billowy cloak. Aiming for his pocket to put it back, he missed and the kerchief went flying through the air. He watched ruefully as it floated toward the pier, where it was caught and gleefully brandished by a small unkempt boy. The earl shrugged.

Adelaide remarked, "Well, maybe he needs it more than you do."

"Thank you, my dear. A most astute observation." He took her arm and followed the others as Richard led them below to inspect the quarters where Joanna and her ladies would be lodged.

"Now you see, Joanna," said Richard, "why they've made this galley so wide. Actually, it was probably at one time a merchant galley, meant to hold cargo. That's why they've been able to fit in this commodious set of rooms here." Behind his back Lady Marian sniffed. "Doesn't look very commodious to me," she grumbled under her breath. True, there were several separate cabins: one for Joanna, one for Lady Marian and Mary, and two even smaller ones to accommodate the three ladies in waiting. All had barely enough room to turn around and the ceilings were so low that they had to bend to enter.

They trooped up on deck again, where six oarsmen were already seated, three on a side. Joanna looked at them with interest. She'd heard that oarsmen on galleys were slaves, chained to their benches. But these looked like any seamen one would see in a port, muscular and talkative. No chains were in sight. They were joking as they settled down for the task of pulling on the long oars to propel the craft downriver.

Alan and Brother Jean-Pierre, who were lodged forward in the crew's quarters, were talking to the captain.

"So you expect to reach Marseilles within a week, do you?" Alan asked. The captain, a lean, sinewy, balding man with a short neat brown beard and a short way of talking, said, "Aye, the good God and fair weather willing."

"And Sicily? How long to Sicily?" asked Jean-Pierre anxiously. He was not a good sailor.

"That's to be seen. I'd hope by mid-January. That's when I told King William to expect us. But we'll have to stay close to shore and maybe put into port for shelter more often than I'd like. It's November. The weather's only going to worsen as we make our way."

Jean-Pierre groaned inwardly and resolved to say a special prayer for calm seas.

Richard had heard the exchange and clapped the captain on the shoulder.

"But you're the canniest captain who's ever sailed the Mediterranean, they say. I've no doubt you'll make good time and be in Palermo by New Year's."

He bent to give Joanna a peck on the cheek and a hug.

"Goodbye, little sister." He whispered in her ear, "And if those Sicilians give you any trouble, send for me." He winked and she giggled. Trouble? That was the last thing she expected.

He turned to Lady Marian and the three ladies in waiting and pressed each of their hands in turn.

"Goodbye, ladies. Take good care of my sister."

"Oh, we will, Prince Richard. That will be our pleasure and our privilege," said Adelaide.

"And we wish you good fortune in your battles," said Charmaine.

Beatrice, who had not said a word since stepping onto the galley and who had avoided meeting Richard's eyes, seemed to tremble when he took her hand. She looked up at him, her lips slightly parted as though she were about to speak. But no words came. Joanna thought she saw tears brimming in Beatrice's lovely blue eyes. "How beautiful she is!" she thought. "How can Richard resist such an appeal?" But he did. After a quick glance at those pleading eyes he dropped her hand and waved a collective goodbye to all. He strode down the gangplank and to his waiting horse. In one swift, fluid, graceful movement he placed a foot in the stirrup, swung into the saddle, seized the reins from his groom and gave a final wave. Horse and rider disappeared up the winding street.

The captain gave the order to raise the sail. Slowly the bulky vessel began to move out into the river as the oarsmen bent to their task. The big square sail flapped briefly and noisily, then caught the wind and held it in a taut embrace. The strengthening tide hastened the galley along to join the other vessels, all getting underway and almost filling the river from bank to bank before they settled into an orderly line.

Joanna looked back at the town and the pier growing smaller by the minute. She looked around her and ahead at the brave fleet, flying southward like a flock of geese in the autumn. Though at the moment she was surrounded by friends, for the first time it was truly borne in on her: I am leaving everything I know and love. My mother. My brother. My England. Will I like King William? And what if he doesn't like *me*? So many questions, and no answers.

Back on the pier, the townspeople straggled off toward home and the day's routine, chattering and laughing. The sudden, brief presence of these noisy, strange but well-paying visitors to Saint-Gilles had given them a winter's worth of material for conjecture and discussion.

Above it all, on the bluff overlooking the harbor, Richard had paused to watch the departure. He would miss Joanna. He wished her well, but he almost hoped the Sicilians would indeed give him reason to come save her from some peril. I wonder what Sicily is like, he mused. I would like to see a land different from the France I know so well. Maybe to do battle with a new foe. And maybe to have Beatrice again. She was sweet. Sweet and compliant, a little too compliant. But when she's grown up a bit she might prove quite a spirited lass.

His horse stamped a hoof, shook its head and snorted. Richard laughed and patted it on the neck. "Right you are, old Silvermane. Why do we stop here musing about what might be, when what will be is waiting for us over in Aquitaine? The sooner I get to Dax, the sooner I'll take the city from that old rogue the Count of Bigorre." He dug his heels into the horse's sides and they were off.

IO

When the fleet sailed out from the Petit Rhône and into the open Mediterranean, Joanna was amazed at the endless expanse of blue water that reached toward infinity, with no land in sight except what lay behind them. She, and most others in the company, had never seen anything like this. When they had crossed the English Channel they'd been able to see not only where they had come from but also where they were going.

Joanna was relieved to find this enormous, encompassing sea relatively unthreatening. At first it seemed Jean-Pierre's prayer for a calm voyage had been answered. They made their way through waters ruffled by just enough wind so the sail could provide nearly all the power, and the oarsmen had it relatively easy. For some days the weather continued to cooperate. Even when the sun disappeared, the sky sent down no showers of freezing rain or blasts of frigid winds. Most days Joanna and her ladies could stand at the rail of the narrow deck, watching with fascination as the unfamiliar coastline rolled by.

One morning Joanna came on deck early to find Beatrice already there, near the stern and gazing at the galley's wake. Joanna had noticed that Beatrice, always quiet and reserved, seemed even more subdued lately. Joanna had a vague idea it had something to do with Richard.

Neither Joanna nor her three ladies in waiting had tried very hard to be friends. Joanna found Lady Adelaide overly talkative and concerned with her impression on others, Lady Charmaine silly and simpering, and Lady Beatrice so withdrawn, especially since leaving Saint-Gilles, that it was impossible to make any overtures. Of the three, Joanna thought she preferred Beatrice. She knew what it was like to have feelings and thoughts that you kept to yourself and to have no taste for idle chatter. Once she had overheard her mother saying to her father, "Henry, how did we manage to produce such a solemn child in this family of show-offs and know-it-alls?"

Now on this peaceful, quiet morning, she wondered if she could cheer Beatrice up, maybe by telling her that she missed Richard too. She walked aft to where Beatrice stood huddled in a gray cloak, holding it tightly closed at her neck, still looking back at the neat V-shaped wake that the galley cleaved in the sea. When Joanna put a hand on Beatrice's arm the young woman, startled, turned, and Joanna saw how swiftly her expression of brooding unhappiness changed to one of closed composure.

"Are you thinking about everything we've left behind, and wishing you hadn't come? I felt that way sometimes too, at first. But now I don't," Joanna said.

Beatrice's lips parted slightly as though she were about to speak. When she didn't, Joanna went on. "But I do so wish Richard could have come with us! He would have loved this galley, wouldn't he? He's never really been to sea. I do miss him—but I know he had important things to do in Aquitaine."

Joanna had to strain to hear when Beatrice replied, in a low voice and with her head averted.

"Yes, I miss him too. But most of all I wish I'd never left Winchester."

At first Joanna didn't know what to say to that. Though she'd been sorry to leave her mother, she couldn't imagine wishing she were back in Winchester, now that they were truly on their way to Sicily. And so swiftly! She felt exhilarated. Her uneasiness about her future diminished with every stroke of the oars, with every wave that passed smoothly under the galley. She was almost afraid the voyage might end too soon.

She still hoped to brighten Beatrice's mood. "But if you'd never left Winchester, you wouldn't be here now having this wonderful adventure. And there'll be even more adventures when we get to Sicily. Maybe you'll meet a handsome signore!"

Beatrice tried to smile at that. "Thank you, Princess Joanna, for being so kind. Now I think I'll go below. And I'll try to look forward to Sicily, I really will."

Joanna wasn't sure how much she'd helped. But she thought per-haps she and Beatrice had established the beginning of a friendship.

For the next few days the coastline was quite dull: stretches of sandy, shrubby dunes, beyond which they could occasionally see what looked like lakes and marshes extending northward. Once, though, Joanna saw a scene she'd remember for the rest of her life. Leaping over the dunes and onto the shore galloped a pure white horse, mane and tail flying in the wind, and behind him, a dozen more. They ran in a line along the beach, as though they were showing off for the spectators in the galley and exulting in their freedom. Even the captain was impressed. He stood beside Joanna to watch. "Don't see that often. Quite wild, they are. Usually they stay more inland." For a while the ship and the beautiful horses kept pace with each other. Then, as though they'd put on enough of a show, the horses trotted up to a break in the dunes and disappeared.

A few days later the galleys approached a gap in the coastline that led to what must have been a busy port, judging from all the vessels making their way in and out. Instead of sailing past, the captain shifted course and led the fleet into the harbor. It was long and narrow and bordered all around by stone wharves where ships were tied up. The galleys threaded their way among dozens of vessels, from seagoing ships like their own to little cockleshells that darted about like waterbugs. As they got closer they could see that market stalls were set up along the shore and crowds were milling about.

Earl Hamelin and Brother Jean-Pierre came aft to where Joanna and the ladies stood, exclaiming and pointing.

"Where are we, Brother Jean-Pierre?" Joanna asked.

"Why, this is Marseilles, Princess. Or as some still call it, Masilia. It's very old—goes clear back to Greek days. The captain says we'll stop here to take on provisions. It's the last big, sheltered port for a long time."

"Oh, I hope we can go ashore! May we, uncle?"

"It would be heavenly to feel terra firma under our feet again," said Lady Charmaine.

"And I'd like to buy some lavender," said Adelaide. "I've heard the very best comes from this part of France, and they say it helps against the seasickness."

"Do say yes, uncle," Joanna implored.

The earl pursed his lips, considering. It might be agreeable to escort Lady Adelaide in search of lavender. The captain intervened.

"Most unwise. King William would never permit it. It's not safe. You'd get no respect and maybe some unpleasantness from the ruffians who roam these piers. They're just looking for somebody to rob or kidnap. Most unwise, Princess Joanna."

"My opinion exactly," said the earl. "Out of the question, I'm afraid."

As soon as the casks had been filled with water and wine, and baskets and boxes of dried and pickled meat and fish were stowed on board, they sailed on. And on, and on.

Gradually the winds increased. Some days Joanna found it too hard to keep her footing on the tilting deck and stayed in her little cabin. Beatrice and Charmaine also spent most of their time below. But Adelaide, at least on drier days, forced herself to go on deck so Earl Hamelin could congratulate her on her sea legs and explain to her the finer points of navigation.

One relatively calm day he pointed to two coils of rope on the deck. "Now this one, Lady Adelaide¾the heavier one, you see?—this one is used to hitch onto the sail and raise it up the mast. You can understand that it has to be very thick and strong to raise such a heavy great sail. And this other lighter one is what they use to tie us up to the dock when we come ashore. It needn't be so strong because when the vessel's at rest, there's not much pull on it."

"Do tell!" said Lady Adelaide, greatly impressed.

A passing crew member who couldn't help overhearing let out a "Haw haw!" and said audibly to his mates, "That's a good one, that is. Doesn't know a halyard from a hawser."

Joanna had just climbed up the steep companionway and heard the whole incident. Though she thought the earl was sometimes ridiculously pompous, she felt sorry that he'd been humiliated in front of Adelaide. She'd noticed how he sought Adelaide's company. She supposed this was what they called courting. Will King William feel he has to court me? she wondered. Probably not. Everything is already arranged and we'll have to get married, whether we like each other or not.

As they approached Genoa the weather worsened. The little fleet was buffeted by terrifyingly high waves, and the ships swayed sickeningly. Sometimes the driving rains made a gray curtain all around them, hiding not only the other galleys, but also the shoreline that was the captain's only tie to knowing where he was. Almost everybody was seasick. Joanna was more miserable than she had ever been in her life. All the way down the coast of Italy she wished she were dead, and begged Lady Marian to have her put ashore so she could die in peace. Her ladies suffered almost as much.

The captain managed to find ports where the fleet could take on water and foodstuffs for the few who felt like eating, but he dared not linger. He knew worse weather was very likely to come and ran for Naples as fast as he could, peering into the mist and the spray for the first glimpse of the looming cone of Vesuvius.

They safely reached the city under the volcano on December 20th, to find the rest of the fleet already there. At last the weary passengers could leave the cursed galley and walk without staggering to keep their balance. But Joanna was so weakened that she had to be carried on a litter up the hill to their lodgings in the Castel Capuano. The two ambassadors walked by her side. They had sailed in a different galley so she had seen nothing of them during the entire journey. Though she knew they were trying to raise her spirits, she hardly heard them as they explained that the castle had been built by King William I, her fiancé's father, and that she would find it very comfortable.

"It's where our King William stays whenever he comes to Naples," said Arnolfo. "And what's more, since Naples is part of the kingdom of Sicily, from now on, while we are here and when we go to sea again you will be on land and in waters that are part of the kingdom of which you will be queen."

She knew she should raise her head and try to show some interest, but she was too weak. She groaned at the thought of going to sea again.

As soon as they reached the castle Lady Marian directed the litter bearers to take the woebegone princess carefully up to their chambers. Earl Hamelin caught up with Lady Marian as she followed behind the litter.

"Lady Marian, please come down as soon as you can. We must make some plans."

Ten minutes later the earl, Lady Marian, Brother Jean-Pierre and Joanna's bodyguard Alan sat huddled in a corner of the great hall, worrying. It was only eleven in the morning but servants were already laying tables and preparing for the afternoon meal.

"She looks terrible," said the earl bluntly. "Skinny, down-at-the-mouth, hair all stringy, no color in her face. If King William were to see her now he'd have the heads of those ambassadors who told him she was a beauty. And very likely King Henry would have my head too, for not delivering a princess in the same condition as when she left." He raised his arm and swung it in a vigorous head-chopping-off gesture. His elbow brushed against Lady Marian's cap and knocked it askew.

She sighed, straightened it, tucked in her curls, sighed again and said, "I'm afraid you're right. And what's worse is that she's had fever as well as the seasickness. That's why she looks so sickly."

Jean-Pierre nodded. He hadn't suffered as much as he'd feared during the voyage, but what with a total loss of appetite, his slight figure had become almost skeletal. He still felt rather fragile.

"I agree. In fact if King William were to see me now, he might send me back to the monastery farm for fattening up." Nobody laughed. After a few moments, Lady Marian's practical good sense reasserted itself.

"Well, there's only one thing to do. We'll just have to put off our arrival in Palermo. We must stay here until she's better. She's a resilient child. I'm sure after a week or ten days of rest and good food she'll get over it and be as presentable as ever."

Jean-Pierre brightened. He took his responsibilities seriously. "And maybe I'll have time to resume our lessons. I only hope the gales haven't swept everything she's learned out of her head."

"Very well, I'll ask Count Florian to go ahead of us and tell King William about the delay," said Earl Hamelin. He stood up.

"There's just one more thing," said Lady Marian. The earl sat down again.

"If Count Florian and Count Arnolfo tell King William the truth about the state his little bride is in now, we might all be in trouble. He might even reconsider the marriage agreement. What king would want a frail sickly child for a wife?"

"That's indeed a concern," said Brother Jean-Pierre. "I noticed they were whispering together after they walked up the hill beside her litter."

"And so did I," said Alan. "In fact, I was marching along just behind them. I couldn't hear too much, but I did hear Count Arnolfo say something about King William and second thoughts."

Jean-Pierre frowned. Lady Marian's sigh was almost a groan. Alan looked stoical. The earl fidgeted, then broke the silence.

"Frankly, I don't see that we can do anything but hope for the best."

Jean-Pierre demurred. "But couldn't we at least ask them to assure the king that we, who know the princess well, are confident this is only temporary and she'll be her usual blooming self by the time we reach Palermo?"

"I don't think we should try to influence them," said Lady Marian. "After all, their loyalty is to the king of Sicily, not the king of England. I'm afraid that this time the earl is right."

Earl Hamelin, pretending not to notice the accentuated "this time," got to his feet and said, "That's that, then. I'll tell the ambassadors about the delay. I expect they'll want to be on their way at once."

11

After the conference Lady Marian went up to their rooms. She was anxious about her charge, but she was also dying for a wash, a change of clothes and a proper meal at last.

She found Joanna being well tended by Mary in a spacious chamber with tall windows that provided a panoramic view of the harbor. Mary had already helped Joanna out of her wrinkled garments that smelled of seawater and sweat, bathed her and dressed her in a clean white gown and a soft blue robe. Mary, blessedly, had not suffered from seasickness and had been of great service during the voyage. She would sit by Joanna's side for hours, sponging her perspiring face and urging her to take little sips of water and to try to swallow bits of dry bread. As often as not they didn't stay down, and Mary dealt with that too.

Lady Marian helped Mary prop Joanna up against a mound of pillows on the high bed. The princess sighed, looked around her and slowly realized that though she felt weak and limp, she was no longer nauseated or feverishly hot.

Lady Marian smiled at her. "You do feel just a bit better, don't you? Haven't I been telling you all along that you would?"

"Yes, you have, ever since we left Genoa. And it was never true."

"But now it is, isn't it, Princess Joanna?" sensible little Mary asked.

Joanna was rather enjoying feeling cross and peevish. It was certainly preferable to the abysmal physical malaise she had suffered for the last fortnight. But she supposed they were right, up to a point. "Yes, I do feel better. A *little* better."

Her three ladies in waiting, similarly cleansed and refreshed, came in, full of chatter about this wonderfully appointed castle. The thick carpets, so colorful! The glorious views! The helpful servants! The big wardrobes where one could hang up one's clothes instead of stuffing them into chests! The bowl of dates and nuts on the table with a carafe of cool water! And best of all, a private room for each.

What with all this good cheer, Joanna revived enough to consent to go down to the hall for dinner. Mary held her arm and supported her faltering descent of the stone stairway. When Earl Hamelin had helped her to her seat, she looked around and saw that the castle hall was about half the size of the drafty great hall at Winchester and far warmer. Tapestries hung on the walls, with wondrous scenes of ladies seated in a garden and huntsmen with their bows and arrows in pursuit of a stag. The room was humming with the approving comments of her traveling companions and their hopeful conjectures about the menu. She hardly recognized them, all so much cleaner and better clothed than she had seen them in weeks. A pleasant whiff of incense came from a brazier in a corner.

Just as she was beginning to feel she might rejoin the ranks of the healthy human race, she caught the odor of roasted meat as servants began bringing in platters heaped with beef and fowl. Joanna shuddered and for a moment her queasiness returned. But she managed to partake, without incident, of a small bowl of beef broth, two chunks of bread dipped in the broth, and a sliver of apple tart.

"Bravely done, Princess," said her uncle, as though congratulating her on a well-run race. He himself had just made away with a brace of guinea hens. "We'll have you fit and fine again in no time." She gave him a small wan smile and retired to her chamber.

The ambassadors left and the royal party devoted themselves to the princess's recovery. It wasn't as rapid as they'd hoped. All signs of seasickness had disappeared, but not the fever. She would revive enough to get up for a few hours in the morning, but every evening she weakened, grew hot and trembly and had to lie down. The best physicians in Naples were called in and prescribed various remedies: hot compresses, cold compresses, infusions of feverfew, poultices of fenugreek. Nothing seemed to help. Lady Marian was discouraged.

"Her brother Richard has had the same thing," Alan told her. "When I've campaigned with him, I've seen him laid low like an oak that's been felled by a woodsman. There was nothing for it but to make him as comfortable as we could in his tent and wait until the fever went away. Sometimes it took two weeks."

"My grandmother used to make a brew of hot water, honey, and fresh hyssop flowers," said Lady Adelaide. "It worked wonders for me when I had coughs and fever."

"Yes, I've had that," said Mary. "But we always put anise seeds in, too."

"Well, it's worth a try," said Lady Marian.

But where to find what they needed in this strange, confusing big city? Mary volunteered that she'd seen a box of anise seeds in the kitchen, and was sent to ask the cook if he had any hyssop.

"He hasn't," came the report. "But he told me there's a special street in the market where the herbalists set up their stands. I think I've seen it."

Earl Hamelin's eyebrows shot up and he leaped to his feet. A search for hyssop in Naples might not be as pleasant as one for lavender in Marseilles but the rewards of success were tempting: Lady Adelaide's admiration and, of course, the princess's improved health.

"I shall be honored to lead the search if you will accompany me, Lady Adelaide." He made her a little bow.

"Gladly, Earl Hamelin."

"And perhaps Mary should go along," said Lady Marian, "since she's the only one of us who knows where the market is."

Mary turned quite pink at being included in the party. But when they set out, the other two paid her no attention beyond keeping her bustling little figure in sight as they navigated the twisting, crowded streets.

They found the right street, lined with stalls offering a bewildering variety of powders, dried herbs, flowers and mysterious crumbly substances. Competing smells assaulted their nostrils. There were no fresh hyssop flowers, but Lady Adelaide followed her nose to a stall with a basket of nondescript dried flowers with a strong minty smell.

"Ah, here they are. The dried ones will do very well," she said.

The earl managed to find in his various pockets a large handful of coins and held them out for the merchant to select what was owing him. They started back.

"Mary," he said, "why don't you go ahead with the herbs, and get cook started making the infusion? We'll be able to find our way."

The girl looked doubtful.

"Now don't worry," said the earl. "I paid particular attention as you led us here." Mary ducked her head, smiled, and darted off.

An hour later the other two arrived at the palace. Lady Marian and Brother Jean-Pierre were waiting in the hall, trying not to worry. The earl looked agitated and Lady Adelaide was flushed.

"These Italians!" exclaimed the earl. "What kind of a city is this, where the streets go around in circles and nobody can speak any English or French to tell us where we are!" He flung off his cloak and let it fall in a heap on the floor. It jangled. A few coins rolled away toward a corner.

"Are you all right, Lady Adelaide?" Lady Marian asked. "You look upset."

"We have had an adventure!" exclaimed Lady Adelaide. "A rude little man in the market grabbed me by the arm, trying to make me look at his gold and beads, and Earl Hamelin pushed him away and threatened him with his fists, and the man almost ran, he made off so fast. The earl was so brave!" She looked at him with such a fond smile that for a moment her long face was almost attractive.

The earl looked up at the ceiling and pretended not to have heard.

"Don't you want to know whether the princess has benefited from her hyssop potion?" asked Lady Marian.

"Of course! Please forgive me, I should have asked at once. How is she?"

"Possibly a little better. She said this was the first medicine we've given her that tasted good. It's all that honey, of course, and the nice mint flavor of the hyssop."

"And she sat up in bed and asked for more," said Brother Jean-Pierre. "And she said to thank you for suggesting it."

"The little love!" said Lady Adelaide. "I'm so glad to hear it, aren't you, Hamelin?"

"Indeed I am. Now my dear, you must rest after our long walk and all the excitement." He took her arm and they started up the stairs. Lady Marian and Brother Jean-Pierre heard her murmur, looking up at her companion, "I was so very lucky that you were with me to protect me!" and his reply, "Lady Adelaide, I would like to be with you to protect you always."

"Oh my, oh my!" said Lady Marian, looking with dismay at Brother Jean-Pierre.

"Oh my indeed! Apparently he hasn't told her he has a wife waiting for him in England."

Earl Hamelin and Lady Adelaide didn't come to dinner and were not seen again that night.

Whether it was the hyssop tea, the other and viler potions her caregivers kept plying her with, or simply the passage of time, Joanna's health returned and with it her good looks and spirits. The physicians, when consulted, agreed that she would be well enough to attend Epiphany mass at the cathedral.

Lady Marian decreed that she should dress up in her finest gown. "That's the white satin, you know, that's been in a chest ever since we left Winchester."

Anticipating objections, she hurried on. "The people of Naples will be pleased to see an English princess honoring their splendid cathedral by appearing in suitable royal splendor. It's what they would expect from the fiancée of their king."

"And besides," said Lady Charmaine, "if that's what you'll wear when you meet King William you'll feel more at ease then for having become accustomed to it."

Joanna was convinced and let Mary and Lady Marian help her into the ceremonial gown. It was high-necked, long-sleeved and full-skirted with a gold sash. As its only adornment, the red-and-gold Plantagenet lions romped around a wide band at the hem and a narrow one at the neck. It was a little loose because she hadn't yet regained all the weight she'd lost, which made it more comfortable. When they placed the pearl-studded tiara on her head she took a deep breath and stood as tall as she could. She felt she was indeed a princess of the realm, no longer a sick bedridden child.

Mary held up a small mirror so Joanna could see herself in sections. But she got a better idea of how she looked from the faces of her ladies. Even shy Beatrice joined in the approbation. "King William will be enchanted!"

"So I'm pretty again, Lady Marian?"

"My dear, you are. Prettier than ever. Thank God for your recovery."

Brother Jean-Pierre had just come in to announce it was time to leave for the cathedral.

"Amen," he said.

12

K ing William, alone in his private study, was waiting for his mother. She'd sent word that she wished an audience. He sat at an ebony table on which rested a massive gold candlestick, an illuminated Latin text, and his elbows. Supporting his chin with his cupped hands, he was studying a history of Apulia, one of the Sicilian possessions on the Italian mainland. He'd had reports of unrest there and thought he should educate himself about the province, in case he had to take action. But his attention wandered.

He looked up and surveyed this room where he felt so at peace. He liked its harmony and simplicity, with its tall arched windows and rich paneling, innocent of the carvings and mosaics that embellished so much of the rest of the royal palace in Palermo. The only furnishings, besides his chair, the table and another chair facing him, were four polished wood cabinets. Tall and austere, lined up against the wall, they held the substantial library of manuscripts that his father had acquired. And he liked the room because he could slip in here from his adjoining bedchamber without having to advertise his movements to all the palace staff and curious visitors who wandered the halls, hoping for a glimpse of royalty.

Restless, he stood up and stretched, then walked over to look out the window. From his second-story vantage point he could see that people were already filing into the square, some with cushions and stools, many with wineskins and sausages. It was hours before the anticipated event of the evening would begin but the citizens were already feeling festive and were plainly intending to make a night of it. He nodded approvingly when he saw that, in accord with his orders, the lamplighters were placing torches on the columns around the square, ready to light when darkness fell.

His mother was late. He wondered what excuse she'd have this time. Maybe her maid had forgotten to wake her from her nap. Or her gown had been torn and she'd had to change to a new one.

A page, so young that he still spoke in a childish treble, knocked, stepped quickly inside and announced, "Queen Margaret to see her son King William."

In she swept, almost engulfing the lad with her billowing skirts. William had observed that as his mother increased in years and girth, so did the complexity and layering of her costumes. Today she looked rather oceanic, with her full-skirted sea-green gown and several filmy white scarves and shawls foaming about her shoulders. The ensemble was anchored by a five-strand necklace of enormous pearls. Above all this splendor her small dark face, plump as a ripe cherry and topped with a wisp of a white lace cap on her black hair, rose like an afterthought.

William couldn't help smiling at the sight. His mother, mistaking this for cordiality, spoke in a rush.

"Oh William, I'm so glad you're not annoyed. I really couldn't get here any sooner. You wouldn't believe how hard we had to look before we found my pearls. I quite thought they'd been stolen, until..."

"Yes, mother, that's good. I'm glad you found them." He spoke firmly but not unkindly. He was accustomed to her flighty ways. He'd lived through her seven years as queen regent after his father died. William was only eleven then, but he'd been old enough to observe how totally unfit she was to govern. Along with most Sicilians he'd been relieved when, six years ago, he'd turned eighteen and had thereupon become king in fact as well as name.

Now that William ruled, his mother was on the political sidelines. She had to find new ways to amuse herself. One of these was to offer advice to her son.

She plumped her well-cushioned posterior down in the equally well-cushioned chair across the table from him.

"William, I'll waste no words. I'm sure you're very busy." She looked disapprovingly at the manuscript before him, then glanced around her. "But William, why do you persist in burying yourself in this musty little hole instead of receiving people in the throne room next door? It's so much more suitable and commodious, and your father made it so beautiful, with that splendid golden throne and plenty of places for his friends to sit."

"Mother, we've been over this before. I'm perfectly willing to use the throne room to receive ambassadors or to hold meetings with my council. But when I need to concentrate or study it's impossible, with servants running in and out and the master of the horse or the archbishop dropping by to interrupt me with whatever's on his mind. Now, to get back, what's on *your* mind?"

"Yes, I was just coming to that. William, I want you to reconsider this marriage to the English princess. You know I've never thought it was a good idea. Now I've had some really disturbing news. I've called in Count Florian to ask his opinion on what kind of match the girl will be. He traveled with her all that way, and he should be familiar with her by now. And I didn't like what he had to say, not at all." She looked at him expectantly, waiting for some evidence of curiosity. But he merely watched her with a slight smile, silent.

"I gather from what he said—though he didn't come right out and say it, William, it was easy to guess what he really meant—I gathered that she's a poor little frail wisp of a thing, who might die on you before she could bear you a child. So I really advise you to send her home again. And it's not too late to negotiate with Emperor Frederick. I still think you were wrong to turn him down when he offered his daughter to you, two years ago. He'd make a much better ally than King Henry. And you'd be so much better off with one of those strong, healthy German princesses. So would the succession."

She sat back and folded her hands in her lap, having made her case.

William stood up, brushed back a lock of hair and walked to the window. It was getting noisier down in the square. Dusk was approaching, and the lamplighters were beginning to kindle the torches.

"Mother," he said, seating himself again, "for one thing, it would be the height of rudeness and most deplorable diplomacy to send the princess back as soon as she arrives. For another, I've talked to Count Florian too, as well as Count Arnolfo. They reported to me as soon as they got here from Naples two weeks ago. They told me of Princess Joanna's illness and her suffering during the voyage. They said they'd been quite shocked when they saw the condition she was in when they arrived at Naples. But they said they'd discussed the matter at length with each other during their journey from Naples to Palermo. They now feel there's every reason to expect that my fiancée will have recovered and will be as pretty and spirited a young girl as the one they first saw in England. Furthermore, just yesterday I received a message from Earl Hamelin, the girl's guardian, telling me that she was quite well, she had attended Epiphany mass in the Naples cathedral, and she was greatly admired. In fact, the townspeople cheered her and called her 'our beautiful English princess.' So, mother, I see no need to take such drastic measures as you suggest and send her home. And if you'll excuse me, I must get ready to go down to the harbor to welcome her and her party."

Queen Margaret, who was used to losing arguments, sighed. "Very well, William, if that's your decision." She hoisted herself from her chair. William stood too and gave her a little bow, then turned his back and walked toward his chamber.

She gathered up her skirts and sailed toward the door, but turned to deliver one last volley. "Don't say I didn't warn you, when your sickly English princess fails to give you an heir." But William had already closed his door and didn't hear.

13

After an easy day of sailing, Joanna and her party were on deck, watching as the harbor of Palermo hove in sight. The fishing boats had already come in and the fleet of galleys had the harbor almost to themselves. They slipped silently over the quiet waters toward a long pier that jutted into the bay. Joanna's galley was in the lead and made for the landward end of the pier. There was no chatter. It was a solemn moment, the end of a long, long journey and the beginning of whatever was to come next.

Joanna was dressed for the occasion in the gown she'd worn to the cathedral in Naples. She smoothed her white satin skirts and looked down with approval at the brightly embroidered band around the hem, with the Plantagenet lions in all their glory. Her pearl circlet was fixed firmly on her head. She felt quite royal.

But the closer they came to the landing the more nervous she became. Until now, the arrival in Palermo and the meeting with William had been a vague event, far off in the distant future. Now it was here. Already they could see a mounted procession wending its way down from the city toward the shore.

When the galley was almost at the pier, the sun set behind the western hills and it suddenly became chilly. Lady Marian sent Mary below to fetch the princess's brown wool cloak, but Joanna objected.

"What's the point of dressing in my finest for King William, if he can't see anything but a dreary old cloak? I won't mind the cold."

"That's all very well, Joanna, but it would not do at all if you fell ill again the minute you got to Palermo. King William wouldn't like that. I'm afraid I must insist."

"Besides," said Lady Charmaine, gazing at the shore from the deck, "it's getting quite dark, and nobody will be able to see what anyone is wearing." She spoke with regret, having put on her crimson brocade for the occasion.

As though to prove her wrong, the approaching procession and the road all the way to the pier were suddenly, dazzlingly, illuminated. King William's well-instructed army of torchbearers had performed admirably.

When the travelers disembarked from the galley they found several horses waiting and grooms standing ready to help them mount. Earl Hamelin, scorning assistance, leaped into his saddle with such vigor than he pitched over on the other side, landing on his feet and looking quite amazed. But hardly anybody noticed—all eyes were on the band of riders that was approaching. Standing there in the dimness and watching as they drew nearer, Joanna could clearly see in the lead a tall young man, resplendent in purple leggings and a purple cape embroidered with gold. The purple-and-gold robe of his magnificent white horse fell almost to the ground. The rider sat gracefully in the saddle. In the light of the torches, his brown hair gleamed and his gold crown glittered. Even from some distance she could see that he was remarkably handsome.

Earl Hamelin, who had managed to get back in his saddle, at once had to get down again when he saw the king dismount. The two men exchanged greetings, then walked to where Joanna stood. William beckoned to a squire who brought up a white palfrey, a smaller twin of the king's horse. It was draped with cloth-of-gold hung with little silver bells that jingled pleasantly.

"Welcome to Sicily, Princess Joanna," William said. "I am so very glad that you have arrived safely." His eyes—a startling, intense blue—looked directly into hers. Seeing him close-up she observed a straight nose, a generous mouth, a square and beardless chin, all perfectly proportioned. She thought he was like one of the Greek gods she had read about, perhaps Apollo. She liked his voice, and the way he looked at her as though he truly was glad to see her. When he took her hand to lead her to her horse, she liked that as well. His hand was warm and clasped hers firmly.

He helped her onto her mount, returned to his own and the procession re-formed to ride up to the city with Joanna at William's side. Later, try as she might, she couldn't remember what she had said in response to his greeting, if anything.

At first she was in a daze. The men stationed all along the way held their flaring torches high. The lights were blinding, but when they flickered and almost went out it was worse. Then the surrounding darkness was terrifying. She wondered what the people who lined the road were shouting about. She couldn't make out a word. She stole a glance at William. He was smiling at his vociferous subjects, waving a hand from time to time. He saw how apprehensive she looked and leaned closer to say, "Don't be alarmed, Princess. They're happy to see you because they've been waiting for you so long."

Then she remembered that Jean-Pierre had told her that when they got to Sicily, she'd be unlikely to hear much French except at court.

"I've been told the inhabitants speak their own brand of Latin," he'd said. "It will be interesting to see how much we understand."

Interesting indeed. Now, listening carefully, she made out "regina"—queen—and then "nova"—new. Were they welcoming their new queen? Whatever it was, they kept cheering lustily, even though she was enveloped in her dark hooded cloak and she supposed it was hard for them to tell what if anything was inside.

She pushed the hood from her face, poked out an arm and waved tentatively. The cheering became louder. She saw that William seemed pleased. That gave her confidence. These people were rejoicing at the sight of her, Princess Joanna. Delighted, she flashed at William the same spontaneous, artless smile that had captivated the ambassadors at Winchester. No longer fearful, she warmed to her new role. She shrugged her way out of the cloak so it fell to her waist. Now, she thought, everybody can see that I did my best to do them honor with my gown. She waved and smiled at the onlookers, now to one side, now the other, as she'd seen her parents do at processions in England. The people shouted even more enthusiastically at the sight of the small figure in gleaming white, sitting so straight in the saddle with her hair flowing to her shoulders. One man, quite close to the procession, startled her with his bellow of "Angelina mia!" William laughed and said, "Did you hear that? He's calling you his little angel." Truly, caught in the torchlight, she did look like a silvery angel riding a milk-white horse.

Earl Hamelin and Lady Marian rode just behind the leaders. The earl was nodding, smiling graciously and waving his arms about as though all this adulation were meant for him as well. Lady Marian, watching Joanna, was so full of pride and joy in her performance that she almost choked and her eyes misted with tears. All the trials they'd been through these past six months had been worth this moment.

Alan, riding behind Marian, moved up to her side, grinned and raised his arm in a salute. "A princess to be proud of, that's our lass, Lady Marian!"

At last they rode into the square in front of the royal palace. The whole expanse was full of light, noise and revelers. Tables had been set up offering a variety of potables and edibles¾ale, wine, roasted fowl, grilled sausages, boiled beets and turnips swimming in vinegar, huge baskets of bread. When the merrymakers saw their king and his princess the hubbub became deafening. The townspeople thumped tankards on tables and stamped their feet, adding their bit to the vocal rejoicing.

I've never seen or heard anything like this in England, thought Joanna, who came from a land where the royal family, though respected and even feared, was not wildly popular. But if this is what Sicilians are like, I must get used to it. And with William, she made a circuit of the square, trying to look like a suitable future queen of this strange nation.

When they approached an enormous palatial structure, where a flight of stone steps led to a beautifully carved tall wooden door, she hoped that this was where the procession would finally halt. She was very, very tired, and found it hard to keep her back straight and her eyes open.

William had noticed. He reined in his horse and she followed suit. "My dear Princess Joanna, I can see that you've won the hearts of our subjects. It's long past time for you to seek your rest, and now we'll leave the people to their amusements and we'll go on to the Palace of Zisa, where your rooms have been prepared for you." She looked dismayed. Why wasn't she to be lodged in the palace before them, so handy and seemingly so capacious? William put a hand on her arm and spoke softly, reassuringly. "I promise you, within ten minutes you'll be there. And you'll be much more comfortable than in this cold old pile, where the noise from the square would disturb your rest."

She was looking longingly at the palace entry when the ornate door opened and she saw two figures standing there. One was a rotund woman with her hands on her ample hips. Joanna couldn't make out what she was wearing because she was silhouetted against the lights inside. But her smaller companion held a candle and its light shone up on the portly woman's face. There Joanna saw an expression of such malevolence that she almost recoiled. The venom seemed to be directed straight at her. She shivered and drew her cloak closer about her as she rode off. She was too tired to try to make sense of the vision.

Within ten minutes, as William had promised, she was dismounting with his help before what seemed, even in the darkness, like a magical palace. She could hear the splashing of fountains. Breezes were singing in the palm fronds. She saw, brightly lit by torchbearers, broad marble steps that led to a pillared portal, door wide open. Eager servants were waiting to help her and her party in. She was barely awake, but felt grateful at the welcome, in contrast to the forbidding palace she had just left.

William bent to kiss her hand. "Now, Princess, this will be your home. I'll come to see you tomorrow, when you've had a chance to recover from what I know has been a trying day. Everybody here wants only to make you happy and see to your comfort. May God watch over you and give you good repose."

She looked up at him, blinking to keep her eyes open. She tried desperately to think of a suitable reply. What would her mother say?

"Thank you, King William, for welcoming me so royally. I shall look forward to seeing you tomorrow."

Lady Marian took Joanna's arm and they started up the steps.

Just before they went through the door, William ran up and stopped them.

"My dear," he said, "you need not call me King William. From now on, to you I am William and to me you are Joanna."

14

The next morning Lady Marian stood at the window of Joanna's chamber in the Zisa palace, not pleased with the view.

"I thought Palermo was supposed to be bathed in perpetual sunshine," she grumbled. Joanna, barely awake and snuggling in her nest of soft goosedown pillows, murmured something and turned over to go back to sleep.

The sky was overcast and the mist shrouded what Lady Marian supposed might be a beautiful park. All she could see were the tips of palm trees and, when the breeze blew holes in the blanket of fog, tantalizing glimpses of brightly-colored, if damp, flower gardens. She sniffed and pulled the draperies closed.

She knew perfectly well why her mood was as dismal as the day. The long stressful journey, during which she had never complained but had tried to keep everybody else as cheerful as she pretended to be, was over. She could relax. She could stop worrying about Joanna's health. She could let her shoulders droop, as they now did, instead of standing straight and moving briskly about, to set a good example to the rest of the party. She could indulge in a little self-pity and even a little bad temper.

And she could, with no trouble at all, find something new to worry about. Lady Marian was an expert worrier, though it wasn't evident from her calm demeanor and generous store of good sense.

First of all there was King William, so far a mystery. Could he possibly be as perfect as he seemed? What did he expect from Joanna? What would the wedding be like? And what then—it was still two or three years before Joanna could fulfill the role of a wife. How would those years be spent? It could be so awkward. She sighed and looked at Joanna, curled up on her side with her cheek pillowed on her hand. She was such a mixture of wisdom beyond her years and innocence. Lady Marian prayed that she herself had the wisdom to help the girl keep the two in harmonious balance.

Meantime, she told herself, there's not much point in agitating myself about all this now because there's nothing I can do about it. We'll know soon enough what King William's plans and nature are. And there are a few immediate problems that need to be dealt with. She must have groaned aloud at the thought of them because Joanna, suddenly wide awake, sat up and asked, "Whatever is the matter, Lady Marian? Are you unwell?"

Lady Marian laughed and went to sit on the bed. "Thank you, I'm quite well.

Good morning, my pet, and I hope you had as good a rest as I did, in this elegant
palace. It's so beautifully quiet, isn't it!"

"Yes, I can't remember when I've slept so soundly. I don't think I would have
heard a trumpet blast. I do believe I heard a nightingale just before I went to sleep,
then nothing more until you let out that awful moan."

"I'm sorry. I was just feeling frustrated at the messy situations your ladies-in-
waiting seem to have gotten themselves into." She was sure that Joanna, who didn't
miss much, knew what she was talking about.

Before she could go on there was a knock on the door. Two girls in black
dresses, stiff white aprons and white caps, who must have been waiting until they
heard signs of awakening, came in. One of them had a mop of red hair cascading
out below her cap. Both were intent on keeping their heavy silver trays level.

"Mary!" Joanna and Lady Marian exclaimed. Mary giggled when she saw their
surprise.

"Good morning! Yes, it's me. And this is my new friend Marina. She's teaching me how to be a lady's maid in a Sicilian palace." She turned to Joanna, "I hope
you had a good rest, and are feeling better? I have a little room just down the hall
so I'll be ready when you wish to get dressed. I know you'll like your breakfast—I
had some in the kitchen."

Marina looked disapproving at this familiarity and shushed her. The girls bore
their trays to a table near the windows where they set everything out. When all
was arranged to Marina's satisfaction, she bobbed her head and said, "If you should
need anything more, my ladies, please come to the door and ask. We will be waiting just outside."

Joanna jumped out of bed, wrapped herself in her robe and ran to the table.
She was suddenly ravenously hungry. She couldn't remember when she'd last
eaten—yesterday afternoon, while they were still on the galley?

When they saw what was awaiting them, both were silent a moment, taking it
in. One bowl was heaped with segmented oranges and bunches of plump grapes,
some purple and some a pale misty gold. In another bowl were sliced apples in a
nectar redolent of honey, lemon and spices. There was a long beribboned basket of
slices of bread, far whiter and finer in texture than they were used to, warm from
the oven, and little round rolls, glazed with honey, powdered with cinnamon. A
strange fat pot with a long spout and a Persian-looking pattern was steaming,
sending out an odor of lemon, ginger and something unidentifiable. Fine porcelain
cups stood by its side as well as several white linen napkins, neatly folded.

Nothing was heard for some time except the occasional "Heavenly!" or "Have
you tried these candied cherries?"

"Why can't our English bake like this?" Lady Marian wondered. "Have you
ever had bread with such a tender crust? One could break a tooth on our English
loaves."

"Mmmm," said Joanna with her mouth full. "I remember that when we stayed
at Fontevraud Abbey they did almost this well, but that was because my mother

kept after them so."

When to her regret she could eat no more, Lady Marian put down her plate and looked appreciatively around the room. It was so welcoming and easeful, with cushions, carpets and —best of all ¾warmth. Instead of a blazing conflagration in a fireplace that put on a great show but did little to warm you if you happened to be on the other side of the room, here were braziers. A half-dozen, some standing on the floor and some suspended from hooks set into the walls, all gracefully con-structed of wrought iron, were artfully placed so that no matter where you stood or sat, you were never far from the comforting glow of the incandescent coals.

Her reverie was interrupted.

"What are the messy situations you spoke of?"

"Oh yes, I did mention that." She paused to brush the crumbs off her lap and to gather her thoughts. She frowned in concentration. Joanna had seldom seen her so serious.

"You, my dear young friend, will soon be a wife and a queen and that will mean new responsibilities. One of them is to deal with 'messy situations,' especially when they concern people who serve you. Now, you can't be unaware that Lady Beatrice shows signs of approaching motherhood."

"Well, I guessed that must be it. Although she kept to herself most of the time since we left Naples, and wrapped herself up in those big floppy cloaks when she did join the rest of us, it's gotten pretty obvious, hasn't it? Poor Lady Beatrice! Back when we were just starting the voyage I thought maybe we could be friends. But now when I try to talk to her she just looks at me without any expression and turns away."

"Yes, I've tried too, same thing." She was silent a moment, looking at Joanna as though hesitating to say more. Joanna laughed.

"I know exactly what you're thinking. You're wondering if I know where babies come from. Well, I do. My mother explained it all to me. She said I had to know certain things before I married. I do think God could have thought of a way to put new people in the world that wasn't so complicated or so hard on the poor women. Anyway, I'm sure I know where Lady Beatrice's baby came from. It was my brother Richard. And I think it was very thoughtless of him."

"And so do I!" Lady Marian snapped out the words and she pressed her lips together as though afraid that other imprecations might escape her. It might not be politic to be overly critical of one Plantagenet to another, no matter how much Joanna disapproved of her brother's conduct. She continued.

"But what's done is done, and we can't alter it now. What we can do, my dear, and this is up to you, is send a message to Richard and tell him the situation. If he's the man of honor we know him to be, he'll admit he's the father, and see to Beatrice's health and comfort and accept responsibility for the child."

"Do you think he'll marry Beatrice?"

"Hardly. Richard's nowhere near ready to settle down with a wife. And anyway, your parents would never permit it. They'll find somebody of much loftier birth when the time comes."

Joanna picked up a cherry and chewed it slowly. "Do you think, then, that I should be the one to write to Richard?"

"I do, and so does Brother Jean-Pierre. It would be your first act as a representative of your royal family. What you say will have far more weight with Richard than what any of us could say. We will, of course, send word to your father and mother. I'm sure they'd agree that Richard should be informed. But it takes much longer to get a message to England than to Aquitaine."

"Then I'll write at once. Or at least as soon as we can find pen and ink and parchment."

Lady Marian said she'd see to that. Neither spoke for a few minutes.

"You said messy *situations*, Lady Marian. Is there another?"

"Oh well yes, not quite so serious. It concerns Lady Adelaide, who I fear isn't setting the example she should. In fact, she has been most indiscreet."

Joanna looked mystified.

"But the real culprit is your uncle. The earl seems to have led her on, letting her believe he had honorable intentions, without bothering to tell her he was married."

"But I thought everybody knew about my Aunt Isabel. My goodness, they've been married as long as I can remember."

"Well, apparently Lady Adelaide hasn't heard that news. And I fear she's somewhat gullible and naïve. She's convinced that the earl means to marry her and she may have let him take liberties. At least that's what Lady Charmaine tells me."

"I hope you aren't going to ask me to talk to Lady Adelaide! Or to my uncle. I wouldn't know what to say."

"No, but Jean-Pierre and I think it best if he goes back to England."

"Yes, it would be awkward for him to stay here. I do think he should go back to Aunt Isabel. But on the other hand…" She stopped and her brow wrinkled in thought. She didn't like to think of the earl's humiliation at being sent home in disgrace. She was fond of him in spite of his peculiarities.

"Couldn't King William let it be known that he's sending Earl Hamelin on a delicate mission, though of course we wouldn't say in public what it was, but it would be to tell Richard about Lady Beatrice? And William could ask him to go on to England to report to my parents on my safe arrival and so forth."

Lady Marian smiled, slowly at first then in growing admiration. "What a good idea! For the king to appoint him as his personal messenger on an important matter would let the earl save face. My dear little schemer, you have the making of a diplomat."

Joanna flushed. "Thank you."

"Of course there are a lot of ifs. The king's cooperation, for one. But I'm sure if Brother Jean-Pierre tells him what the situation is, he'll see the wisdom of the plan." She sighed in relief and sat back in her chair. Post-breakfast torpor was setting in. Joanna looked speculatively at the bed. Lady Marian glanced toward the window.

"I do believe the mist is lifting!" Sure enough, tendrils of golden light were feeling their way through a gap in the curtains. Lady Marian hurried over to pull them open. "Oh my dear, come and see!"

Blinking at the blaze of sunlight, Joanna joined her.

Looking out, she blinked again, hardly able to believe that what she saw was real. It was a fairytale garden. Just below their window a lake shimmered in the glancing sunlight. Golden fish flashed about like shooting stars. Near its shore, a dot of a grassy island held a single cypress and a stone bench. Nothing more. A bridge arched from the edge of the lake to the island. Beyond the lake was the garden where, as far as she could see, tall, slender cypresses stood sentry along broad paths that wound through patches of lush green grass and beds of vividly hued flowers. She'd never seen such flowers—flame-colored, ruby-red, canary-yellow, magenta, purple. As she watched, a brilliant blue bird flew down from the cypress on the island to hop about on the grass. The sun, having vanquished every shred of fog, bathed the whole exotic scene in brilliant light.

"Where is Mary?" Joanna cried. "I must get dressed, we must go out!"

William and two of his courtiers arrived at the palace of La Zisa an hour later. Before entering the gardens the three men stood, unobserved, surveying the scene from the shelter of a clump of palms. They saw a covey of ladies decorating the prospect. Besides Joanna there were Lady Marian and all three ladies in waiting.

"I've never seen so many pretty women in this garden," said Count Florian of Caperota, William's justiciar.

"Or so hideously garbed," said Matthew of Ajello, William's chancellor. Having survived two decades of intrigues and plots under William's father and then his mother, in this new and calmer reign Matthew had settled into the role of elder statesman-curmudgeon. William valued him because he never hesitated to say what he thought.

"I beg to differ, Matthew." Florian shook his head vigorously and his few gray locks bounced about on his balding pate. "It's true, all too true, that Queen Margaret's ladies seemed to favor gowns of more subdued tones. I for one find all these bright colors quite refreshing. Rather like a rainbow come to earth." He stopped there. But all three were probably thinking the same thing. To the amusement of the entire court, Queen Margaret had favored ladies around her who were as old as she or older and who were willing to dress in dull grays and browns, the better to show off her own brilliant plumage.

Today, Joanna's ladies had changed all that. At last they'd been able to take out of their chests the fine gowns they'd brought all the way from England and to come out to enjoy the sunshine.

Lady Marian and Beatrice, who were walking down one of the cypress-bordered allées, were a particularly pleasing duo, with Lady Marian in a rosy-red gown with a gray silk tunic, and Beatrice—who had been persuaded to forsake her all-encompassing dark cloak—in a rather shapeless but colorful wrap of gauzy purple silk. Lady Marian was talking earnestly and Beatrice was listening just as earnestly. Lady Marian had told Joanna that she thought the sooner they told Beatrice about their plan to inform Richard of his impending fatherhood, the better.

Charmaine, in the crimson brocade that she'd worn when they arrived the night before, and Adelaide, decked out in cornflower blue that seemed to reflect the smiling sky, made their twittering way along another walk where almond trees were in flower, each tree like a little cloud of palest pink. Whenever the ladies came to a bed of brilliant, unfamiliar flowers, they would lean over, cup a blossom in their hands, and inhale deeply. Few of the blossoms smelled as lovely as they looked, but the quest continued.

Joanna was the least colorful of them all. In her haste to get down to the garden she'd thrown on a shapeless deep-blue garment that Lady Marian had thought she'd managed to dispose of long ago. From his vantage point William saw that his betrothed was kneeling under the cypress on the little island but he couldn't make out why. He thought, though, that she made a very pretty picture, with her blue skirts flowing like petals spread on the brilliant green grass.

Joanna was captivated by the showy bird she'd seen from her window. She was trying to entice it down from its perch. It was hopping back and forth on one of the lower branches, and she could see now that its jaunty tail and cockaded head were a deep iridescent blue, while its breast was a delicate pale turquoise. She beckoned and cajoled and held out her hand. But she had nothing to offer and the bird wisely kept its distance, squawking periodically with no sense of musicianship.

"I've never seen anything so gorgeous, not in England or in France, have you, Lady Marian?" She looked up but Lady Marian was just disappearing around a corner, out of earshot.

"Oh well, bird, then I'll talk to you." And she pretended she too was a bird and tried to mimic its harsh cry. But the bird knew better.

Out of the corner of her eye she saw someone walking swiftly along the shady path from the palace. It was King William. Before she had time to rise he'd crossed the bridge and was at her side, holding out a hand to help her. On her feet, she was acutely embarrassed at having been found in such an undignified position. She brushed the dew from her skirts, wishing she looked more presentable.

William didn't seem to find anything amiss. He smiled at her.

"Good morning, Joanna. I see you're getting acquainted with some of the local inhabitants. I'm told that bird comes here all the way from Africa to spend the winter, and will go back again before long. So don't take its rejection to heart. All we true Sicilians are very glad to welcome you."

How kind he is, thought Joanna. Last night by fitful torchlight she'd thought him impossibly handsome, like an unknowable mythic god. But today she sensed genuine warmth in his voice and in the steady gaze of his eyes. Today he seemed human. He talked to her as an equal, not as a child. Yet there was something exotic about him. Perhaps it was his voice. He spoke with an almost musical intonation, nothing like the more rapid speech she was used to. She hoped he would go on talking, and he did.

"Joanna, I see your ladies are exploring the park. Would you like me to give you a tour? While the sun shines and there's no wind, it can be quite pleasant, even in winter."

"I'd love to see more of it. I meant to go with Charmaine and Adelaide, but this silly creature has kept me here." She made a face at the bird, which had stopped squawking but was still hopping about in the tree, turning its head this way and that to keep an eye on the trespassers on its island.

"Good! Let's be off." He took her arm and guided her onto the bridge. "And if it won't bore you, I'll tell you a little about this palace and park of Zisa, and why we are so proud of them."

She smiled up at him. "I know it won't bore me. I want to know all about them. We had gardens at Fontevraud that I thought were beautiful, but in the winter everything died down and it was just dry little sticks in the bare ground."

They set off along a path paved with multicolored tiles toward a grove of laurel and pines. Every so often she caught a whiff of something sweet but unidentifiable from the flowering bushes along the way.

"Fontevraud, eh?" said William. "That's the big abbey in France, isn't it? How do you happen to know it so well?"

"I spent a lot of time there with my mother when I was younger. So did Richard. My mother had a whole building there, just for herself and her family. But my father was hardly ever there."

"And why not? Too busy with other affairs, I dare say. From what I know of your father, he'd far rather be leading his troops into battle than cooling his heels in an abbey."

"And which would you rather do?" She was surprised to hear herself asking such a personal question. But the way he spoke to her invited frankness and familiarity.

"Oh, I'm no warrior. Thanks be to God, we've had no reason to fight anyone since I became king. And as for abbeys, I'm not ready to retire to contemplation and seclusion. But I thoroughly approve of abbeys. In fact, I'm already well along in building one not far from Palermo, at Monreale. I look forward to showing it to you. Perhaps you can give me some suggestions, what with your familiarity with Fontevraud."

She looked up, wondering if he was joking. No, he seemed perfectly serious.

They were now in the grove of trees. The sun couldn't penetrate their gloomy canopy. William, who was still holding her arm, felt her shiver.

"It does get cool when we leave the sunshine. Here, take my cloak." He took off his short ermine-lined cape and arranged it around her shoulders. She buried her nose in the soft fur and said, "Oh, that feels good. Thank you."

"And now I'll begin my lecture." As they walked on he told her how his father, William I, had admired the taste for ease and beauty of the Arabs who had ruled Sicily for centuries before the Normans took it over; how he'd built La Zisa in the Arabic style as his retreat from wars and politics, and how he'd died before quite finishing it.

"So it fell to me to complete the palace. My father had begun these gardens too, but I've enlarged them and added a few ponds and walks."

"It's lovely, in fact it's magnificent. And I haven't even begun to see the inside of the palace."

"You've hit on the right word, Joanna. La Zisa means "The Magnificent" in

Arabic. I'll look forward to showing you around inside, and taking you to some of our other palaces. Thanks to those luxury-loving Arabs we have a good supply."

She'd been so interested in what William was telling her that she hadn't noticed that their path had made a loop through the park. Now here they were back at the lake.

Lady Marian and Beatrice sat on the bench on the island. Beatrice's head was bowed and her shoulders quivered as though in an effort to control her sobs. Lady Marian sat upright with the pinched look she wore when she was trying to hold in her displeasure.

Charmaine and Adelaide were approaching along the path, chatting with two men Joanna didn't know—or did she? Yes, as they drew near she saw that one of them was Count Florian, the ambassador and William's justiciar. The other man was older than Florian, very tall, with a long face deeply lined with furrows, the face of a man disillusioned with the world.

William led Joanna to the group. He introduced the tall, dour man as Matthew of Ajello, his chancellor. Matthew gave her a thorough inspection from head to foot and then back again, finally acknowledging her with a nod and a growl. She doubted if she was going to like Matthew of Ajello. But she was glad to see Count Florian again, almost an old friend by now. The count bowed most properly and told her how pleased he was to see that she had recovered from the trials of the journey.

Charmaine cooed, "Oh, Count, it is your heavenly Sicily that has restored all of us. How fortunate we are to be surrounded with so much warmth and beauty!"

"And to have been served such a delicious breakfast!" said Adelaide. "I have never tasted anything like those sweet little cherries."

"But that was some time ago," said William. "I'm sure we're all more than ready for dinner. Shall we go inside and see what the cooks have to offer us? I asked that dinner be served at three, and it's past that now."

William and Joanna led the way and the others followed, with Lady Marian and Beatrice, who had regained her composure, bringing up the rear. When they reached the marble steps of the palace, William paused and pointed up toward a carved inscription that ran around the graceful entrance arch. "There, Joanna, you see my latest addition to the palace, so that all the world will know how dearly I love it."

"But what does it say? I can't read Arabic."

"True. We may need to remedy that. Roughly, it says this is the loveliest possession of the kingdom, the beautiful dwelling-place of the king, a house of joy and splendor, an earthly paradise. Its king is the Magnificent One and his palace is the Zisa—the Magnificent."

The rest of the party were clumped below them on the steps, listening. The scene reminded Joanna of their visit to the church in Saint-Gilles, when the pilgrims listened with rapt attention to Earl Hamelin as he explained the carvings. But Joanna was sure William had a better command of his facts than the earl. He was about to move on when Lady Adelaide spoke up.

"It is indeed magnificent. But can you please tell us, King William, if the king referred to in the inscription is your father, or yourself? He began the palace and you finished it, so which of you is being honored?"

William turned and looked at her like a pedagogue instructing one of his more trying students.

"Indeed, I can tell you. The inscription refers to any king who may occupy this palace: my father, myself, or my son who will come after me."

Joanna smiled inwardly. It had been a rather presumptuous question and deserved the crisp response.

Then it came to her: It was going to be up to her to produce that son.

Life was getting more serious.

16

There was no time to change before dinner. King William, who put a high premium on punctuality, herded his little group into the entrance hall. There they found a few of his courtiers and the rest of their English party gathered. The king conferred with his steward about seating arrangements. Lady Marian, distressed at Joanna's overly casual dress, was relieved when she caught sight of Mary. "Hurry, Mary. Run up and get the princess's blue velvet cape, the one with the silver clasp at the neck." Mary ran so fast that by the time William was finished with his consultation, the cape was securely in place on Joanna's shoulders. "There, at least you'll look presentable from the waist up," whispered Lady Marian.

When, escorted by William, Joanna entered the palace's dining hall she stopped in her tracks and stared. This was like no great hall she'd ever seen. For one thing, it wasn't great—only about a third the size of the one in Winchester. Nor was it, like Winchester's, walled and floored in cold gray stone and unadorned except for a few tapestries hanging on the walls to give an illusion of softening. From the vaulted ceiling to the marble floor, the whole room glowed in warm tones of ochre and tawny ivory. A half-dozen arched recesses around the perimeter had intricately worked ceilings that looked like waterfalls carved in stone. She wondered if it was her imagination that brought the sound of cascading water. Then she saw a fountain that gushed out of the far wall to flow, rippling and burbling, down a marble channel halfway across the room, then disappear into some subterranean chamber.

William watched as she took in these marvels. "Do you like it, Joanna?"

She looked up at him, her eyes wide with wonder. "I do, I do. It's beautiful. Oh, William, are those peacocks?" She pointed at the frieze of vividly colored mosaics that ran all around the room just above eye level.

"Yes, you have a sharp eye. I'm glad you approve of our Fountain Room. Now let's get settled and I'll tell you all about it. And we'll see whether our meal pleases you as well."

They sat down at a long table, covered with deep purple cloths fringed with gold. Gleaming brass and silver bowls and plates awaited the guests. On the other side of the purling stream was an identical table.

Joanna found herself between the chancellor and William. She managed a smile and "I'm happy to see you again, Sir Matthew." Once more, the curt mumbled response. She resolved she would pay him no more attention. Leaning forward, she saw that the seat to William's right was vacant. To her left, beyond Sir Matthew, was Lady Marian, deep in conversation with Brother Jean-Pierre. She wished she'd had a chance to ask Lady Marian about her talk with Beatrice. Across from her at the opposite table were Earl Hamelin and Adelaide. Next were Charmaine and Count Florian. She didn't see Beatrice. Down at the far end were Alan and two English knights.

Food began to arrive. William, attentive, urged her to try the unfamiliar dishes. First came a heap of tiny fried fish. She looked around. Apparently it was acceptable to pick up one at a time and eat it whole. They were crisp and delicious. But she looked suspiciously at the next plate that was set before her.

"You will see, Joanna, that we eat a great deal of seafood here. We are so close to the supply. Are you not fond of fish?"

"Yes, I am, but even though it's covered with sauce, I can see that this…this *thing* seems to have a great many legs for a fish."

"Aha, you're right. Eight, in fact. That's a young octopus, strictly speaking not a fish. They flourish in our Mediterranean. When caught while little, and not cooked too long, they're one of our delicacies. And would you believe, they say the full-grown ones can be bigger than a man? But I suppose those would be rather tough."

Joanna was so divided between pity for the strange baby creature before her and horror that it might have grown up to have eight huge legs and be as big as a man that she couldn't bring herself to take a single bite.

Perhaps to take her mind off her discomfiture, William told her how this room was his father's pride, how he had determined to permit no hint of Norman influence. "He wanted it to be the highest expression of Islamic design. But personally, I think he may have gone a bit too far in decorating nearly every inch."

He was interrupted by a flurry of activity at the door. In came a plump lady in what resembled a glittering golden tent that enveloped her from double chin to tiny gold-slippered feet. Her mouth was puckered like a discontented prune. She was complaining loudly that her maid had failed to appear and she'd had to dress herself, which accounted for her coming to dinner a half-hour late.

She sank into the vacant chair at William's right and exhaled a long, self-pitying sigh. William rose.

"Madame, I wish to present to you Princess Joanna. Joanna, this is my mother, Queen Margaret."

Joanna stood too and tried not to stare.

This was, beyond doubt, the baleful woman she'd glimpsed in the royal palace doorway last night. She didn't look any more friendly now than she had then. But Joanna managed a polite acknowledgment.

"I'm happy to make your acquaintance, Queen Margaret. I've heard so much about you."

"I shouldn't wonder. And I have heard a great deal about you, too." She turned away and Joanna heard her mutter, "And not much of it good."

Dinner resumed. Servers hurried to bring provender to Queen Margaret, who fell to as though famished. In honor of the English guests there were courses of roast beef, onion stew and a prune pudding. It seemed to Joanna that the meal went on for hours.

She was surveying the pudding, wondering if she had room for a very small spoonful, when she was startled to hear from her left the gravelly voice of Sir Matthew, hitherto utterly silent.

"So you and William are to be married."

"Yes, of course. That's why I'm here."

"And before too long."

"Yes, it's very soon. The date was set before we left England. Nobody knew then that the voyage would take so long."

"I expect King William hasn't had time to discuss the wedding with you."

His nosiness annoyed her. She couldn't see what business this was of his. She looked around, wondering if anyone was listening to them. But Queen Margaret had William's attention, and the other guests were occupied with eating, chattering or listening (especially Lady Charmaine, with rapt face and upturned eyes) to the harpist who was plucking a subdued accompaniment to the gurgling of the fountain.

Sir Matthew leaned closer and almost whispered. She could see the malice in his eyes. "I'm sure he will soon. And when he does, you might want to ask him about a certain Arabian princess. You aren't his first choice for a partner for the royal bed, you know."

She wished desperately to close this conversation. How would her mother respond? Whatever she said, she would accompany it with a brilliant, disarming smile. Joanna knew she couldn't manage that. She spoke as coolly as she could.

"Thank you, Sir Matthew. You're very kind to share this information with me."

He produced an almost imperceptible smile in response—a slight curving at the corners of his lips. But there was no gleam of warmth or humor in his faded blue eyes. He turned away.

She tried to regain her composure, staring again at the pudding. She pushed the dish aside. When William urged her to try some of the almond pastries that arrived next, she regretfully refused.

"I'm afraid I can't manage another bite. I had a *very* large breakfast."

"And I'm sure you're tired. I shouldn't have forced you to walk so far today."

"Oh, I didn't mind. It was wonderful to be able to walk about freely and not be shut up on a little boat. But I think I'd like to go up to my beautiful room and rest." He helped her to her feet.

"Very well. And tomorrow I'll give you a tour of my royal palace."

She wasn't too tired to remember her manners.

"I shall hope to see you again soon, Queen Margaret." The queen, jaws working methodically, looked up, nodded, and resumed her assault on a thick slice of beef.

Matthew of Ajello didn't look up.

William escorted Joanna down the table to where Lady Marian, who had been watching, stood ready. They were hardly out the door when Queen Margaret gave a little snort and said to William, not caring who heard her, "Just as I expected. Scrawny, puny, bag of bones. A poor sort of wife for you."

"Maybe we can persuade her to follow your example at table, mother. That should fatten her up in a hurry."

On the way up to their rooms Lady Marian told Joanna all about her talk with Beatrice in the park.

"I know you've been wondering."

"Yes, I have. What could have made her cry so?"

"That girl! That ninny!" Lady Marian sputtered a bit before she could go on, explaining how she'd assured Beatrice that everybody sympathized with her and wanted to help; how she'd told her they planned to inform Richard of her condition and that there was no doubt that he'd see that she and the baby were well cared for.

"But would she listen? No! She started to cry and to moan and to insist that Richard shouldn't be told. Said it was as much her fault as his. Said she didn't want him to think she blamed him. I do believe the little silly is still in love with him, but too proud to beg for help. Oh dear oh dear, what's to be done?"

"What does Brother Jean-Pierre think?"

"He thinks we should send word to Richard anyway."

"So do I. Don't you?"

"I suppose so. It's just that she begged me so hard and tried to make me promise not to tell him."

"She doesn't need to know."

"No, that's true. And she'll be glad enough to have some help after the child arrives, I warrant. She won't be in an easy situation, mother of a royal bastard."

Once in their room—softly lit, cozily warm—they found Mary waiting. While the girl helped Joanna change, Lady Marian paced about nervously.

"I think I'd better go back down to the hall and find Brother Jean-Pierre and ask him to try to arrange a meeting, tomorrow if possible, with King William. The sooner we can get his cooperation and send Earl Hamelin on his way, the better." She turned toward the door.

Joanna was pulling on her long, warm robe. When her head emerged she said, "Wait a minute before you go. I have something to ask you. What do you know about Matthew of Ajello?"

"Very little, except that he's been associated with the royal family for ages. I believe he was an adviser to Queen Margaret during her regency. Why?"

"He talked to me very strangely during dinner, and I think he tried to make me jealous of some Arabian princess in William's past."

Lady Marian thought a minute.

"I shouldn't pay too much attention. I expect when King William gets a chance he'll tell you all about himself."

"Maybe. But he seems to be more interested in educating me about Arab architecture and Sicilian seafood than in talking about our marriage. He might tomorrow though. He's promised to show me the royal palace."

Lady Marian smiled tiredly and started toward the door again.

"I must hurry, or they'll all have scattered."

On her way downstairs she said to herself, "I wonder whatever made me think that once we got to Sicily we could relax and enjoy our leisure."

17

Joanna wasn't present at the conference with the king about Earl Hamelin's fate, or at the meeting when the earl was informed of his mission to Richard and to England. But Lady Marian and Brother Jean-Pierre had promised her a complete report.

The three of them met in the sitting room that connected Joanna's chamber with Lady Marian's. The weather had worsened and it was far too cold to go into the gardens. For a few minutes nobody said anything as they luxuriated in the room's warmth and elegance. It was like an exquisite jewel box, ablaze with color. Joanna surveyed the big pillows—purple, gold, emerald, lilac—that were scattered about on the indigo-blue Persian carpet like exotic waterlilies floating on the sea. She chose to sit on a purple one, decorously spreading her skirts over her crossed legs. Lady Marian sank onto the crimson cushioning of the broad, high-backed bench that ran along one wall. She leaned back and wriggled her shoulders a little, as though settling into a nest.

Brother Jean-Pierre, beside her, was doing his best to sit up straight and not yield to the seduction of the velvety softness. In his black cassock, he was a sobering contrast to the splendors around him but not indifferent to them. He pointed to the tall panels that were set into the ochre walls at intervals.

"King William told me that his father engaged the finest Arabic artists of the kingdom to carve screens for this palace." Joanna jumped up and went to examine their delicate tracery, painted in subdued hues of green and rose.

"Do you think they're meant to be vines and flowers? It's hard to tell."

"I expect that was deliberate. The Arabs aren't supposed to depict any living thing in their art, so they'd have meant these to look purely decorative. But you're right, Princess. I'm sure they introduced some recognizable plants here, subtly of course. The farther they were from Mecca the more liberties they could take."

"In that case," said Lady Marian, "I'm glad Sicily is such a long way from Mecca." She helped herself to a date from a silver filigree bowl. "One could almost imagine oneself in a seraglio."

"What's a seraglio?" asked Joanna.

Brother Jean-Pierre thought it best to change the subject. "It's a sort of pleasure palace for a sultan. But we're here to discuss your uncle and his affairs. I must say, King William is a sensible man. He took in the situation at once. When we told him about Lady Beatrice's condition, and also about Earl Hamelin's behavior, he didn't seem shocked or ready to blame anyone."

"In fact," interjected Lady Marian, "he said something like 'Ah yes, these things happen.' Then he agreed that Richard should be informed and also that the earl should be sent home."

"And then we told him that it was your idea, Princess, to send a message to Richard by Earl Hamelin. 'Is that so?' he said. 'Hmm,' he said, and twiddled his thumbs a bit. 'Well, if she can come up with clever solutions like that, perhaps we should include the princess in future deliberations.'"

"At which," said Lady Marian, "Matthew of Ajello, who was at the king's side, raised his bushy big brows and cleared his throat rather noisily, but he didn't say anything."

"I don't think Sir Matthew likes me," said Joanna.

"Never mind, it's the king's opinion that counts," said Brother Jean-Pierre. "And he now has a high regard for your good sense, that's plain."

"So, to continue," said Lady Marian, "we met again the next day with Earl Hamelin and the king informed him of what we'd decided. He also told the earl very firmly that he before he left he was to apologize to Lady Adelaide and confess that he had a wife in England."

"Was my uncle upset about that?"

"I thought he took it pretty well, all things considered," said Lady Marian. "Of course, he was flattered to be told he was entrusted with a very important and confidential message for Richard. But I would have liked to see him a little more contrite about toying with Lady Adelaide's affections."

"Does Lady Adelaide know about all this? I saw her yesterday evening in the hall and she seemed to be in good spirits."

"She probably didn't know then, but she must by now, because the earl is to leave in a day or two, as soon as a fleet of galleys is ready to sail."

"So soon!" Joanna said. "But I must see my uncle before he goes. Lady Marian, could you please ask Alan to saddle a horse so I can ride over to the royal palace this afternoon? And send word to the earl that I'm coming."

"Wouldn't you like me to come with you, my dear? Or Lady Charmaine?" With Lady Beatrice obdurately remaining in total seclusion, and Lady Adelaide presumably in a state of grief or at least mortification, Lady Charmaine was the only available lady in waiting. But she was not a favorite with Joanna.

"I'll be perfectly all right, Lady Marian. Alan can get me to the palace and back safely and my uncle will see to me while I'm there."

"Very well, but we must protect you from this unpleasant weather." She had Mary bring out boots, a wool vest to wear over her gown, a voluminous cloak and a fur hat. When Lady Marian was satisfied, surveying her well-wrapped charge, Mary put a hand over her mouth to suppress a giggle and said, "She looks like the stump of a smallish tree with a patch of brown moss on top!" Lady Marian frowned, but not very severely.

Joanna was happy to see Alan waiting with the same white horse she'd ridden her first night in Palermo, still fitted with tinkling bells. It reminded her of the galloping white horses they'd seen on the shore as they sailed along the coast of southern France. This one wasn't wild and free, but she seemed to have their same brave spirit.

"Is she going to be my own horse from now on, Alan?"

"I'm sure she is, Princess. Nobody else rides her, and she's kept in a special stall in the same stable as the king's favorite horses."

"Then I shall give her a name. What do you think of Belle Blanche?"

Alan furrowed his brow and pursed his lips, giving the question due consideration. "Very nice. She's beautiful, and she's certainly white. But remember she's a Sicilian horse. Maybe she wouldn't answer to a French name."

Joanna was about to argue, but saw his barely repressed grin. She laughed. Still, he had a point. As they set off she considered names, but before long she was too busy trying to keep from being blown out of the saddle by a fierce cold wind that had sprung up. By the time they reached the palace, she was blessing Lady Marian for wrapping her up so thoroughly.

Once inside the spacious entry hall, they found servants lounging about and gossiping. Those who paid any attention to the visitors looked with curiosity at this strange little mystery and her tall, sword-carrying bodyguard. But when Alan boomed out, "Some attention here to Princess Joanna, if you please!" they sprang into action. A man who appeared to be the house steward, elegantly clad in a purple tunic, ordered a maid to help Joanna remove a few layers. A page was sent running to inform Earl Hamelin of their arrival. Another guided them up a soaring staircase and down a long corridor with a high vaulted ceiling to the earl's chamber. Here Alan, satisfied that he'd done his duty by the princess for the time being, told her he'd wait for her below in the hall.

When Joanna entered her uncle's room she found it in an incredible state of disarray. Garments, boots, bulging sacks, robes, a sword or two were strewn about on the bed, on the floor, in overflowing chests. Amid it all stood the distraught earl, giving orders to his valet and then countermanding them.

"Oh, Joanna, I'm glad to see you. I apologize for the disorder, but I must have all my effects ready to be taken down to the port by tomorrow morning, and…no, no, Peter! The tunics go in the black chest, not that one. But you're packing them in far too tightly, they'll get all wrinkled. Maybe you'd better take them out and put them in the chest over in the corner, it looks bigger.

"So you see, Joanna, we're rather at sixes and sevens here. Was there something in particular you wanted to see me about? Did you come to say goodbye? Very kind of you." He snatched up a white linen shirt from a pile of clothes that Peter had just stacked neatly on the bed, mopped his long worried face and threw the shirt on the floor.

"Yes, there was something. Why don't you let Peter get on with it, and we'll go out and find a quiet spot? You need a rest from all this." She took his hand. At first he resisted, looking doubtfully at Peter, then to her relief agreed.

"Very well, perhaps I do need to let it go for a bit. Now Peter, remember what I told you about what goes where, and don't let them take anything away until I have a chance to make sure everything's as I want it."

Peter nodded but didn't say anything. He intended to get the boxes and chests filled and fastened and out the door before the earl came back.

Back the long corridor they walked, to where it gave onto a sunlight-filled gallery overlooking a courtyard on the lower level. Similar galleries, with tall rounded arches supported by slender columns, ran around the upper levels as well. Joanna walked over to the railing, looked up to see the blue Sicilian sky, looked down to the courtyard, an inviting space paved with colorful mosaics and dotted with palms in huge blue pots. She promised herself that she would explore it later.

The earl sat down on a bench and stretched out his long legs. "This will do, Joanna. I must say it feels good to rest for a bit."

She sat beside him.

"First, uncle, I know King William is sending you with a message for Richard and I'm glad he trusted you with something so important. But besides whatever he told you to say, I want you to tell Richard, from me, that it's his duty to take care of Lady Beatrice and the child. He ought to be glad he can help them. Richard's really a good person but sometimes he's sort of irresponsible. He's probably forgotten all about Lady Beatrice. Make him see how important this is. And tell him I want him to send word to me, soon, about what he's going to do for them. He mustn't put it off." How she wished she could talk to Richard herself. She only hoped Earl Hamelin would pass on her sense of urgency.

"I'll tell him just what you said, Joanna. And I'll remind him there are political reasons for doing his duty as well. He should remember that Beatrice is high-born and her family could make a lot of trouble for the kingdom if they think their daughter has been tossed aside like Richard's worn-out plaything."

Joanna looked at him admiringly. "I hadn't thought of that, uncle. How clever of you."

The earl struggled with his conscience, then admitted, "Actually that was King William's idea. He told me to remind Richard that he might be king some day and he can't afford to make enemies." After a moment's hesitation, he went on.

"May I ask you to do something for me, Joanna? Will you be as kind as you can to Lady Adelaide? She's rather unhappy, because as you know…I suppose you know…I may have led her to believe…"

Joanna rescued him from his embarrassment.

"Of course I will, uncle. And so will Lady Marian. I'll get Lady Adelaide to go walking with me, and my goodness, with the wedding coming up so soon, there'll be plenty to keep her busy."

"You're a good girl, Joanna." The earl rose and patted her on the head. "And when I get to England, I'll be able to tell your parents that you're doing very well indeed here. They'll be pleased to know how you're adjusting and acting like a proper princess."

She looked up at him gratefully, "Thank you, uncle. I'm not always sure whether I'm behaving the way my mother would like. But I think of her all the time. Will you tell her that, and tell her how much I wish she could come visit me?"

On the way back to the earl's room, both silent and thinking their own thoughts, they passed a substantial wood door with an elaborate golden lion medallion.

"Isn't that lion like the one on the coat of arms of the Sicilian kings?" Joanna asked.

"Indeed it is. That's the door to the king's private study and reception room. Would you like to see it? He's gone off to inspect his new abbey at Monreale, I understand, so he won't be back for hours. I'm sure he wouldn't mind."

He opened the door a crack, poked his head inside to make sure the room was empty, then opened the door wider, gesturing to her to follow him. She was surprised. This room wasn't like any of the other palatial chambers she'd seen. No delicately carved screens, no arabesques or curlicues, no color except dark red tiles on the floor and dark wooden furnishings. These too were restrained: a big table, two chairs, several cabinets against the walls, and that seemed to be it.

Earl Hamelin walked around the table, pulled out King William's chair and sat down heavily. He supported his head with one hand. She looked at him with sympathy, thinking of all the changes in his life lately. No wonder the poor man was worn out.

Before either of them spoke, a door behind the earl slowly and noiselessly opened. A woman slipped in, smiling eagerly. She wore a soft violet gown that clung to every seductive curve of her slender figure. The crimson scarf thrown over her glossy black hair was contained by a gold circlet, worn low on her forehead. Olive-skinned, rosy-lipped, with dark eyes rimmed with kohl, she was, Joanna thought, like a vision escaped from some exotic Eastern land.

The earl saw Joanna's look of utter astonishment and turned around.

By then the woman's smile had faded. She clapped a hand to her mouth and her eyes widened. The other two stared at her, too surprised to say a word.

The apparition spoke in hesitant, prettily accented French.

"Oh! I heard someone come in and I thought it was the king. I beg your pardon. I shall leave at once."

And she did, as silently and as mysteriously as she had come.

"Mother of God!" muttered Earl Hamelin.

"Who on earth…?" said Joanna.

They looked at each other, the earl uneasy, Joanna perplexed. After a minute he gathered his long limbs together and stood up.

"Perhaps we should leave."

"I suppose we'd better."

18

After the earl's departure King William mapped out a program that would introduce Joanna to two palaces, one cathedral, one abbey under construction and the tutors he had selected to improve her Latin and to give her a grounding in Arabic.

"First," he said, "I expect you're curious about the royal palace. So we'll start there, this afternoon. That is, if you wish?"

They were sitting in the Fountain Room of La Zisa after the midday meal. Everyone else had left. The king was leaning back in his chair, taking an occasional sip from his wine goblet. Joanna was finishing a small dish of a light, lemony confection. The stream sparkled and talked to itself. Servants were quietly and deftly removing dishes from the tables. Joanna looked around and decided that there was nowhere she'd rather be. She was beginning to feel easier with William and less intimidated by his occasional reserve and his startling good looks. Today he wasn't wearing his crown, and his hair fell in soft waves to his shoulders. In his unadorned blue tunic and leggings with a silver mesh belt, he could be any noble who took great care about what he wore.

But not just any noble would look at her as William looked at her now, with a mixture of attention and affection. As the youngest and least (until John came along) in a large and boisterous family, she'd been used to being ignored. Now for the first time in her life she was being noticed—by a man she hardly knew, yet who she felt would in time be easy to talk to and confide in. Maybe she could even ask him about the mysterious woman. Or maybe he'd bring it up.

"Is that what you'd wish, Joanna? To tour the palace today?"

She realized she'd been daydreaming and hadn't answered his question.

"Very much. I saw a little of it when I went to visit Earl Hamelin, but I'd like to see more, especially that beautiful courtyard in the center."

"Very well, let's be off."

A half-hour later they were walking up the same curving marble staircase she remembered from her previous visit and along the vaulted corridor.

"We'll go first to my private study." He was leading the way and didn't see her look of dismay. She wondered if he knew she'd been there before. She wondered if she'd pluck up enough courage to ask him about the woman they'd seen.

When she entered the room, it was almost as though for the first time. She'd barely had time to take it in the other day.

"Here's where I spend my happiest hours," he told her. Besides the big table that she remembered, she now saw the tall cabinets held books and rolled parchments on their shelves. Everything was well ordered and serene. She remembered that he'd told her he wasn't much of a warrior and that she'd wondered fleetingly what he was, then. Studious, a scholar, apparently. She looked up to see him watching her appraisingly with just the suggestion of a smile.

"Why so solemn, Joanna?"

"I'm thinking how different this is from any of the chambers of our palace at Winchester. There's certainly no quiet, out-of-the-way place there to read or study."

"Well, I suppose your father and mother are far too busy to engage in anything so prosaic and solitary as looking at old manuscripts. Fortunately my kingdom is at peace and I can indulge myself. Besides, a little learning about the past has helped me deal with events of the present. Sit down, Joanna, and I'll show you something beautiful."

She sat down in his big chair and swung her feet, which didn't quite reach the floor. He selected a parchment tied with a red ribbon, carefully unrolled it and spread it on the table. She looked at it, puzzled. He sat beside her.

"It's in Arabic, Joanna."

Then she saw that the letters were like those of the inscription over the entrance to La Zisa. They were graceful, precisely drawn with flowing strokes, and totally incomprehensible. She sighed and brushed a lock of hair out of her face.

"William, I'll never be able to learn Arabic. Brother Jean-Pierre says he isn't even sure I'll ever get very good at Latin."

"Of course you will. Maybe Brother Jean-Pierre he hasn't been pushing you hard enough."

"Will Sir Walter push me hard?" That was the tutor William had selected for her.

"Walter of the Mill? Yes, I expect he will. He wasn't easy on me when he was my tutor." He saw that Joanna was looking glum. "On the other hand, maybe he's developed more Christian charity and forgiveness, now that he's become archbishop of Palermo."

"Oh my! An archbishop for a teacher!"

"It will give you a chance to get to know him before he officiates at our wedding."

"Will that be a very grand affair?"

"Oh yes, I'm afraid so. There hasn't been a royal wedding in Palermo for years, not since my father brought his bride from Spain. The people are already looking forward to it. They love to celebrate, as you saw the night you arrived."

"How old was Queen Margaret when she married your father?"

"I believe she was fifteen."

"Three years older than me."

"Yes." He studied her sober face. "Joanna, I know for a twelve-year-old princess to come to Sicily to marry a man twelve years her senior must be unsettling. I've already observed that you're a wise little thing, and more mature than one might expect. But you must be feeling rather uncertain, wondering what's ahead for you. Am I right?"

She nodded. He reached over, took her hand and looked down on it.

"Such a little, soft hand, and still so white. When you've been here a bit longer you'll be as brown as the rest of us." He looked up into her eyes. "And you'll be one of us. That's my hope, Joanna. That you'll learn to be a queen my people will love and respect. That's why I'll be taking you not only to churches and monasteries and palaces, but also to the towns and into the countryside. I want you and Sicily to get to know each other thoroughly."

She nodded again. It seemed rather daunting, though she did look forward to exploring this exotic island, still so strange to her.

But there was more. He became very serious.

"You'll need to learn the language of the people. You'll want a little schooling but it will come easily to you because it's so much like Latin. At the same time, there'll be Arabic, with Ibn al-Athir. I'd like you to learn as much Arabic as you can so you and I can read it together."

He's beginning to sound like my father when he lays down the law, she thought. She snatched her hand away and looked down.

"It sounds like a lot of work. Why can't I just keep on studying with Brother Jean-Pierre?"

"Much as I admire and respect Jean-Pierre, I fear he's become more like your friend than your teacher. Let him continue to be your friend and counselor, and yield the teaching duties to someone else. I shouldn't wonder but what he'll be relieved."

She looked around the room, considering, then at William.

"I'm just afraid you're expecting too much of me."

"Nonsense, Joanna. I've an idea you've more aptitude for learning than you realize. Let's give it a try and see how it goes. And I assure you, I'll never ask you to do anything you really don't want to do."

"Promise?"

"Promise. And that brings up another subject. Along with all your other uncertainties, you must be wondering what happens after our wedding. Has anybody talked to you about that, your mother perhaps?"

"Yes, she did, a little. She said she hoped you'd wait at least two years before you… before we… before we started living together as man and wife." She was blushing and not looking at him, stumbling over her words. "And she told me about that too."

William smoothed her hand. It was almost a caress and she found it comforting.

"Good. Of course we'll wait, until you're quite ready. There's no need to hurry. A couple of years will give us time to get to know each other better. In the meantime things will go on much as they are now. I'll continue to live here and you in La Zisa. I'll need to go to Italy sometimes, and maybe you'll want to go with me."

Glad of the turn the conversation had taken, she asked eagerly, "Will we go to Naples? When I was there before I was in bed the whole time, except for one visit to the cathedral. All the others kept telling me what a beautiful city it was. I felt very sorry for myself."

"Yes, Naples and maybe Rome."

"Rome! Will we see the pope?"

"Of course. He's the only reason I ever go to Rome. It's good diplomacy. I want him to think I need his advice about affairs here."

"And don't you?"

"Sir Matthew and Archbishop Walter manage between them to keep affairs of the kingdom and the church running smoothly without much counsel from the Holy See."

He stood. "But enough of this serious talk. Come. Let me show you the chapel where we're to be married." He helped her to her feet.

While he rolled up the scroll and carefully retied the ribbon she looked around this severe room where he said he felt so comfortable. Maybe, she thought, he needs to get away sometimes from the palace and its decoration of every inch. She was beginning to understand how that might be.

Her eye fell on the door behind William's chair. As casually as she could, she asked, "Where does that door lead, William? To another corridor?"

From where he stood by the cabinet he shot her a look as though she'd reminded him of something unpleasant.

"Oh no, that's just to my bedchamber. Now, shall we continue our tour?"

He knows that I saw her, she thought. And then: His bedchamber!

William walked quickly out the door, toward the gallery over the courtyard and halfway around it to another corridor without a word. Then he took her hand, looked down at her and smiled. The awkwardness was behind them.

"I'll tell you a little about our wedding ceremony. It may go on for three hours. There'll be a good deal of kneeling and praying and jumping up and listening to the archbishop lecture you about being a proper consort to your king. When Archbishop Walter gets going, he becomes quite enamored of his own voice. Then there'll be the ceremony of placing the royal crown on your head. But I'll be right beside you all the time. Lady Marian will represent your mother so she'll be nearby too. I'll ask Sir Walter to include Brother Jean-Pierre in his attendant clergy. It's too bad there's nobody here to represent your father. That would have been Earl Hamelin's role."

"Maybe it's just as well. He might have tripped over his sword or jumped up when he should have been kneeling." She giggled. William smiled too and looked at her quizzically. "You know your uncle well. But he's basically a good sort, don't you agree?"

"Of course. I've become fond of him and I'll miss him. But I'm so glad you've given him that mission to Richard and to England, so he won't feel he's been sent home in disgrace."

"Ah, but Joanna, I know it was you who came up with that idea. And I congratulate you. Very ingenious."

At the end of the corridor she saw a glimmer of golden light that became brighter the closer they came.

She'd been expecting a chapel something like the family chapel in the palace at Winchester, which was small and dark with little adornment except a statue of the Virgin Mary in a blue gown on one wall and another of Christ on the Cross opposite.

No—the Palatine Chapel was so dazzling and so immense that she stopped short, unbelieving.

"William!" she breathed.

Mosaics, almost blinding in their brilliant color, adorned the walls, the floor and the domed cupola. Tall, graceful, marble columns supported the arches that ran the length of the vast chamber. Gold leaf was everywhere—surrounding the image of Christ over the altar, in the haloes of the holy family, decorating the carvings on the high ceiling. She thought they were like golden icicles hanging from a heavenly blue sky.

"I see you're impressed. I know just what you're experiencing. I still have to stop and stare every time I come in here, though I've known it since I was a child. And I never cease to feel grateful to my grandfather, King Roger, who built it. I never knew him but he was a great admirer of the Arab idea of beauty. Somehow he managed to blend all that with what he remembered of his Norman heritage. Those rounded arches, for instance, are just like the ones in your northern churches."

Joanna wasn't really listening. She was getting used to William's disquisitions on architecture. All she wanted to do was to let her eyes roam over the magnificence before her. She tried to imagine herself a week hence, standing there at William's side before the archbishop. She was already nervous about the ceremony and her central role.

She could only hope that with all the rich decorations and important churchmen to look at, maybe people wouldn't pay attention to her. She said as much to William.

He laughed. "Oh, they'll be observing you very closely. All the nobles and churchmen are full of curiosity about the English princess who's come so far to marry their king. But don't worry, my dear. They'll be enchanted with you. Also, by the time your ladies get you all gowned and bejeweled, you'll look fully as splendid as King Roger's chapel. You may not know it, but you're really a very pretty girl."

She flushed and could think of nothing to say. Few in her short life had called her pretty.

He went on. "So much for the royal palace—enough for one day, no? Tomorrow or the next day I'll take you to Monreale to see my new abbey and its cathedral."

Down in the entrance hall he turned her over to Alan, who had been amusing himself while waiting by joshing with the maids and exchanging battle stories with one of the older footmen, who was a veteran of William's father's army. Alan came to attention when the king and Joanna entered.

"The horses are ready and waiting, my lord King."

"Thank you, Alan," said William. "One last thing, Joanna. Will you please ask Lady Marian if she would be so good as to come see me later this afternoon, any time before dusk?"

"Of course. And thank you very much for showing me your wonderful palace."

On the way back to La Zisa she puzzled about why William wanted to talk to Lady Marian. It must have to do with the wedding arrangements.

That night, when Mary had finished helping Joanna get ready for bed and had left, Lady Marian knocked and came in. She looked unusually serious.

"Come into the next room with me, Joanna."

She led the way to the elegant little sitting room, sat on the crimson-cushioned bench and patted the seat beside her.

"Sit here, my dear, and listen carefully."

Joanna obeyed.

"Joanna, do you know what a concubine is?"

19

Joanna had a hard time taking in what Lady Marian told her about King William's concubine. Somehow she could hardly connect kind, open William—who seemed more like an affectionate uncle than a man with carnal appetites—with what she was hearing. She knew, of course, that men were not always faithful to their wives. She'd heard servants and courtiers gossip about her own father.

But William, after all, wasn't even married. He'd been a bachelor for years and still was. Certainly his personal life was his own business. And yet…

"Men need female companionship more than women need men, that's the way it is," said Lady Marian. "My own husband, may his soul rest in peace, strayed once or twice. But I chose to ignore it, which kept things much more comfortable."

The worry lines on her face softened as she remembered what must have been, Joanna decided, a marriage that had been mostly quite satisfactory.

"But that was long ago. As for King William, his father adopted many Arabic customs and had concubines. It was probably thought quite natural that his son would too. At least until he married."

They talked a little more. Joanna asked if the "Arabian princess" Sir Matthew had hinted at might have been the woman she'd seen.

"I suppose so. When we met this afternoon, King William didn't say much about the woman except that her name is Yasmin and that she belongs to an old and distinguished family that goes back to the time before the Normans conquered Italy."

"I wonder—do you suppose William would have told me about her eventually if we hadn't surprised her in his rooms the other day?"

"I think he might have. He did say one curious thing: that he'd considered introducing the two of you, because he thought Yasmin could be helpful in your learning Arabic. I must say I thought that quite an extraordinary idea."

Joanna at first was inclined to agree. Then when she thought of Ibn al-Athir, the unknown and doubtless terrifying scholar who was designated as her tutor, she felt that lovely smiling lady might be preferable.

It was getting late, and her brain was tired with trying to sort it all out. She yawned. Her head fell back against the cushions and she closed her eyes.

"Yes, it's long past our bedtime. Are you as easy in your mind as can be, my dear? King William wanted me to assure him that you weren't unduly upset."

"I don't think I'm *unduly* upset. It's just that I never thought of King William as having that kind of women friends." She yawned again.

As they parted, Lady Marian gave the girl an affectionate hug.

"Sleep well, Joanna."

Joanna doubted if she would. She expected to lie awake for hours, going over what she'd heard. It wasn't that she was shocked or repelled. Rather, she was uncertain about how the easy, comfortable relationship she and William had built would be affected. She was afraid she'd be tongue-tied and embarrassed when she saw him again. But she went to sleep almost at once. And she dreamed that she and Yasmin were seated at the table in William's study. Yasmin wasn't wearing her seductive violet gown, but a nun's habit, complete with white wimple. Only her pretty face was uncovered. She was pointing at a line in the manuscript before them.

"Yes, Joanna, you have translated it exactly, except for this word here. It means east, not west. But you are doing very well!" Joanna felt a surge of self-confidence. Just then William appeared at the door and saw them working.

"I won't disturb you," he said.

"No, you had better not," said Yasmin. "We still have two pages to read. But King William, your little queen is making great progress!"

When Joanna awoke the next morning she could remember the dream vividly. And she still felt the euphoria that had spread over her at Yasmin's compliment.

The flurry of preparations for the wedding, now fast approaching, intensified. There were endless clothes to try on, jewels to locate and polish, demands that Joanna practice walking up and down stairs in this or that elegant but unwieldy gown. On the day before the wedding she managed to escape for a walk in the gardens. Remembering her promise to Earl Hamelin that she would be kind to Lady Adelaide, she invited her to come too.

"I suppose it would do me good," Adelaide said doubtfully. She had been subdued since the earl's departure and Joanna wasn't expecting much in the way of conversation. But hardly had they set out along one of the leafy walks than Adelaide stopped and took Joanna's hand. Usually so loquacious, she stumbled over her words and bent her head to look at the path rather than at Joanna.

"Dear Princess, you've been so kind and understanding in spite of my unsuitable behavior. I've wondered how to ask you to forgive me for being so foolish and gullible. I assure you, I've learned a great deal from the experience."

"But Lady Adelaide, the fault was really my uncle's. He deceived you."

When Adelaide looked up, Joanna saw that her long, sallow face was flushed with her emotion and her eyes sparkled with tears. My goodness, thought Joanna, she could almost be pretty, if she didn't usually look as though she were chewing on a lemon.

"He did. But it wasn't so much deliberate deceit as thoughtlessness on his part. And I permitted myself to be deceived. I should have known better. But it was the first time I'd had so much attention from a man, and…" Her voice trailed away and she wiped her eyes.

They walked on. After a cloudy, damp morning the sun had come out, and everything basked and blazed in the warmth and light, from the jets of crystalline water spurting from the fountains to the clumps of ruby-red and coral cannas along the walk. At the lake they crossed the bridge and sat down on the bench. The golden fish darted about tirelessly. With every twist and turn each reflected a sunbeam.

Adelaide broke the silence. "I've learned a great deal from this and I've been thinking a lot about what to do now. I've been praying to the Blessed Virgin to give me guidance and teach me humility. With her help, I've decided to retire to a religious house that offers shelter to Christian women. I'm not really meant for the worldly life at court."

"Oh! What a change that will be for you! Are you sure, Lady Adelaide? And where? Certainly not in England, where you'd be so likely to meet Earl Hamelin!"

"That wouldn't bother me. I'm really, truly, over all that. But no, I've been thinking of the Abbey of Fontevraud. I know your mother is a good friend of the abbess. Do you think she could help me find a place there?"

"I'm sure she could. She's given so much to the abbey that they can't refuse her anything. We'll write to her and see what she says. But don't be in a hurry to leave. Wait until the weather's better and the voyage will be smoother than when we came."

Lady Adelaide took her hand again and smiled in genuine gratitude, and Joanna smiled back.

"That's that then. But we'll miss you." They rose and started back toward the palace. A page met them as they reached the steps.

"Princess Joanna, I'm sent to tell you that Brother Jean-Pierre is waiting for you in your reception room."

"Oh dear! I completely forgot. Please tell him I'm on my way."

The king had asked Brother Jean-Pierre to go over the order of the Latin marriage and coronation service with her, so she would have a good understanding of what was going on and what was expected of her. She'd come to look forward to the sessions as a welcome respite from the wedding preparations. She found Jean-Pierre looking at a book spread open on the table before him and drumming his fingers. She sat down beside him and they fell to the task—Jean-Pierre reading aloud, Joanna chiming in with the appropriate responses.

There was a knock, and William came in.

"Ah there, I found you. How goes it, Brother Jean?"

"Very well. We've almost reached the benediction."

It was the first time Joanna had seen the king since Lady Marian's disclosures. She was disconcerted by his sudden appearance, unsure how to behave. She kept her gaze fixed on the book, but she saw only a blur of words and spots of blazing color that were the illuminated initial letters. She sensed William was watching her.

"And Joanna, how goes it with you?"

She forced herself to look up and meet his eyes.

In an instant all her uneasiness melted away. This was the William she'd learned to know and like, William with the kind eyes and the face full of understanding and good humor. Without a word he was telling her that though she must have been confused and uneasy, nothing had changed between them. A smile of welcome lit up her face. Involuntarily she reached up a hand to take his.

"Yes, Brother Jean-Pierre's right. It *is* going well. Would you like to hear what I say when the archbishop asks me if I promise to be a good queen and to always have a regard for the welfare of the Sicilian people?"

He squeezed her hand and held it a moment before releasing it.

"Oh no, I'd rather be surprised when I hear your excellent Latin in the cathedral tomorrow. Now Brother Jean, don't keep the princess here too much longer. She'll need her rest tonight."

He put his hand on her head and smoothed her hair. "Until tomorrow, Joanna. Sleep well."

She looked up with a happy smile. "I will. Thank you, William."

She watched as he left the room. *Still friends.*

20

Six weeks later and a thousand miles away, Queen Eleanor of England settled herself in her favorite spot, an alcove in the reception room of her private apartments at Winchester Palace. From here she could look out on her garden, which she'd carefully designed to provide a harmonious prospect throughout the year. Today in March, bathed in pale spring sunshine, it was full of promise if not of actual bloom. Neat low hedges of boxwood lined the stone-flagged walks and bordered the square beds. In one bed, green spears of daffodils had pushed up through the brown earth and some showed yellow buds about to burst forth. In another, clumps of violets had already produced a few blossoms, hiding modestly in the leaves. From where she sat Queen Eleanor couldn't see them, but she had observed them during her morning walk and it pleased her to picture them there. Two kitchen maids were returning from the herb and vegetable gardens beyond, their baskets filled with leeks, turnips, and the curly dark-green leaves of kale.

Satisfied that everything was in order outside, Eleanor turned her attention to the interior. Yes, the fire, recently replenished, blazed discreetly and efficiently. Its light flashed off silver wreaths that festooned her two polished wood chests. More light brightened the room from candles in tall gold candlesticks set in each corner. Her feet in their soft leather slippers rested lightly on the Persian carpet. At her side was an ebony table that held a silver flask of wine, another of water, a chased silver goblet and a rolled parchment.

Queen Eleanor had always seen to it that her surroundings were as elegant as she was herself.

She picked up the parchment. It had been delivered only half an hour ago, and she had seen from the handwriting of the superscription that it was from her old friend Lady Marian de Beauchamps. She could tell from the thickness of the roll that it was a long letter. Along with all the other instructions she had given Lady Marian before she left was that she serve as the queen's "eyes and ears" in Sicily. Now she would learn what Lady Marian had seen and heard. She untied the black ribbon, unrolled the parchment and began reading.

To my lady, Queen Eleanor:

I trust this finds you and my lord, King Henry, in good health. God be praised, all here are well. The last word you have had from me was from Naples, whence I sent the news of Princess Joanna's recovery from the ills she had suffered on the voyage. Now we are comfortably settled into our new life in Palermo, and the princess two days ago became the wife of King William and was crowned queen of Sicily. I will try to describe the scene for you.

The chapel in the Norman palace is a marvelous place, very large and with high ceilings, but for my taste overly decorated with gold and those bright-colored mosaic tiles people in this part of the world are so fond of. I had the honor of representing you, my lady, during the ceremony so I was just behind the princess and could observe her well. She comported herself excellently, with great dignity for one so young. She entered the chapel on the arm of Matthew of Ajello, the king's chancellor (of whom more later). It was unfortunate that there was no member of her family to escort her, since Earl Hamelin had departed. She wore the wedding gown we brought all the way from England, and it was greatly admired. You will remember it—pale green satin, with a rather full skirt and rose-colored embroidery around the neckline and at the wrists. The wedding was a grievously long affair with a great deal of chanting and swinging of censers. It required one to stand for lengthy periods and kneel frequently for Archbishop Walter's interminable prayers. You may recall him as Walter of the Mill when he was a much more humble cleric in England. He has risen here to become a leading member of King William's council and a very powerful man.

In spite of the tiring nature of the ceremony, your daughter stood straight and did not lose her composure. Furthermore, my lady, she looked very much the little queen. I heard more than one comment from the nobles and their ladies who were assembled in the chapel about her beauty and how well she bore herself. Only once did she appear a little discomposed, as anybody would have done under the circumstances. It was during her coronation, which followed the wedding ceremony. After the archbishop removed her diamond tiara, he sprinkled a few drops of holy oil on her head. Than he took the crown of the queen of Sicily from the red cushion that an assisting priest was holding. (And only then, my lady, did I realize that the priest was our Brother Jean-Pierre, looking quite splendid and a little uncomfortable in a red cope and a snowy white surplice over his customary black cassock.) The archbishop placed the crown, which was all of gold and laden with jewels, on Joanna's head. Because it was so large and heavy (and, I suspect, because the oil on her hair sped it on its journey), it slipped right down over her forehead and came to rest supported by her little nose. I saw her start and begin to reach up to push it away, but in a trice King William took it off and placed it back on the cushion that Jean-Pierre was still holding. The archbishop, quicker-witted than I would have thought, inserted something in the ritual words he was delivering to the effect that now the queen had been symbolically crowned. He went on to ask her to acknowledge her sacred duty to serve her lord the king loyally and to care for the welfare of his people. She spoke up as though nothing had happened, in a voice audible to all, that she did so promise. This was almost the end and after another prayer (for which we all knelt yet again and heartily glad were my knees that it was the last time) and the benediction, William took Joanna's arm and led the procession out of the chapel.

Then, of course, there was a long banquet in the Fountain Room. I will not describe that splendid chamber to you, since by the time you read this I am sure Earl Hamelin will have arrived and told you about the beautiful palaces we live in here.

Eleanor looked up, exasperated. No, Earl Hamelin had not arrived. Where was the man? She knew he was on the way. Although she herself was confined to Winchester at Henry's orders, she had a trustworthy network of informants who kept her aware of what was important to her. She knew the earl had reached Bordeaux where he was to take some matter up with Richard. But he should have reached England by now.

She resumed reading.

Joanna was, understandably, quite tired when it was all over. But she was as happy as I have seen her. I believe she fully realizes the honor and good fortune she enjoys in being the queen of Sicily. Also, she and King William have, even in the short time they have known each other, become good friends.

Now, my lady, though this letter is already over-long, I must add a few words about a matter that is not so pleasant. I mentioned Matthew of Ajello, the king's chancellor. By tactful questioning and listening here in the king's court, I conclude he is a wily man and in league with Queen Margaret, who despite having given up her position as queen regent, still wishes to be influential in the kingdom's affairs. Brother Jean-Pierre and I are convinced that she has taken an intense dislike to Joanna, probably because the king did not consult her about his choice of a queen. We fear that she and Sir Matthew may make trouble for Joanna. To be blunt: we believe Sir Matthew intends to revive the old Thomas à Becket affair, when King Henry was falsely accused of ordering the murder of Archbishop Thomas of Canterbury. Jean-Pierre has acquired reliable information that Sir Matthew intends to publicly brand King Henry as a murderer, and thereby to defame his daughter.

None of this may be imminent. Sir Matthew is preoccupied now with his rivalry with Archbishop Walter for the king's favor and for power in the kingdom. However, I beg of you, my lady, to acquaint King Henry with this situation. It would be most helpful if he could send someone—or come himself—to look into whatever mischief Sir Matthew and Queen Margaret may be plotting, and to see how they can be controlled. I suppose that if Earl Hamelin were still here he might have been of help. But perhaps it is just as well, because the situation seems to call for a man of more standing —shall we say a man of judgment and discretion?

I have kept you reading too long, my lady, and your eyes must be tiring. Adieu, from your loyal servant, Marian de Beauchamps.

An afterword: When I told Joanna I had written you and described the wedding, she asked me to send you her love and to say that she looks forward to the day when you may visit her. How pleased she would be if King Henry were to send you to deal with this matter!

And so would I, thought Queen Eleanor. And so would I.

But now there was work to be done. She rolled up the parchment and tied the ribbon. She walked to the door and told the page outside to send her a messenger at once. By the time the man arrived she had written ten lines to King Henry, who was at Westminster:

My lord:

I have just received the letter that accompanies this from Lady Marian de Beau-champs in Palermo. Not only does it contain news of the marriage of our daughter—apparently a successful and joyful occasion—but at the end some alarming cautions about the political situation in Sicily. As we are both aware, Sicily is one of England's most powerful allies and we had hoped this marriage would strengthen the alliance. We cannot afford to see any cracks appear in the relationship, nor can I bear to think of danger to Joanna. Lady Marian must be answered—can you come to Winchester soon so we can take counsel together about this?

Eleanor

She hardly dared hope that Henry would come, much less soon. He seldom asked for her counsel in anything nowadays. To her surprise he arrived three days later, greeted her with an embrace and a kiss on the cheek and said, "You are looking remarkably handsome, my Queen. I've come at your bidding, to discuss Sicily and Joanna and all the possible disasters that may befall us if we fail to take action at once." He was laughing, he was almost the old Henry with whom she'd fallen in love all those years ago. She doubted if this rapport would last but welcomed it none the less.

They dined in her private dining room early in the afternoon. Clouds were scudding across the sky, often blotting out the sun so the room swung from brilliantly alight to dark and gloomy. Eleanor ordered the candles to be lit.

She had forgotten how enthusiastically Henry could attack a meal and watched in amazement as he made away with half a roast chicken and a bowl of stewed beef before she'd had more than a few mouthfuls of her own chicken. Finally replete, he pushed his chair back from the table and sat watching while she ate. He stroked his brown-bearded chin. He sipped from his goblet.

"As to this pother in Sicily, of course we must look into it. But I can hardly believe anybody would seriously accuse me all over again of murdering the archbishop."

As he continued, Eleanor could see the signs she knew all too well that his temper was rising. He was biting off his words and shaking his head in anger, his voice becoming strident.

"All Europe knows by now, in fact has known for seven years, that when those renegade knights killed Thomas in Canterbury Cathedral, it wasn't on my orders. They just assumed..." He began to sputter and his face was mottled with an alarming flush. The sputter turned to a roar. "How could they be so rash and stupid? They assumed that simply because I'd complained about my differences with the archbishop I wanted him put out of the way." He jumped to his feet, overturning a stool in his vehemence, and shook his fist at the ceiling as though to enlist a just God to his cause—or to rail against an unjust one. "And didn't I crawl on my knees to do penance for a deed I hadn't done? Didn't I let the cardinals scourge my bare back? Didn't I beg the pope to make Thomas a saint?"

Eleanor, accustomed to his rages, watched in admiration. It was something like witnessing a thunderstorm. There was nothing to do but wait until the thunderer tired and calm returned.

Henry kicked the stool out of his way and sat down, breathing heavily. His hands were shaking. Eleanor poured him more wine.

After a few minutes his breathing became normal. He resumed their conversation.

"Yes, we must look into the situation. Lady Marian's analysis seems sound. You may compliment her on her wisdom and on her loyalty to us. She was a good choice to send with Joanna. What a pity she isn't a man, she might have served as our agent in Sicily." He took a sip of wine. "Too bad the other ladies didn't turn out so well. I hear that the duenna resigned her post in Saint-Gilles, that one of the others was seduced by our Richard with unfortunate results, and still another permitted herself to form a liaison with Earl Hamelin, though he seems to feel very little remorse."

Eleanor's eyes widened in astonishment. "Has he returned, then?"

"Yes, he arrived in London a week ago. Do you mean to tell me you, with all your sources of the latest news, were ignorant of that?" Now he had reverted to the malicious, insinuating Henry, the husband who had kept her prisoner for four years and took pleasure in baiting her.

"Never mind, I'm sure he'll call on you before long. I believe he has a message for you from Joanna. Something about asking you when you'll be coming to Sicily."

This was her opportunity, but she mustn't sound too eager.

"And what a good time this would be for me to go. I could find out what Chancellor Matthew is up to, and perhaps enlist Archbishop Walter to help me. I knew him when he was a priest at Winchester Cathedral."

"So you could, Eleanor." He picked up his goblet, stared into it and downed the last few drops. He rose and stood in front of the fire, his hands clasped behind his back. "You never stop trying, do you? But I'm not ready to grant you your freedom. The minute you crossed the Channel you'd start stirring up rebellion and encouraging my sons to rise against me."

She knew better than to argue. She looked at him standing there, stocky, square-jawed, booted feet planted well apart: still a fine figure of a man, a man as confident of the strength of his will as of the strength of his sword arm.

"What's more, you're a bit late. I've already arranged for Archbishop Richard to go to Sicily. I spoke to him when I arrived in Winchester this morning. He'll travel back to Westminster with me tonight and I'll instruct him on how he is to represent me in Palermo. Or rather, to represent us. I take it you concur in this choice?"

He was pretending to solicit her assent. She was pretending to be thinking of whether to give it, staring at him thoughtfully. She nodded. "Very well, my lord. I shall write to Lady Marian, shall I? And explain to her what we plan?"

"Please do. But I believe you should caution her against telling Joanna anything about all this. There's no point in alarming the child about something that may not happen."

For once they were in agreement. Eleanor rose.

"You will want to leave soon while there is still daylight."

Henry left, the candles guttered in a blast of cold air that blew through the open door, and Eleanor stood staring into the fire. Twelve years would pass before she traveled to Sicily and saw her daughter.

21

Except for a move from one palace to another, very little changed in Joanna's life after her wedding. She now had her own apartments in the royal palace, every bit as sumptuous as the ones at La Zisa. Rooms for Lady Marian and the other ladies were nearby. William continued to be attentive and friendly, though more like a brother or a teacher than a husband. Joanna was perfectly content with that.

Archbishop Richard of Winchester, dispatched by King Henry to investigate the subversive plotting of Matthew of Ajello, arrived in due course. Joanna had never been particularly fond of the archbishop, but she was glad to see a familiar English face. Nobody had told her why he was there. She supposed it was one of those state visits that monarchs and their deputies make, just to remind their allies that they're still allies.

Aside from the archbishop's rather perfunctory transmittal of her parents' greetings, she saw very little of him during his three weeks in Sicily. First he had to recover from the rigors of the sea voyage, which had left him bilious and nearly bedridden. Next he was present at a series of state dinners in his honor. There he divided his time between conversation and consumption, the former looking to Joanna like polite but desultory talk with various notables and dignitaries, the latter a serious effort to make up for the reduction of his girth due to seasickness.

Once when she was seated on the balcony of the courtyard, waiting for Lady Marian, Beatrice and Adelaide, she heard a door close, then hearty masculine laughter from the corridor. She recognized the voices of Sir Matthew of Ajello and Archbishop Richard. They must have just come from William's private study. She couldn't help overhearing their conversation as they drew closer.

"That's that, then, Sir Matthew," said the archbishop. "I'm so glad we see eye to eye. This has been a most interesting and, I trust, productive visit. I'm only sorry I must leave tomorrow. I've grown quite fond of your Sicily. I've never had such fine capons in wine sauce."

They'd reached the balcony, but to Joanna's relief turned to the right rather than to the left where she was seated. They didn't see her.

Sir Matthew was more cordial and outgoing than she'd ever seen him. He clapped the archbishop resoundingly on the back, which caused the latter to wince and recoil. Sir Matthew didn't notice. They sat on a bench not ten feet from her, but a stout pillar kept her hidden from their view. She couldn't help but eavesdrop.

"Yes, Richard, as you say, interesting and productive. I hope you'll tell your king that he need have no further concerns about the matters we've discussed."

"So I shall. Where he got the idea that anybody hoped to cause a split between Sicily and England, I can't imagine." The archbishop belched discreetly. One too many capons, Joanna thought.

"Oh well, the common folk will make up foolishness when they've nothing better to do. Perhaps some of that idle talk reached King Henry. Come, shall I see you to your chamber?"

They descended to the courtyard and were lost to sight.

Joanna sat on, puzzling about what she'd overheard. Presently Lady Marian arrived and Joanna told her about it.

"I can't say I'm surprised. That archbishop's a useless sort of man, in my opinion. Might as well have stayed at home."

Before Joanna could ask her what she was talking about, Lady Marian hurried on.

"But never mind that now. Adelaide and Beatrice are coming to say goodbye."

Joanna knew Adelaide would be leaving for the abbey of Fontevraud in France and that Beatrice wished to be with her family in England when her baby was born. But so soon? "I thought they'd be here another month."

"Apparently King William has sensibly decided it's best for them to join the archbishop's party, which will have seven galleys staffed with skilled captains and seamen, rather than going later on transport that's possibly less reliable."

When Beatrice and Adelaide appeared Joanna realized how much she was going to miss them. She'd always liked Beatrice for her gentleness and lack of pretense. Immediately after Richard's desertion she'd become even more reserved, turning aside Joanna's overtures of friendship. Yet in time she seemed to have gotten over her broken heart. Lately she'd responded gladly to suggestions for a walk in the park or a visit to the bazaar. As for Lady Adelaide, her misadventures with Earl Hamelin had left her chastened and far less assertive.

Joanna sometimes wondered if an unhappy love affair made one a nicer person than before.

"I hope this isn't *really* goodbye," said Joanna, giving each a hug. "Surely we'll meet again some day. Beatrice, maybe after your baby comes, you could bring him back to Sicily, at least for a while."

Beatrice's blue eyes grew misty. Joanna thought that her approaching motherhood had made her even more beautiful, with a calm contentment that softened her features.

"I don't know, my lady. Maybe. But all I look forward to now is to be back in my father's house and to see him and my mother and—soon—to bear my child." She took Joanna's hand and, near tears, clasped it in both of hers. "I shall never forget how good and kind you've been."

"Oh dear, if you start crying I will too." Joanna turned to Adelaide, who was standing with bowed head, surreptitiously wiping her eyes with a corner of her sleeve. Lady Marian passed out handkerchiefs to all.

"Dear Adelaide, I feel sure we'll meet again, too. Let me hear from you after you're well settled at Fontevraud Abbey. I know you'll be happy there. And who knows, maybe I'll come to visit you some day!"

"Oh, I hope so. After everything you've told me about the abbey I expect to find it's just what suits me. But I'll never, never forget you and this beautiful land of Sicily."

And with more tears and protestations of friendship, they parted.

Joanna did miss them, but not as much as she'd expected. William kept her busy, asking her to accompany him on various expeditions. She particularly liked it when they went several times to his new abbey and cathedral at Monreale, an ambitious project and very dear to his heart, though still some years away from completion. William took an intimate interest in every aspect of the construction.

"It will be my legacy," he told Joanna, "just as the Palatine Chapel where we were married was my grandfather's and La Zisa was my father's."

Joanna tried to think of some comparable achievement in her family. Her father had certainly built no cathedrals, though he had a respectable list of refortified castles to his credit. Then she remembered something she'd heard once.

"I believe an ancestor of mine built Westminster Abbey," she said. "Then he was buried there and they made him a saint."

"Would that have been Saint Edward, called the Confessor?"

"I think so. My mother and father took me there when I was very small, and I saw his shrine. It's a beautiful church, but I thought it was very dark, like an enormous cave."

"Ah yes," said William. "I've heard a great deal about Westminster. I'd like to see it. Maybe I'd get some ideas for my cathedral. But mine won't be dark. It will gleam and glitter!" And he explained to her how he would bring about this splendor, through generous application of gold leaf and mosaic tiles.

With such conversations and instruction they would pass the time during the three-hour ride to Monreale. Sometimes it took longer, because William often reined in his horse, whereupon all the others in the cortège had to stop too, from queen to courtiers to grooms. William, in his zeal to acquaint Joanna with Sicily and vice versa, would pause to point out notable sights to her, or to greet well-wishers who came out to see them pass. William's subjects loved him and were learning to love her too. Sometimes she heard the same cheers that had greeted her on her first night in Sicily—"Welcome to our new queen!"

But toward the beginning of 1178, when she'd been married nearly a year, she thought she noticed less enthusiasm from the populace when she wasn't with William. There were even sullen looks and muttered remarks. She couldn't catch the words but the tone was unmistakably hostile. She worried and resolved to tell William about it.

Before she could, she found out with a jolt just how unpopular she'd become. She and Lady Marian were returning from the gardens at La Zisa where they'd spent the afternoon. Alan was as usual in attendance. They'd almost reached the royal palace when they saw, scrawled in huge letters on the wall of a house, "Joanna . . ."and some more words she couldn't make out. She asked Alan what they were.

"I'm afraid it says something like 'Daughter of a murderer! Go home.'"

While Joanna stared at the words. a slovenly looking man with a bucket and a brush, heading for the corner, turned to send her a look of such scorn and hatred that she shuddered. Speechless with dismay, they rode on. When they reached the palace Alan helped her dismount.

"You'll want to see King William about this, my lady. Shall I find him and send him to your chamber?"

"Yes, yes, please do, Alan."

"And quickly," said Lady Marian.

William appeared within five minutes. Joanna was standing by the window, her slight, motionless figure outlined by the slanting rays of the setting sun. William reached her side in three long steps. When she told him what she'd seen, his lips tightened.

"This is monstrous!" Joanna had never seen him so angry.

"William, who would want to attack me so? And what does it mean?"

He saw that she was trembling and pale. He put his arm around her shoulders and she took comfort from its protective pressure.

"My dear Joanna," he said, "of course you're frightened and confused. I'm so sorry you had to undergo such an insult, all innocent as you are. I think I know who's behind the calumny, though I wish I were mistaken."

"But what does it *mean*, William? Do they resent me because of that old business of Archbishop Thomas of Canterbury? That was eight years ago! Surely nobody still thinks my father killed Thomas à Becket!"

"No rational person does. But it takes very little to revive ugly rumors in the minds of the people. You know, I know, all the rulers of Europe, all the churchmen—even the pope—know that your father didn't order Thomas à Becket's murder. And they know he voluntarily did public penance for the crimes of those misguided lords who did the wicked deed."

"And what's more," said Lady Marian, "he pressed as hard as anyone for the elevation of Thomas to sainthood four years ago."

Joanna remembered that. And she remembered her father telling her never to forget to include St. Thomas of Canterbury in her prayers.

She felt her legs weaken and sat down on the windowseat. "I don't know what I can do to make them see how wrong they are."

"You need do nothing," said William, "except go on as you are and try to forget this outrage. And soon enough, you'll see, it will all die down and the people will find something else to clamor about. I shall get to the bottom of it, I promise you. And I shall start now." He strode out of the room. They heard him snap to the page at the door, "Find Queen Margaret and ask her to come to my study at once."

Joanna remained seated with her head bowed for a moment, then sat up straight. "Lady Marian, I think you know more about all this than you've told me."

"Yes. I suppose I should have been more frank with you from the beginning. It all started with Queen Margaret's being so insulted that William had chosen to marry you instead of the German princess she favored."

She continued with the account of how the old queen had enlisted Sir Matthew in her campaign to denigrate Joanna; how she—Lady Marian—had written to Joanna's mother; how King Henry had sent Archbishop Richard to investigate Sir Matthew; how the latter had obviously duped the archbishop into believing it was all a tempest in a teapot; and how Sir Matthew had recirculated the long-forgotten evil rumors about King Henry and Thomas à Becket, with the results they had seen today.

Joanna listened carefully to the end of the sorry story.

"Why didn't you tell me any of this while it was going on?"

"My dear, I didn't want to worry you. Brother Jean-Pierre and I decided it would be unkind to trouble you about something we hoped would soon blow over."

"But it didn't."

"No, it didn't."

Joanna stood up. The room was now quite dim. But Lady Marian could see from the girl's rigid stance and the firmness in her voice that something about her had changed.

"I am no longer a child. I'm thirteen years old. You needn't be afraid of upsetting me. From now on, be so good as to keep me informed of anything you see or hear that has to do with me, my husband the king, or the Sicilian people. And you may tell Brother Jean-Pierre the same thing."

William was right. After stern interviews with his mother and with Sir Matthew, including the threat of demotion and even exile to the latter, the attacks on Joanna dwindled, then ceased. The people took her back into their hearts and before long, they were swept up in noisy protests about a new tax on wine.

Queen Margaret still made *sotto voce* derogatory remarks about her daughter-in-law in the dining hall but Joanna learned to ignore them.

William's preoccupation with his new cathedral intensified, if possible. One morning in April of 1178 he and Joanna left Palermo quite early, along with a half-dozen courtiers and Florian, the justiciar, who possibly wanted to see whether all this money the king was spending was getting results.

They rode quickly through the little village of Monreale, where people were just emerging from their cottages to go to the fields. Then it appeared, an enormous structure of thick stone walls rising to dizzying heights, pierced by arched windows, but still lacking a roof. They left the fresh, sunwashed spring day to enter the cavernous interior. Joanna shivered and drew the fur collar of her cloak closer.

William had come to address a group of skilled artists he had invited from Constantinople, masters of the Byzantine techniques of creating images with tiny pieces of colored glass and stone.

"All along this south wall," he told them, "I shall have stories from the Bible.

I wish you to use all your skill, so that the people can instantly understand the life of our Lord from the pictures you build with your mosaics. Do not hasten the task. Be careful and be inventive. Generations to come will make pilgrimages here to admire your work."

"And have you selected the stories you wish us to picture, my lord King?" asked a bearded ancient, apparently the leader of the group.

"I have, but I will be glad to hear others' suggestions. I would like to see the Washing of the Feet, the Miracle of the Loaves and Fishes, the Last Supper, the Betrayal, to start with."

"And perhaps," said Florian, "Christ Driving the Money Lenders from the Temple?"

"By all means. You, my lord justiciar, as the man in charge of safeguarding the king's treasury, naturally have an interest in putting a stop to any unseemly financial behavior." William smiled, whereupon the others in the party chuckled discreetly.

After further discussion with the Byzantine artists, and having made sure they would be well lodged and fed, William and his chief of construction made a tour around the outside of the cathedral. Satisfied that it was not about to tumble down and was progressing according to his wishes, he re-entered to tell Joanna it was time to start back. She was standing at the center of the vast space, looking up toward the sky.

"William, will you cover all the walls with mosaics of Bible stories? And the ceiling?"

"I'm not sure. The walls, certainly. But I'm thinking that just there where you were looking, at the center of what will be the dome over the apse, I'll have a very large Christ, as though he were looking down from heaven with his hands out-stretched to embrace all who enter here."

"That would be wonderful." She gazed up, trying to imagine it.

"I'll have to confess, Joanna, that it wasn't an original idea. My grandfather, King Roger II, created such a Christ in the dome of his cathedral at Cefalù. I'll take you there soon. You'll see how glorious a great cathedral can be—and how I hope mine will be."

"Will you have the artists picture some saints, too?"

"Saints, angels, archangels—the whole host of holy folk."

They began walking out toward the bright afternoon.

"Then I'd like to make a request. Would you find a place somewhere for St. Thomas of Canterbury? And let me pay for that? My father gave me a rather large sum of money when I left home, and I haven't had much to spend it on. I would dearly love to do this."

William stopped, placed his hands on her shoulders and looked down at the earnest face turned up to his.

"Joanna, what a splendid idea. You've surprised me again with your good sense. Think of the effect on the citizens when they know their queen has honored St.

Thomas."

"I'm not suggesting it because of that, but because I truly do venerate Thomas. But I suppose"—she smiled at the thought—"it wouldn't hurt anything if people knew I paid for it."

"And we'll see that they know. Maybe we can hire some of Sir Matthew's rumormongers. If they could spread falsehoods so quickly, they should be able to spread the truth even faster."

22

On a warm, steamy July evening in 1180 King William stood, arms akimbo, and surveyed the antechamber of his apartments in the royal palace. His justiciar, Count Florian, who was ten years older than the king and not as fit, had sat down to rest. They had been preparing for departure the next morning for Italy.

Though the room appeared cluttered, to William's eye it was in perfect order. Royal robes, boots, tunics, jerkins, capes, crown and jewels were secured in a half-dozen stout chests, strapped and locked. William and Florian had selected the documents they'd need when conferring with the envoys of the emperor of Germany. They'd seen to their placement in a leather satchel, also securely locked. This, and the pouches of gold and silver they would need during the next six weeks or so, were entrusted to Count Florian.

The valet, Peter, was just finishing stacking the bags and boxes that the draymen would take down to the galleys that awaited them in the harbor.

William's face was glistening with sweat. Peter handed him a linen cloth to wipe his brow.

"Thanks, Peter. You have managed very well, You may go." Peter bowed and left.

"I believe, Florian, we've earned a few minutes' rest," William said, seating himself on a chest. "We seem to be as ready as we can be."

"I believe we are, my lord King. But before any more time passes, may I say that I greatly appreciate the honor of accompanying you? I hope to justify your trust in me." William had usually taken his chancellor, Matthew of Ajello, on his diplomatic missions. Florian's role had been to stay at home and see to the day-to-day business of the kingdom during his absence.

"I do trust you, Florian. You've served me loyally for many years. I'm afraid I don't remember to thank you often enough."

Florian's thin face, his beaked nose and the bald spot on top of his head turned pink with pleasure. He wasn't used to praise from his monarch. Their relations had always been extremely businesslike, but now William seemed disposed to speak more freely. He poured each of them a goblet of water from a pewter pitcher. Florian drank deeply and settled in his chair with a tired sigh.

"In fact, Florian, you're one of the few people I can talk to frankly without fearing you'll turn it to your advantage. I've ceased to trust Sir Matthew as much as

I'd like. He and Archbishop Walter are at such loggerheads over so many matters that they seem to be putting their own interests first instead of those of Sicily."

"Yes. I'd hoped that after the archbishop of Winchester came two years ago and looked into the chancellor's activities, Sir Matthew would have seen the error of his ways. And maybe he did, for a while."

"But he can slide back into his devious paths as smoothly and quietly as a snake."

Florian reflected that it wasn't easy being the king of Sicily. He tried to think of some less discouraging subject.

"At least, my lord, he seems to have stopped plotting to discredit your queen. That was disgraceful."

"True. But I worry that while we're gone we'll have few to keep an eye open for signs of further intrigue except Queen Joanna and Brother Jean-Pierre."

"Still, Jean-Pierre is very good at learning what's going on. He looks so meek that everybody thinks he's just a harmless monk and people say things in front of him that they'd best not."

"I hope you're right. And it isn't just Matthew, you know. I'm concerned about Archbishop Walter as well. He sees my new abbey and cathedral at Monreale as a threat to his primacy in the kingdom. He's already enlisted most of the bishops and priests of Palermo on his side. If he goes much further, Sir Matthew may see his own power waning and who knows what he might do in reprisal."

Florian's shoulders were hunched and he looked so dejected that William had to laugh. "Yes, my friend, it's a dismal prospect, but don't despair. We've been through worse, and I much prefer a battle of wits than one on the field of combat. And let's be grateful for Jean-Pierre's powers of detection, and for Queen Joanna's watchfulness and wisdom."

Florian brightened. "Yes, our queen is a wise one. I've been convinced of it since I first saw her as a child at Winchester. Sicily is fortunate that you chose so well."

"And so am I, Florian. Now I must go down. She's been waiting for me to join her, and I have a great deal to discuss with her—a great deal. Some of it affecting our court here, including a very important addition that should help us keep better informed of what the mischief-makers might be plotting." He rose and stretched. "So I'll be off. You and I will have plenty of opportunity to talk about these matters during the voyage. If all goes well on this trip, Florian, don't be surprised if you find yourself vice-chancellor when we return. Good night, my friend, and get a good night's sleep. Remember, we sail at first light."

Florian was left to absorb this news of his prospects for promotion. It was all very flattering, but also promised to entail new responsibilities. Was he up to them?

And what, he wondered, is this step that William has taken that affects the court?

He doubted that he would get a good night's sleep.

23

When William walked into the atrium, he found Joanna and Lady Charmaine fanning themselves idly. Their embroidery lay in their laps, ignored. Though the sun had gone down it was still too warm for serious endeavor. Not a breath of air stirred. The stately palms in their blue pots were as motionless as though they had never known a breeze.

Joanna was wearing a loose gown of lacy white cotton. "Just looking at you, my dear, makes me feel cooler," William said.

He sat next to Joanna and rested his head against the back of the bench, closing his eyes. She rose to stand behind him and gently massaged his neck and shoulders. He looked up at her gratefully.

"No wonder you're tired, my lord," chirped Charmaine. "Getting ready for a long journey takes so much planning and concentration. Why, I remember to this day how it was before we left England all those years ago. I was quite exhausted by the time we set out. I could hardly put one foot in front of the other. And then…" Joanna cleared her throat audibly and looked at her meaningfully. Charmaine stopped in mid-sentence. "But what am I thinking of? I told Lady Marian I would help wind some yarn this evening. She must be wondering where I am." She gathered up her work and hurried out.

William put his hand up to rest on Joanna's and squeezed it. "Thanks, my sweet. You always know what I need. Let's go out to walk in the park. It must be cooler there."

With arms about each other's waists they walked along an avenue bordered by palms and cypresses. The breeze from the sea was freshening and it ruffled William's smooth cap of hair and set Joanna's ringlets dancing.

A tantalizing scent drifted toward them from a trellised gateway where roses were in full flower. They sat on a bench within the arbor and William put his arm around her shoulders. Joanna reached up to pull down a blossom so she could inhale its sweetness. Suddenly she was overcome with a wave of nostalgia for her mother's rose garden at Fontevraud Abbey. It was the same rose, pale yellow with a blush of peach, and the same spicy fragrance. How long it was since she'd played in that garden as a child! And how her life had changed! Here she was, queen of Sicily, with a loving husband—who was about to leave her for a long time.

"I do so wish you weren't going away," she said almost inaudibly.

"But I must. The situation in Italy is even more delicate than what's facing us here." He tilted her face up so he could look into her eyes where tears were welling.

"I shall miss you, Joanna. I wish you were coming with me." She'd often accompanied him on his travels, but lately she had been feeling unwell with some vague indisposition. William had decreed that she must remain at home and rest.

"How have you been today—better?"

"Yes, on the whole, though I still can't bear the thought of food when I get up in the morning. My appetite seems to recover by dinnertime, but I'm easily tired."

"Perhaps we had better call in the physicians. I'll leave instructions for them to come tomorrow."

Her mind was still in the past. She smelled the rose again, then looked up at the tall palms. With their scaly trunks and their topknots of drooping fringes moving gently in a slight breeze, they still looked outlandish to her, just as they had when she first came. Nearly four years ago! It seemed much longer.

"Did you think, William," she mused, "when we met each other in the port that first night, that I'd ever be a proper queen for you?"

He caressed her cheek.

"I had no doubt. You were young, but I knew you'd have plenty of time to grow into your role. But I wasn't thinking about you as a future queen when I first caught sight of you that night. You were so tired, poor little Joanna, yet you stood so straight, all wrapped up in your cloak with your head held high and your crown in place. I thought to myself, there's a girl with pluck, determined to live up to whatever's expected of her. I must help her to feel at home here. I remember also thinking that you had an interesting face, you looked so alert, taking it all in. I didn't see till later how very pretty you were."

"But I saw at once how handsome you were, William, and how kind. I think I was smitten with you from the first moment."

"I can't say when I became smitten with you," William considered. "It was so gradual. I liked you enormously, and the more we saw of each other the fonder I became of you. But when did that become love?"

"I know exactly when you first *said* you loved me. It wasn't so long ago—on my fifteenth birthday, last fall. Remember, William, after the banquet, when we'd just left the Fountain Room and you asked me if I felt any different, now I was fifteen? And remember what I said?"

"I do remember, but I want to hear you tell me again."

"I said, 'Yes, I feel different. I feel ready.' And you knew at once what I meant. And you kissed me and told me you loved me."

"Are you sure that was when I said it? I thought it was after we ran up the stairs and into your bedroom, and I slammed the door and took you in my arms. Like this."

Cradled in his embrace, she laughed up at him. "Maybe you said it twice. But I don't care how often you say it." So he told her again that he loved her and they kissed as though it were her fifteenth birthday all over again.

William pulled away reluctantly.

"My dearest queen, I need to discuss a few matters that may come up while I'm gone, and if you keep distracting me I might forget."

She folded her hands in her lap and looked at him demurely. "I await your instruction, my lord."

"The first has to do with Archbishop Walter and Sir Matthew of Ajello. One or both is likely to do some mischief the minute my galleys are over the horizon. I'm thinking especially of the archbishop."

"Well, I'm worried about Sir Matthew. He's never liked me. What if he took advantage of your absence to start those attacks on me again?"

"I hardly think that's likely now. My mother encouraged him in that but now, poor soul, she's more concerned with her own frailties than with a daughter-in-law not of her choosing."

"I truly hope you're right."

"Brother Jean-Pierre agrees that at the moment she's not a threat. No, it's the proud archbishop who's more likely to be a troublemaker. So please be watchful, and keep in touch with Jean-Pierre. If the two of you agree that there's danger of an uprising, that one or the other of the rivals may arouse the citizenry, you must send word to me at once."

He had become very serious.

"My love, think of this as your chance to prove to yourself and our people that you're as much a queen as I'm a king. I'm depending on you."

"I'll try, but I'm afraid you're depending on a rather weak reed."

"Nonsense. You have more good sense than a woman twice your age."

She laughed uncertainly, then saw that he meant it.

"And speaking of women with good sense, or lack of it," he went on, "don't you think it's time to find somebody more suitable than Lady Charmaine? You can't really enjoy her company."

"I don't. She does prattle so. But I can't hurt her feelings by telling her the truth—that I'd rather be alone than have her trailing after me. She thinks it's her duty, since Beatrice and Adelaide have gone back to England."

"Ah yes. The unfortunate ladies whose affections your brother and your uncle trifled with. Have you had any news of them lately? Anything since we heard that Lady Beatrice had been delivered of a son?"

"Not really. My mother wrote that Richard was sending them support. She wants him to do more—maybe endow the boy with a title and an assured income. But Richard has so much on his mind, keeping things under control in Aquitaine."

"Do you think it would help if I urged him too?"

"Oh, I do! He'd certainly pay attention to you. And William, I've been thinking how nice it would be if we could persuade Lady Beatrice to come back to Sicily. I did like her, and I think she liked me."

"A good suggestion. We'll keep it in mind."

It was getting quite dark. Joanna rose.

"It's hard to believe, but I'm actually a little cold. Shall we go back?"

"Yes, but I haven't quite finished discussing your ladies. Even if Beatrice comes, that won't be soon. I'd like to think of you with congenial company while I'm away, besides Lady Marian of course. So I have something to tell you."

She sat down again.

"I've asked Lady Yasmin and her husband to join our court."

Joanna drew in her breath sharply. In the twilight she could hardly see his face, but she felt he was making an effort to sound casual. It seemed almost like a speech he'd practiced.

"You know, of course, that Lady Yasmin and I were once very good friends. What you may not know is that, shortly before you and I were married, she went back to her parents' home in Messina. I haven't seen her since. But I know that she has married a nobleman, of Arabic blood equal to her own. I met him a few weeks ago when I was in Messina. I had a long talk with him. He strikes me as a man with a good head on his shoulders. He understands the touchy situation here, with the chancellor and the archbishop trying to outfox each other. The couple would make a valuable addition to our court, which at the moment is rather overloaded with Normans, many of doubtful loyalty." He stopped, waiting for her comment. None came.

"Even more important to you, Yasmin would serve as a much more suitable companion than Lady Charmaine. Yasmin is clever and astute. Your Arabic has reached a point where you need no more instruction, but with Yasmin to keep you company you could get practice in conversation." He seemed to have come to the end of his speech. Joanna couldn't think what to say. She needed time.

A servant with a torch had approached and was waiting to light their way back to the palace. They rose and started along the dim path. Joanna was unable to break the silence. The memories that had been buried for years rushed back: how she'd learned of William's concubine, how she'd agonized that he might think she'd been spying on him when she went into his study with Earl Hamelin, then the painful waiting to see if their friendly but fragile relationship would be damaged. And finally, her tremendous relief when it endured and strengthened. Gradually, the very existence of somebody called Yasmin had faded from her consciousness.

And here she was, alive and, apparently, imminent.

Then another long-buried memory surfaced. That dream! When she was the pupil, Yasmin the teacher, and the subject was Arabic. She'd never told William about it. Now she would.

"Maybe that dream I had was a good omen."

He stopped. So did the torchbearer, wondering why these royal personages couldn't just keep walking, without all this pausing and chattering. He was eager for his bed.

"What dream?"

"It was the night after Lady Marian, on your instruction, told me about your … your…concubine." She stumbled a little over the word. "She said that you'd surprised her by saying that you'd considered having Yasmin teach me Arabic. She said she thought it a very strange idea. I suppose that stuck in my head and that's why I dreamed Lady Yasmin and I were working away at the Arabic, and having a good time too, when you came in and asked how we were getting along. And Lady Yasmin told you I was an excellent pupil. I remember I felt so pleased and puffed up."

"Then let's say it was indeed a good omen. I hope, I believe, that Yasmin will prove a good friend to you and that Lord Hassan, her husband, will be a loyal and useful courtier for me."

They walked on. The torchbearer stepped up the pace, hoping to set them a good example.

"When are they coming?"

"I'd hoped they'd arrive before I left. But unfortunately, it won't be for a week. I'll depend on you and Sir Matthew to make them feel welcome."

So, Joanna said to herself, I'm to welcome her officially and accept her as a companion whether I like her or not. The more she thought about it, the more she resented the fact that William still seemed so unwilling to talk frankly to her about Yasmin. Three years ago she'd persuaded herself that since he seemed to think his private life before he met her was his own affair, she would too. But now—couldn't he say, right out, that though Yasmin and he had been lovers, that was all in the past and now, this moment and from now on, she—Joanna—was his only love? In her head she believed that to be true. In her heart she was not so sure.

But she couldn't let doubts spoil this, their last night together for a long time. By the time they reached the top of the palace steps she had resolved to do all she could to make William reluctant to leave her and eager to return.

William took her hand and looked searchingly at her in the light of the torch that the servant still held patiently.

"Shall we say goodnight now? I don't want to leave you, but I think you need your rest, and I must be up and away by cockcrow."

She moved closer to him. "No, come to me for at least a little while. I'll be waiting in my chamber, but give me time so Lady Marian can repair some of the ravages of this torrid day. And shall I send for fruit and cool wine?"

"By all means. But you don't look ravaged to me, my love. Well, perhaps your nose is a little pink. You must have been in the sun." He kissed her on the nose. She put her arms around him and her lips sought his mouth. She pulled him to her, prolonging the kiss. She felt a familiar stirring mount through her as his embrace tightened. They held each other close, closer, and she was acutely aware of the pressure of his body and of his smell. What was it—sandalwood? They clung together, unwilling to part even for a few minutes. Gently, Joanna pulled away. "Come soon, William," she said over her shoulder as she left him.

Lady Marian was waiting.

"You look tired, my dear. I've sent Mary off to bed, but before she left she brought this basin of water to bathe your face. Let's get you out of that dusty rumpled gown and into something to make you more easeful—perhaps the blue robe?"

"Yes, William will like that. It's one of his favorites. I'll wear it without the sash. That will be more comfortable. I am tired."

She sank gratefully onto a chair and Lady Marian brushed her hair.

"Thank you, that feels good," she said. Then after a moment, "Why do you suppose there seems to be no end to what I have to learn in order to be a good wife and queen? Sometimes I just don't understand William."

"My poor lamb, that's likely to go on for a while. You're married to a good man, but he's complex, with much more to him than appears on the surface. What did you learn today?"

"I learned that in a marriage, apparently one has to take a good deal on faith. And when that isn't enough, on hope."

She stood up and smoothed down her skirts, so silky and soft. She felt revived by the few minutes of rest. She looked at Lady Marian sidewise, with a sly little smile.

"And when faith and hope aren't enough, there's always…"

"Charity?"

"Well, that too. But maybe then it's time for hugs and kisses."

"Wise words!" There was a knock on the door. "Now I'll leave you to practice what you've learned. Good night, my lady."

24

Joanna was inspecting the throne room of the royal palace in Palermo on a mild autumn day in 1181. Here King William would meet soon with his council and court to report on his trip to Italy. His galleys had been sighted the evening before off Cefalù on the northern Sicilian coast, which meant he should arrive by midafternoon. He'd been gone seven weeks and it was the longest Joanna had been separated from him in the four years of their marriage.

The throne room didn't blaze with the gold leaf and ostentatious carvings of the Palatine Chapel, which was why Joanna liked it better. Though she was awed by the chapel's gleam and glitter, her northern sensibilities were still not comfortable with it. The throne room had been built by and for William's father, a king who adored the chase—whether of accommodating ladies or wild beasts. Its walls were alive with images of the latter, real and imaginary. No icons of saints or benign Virgins here, but stags pursued by archers, peacocks with fanned tails in flaring display, centaurs, lions and leopards slinking through the forest—all in brilliant blue and green and gold. What patience those long-gone Byzantine mosaic artists had, she thought. And what an admirable disregard for reality.

She was pleased to see that everything seemed to be in order. William very much liked things to be in order. His gilded throne had been artfully draped with crimson velvet, the folds falling just so. Four lesser but still magnificent chairs were precisely placed, two on each side and slightly behind the king's throne. One was for Joanna, one for Chancellor Matthew of Ajello, one for Archbishop Walter and one for Queen Margaret.

The queen mother had grown so corpulent that she had trouble dragging her tired, awkward old body around. Still she insisted on attending all the court ceremonials, where her muttered comments were like a muted accompaniment to the proceedings. Nobody paid much attention to her except Sir Matthew, who occasionally caught her eye and nodded reassuringly. He hadn't forgotten that, not so long ago, they'd been allied, conniving closely if not always successfully to influence events in the kingdom. Had been, might be again.

Joanna examined her mother-in-law's chair—recently modified to accommodate the queen's larger girth—and shook it a bit to make sure the legs were sturdy and securely attached.

Suddenly feeling a throb of the backache that had been plaguing her lately, she sank into the nearest seat, which happened to be the king's throne. She leaned back and closed her eyes. Two servants who were still sweeping and polishing glanced at her speculatively.

"Looks like a child playing at grown-up," whispered one. "What a little thing she is."

"Ah, but nothing like what she was when she first came. You weren't here then. The old queen called her a bag of bones. She's filled out nicely, and she must have grown half a foot."

"And I must say, she's a pretty one. King William picked himself a looker, all right."

"Now did you see that? She's smiling. Must be dreaming of her man."

Yes. Joanna was imagining what it would be like when William came. She'd be waiting at the palace door with her ladies and the more important members of the palace staff ranged in their finest behind her. She could see him running up the steps and taking her in his arms. She could feel the warmth of his lips on hers, hear his whispered, "My love, how I've missed you!" And then she'd tell him the wonderful news—that she was carrying his child.

It was at that point in her dream that the servants saw her smile.

She was startled by a touch on her shoulder and a murmured "My lady!"

It was Mary.

"My lady, wouldn't you like to come back to your chamber so I can help you to dress? Lady Yasmin told me you hadn't come for your lesson today. Nobody knew where you were. It's growing quite late."

Yasmin! thought Joanna crossly. The friendship William had predicted between the two women hadn't happened. Since Yasmin's arrival they'd been like two dancers moving around each other, smiling warily, waiting to see who would be the first to hold out a hand so they could dance together. They hardly saw each other except at the sessions that Brother Jean-Pierre scheduled for Arabic conversation. Both were polite, neither was forthcoming. Joanna knew she should make an overture, she should forgive and forget so they could start over without any demons from the past getting in the way. So far she hadn't been able to force herself to take the initiative.

But Mary was right. It was time to rouse herself. She brushed her hand across her eyes and smiled up at her maid. Good Mary! So faithful, so dependable, so indispensable. Who'd have thought the bouncy, scatterbrained little redhead would grow up to become this capable young woman? Her freckles had faded; she'd tamed her mop of unruly curls by tucking them under a frilled white cap. Under Lady Marian's tutelage she'd also tamed her tendency to say the first thing that came into her head. Surprisingly, she'd developed a useful sense of style when it came to costuming the queen.

"Thank you, Mary. And I expect you've decided just what I should wear, to please my husband and dazzle the court?"

"Indeed I have. I've laid out your pale rose silk and, to go over it, the sleeveless tunic in darker rose. King William always likes you in pink."

"Yes, that will do very well. Now how about the dazzling? I don't think my emeralds would look right with the rose. Maybe just my silver chain with the cross?"

"Or how about the pearls King William brought you from Venice last year? They'd look so pretty, with the low neck of the gown. And you could wear your lovely gold ring with the three pearls."

Joanna laughed ruefully. "Just listen to us, Mary. Who would have thought four years ago that you and I would have such a serious discussion about gowns and jewels? My goodness, back then I didn't care what I wore, just so it was comfortable."

"But you didn't have the figure then that you do now, my lady. And you weren't so concerned with what King William would think."

A page, breathless, almost ran into them as they were going out the door. "My lady Queen, you asked to be told when the king's ships were sighted coming into harbor. They've just rounded the point."

"Thank you, Guido. Mary, we must really hurry now."

Within an hour she was ready. She hurried to the palace entrance, getting there just as the herald's trumpet call announced that the king's party was entering the square. Excited and with cheeks as rosy as her gown, she watched impatiently as the square filled with horsemen. Grooms came running. William was the first to dismount. He didn't run up the steps as Joanna had envisioned in her dream, though he did mount them with perhaps a trifle more speed than his dignity ordinarily allowed. He didn't take her in his arms but raised her hand to his lips, kissed it and said, "My lady Queen." To an observer it may have seemed quite formal and proper. But the private look that the two exchanged gave mutual promise of informality to come.

With Joanna at his side he walked along the corridor to the crowded throne room. When they entered, those who were seated rose and everybody bowed respectfully. William acknowledged their greetings, saw Joanna to her seat and stood in front of the golden throne.

He turned first to the others on the dais, nodding to each as he spoke. "My lady mother, Queen Joanna, Sir Matthew, Archbishop Walter," then addressed the assembled courtiers and their ladies.

"I am pleased to report, my friends, that our meeting with the envoys of Emperor Frederick went just as I had hoped. He is holding to the conditions of our truce and, in fact, is withdrawing all the German troops from Italy. We assured them that we too had no troops on the ground except a token force on the borders of our lands in Calabria. I have every expectation that the truce will hold unless Frederick revives his disputes with Pope Alexander, which would complicate the situation. As you know, we have pledged our support for the pope should the Holy See be threatened."

Archbishop Walter broke in. "And did you, my lord, find time to stop in Rome to call on the pope?"

The corners of the king's lips twitched slightly in annoyance. Like most in the room he knew why the archbishop asked. Consumed by his hunger for power, the prelate still hoped the pope would oppose William's new archbishopric at Monreale. Walter and his followers, who included most of the priesthood in Palermo, had been petitioning the pope not to sanction William's ambitious venture but to give his blessing instead to the cathedral they'd begun building in Palermo. Their hopes of prevailing in the contest would be dashed if William had been able to plead his case in person. And if Walter's star fell, that of his archrival, Matthew of Ajello, who had encouraged William in the Monreale scheme, would rise.

"Unfortunately, I was unable to call on Pope Alexander in Rome." The king paused. The archbishop sat back with an audible grunt of relief.

"No, I could not call on him in Rome, but I saw him at his new residence in Civita Castellana. I'm happy to say we had a friendly and productive meeting. He promises to send an emissary when we consecrate the new cathedral at Monreale."

"Ha!" came a triumphant bark from the direction of Queen Margaret. The archbishop glowered. Matthew of Ajello looked smug. Joanna beamed. How clever of William!

William continued. "Count Florian of Camerota was with me at all these conferences, as well as when we met our vassals in Calabria." He nodded toward the justiciar. "He is writing a report on the proceedings for the royal archives. Any of you who wish to consult it are of course welcome to do so."

He ran his eyes over the room. His gaze rested on a couple standing a little apart.

"Now may I publicly greet Lord Hassan ibn-Hawas and his wife, Lady Yasmin, who have joined our court. I am sorry I was not here when they first arrived. By now many of you are acquainted with them and I hope you have been making them feel welcome." Then, speaking directly to the couple, "I trust you will not regret leaving your comfortable estates in Messina to serve us here in Palermo. Welcome, my friends."

Lord Hassan, tall and wiry, black-haired and black-bearded, sober-faced, nodded his head and said, "Thank you, my lord King."

Yasmin looked down modestly and said nothing. Joanna, watching closely, was quite sure her eyes and William's hadn't met. Yasmin looked beautiful in a close-fitting dress of glimmering midnight-blue silk, adorned only with a silver necklace. She raised her head, saw Joanna's eyes on her, and smiled. Joanna could detect no duplicity in the smile.

"One more announcement, my friends," said William, "and then we'll adjourn to the banquet hall. My longtime justiciar, Count Florian of Camerota, who served me well during this difficult journey, merits advancement to a higher post. I am pleased to appoint him as vice-chancellor in our royal council."

Florian, standing at the front of the assembled nobility, looked flustered but proud, and bowed to the king. Murmurs of congratulation broke out, punctuated by some unintelligible grumblings from Queen Margaret.

William stepped down to take Florian's hand and accept his thanks for this very public sign of favor. Joanna and the others on the dais followed and mingled with the throng that was slowly making its way out the door toward the banquet hall. Joanna found herself next to Yasmin. Impulsively, she spoke.

"How lovely you look, Lady Yasmin. That's a beautiful gown, just the color of your eyes."

"I was about to compliment you as well, Queen Joanna. An inspiration, to combine those two shades of rose! They suit your complexion perfectly. And the pearls—they have a little rosy tinge too, haven't they?"

"Thank you, but to be honest, I must give most of the credit for my appearance to my maid, Mary. She's made it her mission to watch over my wardrobe and she always senses what's right. If it weren't for her I'd very likely be here in last year's threadbare brocade."

"What a pity none of the other ladies have such a treasure." Yasmin gestured around the room, dotted with elaborate, multihued costumes, gaudy enough to put even the peacocks on the walls to shame. "Did you ever see so many ruffles and laces and colors and jewels?"

They surveyed the scene and Joanna reflected on how anything so trivial as the attire of the ladies at court could have brought her and Yasmin to this turning point. They were conversing as easily as friends who had seen each other only yesterday.

She was startled when she caught sight of Queen Margaret. There stood the queen, encased as usual in multiple layers and flying attachments. Today she'd added a new feature: a broad, fluttery white scarf that ran from her left shoulder, diagonally down across her midriff, and around her ample hips to fasten somewhere on her backside. When she moved it billowed. She was coming now in their general direction, slowly navigating through the crowd.

"A ship under full sail!" whispered Yasmin. The old queen's eyes were fixed on them as she approached but when she arrived she ignored Joanna.

"I see you've been admiring my gown, Lady Yasmin. My maid took particular pains and I think she showed a great appreciation of my unique style. Tell me, who dresses you?"

"I myself generally select my gowns, Queen Margaret. But I do get excellent counsel from my husband." She smiled up at Hassan, who had just appeared at her side. "He has very definite ideas of what his wife should wear."

"Of course. Every precious jewel should be enhanced by its setting." Hassan looked approvingly at Joanna. "And judging from the evidence, King William would agree. Which brings me to why I'm here, my lady Queen. Your husband asked me to find you in this tight press of people and to escort you to where he's waiting by the door yonder."

"Thank you, you're very kind." Joanna placed her hand on his arm.

Before they had taken two steps Queen Margaret said, not loudly but more distinctly than in her usual mumble, "I'd think twice, Lord Hassan, before I was seen in public associating with that hussy on your arm. But of course, she won't be around much longer."

Very few could have heard. Those who did stared in shock. Hassan stiffened. Joanna's cheeks flushed a bright red.

She turned and looked her attacker in the face.

"If you have anything to say that concerns me, Queen Margaret, you may address me directly. I am right here, well within hearing."

Without waiting for a rejoinder she tightened her hold on Hassan's arm and they walked on. Lady Yasmin took her other arm. Joanna was trembling. In a shaky voice, she said, "Thank you both. Please, don't say anything to William about this, I'll tell him."

They threaded their way slowly through the crowd. By the time they reached the door she felt calmer. William hurried to her and led her along the vaulted corridor. Looking down, he saw the tenseness in her face. "I'm sorry if this is tiring for you. But be patient." He bent and whispered in her ear, "It will soon be over and then..." The rest was lost as the trumpeter at the door to the banquet hall produced a deafening blast to announce the arrival of the king and queen.

The sounds of hurrying footsteps, shouted orders, benches being shoved into position and silver platters and goblets clanging onto the tables heralded the state banquet that was about to begin. Joanna braced herself and stood as straight as she could in spite of her aching back. On William's arm she stepped proudly into the room.

25

It was too much. Too much heat, too much noise, too much suckling pig, too many treacly tarts. And too little of William. Joanna had learned to accept the way her husband compartmentalized his life, but really! On being reunited after so long, for him to devote himself to earnest consultation with Matthew of Ajello on his right, which left her no one to converse with except taciturn Count Florian on her left! It was too much.

"I've not heard anything yet about your journey, Sir Florian. Did you by any chance get to Naples?"

He looked up from his methodical assault on a rather tough mutton chop. He brushed his cuff daintily across his mouth.

"We did, my lady Queen."

"I remember Naples because I was so glad to get there and to step on dry, firm land after being so terribly seasick. But of course I saw very little of the city—it took me so long to recover. Wasn't that a dreadful voyage?"

"Indeed, it was not pleasant."

"But you came through it very well. Do you never get seasick, Sir Florian?"

"Very seldom."

The new vice-chancellor had many fine qualities but an aptitude for small talk wasn't among them. Joanna gave up and looked about her. She wasn't fond of the banquet hall in the royal palace, so much larger and less charming than the Fountain Room at La Zisa, where the stream's murmur made such a pleasant backdrop to music and conversation. Here there were no graceful arches and only a few mosaics. The loud conversations of three dozen diners bounced off the stone walls. It was hard to make oneself heard over the banging of heavy platters onto the tables.

She looked with sympathy at the harpist in the corner who was bravely trying to compete with the chatter and clatter. He was in black velvet from head to toe with a little black cap perched on his chestnut curls. His fingers flew over the strings, his mouth opened and closed, but he and his song could have been mute for all Joanna knew.

Hearing a familiar querulous voice, Joanna glanced down the table. Four or five places along on the other side she saw her mother-in-law, pointing at her and addressing the lady next to her. "See that? That's where I should be seated, next to the king, instead of that upstart." Oblivious to the uproar, she stared fixedly at Joanna while her jaws worked steadily.

What can be going through her head, Joanna wondered. Her look wasn't so much one of hatred as of cold conjecture—like a huntsman training his arrow on a deer, waiting for just the right moment to let the arrow fly.

She looked down at her plate. She pushed the food around so she'd appear to be eating. But her back was paining her so much that she could hardly continue to sit up straight and look bright. She touched William on the shoulder.

"I feel I've had quite enough. I'll wait for you upstairs." He looked surprised but smiled affectionately and said, "Very well, my love. I won't be long," and turned again to Sir Matthew.

Back in her chamber, feeling cleansed and refreshed thanks to Mary's ministrations, she sat down to wait for William. She considered whether, or how, to tell him about Queen Margaret's attacks—two within two hours. She decided she wouldn't, at least not now. This was to be their night for reunion and rejoicing. Later, perhaps. Or perhaps not. Wasn't she sixteen—old enough to fight her own battles? Surely she could figure out some way to deal with the old queen. Maybe she could arrange a meeting, just the two of them. Maybe they could talk about William and she could ask what he was like as a little boy. Maybe when Joanna told her about the baby on the way she'd become less hostile.

She sighed. What a lot of "maybes." She'd think about it later.

She fidgeted, she fingered the edge of her robe—the same blue robe she'd worn the night William left. Unable to relax, she walked about the room. Its ambience soothed her. When she'd first moved to the royal palace she'd tried to achieve, here in her own private space, a blending of exotic Arabic elegance and familiar English decorum. At her first home in Sicily, the La Zisa palace, she'd been captivated by the lushness of thick carpets, the bright colors of soft pillows strewn about, and the delicacy of carved screens. She'd lavished these new apartments with such seductions. But as a salute to her English heritage she'd acquired a huge four-poster bed draped with burgundy velvet, as well as a few carved chests and tables that were as serious and dignified as the ones she remembered from her childhood. William indulged her but teased her, especially about the bed.

"I hope this doesn't mean, my love, that when we're lying on that lofty eminence you're secretly wishing you were back in Winchester Palace. What a monster it is, and so much trouble to get in and out, what with having to step on that stool. And don't you feel suffocated, closed in by those heavy curtains?"

Nevertheless, she'd reminded him, they'd spent some very pleasurable nights in that monster bed. But she'd considered what he'd said, and while he was gone she'd had half a foot sawed off the legs, and had done away with the velvet canopy. Now the bed was draped in white silk gauze, so airy and diaphanous that it looked as though a wispy cloud had settled in the room.

She was tempted to climb up and stretch out within the cloud right now. Her back was still bothering her. But she wanted to be fresh and wide-awake when William came. She looked speculatively at the divan by the window, another of her acquisitions during his absence. Covered in finespun fawn-colored wool, with pillows of daffodil yellow, it invited her to come lie down. Maybe for just a few minutes?

When William came he found his queen curled up on the divan, sound asleep. Her lips were parted in a half-smile. Her lashes rested lightly on her cheeks. Her hair, shining russet-brown in the candlelight, fell across the pillow. He stood looking at her, admiring such innocence and repose. He also admired the new divan—roomy enough for two, he noted. He removed his tunic and boots and carefully lowered himself to lie beside her. Her eyes flew open.

"Oh, I'm sorry! I meant to be waiting at the door to greet you."

"I much prefer this arrangement." He kissed her, then slipped his hand inside her robe and slowly, lovingly, his hand journeyed from neck to knee, with many side trips along the way. She held her breath and tried not to giggle when it tickled. The hand returned to the smooth swell of her stomach—rounder than he remembered—and rested there. She heard his indrawn breath. He raised himself on an elbow.

"Joanna! Are you with child?"

"I am! And you found out all by yourself, I didn't even have to tell you. Are you glad, William?"

For answer he kissed her gently and folded her into his arms. She rested her head on his shoulder and they lay there, talking softly, marveling at the incredible fact: two who had become one would soon become three.

"I should have guessed, shouldn't I, when you weren't feeling well back in July? Tell me, when did you know?"

"The very day after you left, when the physicians came and examined me. I could hardly believe it at first. But Lady Marian, and Mary too—they told me they'd been suspecting that I was pregnant because of the way I couldn't keep my breakfast down."

"And did the physicians say when the child will come?"

"They think after the new year, around Epiphany."

"Four months and a bit more. Joanna, you must promise me to behave yourself and do everything the physicians say, get your rest, and not let anything upset you."

"I promise."

The next day William ordered that Joanna have a thorough going-over by the physicians, who shortly appeared: a trio of tall solemn Muslims, wearing long black cloaks. They poked and prodded, looked at her tongue, placed their ears at her navel or where they guessed it to be since she was fully clothed, and requested a sample of her urine to peer at and smell. They asked her how much and when her back pained her, and whether she had an aversion to or strong desire for any foods. She thought hard and said at the moment she'd enjoy a pickled onion. They made painstaking notes of that and other matters on the clay tablets they pulled out of their deep pockets, scratching away busily with their little styluses. They murmured to each other in Arabic and consulted the bound manuscripts they'd brought with them.

The verdict was that the patient should remain in bed as much as possible. Frequent doses of soothing teas should be administered. Highly spiced foods should be avoided. (So much for the pickled onion.) Short walks within the palace would be permitted.

From then on Joanna received her visitors from her divan, where she lay wrapped in shawls and blankets and propped up by pillows.

William came as often as he could. He'd sit beside her and hold her hand and tell her about the foreign ambassadors and the churchmen he'd been entertaining and how solicitously they'd asked about her health. Joanna wondered privately if some of these dignitaries had a substitute queen in mind, in case she should decline and die.

One day he arrived full of enthusiasm after an inspection visit to Monreale.

"How I wish you could see it, Joanna! They're beginning the mosaic of the Christ Pantocrator—it will fill nearly the whole dome. I've seen the sketches. He'll be reaching his arms out as though to bless the entire church."

"Couldn't I go, William? Please? I feel so well now, and I don't see how it could harm me, a little trip like that."

"No, the doctors say absolutely no horseback travel. And the way is so steep that a litter wouldn't do, you'd be bouncing about and in danger of falling out. No, I'm sorry. But let me tell you about your Thomas à Becket portrait. It's coming along nicely. It should be completed by this time next year. Which reminds me, the mosaic artists have a question for you. They've almost finished Thomas's head and his halo, but they aren't sure how much hair he had, if any. I told them you'd seen him when you were very young—can you possibly remember what the top of his head looked like?"

She closed her eyes tight and tried to picture that long-ago day in Canterbury. She opened them. "No, I'm quite sure he was wearing his miter so I wouldn't have seen how much hair he had. But I do remember that he had a flourishing brown mustache as well as a beard."

"You don't say! A mustache! They've given him a beard, and I'm sure they can easily add a mustache. They'll be delighted to hear this. They're absolutely obsessed with accuracy, especially when the figure is of someone so recently dead."

"In that case, I'll write to my mother and ask her about the hair. She'll remember, I'm sure. But it will be some time before we get her reply."

"That's no matter. The artists have plenty to keep them busy. They've barely begun the Mary and Jesus who'll be above St. Thomas, and there are several more saints yet to do in that same section."

"What an age it takes to build a cathedral! How much longer, do you think?"

"I'm guessing two or three years at most. We must complete it and have it consecrated before Archbishop Walter finishes his cathedral here in Palermo." The worry lines that Joanna had begun to notice lately on her husband's forehead appeared.

She reached up to smooth them away. "That means that when our little one is

able to walk we can take him there and show him his father's glorious creation."
From the beginning William had assumed they'd have a boy and Joanna went
along with it. Actually, she wouldn't have minded if this first child were a girl.
Plenty of time for boys later.

William brightened. "So we can. Now I must be off. Rest well, my love." He
kissed her and patted her stomach. "Take care of our son." He held her hand a moment longer, then left.

So far there hadn't been any official announcement that the queen was
pregnant. King William was superstitious and didn't want it talked about. Only
Joanna's inner circle knew: Lady Marian, Mary, Brother Jean-Pierre, and Mary's
uncle Alan—now Sir Alan. King William had knighted him to recognize his years
of loyal service as the queen's guard and escort. The physicians had been ordered to
say only that Joanna was run down and needed a complete rest. When that word
spread, some of the lords and ladies of the court dropped by to offer sympathy.
Lady Charmaine came more than most. She'd hold forth on whatever wandered
into her head, whether her wardrobe, what was served at dinner, or reminiscences
about her childhood in Normandy. Joanna wasn't annoyed at the flow of words
and in fact found it soothing. She didn't need to respond and she could lie there
dreaming of the child she would bear. If it was a boy, what would they call him?
She couldn't decide between Paul, her favorite disciple, and Richard, her favorite
brother. If it was a girl there was no question. She'd be Eleanor.

Presently she noticed frequent references in Charmaine's monologues to a Sir
Mario. "Sir Mario thinks that the melons from the south are far sweeter than the
ones we get here." Or "Sir Mario's promised to take me to Agrigento to see the
Greek ruins."

"How I would love to see Agrigento!" said Joanna. "William will take me
some day, I know. He says the temples there are as fine as anything to be seen in
Rome."

Charmaine, unused to interruption, was silenced but only momentarily. "And
I'm sure you will go, my lady. Maybe one of these days when you're feeling up to it
you could join Sir Mario and me on an expedition."

"Perhaps," said Joanna, and fell into a doze. She dreamed that she and William, each holding the hand of a little boy who stood between them, were staring
up at the white marble columns of an ancient temple on the shore of an impossibly
blue sea.

26

Lady Yasmin visited often, the first time only a few days after the banquet. She came straight to the divan. "How are you, my lady? I must say, you look fetching! I hope that means you're improving. And none the worse for your jousting with the queen mother?"

Joanna held out her hand to clasp Yasmin's.

"How kind of you to come! I was feeling quite bereft. Lady Marian was here but she had to leave to see about something. So I tried to embroider but as you see, the threads got all tangled up. I was almost ready to ring the bell and call the page to talk to me! But do sit down, get comfortable."

Lady Yasmin sank gracefully onto a pillow on the floor, tucked one leg under her and looked at Joanna expectantly. "So? Are you feeling as well as you look?"

"I do feel quite well, thank you. My back hardly bothers me. My appetite is excellent—too much so, look how plump I'm getting! The physicians say that if I have no setbacks I may get up soon and walk a bit."

"Wonderful!" said Lady Yasmin. "I'll volunteer to keep you company. And if we should come across the mean old queen, I'll do my best to defend you."

"You're kind to offer, but I doubt if you'll need to bring your sword. William has told me that Alan must be with me whenever I leave my rooms. But your moral support will be appreciated. Thank you."

"You're welcome. Now forgive my curiosity, but I can't take my eyes off your lovely blue shawl. Do I detect the fine hand of your priceless Mary?"

Joanna laughed and told her about Mary's determination to keep her mistress in fashion. "She even goes out into the city to shop at the bazaars. She told me this shawl came from Samarkand. Where do you suppose that is?"

"I believe it's far to the East, in Asia. It's on the road the silk merchants from China follow. What a lot of traveling that shawl has done! From China, all the way across Asia and over the sea to us here in Sicily."

In no time they were chatting easily, just as they'd begun to do the night of the banquet. It was as though everything that had been tormenting Joanna about Yasmin and William had never happened. When Lady Marian came in to announce it was time for her lemon balm tea and her nap and Yasmin left, Joanna was astonished that so much time had passed.

"Lady Marian, I do believe that Yasmin and I can become friends. Who would have thought it?"

"Yes, it would be quite surprising, considering everything. Also since she's five years older than you. But she does seem a nice person, basically. I hope for your sake it turns out that way. You've never really had a friend, my pet."

It was true. As a child Joanna had been mostly in the company of her elders. Her two older sisters left England while very young for the lands of their royal fiancés. Richard was a favorite companion but he was hardly ever there. Her younger brother John was about as friendly as a baited bear. If any of Queen Eleanor's ladies had young children they wouldn't have been allowed in the palace, for fear they'd break something or make too much noise for Eleanor's highly developed sense of decorum.

Later, Joanna had hoped Lady Beatrice and she might be friends, but those hopes had withered. It was less and less likely that Beatrice would ever come back to Sicily.

Now here was Yasmin. Warm-hearted, outgoing, nimble-witted, amused by the same things that amused Joanna. The difference in their ages didn't seem to matter. Maybe Yasmin too had never had a friend.

The time came when she was permitted to take little walks along the palace corridors with Lady Yasmin, while Alan paced gravely behind them. But she was always glad to come back to her warm, pleasant rooms. Increasingly, she was focused on the life that was growing within her. She contentedly spent her days dozing or dreaming, waiting for William's visits, gossiping idly with Lady Marian or Mary about the life of the court. Lady Marian was teaching her to knit, and despite considerable ripping out and starting over, she'd completed three fairly presentable rows of a tiny baby blanket.

Sometimes, though, her placid calm would be interrupted. She'd be lying on her couch, thinking of nothing in particular, when Queen Margaret's heart-chilling words—"She won't be around much longer"—would echo, unbidden, in her ears. She wanted to believe that they'd been the maundering of a spiteful, idle old woman and were not a real threat. She worried for a while that she hadn't told William about it, but as time passed it would have been awkward to bring it up, so long after the fact. So she succeeded in putting it out of her mind. Most of the time.

In the early afternoon of a mid-October day, she sat down to examine a psalter Brother Jean-Pierre had brought the day before. She was alone. Lady Marian had gone to confer with the cook about Joanna's dinner and Mary had gone out on some errand.

Autumn sunlight poured through the windows. It brought more light than heat but Joanna's slippered feet were warmed by the brazier under the table, and the rest of her was snugly encased in a wool robe.

Brother Jean-Pierre had told her to look in Proverbs 22 for some good advice on bringing up a child. But as she leafed through the little book, she was distracted by the brilliance of the illuminations. When the sun fell on the ornate initial letters, red or gold or sapphire-blue, they glowed like jewels. Many of them were wreathed with vines or flowers or accompanied by minute animals and birds. Totally absorbed in the scribe's artistry, she was startled by a knock on the door. The page on duty poked in his head and announced "Lady Maria Cristina asks if you will receive her."

Joanna hardly knew the lady except that she was Queen Margaret's companion and had come with her to Sicily from their native Spain many years ago. The two were often seen together at dinner. In fact, Joanna remembered now, it had been Lady Maria Cristina to whom Margaret had directed the complaint about her seat at the table, back in September.

"Yes, Guido. Show her in." She rose and moved toward the door, wondering what could have prompted this visit.

Lady Maria Cristina was tall, thin and all in black except for a gray wimple. She had a pinched face and dark eyes that roved about the room, taking in every detail. Joanna held out her hand in welcome.

"I'm so glad to see you. Please, come and sit down. May I call for some refreshments?"

"No, thank you. I am here only for a moment." Her voice was raspy and heavily accented. "I come at her majesty's request to ask if you would be so good as to call on her. If you are feeling up to it, that is. We have heard you are not well. But it's only a short walk to the other side of the palace."

Joanna, uncertain, played for time.

"Yes, that's true, that is, yes I have been unwell, but nothing serious, just some kind of stomach upset. But indeed I'm much better now. The doctors seem quite sure that before long I'll be able to be as active as I like."

She knew she was babbling. But how should she respond? Lady Maria Cristina wasn't helping. She simply stood there, waiting. Only her eyes moved, darting from Joanna to the psalter on the table to the braziers in the corners, from the rumpled blankets on the divan to the white-curtained bed. And back to Joanna.

Joanna made up her mind. Whatever the queen's purpose, this might be her best chance to mend the rift—to talk to her adversary and persuade her that they could be friends.

"When would the queen like to see me?"

"Now, this afternoon, if that is convenient."

Another surprise. Why the hurry? But she must seize the moment

"Then I'll be happy to come. I hope Queen Margaret will forgive me if I don't change from my robe. I've been ordered to avoid drafts and chills."

She instructed the page to watch for Lady Marian's return. "Tell her where I've gone and say I'll be back soon."

Lady Maria Cristina held out her sharp-elbowed arm, Joanna took it and they set out.

Joanna was so flustered that she completely forgot that she should have sent for Alan to accompany her.

27

L et her come!

Queen Margaret was ready to receive her daughter-in-law.

She sat in her favorite chair. It was oversized and very soft. Sinking into it, she felt cradled, secure and—in relation to the chair—quite small.

Around her shoulders she wore a blue velvet cape embroidered with the royal golden lions. The table before her was draped with a fine white silk cloth emblazoned with more lions. Arranged on it were three silver goblets, a bowl of dried sugared cherries, and several tiny lacquer bowls of powdered spices. An ebony tray held nutmegs, a silver grater and a long-handled silver spoon.

She'd given her chambermaid precise instructions as to the refreshments to be served: sweetened, heated red wine, to which the queen would personally add condiments. After settling herself in her chair she'd reached into her bosom and pulled out a gold locket. She opened it and carefully shook out a small amount of grayish powder into one of the bowls of spices and stirred it well.

As the final touch she'd ordered her maid Marie to bring to bring her crown. "Not the crown of state but the second-best one, Marie." No point in wasting her finest on an ignorant girl who wouldn't appreciate it.

Now, royally clad and crowned, she waited. She was feeling clear-headed and focused, for which she was grateful. So often nowadays she found it hard to keep her mind on the matter at hand. She'd seen how people looked at her strangely when her unspoken thoughts unexpectedly came out as muttered imprecations. She was resolved that today she'd be calm, judicious and careful in her speech.

As usual, the door to the main corridor of the palace was open. From her seat she could keep an eye on who was out and about.

If any passerby had cast a furtive glance into the apartment, he would have seen the queen in the center of a pool of light issuing from two tall candelabra behind her. The rest of the room was a vague dim jumble of shapes—chairs, couches, tables, chests. Most who passed had learned not to catch her eye. It ordinarily led to a royal summons and a relentless questioning until she could elicit a morsel of palace gossip.

But today she wasn't interested in enticing stray visitors into her lair. She was waiting to hear the sound of Lady Maria Cristina's cane.

There it came—tap tap, louder and more staccato as it approached along the marble-floored corridor.

The queen arranged her crumpled face in what she trusted was a look of benevolent welcome when the page announced from the door, "Queen Joanna and Lady Maria Cristina."

"There you are, my dear. Come in, come in." She hoped her voice sounded cordial. She was unused to offering ingratiating greetings. "Do sit here beside me."

Joanna obeyed. Lady Maria Cristina, as previously instructed, closed the door and seated herself on the queen's other side.

What a sorry excuse for a queen for my William, thought Queen Margaret. Puny. Pale-faced. And why is she wearing such an unbecoming robe? She looks quite lost in it. Oh dear, why didn't William listen to me and marry one of those strapping German princesses instead?

She caught herself. Had she been thinking out loud? Apparently not. Joanna was looking at her politely.

"Wouldn't you like to take off your robe, Joanna? I always insist that my rooms must be nice and warm. I'm sure you'd be more comfortable."

The old queen had given much thought as to what to call her daughter-in-law. Certainly not Queen Joanna. It was unthinkable that there could be two queens of Sicily, and she still saw Joanna as a queen without the proper credentials. She certainly wouldn't call her daughter, as some witless mothers-in-law might. So it came down to simply Joanna.

The girl seemed to see nothing strange in the familiar address. She smiled and Queen Margaret saw with surprise how that ingenuous smile transformed her face, heretofore so grave. It was a wide, spontaneous smile, revealing two rows of perfectly even, white teeth. Even her eyes seemed to take on more liveliness. The queen could see flecks of gold in them that caught the candlelight Why, she was a little beauty! Margaret, even in the first blush of youth, had never been a beauty. A surge of jealousy joined her other reasons to dislike Joanna.

"I'd indeed like to take the robe off, but the doctors have ordered me to wrap myself up like a mummy and I've given them my promise."

"Yes, we've heard that you've been ill. And I suppose one must listen to the doctors. But I do think sometimes we who have actually had ailments and have recovered from them know as much as the doctors about what's good for us. Haven't I always said so, Maria Cristina?"

The lady-in-waiting, perched on her chair in semi-shadow, had been watching and listening but saying nothing since she entered. She recognized her cue. With her hands folded on her cane she leaned forward.

"You have, my lady Queen. And so often you've been proved right. I remember well that time when your little William was suffering from a fever, and the doctors said he should be put on a strict diet of thin broth and toasted bread, but he didn't improve. And you were so worried until you remembered how your old nurse had cured you when you were a girl in Spain and fell sick. So you did just what she did. You gave William nourishing stews of beef and chicken and had him drink possets made of good red Spanish wine. Diluted of course. And he had a remarkable recovery." She sat back, performance over.

"What a happy ending to the story! Thank you, Lady Maria Cristina," said Joanna. She asked Queen Margaret, "Was William often sick as a child?"

"No, on the whole he was a healthy lad. His father, my husband, started him early on hunting and jousting and archery. He loved all that. I'm sure it helped him to keep strong and well. But I didn't ask you here to talk about William. I was so grieved to hear of your illness and I thought, why not see if an old remedy I was brought up with might help? It certainly can't do any harm—nothing but wine, water, honey and spices."

Before Joanna could reply a tantalizing aroma of mulled wine filled the air. The maidservant brought a jug and placed it carefully on the table. The smell was almost as intoxicating as wine itself.

Queen Margaret poured each of them a goblet of the steaming potion. "As I remember, you like only a little cinnamon?" she asked Lady Maria Cristina. The latter nodded. The queen stirred a small spoonful of the spice into her goblet.

In her own, Margaret grated some nutmeg and stirred in cinnamon.

"But for you, Joanna, we'll do it just as my old nurse did—with all three, cloves as well as the others," and she proceeded to measure small spoonfuls of the powdered spices and a generous grating of nutmeg into the third goblet. Joanna was looking doubtful. She picked it up and brought it toward her nose. She put it down.

"It smells so good! But I'd better not drink it. I've been told I should avoid wine for the time being."

"Nonsense! It's perfectly harmless, mostly water. And I know for a fact it's safe for delicate stomachs. Which is what you apparently have."

Margaret was getting irritated. Why was the silly girl being so fussy?

Joanna bent her head and stared at her folded hands in her lap, as though in thought. She came to a decision. She raised her eyes to look at the old queen, whose face was not quite so benevolent now.

"I've been wanting to talk to you about this and I was just waiting for the chance. So I'm glad you've asked me to come see you. You see, we've known for some time why I've been unwell. It's not at all mysterious. I'm going to be a mother, and you'll be a grandmother!"

If she expected crows of delight and maybe a hug, she was sadly disappointed. Queen Margaret stared at her in stunned silence. She looked at Lady Maria Cristina, whose face was a thinner, craggier version of her own. Things were not working out as they'd planned.

She completely forgot her resolve to be nice.

"Well! Aren't you the crafty little one! Whose idea was it to keep it a secret? Not William's, I don't think. You must have persuaded him not to tell anyone, not even his own mother, just out of vanity. You didn't want people staring and whispering. No wonder you've been wearing those floppy cloaks that hide everything."

She snatched up her goblet and drained half the wine. She looked angrily at

Joanna. The girl was crying and trying to tell her something while the tears ran down her cheeks.

"You don't understand. I wanted to tell you but William kept saying, not yet. He's so superstitious, he wanted to wait to announce it until we were sure I was going to get through the pregnancy all right. But I'm in my seventh month now and really feeling fine. I did so hope you'd be glad to have the news." She found a handkerchief in her pocket and wiped her eyes. "I think I'd better leave now."

Queen Margaret eyed Joanna's untasted wine. Maybe all was not lost. But she'd have to turn honey-toned again.

"Well well, I suppose I was hasty to get so upset. You must forgive me. It was such a surprise, I hardly knew what I was saying. Please don't go yet. Of course I'll be happy to be a grandmother. It will take me back to the days when my William was a baby. Why don't we drink a little toast to the child—and of course to your health?"

Joanna looked uncertain. "I suppose just a few sips won't hurt," she said.

"Of course not. You too, Maria Cristina. Now let us all drink to the future of the royal house of Sicily!"

Joanna reached for her goblet but before she could pick it up the door burst open. Startled, she turned to see who it was. Her arm upset the goblet, and the wine spread over Queen Margaret's precious tablecloth, dripped onto her white damask skirt and down to her costly Persian carpet.

Alan had pushed past the page and stood inside the door. His face, usually so amiable, looked uncommonly stern.

"Queen Joanna, I'm sent by Lady Marian to see you back to your chamber. The king is on his way and he'll expect to find you there."

Joanna rose and looked in dismay at the mess she'd made. The old queen was looking at it too. Joanna's tears flowed again.

"I'm so very, very sorry. Oh dear, how could I be so clumsy?"

"How could you indeed! Go now, go." Margaret was so furious at how her careful plans had been shattered that she could hardly speak. She sank deeper into her cushions and began to mutter and mumble. "Idiot girl. Stupid. Stubborn."

Joanna, hurrying out with Alan, heard the mumbling but not the words.

Lady Maria Cristina hobbled away to find the maid to bring cloths to mop up the wine, and salt to sprinkle on the rug. Queen Margaret, still sputtering, retired to change her gown.

Half an hour later the two old cronies settled down by the fire in the queen's bedchamber to assess the situation. Margaret had put on a black gown to suit her mood.

"A disaster, that's what it is. All my planning, for nothing."

"We'll never get her to come back now."

"I can hardly remember what I said. Was I quite unkind?"

"I'm afraid you were."

"Well, she deserved it, the ninny. Making all that fuss about drinking a little wine. And then spilling it, after I'd been so clever with the poison."

"Yes, true. We'll just have to think of something else. Even if she does come back she'll be suspicious if we try again to get her to disobey her doctors."

They sat there like a pair of crows croaking to each other about their chances of finding a mouse or a baby bird for dinner. Queen Margaret fell to grumbling to herself. Maria Cristina sat looking at the fire, waiting for her lady to make sense again. It didn't take long.

"I have it!" she exclaimed. "Maybe, Maria, this was all for the best. Really, the news that there's a baby on the way changes everything. If I take charge of raising him maybe I'll get some respect again in the court!"

"But how could you... Joanna wouldn't ..."

The queen paid no attention.

"They'll see that I'm still someone to be reckoned with, just like the old days!" She chortled. "That'll show them! And I'll bring this child up right, not the way that nincompoop of a girl would."

"But my lady, surely Joanna would never give up her baby!"

"Of course she wouldn't, you stupid old thing. But she won't be here. And King William will be glad enough to turn the child over to me, mark my words."

Maria Cristina still looked bewildered. Her powers of contriving mischief lagged seriously behind her lady's.

"Don't you see? As soon as the child is born, we'll find a way to get rid of Joanna. It shouldn't be hard. Everything will be in such a state of confusion. Nobody will suspect anything; women so often die in childbirth."

"Oh yes! They do!" Maria Cristina had begun to understand.

"And everybody will be grateful when I offer to take charge of the baby."

"How kind of you, my lady! To sacrifice your own comfort in your old age, to care for that poor little motherless child."

The two old crows had found their prey. Now it was just a matter of waiting for the moment to swoop down on it.

28

Relations between the king and queen of Sicily turned frosty after the queen's impromptu visit to her mother-in-law.

Alan told William immediately what had happened. William arrived in Joanna's chamber shortly after her own return. He planted himself before the divan where she was sitting, his feet firmly together and arms folded. He was so cross that he forgot to be civil. In fact, he very nearly shouted. Joanna had never heard him shout.

"You deliberately ignored my orders, Joanna. You went out without an escort and without Lady Marian's knowledge."

"But William..."

"Furthermore, of all places, you went to my mother's. We've talked about this, Joanna. She resents you and she's erratic enough in her behavior not to be trusted. You were foolhardy to place yourself in what might have been a dangerous situation."

"No, I..."

"Let me finish, please. Most serious of all, you not only took a chance on your own safety, you endangered our unborn child. Don't you care? Have you no idea how important it is for me to have an heir? Sicily's future depends on an orderly succession. If anything happened to the child—and to you, of course—there'd be no lack of other claimants to the throne to start maneuvering. I hope, Joanna, that you're sorry for your foolish behavior." He stopped for breath.

Joanna, looking about as penitent as a pugnacious bulldog, leaped in.

"I don't agree that I was foolish. This was the first time in all my years here that Queen Margaret has made an overture to me. You apparently don't understand how it's hurt me all this time that your mother never accepted me and that we couldn't be friends. So when I saw a chance to change all that of course I welcomed her invitation. And Lady Marian knew where I'd gone, I sent word to her. I didn't see why I had to have Alan come with me, since it was only to the other side of the palace and Lady Maria Cristina was with me."

"Nevertheless..."

"And William, nothing terrible happened. She was really quite kind and cordial, except for a couple of times when she flew into a bit of a rage. But she's always doing that, and she got over it right away, except maybe right at the end."

"But Joanna..."

"Now let *me* finish." She stood up and faced him, with her hands straight down at her sides and her fists clenched. Her eyes were flashing and her cheeks were flushed with agitation. "It's not fair to say I don't care about the baby. I care terribly. I've been as good as I can be to make sure nothing goes wrong. I look forward to the birth of our child more than I've ever looked forward to anything in my life."

They stared at each other. Joanna was as surprised as William at her vehemence. She'd never even argued with him, much less quarreled. She sank onto the divan. After a moment he sat beside her. He put his arm around her.

"My love, we've both been hasty. I'm sorry I spoke so harshly. Let us mend matters. I want you to tell me in detail everything that happened this afternoon. Then we'll decide whether there was, or will be, any threat to you and the child."

She complied, from Maria Cristina's arrival at her door to Alan's appearance at the queen's. William questioned her closely about the wine.

"So all the wine came from the same pitcher, but each of you had a different selection of spices in your serving?"

"Yes—or would have had if I hadn't spilled mine and set the queen off on another tantrum." She grimaced in mortification at what she'd done.

"And my mother doled out those spices and stirred them into each goblet?"

"Yes. They were in little bowls in front of her."

"Hmmm."

"What do you mean, 'hmmm'?"

He became, if possible, even more serious. His eyes darkened and his gaze grew more penetrating as he looked at her for a moment, choosing his words.

"Joanna, I must talk to you now about a subject I'd hoped we wouldn't have to discuss. Do you remember, not long after we were married, when you were cruelly maligned in graffiti you saw on the walls in the city? And how I promised to find out who was responsible, and I discovered that my mother and Sir Matthew of Ajello were behind it?"

"Yes, it was terribly upsetting. I hated it. But you must have taken care of it because the ugly messages disappeared and there haven't been any since."

"No, thank God. But I didn't tell you the whole story at the time. You were still very young and I wanted to shelter you from evil and unpleasantness. When we were looking into the source of the graffiti we discovered that my mother had asked Sir Matthew to find men who could be hired as assassins. And he did."

She caught her breath. "You mean…?"

"Yes, my love. We tracked the men down and imprisoned them. I think it was then that my mother's mental state really began to deteriorate into madness. I reasoned with her and though she expressed remorse for what she and Sir Matthew had done, I never quite knew what she was really thinking. Fortunately, she lost her ally. When I threatened to banish Sir Matthew he did a complete turnaround, promised me faithfully to call a halt to his conniving with my mother, and has in that respect at least been a loyal chancellor; though we don't always see eye to eye on other subjects."

"And why are you telling me all this now?" But she was beginning to guess why. She tensed.

"You've grown up. I owe it to you, as my wife and the mother of my child, to talk to you as an adult, freely and frankly, about everything that concerns us both."

She waited.

"My love, it's quite possible, though it grieves me to even think it, that my mother hasn't changed. I believe she meant to give you poisoned wine."

Joanna gasped. It was as though a monstrous cold wave had washed over her. Somebody wanted to kill her! She couldn't think, she could only yield to the numbness of terror.

She'd never felt such fear. Even during the worst storms and perils of the voyage to Sicily, when she was convinced her life was coming to an end, she'd still put her trust in God and prayed to him to be merciful to her and to all on the ship. But if he could not spare them, "Thy will be done," she'd prayed.

Now it wasn't a matter of God's will but the deadly intrigues of man—or rather, of woman.

Later that afternoon Alan Broadshares, Joanna's bodyguard, met her maid, Mary, for a chat in a nook just outside the palace kitchens. When they had time, uncle and niece came here to relax, to talk of home and family and to gossip about goings-on in the palace.

There was room for only one bench in their cranny and there was a great deal of noise from next door—raised voices, spoons banging against metal cauldrons, logs dropped heavily, squawks from indignant fowl being dragged by the neck. But that was why they liked the spot. Nobody could intrude on their privacy, and nobody could hear what they said. Besides, the kitchen with its ready supply of wine was handy, in case Sir Alan felt a pang of thirst.

On this particular afternoon Queen Joanna's daring foray into enemy territory was on both their minds. They compared notes.

"Of course I went to tell the king, the minute I got the queen safely back," said Sir Alan. "I didn't want to be blamed for letting her go about unescorted."

"But nobody could think it was your fault, uncle, when she didn't send for you or tell you what she was up to."

"True. And as it turned out, the king didn't go after me very hard. I fancy he didn't let Lady Marian off so easy though."

"Or Queen Joanna either. Uncle, you should have heard the talking-to he gave her and how she answered back!" Her face was awestruck with the memory.

"Do you mean to tell me, Mary, that you were there?"

"Well, not exactly. I'd taken a load of linens to the washerwoman, and as I came back into the queen's antechamber I heard the king in the next room. He must have just come in through her private entrance. I've never heard him so loud or so angry. He wouldn't let her get a word in edgewise. Then she started in on him, defending herself, every bit as cross as he was. I didn't know what to do. The door was ajar but I didn't dare close it, they'd have noticed. So I had to stand there, listening in spite of myself."

"Who won?"

"If it were up to me, I'd say the queen. But all of a sudden they stopped shouting at each other and began murmuring. I couldn't make out any more and I kept quiet until King William left. Then I pretended I'd only just arrived and went on into the queen's chamber. She was sitting there, looking dazed. She looked up at me as though she didn't recognize me. I don't know what was the matter and I still don't. It couldn't have been because of the quarrel. I distinctly heard King William say very kindly as he left, "But you are not to worry, my love. I'll deal with this. Now rest.""

Sir Alan pursed his lips, stroked his grizzled beard and furrowed his brow. "It's a puzzlement, that's what it is." He went out to get a mug of wine to lubricate his thinking capabilities.

But after draining the mug he was no closer to figuring out the puzzlement.

"Well, no point in worrying my poor old head. The king has asked Brother Jean-Pierre, Lord Hassan and me to come to his chamber after supper. I expect we'll know soon enough what's going on."

"And you'll tell me, won't you, uncle?"

"I will, because I know I can trust you not to go blabbing what you hear. You're a good girl, Mary. And you are to tell your mother and father I said so, next time you write."

"If that's an order, of course I will." She blushed with pleasure. Few people thought to praise her. Alan kissed her on the cheek and they said goodnight.

King William's meeting was short and productive. He'd asked his vice-chancellor, Count Florian, to join the other three.

They met in his private study, a setting so austere as to discourage any inclination to lightmindedness. The four men—solemn, worried men—sat in chairs ranged around the king's bare, polished table, behind which he sat in his own slightly more royal chair.

He told them of his suspicions, and of the need for watchfulness to prevent the old queen from contacting anyone who might connive with her in further schemes.

"You may be sure it pains me enormously to have to suspect my own mother of being a murderess. My only consolation is that the unfortunate woman may have reached such a stage of dementia that she doesn't realize the seriousness of what she's doing. We'll say no more on that subject."

Alan, when he took in the import of the king's words, saw at once the meaning of what Mary had overheard. He struggled between anger and remorse—anger that anybody should plot to kill Joanna, and remorse that he hadn't been more watchful. The king told him the page at Joanna's door was to be replaced by a knight from the palace guard. "And I will share the duty, my lord King," said Alan, resolved to redeem himself.

William also asked him to place an armed guard at Queen Margaret's door.

"And the guard is to demand of every caller his name and his business, and he is to have the person discreetly followed when he leaves."

Lord Hassan was to provide the followers.

"You are acquainted, I believe, with persons in the city who could put you in touch with men both trustworthy and guileful?"

"Indeed I am." Lord Hassan's lean, dark, guarded face relaxed into an expression of eager anticipation. On arriving in Palermo he'd accepted the king's directive to keep him informed of any incipient mischief in the kingdom. This was the most interesting incipient mischief he'd heard of yet.

As for Brother Jean-Pierre, his assignment was the most delicate. As a man of the church he was to attempt to ingratiate himself with Queen Margaret, get her confidence and learn what he could of her plans and plots. Failing that, he was to pursue the same goal by conversations with his fellow members of the clergy. Ideally he'd become intimate with the queen's confessor.

At this suggestion Jean-Pierre bridled.

"My lord King, I could never ask a priest to betray the sacred privacy of the confession." He shook his head decisively.

"Of course not. But in conversation with him you might well glean a few useful tidbits about Queen Margaret's habits, state of mind and so forth."

"With all due respect, sir, could not you, as her son, accomplish the same thing more easily?"

This question had been nagging the others as well.

"I wish it were so. But unfortunately my mother will hardly speak to me these days. She has so much animosity toward Joanna that a good deal of it becomes attached to me."

He looked at each of them in turn. "So. We understand each other?" All nodded. He rose.

"Very well. Thank you, on behalf of my queen and myself. We'll meet again soon."

And so they did, but to very little purpose. Queen Margaret had become a recluse. She stopped attending court functions and shunned the dining hall. She sent no messages, received no one except Lady Maria Cristina. When Brother Jean-Pierre tried to get a foot in the door he was rebuffed. "The queen is sorry, but she is too tired and ill to see anyone," came the reply.

William dutifully dropped in on her regularly and found her no more unwell than usual but curiously lethargic. She didn't scold. She didn't ask for or volunteer any gossip. She sat looking at him, waiting for him to leave.

Once she inquired about Joanna's health. When William reported that she was feeling as well as could be expected and prayed daily that her child would be born safely and soon, his mother said, almost as though she meant it, "As do we all." William was perplexed—where was the old malice?

After he left, the queen called Maria Cristina to sit with her by the fire. The old malice was back in force. "It won't be long now. We must start our planning. I think we'll wait until the child is a week or so old. You'll have to drop in often, to send my best wishes to Joanna and to say how sorry I am that I don't feel well enough to come myself. You'll admire the baby. Then when they're used to seeing you there, it won't be hard for you to find a moment to drop the poison in her tea or her wine."

Maria Cristina was used to a more passive role, as audience for Queen Margaret's rampages and complaints. She was nervous about playing such an active part.

"I still don't see why you can't do it yourself."

"How I wish I could!" Her little eyes, almost hidden by the fat wrinkled cheeks, blazed in the firelight like black diamonds. "But William has people watching me like a hawk. There's no way I'd be permitted in Joanna's apartments. But don't worry, it will be easy. You're such a perfect nonentity that you'll blend right in. You can do it."

Maria Cristina, who didn't quite know what a nonentity was, began to think that maybe she could indeed do it.

The weeks passed. At last came the morning when Joanna felt a sharp pain, then two more, as though her stomach was trying to explode. She cried out, Lady Marian and Mary came running, and messengers were sent to bring the doctors, to find the nurse, to tell William. Joanna was hardly aware of all this. In fact for the next six hours she was hardly aware of anything except her excruciating pains, each spasm worse than the one before, and the refusal of the doctors to do anything to help her though she shrieked at them.

At four in the afternoon of January 15, 1182, the baby was born. He was very small and after one short wail very quiet. When Joanna had been cleansed and was resting, they brought him for her to hold and told William he could come in.

He kissed Joanna, then gingerly took his son from her arms.

"How tiny he is! Are all babies this small? I haven't met many babies." He tickled his son under the chin but got no response beyond a solemn stare.

"He has your eyes, Joanna, the very same intense brown eyes."

"And your nose, I think, so straight and noble."

"We'll call him Bohemund," said William.

I'd really have liked him to be named Richard, thought Joanna. But she was too tired to argue and smiled a weak assent.

"Bohemund was my ancestor and Prince of Antioch, you know. A hero of the Crusade, long before I was born but I heard tales of his deeds all during my youth. They say he was taller and stronger than any man in his army. So that gives this little prince something to live up to, eh Bohemund?" But the little prince had closed his eyes and seemed to be asleep.

Baby Bohemund hardly cried and was almost indifferent to the wet nurse's nipple. He slept through his own baptism in the resplendent Palatine Chapel, except for a whimper when he felt the priest's cold hand on his forehead. Back in Joanna's chamber, lying in his cradle or in his mother's or his father's arms, he'd look up with his dark unblinking eyes at the face hovering over him, then close them again.

After three days in the world, quietly, uncomplainingly, he left it.

29

After the death of her baby, Joanna shunned palace dinners and court activities. She cried often, almost inaudibly, while lying in bed or propped up on the divan. Lady Marian kept a supply of soft handkerchiefs in Joanna's reach and was getting well practiced in murmuring, "There, there."

Other than such minor measures, Lady Marian didn't know how to cope with this prolonged depression. Neither did King William. No matter how much he sympathized with Joanna, how lovingly he told her they had both suffered a grievous loss and must now take strength from each other, she wouldn't be consoled. When he suggested that they could still hope for children, she shuddered and didn't answer.

Brother Jean-Pierre reminded her of God's promise to comfort the afflicted. He urged her to go to mass and to pray for submissive acceptance of her loss.

"If that means attending mass in the Palatine Chapel I cannot—I *cannot*—bear the thought. That was where my Bohemund was baptized, only to die the next day."

"Then we'll go elsewhere. There are many more churches in Palermo, some quite beautiful. I'd be honored to introduce you to them."

"I'll think about it. You're very kind." And she turned her face to the wall again.

Lady Charmaine with Sir Mario in tow came once but they didn't stay long. Joanna hardly acknowledged Charmaine's effusive introduction of her companion, a foppish gentleman with a tiny blond beard that didn't quite conceal a receding chin. He was superficially handsome but somewhat the worse for wear. Joanna guessed he was Charmaine's senior by at least fifteen years.

"I've told you so much about Sir Mario, my lady, and of course I've told him about you. We were both very sorry to hear of the death of your baby, and we thought we'd call on you and try to cheer you up."

To cheer me up, thought Joanna bitterly. What could they possibly say that would cheer me up?

"And we have the most wonderful news, haven't we Mario?" She looked at him adoringly and took his hand. "You'll never guess what it is, my lady!"

Joanna thought she could.

"We're going to be married, aren't we Mario?"

"Indeed we are, my love. You are going to make me the happiest man in the world." He kissed her hand, then shot a glance at Joanna to see how she was taking this astonishing turn of events.

She was taking it with a distressing lack of enthusiasm.

"I'm very happy for you." But she didn't look happy and had nothing more to say, even when they told her that though they'd make their home in Messina they'd come often to Palermo to visit their old friends.

They left soon after that. Lady Marian heard Sir Mario growl on their way out, "I thought you told me she was pretty and pleasant."

Lady Yasmin called too. Lady Marian was glad. Surely Joanna would cheer up at the sight of this good friend.

"I waited a few days, my dear, because I knew you'd need some time to get over the dreadful shock. Of course you'll never really get over it. There must be nothing more heartrending than to lose a child." She sat beside Joanna on the divan and looked at her affectionately. Joanna smiled, weakly, for the first time in days.

"Thank you, Yasmin. Thank you for coming, and thank you for understanding. Right now I don't think I'll ever get over it, no matter that everybody tells me I will in time."

"And I'll be here whenever you need someone to keep your spirits up. May I start now, with the latest court gossip?"

"Yes, please do." Joanna adjusted her pillows and sat up. "But you needn't tell me about Lady Charmaine and Sir Mario. They've already come and gone. I told them I was happy for them, but honestly I'm happier for myself. It's always been on my conscience that I couldn't like Lady Charmaine more. Now Sir Mario has relieved me of the duty."

"Very well, and shall we be charitable and agree not to remark that Lady Charmaine, who must be all of twenty-seven, should count herself lucky at such an advanced age to snare a husband—never mind that he's a bit desiccated and more than a bit impressed with himself."

Joanna laughed. Lady Marian, busy with her embroidery on the other side of the room, could hardly believe it. She listened with half an ear as the two chatted on.

"What about Queen Margaret? Has anyone seen her at all?"

"Not since your little one was taken from you. Her maid told my maid that when the queen heard the news of the baby's death it sent her even further out of her mind. She won't see anyone but Lady Maria Cristina and even lashes out at her, the poor long-suffering soul. Strange, isn't it? For someone who wanted to kill you to take it so hard when your child died."

"Yes, it is strange. But I've long ago given up trying to understand Queen Margaret."

"Me too. So let's move on. I'll confine myself to three items that may interest you. I'm sure you're dying to learn that Lady Genevieve's little dog has refused to eat for four days, and she paid one of the court physicians an exorbitant sum to examine him. "

"And what was the verdict?"

"That she should change his diet from chopped lamb to mashed boiled white-fish with plenty of garlic."

"Ugh. Poor dog."

"And the next big news is that the astrologers are predicting that Mt. Etna may erupt again this summer."

"How I'd love to see that! But I suppose it could be dangerous."

"Oh, it could. Hassan was in Catania last year when there was a great spurt of fire into the sky and he said that all the villagers on the north side of the mountain had to run for their lives. A great many of them, unfortunately, lost their homes and fields when the lava poured down so fast. But he said it was a marvelous sight, if you weren't too close."

After a bit the chatter stopped suddenly. Lady Marian glanced up to see Yasmin look at Joanna uncertainly and put an arm around her shoulder. Joanna shook her off. In a strained voice, she said, "Of course that's wonderful for you. How happy you must be! But I can't…I can't…" and she sobbed aloud and bowed her head. "Maybe you should go now, Yasmin. I'd like to be left alone."

Lady Marian met Yasmin at the door.

"What on earth…?"

"Oh dear, I'd no idea she'd take it like that. I told her I was expecting a baby. She was absolutely stricken. I should have thought. It must have been a terrible reminder of how happy she was not long ago, just as I am now. I'm so sorry, Lady Marian." She looked back at Joanna, who was sitting motionless, bent over, with her head in her hands.

This can't go on, thought Lady Marian. But what to do?

King William, a patient man, loved his wife and indulged her in her grief. But patience and indulgence have their limits. He visited her often, hoping to find her in better spirits and urging her to come out of seclusion, but to no avail. When this had no effect his visits shrank to one a week if that.

On the six-week anniversary of the baby's death, she forced herself to go to the Palatine Chapel to hear mass and to say a prayer for his soul, but it gave her no comfort. She came back to her chamber to resume her solitary mourning. Before she could climb up onto the four-poster bed where she'd taken up near-permanent residence, Lady Marian took her firmly by the hand and sat her down in a chair.

"Joanna, I'm going to talk to you as I believe your mother would. She'd tell you that no matter how you feel now, this isn't the end of the world. She'd tell you that she herself lost her first son in infancy. She grieved, as you do. But she knew the importance of looking ahead, not back."

Joanna's expression was as woebegone as ever. But she was listening. Lady Marian warmed to her subject. She even began to sound as firm as Queen Eleanor at her most imperative. Instead of her usual gentle tone she spoke sharply, articulating each syllable precisely.

"She'd remind you that you are the queen of a king who depends on you to give the royal family an heir. You must think beyond your own anguish and put yourself in your husband's place. He loves you, Joanna. He's been waiting for you to pull yourself together and remember that you're a wife as well as a bereaved mother. But he may not wait forever. He's a man as well as a king. Your mother would tell you in no uncertain terms that it's time to get hold of yourself, to stop wallowing in self-pity, to get up and get dressed, and receive your husband with wifely welcome." She stopped and took a deep breath. She was amazed at her audacity in speaking so to the queen, but also rather proud.

Joanna, equally amazed, stared at her wide-eyed. She swept her hand across her forehead as though brushing aside a spiderweb.

I do believe, thought Lady Marian, that she really listened.

Joanna felt she was waking from a dream. She stood up. She asked Lady Marian to send for Mary and to send word to King William that she hoped he could call on her in an hour. Mary, delighted to be useful again, dressed her lady in a white gown with a rose-colored velvet cape. When King William arrived, in exactly one hour, he found Joanna not reclining listlessly on her divan but sitting up in a chair before the fire, with a happy smile of welcome. Lady Marian observed with satisfaction his look of glad surprise to find Joanna herself again. She slipped out to muse on the changing nature of a young woman's humors.

She discussed it with Jean-Pierre later in the dining hall. Most of the others had left, but the two old friends were still at table with their glasses of sweet wine and bowls of dried apricots and almonds.

"I can hardly believe how quickly she seemed to come to herself. But she has always wanted to please her mother. So I'm glad it occurred to me to speak as a surrogate for Queen Eleanor, as it were."

"A powerful shaper of events, our English queen, even from half a world away," said Jean-Pierre.

"When I write to her and tell her about all this I'll beg her to pray to the blessed Virgin—as I shall—that our little queen isn't dealt any more such punishing blows."

"Amen. My prayers will join yours." Brother Jean-Pierre, feeling he'd now earned his nap, took his leave.

30

"He looks very like the archbishop that I remember, William. How skillful your artists are! See how his hand is raised just so, and he has such a wise and intelligent expression—as though he knew something we don't."

They'd come to Monreale so Joanna could admire the progress at the cathedral since she'd last been there, nearly a year ago. She'd gone straight to the Thomas à Becket portrait. William enjoyed her enthusiasm. He'd been greatly heartened at her request to make the trip. He didn't understand how her state of mind could have reversed itself so quickly, but it was a tremendous relief. Once more he was welcomed into his wife's bed. His worries about the succession, dashed by Bohemund's death, receded. Once more his marriage seemed on an even keel.

They surveyed St. Thomas critically. William put his arm around Joanna's shoulders and asked, "And the head, my dear, the hair. How do you like it?"

Queen Eleanor, in reply to their query, had promptly written that she recalled the archbishop with a healthy head of hair, brown and bushy, though with a bald spot in the middle. And thus he now appeared.

Next Joanna asked to see the soaring dome over the apse, with the immense mosaic of Christ Pantocrator—Christ, Ruler of All. But it was far from finished.

"That's the most difficult mosaic work of all," said William. "Look at them up there, working from those rickety platforms suspended from the ceiling. And how they have to reach up to set the tiny cubes of glass in the cement before it hardens. I asked to be raised up on the pulley once, just to see what it was like. The artists let me place several bits of brown glass in Christ's beard. I got quite dizzy when I looked down at the floor so far below."

Joanna was aghast. "William! You must never do such a thing again! How foolhardy!"

"Perhaps it was. But I wanted to feel I'd had a small part in creating all this beauty." He stood with his head tilted back, gazing in approval at Christ's beard.

Joanna, having inspected one cathedral, prevailed on William to take her to see another: Cefalù, which had been built by William's grandfather, King Roger II.

"You've said so often it was your inspiration for Monreale, but you'd never be able to equal it. But I can't imagine anything more beautiful than Monreale."

On a fine day in early April they set out. Joanna was glad to be reunited with her dainty white mare, Belle Blanche, whom she hadn't ridden since the early days of her pregnancy. The feeling was mutual. The little Arabian nuzzled Joanna's shoulder when they met.

Several courtiers and their ladies had joined the party, including Lord Hassan but not Yasmin, whose child was due any day. Brother Jean-Pierre came and so did Lady Marian, who had at first declined, unwilling to subject her stiffening joints to such a long and bouncy journey. Joanna persuaded her. "You've always said you longed to see Cefalù and the cathedral. We'll ride slowly, and I'll want your company."

Joanna rode at the head of the procession at William's side. When they left the confining streets of the city behind and moved into the open countryside under the wide blue sky, she let her thoughts roam where they wished. She expected that the familiar sense of loss, never far below the surface, would envelop her. She'd schooled herself to appear animated and cheerful to others, no matter how much desolation filled her heart. But today she found herself looking around with genuine interest and a sense of discovery. Dull wintry fields had given way to freshly plowed plots. In others, stolid peasants plodded behind their oxen, guiding the plow as it parted the rich brown furrows. Here and there a patch of startling green appeared where the first shoots of grain were already rising in orderly rows. In the orchards, cherry and peach trees were in leaf and in bud but so far showing no blossoms. Off to the south, the hillsides, too, were greening. She breathed in the fresh cool air and sat up straighter in her saddle.

Hope! That was the message of this verdant land, signaling with every leaf and blossom that spring had arrived. She felt hope creeping into her heart like tendrils of a vine, filling her with an almost tremulous sense of well-being. She looked at William, wondering if she could explain to him what she felt. No, not now. It was too intimate. Too mixed up with her realization of how patient he'd been with her and how sorry she was for her selfish concentration on her own grief without talking to him about his own. She reached over to take his hand. Her smile spoke for her. "I love you, William, and I'm happy to be here at your side. Later when we're alone together I'll tell you more of what's in my heart."

Presently they came in sight of the sea. Sapphire-blue and sparkling in the sun, the Mediterranean stretched northward to the horizon. Their road ran along a cliff, and below them waves washed onto the rocky shore and flowed placidly in and out of secluded coves. It was picturesque but not alarming. Joanna could hardly believe this was the same sea that had made her so miserable on her voyage to Sicily.

When they drew near Cefalù on the second day, William rode ahead to make sure the royal standard with the royal lion was being borne well in advance, and the royal trumpeter was ready to announce their approach. William set great store on ceremony whenever he toured his kingdom.

Alan took William's place beside Joanna.

"How splendid you look, Sir Alan," she greeted him. He beamed. King William had recently knighted him in recognition of his years of loyal service to Joanna. He was as proud of his new title as he was of his polished armor. Though there wasn't the slightest chance of battle on this journey, he felt more himself with a burnished breastplate and a well-honed sword in his scabbard.

Cefalù captivated Joanna immediately. It wasn't nearly as big as Palermo, where thousands of people lived amid the temples, squares, markets, gardens and palaces—as well as in modest homes and hovels crowded along dark twisting streets. But Cefalù's setting was spectacular, tucked below a fearsome crag. "That's the *Rocca*," William told Joanna as he rejoined her and found her staring up in awe.

The cathedral rivaled the *Rocca* in fearsomeness. From the outside it looked like a fortress, rearing up to protect the little town that clung to the slope between cathedral and sea. Down beyond the red rooftops of the town ran a golden, curving beach, fringed by palms and pines. In a cove farther to the east she could see fishing boats coming and going.

They'd heard the cathedral bells as they entered the town. "Aha. That's for the noontime mass," said William. Soon they drew close enough to take in the whole immense structure. They walked their horses into the square, looked and listened.

"Mass must be nearly over. Would you like to go in now, or after we get settled in the palace?"

"Now, please, William. I've waited so long to see it."

Most of the rest of the party went off to find their lodgings, but William, Joanna, Hassan and Brother Jean-Pierre walked up the steps and into the twilight of the long nave. They stood at the rear and watched the bishop officiating at the altar. A dozen worshippers were gathered before him. Joanna found the chanting and prayer, the incense and the candles, soothing, as though she'd come home to a familiar place. She saw the mosaic portrait of the Madonna and the archangels, smaller than at Monreale but no less colorful. She smiled as she recognized the apostles, so true to life, as though they'd just stepped in from the town.

After the worshippers left, the bishop walked down the aisle to pay his respects to King William. Then he, the priest and the acolytes filed out. William led his little group around to examine the mosaics more closely.

"What a vision your grandfather had!" said Hassan. "And what a compliment to my people's heritage he paid by incorporating so much of the Arabic decorative tradition. Those delicate arches! The finely detailed work on the mosaics! I've heard that he intended to continue them from the apse all the way into the nave, but he died, did he not, soon after the cathedral was completed?"

William nodded. Joanna wished Hassan would stop talking. She wanted nothing to interfere while she drank in the beauty that surrounded her. She looked up to the vaulted ceiling over the apse, where her gaze met that of the Christ Pantocrator. The mosaic filled a curved recess that took up about a quarter of the great dome. Christ wore a sky-blue cloak over a brown tunic. His halo was gold and so was the background, as though he were looking down from a glowing heaven. His right hand was raised in blessing and in his left he held an open book. Joanna imagined she could make out the Latin words "I am the light of the world." She sat down, transfixed.

"William, I think I'd like to just sit here for a while in this peaceful, beautiful, holy place. Would you mind?"

"Of course not." But he wondered. Her church-going didn't usually go much beyond normal attendance at mass and daily prayers.

"Would you like me to stay with you?" asked Jean-Pierre.

"No, thank you. I'd like to be alone. But I won't be long."

William kissed her on the cheek. "Certainly, my dear. Sir Alan will be waiting at the entrance to lead you to the palace."

Totally alone in the silent church except for a pair of sweepers far to the rear, Joanna sat for a moment with her head bowed, then looked up to the Christ again. Majestic yet compassionate, he seemed to be returning her gaze. She was touched by the sorrow in his eyes, the way both arms were held out as though to bless all the world. She lost herself in an almost mindless contemplation, letting peace flow over her. The anguish of the weeks since the death of her baby melted into acceptance. She felt that Christ was telling her, "Yes, you have lost your beloved son. But do not grieve. Your child is safe with his heavenly father, in a far better place than the world he was born into. He will wait for you until your time comes to rise into heaven. Meantime, trust in God's mercy and wisdom and love for all his creatures."

For a quarter of an hour Joanna sat there, looking up at the face so full of love and understanding while she absorbed the message of consolation. At last, with a sigh not of sorrow but of gratitude to be cleansed of her consuming angry grief, she stood up and, dazed by the transformative experience, walked slowly out of the dim cathedral.

Blinded by sunlight that flooded the square, she blinked and looked around. No Alan was to be seen. But out of the shadowed portico stepped Hassan.

"Ah my lady, unfortunately Sir Alan was called away—something to do with one of the knights' horses having thrown a shoe. So I volunteered to escort you to the palace. But you seem not quite yourself—are you well?" His dark handsome face was all concern.

"Yes, thank you, quite well." She didn't want to talk. But she had to be polite. "It's just the brightness of the day, after the darkness inside."

"What would you say to a stroll down to the shore? We have plenty of time before dinner, and it may be your only chance to see more of Cefalù. I've been here often and I know the way. It isn't far. And you might find it relaxing, after our day in the saddle." He took her arm and before she could think how to decline the invitation they began the gentle descent from the cathedral square, down a cobbled street, past neat stone cottages, until the glorious Mediterranean came in view. She permitted Hassan to lead her all the way to where land met sea, where wave after wave curled ashore and caressed the sandy beach before retreating to make way for the next. There was no one else in view except some fishermen mending their nets far to the south.

Joanna gazed out to sea, hypnotized by the inexorable rhythm of the waves. The clean, salty air filled her nostrils. Still in the spell of the euphoria she'd felt inside the church, she fell into a reverie. Perhaps, she thought, this is God's way of showing me I should pay more attention to the real, beautiful world I live in instead of longing for what might have been.

She smiled at the thought and turned to see Hassan staring not at the sea but at her. He stepped closer.

"My dear Joanna, what are you thinking, to bring that beatific expression to your face?" He moved closer still. "Oh Joanna, do you have any idea how enchanting you are? How desirable?"

She was confused. He'd never spoken to her like this.

Before she knew it he'd thrown an arm around her and pulled her roughly toward him. He tried to kiss her but she struggled, turned her face aside and managed to slap him as hard as she could.

"How dare you!" She staggered back, trying to distance herself from him, but she stumbled in the loose sand and one of her shoes came off. She watched in dismay as it was carried away by a retreating wave.

Hassan watched too. He ran his fingers over his cheek where the imprint of her hand was still visible. He sighed as though this weren't the first time a lady had rejected his advances.

Gallant even in defeat, he waded out to retrieve the shoe, handed it to her and held out his arm for her to hold while she put it on. Neither of them had spoken since her cry of outrage.

A little calmer, she said, "Hassan, what possessed you? Have I ever given you the slightest indication that I would welcome such behavior?"

"Sometimes I imagined you did. I see now it was wishful thinking." He touched his cheek again. "But haven't you ever thought, Joanna, of the exquisite revenge you might take on William and Yasmin if you and I became...more than friends, shall we say?"

"But why should I want to take revenge now for something that happened so long ago, before William and I were married? I put that attachment out of my mind years ago."

"But Joanna, the attachment didn't end. Do you mean to say you don't know that? You must be the only person in the palace who doesn't. Why do you think William sent for me and Yasmin to come back from Messina and join his court? Not from any overpowering need for my talents, though I will say I've been very useful to him. No, he missed his little plaything."

Her face went white.

"And they're still the best of playmates."

The sun had long ago sunk behind the crags of the *Rocca*. The sea had turned from shimmering blue to dull leaden gray. A cold wind whipped Joanna's unbound hair about her anguished face. Dazed, unbelieving, she stood perfectly still as though frozen. Suddenly an awful question entered her mind.

"Hassan, your child, the one that's soon to be born—is he—could he be..." She couldn't go on. He laughed, sharply and without humor. "Oh no, my dear, don't worry. Yasmin tells me that I'm the father and I believe her."

Wearily, she brushed the windblown hair off her forehead. She wanted only to escape from this cold, forsaken spot to someplace warm where she could pretend the encounter with Hassan had never happened. But she had one more question.

"Hassan, how could you still live with Yasmin, knowing that you were sharing her with someone else?"

"Oh, we have an understanding. I don't demand fidelity from her, nor does she from me. It's worked quite well. We're really very fond of each other." He paused. "And, my dear, I'd hoped that you and William could arrive at such an understanding, and I could be the instrument of your liberation from your marriage vows. I was captivated by you the moment I saw you, and I still am. Perhaps you'll change your mind. I'll wait."

She turned blindly to leave. Hassan offered his arm in support but she brushed him off angrily and began to climb toward the town. He followed close behind. The townspeople looked with curiosity at this strange pair, obviously nobility, but what had they been up to? Her hair was in tangles, there was sand all over her shoes and her face was aflame. His leggings were wet up to the knees. His fine leather boots were sodden. Neither of them said a word.

When they reached the palace she was relieved to see that William wasn't waiting for her at the entrance. However, Lady Marian was. She was shocked to see the disheveled state of Joanna's hair and gown, and the distress and confusion on her face, like a child who has been punished without knowing why. Instead of scolding her for going off without telling anybody where or with whom, Lady Marian took her firmly by the arm and led her into the palace. But first she looked suspiciously at Hassan, who waved, bowed and headed for a nearby wineshop, squishing as he walked.

Joanna poured out her story the minute they were alone, but she began at the end, adding Sir Hassan's atrocious attempt to kiss her almost as an afterthought. It was some time before Lady Marian sorted out the sequence of events.

"What shall I do?" Joanna wailed. "I must talk to William, mustn't I? Maybe Hassan had it all wrong." She'd bathed and changed and was sitting before the fire while Lady Marian brushed her hair. Word had been sent that Joanna was tired and would have supper in her room.

"I fear there may be some truth in what Hassan said," Lady Marian replied. "But how despicable to blurt it out to you like that!" She put the brush aside and sat beside Joanna. "Again, my dear, you must think of your mother's example. Do you remember being so upset when you first learned that Yasmin was William's concubine?"

"Oh yes, but that was different. Then, I had to forgive William for something I thought was long past. Now, apparently, it's still going on. And William's been deceiving me all this time."

"I'm not so sure that's so. More likely, Hassan is leading you on."

"But why would he make up such a story?"

"Why? To make you so angry at William that you'd be more likely to accept his—Hassan's—advances."

"Oh." A pause. "But what were you going to say about my mother?"

"Only this: Your father, King Henry, was unfaithful from the beginning. At first Queen Eleanor took it very hard, as you're doing now. She railed at Henry and even tried to confront some of the women involved. But in time she saw how useless this was. It only made her more unhappy, did nothing to change Henry's behavior and made an already rocky marriage even more unstable. So she decided to ignore it and never to bring up the subject with Henry. And that, my dear, is what you should do. It won't be easy, but you have one advantage your mother hasn't had for years. Your husband truly loves you."

"Yes, I believe that with all my heart. But if he does, how can he go off and..." She fell silent.

"Because, my pet, that's the way men are."

Maybe Hassan told Yasmin about his unsuccessful assault on Joanna's virtue and Yasmin told William. Maybe William had tired of Yasmin. Maybe he needed Hassan's services more in Messina than in Palermo. Joanna never knew why and never asked William, but it soon became known that Sir Hassan and Lady Yasmin would move back to Messina as soon as their child was born.

31

King William thought perhaps he should send an armed force to Byzantium. The rich and powerful eastern empire, where the Greek Orthodox Church ruled supreme, had been in turmoil for three terrible years, ever since the cruel despot Andronicus Comnenus had declared himself emperor in 1182.

"And there he sits in Constantinople, torturing and killing his subjects, enriching himself, while nobody dares to rein him in. Something must be done!"

William was orating not to his council but to his wife. He'd formed the habit of trying out his ideas and formulating his plans with her as audience. He never really expected a comment, though, of course, he paused courteously if she replied to one of his rhetorical questions or expressed an opinion. Sometimes he even listened. Joanna was proving to have a quick grasp of the kingdom's problems and William's policies. Her suggestions often made a great deal of sense. William found this surprising but, being of a pragmatic nature, he welcomed it.

On this occasion they were taking a pre-bedtime stroll around the atrium of the royal palace. It was dusk. A servant, having noticed the royal couple, was placing candelabra here and there to create pools of light in the encroaching darkness.

Joanna had made it her project to turn this large, rather sterile space into an indoor garden. When she'd first come to the palace, the courtyard was graced only by one tall palm in each corner as well as a few placed haphazardly near the center, all in enormous pots. She'd added numerous smaller pots and planters overflowing with greenery and flowers. These were arranged on the marble floor to create pathways. She'd even cajoled the architect of the royal gardens to devise a way to bring water in for a fountain and to surround it with a circular bench. More than once Queen Margaret had been heard to sneer at the very idea of such a useless extravagance. But most who lived in or visited the palace welcomed it, especially on summer days when they wanted to escape the scorching sun. And Joanna took private pleasure in the knowledge that, like her husband and his forebears, she was adding a bit of beauty to the Kingdom of Sicily.

This evening the two of them had the atrium all to themselves. They strolled along a flower-lined path to the fountain and sat on the bench.

William looked around rather absently. "You've made such a difference here, Joanna. I do appreciate it."

"Thank you. I think I may have inherited my mother's love of gardens. I wish you could see the rose garden at Fontevraud Abbey!" She was hoping to change the subject. But William's mind was not on roses. He was still caught up in his battle plans.

"Yes, the tyrant must be stopped! And who will take on the task if I don't?"

"William, I don't see why it has to be you. I don't want you going off into battle. I have enough worries about Richard, risking his life every day while he and his soldiers march about Aquitaine."

"Never fear, I wouldn't lead the expedition myself. I have two excellent commanders in mind for that, one to lead the naval forces and another for the army. I know my limitations. I'm no soldier. But I will say I know how to plan and supervise."

"Yes, you do. But why must this be a task for Sicily? Rome is ever so much closer to Constantinople than Sicily is. Why can't the pope do something?"

"He could if he would. But the main concern for the pope these days is how to hold onto the little patch of Italy that Rome controls. He'd be most unwilling to start a quarrel between the Latin and the Greek churches. Because that's what it would come to."

"Well then, what about Frederick Barbarossa of Germany? As Holy Roman Emperor, surely he has as much reason to control this tyrant as you do."

"Yes, good point, Joanna. He should get involved. But he won't. He maintains he must stay close to events in northern Italy. He's been trying for years to incorporate those independent towns in Lombardy into his empire."

"But I still don't see why you or anyone has to send an army at great expense to settle the problems of a land so far away. Why can't the mistreated people who live there rise up and get rid of Andronicus?"

"Because they're demoralized and terrified. While this pseudo-emperor is in power, nobody's safe. His minions kill anyone they suspect of disloyalty. He's a madman. No matter what the differences between Greeks and Latins are, it's our duty as good Christians to intervene."

She considered this and sighed. Why, she wondered to herself, did being a "good Christian" so often require going into battle and killing one's fellow Christians?

William heard the sigh. "But Joanna my love, it's not as though I were leaving tomorrow. It will take months and months to assemble a fleet and train recruits. And I'll need to travel about the kingdom to build up popular support for the expedition. For any endeavor of this nature, thorough preparation is half the battle."

"I'm sure it is. But tell me, dear William"— she took his hand and looked into his eyes—"could there be still another reason you want to do this? Something to do with pride and reputation and your place in history?"

"Joanna, you know me too well. There is one other reason. I keep thinking of what my grandfather Roger accomplished. By the time he was thirty-three he'd conquered both Apulia and Calabria on the Italian mainland and united them to Sicily. Roger was the founder of this great kingdom that we are fortunate enough to rule over today."

"Yes, I know. Your grandfather's memory is so much alive that sometimes when I'm out in the city I expect to see him walking along the street toward me. But I didn't know he'd done all that while so young."

"And that's just it. Here I am, almost as old as he was when he created the kingdom, and what have I done? I've built a cathedral, but it will never rival the one he built at Cefalù. I've launched a few naval assaults on the Muslims in North Africa but I've added nothing to our possessions. And I sense a growing boredom and cynicism in the army, as though my soldiers and generals believe me incapable of bold action and may be losing respect for me. I wish to prove them wrong."

"Very well, it would indeed be a bold action that your people could applaud— at least all those you don't conscript for the army!" William ignored that.

"But never mind," she added, "I'll join you in praying for success. I'll also give thanks that you're sensibly not insisting on leading the forces. If you were gone so long with your life in constant danger I don't think I could bear it." There was a catch in her voice. He could see a tear on her cheek. He gently wiped it away with his fingers and she seized his hand and kissed it.

"Don't ever leave me, William."

Arm in arm, they walked slowly up the marble steps. Halfway up William paused and Joanna looked at him questioningly. He kissed her and held her close. "I'm so glad to have you back," he whispered.

She knew what he meant. After the death of the child, she'd put him off. Then, after Lady Marian had scolded her for neglecting her duties as a wife, she'd welcomed him but with a kind of frantic haste, as though she were hoping to have the whole thing over with as soon as possible. But now, she'd found comfort and strength in the cathedrals of Monreale and Cefalù, those calm, holy places. She'd gotten over the panic she'd felt at Hassan's crude attempt to alienate her from her husband. She'd become more relaxed with William. Their lovemaking had become more mutually considerate and ultimately more passionate than ever before.

"And I'm glad to be back," she said. They walked on to her chamber where her lofty bed with its airy white curtains awaited them.

Before William could get seriously into planning for his eastern expedition, he was distracted by the illness of his mother. People had begun to think that Queen Margaret, by some dark sorcery, had found a way to live forever. But now she entered on a serious decline.

After the death of Bohemund, she'd stopped plotting to become a person of consequence in the palace again. She went into even deeper seclusion. For a while, she'd occasionally totter down to the banquet hall, leaning on a cane and with Maria Cristina hovering nearby. She'd given up her flouncy colorful garb and wore only black. She shrank, her fat face grew gaunt and her pointed nose protruded like a beak.

Mostly, however, the old queen kept to her bed. When William called on her she'd hardly listen while he tried to make conversation. She'd babble on incomprehensibly about something that happened when she was a much-admired young queen or even farther back when she was a princess in Spain.

Once he asked her if she'd like Joanna to come, hoping her old enmity had died away and the two could be reconciled before she died. Suddenly she became lucid.

"No! Stupid girl! Spilled the wine I'd specially prepared for her! Then let her baby die but she didn't die! It wasn't supposed to be like that. I'd so wanted to have another little William to bring up." She began to whimper. It was as close to a confession as she'd ever made. A confession but not an apology. William, shocked and saddened, left her.

That same night she died in her sleep.

He gave her a state funeral with all the pomp befitting a queen of Sicily. She was buried at Monreale. Thousands turned out to watch the funeral procession. The Sicilians always enjoyed a grand funeral. It wasn't quite as good as a royal wedding, of course, when free food and drink were liberally provided in all the city's squares and plazas. But there was usually a distribution of money so the citizens could buy a candle and pray for the soul of the departed. And if you spent the money on a bottle of wine instead, who was to know?

32

It was an oppressively hot day in July of 1184. All Sicily was baking under a merciless sun. But the world's work had to go on: peasants scything the prickly golden hay in the fields; fishermen at sea where there was no shade or breeze and there were precious few fish; bakers and cooks laboring by their blazing hearths and red-hot ovens, for the people must have their daily bread; tradesmen trudging dusty roads laden with heavy packs —all these, unable to escape the heat, could only wipe the sweat from their brows and pray for sunset.

Far from the common folk, two men were walking slowly, not speaking, along a seldom-traveled path of the walled park of Palermo's royal palace. The path led them to a secluded dell with a small pool. In the middle of the pool, a marble faun tirelessly spewed jets of water from his laughing mouth. Thanks to the shade provided by tall laurels and the musical splashing of the fountain, it was possible here to forget the hot city, but not the stability of the kingdom.

"Sicily needs an heir," said Archbishop Walter, lowering his bulky body awkwardly onto a bench and trying not to wrinkle his crisp white robe.

"You are absolutely correct," replied Chancellor Matthew of Ajello. He sat down on a bench opposite with a thump and a sigh. A thickset man but muscular, Sir Matthew was feeling his sixty-four years these days.

The need for a royal heir was probably the only thing the archbishop and the chancellor had agreed on in twenty years. They were still bitterly at odds over the cathedral affair. King William, with Matthew's support, had completed his stupendous monument, the cathedral at Monreale, and the pope had established its legitimacy as an archbishopric by a papal bull. Archbishop Walter's rival cathedral in Palermo was at least a year away from completion. Matthew had won that battle.

But they weren't here to breathe new life into those smoldering old coals. They had more urgent business on their minds: how to forestall the civil war that they feared would break out if King William should (God forbid) die without an heir.

"We may continue to hope that the queen will bear a son, but it's looking less likely," said the archbishop. "It's three years since she lost the first one. Something should have happened by now."

"Agreed," replied Matthew. "I've talked to the royal physician but he shilly-shallies and won't give an opinion, beyond saying the first birth was perfectly normal and shouldn't have precluded future pregnancies."

"And I've talked to the king and tried to inquire—delicately of course—if he or the queen would like some counseling as to their marital duties. But he assured me they were both well aware of their duties and needed no urging from God or anyone else to live together as loving man and wife. He seemed rather irritated that I should have brought up the subject. He just brushed me aside when I said that his subjects are understandably nervous, as long as they see no heir on the horizon."

"Ah well. He has so many overseas matters on his mind these days that I fear he may have lost track of what's going on here at home and the mood of the people. Why is he so set on this misguided notion of an assault on Constantinople?"

Walter suspected that Matthew's annoyance had as much to do with resentment that he hadn't been put in charge as with disapproval of the king's planned expedition.

"Never mind all that now, Matthew. We're here to talk about an heir to the throne of Sicily. If we can agree on a recommendation it will have more force than if we each support different candidates."

"So far I am with you." Matthew fixed his world-weary gaze on his adversary. He waited. He knew the advantage of letting the opponent strike the first blow.

"Good. I urge you to join me in favoring the king's aunt, Constance. You must agree that, as the daughter of William's own grandfather, Roger, she has impeccable lineage. She's only thirty—young enough to bear a respectable brood of children, once she's fitted with a suitable husband. From my own knowledge, she's modest, tractable and God-fearing. She'd have the people's trust and, in due course, their support and affection."

"And in the meantime? While we wait for the suitable husband to appear, and wait still longer for the respectable brood of children? What if King William dies before all that? Will the people of Sicily accept an unknown like Constance as their queen, as someone able to hold the kingdom together? I think not. Sicilians have never held with women as rulers of the kingdom and aren't likely to change their minds now. Even Queen Joanna, popular as she is, would be opposed."

The archbishop raised a hand, palm outward, in priestly reproof. "Not so fast, Matthew. Constance is hardly unknown, at least to those who have kept in touch with her. Just because she's been living quietly in a convent doesn't mean she's in another world. It's only half a day's ride from Palermo, if you'd ever taken the trouble to go see her. Plenty of people do, and they'd support her as Queen Regent until her son becomes old enough to assume the throne." In his vehemence, the archbishop's voice had risen and so had his temperature. He subsided and fanned himself vigorously. Gradually his plump face resumed its placid self-righteousness.

"My turn now?" Matthew's thin lips curled. "Whether Constance or Joanna, it will be years before either produces a son—if ever. In the meantime we'd risk anarchy. What Sicily needs isn't an inexperienced woman but a strong, proven leader to be recognized now as William's heir. Fortunately just such a man is available: Tancred of Lecce, the king's nephew, would command the people's respect. The king trusts him. And as for lineage, he too is directly descended from King Roger."

"Ah, but you don't mention one obstacle, my friend. Tancred's a bastard. His father, the king's brother, never bothered to marry his mother. His lineage is flawed. Many in this Christian land will hold that against him. And many more, if I'm not mistaken, will remember how he rebelled against King William's father, a score of years ago. What's to keep him from repeating the deed, if he takes a notion?"

"His own self-interest. He's in a position of power now and isn't likely to do anything foolish to jeopardize it. As to the rest of your argument, sometimes toughness and ingenuity in a leader are more important than character and reputation."

They sat staring at each other, deadlocked. Neither had really hoped to change the other's mind. The test would come when they made their cases to the king. They were already mentally rehearsing their speeches.

A rustling in the shrubbery made them start. They'd chosen the spot for its privacy, where eavesdropping would be most unlikely. Was it a spy? Sir Matthew's hand went to his sword. Was it a bloodthirsty beast escaped from the royal menagerie, on the prowl for a juicy archbishop? Walter clutched the gold cross that hung around his neck and muttered a prayer.

A doe emerged from the bushes and stepped daintily down to drink from the pond. Matthew snorted. The archbishop let go of the cross. Both rose.

"Shall we return?" growled Matthew. Off he went without waiting for a reply. They retraced their steps, walking without speaking, as the sun finally sank below the walls of the park and the palm fronds waved gently in a hesitant breeze.

Meantime, in the Zisa palace another colloquy was in progress. The king and queen had decided to dine here rather in the close, windowless dining hall of the royal palace. Dinner was over and the tables had been cleared except for a bowl of grapes and a decanter of white wine that had been brought up from the cellar. All the diners had left except William, Joanna, Count Florian, Lady Marian, Brother Jean-Pierre and Lady Charmaine, who was visiting from her new home in Messina. Joanna's hair was coiled in a loose knot at her nape. This and her azure gown that fell in soft pleats from neck to hem gave her, William thought, a classic Grecian look. He and Florian too had dressed for the warm day, in loose white linen tunics over cotton hose. Only Jean-Pierre had made no concessions to the heat, other than leaving his brown robe unbelted.

The group leaned back in their chairs, plucking a grape from time to time, letting digestion take over and discussing what William had just told them. He'd said that he planned a ceremony at Monreale on the following Sunday to mark the first anniversary of his mother's death and also to celebrate the transfer of his father's remains from Palermo to a new tomb adjoining hers at Monreale.

"I intend to make Monreale Cathedral the royal burial place. You and I will be laid to rest there, Joanna, and all the kings and queens of Sicily who come after us."

"A most worthy plan, my lord King," said Brother Jean-Pierre. "Future generations of Sicilians will thank you for leaving them this magnificent cathedral, where they can come to pay their respects to the royal line that has brought honor, glory and prosperity to the kingdom."

The others looked at him in surprise. He was not ordinarily so eloquent. Perhaps he had taken just a bit more wine than usual.

"Thank you. I hope your prediction will come to pass." William took a sip from his glass. "And it may be that the ceremonies at Monreale will prove entertaining to the noble visitors I expect in two days' time."

"Noble visitors?" asked Count Florian, as confused as the others about whom the king referred to.

"Yes, two emissaries are on their way from Germany with a message from Frederick Barbarossa Their arrival date has just been confirmed."

"I wonder what the emperor has in mind," said Florian. "I thought he was your enemy."

"I wondered too. But of late he's been acting more like a prospective ally. My informants tell me that the emissaries will propose on Frederick's behalf that his son and heir, Prince Henry, should marry my kinswoman, Constance."

"Constance? Your old aunt who's spent her whole life shut up in a convent? Why would an emperor's son want to marry her?" Charmaine asked.

"She's not my old aunt, she's actually a year younger than me. We were both brought up in the royal palace. We were playmates and became good friends and still are. And it's true she's been living in a convent for the past twenty years. But she went there to further her education, not as a member of the order. She hasn't forsworn the world."

"In fact, she's well-informed and quite nice," said Joanna. "William took me to see her once soon after we were married. She was interested in everything we had to tell her about goings-on at court. She was very kind to me, at a time when I was still feeling rather lost in my new home."

"But why she isn't here in Palermo, living in the palace as she used to do?" Charmaine asked.

Joanna knew why. The minute Queen Margaret had become queen regent on the death of her husband she'd banished from the court both the child Constance and her mother Beatrix. This was common knowledge, part of the vast store of unsavory lore that had accumulated about Queen Margaret over the years. Margaret hadn't wanted any attention deflected from her own son or any possible notion that there might be another claimant to the role of rightful heir.

But Joanna didn't answer Charmaine. She didn't want to lay still another accusation at her late mother-in-law's door. Count Florian rescued her.

"Never mind that now. We should be concentrating on this upcoming visit by these important visitors. I assume, my lord King, you've decided what you'll say to them?"

"I have. I shall give my assent. And I've already invited Constance to come to Palermo to prepare herself for her new role."

"Shall you discuss this with your council?"

"I shall. But I know exactly what they'll say. Chancellor Matthew will oppose it, on the grounds that it would give Emperor Frederick a stake in Sicily. Frederick has coveted Sicily for years. Even as Holy Roman Emperor with a dominion that reaches from the North Sea to the northern border of Italy, he's hungry for more."

"So would this alliance not help him to claim that stake?"

"Theoretically, yes. But it's very unlikely any time soon. He's far too busy reining in his uncooperative lords in Germany and consolidating his hold on his demesnes in Tuscany. As to the rest of the council, Archbishop Walter will support me because of his friendship with Constance. She's always been a devout Catholic. He'd see this as a splendid opportunity for her. And he'd support my suggestion that she spend time in Palermo before leaving to marry Henry. She'd be very popular here because of her direct descent from King Roger. The people still revere his memory."

He paused and looked at Florian with a slight smile. "Vice-Chancellor Florian will support me as well, I'm sure." The latter nodded. "As for the others, they're insecure enough in their positions to be unlikely to go against my wishes."

Joanna was impressed. How well William had thought everything out! Then it struck her. He was seeking this alliance because he feared she would remain childless. If so, and if Constance and Henry produced a son, that son would be in line to become king of Sicily. William was making sure that the next king would still have Norman blood in his veins—if only through the mother.

She had failed William, her parents and everybody who'd had such high hopes for this marriage.

She couldn't help it; tears welled up in her eyes as conflicting emotions overwhelmed her. She loved William for his wisdom, she despaired of her own role, she railed at the God who had disdained her prayers for a child. And she resented being replaced by Constance as provider of the heir.

She rose, mumbling something about feeling unwell. "I think I may have had too much of that garlic sauce on the lamb."

William half rose and looked at her with concern. Lady Marian asked "Would you like me to come with you, my lady?"

Joanna averted her head to hide her tears

"No, thank you, I'll be fine in a minute. "

She escaped to run up the stairs to the quiet comfort of her old room, the room where she'd lived when she first arrived in Palermo. She sat down, dried her eyes and resolved to deal logically with her distress.

First of all, Constance. None of this was her fault. When they'd first met Joanna had seen her as well-meaning, genuine, outgoing. She was calm and spoke little but when she did speak it made sense. And she'd treated Joanna as an equal, not as a child, in spite of being a dozen years older. She wasn't quite a beauty; her chin was too long and her nose pronounced (what William called "the Norman nose"). But she was attractive—tall, slender, with fair hair and blue eyes and a wide, generous mouth. So what if she married Henry of Germany? There was nothing Joanna could do about that, so why worry about it? And perhaps when Constance came to Palermo they would become friends.

And I would dearly love a friend, she thought. Someone I could talk to freely about things that matter.

For a time she'd thought of Yasmin as that friend. Now she saw how mistaken she'd been. Even before the revelation of her duplicity about her relations with William, Joanna had begun to see through the superficial charm and beauty. Beneath the good humor, the idle chatter about fashion, the amusing gossip, there was a rather empty head.

But these musings had nothing to do with the subject she'd been trying to push out of her mind. She forced herself to confront it: William's desire for a son. I've been praying to the Virgin Mary, to God the Father and God the Son and to all the saints for a child. What more can I do?

She stood up wearily and stretched. It was very warm. Late-afternoon sunlight slanted through the open window. Not a breath of air stirred. There was a basin of water on a nearby table, with a scattering of pale pink blossoms floating in it. She dipped her hands in the water and bent over to bathe her face, then wiped it with a linen towel. That felt better, as though she'd washed away the doubts and questions that consumed her. But she'd hardly sat down to continue her search for constructive action when there was a knock at the door.

"Come in," she called. It was Brother Jean-Pierre, quite his sober self again.

"My lady," he said, "the others will be starting to walk back to the royal palace shortly, and I said I'd come ask how you are feeling and whether you'd like your horse brought around."

"I'm feeling much better and I'd prefer to walk too, just so we go slowly, what with this heat."

Jean-Pierre assured her he too was in no hurry. When they joined the others, William looked at Joanna. "All right now, my love?" She slipped her hand in his and said, "Much better. I just needed to rest a bit and let my dinner settle."

Their route led them along narrow, shady streets lined with substantial houses. Joanna found herself walking beside Jean-Pierre as they came out into a square dominated by a lofty church with a glorious three-tiered bell tower, each tier supported by graceful marble columns. Next to it was a more modest church with three neat round cupolas.

"What a lot of churches there are in Palermo!" exclaimed Joanna. "Jean-Pierre, do you remember that once you offered to introduce me to the city's churches, back when I was so inconsolable about the loss of Bohemund?"

"I do indeed. You said you felt uncomfortable in the Palatine Chapel with all its brilliance. So I told you Palermo was blessed with a number of more modest churches that I'd be glad to show you. But you put me off."

"So I did. How insufferable everybody must have thought me during those days. Now I think the time's come. I still don't feel God really hears me in the chapel; I'm too distracted by the blazing gold and the glitter of the mosaics to concentrate properly on my prayers. But there, for instance"—she pointed to the smaller church—"perhaps I'd find the peace and calm I'm looking for. It reminds me, somehow, of our country churches in England."

Jean-Pierre smiled like a child who's been given a sweet. "That's San Cataldo. It's one of my favorites. Nothing would give me more pleasure than to accompany you there. You have but to name the day."

"I will, and soon."

William appeared at her side and she took his arm and they strolled on. The heat was lessening at last with the decline of the sun. For the first time in months, in years, she felt a glimmer of hope that God might hear her prayers for a child.

33

Summer waned and presently Constance arrived. At first she found it disconcerting to be again in the palace where she'd romped with William as a child. It had seemed enormous to her then, with so many high-ceilinged corridors to run down, so many chambers to explore, so many walls festooned with fantastic beasts and birds created with brilliant mosaic. And of course there was the great park. How fearfully the children had approached the cages where William's father's prized collection of exotic creatures prowled, roared, whistled, hooted, growled and sulked.

"If the lion gets loose," eight-year-old William had cautioned her one day, "we must run as fast as we can and climb a tree."

"But there aren't any trees except those palms and they don't have any branches low enough to hold onto," objected nine-year-old Constance.

"It isn't hard. I've never done it but I've watched the men climb up to get dates. You have to use your knees and put your arms around the trunk and pull yourself up. Come on, let's try."

They tried, with considerable damage to Constance's skirts and William's leggings. In ten minutes they managed to get three feet off the ground. The lion watched the exercise from his cage with infinite boredom.

Constance was remembering those carefree days now as she set off from her chamber in the palace—far more sumptuous than the rooms she and her mother had occupied, all those years ago, until Queen Margaret pushed them out. Joanna and Constance had arranged to sally out into the city this morning for shopping and strolling. She looked forward to the expedition. The two women had taken to each other in spite of the eleven-year difference in their ages. Constance, accustomed to the serious, sedate life in the convent, was enlivened by Joanna's enthusiasm, her artless charm and her quick intelligence. Joanna admired the older woman's broad range of knowledge, her calm, and the way she listened to whatever Joanna said and considered carefully before replying.

But when Constance arrived at the palace entrance for what she thought would be a walk for the two of them, she was greeted by what looked like a crowd.

"I'm afraid the party has grown," said Joanna. "Brother Jean-Pierre wants to show us San Cataldo. William has business with the bishop of Santa Maria on the same square. And Mary can point out the best stalls for silks and laces."

Lady Marian appeared with a shawl for Joanna. "It looks warm, my pet, but you never know when a breeze will spring up." After some dithering, she decided to accompany them because she needed blue embroidery thread. "But I don't want to slow you down. You know I can't walk as fast as I used to."

Then William decided that Sir Alan and two of the palace knights should do guard duty, one ahead and one behind.

Hardly had the party dawdled across the square than it fell into serious disarray. Lady Marian decided to sit on a bench in the sun for a few minutes. "Don't worry, I'll catch up with you," she said. Then William and Jean-Pierre, who were engrossed in a discussion of which of the city's churches had the finest Arabic frescoes, didn't notice that the others had turned a corner and kept going straight ahead. Mary darted into a shop where a skein of blue silk had caught her eye—just the color Lady Marian wanted. When it was noticed that Mary was missing, one of the guardsmen went back to look for her. Sir Alan sent the other guardsman to round up William, Jean-Pierre and Lady Marian. That left Joanna and Constance to stroll along behind Sir Alan, which was the kind of sortie Constance had in mind in the first place. She smiled when the exasperated knight turned and growled—but it was a respectful growl—"Begging your pardon my lady Queen, but this reminds me of nothing so much as when I was a lad herding a flock of heedless sheep on the moors."

They'd reached one of the busiest streets in the city. It was crowded with townsfolk hurrying to buy or to sell or to get home for dinner. Everything was just as Constance remembered: passersby chattering and shouting in Arabic, Greek, French and the local patois. Hurrying, dark-skinned men in burnooses, pairs of women in veils gossiping animatedly, wealthy merchants in furred cloaks, their wives strutting in sumptuous gowns of velvet and silk while servants walked behind to hold up their trailing skirts and keep them out of the mud and dust. Soldiers marched or sauntered by, the former guarding an important person in a closed litter, the latter off-duty and making their noisy way to an alehouse. Farmers dragged carts of vegetables and fruits to the market. The shops and stalls displayed a bewildering variety of wares that had come from far and near to this polyglot city, crossroads for tradesmen from Asia, Africa and Europe. The scent of cinnamon and cloves wafted from one open doorway. From another, squawks and squeals were heard and customers came out bearing a chicken by the legs or a piglet in a bag.

"How it takes me back!" said Constance. "Everything is so much the way it was. Oh look, here's Simon's shop!" She'd stopped at a tiny hole-in-the-wall shop, open to the street, where shelves were stacked with silk fabrics. Turquoise, purple, crimson, magenta, apple-green—all were piled up helter-skelter and with no regard for harmony. The proprietor's head popped up from behind the counter as they entered. His wrinkle-seamed face looked puzzled and he stared at Constance, trying to place her in some distant memory.

"Yes, Simon, it's Constance, daughter of King Roger. Twenty years older, though, than when you last saw me." He grinned in sudden recognition and ran around the counter to clasp her hand. He hardly came to her shoulder—a very small man with a great deal to say.

"Oh yes, Princess. You and your mother, Lady Beatrix, used to come in so often, when you were just a tiny girl. And you're even prettier than you were then! Tell me, how is your dear mother?" Constance explained that her mother had died. His face changed in an instant from merriment to sorrow. "Oh me oh my, a fine, generous lady she was. I remember her so well. Her favorite color was blue and she was especially partial to the silks from our own silkworks, right here in Palermo. But so it goes, and we must accept our losses. Make the most of today, for who knows what God has in store for us tomorrow, I always say." Taking heart from his own philosophy, he spread out a length of gold-embossed ruby-red brocade from a roll on the counter. "So, Princess, you've come at a very good time. Do look. We've just received this beautiful silk…" He broke off in confusion, having at last noticed Joanna standing behind Constance. "But forgive me—can this be our queen? I've heard so much about you from your maid Mary. She comes in often. And now you yourself honor my humble shop!" He bobbed his head several times and danced from foot to foot in his delight at such distinguished visitors. Before they could stop him he was pulling samples of his wares down from their shelves and strewing them across the counter. "He's like a merry little monkey!" Constance whispered to Joanna. Simon urged them to look and feel but they explained they'd have to come back when they had more time.

"What a dear man!" said Joanna on their way out. "I'll have to come with Mary soon and buy reams of silk."

They emerged to find that Sir Alan had managed to collect Lady Marian and Mary. In a few minutes they reached their goal, a spacious square with one whole side bordered by two churches that couldn't be more unlike: extravagant Santa Maria del Ammiraglio and unassuming San Cataldo. They joined King William and Brother Jean-Pierre, who were standing in the middle of the crowded square, gesticulating and talking loudly to be heard above the noise.

"Do you see what I mean, Jean-Pierre?" William asked, pointing toward the larger church. "There you have the Islamic style at its most sublime. That belltower is the perfect flowering of the eastern architects' creativity." The whole party looked up at the tall slender tower, surmounted by a graceful dome.

"Indeed, I see," said Jean-Pierre. "It balances the monumentality of the church itself, quite exquisitely too. Whereas the little church next to it, San Cataldo, is a different thing entirely. It's more like a Norman church."

"Exactly, my friend! San Cataldo came later than Santa Maria, during my father's reign, and is a fine example of how the Norman influence began to take over. The three red domes are Arabic, to be sure. But the arched windows are pure Norman."

Once again disorder befell the party as various members wandered around and into one or the other church. Sir Alan and his guardsmen stood in the square, mentally noting who was where. Constance and Joanna headed for San Cataldo.

"Brother Jean-Pierre told me it was his favorite in all Palermo. I want to see why," said Joanna.

"I can hardly remember it, though I must have been there as a girl. Let's go in."

They found themselves in a serene, almost austere space. They sat on a bench near the entrance and looked down the nave to the altar, its gold leaf gleaming in the light of a few candles. The only other illumination was from slivers of sunlight that filtered through the honeycomb windows in the ceiling domes. In the dimness they could make out a few frescoes of Biblical scenes—the Nativity, Christ preaching to the multitudes, the annunciation. A whiff of incense, lingering in the air from some recent service, almost dispelled the musty odor of a little-used church.

"I like it," said Joanna. "It's peaceful, and it doesn't intimidate me with blinding gold and blazingly bright mosaics."

"I know what you mean. You're comparing it to the Palatine Chapel, and I've always felt the same way. It seemed that the idea there was to pay tribute to man's works, not to God's."

They sat quietly for a few minutes, each wrapped in her own thoughts. Joanna was first to break the silence.

"I feel in this church just as I did at the cathedral of Cefalù, yet the two couldn't be more different."

Constance looked at her, curious.

"When I was there, Constance, I felt for the first time in my life that Christ cared for me, for me, and that if I listened to him and prayed with an opened heart he would bring me the comfort I longed for."

"Why did you so especially need comfort, Joanna?"

After a moment of uncertainty Joanna found herself confiding in Constance. She poured out the story of her joy at the birth of Bohemund, her anguish at his death, her months of despair, her turning aside of every effort to comfort her, her coldness to William—until at last she came face to face with the compassionate Christ at Cefalù.

Constance clasped her hand. "My dear girl, I knew nothing of all this. What a very sad time for you! And though it's not exactly a happy ending, at least you now seem to have found strength to face the future more calmly."

"Yes, and with hope and with trust in God's wisdom. And with a greater realization of how blessed I am, with a loving husband and with so many close to me who wish me well. Like you, Constance. Already I feel we've been friends for ages."

"As do I. I'll be sorry to leave, now that we're getting to know each other. But Prince Henry's waiting for me in Germany so I expect that one of these days the summons will come."

"What do you suppose he looks like?"

"I can't say. I've seen a miniature portrait that must have been made several years ago. He seems to have a great deal of hair but no beard, and big staring eyes with big black eyebrows, and quite a proper nose. Oh, and a crown that looks wobbly, too small for his head."

"Have you any idea of his character, his disposition? I hope they don't turn out to be wobbly too!"

"None whatsoever."

"I didn't know much about William either when I came here to marry him. I'd been told he was handsome and wise. That was certainly true. But I wasn't prepared for discovering how easy it was to love him, and that we'd be so happy together. I hope it's like that for you, Constance."

"Time will tell," Constance replied, sounding less than hopeful.

The church door creaked. They turned to see Lady Marian come in. She peered around, adjusting her eyes to the gloom after the brightness outside, then caught sight of them on their bench.

"Oh, there you are! King William says we must hurry back if we're to have dinner before the cooks give up on us."

Back in the palace and after dinner—which consisted largely of cold meats and cheese, the cooks having indeed nearly given up—King William asked Joanna and Constance to accompany him to his study.

"You aren't going to scold us for staying so long in the church, are you?" Joanna asked, sitting primly in her straight chair before his desk.

"Not at all. It's the future we're here to discuss. Constance, a messenger came this afternoon with word from your future father-in-law, Emperor Frederick. He intends to send emissaries from Germany to Rieti in Italy, from where they'll escort you to Milan for your wedding to Prince Henry. He expects them to arrive in Rieti by the end of August. So you'll need to start your journey from Sicily within four weeks."

"So soon!" Though she'd known for a year that she was to marry Henry, this setting of a date brought it starkly home. To leave this sunny island where she'd lived all her life, quietly and contentedly; to say goodbye to her old friend William and her new friend Joanna; to start over in a land that might prove cold and unwelcoming; and to marry a man she knew nothing about except that he was ten years her junior and would almost certainly succeed his father as Holy Roman Emperor before long—it was an overwhelming prospect. William saw how stricken she looked and that Joanna too appeared dismayed.

"Yes, so soon. Sooner than I'd anticipated. We'll barely have time to assemble your dowry and organize its transport. The emperor drives a hard bargain—we may need to conscript half the packhorses in Sicily to carry all the gold and jewels and finery he's requesting."

"Am I worth so much, then?" asked Constance, trying to keep her tone light. But when she saw that tears had come to Joanna's eyes, she put her arms around her. They clung to each other, wordless.

"Now, now." William spoke quickly. "Don't be so downhearted. There's more. I'll escort you myself on your journey, Constance. Furthermore, I've decided that Joanna shall accompany us. And it's very likely we'll be able to continue with you to Milan for your wedding."

This postponement of the farewell was immensely heartening and within minutes they were peppering William with questions.

"We'll have to go through Messina, won't we?" Joanna asked. "It's so close to Mt. Etna—will we have time to see the volcano before crossing to Italy?"

"And surely, William, we'll stop in Rome? I've always dreamed of seeing the pope's palace and maybe even the pope himself," said Constance.

The mood was rapidly brightening. Before long they were arguing amiably about the proper costumes for volcano-viewing or for an audience with the pope. William left them to it.

34

The scene in the queen's chamber was one of delectable domestic felicity. Joanna reclined against a pile of soft saffron-colored pillows, reluctant to leave the bed where she and William had spent such an agreeable night. Still in her white nightgown, she'd thrown a stole of feather-light wool around her shoulders, the color of the first tender leaves of the almond tree in spring. William in his robe of royal purple sat nearby in a chair, legs stretched out toward the glowing coals of a brazier.

Mary appeared with breakfast trays and placed one on a table by William, then looked at Joanna. "Would you like yours up there in bed, my lady? I could find a nice flat pillow to put on your lap."

"No, thank you Mary. I'm sure I'd manage to spill something or lose the cheese in the bedclothes." She descended from her aerie and joined William at the table.

They surveyed with approval what lay before them: thick slices of bread, baked that morning; chunks of golden cheese; bowls of oat pottage, and a mug of ale for William, a goblet of watered wine for Joanna. For a few minutes they ate in companionable silence.

"I've grown quite fond of your Aunt Constance," remarked Joanna. "I'm so glad we'll be together on the journey and won't have to say goodbye just yet. It was rather awkward talking to her when she first came. But we've become more at ease with each other. She seems very intelligent and she puts on no airs whatsoever."

"M-hm," said William, with a mouthful of bread and cheese.

"And I do like the way she dresses—simply, no fussiness, but so elegantly! I thought your council members were quite impressed with her."

The day before, William had gone through the formal ceremony of naming her as his heir before his council and the highest dignitaries of church and city. This was no surprise to most. Rumors had been flying and William's pronouncement only confirmed what they expected.

"Yes, I believe they were impressed. I was especially gratified that Sir Matthew refrained from rising to object. He glowered and disapproved, of course. But at least he kept his disapproval to himself."

He took a spoonful of pottage and Joanna distinctly heard a crunch.

His jaws had stopped in mid-chew. "What's this!" he exclaimed. "A bone! A bone in my pottage. The cook knows I like neither fish nor flesh nor fowl in my breakfast pottage."

"Maybe a mouse fell into the kettle when nobody was looking."

He looked startled, then he grinned. But he pushed the bowl away.

"Never mind. As to Constance, I'm glad to say I've finally come to a satisfactory agreement with Emperor Frederick on her dowry when she marries Henry. I had to talk him down a good deal from his first demands. He must think Sicily has an unlimited supply of gold and silver."

"Why do you pay it, then?"

"I suppose you might say it's a kind of bribe. To keep him from poking about and interfering in our possessions in Italy while my army and navy are otherwise engaged."

"You mean while they're chasing after that dreadful Andronicus in Constantinople? I do wish you wouldn't go on with that, William. To risk so much on such a hazardous and uncertain adventure! Can't you reconsider?"

"Hardly. The preparations are well under way and it's high time I consulted with my admiral, Tancred de Lecce. He should have arrived in Messina by the time we get there on our way to Italy."

She said nothing. She sat with head bowed. The set of her shoulders showed not submission but stubbornness.

"So, my dear, while I'm meeting with Tancred, you and Constance will have plenty of time to examine Mt. Etna."

Even this tempting prospect failed to move her. William pushed his chair closer to hers and took her hand.

"My love, the expedition makes more sense now than ever. Only yesterday I talked to a nephew of Manuel, the last legitimate emperor. He came all this way to let me know how desperate the situation is. He says the people are getting more restive and Andronicus's days are numbered. Whether the tyrant's subjects rise up and depose him or we do it, I want Sicilian forces to be there to act as a stabilizing influence. When he does fall, the Greeks will have to choose a new emperor."

He stood, paced up and down as though planning his next words, and stopped in front of her.

"Who do you think would make a fitting emperor of Byzantium, Joanna?" He stared at her intently like a teacher willing his pupil to give the right answer.

A pause. Then a realization.

"You, William? Is that what this is all about?"

He sat, he stood, he sat again and drummed his fingers on the table. For William these were signs of extreme agitation.

"Yes. And why not?"

"I'm not disputing you, William."

"No, but you're wondering. I know that wondering look. I'll try to explain. I've been thinking about this for a long time. It makes perfect sense when you look at history. Byzantium, before the Romans came, was Greek. And Sicily, before the Muslims came, was Greek. There's still a strong Greek heritage in both kingdoms. With the King of Sicily on the throne in Constantinople, we reunite the kingdoms and build a firm foundation for peace in the eastern Mediterranean. We might even begin to mend relations between the Greek and Roman churches."

"Aha. And at the same time you outdo your grandfather in adding to Sicily's land and glory. What lofty goals!"

"Too lofty, you think?"

"I suppose not. It seems to me you generally get what you aim for. If you want so much to be an emperor, I'll try to want it too."

"We'll see, we'll see. But for now, let me toast the lady who may be the empress of Byzantium!" He raised his pewter mug of ale and saluted her as though it were a crystal goblet of the finest wine.

"And I'll drink to the emperor." She tried to match his conviction but she couldn't repress the thought that they were playing games. Oh well, she reflected. As William said, why not?

Preparations for the journey became more frenzied as the August days passed. Both Constance and Joanna had splendid new wardrobes, which had required many visits to Simon's shop and many long days and nights for the seamstresses of Palermo.

William had dipped deeply into the royal treasury to provide Constance's dowry. Gold and silver; rubies, emeralds and diamonds; perfumes, spices and silks from the Orient; precious, carefully packed porcelains—all added to the wealth in the hundreds of bags and chests. Constance's supply of costly fabrics and furs was enough to keep her sumptuously and warmly clad for several lifetimes. As the only surviving child of King Roger, she was one of the wealthiest heiresses in Europe—a fact that canny Emperor Frederick was well aware of.

Then only four days before they were to set out Joanna came to an inescapable conclusion.

She was pregnant.

She told William the news in the garden at La Zisa. They were sitting on the same marble bench on the same little island where she and William had had their first real conversation, the morning after her arrival in Palermo eight years ago. The cypress on the island was reflected in every detail in the still waters of the lake, just as it had been then. Only the showy, quarrelsome blue bird was missing.

After William's initial amazement, he held her close and kissed her. But he couldn't stay still. He jumped up and looked down at her.

"Dear Joanna—are you sure? Have you seen the physician? How do you feel? Shouldn't you go in and rest?"

He sat down again and put his arm protectively around her shoulders.

"I've never felt better. And yes, good Doctor Ibn Hakim has examined me and assures me that all's well. I know what you're going to ask next. He expects the baby to be born next spring, possibly as early as February."

"Aha. I'll be well back from my travels by then. As to that, I hope you agree with me that it would be foolish, now, for you to take this trip?"

"Of course. I've already come to terms with that, though it gives me great sorrow. I'd been so looking forward to it. But I'd do nothing, *nothing*, to endanger this child we've hoped for."

He kissed her tenderly. "My dearest love…" There were tears in his eyes, a sight she'd never seen. They sat a moment in silence.

"This will require some changes in the arrangements,"said William. "And you'll want to tell Constance. She'll be happy for you, I know, but the loss of your companionship on the journey will be a blow."

"It is to me too. It's really my only regret."

They walked across the little bridge and back along the sunny path.

"And while you're gone, William, I shall go at least once a week to San Cataldo and give thanks to God. I'm convinced it was in that church where he finally heard my prayers and granted me this gift."

"Very well, splendid. But while you're spreading your thanks around, could you spare a few for me? I don't believe God would mind if you gave me at least a small amount of credit for your current condition."

35

William returned eagerly to Palermo on a blustery day in October, 1185. He felt his trip had gone quite well. First he and Constance had stopped at Messina so he could supervise the departure for Constantinople of his army and his fleet, which were under the command of his cousin Tancred. Then he'd conducted Constance across the strait to Salerno and thence to Rieti, where Emperor Frederick's ambassadors took over.

The parting had been hard. William and Constance had known each other most of their lives and in childhood were almost like brother and sister. He felt a pang at having torn her away from her home and plunged her into a new and unfamiliar world. But she was a mature and sensible woman and surely she would adjust. As for Constance, in spite of her own misgivings about the demanding new role she'd be called on to play, she managed to put on a brave and optimistic face. Her parting words were, "And tell my dear Joanna that I'm sure we'll meet again some day."

During his homeward journey, William was encouraged by early reports of the progress of his expeditionary force. And soon he would be reunited with Joanna.

Rain was spitting as his galley approached the harbor. A gusty east wind had been pursuing them all day, now filling the sails so they were stretched taut, now weakening so they fluttered and the ship barely made headway. Once beyond the headland and in sheltered waters, the crew lowered the sails and the oarsmen took over, propelling the vessel smoothly over the rain-dimpled waves. As they neared the pier in the lowering half-light of late afternoon, William threw back the hood of his cloak and scanned the shore anxiously, hoping to see Joanna. She was not there. But of course, he told himself, in her condition she'd been sensible enough to stay indoors on such a horrid day.

Even before the galley had been secured at the pier, he leaped ashore. His horse was waiting. He rode at a gallop up to the town and dismounted before the palace steps. The sense of foreboding that had been gnawing at him increased when he saw Lady Marian, Brother Jean-Pierre and several servants at the top of the steps, but no Joanna.

He took the stairs two at a time. One of the servants held out a dry cloak and quickly removed William's soggy garment, while another pulled off his wet boots and placed dry slippers on his feet. He paid them no heed. He saw the somber expressions of Lady Marian and Jean-Pierre.

"Where's Joanna? What's wrong?"

He clutched Lady Marian's arm.

"Is she ill? Is she…"

Lady Marian struggled to answer.

"No, she is well—or as well as can be expected. But…" She couldn't go on. Brother Jean-Pierre took over.

"My lord King, she has lost the child. Only yesterday. She asked us to tell you as soon as you arrived. She wanted you to hear the news from us, before you saw her."

"But she's waiting for you and begs you to come as soon as you can." Lady Marian, filled with pity at the sight of his stricken face, wished desperately she could think of some words of comfort. But William wouldn't have listened. He pushed his way through the group and rushed up to Joanna.

After her miscarriage Joanna didn't give in to the same deep depression that had followed Bohemund's death. She felt bereft, she wept, but before long she was able to accept this second loss as God's will, for his own mysterious purposes. She recovered, physically and emotionally, more rapidly than anyone had dared hope.

She was far more concerned about the effect on William, and it was grave.

After his profound relief that Joanna was all right, he began worrying about the future. If he had no son, then a son of Constance and Henry could inherit his kingdom. Had he been wise to open the door to that possibility? To be sure, the child would have Norman blood through Constance. But in reality, the royal line of Germany would displace the Norman kings who had ruled so brilliantly for two centuries.

Looking back, he realized it had been an impulsive decision. He'd been dazzled by Emperor Frederick's offer to betroth his son and heir to Constance. It would mean peace between Germany and Sicily, two of the greatest powers in Europe. Thus allied, Frederick wouldn't meddle with Sicily's possessions in Italy while William's forces were pursuing his cherished goals in Byzantium. Finally, it would offer to Constance a resplendent future. In due time she'd be an empress. He was fond of Constance, and it had pleased him to be able to present her with this magnificent gift.

But all that had been back when he still had realistic hopes of having an heir. Now those hopes were dimming. And yet—the doctors maintained there was no physical reason that Joanna couldn't bring a pregnancy to term.

He confided in no one about his concerns, but spent hours in his study walking up and down, arguing with himself. It was urgent that he father a son. He owed it to Sicily, to posterity. Yet wasn't it this desire that had led to Joanna's two disastrous pregnancies? Could he risk her undergoing another?

While he wrestled with these matters he tried to avoid being alone with Joanna and denied himself the pleasure of going to bed with her.

This state of affairs didn't suit Joanna. Day after day passed while she waited for William to see sense. But she also remembered how, two years ago, she'd rebuffed him for weeks.

As so often when faced with a dilemma, she tried to think what her mother would have done.

"Didn't you tell me, Lady Marian, that my mother had several miscarriages?"

"Indeed she did, poor lady."

"How did she deal with them? And did it make my father less attentive?"

"I wasn't in Queen Eleanor's service then so I can't say." She'd assumed her prim expression to show her discomfort at such intimate questions.

Joanna assumed her guileless expression to show she considered these to be simple matters any woman would be glad to discuss with another.

"But surely her other ladies who *had* been there talked about it. What did they say? You must remember."

Lady Marian relented. She knew why Joanna was asking. She remembered perfectly well the way the ladies had gossiped and conjectured about the royal marital relations.

"To the best of my memory they said Queen Eleanor recovered her vigor and her spirits quite soon after the unfortunate losses. She's always been one to look forward, not back."

"And my father?"

"I believe he regarded them as temporary setbacks and was undeterred from his task of procreation."

Joanna laughed. "My dear friend, how marvelously discreet you can be! Well then, I guess it's up to me to remind William of his task." She mused a moment. "I'll send an invitation to him to join me for supper. Let's have Mary in to find something particularly fetching for me to wear. And she can do my hair pulled back in a knot the way William likes it."

Lady Marian went to find Mary. On her way back she discovered William standing in the corridor outside his study as though he'd been waiting to intercept her. His air was almost furtive and decidedly nervous. He smoothed down his hair, which was already in flawless order.

"I'm so glad to see you, Lady Marian. I've been wanting to ask you something. Will you step inside for a few minutes?"

He ushered her in and gestured toward a chair. Lady Marian had seldom been in the king's private rooms and looked around at the lack of ornamentation, so unlike the rest of the palace. She found it restful. But the king was in no mood for repose and stood behind his table, clasping and unclasping his hands.

"I know that your first loyalty is to Joanna, and I wouldn't wish you to betray any confidences. But can you tell me frankly whether you think she would... whether she is ready... " He started over. "May I consult you on a matter that bears on the queen's state of mind in regard to..."

Lady Marian took pity on him.

"I think I know what is on your mind, my lord King. I can assure you that your wife would welcome a return to the intimate relations you have previously enjoyed, and is still desirous of giving you an heir." There, she thought. That's plain enough.

King William thought so too. He stepped quickly around the table and pressed her hand.

"Thank you, thank you. You've relieved my mind."

"Then I may add that she's sent you a message inviting you to supper in her chambers, this very evening."

His tenseness melted into pleasure and anticipation.

"Please tell the queen that I shall be at her door within an hour."

Hurrying back to Joanna's chamber, Lady Marian thought maybe Mary's assistance wouldn't be needed after all.

For some time tranquility reigned in the royal bedchamber and optimism increased in the council chamber. Reports came in that the fleet of two hundred vessels, commanded by Tancred de Lecce, had reached the eastern Mediterranean and was nearing the Dardanelles—almost in sight of Constantinople. The news of the army's progress was even more exhilarating. The five thousand mounted knights and still more thousands of foot soldiers had moved from Durazzo on the Adriatic into Macedonia, meeting no resistance from the despot Andronicus.

Thessalonika, second city of the Byzantine Empire, held out briefly but fell to the conquerors. The triumphant army proceeded eastward, while the scattered forces that Andronicus finally sent out soon retreated into the hills and, whether through cowardice or lack of leadership, watched the Sicilians make their way unimpeded across the parched plains.

There was every reason to expect a resounding victory and the downfall of the hated tyrant.

That was the last word William had for several weeks. In December, 1184, he received a messenger from Tancred.

The messenger, who had been riding night and day, was dust-covered and weary but refused any refreshment or rest until he had told his tale to his king. William hastily summoned his chancellor, Sir Matthew of Ajello, and the vice-chancellor, Count Florian de Camerota, to join him in King Roger's throne room. Joanna and William sat on their gilded thrones. Nobody had had time to change into ceremonial garments, though the king and queen wore their crowns as they always did in this magnificent room that was dedicated to royal power.

The messenger's somber face and his drooping, dejected posture spoke of bad news before he said a word. In five minutes he dashed the hopes William had been nurturing for years. He told his tale doggedly.

"Five weeks ago the Emperor Andronicus accused his cousin, Isaac Angelus, of treason and threatened to arrest him. But Isaac took the initiative. He urged the citizens to rise, which they promptly did. They even broke open the prisons and released all those the emperor had unjustly confined. Andronicus escaped with his wife and his favorite concubine but the mob captured him. I'll spare you the details, my lord King, of what they did next but eventually the unfortunate man died."

He paused, took a deep breath, and drank from the goblet of water on a table at his side.

So far so good, thought William, still hopeful. The tyrant is gone. I'd have preferred that my army deposed him, but at least he's out of the way and the people will be eager to accept a ruler who governs with fairness and kindness.

The messenger went on, however, to report that the citizens of Constantinople had at once chosen their liberator Isaac as their new emperor and he had been promptly crowned in Hagia Sophia.

"This was before our army arrived?" William asked.

"Alas, the Sicilian army never arrived. Emperor Isaac saw them as invaders, not rescuers, and sent a force of many thousands to repel them. Which they did, driving our army back and killing most or taking them prisoner. Those who could escape managed to reach Durazzo where some of the fleet had remained, and they're now on their way home."

William, searching for a straw to clutch, asked, "What of the rest of the fleet? Was it too destroyed?"

"No, fortunately, most of the fleet, which had been lying off Constantinople waiting for the army, was able, under Admiral Tancred, to sail off through the Sea of Marmara to safety in the Mediterranean. By now they'll be well on their way to Sicily."

"Thank God at least for that," said Sir Matthew.

But William stared wordlessly at the messenger without seeing him. Instead he envisioned scenes of slaughter, blood and sweat, dying men, screaming horses, rampaging enemy soldiers brandishing their banners and their swords as they pursued his brave, outnumbered troops. His face was blank but his heart was burning with rage and helplessness.

The messenger broke the awful silence.

"And that is all I know, my King." He was swaying with weariness. Joanna, since no one else made a move, stepped down from her throne and led him to the door where she instructed the page to see that he was given food, drink and rest.

Meantime the others had risen and were talking.

"I must go to Messina again," said William. Suddenly he was all business. "I must be there when the men who escaped arrive, and when Tancred comes with the fleet. Sir Matthew, you will accompany me. We will leave tomorrow. Count Florian, you will act as chancellor in our absence." In short order it was decided who would join the party and that Count Florian would convene the rest of the council and tell them what had happened.

"And one more thing. Count Florian, please see that the messenger is well rewarded. It wasn't his fault that the news he brought so swiftly was so dire."

Joanna and William left the room and walked slowly down the corridor. She took his arm, wishing she could think of something to say that would help him deal with this tragic development. William sighed deeply, then managed a tired smile.

"At least, my love, I won't have to uproot you from your comfortable home and take you off to be the empress of Byzantium. You never really wanted that, did you?"

36

William wasn't the only one worrying about the future. While he was still in Messina and she was wishing he'd return, Joanna found her thoughts turning more and more toward the days, the years, ahead. What if she remained childless? And then, what if something happened to William? Goodness knows, she thought, plenty could happen, what with the way he dashes about on his many ventures: a storm at sea, shipwreck, pirate attack, a fall, a fever... Without William she'd be completely on her own, a queen without a king, without a child, without position. She'd probably have to go back to England, or to France, or to wherever her mother was.

Or possibly to Richard, wherever he was. She still thought of him as her protective big brother. Of course he'd grown older, more famous and, from what she'd heard, more fierce since she'd seen him, eleven years ago. But surely he'd find her a refuge if she needed one, wouldn't he?

Wrenching herself out of such fruitless worrying, she told herself she must give her mind something else to do.

She decided to resume her study of Arabic, but on her own. She didn't need Yasmin anymore. She could always go to Ibn Hakim, the physician. He'd often let her practice speaking Arabic to him and offered to help if she had questions.

With the doctor's guidance she perfected the greeting she'd give William on his return:

"Welcome, my dear lord. I have missed you sorely and I trust you will not leave me again soon, God willing."

This was all very well, but it wasn't enough. She still felt the lack of something worthwhile to fill her days. Most unexpectedly, Brother Jean-Pierre gave her the answer.

The two had formed the habit of going together to services at the Church of San Cataldo once a week. One morning when they met in the palace entry hall, Jean-Pierre remarked that he was glad the weather was so fine because he was planning to walk down toward the harbor that afternoon.

"Why to the harbor?" asked Joanna. "Are you searching for a ship to take you back to England? Have you had enough of Sicily's balmy days? And you long for our northern damp and chill?"

"Not at all. In fact, I've found a new way to do God's work right here. I'm trying to alleviate the dreadful poverty that blights the lives of so many in Palermo."

"I don't understand. Are there so many poor people in Palermo, needing help? I must say, when I go into the city everybody seems well fed and well clothed. Some of those ladies must spend far more on their wardrobes than I do."

"Let's sit down and I'll explain." They seated themselves on a nearby bench. Around them the business of the palace swirled. Servants and their masters, ladies and their maids, and preoccupied, frowning men with their minds on important matters came and went. Nobody was paying much attention to the queen and her friend the monk. Joanna's gown was a discreet dark brown, unadorned except for narrow bands of silver braid at the neck and hem. She always avoided ostentation for these visits to the unassuming San Cataldo.

"It's true," said Jean-Pierre, "that there are plenty of well-off citizens. But Joanna,"—when addressing his queen as teacher to pupil, as he'd done when he first began instructing her, Jean-Pierre reverted unconsciously to the familiar address— "Joanna, you've never ventured beyond the busy center, where people with money and leisure gather. Though even there you'll see the occasional beggar. You have seen an occasional beggar, haven't you?" He fixed her with a stern gaze. She felt again like the little girl who hadn't done her lessons.

"Of course I have. And if they look ill, or old, or thin and starving, I always give them a few coins. But if they're young and able-bodied I don't."

"Well and good. You're to be commended. But that's not where poverty is visible. Well beyond the center, down by the port and off to the east, families of four, six or more are crowded into cold, leaky hovels. They're always hungry, hardly ever warm and dry."

"They must be lazy. Can't they find some way to earn enough to live better?"

"The lucky ones may have a little plot of ground where they can raise a few turnips and cabbages, maybe even have a couple of chickens. But for the most part they live by scrounging. They search the gutters, the waste heaps and around the market after the vendors go home, looking for a morsel to eat or rag to wear."

He paused, realizing he'd gotten carried away. His face had reddened from his beardless chin to the bald spot on his pate. His eyebrows went up and down with indignation. His hands were clenched in his lap.

"And some become robbers, I suppose," she said.

"Some do."

Calmer, he went on. "And some are enterprising enough to be in the right place at the right time, when a merchant needs goods delivered or picked up. The ones with halfway decent clothing can earn a few coins as litter bearers for merchants' wives who are afraid to soil their dainty feet in the dust of the streets. We need to encourage all those who are honestly trying to find any way at all to earn a living. But we also need to provide alms for those who are too ill or old to work and those who, try as they might, can't find enough food to keep their children alive. I've been working with the Benedictine Abbey here in Palermo to gather food and clothing and distribute it where it's most needed. As a Benedictine lay brother, thanks be to God I have a good deal of experience with this kind of thing."

She looked pensive, then stood up decisively. "We'd better go or we'll be late for the service. But may I go with you this afternoon? I had no idea there were such conditions in our city. I must see for myself, if what you say is true."

He considered this while they walked down the steps and out into the square.

"Of course, as far as I'm concerned. But I'm not sure what King William would think. You'd be in a rather unattractive and sordid part of town. I can't imagine there's be any danger but he might not see it that way."

"Never mind, he isn't here to object. And I'll ask Sir Alan to have one of the palace guards go with us."

When he heard where the two were going Sir Alan decided to accompany them himself. He also advised them to ride rather than go on foot. "It's not only safer, it's more seemly, my lady," he told her, his stiff soldierly bearing tempered by the solicitous concern in his voice. "You are, remember, the queen of Sicily. Your people expect you to show yourself as such. And so would King William."

Around two in the afternoon of that mild winter day, they rode sedately down the broad avenue toward the harbor. Taking advantage of the almost springlike weather, many citizens had come out to stroll, and Joanna received recognition, smiles and bows as the little party rode along.

Just before reaching the port they turned to the right on a narrow, twisting, cobbled street. Joanna looked curiously at the humble shops, offering the most basic of necessities: long loaves of black bread; baskets of onions; dried fish spread on a table, so desiccated-looking that even the flies weren't interested; yellow turnips as big as a man's head with the soil from the field still clinging to them. Scrawny chickens scratched disconsolately for something edible in the dirty straw that lined their cages.

Of these last, "They don't look very happy," she commented.

"They'd look even less happy if they were aware their necks could be wrung at any moment," said Sir Alan.

It was noisy. Shopkeepers cried their wares and women in black shapeless gowns, with baskets on their arms, bargained vociferously. Most had a child or two in tow and many another had a sling about her neck from which a tiny face solemnly surveyed the bustle, or squalled in disapproval.

The three riders, their horses at a slow walk, moved in single file down the center of the street. A few of the people they passed bowed their heads in respect when they saw Joanna. They may have known this was their queen, or more likely they supposed it was some noble lady, visiting their out-of-the-way enclave for whatever reason a noble lady might dream up. But many, when they saw Jean-Pierre, smiled and greeted him.

"You're well known here! Do you come often?"

"Of late, I've done so. I must talk to the people so I can report back to the abbey about where we need to direct our efforts."

Presently the street petered out in a small, dusty square surrounded by a jumble of wooden hovels so unstable that Joanna was sure they'd all fall down if they weren't propping each other up. Several boys in ragged, skimpy garments were playing a game with pebbles in the scanty shade of a discouraged-looking tree. They were very thin and very dirty. An emaciated black-and-white-spotted dog approached them hesitantly and sniffed hopefully at the pebbles. The biggest boy kicked the dog viciously and it slunk off. But another boy, smaller, with a mop of curly black hair, protested. Joanna couldn't make out the words but he was clearly on the dog's side; he ran after it and petted it and murmured in its ear. The dog licked the boy's hand and lay down in a patch of sunlight near an old man who was sitting in a chair outside his door. The game resumed.

A movement on the far side of the square caught Joanna's eye. She saw an ancient, straggle-haired woman whose back was so bent that she seemed almost on all fours, pulling a rickety two-wheeled cart attached to a cord around her waist. In the cart sat a vacant-faced old man with his bony knees drawn up and his skeletal arms hugging them. Step by labored step, the old woman pulled her burden into a dark alleyway and was lost to sight.

Joanna was stunned. She'd never seen anything like this—not in England, not in France, certainly not in this city where she'd lived for ten years.

Jean-Pierre dismounted. The old man in the chair raised a hand in greeting and started to struggle to his feet but Jean-Pierre gestured to him to stay seated.

"How are you today, Pietro?" he asked.

"Not much worse than yesterday, I suppose, but better than tomorrow." He cackled and fell into a fit of rasping coughs that seemed to be tearing his insides apart. Jean-Pierre waited. Meantime, Sir Alan helped Joanna to dismount and they moved to stand beside Jean-Pierre. In time the coughing subsided.

"I've come to ask your help," said Jean-Pierre. "Will you please see that all the other families around the square are told that if they'll come to the San Benedetto Monastery tomorrow, we'll be serving bread and meat broth all day? And maybe if the bakers keep their promise there'll be enough bread for everybody to take a loaf or two home."

Pietro nodded. "I'll make sure they get the word. They'll be glad…" His last words were lost as a swarm of children burst out of the house. They surrounded Jean-Pierre and looked up at him like a nestful of baby birds eager to see what their parents had brought. Joanna counted: seven children, from toddlers who could barely walk to a girl of perhaps twelve. They were barefoot and their clothing was threadbare but looked reasonably clean.

Jean-Pierre introduced the oldest girl to Joanna. "My lady Queen, this is Anna-Teresa, the granddaughter of Pietro here. While the mother of all these children is away, Anna-Teresa is in charge."

Anna-Teresa was so flustered to be meeting the queen of Sicily that she was tongue-tied. Joanna tried to put her at her ease.

"You have a great responsibility, indeed! Is your mother away often?"

"Every day except Sunday. She's a washerwoman at the royal palace." She smiled shyly. "That's where you live, isn't it? Mother says it's very big and very beautiful, at least the little bit of it she's seen. How I wish I could see it some day!"

"Well, perhaps you will."

Some of the younger children were jumping up and down, their eyes fixed on the pouch hanging from Jean-Pierre's belt. He smiled around the circle of hopeful faces and opened the pouch, handing a small brown nugget to each child. They scampered off, sucking on their treats.

"What are those strange, unappetizing-looking objects you're distributing, Brother John?" Sir Alan asked. "Are they really edible?"

Jean-Pierre laughed. "The Sicilians call them *ciottolini*—little stones. They're hardly more than bread dough sweetened with plenty of honey and baked to a considerable degree of hardness. The idea is to see how long you can suck on one before it begins to crumble in your mouth."

While he was handing out the little stones, the gaggle of ragamuffins who had been playing under the tree approached silently and stood a few yards off, watching. The pouch appeared to be bottomless. Jean-Pierre reached in and, just as impartially as with Pietro's grandchildren, gave each boy a sweet, even the one who'd kicked the dog. They ran off, whooping. But one—the black-haired boy who'd defended the dog—looked up at Jean-Pierre and said "Thank you, Father." Joanna saw that beneath the grime he had the face of a cherub. He smiled so angelically that she caught her breath. Jean-Pierre ruffled his black curls and said, "You are very welcome, Federico." The boy ran to join his companions.

"My goodness!" said Joanna. "Do you know them all by name?"

"Not all. But that one's caught my eye before. His mother's dead but she must have taught him some manners before she went."

Sir Alan, like a horse eager to get back to his barn and his oats, was getting restive. "The afternoon's advancing and I do believe we should be starting our return journey. Are you nearly finished here, Brother John?"

After a final word with Pietro and a wave and a smile for all the children in sight, Jean-Pierre remounted. Joanna and Sir Alan were already in their saddles. Joanna would have liked to say goodbye to Anna-Teresa, but the girl had disappeared into the house. The three of them walked their horses out of the square.

Almost all the way back she was silent, trying to understand what she'd observed. She'd known the world contained poor people as well as rich. Hadn't Jesus preached that the poor are always with us, and that good Christians should be charitable to them? And when she'd gone with her parents to Westminster she'd seen among the throngs on the London streets many who were ill-clad, scrawny and not very clean. King Henry and Queen Eleanor had paid no attention to them so she didn't either.

Never until today had she given a thought to where such people lived, and how.

How sheltered I've been, she mused. And how blind! I must find a way to help.

Jean-Pierre had glanced at her occasionally, guessing at what was going through her head. When they'd almost reached the palace she spoke.

"I suppose, from what you've said, that the city contains many other districts where the people are just as ill-provided as in that one little square we saw. Do you think King William knows how much poverty there is in Palermo?"

"I'm sure he does, in theory. I doubt if he's observed much of it firsthand."

"But wouldn't he do something about it, if he knew?"

"Oh, he does. Or at least the Royal Treasury does. The kings of Sicily have always seen that a certain amount is allotted to serve the poor. I've talked about this to Count Florian. He says the money goes directly to the monasteries and churches that are best equipped to dole out alms and food. But he concurred in my suspicion that along the way a certain amount is siphoned off. Unfortunately, not only are the poor always with us, so are those who prey on the poor."

"I must talk to William about this. But Jean-Pierre, I want so much to do something right now. I was wondering—could I take little Anna-Teresa under my wing, and find something for her to do at the palace, maybe in the kitchen or as a helper for my lady's maid, Mary? She seemed quite bright and I think she'd learn quickly. And it would be one less mouth for her mother to feed."

They'd reached the palace steps. They dismounted and Sir Alan called a groom to lead away the horses.

"Thank you, Sir Alan," said Joanna. "Once more you've kept the forces of evil at bay and we're safely home!"

He didn't smile. "No matter what you think, my lady, if I hadn't been there with my sword ready to draw, who knows what villains might have sprung out on us, along those dark streets!"

"Yes, I shouldn't make light of it. I do truly appreciate your vigilance and protection."

Somewhat mollified, he touched a hand to his brow and left. The other two mounted the steps and by common consent sat on the same bench in the palace entry where they'd conferred only a few hours before.

"As to bringing Anna-Teresa to the palace to live, I'm not sure it would be a good idea, though I appreciate your motives. It's true, it would be one less for her mother to feed; but she's very useful to her mother, watching over the younger children as she does and keeping the little dwelling in order and tending to the grandfather."

Joanna looked disheartened. She'd already begun to visualize Anna-Teresa in a neat gown and proper shoes, helping Mary with the sewing and learning how to care for the royal wardrobe.

"However, let me make a different suggestion. Thanks to the mother's employment, at least that family manages to keep body and soul together. But there are many others, young and old, with no homes, no way to earn a penny, no future. For example, the boys you saw in the square today. They live by handouts, they sleep in alleys and in a few years I have no doubt every one will have taken to thievery. By rescuing just one from that kind of life you'd be going a long way to insuring yourself the place in heaven that our Lord promised to those who give to the poor."

She looked doubtful. "But what do you mean, 'rescue'? What would I do with a little boy?"

"Just what you'd do with Anna-Teresa. Bring him to the palace and see that he's trained in some useful trade or occupation. He could work in the stables, in the kitchen or even, if he looks like good material, as a page."

Her mind had raced ahead. "Yes! A splendid idea! And could it be the child you called Federico? You said his mother was dead. Do you think there's any other family?"

"I'm pretty sure there isn't, but I'll ask around. And of course I'll explain to him what we have in mind and give him a chance to think about it. But, young as he is, he's smart enough to see the attraction of trading a life in the streets for a warm bed and a full belly. I expect we'll see him here in the palace within a day or two. I applaud you, my lady."

She pressed his hand. "What a good man you are, Jean-Pierre. Thank you for opening my eyes to what the real world is like. It's been a most instructive afternoon. And I hope you'll let me do what I can to help in your charitable work. Maybe I could come and ladle soup tomorrow!"

He chuckled. "I don't think that would be quite the thing, but be sure I'll find some task for you. Meantime, you'll be quite busy supervising the transformation of the child Federico."

"So I shall." She rose. "I must go. But the more I think of it, the more I can see him as a page. It would be a pity to waste that sweet face and those black curls on horses in the stable or cooks in the kitchen."

"We'll see, we'll see. Meantime, I'll let you know as soon as soon as he arrives. Good evening, my dear lady."

He watched her affectionately as she plucked up her skirts and ascended the stairs. I believe she's right, he thought. I've opened her eyes to the real world. And she's just the kind who can help to make it a better one.

37

William arrived home from Messina two weeks later. It was nearly noon of a dark, overcast February day. He went straight to Joanna's chamber where he knew he'd find warmth, a loving greeting and an attentive ear. They embraced, holding each other close, glad to be together again. Joanna took his hand and led him to a bench just big enough for two, in front of the tall window that overlooked the park. William kicked off his boots, stretched out his legs, wiggled his toes, and leaned back. Joanna curled up beside him. He put an arm around her shoulders and sighed with satisfaction.

"I have so much to say to you, love. I'll start by complimenting you on that fetching green gown. Is it new?"

"Oh William, you always ask that. I've had it for ages. But thank you. Now before you begin you must listen to me for just a moment." She closed her eyes° briefly, concentrating, then opened them and recited the Arabic greeting she'd memorized, welcoming her husband and hoping he wouldn't leave her again. She gave special emphasis to the last word, *Insha'Allah*—God willing. She liked it: such a useful expression in so many circumstances.

He sat up, surprised. "Excellent! You've been working on °your Arabic?"

"Yes, but we'll talk about that later. I have so much to tell you! But I must have your news first."

"Very well. To start with, I was already in Messina when Tancred returned. He made a most heartening and informative report. You've never met him, have you?"

"No, though sometimes I feel I have, he's so much spoken of."

"Well, some day you will. I hope to keep him in my service. But I wish you could have heard from his own mouth how he kept this whole Byzantine campaign from being the total disaster it might have been."

He stood up and began pacing up and down, declaiming like a Roman general relating his conquests to the Senate.

"His performance as fleet commander was absolutely brilliant. He brought the ships almost to Constantinople but not quite in sight of the city. There they waited for our army to arrive and take the city. Which, alas, they could not. But the moment Tancred received the news of our army's rout by the Byzantines, he ordered the fleet to weigh anchor. If the emperor's forces had been paying more attention they could have bottled up all our ships in the Sea of Marmara. But Tancred managed to elude them and sailed on through the Dardanelles and into the Mediterranean. The weather was mean, but he's a skilled sailor and he knows those seas well. In short, he got every one of the three hundred galleons safely home." He resumed his seat beside her. "And that's exactly what I'll tell the council tomorrow."

"He does sound like a man you'd want to keep on your side. I'd be happy to make his acquaintance. Is he as pleasing to look at as he is brave in battle?" She was imagining a tall, commanding man in spotless admiral's dress, with a flowing mustache and piercing blue eyes.

William smiled ruefully. "I'm afraid not. He's very short and you might say ugly, with a pinched little face; in fact some unkind folk have given him the nickname 'The Monkey.'"

"Really! So he doesn't take after the rest of the family. Wasn't your Uncle Roger his father? And wasn't Roger a tall, good-looking man, like all you Hautevilles?"

"Yes, he was. So Tancred must resemble his mother, whom nobody knows much about. And if that's the case it makes one wonder what Roger saw in her, though come to think about it, it may explain why he didn't marry her. Well, all that's neither here nor there. While I tell you the rest of my news shall we have some wine? And perhaps something to nibble on to keep me going until dinner?"

"Indeed we shall." She rang a little silver bell and the door opened at once. William looked up to see a very young page who bowed to them both, and stood awaiting orders. He looked nervous, and Joanna nodded at him encouragingly. "Federico, will you please go down to the kitchen and bring us a decanter of wine and a bowl of almonds? And ask the pastry cook if she has any of the anise cakes that King William likes?" The boy frowned and narrowed his eyes, committing all this to memory, then smiled timidly, bobbed his head, and hurried out.

"New, isn't he? I've not seen him. He looks very young for a page."

"Yes, he's only nine. But I'll tell you about him later. Do go on—are we finished now with the paragon Tancred? May we hope he'll pay us a visit soon?"

"I'm afraid not. I've sent him to Apulia where he's justiciar, to see to affairs there. But as luck would have it, now when I need someone to take charge of an expedition to Cyprus, Admiral Margaritus of Brindisi appears. Precisely the man I need—bold and fearless and a veteran of many a naval battle. We had a long talk before I left Messina. I believe he may have gotten his sea legs as a pirate, but he's given all that up, and he rose quickly to admiral in the Sicilian Navy. I expect him to make short work of that ridiculous, overbearing Isaac Comnenus who's proclaimed himself emperor—emperor, of all things—of Cyprus."

Joanna groaned. William looked at her in concern.

"Whatever's the matter, my love?"

"William, surely you're not going to try to save another country from a despotic ruler! Wasn't Byzantium enough? Why should you go to the rescue of the Cypriots? What has this Isaac ever done to you?"

Before he could answer there was a knock and the page came in with a well-laden tray, which he carefully set on a table. He looked at Joanna. "Will there be anything else, my lady Queen?" Joanna surveyed the tray quickly and smiled at him.

"No, you've done very well. Thank you, Federico."

As soon as the boy had left, closing the door noiselessly, William resumed his justification of the Cyprus intervention.

"But don't you see, this so-called emperor is illegitimate. He has no right to rule Cyprus. No one's crowned him, except a pseudo-patriarch he created himself. But worse than that, he's ravaged and impoverished the whole island. He's plundered the rich and sent them into the streets and then raped their wives."

"So you plan to send an army to defeat him, then you'll declare yourself emperor in his place?"

"Of course not." He poured them each a glass of wine. "Only the pope could confer such a title, and I wouldn't want to waste whatever goodwill Pope Gregory feels toward me on such an unnecessary request. But if we rid the Cypriots of this impossible Isaac, we could establish some of our own people there to maintain order and govern with justice."

He scooped up a handful of nuts and munched. She sipped her wine and waited, trying to look noncommittal. He resumed.

"And then, my dear, Sicily would have a huge advantage in whatever Mediterranean conflict comes next. Whoever controls Cyprus controls the most strategic steppingstone to both Byzantium and the Holy Land."

"So you think there'll be more trouble in the East?"

"There may well be. Constantinople seems calm for the time being, but in Palestine the Christians are barely hanging on by their fingernails. Saladin's gathering more troops and making more forays all the time in the direction of Jerusalem. We, not to mention the rest of Europe, may be called on to drive him out."

Joanna decided to change the subject. She'd learned how hard it was to argue with William when he'd decided on a course of action.

"God grant it doesn't come to that. Now William, you are pleased that I'm studying Arabic, aren't you? Doctor Ibn Hakim has been so helpful. He's tutoring me in writing the script too, though I'm only stumbling now."

"I'm not only pleased, I'm proud of you. I myself have never gotten very skilled at the writing. Maybe you'll show me up."

She laughed. "*Insha'Allah!*"

He stretched, leaned back and said lazily, "So good to be here again with you, my love."

He sat up suddenly. "But I'm almost forgetting! A few days before I started home I came across the archbishop of Messina at the cathedral. He'd recently come back from Milan where he'd helped officiate at Constance's wedding."

"Oh, do tell me what he said! How did she seem? What was her wedding gown like? What did he think of her new husband, King Henry?"

"I'm afraid he hadn't much to report on such matters. I should have thought to ask him. He did say there were many dignitaries in attendance, though not Henry's father, the emperor. But at the banquet after the ceremony he had occasion to talk to Constance. He told her he'd soon be returning to Sicily and she begged him to deliver a message to us if he possibly could. It wasn't much—just that she asked to be remembered to both of us, that she was very well, and that she'd soon be on her way to Germany."

Joanna sighed. "That's all?"

He wrinkled his brow, thinking. "Ah, now I remember. She also asked him to tell you that she'd write as soon as she's settled."

"I'll look forward to that, then."

After a knock, Mary came in. "They'll be serving dinner soon, my lord King and my lady Queen. I've just come from the kitchen. The cook has been preparing roast suckling pig and some more of the king's favorites and he'll be in a state if he can't serve promptly."

Mary had never quite learned how or why she should curb her natural good cheer and chattiness when talking to her betters. William found this lack of servility refreshing. He smiled.

"Thank you, Mary. We promise to be there in good time, and you may reassure the cook. Have you perchance heard him drop a hint as to what else he's cooking? I haven't had a decent meal in weeks."

"I believe there'll be roast pheasant and onion tart."

William's eyebrows shot up in anticipation.

"And octopus, the little ones, stewed in wine with fennel and thyme."

"Better and better," said the king.

"Worse and worse," said the queen, who'd never learned to abide octopus. "Oh well. Mary, will you please stay and help me with my hair while the king goes to change?"

While Mary was brushing out her hair, finding the silver-embroidered green stole, and giving the silver tiara a quick polish, it occurred to Joanna that she'd never gotten around to telling William her news—what she and Brother Jean-Pierre had been doing for the poor, and where Federico had come from.

But perhaps it was just as well. She was uneasy about his reaction to her going into the poorer parts of the city, as she'd done more than once since her first venture. It might be wise to wait to tell him when he was in a mood to be cajoled. Tonight, when they retired. She smiled to herself in anticipation.

38

In October 1187 Jerusalem fell to Saladin, the dread sultan of Egypt and Syria, whose unshakable purpose was the unification of the Islamic world.

For eighty-nine years the Kingdom of Jerusalem had been under the control of European Christians. At its peak it embraced most of Palestine and the Syrian coast, including proud cities like Antioch, Tyre, Tripoli and Beirut. But fractures broke out in the Christian ranks. Saladin was quick to take advantage of the weakened condition of his squabbling enemies. After a victorious sweep through southern Palestine, Jerusalem was his.

When the shocking news reached Europe, Pope Gregory at once sent out a call for a Crusade, while reminding his Christian flock that though the enemy was sinful, so were they.

"The goal of those who profane the holy places is nothing short of sweeping away the name of God from the earth... But we should first amend in ourselves what we have done wrong and then turn our attention to the treachery and malice of the enemy."

He went on to promise that once they had truly repented their misdeeds and vowed to undertake the perilous journey to the Holy Land, they would be granted indulgence for their sins and promised eternal life.

When King William heard of the fall of Jerusalem, he was so overcome that he retired to his private chapel to pray, reflect and repent. William was a truly pious man. But his piety was so closely intertwined with his zeal to right all wrongs against Christians that it was hard to tell where the one stopped and the other began. After a day of prayer and repentance he began planning Sicily's response to the pope's call. It would be on a massive scale. The expedition to Cyprus was cast aside.

Maybe he'd join the Crusade in person! The pope's promise that those who took part would be forgiven their sins was a powerful incentive. If he did go it would be the first time he'd taken an active role in a war. But why not? It would impress his people. He'd sometimes worried that they respected him less because he never went into battle. But he hadn't been brought up as a soldier, nor had his father before him. He preferred to rely on diplomacy and, when that didn't work, to plan the campaign, set up chains of command and dispatch the forces. The fact that few of his campaigns had succeeded only spurred him to keep trying.

Whenever he'd had doubts about whether he should go or stay, Joanna urged the latter. "It's very important for your people to have their king nearby and visible. It maintains their faith in the strength of the monarchy and keeps the nobles and bishops from getting wild ideas about usurping power."

On the day after emerging from his retreat he came to her chamber shortly before dinner, intending to discuss his plans with her, though not the notion that he might go himself. He was prepared for her objections and looked forward to rebutting them. Usually this only strengthened his determination to do what he'd planned to do in the first place.

But this time Joanna was fully supportive of the ambitious scheme. She too had been deeply moved by the fall of Jerusalem. The loss of the most holy place in Christendom to unbelievers was unthinkable.

"Of course we must fight to get the Holy City back!" she said when he told her what he meant to do. "That wicked Saladin!"

She was standing so Mary could finish dressing her for dinner. William watched as Mary tied a sash around her mistress's slender waist and fastened the clasp of the pearl necklace William had given Joanna on her sixteenth birthday. The pearls seemed to glow from within, and the necklace's curve fell just above the rounded neckline of her gown. After Mary carefully placed the queen's pearl-studded tiara on her head, she stood back in admiration. "What do you think, King William? Is she presentable?"

Joanna, still caught up in her enthusiasm for the Crusade, was glowing—rosy-cheeked, eyes shining, her whole being a bundle of suppressed emotion.

"Not just presentable—more beautiful every day." He kissed Joanna on the ear. "And you, my dear Mary, are more invaluable every day, finding new ways to improve on perfection."

Mary flushed with embarrassment. William didn't often bother to express his gratitude. She managed, "Thank you, my lord King," and was rescued when a piping voice was heard from the open door. "Word has been sent that dinner will be served in five minutes, my lord and lady."

"Yes, we're on our way, Federico," Joanna called.

"But first, my love," said William, "let me tell you what I intend to do. I shall send Admiral Margaritus at once to take as many ships and men as we can muster to defend the ports of the Holy Land. When Saladin tries to take those ports and control the coast, as he undoubtedly will, we'll be ready for him."

"Excellent! Such forethought. And the sooner the better."

He took her arm and they stepped into the corridor. "Yes, the sooner the better. I'll talk this over with my council after dinner today, so we can begin planning."

As they made their way along the corridor, a small procession of courtiers fell in behind them.

William took up his remarks where he'd left off. "And then I'll write to all the kings and princes in Europe and urge them to join me in organizing a mighty army to regain Jerusalem."

She stopped so suddenly that those walking behind them nearly crashed into the royal couple. Joanna tightened her hold on William's arm and looked at him eagerly.

"Does that mean you'll write to my father and to Richard? I know my father will support the Crusade. He vowed years ago to make a pilgrimage to the Holy Land before he died. Now that he's so much older, he may not be up to it, but he'll see that England sends an army. And I'm sure Richard will answer you. It's just his kind of adventure."

The stroll toward dinner resumed.

After the meal, William convened his inner council. They met in his study rather than in the more splendid setting of King Roger's throne room. Besides William and Joanna, only four were present: the archbishop, Walter; the chancellor, Matthew of Ajello; the vice-chancellor, Count Florian; and the king's new secretary, Umberto. The last was a mild-mannered man so retiring that one could almost forget he was in the room. But he paid attention to who said what and carefully wrote it all down.

Replete from dinner, the council might have preferred a siesta to this meeting. William's study was illuminated only by two candelabra in corners and a single tall candle on the long polished table. The chairs were straight-backed and hard. "At least in King Roger's throne room we'd have something soft to sit on and something bright to look at and keep us awake," Sir Matthew grumbled to the archbishop. The aging chancellor suffered from gout. He grimaced and rubbed his throbbing leg. Umberto noticed, brought a padded stool from a corner and gently lifted the leg to rest on it. Sir Matthew was so surprised that instead of acknowledging the aid with his normal noncommittal grunt, he said, clearly enough for all to hear, "Thank you, Umberto."

William, with Joanna at his side, sat behind the table, the others in front. He rose and his first words roused the group from any tendency to nod off.

"My lady Queen and gentlemen, we are about to launch the most difficult and ultimately the most rewarding endeavor in our kingdom's history." William's tone was solemn, but his manner betrayed his excitement. He brushed a hand repeatedly through his hair until it rose to the occasion, tousled and disheveled. His words almost fell over each other in his enthusiasm.

"As you know by now, Pope Gregory has sent out a call to all Christian men to join in a Holy Crusade to free Jerusalem from the infidels. We have already sent word to him, expressing our intention that Sicily shall be in the forefront of those responding to the call and promising our diligent efforts to rally our fellow monarchs to join us. I shall send messengers to England, France and Germany to this effect. I welcome your counsel."

For a half-minute no counsel was forthcoming.

"A difficult endeavor indeed, but as you say, with the potential for great rewards." Archbishop Walter felt it was safe to commit himself to this extent.

Count Florian was more constructive: "Before we discuss the messages to your fellow monarchs, we should perhaps come to a rough estimate of what Sicily is prepared to provide in manpower and ships. The more substantial our commitment, the more likely they'll be to be generous in theirs."

"True," said William. "And tomorrow you, Sir Matthew and I will meet to plan the extent of what we can muster."

"And who will be in command of the expedition?" asked Sir Matthew. "I should think Tancred of Lecce would be the man." He sent a venomous glance toward the archbishop, who returned it in kind. Neither had forgotten their bitter disagreement over whom William should name as his heir, Tancred or Constance.

"Yes, Tancred would be my first choice to lead the ground forces," said William. Sir Matthew concurred with a gruff "Very wise."

"I believe Tancred will shortly return from Apulia," William went on. "I shall send him a message at once. Will you begin composing the message, Umberto?" The secretary nodded, having just made a note to do so.

William then explained his intention to send Admiral Margaritus to patrol the coast of Palestine, even before any crusading armies were on the move.

"And I'm happy to tell you that this plan has my queen's enthusiastic approval. In fact, I wouldn't be surprised if she asked if she could go too, perhaps as vice-admiral." He looked at her with an affectionate smile and she replied, "Oh no, I wouldn't aim so high. Maybe as cook. Though I'd have to learn to cook first, wouldn't I?"

The others, unsure if they were meant to be amused, decided to laugh, though uneasily.

"It's not such an outlandish idea," said Joanna. "You may not know it, but my mother went on the First Crusade, while she was married to King Louis."

"Yes, so I've heard," said the archbishop. "And she came home unscathed." In person if not in reputation, he thought to himself. The tales of how the beautiful young queen and her ladies had comported themselves had scandalized Europe, forty years ago. "But my lady Queen, I'm sure you'd be of much greater service if you stayed home and represented the king during his absence."

"My opinion as well," said William.

"May I bring up another matter, my lord?" asked Count Florian. "It's none too soon to discuss the routes of the various armies and navies. This will be an enormous force, and it will be important for all the armies to meet and coordinate their plans so they can launch a concerted attack when the time comes. I'd suggest Brindisi as a logical meeting place."

"I agree," said Archbishop Walter. "It's on the east coast of Italy, and the voyage from there to Palestine would be direct. It's not too far from Rome. The Holy Father could come to bless the troops before they sail."

"On the other hand," said Sir Matthew, "Durazzo or Thessalonika would be even closer to the Holy Land, and I believe would offer much more space for the troops to set up their encampments than Brindisi."

"Ah," said the archbishop. "Yes, perhaps. Though we'd need to be sure of the cooperation of Emperor Isaac in Constantinople. He still controls all that coastline.

And not long ago he was our enemy."

William pursed his lips and considered. Umberto sat with his pen raised above his inkwell. Joanna spoke.

"May I make a suggestion? Wouldn't the best launching point be Messina in our own Sicily? For the English and French at least, it would be far easier to sail here than to take the long overland journey to the eastern ports. Especially if they come soon rather than wait until winter when the seas can be so rough and dangerous. As I well remember."

"And so do I," said Count Florian. "I believe that's a sound suggestion. Not only does it make sense logistically, but think of the honor it would bring to Sicily and to our king." He turned to William. "My lord, it would establish you as the leader of the Crusade."

"So it would," said Sir Matthew, surprising all by his ready acceptance of an idea that wasn't his own. "Not to mention the wealth it would bring into the country. Think of what we could make, supplying thousands of troops, building and outfitting ships, providing the stores to go into the ships' holds."

Even the archbishop gave grudging approval. After some discussion, it was agreed that King William would write at once to King Henry and Prince Richard of England; King Philip of France; Emperor Frederick and Prince Henry of Germany, urging them to join him in a Holy Crusade, suggesting Sicily as the staging area, and promising to send information soon as to what Sicily was prepared to offer in troops and ships while they considered their own contributions.

Finally he thanked them all for their wise and helpful counsel. "In particular I must acknowledge the valuable participation of Queen Joanna, who has shown again today how dear to her heart are the interests of Sicily."

There were murmurs of approval, and "You speak for us all!" said the archbishop. Umberto duly noted these final remarks, and the meeting was over.

Far to the north in France, Richard needed no urging to join the Crusade. At thirty, he was a seasoned warrior. He gloried in the prospect of a holy war against such a formidable foe, for Saladin's reputation as a military genius had spread over Europe. Even before Richard received William's letter, he responded to the pope's call. In the magnificent new cathedral of Tours, Richard fell on his knees before the archbishop and gladly promised to join the battle to regain Jerusalem. The archbishop raised him and slipped over his bowed head a white surplice, with a scarlet cross emblazoned on front and back.

"Now, Prince Richard, you have taken the Christian Cross, to wear in battle until Jerusalem is ours again."

A month later, in January 1188, King Henry of England and King Philip of France followed suit. They had met in Gisors intending to negotiate a new truce in their endless wars. But the devastating news from the Holy Land took precedence. After hearing a moving call to arms from Archbishop William of Tyre, who had come to France to drum up support for the Crusade, both kings vowed to do battle for Christ in the Holy Land. Spurred on by William's letter, they agreed to begin at once to assemble their armies and to be ready to set out within a year.

Frederick Barbarossa, the Holy Roman Emperor, was not far behind. He too heard the eloquent archbishop's plea, at the Diet of Mainz in March. Both he and his son Henry, Constance's husband, took the cross.

Thus was the Third Crusade launched.

39

For the rest of 1188 and well into 1189, William chafed at the snail-like progress of the English and French preparations for the Crusade.

In his own country, enthusiasm was high. He had no doubt he'd be able to raise a sizeable army quickly. Men were mightily attracted by the triple lures of adventure, earthly gain (Islam's wealth would be theirs for the taking) and heavenly salvation (as promised by the pope). William, his council and his aides were busy overseeing troop training as well as the building of new galleys and cargo vessels.

But King Philip of France and Joanna's father, King Henry of England, had become distracted after their initial zeal. Henry's once firm control of his kingdom, especially his French possessions, was slipping away as he aged. His ambitious sons, anticipating his death, had staked out claims to this and that territory—Brittany, Poitou, Aquitaine—and to the English throne itself. King Philip, who could break a truce as easily as sign one, watched in glee and intervened whenever it was to his advantage.

Joanna learned of these developments in January 1189 in a letter from her mother. Though Henry still held his wife captive in England, he couldn't stop her from keeping in touch with her children, her various agents and her friends in high places. A stream of messengers went out from Queen Eleanor to Aquitaine, to Sicily, to Ireland, to Paris, to Spain, to her steward at her palace in Poitiers, to the archbishop of Canterbury, to the pope. They went forth carrying her counsel and came back bringing news.

Federico delivered Eleanor's letter to Joanna in her chamber. She was working on some Arabic exercises that Ibn Hakim had given her. While William was absent, having gone to Syracuse to check on the shipbuilding underway there, she was trying to make enough progress so that when he returned she could impress him.

Federico knew what he brought must be very important. Sir Alan had told him to give it to nobody but Queen Joanna. But he had no idea what it was. The rolled-up something-or-other was tied with a leather cord and sealed with a great splash of red wax that seemed to have an image stamped on it. It looked like a big dog or maybe a lion, like the ones he'd seen in the cage in the park.

He carefully handed it to Joanna and stood as he'd been taught, with feet together and arms at sides, awaiting further orders. He watched curiously while she untied the cord, looked at the seal and cried, "Oh, it's from my mother! Thank you,

Federico. You have brought me something very precious."

"But what is it, my lady?"

"Why, it's a letter, that's come all this way from my mother in England. But I suppose you've never seen a letter, have you? Come closer and look." She unrolled the scroll and he saw rows of black marks, totally incomprehensible. But he'd heard of reading and writing.

"And can you read this, my lady?"

"Indeed I can. Look, Federico," and she pointed to the first line, "This says 'My dear daughter.'"

"Oh my," he breathed. He touched the parchment gently and brushed his finger along the line.

"Would you like to learn to read, Federico?" She ruffled his black curls and watched him affectionately for the few seconds it took him to think this over. "Yes, I would!" Then he had second thoughts. "But won't it be too hard for me? Maybe I should wait until I'm bigger?"

"No, no, the younger you are the easier it will be. And I'll help you. I'll talk to Brother Jean-Pierre about it. But now I must read my letter. Thank you again, my dear. And please ask Sir Alan to have the messenger stay until I decide whether to send a reply."

A smile spread slowly over Federico's face as he envisioned this new adventure. His short life had been so full of adventures in the past few months! He made it to the door almost sedately but then ran to share his news with Sir Alan or Mary or whoever would listen. He was going to learn to read!

Joanna sat down with her letter.

My dear daughter,

I send you this word from the old castle at Sarum, near Salisbury. The castle is bleak and isolated but I have managed to make my quarters quite comfortable. However, I would much prefer to be at Winchester. I believe King Henry ordered me to be removed here as punishment for some imagined part he suspects I played in the recent unfortunate events in France. Since news of this may not yet have reached you, I will tell you briefly. As you know, ever since your older brother Geoffrey died three years ago, Richard has been next in line for the throne. Yet Henry has refused to name him as heir to the kingdom. Age has not made your father less stubborn or devious. In fact, of late he has let it be known that he may decide to name as his heir your younger brother John instead of Richard.

At this, Joanna gasped and looked up. John—king of England? Surly, untrustworthy, unloved John, instead of brave, noble Richard? It was unthinkable. She read on.

Last November, Henry, Richard and King Philip of France met in Normandy. Richard demanded that his father stop equivocating and name him as heir. Henry refused. Richard thereupon renounced his allegiance to Henry and knelt before Philip as his liege lord. I cannot condone this but I can understand it. For your father, it may have been a death blow. He has withdrawn to Le Mans and sees almost no one, not even the papal legate who is trying to revive preparations for the Crusade. He is despondent and though he has drawn many of his troubles on himself, I feel compassion. It might cheer him if you could send a message expressing affection and respect.

I am also informing your sisters, Queen Eleanor of Castile and Duchess Matilda of Saxony, of these matters. I hope they too will write to their father.

Up to that point the letter had been in the small, neat hand of the queen's secretary. Now Eleanor had taken up the pen herself and wrote in her sprawling, unfettered style.

Finally, a special word to you, Joanna. I have been praying that you would tell me that you are again expecting a child and that God will bless you and William this time with a healthy son. Matters of royal succession are much on my mind these days. If your father should die soon, as seems possible, and Richard should assume the crown, England would be ruled by a king without a direct heir. I have urged Richard to marry but he shows no interest and prefers to busy himself battling our enemies in Aquitaine. Here again you might help. Will you write to him and impress him with the seriousness of this matter? I have already started negotiations with King Sancho of Navarre about a possible betrothal of his daughter Berengaria to Richard. It would be well for England to have a powerful friend like Navarre near the southern borders of our French possessions. However, you need not mention this to your brother. But anything you can say to him in general to make him see marriage as his duty will be helpful. He is fond of you and might pay attention. Thank you, my daughter.

Your affectionate mother,
Eleanor, Queen of England, Duchess of Aquitaine.

Joanna put the letter aside and sat perfectly still. Her mother had given her a great deal to think about. And to do. She rose, walked to the window and looked out at the cheerless scene. A hard rain was falling, and the big drops bounced off the paving of the courtyard like dancers. Beyond, gusts of wind seemed bent on tearing the palm fronds off their trunks and flattening the shrubbery in the park. She shivered, pulled her shawl closer about her and went to stand in front of the fireplace.

The easiest part, she decided, was the letter to her father; though that would hardly be easy. But it need not be long—just enough to let him know she was concerned about his health, that she wished she could see him, and perhaps to tell him something of what William was doing. William would be pleased if she encouraged her father to increase the pace of England's preparations for the Crusade.

She walked briskly to the desk where she'd been working, pushed the pages of Arabic aside and set out inkwell, quill pen and a fresh sheet of paper. At a knock, she turned to see Lady Marian come in.

"Just the person I need! Come, my friend, read what my mother has to say, and then you must help me with my letters."

Lady Marian sat beside her, tucked back a strand of hair—by now quite gray—that had escaped from her wimple and picked up Eleanor's letter. She read it slowly, with the occasional "Hmmm," or "Oh dear," while Joanna watched her kind, concerned face. What a good friend she'd been all these years! Always there when needed, even now when she was growing more bent and afflicted with pains in her knees. But she never complained.

"Poor King Henry," she said. "He must be feeling quite friendless."

"Yes. I shall write to him first. But I don't want to sound too sorry for him. Maybe he's better by now and wouldn't appreciate my implying that he's at death's door."

Together they concocted a short message that they decided struck the right note, expressing filial regard, hope for his well-being and regret that they were so far apart.

"And I wish to bring William and the Crusade into it." She nibbled the end of her pen and thought a minute before finishing the letter.

"Finally, father, I know you will be glad to hear that William is moving ahead rapidly on Sicily's preparations for the Crusade. Even now he is in Syracuse to see about the new galleys that are being built. He still hopes that you and King Philip will have your armies assembled by the end of this year. It is such a very important cause and I support it with my whole heart."

She sat back and they read the letter. "Just right, I believe," said Lady Marian.

"I do hope so. Now I must write to Richard."

She dipped the pen in the inkwell and set to work. She'd thought this would be harder but the words flowed. It didn't take long to produce what she thought was a reasonable appeal to his good sense and his responsibility to the kingdom. She even brought up the possible undesirable consequences if he remained single. "If you should become king, and if then, God forbid, something happened to you, would you rather have our brother John succeed you, or your own son?

But she finished on a brighter note. "William hopes the French and English forces will meet in Sicily before sailing to the Holy Land. I too hope for this, because then I would see you, and that would give me great joy."

"There!" she said, relieved to have finished. She handed it to Lady Marian. "What do you think?"

"I think you've written with skill and intelligence. Surely Richard will take your advice seriously. I also think you've written with commendable brevity. If you'd gone on much longer it would have required a second sheet of paper."

"But you keep forgetting, paper isn't nearly as costly as the parchment we used to write on and as my mother still does. We can get plenty of fine paper like this from the Arab merchants in the city. Jean-Pierre says they just received a new shipment from Spain."

"New-fangled, flimsy stuff," sniffed Lady Marian. "But let's get these messages on their way."

The messenger was instructed to deliver Prince Richard's first, then King Henry's, and finally to go to England and inform Queen Eleanor that "Queen

Joanna has received your letter with gratitude. She has done what you asked her to do and sends her affectionate respects."

Joanna could now devote herself to the education of young Federico.

The lively little nine-year-old was a far different child than the bedraggled, dirty urchin who'd come to the palace six months ago. As soon as she saw him Mary had taken him on as her special charge. Within ten minutes she'd gotten him out of his old ragged clothes and into a large copper bathtub. She gave him a thorough scrubbing, which he greeted with squeals—first of outrage, then of delight as he discovered how much fun it was to wiggle and splash in warm water.

Next, new clothing. At first he had to wear hand-me-downs from the other pageboys, but shortly Mary and Lady Marian had created a suitable wardrobe. He had two suits, one of forest green, the other of russet brown, each consisting of tunic, belt, leggings and, for chilly days, a short wool cape.

"I haven't enjoyed sewing so much since I used to make dresses for Joanna's dolls!" said Lady Marian.

Sir Alan, who was in charge of the palace staff of knights and pages, undertook to school the lad in his responsibilities. When he was on duty outside the queen's chamber, he was never to desert his post. If the queen's intimates came, such as Brother Jean-Pierre or Lady Marian or, of course, the king, they could knock and enter without being announced. But for all other visitors, he was to knock and announce them, but to admit none until the queen agreed to see them. He was to keep himself informed of the whereabouts of Sir Alan and the other knights in the palace.

Meantime his schooling commenced. Sir Alan had agreed that Federico could be spared from his other duties for an hour a day. The boy was eager to absorb as much as he could, as fast as he could. "I've never had such a willing pupil!" said Brother Jean-Pierre. "Except perhaps for you, my lady," he added hastily.

"On the contrary, as I remember it they had to practically drag me to my lessons at first. But you persevered, bless you, and you finally managed to show me the rewards of serious study."

They were in Joanna's chamber waiting for Federico. Though it was mid-afternoon, dreary clouds had obscured the sun all day and not much light came through the window. But the fire on the hearth sent out a cheerful glow and comforting warmth. A tall, fat candle on Joanna's desk shed a circle of bright light on a blank clay tablet and a stylus. A high stool for Federico was drawn up to the desk with Brother Jean-Pierre's chair at its side. Joanna was seated on the divan, wearing her "work clothes"—a shapeless, loosely belted gray gown that Mary had more than once tried to discard, in vain. Joanna picked up her embroidery. She intended to be only an observer at these sessions.

There was a knock on the door and the boy came in almost at a run. He wore his green costume with, Joanna noted, a couple of additions—a green cap and green tassels on his shoes. Mary had been inventive.

He was out of breath and asked anxiously, "Am I late? Sir Alan told me I must wash and change my clothes before I came. That's because I've been out in the courtyard, helping one of the grooms. Sir Alan says every knight should know how to care for his own horse, and he says if I behave myself and pay attention to my elders I might be a knight some day!" His eyes shone in anticipation of such good fortune. Then he looked crestfallen. "But that couldn't happen for a very long time. I'm still only nine. And Sir Alan says nobody ever gets to be a knight before he's sixteen."

"Ah, but you'll hardly notice the time passing," said Jean-Pierre, "because you'll be so busy learning about horses, and jousting, and weapons, and chivalry."

"And reading and writing," said Joanna.

"Indeed. Now Federico, sit here and tell us what you remember from the last lesson."

He climbed up on the stool. "I can write my name." He picked up the stylus and proceeded to do so, biting the tip of his tongue in his concentration. He had to rub out some of the letters and after some thought correct them, but finally put down the stylus and looked up at Jean-Pierre anxiously. "Is that right?"

Jean-Pierre made a pretense of studying it very closely, uttering "Yes" or "Ah" from time to time, before pronouncing, "Yes, that is right. It is, in fact, perfect. Congratulations."

Joanna walked to the desk and inspected the work. "I agree. Very good. A fine beginning. What's next, Brother Jean-Pierre?"

"I think we're ready to attack the alphabet."

"What's an alphabet?" asked Federico apprehensively. "Is it dangerous?"

"On the contrary, it's the best friend you could have for learning to read and write. It's all the letters you need to write all the words in the world. And you've already learned seven of them," pointing to the tablet with Federico's name and pronouncing the letters. "You're well on your way."

The lesson continued. Joanna resumed her seat and her embroidery. She'd never experienced this kind of happiness—seeing one she loved, for she had truly come to love Federico, grow and thrive while she offered him encouragement and affection.

Sometimes William would visit them during a lesson, but he was preoccupied with larger affairs and remained only long enough to pat Federico on the head, glance at his work and tell him he was coming along very well. Nevertheless, Joanna sensed that William was glad of her attention to Federico. She was sure he realized, as she herself was beginning to admit, that in some ways the boy had become a substitute for the child she'd never had.

By tacit agreement, William and Joanna never spoke any more about their hopes for an heir. Both had ceased to see it as a likely event, though Joanna occasionally reminded God that she was doing all she could to serve him and he could so easily show his gratitude by granting her this one thing.

But apparently God, like William, had other things on his mind. Namely, the Crusade.

The morning after Federico's lesson, William suggested that she join him in an after-breakfast stroll in the inner courtyard.

"I have something to tell you," he said. She felt a pang of unease.

Neither spoke as they descended the broad marble steps into the airy atrium. Sunlight streamed down through the open roof far above. They walked along the tiled pathway bordered with pots of greenery. In some, almost hidden in clusters of spear-like leaves, pale narcissi were in bloom, though it was only March. In others, bushy lavender plants flourished. Joanna picked a sprig of the feathery gray-green foliage, pinched it, held it to her nose and inhaled deeply. "Ahhh—how I love the smell. Ibn Hakim says lavender has a tranquilizing effect and I believe him. I feel calmer already, though I'm so eager to know what you have to tell me."

They'd reached the fountain in the center of the courtyard. They sat on the bench and she took his hand. "Now, William, what is it?"

"I have decided to go with the Sicilian forces on the Crusade."

She felt a sinking in her stomach and bowed her head for a moment. She'd been suspecting he'd want to do this, but hoping desperately that he'd decide against it. She turned to look him in the face.

"I won't try to dissuade you. But how shall I bear it, knowing you're in danger every moment?" She clung to him.

With one arm around her, he tilted her head up and looked into her eyes. "I promise you, I'll take no foolish chances. I've no experience in drawing up plans of warfare and don't intend to lead troops into battle. I shall accompany them not as their general but as their king, around whom they can rally. My presence, I hope, will remind them of the importance of our mission and inspire them to press on. Can you understand that?"

"Yes, I think so. Or I'll learn to. But oh, William, if only I could go with you!"

"I know, I know. But without you here at home to keep the kingdom on an even keel, I wouldn't dare to leave. I shall depend on your wisdom and good sense."

She sniffed, wiped her eyes and kissed him, a gentle, wifely kiss. "I shall try to be wise and sensible."

"Of course, it's still months before I can leave. If only Henry and Philip would forget all their differences and concentrate on this far more important war! But I'll need some time to prepare myself so perhaps it's just as well. I must see to my armor, I must review the manpower requirements with Tancred, and practice my horsemanship. And I'll need to find a proper steed soon, so we can get used to each other."

Already his mind was leaping ahead to a vision of the king of Sicily, mounted on a magnificent stallion, lance at the ready, exhorting the troops to attack the enemies of Christendom. There would be danger, there would be bloodshed and carnage, but eventually there would be a glorious victory. And leaping even farther ahead, he saw a brilliantly colored new mosaic portrait at Monreale of William, the Crusader King.

Like all mortals, William knew that some day he would die. But like all mortals, he was sure it could not happen to him before he accomplished all that he intended to do.

40

At last the far-famed Tancred arrived, the brilliant general who had saved the day for the Sicilians at Constantinople. Who better to lead them to victory against Saladin?

William arranged a banquet in his honor. He conducted Joanna into the dining hall, where tapestries depicting naval battles and warriors on horseback had been hung to honor the guest and keep out November drafts. Joanna looked her most queenly in a white satin gown and her state crown with its six points, each bearing a diamond.

She wasn't expecting the hero's appearance to match his achievements. She'd heard he wasn't prepossessing. But when William introduced her to him, she saw with a shock how apt was his nickname, "The Monkey." He was short, hardly taller than she was. His head was round as a ball and covered with tight black curls. His dark-complexioned face was broad and looked as though someone had placed a hand on top of his head and another under his chin and squeezed. A flourishing black mustache drew attention to the lower part of his face, with its receding chin ungraced by a beard. But his broad smile—and he smiled at her as William introduced them—redeemed the initial impression of hopeless ugliness.

She smiled in return. She wanted to like him because William thought so highly of him. But when she found herself seated next to him, she wondered what they would talk about. What did they have in common?

She needn't have worried. After her initial "A good evening to you, Sir Tancred," he took charge of the conversation.

"Yes, a very good evening, especially since at last I meet the beautiful lady that King William was fortunate enough to marry. He's told me more than once how blessed he is to have you as his queen. It was an arranged marriage, was it not? Or had you met and decided you were meant for each other?"

She was displeased by the intrusiveness of the question, but charmed by that open guileless smile.

"No, we hadn't met. My parents came to an agreement with William and then they told me about it."

"And off you sailed from far-off England to meet your bridegroom on his island in the sunny south! How romantic! You were still quite young—twelve, I believe? Were you apprehensive about your marriage, may I ask?"

She was just saved from answering "No, you may not!" when a servant placed an oval silver platter before her with a flourish and carefully adjusted the spray of rosemary encircling a thick slice of something pale and pink that looked as though it had once swum in the sea. It was studded with cloves and peppercorns and reposed on a bed of tiny shrimp. What was it? Joanna had never quite learned to appreciate the Sicilian idea of edible seafood. She looked up to ask but the servant had moved on.

"I believe this is what in your country would be called tunny," said Tancred. He cut off a chunk from his own platter, impaled it on his knife and transferred it to his mouth. "Yes, that's it. And very nicely pickled it is, too." She still looked uncertain. "You need not fear it, my lady. It's quite dead and won't fly up and attack you."

She couldn't help laughing.

William, on Tancred's other side, heard her. Good, he thought. They're getting along. He resumed his discussion with Count Florian about his plans for the next few days. A galleon had just arrived with three young horses that William had ordered from Frisia.

"That's where the strongest, most reliable warhorses come from, you know." Florian looked blank. "Frisia?"

"I wouldn't have known about it either if I hadn't been looking into these matters for some time, ever since I decided to go on the Crusade. It's far to the north, just beyond Holland."

"I see." Florian tried to envision what might lie just beyond Holland. "Cold there, I expect."

"No doubt. Maybe that's why the horses are so powerful—they have to keep moving to keep warm. Anyway, I'll go down and have a look at them tomorrow, ride them around a bit and choose the one that suits me best."

He paused to sip from his goblet. "And I'd like you to come with me. You're said to be an excellent judge of horseflesh."

Florian cleared his throat. "Ah—I don't know about that. But I have had some experience over the years and I'll be glad to help if I can."

"Good. Now, listen to what I have in mind for the next day. I plan to lead a procession from the port to the palace square. I'll be mounted on my new horse. I'll want all the palace knights mounted as well, and in full armor. Can you arrange that with Sir Alan?"

"Yes, I'll do so."

"We'll ride around the square to show ourselves to the citizenry and to salute my queen and the court. From there we'll proceed to the cathedral, where I'll formally take the cross."

Florian looked at him with dawning realization of the importance of this ceremonial royal progress.

"I applaud you, my lord! This will send a signal to those procrastinating French and English and Germans that Sicily is ready even if they aren't. And to make sure they're aware of it, perhaps we should immediately send messengers to the European courts, men with the ability to describe the scene and reaffirm your invitation to all armies to meet in Sicily for the launch of the Crusade."

"A wise suggestion. I'll speak to Umberto about it. Now Florian, of course I'll want you in the procession, and Sir Matthew if we can hoist him into the saddle. And Tancred, naturally." He turned to his left and began to explain to Tancred what he was planning, but Tancred was ahead of him.

"I'll be honored, my lord king." He must have heard the whole conversation. It seemed, Joanna thought, that his ears operated independently, one listening to her, the other to William and Florian.

The latter was still concerned with the details of the procession. "Would you like a herald to precede you, and a trumpeter?"

They were interrupted, as though on cue, by a blast from a trumpeter who led in a line of servants bearing huge platters with the main courses of the banquet. Everybody stopped talking to watch, then to exclaim. First came roasted partridges—six of them, each snuggled into a realistic-looking nest of twigs and grasses. Next was a roast kid stuffed with chestnuts, surrounded by mounds of saffron-colored rice. Bringing up the rear marched three men, each bearing an enormous pie. These proved, when the diners' plates were heaped with all this bounty, to be filled with a savory concoction of pork, apples and onions.

Comments and conversation died down as the diners devoted themselves to the serious business of the evening. To spur them on, two musicians settled themselves on stools in a corner and began to play. The flutist produced a cheery tune while his companion beat out a catchy accompaniment on his tabor. With this encouragement, Joanna did her best to make inroads on the partridge and was just considering the roast kid when Tancred, who had been silent for at least five minutes, resumed their conversation where he'd left it, with her arrival in Sicily.

"So you and William were married, and quite happily it seems. Yet no children have been born of this union? Except, alas, the little son who died so soon?"

"That is true."

"Ah well, you're still young. There's time. I wonder, did your mother Queen Eleanor and her husband King Henry have many children?"

"Eight." She'd decided the best way to deal with this inquisition was to answer him as briefly yet politely as she could.

"I was sorry to hear of King Henry's death last summer. A sad loss for England, and for you of course. But apparently Prince Richard wasted no time in assuming the crown. I wonder what kind of king he'll be."

She glared at him with her lips pressed together to hold back an angry retort. But he was busy with his pork pie and didn't notice. It was true, her father had died in July, and she had mourned him, in spite of feeling she'd hardly known him. She hoped her letter had reached him safely and given him some comfort. But Tancred's leap from sympathy to conjecture about Richard was crude and tasteless.

Oblivious to her displeasure, he kept at her, as the courses succeeded each other. Had she seen Richard lately? Was he likely to come to Sicily to join the Crusading forces? Did she have any idea when that might be? With each query came the disarming smile, as though to say "Please forgive me for being so inquisitive, but it's only that I like you so much and I want to know all about you."

When he had just poked a large spoonful of pork pie into his mouth, she saw her chance.

"You've learned so much about me, Sir Tancred, but I know so very little about you, except for your service as my husband's brave general. Have you a wife, a family?"

"I have, God be praised." He chewed industriously and swallowed, then turned on the smile. "My wife Sibylla and my two young sons, Roger and William, are in Lecce, my native county in Italy. I hope you and Sibylla will have a chance to get to know each other someday."

Roger and William, she thought. Named for Norman kings of Sicily.

Before she could comment, Tancred fixed her with his black, hypnotic gaze and resumed his questioning.

"And speaking of our families, you were well acquainted, were you not, with Constance, your husband's aunt, before she left to marry Prince Henry?"

"Yes, very well acquainted."

She thought she detected a hint of irritation with her brief answers. The smile had been abandoned.

"Well enough, perhaps, to tell me this. In the unlikely event that King William should die without a son, do you think she would claim her rights as his designated heir?"

It was Joanna's turn to smile, brightly and without warmth. "Sir Tancred, I see now how you have earned your reputation as a master of the attack. You are not to be deterred in your relentless pursuit of your objective. But I have wearied of the engagement. Now, if you will excuse me."

She rose swiftly, put her hand on William's shoulder and whispered a few words in his ear, received his smile and pressure on her hand, and left the room.

Lady Marian, seated across the table from Joanna and a few places down, had observed all this though without catching more than a few words except for the parting salvo. She followed Joanna up to her chamber and laughingly took both her hands.

"My dear, tonight I have seen you as a true daughter of Queen Eleanor. Maybe she would have lost patience with that toad a little sooner, but how resoundingly you trounced him in the end!"

Two days later, William's ceremonial progress from the port to the palace went just as he'd planned. The horse he'd chosen was a three-year-old stallion, tall and sturdy, with all the strength and spirit of youth and with a high-stepping trot. He was completely black except for a small white star on his forehead. William named him Black Warrior.

"If it were up to me," Sir Alan muttered to one of the knights, "I'd call him Pretty Boy. Just look at that long black mane, as curly and wavy as a lady's hair when she's going to the ball." Sir Alan himself rode a strong English shire horse with no pretense to elegance.

"It will be a little while before we are completely comfortable with each other," William said to Tancred while they were mounting, "but I've ridden him enough by now to know his ways pretty well. He has his own ideas sometimes, but he responds to a firm hand on the reins."

It was a crisp, dry November day, ideal for a show of royal might and purpose. Up the avenue toward the town the procession rode, with the scarlet-clad trumpeter in the lead, blowing with all his might, his cheeks puffed out like ripe red apples. His silver instrument flashed in the sunlight, and its loud, far-reaching blare brought the citizens to the streets to watch and cheer.

Behind him came the herald, also in scarlet. The pennant that he held aloft didn't bear the usual royal heraldry, the golden lion striding across a field of peacock-blue. Instead it was the battle standard that went with the Sicilian kings on their holy wars: a gold cross on a field of crimson.

Ten paces behind the herald rode William on his magnificent black steed. He wore a white cloak over his black velvet tunic and leggings. One hand rested on the silver hilt of the sword at his side, the other held the reins. The jewels in his crown caught the rays of the sun and shone like stars. Black Warrior was as royally garbed, in a fringed purple robe that fell almost to the ground.

The spectators shouted lustily, first for William and then for those who followed: Tancred, Florian and Matthew of Ajello, then Sir Alan and a troop of two dozen armored knights riding at a brisk trot.

The queen and the court, seated at the top of the palace steps, heard the trumpet and the shouting long before the procession entered the square. Joanna's golden throne had been brought out. Her costume echoed William's though in reverse—a white satin gown, over which she wore a black fur robe. Federico stood at attention behind her. When he'd first come to court, he couldn't see over the high back of the throne but now, a year later, he'd grown so tall that he had a full view of the square.

Presently, the procession came into view and rode once around the square before pausing before the palace. Joanna had never been prouder of William. He looked solemn yet exalted. Black Warrior was tossing his head and prancing, but William put a hand on his neck and spoke soothingly, and the horse stood still. William raised his sword in a salute. Joanna wasn't sure what the proper response should be, but stood as though at attention, clasped her hands in front of her, bowed her head and then raised it, looking steadily at William.

The riders moved on at a ceremonial pace.

Suddenly Tancred's horse, just behind William, bucked as though startled, perhaps by a scarf waved by an enthusiastic citizen, then lunged ahead and crashed into Black Warrior's side.

Joanna gasped. Frozen, unable to move, she saw William tilt sideways from the force of the collision. She saw his left foot lose the stirrup. She saw him fall from the saddle and land heavily on the stone paving.

It seemed to have taken forever but it was over in a few seconds. Joanna screamed, leaped to her feet and ran down the steps. She flung the cloak from her shoulders and ran across the square to where William lay motionless. He was surrounded by stunned men. Tancred was trying to stanch the flow of blood from his forehead where he'd struck the paving. Joanna knelt, cradled his head on her lap and cried "Somebody go get the doctor!" Federico, who had been just behind Joanna, took off like an arrow.

William's face was ashen. His eyes were open but unseeing. Joanna, weeping now, implored, "William, speak to me!" and caressed his cheek with one hand while with the other she pressed the skirt of her white gown against the gushing crimson blood.

When Doctor Ibn Hakim arrived at a run, he strode through the throng, pushing men aside, and knelt beside Joanna. He examined William's bleeding forehead. He felt for a pulse in his neck while she watched, pale and trembling.

He looked at her, his wise old face full of compassion. "My dear lady, I am sorry. Your noble husband has breathed his last."

Only Matthew of Ajello had seen Tancred dig his spurs savagely into his horse's side just before the maddened beast charged into Black Warrior. And Matthew kept his counsel.

41

After the customary three-week mourning period Joanna began going out in public again, always in white as befitted a widow. Her grief was always with her, asleep or awake. Night after night in her dreams she relived the same fearful scene. She watched, helpless, as the black horse staggered with the impact of Tancred's lunging steed, as William was thrown sideways and began what seemed an agonizingly slow descent to the stone paving. She struggled to rise from her throne, to run and catch him before he fell, but could not move. She would awake screaming and tangled in the bedclothes. During the day as well she had only to close her eyes to see it happen again.

Nine months after the tragedy, she was in her chamber and recognized the knock on her door as Federico's—three taps, just loud enough to be heard but not so loud as to be alarming. She rose from the divan by the window. "Come in, Federico," she called. But when the door opened, a man she didn't know pushed past the indignant boy. The stranger wore the royal livery.

"I bring you these orders from King Tancred, Madame." He held out a scroll with the royal seal.

Joanna didn't know whether to laugh or stamp her foot. "Orders"! Who was this self-proclaimed king to give her "orders"? And "Madame"! Why couldn't the fellow use her rightful title, "Queen"? He was quite short. She supposed the undersized Tancred preferred not to have to look up at those who served him.

"I am to wait for your reply and take it back to the king."

She took the scroll. "You may tell your master that I shall send a reply in due course. You may go."

She saw him preparing to object, but he thought better of it. Straight-backed, chin high, he strutted out.

Federico had watched the exchange nervously.

"I'm sorry, my lady. I tried to keep him from bursting in like that. But he pushed me. I pushed back but he's a lot bigger." Then he grinned. "But you managed to send him on his way, you did!"

She was reading the scroll with increasing indignation. She looked up.

"Yes, I suppose I did. But much good it will do me. Federico, please find Sir Alan and send him to me, quickly." While she waited she paced up and down, crushing the parchment in her agitation, smoothing it out to read it again.

It informed her that she and her people were to move from the royal palace to

La Zisa. Tancred required the palace as residence for himself and his family. Furthermore, she was forbidden to travel outside of Palermo. Guards to enforce this would be posted around La Zisa. If she left La Zisa to go into Palermo, the guards would accompany her.

It was, in a word, imprisonment.

Sir Alan arrived when she was reading the directive for the third time, with growing anger. She handed it to him and watched grimly as he took it in. His face turned alarmingly red.

"What can we do, Sir Alan? Must we accept this?"

"My lady, I'm afraid we must. Ever since he declared himself king he's been consolidating his control over the army so they're all now at his beck and call. Matthew of Ajello has been his willing agent in all this and we know what a crafty villain Matthew is."

She sighed. "Indeed we do. They seem a well-matched pair. Well, let's make the best of it. The sooner we move out, the better. At least we're going to a place we know and where we once lived very happily."

After he left, promising to alert the palace staff that they'd be needed to help with the move the next day, she sank down again on the divan. She sat hunched over with her head in her hands. Since William's death nothing, *nothing* had gone right. She went over the dreary history of the past few months.

First was the matter of William's burial.

He'd been entombed at Monreale just as he he'd planned, near the tombs of his mother and father. His motive for building the cathedral in the first place was to provide a glorious edifice that would serve as the final resting place for the kings of Sicily. But Archbishop Walter took it upon himself to order William's sarcophagus transferred to his own cathedral in Palermo. The archbishop was aging and in poor health, but his memory of the affront to his pride when William built his audacious new cathedral hadn't faded. Joanna begged him to reconsider, but Walter claimed that as archbishop of Palermo he had the authority to make the decision.

Next, Tancred had had himself crowned king of Sicily. Archbishop Walter officiated. Though Walter had championed Constance as William's heir, Constance was far away in Germany while Tancred was on the spot, powerful, swift to act. Walter recognized that in this case principle was less important than expediency.

Joanna had been shocked by the irregular manner and haste with which Tancred had put on the crown. Yet she knew he had almost as good a claim to the throne as Constance. She'd hoped that he'd want to reign, as William had, responsibly and honorably.

She'd waited for him to give her the revenues due her under her marriage settlement. When weeks passed and he hadn't done so, she sent a formal request. He didn't respond.

Nor did Sir Matthew, now confirmed as Tancred's chancellor, when she sent a second request.

And now this! This ignominious eviction from the royal palace where she'd reigned at William's side for fourteen years—more than half her life.

She walked up and down the room, trying not to yield to despair and grief. She stopped her pacing, wiped her eyes and scolded herself. "You aren't going to change anything by weeping and wailing. Now get busy and do what has to be done."

Two days later she and her diminished household were settled in La Zisa. Here there was none of the bustle of the royal palace. It was eerily quiet—no courtiers in residence now, no festive dinners in the Fountain Room. She walked in the park, which was as lovely as ever but with too many memories. She went every week to San Cataldo to pray for William's soul.

She took comfort in the presence of Lady Marian, Mary, Federico and Sir Alan. The loyal British knight still served as her bodyguard and as head of a greatly reduced contingent of palace knights. Apparently Tancred didn't fear that she'd need to be forcibly restrained.

She rejoiced in visits from Brother Jean-Pierre whenever he could manage them. Tancred had installed his wife Sibylla, his two sons and his new baby daughter in the royal palace. When he heard of Jean-Pierre's reputation as a teacher he commandeered him as his sons' tutor. With the army behind him and Matthew of Ajello's powerful support, Tancred had the upper hand and Jean-Pierre had to comply. ("But sometimes I teach them the wrong forms of the Latin verbs," he told Joanna.)

On the ten-month anniversary of William's death, a golden autumn day, she looked forward to Federico's lesson—anything to keep herself busy and avoid the brooding and lethargy that so often overcame her. Since Jean-Pierre could never be sure of coming, Joanna had taken over the boy's schooling. Today she would ask him to read aloud a few sentences she had copied from her psalter, a prayer for St. Cecilia's Day.

He arrived on time, bounced into the room and ran to where she stood by the work table. She leaned down to put her arms around him and rested her cheek on his soft curly hair.

"And how is my little scholar today?"

He looked up at her with the eager, trusting expression that always gave her a shock of joy.

"I'm very well, thank you. Today Sir Alan told me that since I'm eleven now, and so much taller, I could try to mount a horse without any help and I did! It was quite a big horse too."

"Bravo! Now let's see if you can do as well with your lesson."

He perched on his stool and she stood beside him. She remembered how everybody—her mother, Jean-Pierre and later William—had insisted that she perfect her Latin, and she was determined to be just as strict with Federico. He began to read with enthusiasm, getting through "Oh blessed Mary, Mother of God," but faltered when he came to "Be merciful." She helped him through the syllables until he had it perfectly. "But what does mer-ci-ful mean, my lady?" She explained as well as she could about compassion and kindness. He listened carefully. "But if Blessed Mary were really merciful, she wouldn't have let God take King William away from us."

She was stunned at how he'd echoed her own thoughts. After a moment she replied, "I sometimes feel the same way, Federico. But then I remind myself that God has his reasons, and we mortals must learn to accept them even if we don't understand them. Now let's go on."

Usually a session with Federico made her forget her troubles. But not this time. After he left she sat for a long time in the darkening room, trying to pray but giving in to overwhelming despair. At last, she forced herself to leave the past and look ahead. When Richard came to Sicily on his way to the Holy Land he'd find a way to end this miserable imprisonment. And what then?

Perhaps he'd encourage her to go back to England. The idea had its attractions. She'd see her mother again. Since King Henry's death, Eleanor had been free to travel, so they might divide their time between England and France.

But it would be hard to leave Sicily. It had become her home. Surely Richard could put pressure on Tancred to leave her alone so she could live here quietly as William's royal widow. She could resume her work with Jean-Pierre to help the poor. She could watch over Federico as he progressed from boyhood to manhood. She could visit places in Sicily she'd never seen—Agrigento with its Greek temples, Taormina in the shadow of Mt. Etna. It wouldn't be too bad a life.

The thought of remarriage never entered her head.

42

A citizen of Messina who was at the harbor on September 22, 1190, described Richard's arrival.

The populace rushed out eagerly to behold him, crowding along the shore. And lo, on the horizon they saw a fleet of innumerable galleys, filling the Straits, and then, still far off, they could hear the shrill sound of trumpets. As the galleys came nearer they could see that they were painted in different colors and hung with shields glittering in the sun. They could make out standards and pennons fixed to spearheads and fluttering in the breeze. Around the ships the sea boiled as the oarsmen drove them onwards. Then, with trumpet peals ringing in their ears, the onlookers beheld what they had been waiting for: the King of England, magnificently dressed and standing on a raised platform, so that he could see and be seen.

Joanna knew nothing of this until she received a messenger from Richard a few days later. The man spoke slowly and carefully as he delivered the message:

"My beloved sister: As soon as I arrived in Messina I learned of the monstrous treatment you have received from Tancred, who calls himself king of Sicily. I have sent to him in Palermo my demand that he release you immediately and provide transport for you to Messina. Later I shall see him in person and require him to re-store your dowry and your inheritance. I believe he recognizes that my forces could easily defeat his own and that he will see reason. I would come to Palermo now but I must be here to parley with King Philip of France. He is raising difficulties that do not portend well for our joint leadership of the Crusade."

Not many words, but so welcome! Joanna felt like embracing the messenger. Instead, she directed him to deliver to Richard her reply: "Thanks, a thousand thanks, to my dear brother from Queen Joanna."

She wondered how Tancred would take this turn of events. But even before hearing from him she began to pack her belongings. No matter where she found herself next she wanted to have with her the furnishings, the clothing, the jewels —everything that would remind her of the place where she'd been so happy for so many years.

The day after receiving Richard's message, Joanna, Lady Marian and Mary were hard at work in her apartments in La Zisa, going through her gowns, robes, capes and linens, relegating them to various chests—those that she'd need access to first, and those that could be stowed for later use. Emilia, whom Jean-Pierre had rescued from a miserable life of beggary and near-starvation, was there as well.

Jean-Pierre had brought her, a scrawny, yellow-haired orphan, the day before and prevailed on Joanna to try to find something useful for her to do in the palace.

"You were so kind to take in Federico," he said, "and I'm sure you'll want to do as much for this waif. I think she may be about thirteen, and she seems bright."

Now that Emilia had been bathed and was in clean clothes, Joanna saw that she was quite pretty. But how thin she was! They'd have to concentrate first on putting some meat on her bones. In time, Joanna imagined, she might be trained as a lady's maid.

The girl was eager to help and quick to learn. The others made up little jobs for her—carrying an armful of folded garments to place carefully in a chest, bringing Lady Marian a cup of water, taking all the shoes out of the wardrobes and lining them up so Joanna could decide which she might discard.

The work was tiring. After an hour, Joanna called Federico and asked him to take Emilia down to the kitchen for some soup and suggested to the others that they stop for a bit to get their breath. The pillows scattered on the floor looked inviting. Joanna chose her favorite purple one and Mary settled on one of daffodil-yellow. Lady Marian lowered herself carefully into a chair.

Joanna sat with her arms around her knees and looked idly around the room. Her gaze rested on the delicately carved screens set into the walls, the alcoves with cushioned benches, the graceful wrought-iron stands for the braziers.

"Do you remember when we first came here, my friends? And how we marveled at the Sicilians' strange idea of proper furnishings for a lady's rooms? And now, I can hardly bear to think of living without all this."

"Will you take the bed, do you think?" Mary was looking through the door to the next room where the enormous bed with its gossamer white curtains reigned.

Joanna considered it. "I don't know. It's really more English than Sicilian. If I go to England I'm sure I'll find beds like that." And besides, she thought, every single night it makes me unhappy, wishing William were beside me.

"But one piece of furniture I shall certainly take is my golden throne. William formally presented it to me as his gift at my coronation. I know he'd want me to keep it."

"And so you should," said Lady Marian. "You're a queen and will be until the end of your days. And a queen must always be properly seated."

"Which reminds me of something," said Joanna. "A queen also must have attendants. Yet here I am with only one, which has been all very well, the way we've been living. But it won't do if I go back to England. Mary, I've discussed this with Lady Marian. She agrees with me that it would be appropriate for you to serve me from now on not as my maid but as my lady-in-waiting. You've certainly earned it after all these years. What do you say to that, Lady Mary?"

Mary was untypically speechless. She turned red, she seemed about to burst into tears, she fell on her knees before Joanna.

"My lady, I don't know what to say! Such an honor! Are you sure? I'm not highborn as a lady should be, I'm only a farmer's daughter. Are you really sure?"

"Of course! We've given it a great deal of thought. You've served a very long apprenticeship and now it's time for you to move on."

Mary stood up and looked with distaste at her unadorned brown dress—neat but far from elegant.

"I'll have to get new clothes, won't I?" Tearfulness gave way to anticipation.

"I expect you will. But there's plenty of time for that. Your first task will be to train somebody to take your place. Now that Emilia's here, it occurs to me that she might do very well. At least let's give her a chance. So what you must do is to teach her what will be required of her, just as Lady Marian trained you." Joanna smiled up at her and rose. "And if you do as well as your Uncle Alan did with Federico, I'll be happy. Now we'd best get back to work."

But before they could, Federico knocked and came in, looking flustered.

"My lady, Lord Tancred has just arrived and sent a request that you receive him." Federico, like many in Joanna's entourage, stubbornly refused to give Tancred the royal title. "Lady Sibylla is with him. He was not very polite. I told him you were very busy but he didn't even listen. He just said, 'Go on now, tell her.'"

All her resentment at the way Tancred had imprisoned her boiled to the surface. Her face grew hot and she was tempted to refuse his insolent demand. But she couldn't. He was her only means of escaping to Richard.

"I shall have to see him, of course. But not here and not until I'm good and ready. Please tell them to wait in the throne room, and that I shall come as soon as I can, perhaps in half an hour. And ask somebody to bring them wine and fruit."

Within forty minutes she was suitably dressed to meet royalty, legitimate or not. She wore the state crown and a purple cloak trimmed with ermine over her white gown. At the last minute she found William's scepter, which he'd used on only the most formal occasions.

When she entered the throne room, Tancred was pacing up and down with a goblet of wine in his hand. Sibylla, whom Joanna had not yet met, sat at a table frowning into her goblet. Joanna walked to her throne and seated herself, holding the scepter upright as she'd seen William do.

Tancred stopped pacing and Sibylla stood up. In contrast to her husband's broad monkey-like face, hers was thin and pinched. She wore a gown of stiff brocade, yellow with a border of pearls. It did nothing for her sallow complexion or her drab brown hair. She stood stooped over, as though trying to squeeze herself down to Tancred's height.

Tancred's ingratiating ways were not in evidence. He wasted no time on compliments, grins or small talk. This is the real Tancred, Joanna thought.

"I believe you've heard from your brother, King Richard. I too have heard from him, requesting that I permit you to leave Palermo for Messina, and that I provide transport. Can you tell me what message he sent to you?"

Sibylla tapped Tancred on the arm.

"Oh yes, May I present my wife, Queen Sibylla."

Joanna managed a smile. "I'm very pleased to meet you. I hope that..."

Tancred interrupted.

"And what did Richard tell you?"

"That I'm to join him in Messina."

"And that was all?"

"No, he plans to talk to you about my marriage agreement with King William. You are to give me my dower and the inheritance due me, as I have twice requested from you."

His thick lips curled in contempt. But he must have been expecting the request because his sneering reply came at once.

"You will receive what is due you. And galleys will be ready for you in three days."

He gestured to Sibylla and was turning to leave when Joanna stepped down from the throne to stand between him and the door.

"One more thing, if you please." She forced herself to speak firmly, but she was trembling with anger. "Will you see that there are suitable quarters in the galleys for Brother Jean-Pierre, my companions Lady Marian and Lady Mary, my maid Emilia, my page Federico, Sir Alan, two palace knights, my cook and several more maids and servitors?"

Ha! That stopped him in his tracks, she thought when she saw his surprise at this assertiveness. Sibylla was sidling toward the door, looking worried.

He recovered quickly. "Certainly, as you wish, with the exception of Brother Jean-Pierre. He will remain in his post as tutor to my sons."

"Sir Tancred, Brother Jean-Pierre came to Sicily with me at my mother's instructions. She'll expect him to return with me. He serves Eleanor of Aquitaine, not Tancred of Lecce." She walked out of the room before he could reply.

Three days later, as scheduled, a fleet of four galleys sailed out of the harbor.

Federico, who'd never dreamed he'd go to sea, was hopping with excitement. As the ship was rowed out of the harbor to catch the easterly wind that would fill the sails and carry them to Messina, he stood on deck, entranced by the waves that curled from the prow as it sliced through the water, the smooth strokes of the oarsmen, the view of Palermo growing tiny behind them. He was probably the only one in the party who was unconditionally happy.

Joanna stood beside him but she couldn't share his joy. She was worried about her future. She was anguished at leaving Palermo, perhaps for the last time. Most immediately, she was fearful that she might suffer from seasickness. But as time passed and she adjusted to the gentle roll of the ship with no discomfort, she began to enjoy the experience as much as Federico. The sky was a limitless expanse of azure blue, melting at the horizon into the deeper blue of the sea. A procession of innocent white clouds moved across the sky low in the south—like a flock of obedient sheep, Joanna thought.

"Are you thinking back to when we sailed along this coast in the opposite direction, my lady, all those years ago?"

Lady Marian had come on deck to stand beside her, leaning on her cane and holding fast to the rail.

"No, if I was thinking at all, it was about what happens next. Do you suppose Richard has sent word to my mother that I'll be coming back?" Her thoughts raced ahead to the meeting with Richard. Would he have changed much? Surely not—her brother would be as handsome and imposing as ever, even though fifteen years had passed since she'd seen him.

The wind was freshening. The captain signaled to the oarsmen to ship their oars and ordered the crew to raise the sail. Now they sped even faster. When the ship rose to meet an unusually large wave, then plunged down the other side, Federico squealed with delight. But Lady Marian staggered and clutched at Joanna's arm.

"Federico, will you come stand on Lady Marian's right and be ready to help her if she needs it?"

"I shall, with pleasure." He ran to take his place, proud of the responsibility. Lady Marian laughed and patted him on the shoulder. "Well spoken and well obeyed. Federico, I'd say you're on the way to becoming a true knight, always ready to help a lady in distress."

Joanna looked at them both with affection. Lady Marian had aged greatly since she'd entered Joanna's service. Her brown hair was now gray and her face had acquired an intricate network of wrinkles. Her knees gave her constant trouble and walking was painful. But she was as doughty, as sensible and as loyal as ever. She must be sixty, Joanna thought. How fortunate I've been to have her at my side all this time!

And Federico—dear Federico. It amazed her how he'd grown in only two years. He'd soon be as tall as she was. His face was no longer that of a plump-cheeked child. She thought she saw glimmers of the handsome, self-confident young man he would become.

And of course I've changed too, she mused. When I look in the mirror I sometimes wonder who that woman is. Often there's a serious, worried look in her eyes. Other days she's serene, even happy. On the whole, not bad for a woman of twenty-five. No wrinkles or double chins yet, and her hair's still brown as ever. And it shines, thanks to Mary's brushing. If Mary comes on deck, she'll probably let me know how displeased she is that I took off my cap. But I love to feel the wind in my hair.

Mary came on deck. "My lady! Where is your cap?"

Before Joanna could reply they were joined by Brother Jean-Pierre and Sir Alan, who had been talking to the captain.

"The captain respectfully requests that the passengers move to the leeward side to keep the ship on an even keel. The wind is shifting to the south."

"Why Sir Alan, you talk like an old sailor," said Lady Marian. "But I believe I've had enough of this bracing sea air and I'll go below. Will you help me down the steps, Federico?"

The others reassembled at the rail on the other side. Joanna was still in a reflective mood. "I wonder who we'll find at Messina. Richard, of course, and all his army. And King Philip. I know so little about him, except that he was my father's enemy for years, and Richard wrote that he was making difficulties."

"He may still be dealing with the loss of his wife," said Jean-Pierre. "It was a tragic affair. She bore twin sons but they died soon after birth. And she succumbed too."

Joanna was touched. So like my own sad story, she thought. Yet the queen of France died, while I live on. Why?

"The poor lady," said Mary. For a few minutes they all pursued their own thoughts. Mary looked forward to Messina, where she'd never been. She hadn't had much time or opportunity for romance in Palermo, and she daydreamed of finding a bold Crusader who would throw himself at her feet and declare his undying love. It's not so outlandish, she thought. I've kept my looks in spite of reaching twenty-four. To be sure, she might not accept his undying love. But it would be nice to be asked.

Jean-Pierre was thinking about Jerusalem.

He'd always dreamed of making a pilgrimage to the Holy Land. Now, perhaps, it could happen, if Richard would let him accompany the Crusaders. Yet did he owe it to Joanna to stay with her? Surely not; she was a capable, self-possessed woman and besides, the indomitable Eleanor would take charge of her daughter's life, probably find her a new husband. But perhaps Eleanor would have some new endeavor she wished him, Jean-Pierre, to undertake? I think, he said to himself, I would be well advised to stay with Richard.

Sir Alan had some of the same qualms. He greatly looked forward to seeing King Richard again, under whose leadership he'd fought long ago in Aquitaine. He hoped against hope that Richard would ask him to join the Crusade. In spite of his fifty-one years he felt as able to wield a sword as at twenty. Yet his loyalty to Joanna weighed against deserting her. She might need a strong arm after Richard left.

The sun was sinking below the mountains to the southwest. Palermo had disappeared long ago. Joanna suddenly felt tired—tired of standing so long and bracing herself against the unpredictable lurching of the vessel, tired of fruitless conjecture about he future.

"I think I shall go below," she said.

Federico reappeared. "My lady, the cook asks me to tell you that he has prepared dinner, and if you want a hot meal you had better hurry because he has no proper stoves or ovens to keep things warm, only puny little braziers."

In the other galleys, the knights and servants in the party had also been discussing what lay ahead. They were understandably perturbed at being uprooted from their familiar surroundings for who knew what fate. But they'd seldom been masters of their own destinies and waited philosophically to see what would happen.

On the fourth day they sailed into the harbor at Messina. Now all were on deck, straining their eyes to make out what lay before them. There was the lighthouse; there was the Crusaders' camp stretched along the shore, with campfires already alight and sending columns of blue smoke skyward in the quiet evening air. There was the pier, fast approaching.

And there was Richard on the pier, raising a hand in greeting. To Joanna he looked as she remembered him, with his shock of red-gold hair and stalwart figure—perhaps just a little stouter.

The oarsmen brought the galley smoothly to rest against the pier. Sir Alan handed Joanna down to Richard's outstretched arms. "My little sister!" he cried. He lifted her up in the air and laughed. "Maybe not so little now as when we were last together, but see, I can still hoist you, just as I used to." She hugged him and he set her down. She hugged him again. "Richard, I am so very, very glad to see you!"

She noticed a man standing near them who seemed to be waiting to be introduced. She straightened her cap and smoothed down her skirt. This must be King Philip. He didn't look like a troublemaker, in fact he looked quite pleasant, though shorter and darker and far less handsome than Richard. Richard said, "Joanna, this is King Philip Augustus of France, whom I don't believe you've met." Philip smiled and bowed over her hand.

She smiled in return. "I've looked forward to meeting you. If you are a friend of Richard's, you are a friend of mine."

"At the moment," said Richard, "we are friends. But who knows what the morrow will bring?" He grinned at them both to show he wasn't in earnest, but Joanna wasn't sure.

"In any case," said Philip diplomatically, "I am pleased to make the acquaintance of such a fair lady. Richard has sung your praises incessantly. I see now he had reason."

She blushed slightly and turned to Richard. "Brother, we are all so weary and in need of a proper meal. Where do you propose to lodge us? Not in your camp, I hope."

"No indeed, quarters have been prepared for you and your party in the palace. The cooks and servants have been instructed to see to all your needs." He signaled to a groom who was waiting nearby. "Please bring the horses." He hugged Joanna again and kissed her on the cheek. "We'll talk more tomorrow, little sister. Now get your rest. And welcome to Messina."

As Joanna rode up the palm-lined avenue Philip appeared at her side.

"I too am lodged in the palace, though in the other wing, far from yours. But if you have any questions or requirements, I hope you will send word to me." He rode on.

Hours later, when Joanna had bathed, dined and gone to bed, she expected to lie awake as usual, a prey to grief and anxiety. But the reunion with Richard had cheered her enormously. She sighed luxuriously. Just before falling asleep, she remembered how gallant King Philip had been. It was a long time since any man had admired her openly, and said so.

43

"Griffons?" said Joanna. "Griffons are fighting with your soldiers, Richard?"

"Yes, that's what our men call the Greeks."

"Oh, you mean the local people, the ones who follow the Greek Orthodox faith. But they're all Christians—both your English and the Griffons. Why can't they get along?"

He sighed, stretched out his legs, leaned his head against the back of the bench and closed his eyes, letting the breeze cool his face and ruffle his hair. They were in the courtyard of the palace in Messina. Joanna had been there two weeks, but only now had Richard found time to come see her for a proper visit.

He looks tired, she thought. And no wonder. Managing a huge endeavor like the Crusade, with his thousands of troops on the loose, without enough to do. There were a few creases in his forehead she hadn't seen before. She signaled to the palace servant who was on duty to bring refreshments.

Richard opened his eyes and sat up straight.

"Why do they fight? God knows. I suppose the Greeks have some grounds for complaint. Our men lord it over them and chase after their women. And then there's the cost of bread, gone sky-high with so many extra mouths to feed. So the Greeks take their anger out on our English."

"Dear me. What a pity you can't just sail off to Palestine and leave all this behind you. Why can't you, Richard?"

"How I wish we could. But we can't, for three reasons." He ticked them off on his fingers. "First, we're still waiting for more ships and troops from England. Second, about half the ships your husband pledged for the Crusade aren't ready. Apparently, after William died there was nobody to keep pushing the shipbuilders to finish them."

"That doesn't surprise me. Tancred lost all interest in the Crusade as soon as he put on the crown."

Two servants arrived, set up a small table before Joanna and placed on it a flagon of white wine, crystal goblets and a platter of tiny honey cakes dusted with cinnamon. They poured the wine. Richard watched them out of sight and then erupted.

"And number three, and most maddening of all, there's Philip." He gulped half his wine quickly and set the goblet down with such a thump that wine splashed onto the table. Joanna remembered how quickly he used to fly into a rage. Apparently he still could.

"What about Philip? I've been wondering about him. We haven't seen him since that first day. I thought perhaps he'd left."

"No such luck. He's still here, raising one difficulty after another. Right now he's threatening to back out of the Crusade unless I marry his sister Alice." An angry red suffused his whole face. He drained his goblet.

"Alice!" exclaimed Joanna. "Yes, our parents arranged that marriage when the two of you were still children, didn't they? I hadn't thought of her in years. I'd supposed it was long forgotten. I remember she came to stay at the palace in Winchester when I was only five or so. She was a pretty girl but a lot older so we didn't get very well acquainted."

"I suppose she was pretty then. Pretty enough to catch King Henry's eye anyway. And simple enough to yield to him. Which resulted in a child, of course."

She drew in her breath. "Our father?"

"The same. And now Philip expects me to keep that old agreement and marry my father's trollop." He popped one of the little cakes in his mouth and chewed. "Hmm. Nuts. Excellent." He took two more. "This all happened after you left, so you wouldn't have heard about it. Everybody tried to hush it up."

"Our poor mother." She remembered Lady Marian's guarded revelations of her father's infidelities, but she'd never mentioned anything as close to home as this.

"Indeed. She had a lot to put up with. And I'm happy to say that no matter how she's pushing me to get married, she's never once urged me to marry Alice." He laughed, but without much humor. "Well, sister, enough of that. I didn't come today to reminisce about the good old days." He filled both their goblets. "Let's drink to the future!"

"Gladly, though mine looks uncertain. Will it be England? France? Stay in Sicily and try to keep out of Tancred's view? What do you think, Richard?"

"As to Tancred, I'll take care of him. As soon as I have the time, we'll parley and I'll make sure he fulfils William's marriage agreement with you and doesn't meddle with your life."

"Thank you! That's been so much on my mind. When it's settled, I believe I'll pay a visit to our mother while I decide what to do next. I'll send word to her that I'll be ready to leave as soon as she tells me whether to go to Winchester or to her palace in Poitiers."

"Very good plan. She'll be glad to see you. And when you go I'll see that you have a guard of half a dozen knights. Not Sir Alan, I'm afraid. He has most eloquently argued that he deserves to join the Crusade, and I've agreed."

He signaled for more wine, dispatched the last honey cake, and continued.

"However, it's the immediate future that's on my mind. You may not like this, but I think for your own safety you will have to leave Messina for a few weeks. The disputes between the Greeks and the Crusaders are getting ugly here and may get worse. I'm afraid I'll have to take the army into the city and restore order. You and your people will be much better off well away from the scene."

To Joanna this seemed unkind, just when she and her party had gotten nicely settled in such a lovely, luxurious palace. But she wasn't going to argue with Richard. If it weren't for him she'd still be imprisoned in Palermo. Besides, all her life she'd trusted his judgment. If he said they'd be in danger here, so be it.

"All right, if you think that's best. Where will we go, and when?"

"You'll be lodged in a monastery up in the hills at Bagnara, just across the strait in Italy. I've sent men to look it over and see if it's suitable, and to persuade the monks to accept you and your people as their guests for a few weeks. A purse of gold persuaded them very quickly."

"That seems hard, to go so far. Aren't there safe refuges here in Sicily?"

"With all the unrest and ill feeling, I wouldn't vouch for your security anywhere on the island. Trust me, Joanna, this is for the best." He stood up, and she rose to embrace him.

"Thank you, Richard. It's good to have my big brother looking after me. I've felt so alone ever since..." She was suddenly overcome. She buried her face in his shoulder.

He patted her head. "I understand. Of course you miss William. I wish I'd known him, he must have been a fine man. And I'm sure he'd agree that sending you across the strait is the wisest course."

She sniffled, blinked the tears out of her eyes and nodded.

"Now, let's get practical. I suggest that besides your two ladies and that pretty little page who follows you about, you should take half a dozen servants. I'm sorry but Brother Jean-Pierre will have to stay here. I know he's your good friend, but I need all the holy men about me that I can find, to put the fear of God into my troops. And you must take your own cook so you don't have to depend on those abstemious monks for your meals. You'll want something more substantial than bread and water. My men went into the town while they were there and advised the merchants to lay in some supplies for you. I expect you'll have plenty of fresh meat. I've heard there are fine wild boar in those beech forests. I'll send a couple of knights; they'll be your huntsmen as well as your bodyguards."

"You've thought of everything, Richard."

So it was decided. They would sail away to their new home in two days. Joanna didn't look forward to telling Lady Marian and Mary and the others that they'd have to start packing again.

A week later, Joanna and her entourage were settled in the guest quarters of the Bagnara monastery. They saw very little of the brown-robed monks except from a distance, as they walked sedately along in pairs, their faces hidden by their hoods. Lady Marian was the party's emissary to confer with the abbot when necessary.

The general mood was not a happy one. The servants missed the relative spaciousness and comfort of their lodgings in Messina compared with cramped quarters and hard beds in the monastery sleeping rooms. The cook complained at having to work in such an ill-equipped kitchen, cheek by jowl with the monks' cook. The latter would cast furtive, disapproving glances at the former's unnecessarily rich concoctions when he himself was putting together a perfectly nutritious meal of barley soup and boiled turnips.

Lady Marian, as was her nature, didn't complain and kept busy. She made great progress on her embroidery. She had decided to give the monks a fine altar cloth for their chapel. When she told the abbot he demurred, saying the plain white ones they had were quite good enough. "We don't want anything bright and gaudy, like those in your big cathedrals." She promised it would not be gaudy.

"So," she told Joanna, "I shall make it all one color, a pale blue, but I'll use my fanciest stitches to work a pattern of birds and flowers. The abbot is rather near-sighted and I doubt if he'll even notice."

Mary chafed at the exile most of all. Precisely as she'd dreamed, she'd met a gallant Crusader. But just as their acquaintance was ripening into romance she'd been torn away from him.

"We might as well have stayed in Palermo," she said crossly a few days after their arrival. She was mending the hem of Joanna's crimson robe. She jabbed the needle in so hard that she pricked her finger. "Ouch!" She popped the finger into her mouth.

Lady Marian, sitting beside her with her embroidery, glanced at the drop of blood on the garment. "Good thing you weren't working on the white one."

Joanna walked to the narrow window in the stark stone wall and looked out at the forested slope running down to the sea.

"Yes, it's too bad to be cooped up like this, when we'd barely gotten comfortable in Messina. But you'll have to admit the setting is lovely. Besides, we aren't prisoners as we were in Palermo. We're free to come and go as we please."

"Yes, my lady, if there were any place to go to," Mary said, still grumpy. "We can take walks, and we can ride into the town, such as it is, and ride back again. We can walk around the cloister garden, but that takes only five minutes. And that's it."

"Never mind, Mary. Richard said it would be only a few weeks, and then we'll be back in Messina and you'll be reunited with your Stephen."

Only Joanna and Federico welcomed the experience. The two of them took frequent walks in the forest with one of the knights and with Mary when she could be persuaded. For Federico, it was a totally new world to explore. He'd never been outside of a city, much less in the company of so many trees, so tall he couldn't see their tops and so leafy that they barely let the sunlight through. He'd scamper about like a puppy, finding all kinds of marvels from deer tracks to fallen chestnuts. Then he'd remember that he was the queen's page and he'd march ahead of her, on the alert for wild beasts or brigands or branches in the path.

As for Joanna, being here was a blessed respite from the sorrows and worries that had oppressed her for the past year. Not only was she physically far removed from her tormentors, Tancred and his partner in mischief Matthew of Ajello. She'd also left behind the pressure of virtual imprisonment in Palermo and the hopelessness of knowing there was no way she could escape. Now, with Richard's arrival and his care for her safety and well-being, she felt secure, content to wait until he summoned them back and she could prepare to leave Sicily.

The few weeks stretched into six, seven, eight. October became November, then December. They were not as hardy as the monks and were only skimpily supplied with bedclothes or anything to temper the chill. Lady Marian decided enough was enough and sent a man into the town to see what he could find.

"And Federico, you will go with him to help. Be sure you get enough blankets for all of us, and see if you can find some rugs for these cold stone floors."

Federico's pride in the assignment propelled him into his saddle in an instant. He sat as tall as he could, eager to be off, watching with impatience as the servant took his time in mounting.

In three hours they were back, accompanied by a mule they'd hired to carry a mountain of furry and wooly coverings and rugs.

"The best are the sheepskins," the servant told Lady Marian, pulling a few off the pile and displaying them for her. "See how thick and soft they are, and they'll do for the beds and the floors too."

Federico picked up a small black lambskin. He brushed his hand over its tight curls and looked up at Lady Marian. "Do you think I could have this one?"

"I don't know why not. It would go nicely with your hair."

He grinned, wrapped himself in it and pranced about like a gamboling lamb.

"What about the packet, lad?" the servant muttered to him.

"Oh yes!" He gulped. "I almost forgot. While were in the market a man rode up and asked if anybody knew how to get to the monastery where Queen Joanna was lodged because he had a message for her. So we told him we were going there shortly and he could come with us. And then he said in that case we could take the packet and he'd hurry back to the harbor so his boat could catch the evening tide." He pulled from his pocket a small linen-wrapped parcel, bearing the bright red seal of the kings of England.

"Take it to Queen Joanna at once," said Lady Marian. "I believe she's in the cloister."

Joanna nervously broke the seal. Was it bad news? She found a single thick sheet in Richard's sprawling hand. Her worried frown disappeared as she read the first line. She looked up to see not only Lady Marian, Mary, Federico and her maid Emilia, but the cook and all the servants, everybody eager to hear what King Richard had to say.

"We're to come back to Messina, all's well there now!"

Something like a cheer broke out. The cook's shout was the loudest. Mary's smile was the broadest.

"How soon does he say?" she asked.

"He will send galleys the day after tomorrow."

"So at least we'll be warm our last two nights," said Mary, once more her cheerful self. "And maybe the monks will relax their rule of self-denial and will be glad to have all these rugs and robes."

Federico plucked up his courage and asked, "Lady Marian, do you think I could keep my black lambskin?"

"Of course you may. Now we must all get busy. Come, Emilia, and I'll help you get started."

When everybody had dispersed, Joanna went back to the letter. There wasn't much more—only that he'd succeeded in subduing the rebellious Griffons and had taken possession of the town. And he was building a castle near the harbor.

A castle? Why a castle, she wondered. She read on. It was designed to be dismantled when they left and reassembled in Palestine as a siege engine. He'd named in Matagriffon—Kill the Greeks. "To remind them they'd better not start any more trouble."

She was about to refold the letter when she noticed writing on the back.

"You will arrive in good time for the Christmas banquet I plan to hold in Matagriffon. You will be guest of honor. The other notable guests will be King Tancred and King Philip—assuming I remain on good terms with them, as I am at the moment."

She stared at the words as though wondering if she had read them correctly. She would share the festive table with the loathsome Tancred and the enigmatic Philip.

Christmas in Messina promised to be most interesting.

44

"That doesn't look like much of a castle to me," said Lady Marian. "More like a monstrous woodpile."

Joanna and her party, having been liberated from Bagnara, were riding up to the palace from the harbor at Messina. King Philip and Sir Alan had met them at the pier. It was a cold, windless day, with lowering gray clouds and a biting chill in the air. In his long, black fur cloak, Philip looked like a figure announcing doom. His dark-bearded face was as hard to read as ever. But his manners were as impeccable as ever. He bowed over Joanna's hand and said, "I bear greetings from King Richard, Queen Joanna. He was unable to be here so I shall do my best to make you welcome and conduct you to the palace." He'd then taken his place at the head of the procession.

He heard Lady Marian's words and reined in his horse to look where she was pointing. Joanna let down her hood and looked too. She saw a tall, square, ungainly structure that dwarfed the surrounding one-story houses and shops that crowded the hillside. So this was Richard's Matagriffon. It seemed to have four walls but no roof. Though they could hear and see workmen busy with hammers and saws, it had not yet assumed any resemblance to any castle she had ever seen.

"You're right, of course, Lady Marian," said Philip. "I believe he calls it a castle in jest. But remember that it's not a permanent structure. Richard must take it all apart when he leaves so he can rebuild it in Palestine. It will help us to besiege the cities we'll need to take."

While they surveyed the scene, a head of red-gold hair caught Joanna's eye. Richard, towering above the workmen, was apparently discussing the placement of a huge timber that three men bore on their shoulders.

Sir Alan said, "He's there every day, morning to night, urging them on and lending a hand. He's set on finishing it in time for his Christmas banquet. Would you like to ride over for a closer look?"

She shivered and clutched her cloak about her. "Not now, thank you. Maybe tomorrow."

"Very wise," said Philip. "I believe it's beginning to rain and I'm sure you've had a long hard day."

She sent him a look of gratitude for his understanding, raised her hood and rode on. It had indeed been a long hard day. During the trip across the strait, their galley had been buffeted by winds that came now from one direction, now from another, so they bounced about like a puppet on a string. All Joanna wanted now was to get inside, get warm and lie down.

She didn't inspect Matagriffon the next day or the next week, being confined to her bed with a fever, a cough and a feeling of general misery. Richard came to see her, but after he was assured that she wasn't at death's door and only needed time to recover, he pressed her hand affectionately, told her she must get well by Christmas (only five days away) and went back to his labors.

Philip didn't appear but he sent an enormous basket filled with exotic temptations: golden globes of oranges, blushing apricots, figs almost bursting with plumpness, bunches of rosy grapes still clinging to the vine, shiny brown dates with seeds removed and stuffed with walnuts. His message: "My physicians tell me that fruit is an excellent antidote to the ill humor you are suffering. I hope these will prove of some benefit."

Whether it was fruit or simply the passage of time, Joanna felt much better by Christmas morning. She was quite hungry, but she knew the banquet would be long and lavish, so she had only a bowl of milk and a chunk of bread for breakfast. Then she called for Mary and Emilia. It was none too soon to begin the serious task of dressing. This involved far more than choosing a gown and jewels. First came the bath. She'd not had a proper bath all the time she was in Bagnara. The monks were as abstemious in their bathing as their eating and saw no reason to provide their guests with towels, sponges and facilities for heating multiple basins of water, much less tubs to accommodate the water and the bather.

Emilia had never assisted a lady to bathe. Mary instructed her carefully. First a large wooden tub would be borne into Joanna's chamber. Then servants would bring basins of hot water and pour them in until it was at least half full. Emilia was to test it with her elbow to make sure it was not too hot, not too cold, and sprinkle into it a few drops of lavender oil. When all the servants had left, she was to help Joanna get undressed (keeping only her cap on) and assist her onto a stool and thence into the tub, where a cushion for her head was to be placed. She would sponge her lady head to toe, or if Joanna preferred to wash herself, Emilia would only offer to do her back. Finally, she would help her out of the tub and into a robe that had been warming by the fire.

"Now, do you have all that in mind? Can you assist the queen just as I've instructed?"

"Oh yes, Lady Mary, I'm sure I can!"

Mary still felt a little start of pleasure and surprise at being addressed as "Lady." With new authority, she spoke to the puffing servant who had just emptied a large ewer into the tub. "Are you almost finished, Arnold?"

"One more trip should do it." He hurried out.

One more trip did it.

Presently, thoroughly cleansed and still tingling from Emilia's brisk ministrations, Joanna leaned back to rest her head on the cushion. Lazily, she stretched, flexed her muscles, wiggled her fingers and toes, letting her whole body relax and respond to the blessed warmth.

Not a bad body for a woman of twenty-six, she mused, taking stock. Skin white and smooth, not a sign of a wrinkle. Stomach still flat, no fat around the waist, breasts as nicely pointed and upstanding as ever—though I do wish they were just a little bigger. I think I'll wear the green velvet gown tonight, the one with the snug fit and the low neckline. I wonder if Philip will notice. It's hard to know with Philip. He never seems to permit his eyes to stray below my face. But William would have noticed. He would have stood behind me, let his hands glide up from my waist to close over my breasts with gentle pressure, like this. He would have leaned over my shoulder to kiss me just where the vee of the gown reveals a hint of cleavage. She closed her eyes, remembering.

William! She sat up, realizing that she hadn't thought of William for days. Should she feel guilty? She leaned back again and gazed at the ceiling, considering. No, she decided. William wouldn't have wanted her to grieve forever. He'd want her to be happy. She wondered if Philip was the one who could make her happy. Anyway, she was still young and the world was full of men. She knew from the way they looked at her that they still found her desirable. Maybe the future needn't be as bleak as she'd feared.

But her immediate future had deteriorated seriously. The bath water was cool, almost cold. She shivered and stood up, wrapping her arms around her.

"Emilia!" she called. The girl hastened to help Joanna out of the tub and into the warm robe and felt slippers.

"Thank you, Emilia. I feel so much better." Joanna snuggled in the robe and sank into a chair by the hearth while the servants drained and removed the tub. She took off her cap and shook out her hair, curly from the damp.

Lady Marian had been bustling about, laying out undergarments and chemises, urging the servants to hurry, telling Emilia to find a hairbrush and a mirror, consulting with Mary about jewels and hair arrangements. There was polite but impassioned discussion about the merits of the green velvet versus the blue satin. The green velvet won. When she'd slipped it on and all the fastenings had been secured and the jeweled girdle encircled her waist, Mary placed the emerald necklace around her neck and fastened the clasp. Joanna stretched out her arms and pirouetted.

"How do I look?"

"Absolutely beautiful, my lady Queen!" breathed Emilia.

"Perhaps I could add a bit of lace at the decolletage for modesty's sake?" said Lady Marian.

She was outvoted.

Next came the subject of her hair. Since her period of official mourning was over, she'd forsaken her white wimples. Could she dare to wear her hair unbound? Lady Marian thought not; she recommended pulling it up into a knot on the top of her head. "But that will make the tiara unsteady," said Joanna. Mary nodded. Emilia, who had been listening enthralled to the give-and-take, chimed in, "Yes, you wouldn't want it to fall off in the middle of the banquet." The majority won. The tiara sat securely atop the cascade of honey-brown hair, unbound.

Meantime, a frenzy of activity was in progress to transform Matagriffon into a suitable banquet hall. It now had a roof of sorts. Tapestries were still being hung on the walls to conceal the raw wood and to keep out the drafts. Carpets covered the splintery floor. Servants arranged a crimson cloth on a long table that would seat twenty-four, all the room could hold. Others scurried about, bearing trays laden with silver goblets, plates, bowls of nuts and sweetmeats, and baskets of fine white loaves. Candelabra were ablaze, all along the table and in the corners of the room. From an adjoining hastily assembled kitchen, created by combining the two houses nearest to Matagriffon, came the roar of the cook: "More wood on the fire there! Stir that soup kettle! Take that bird out of the oven before it turns to cinders! Do I have to do everything?"

Chaos had subsided into a semblance of order by the time Joanna arrived. A page standing at the entrance pulled aside the red velvet curtain that served as a door and she walked in, paused and looked around. Her cheeks were rosy from excitement and her eyes shone with anticipation. It was the first time in many, many months, not since before William's death, that she had attended a grand state banquet. Almost all the guests were unknown to her, nor was she known to them. She supposed most were local dignitaries, and a few of the military-looking types must be officers from Richard's army. She saw one churchman, a dumpy little man with a glum face. His magnificent scarlet cloak was embroidered neck to hem with gold scrollwork. Undoubtedly this was the archbishop of Messina. She didn't see Philip.

Everybody regarded her with immense curiosity, this intriguing queen who had come from far-off England to marry their king, then lost him—so young!—in such a tragic accident. She felt self-conscious and was glad when Richard appeared at her side and squeezed her arm. "You're looking uncommonly lovely tonight, little sister."

She thought perhaps she was but it was good to have his concurrence. He led her to the seat on his right. She smiled at Federico, standing stiffly behind her chair. But she was dismayed to see that the seat next to hers was occupied by—Tancred! However, no sooner had she settled herself and heard his mumbled "Good evening, Lady Joanna," (not Queen Joanna), than he muttered something unintelligible, rose, and brusquely ordered his wife to change places with him. Joanna supposed he felt as uncomfortable as she did about the prospect of making conversation during a long banquet. She was so relieved that she greeted Sibylla more warmly than was warranted by the negative impression she'd made when they'd met so briefly in Palermo. She could hear Tancred quizzing the archbishop, his new neighbor, with the same pseudo-deferential inquisitiveness she remembered from her first meeting with him.

Sibylla seemed delighted with the change. Joanna remembered her as looking sour and uncommunicative, but now her thin face was brightened by a smile as genuine as her husband's was false.

"I'm so glad to see you again. I'm afraid our last meeting at the palace in Palermo was far too brief and not very pleasant—my lord husband was so preoccupied with his negotiations with King Richard and the task of seeing you safely to Messina. But here we are in your brother's fine banquet hall, all friends. I wonder, will they be bringing the food in soon? I'm quite hungry." How she does run on! thought Joanna. But no wonder; I'm sure Tancred cuts her off before she can finish a sentence. And I believe she truly means to be friendly.

"I expect they'll serve as soon as King Philip arrives. Meantime, we could have a drop of wine." She turned to ask Federico to bring wine, but he had anticipated her and stood with a decanter at the ready.

Joanna tried to bear in mind her mother's example of maintaining a courteous conversation even with those one is disposed to dislike. She raised her glass.

"I'm pleased to see you again, too, Lady Sibylla. Tell me, how are your children?" They'd just embarked on a chat about the children's new tutor—who had been found by Brother Jean-Pierre—and how well they were doing in their studies, when a trumpet blast silenced all conversation. A tall slim youth in the gold-and-purple livery of the kings of France stood at the entry. A white satin pennant embroidered with a fleur-de-lis hung from his gleaming instrument. He looked superciliously around, then blew another two-note announcement.

He pulled the curtain aside and Philip entered.

Richard rose to conduct him to the seat at his own left. Joanna, watching, thought the two kings could not have been more different. Richard was tall, sturdily built, broad-shouldered, ruddy-cheeked, with a sunny smile as though Philip were his long-lost best friend. He wore his crown with regal authority. He was all in crimson and black—crimson tunic, black hose, and shoes of supple crimson leather with golden tassels. His hand rested nonchalantly on the hilt of the sword at his belt.

Philip was less spectacular. Of medium height, he was plainly but richly dressed in tunic and hose of silvery-gray and a short black cape embroidered with silver fleurs-de-lis. His swarthy face had none of Richard's animation, but his heavy-lidded black eyes missed very little. His smooth dark hair reached just below his ears. He too wore a crown, less massive than Richard's but sparkling with more jewels. A silver cross on a silver chain hung about his neck. What he lacked in stature he made up for in assurance. He held his head high and surveyed the room impassively before sitting down. When his glance fell on Joanna, he made a slight bow and produced a slight smile.

Richard signaled to the steward to order the parade of servants into the hall, each bearing a heavy platter. The guests' noses fairly twitched in anticipation as the aromas of roast pork, beef in wine sauce, capon with ginger, and many another delicacy filled the room.

In a corner a trio of musicians struck up a tune.

The banquet had begun.

Two hours later, Joanna languidly picked up a square of candied apple jelly, looked at it regretfully and put it back on the plate.

"No, I can't possibly eat another morsel, though I know they're delicious."

"Nor I," sighed Sibylla. She leaned forward and across Joanna to address Richard. "King Richard, you've given us such a marvelous dinner! Thank you!" Richard, who had been carrying on a shouted conversation and exchanging toasts with a knight across the table, paused to acknowledge her with a nod and a smile. Sibylla took a sip of wine and hiccupped delicately. Both she and Joanna had drunk more wine than usual, thanks to Federico. He took his duties seriously and the moment the level in their goblets fell by half an inch he was there to refill them.

The musicians were still hard at it, but had shifted to slow, almost elegiac tunes. They were tired and hoped the banquet would break up.

So did Joanna. She felt hot and a bit lightheaded.

"I'll say goodnight now, Sibylla. I long for my bed."

"As do I, but…" she looked doubtfully at Tancred, who seemed to be settling in to make a night of it. "I expect we'll be leaving soon, too. Goodnight."

Joanna touched her brother on the arm. "Richard, I believe I shall retire."

"Of course. God's teeth, how red you've turned! You must get your rest. We'll find a couple of knights to accompany you to the palace." Somewhat befuddled by wine, he looked around as though expecting a couple of knights to materialize before him.

She rose, staggered and nearly fell, clutching at her chair. Federico caught her and in an instant, before Richard was on his feet, Philip was at her other side, supporting her.

Joanna leaned on him for a moment then straightened. "Oh, dear—I'm so sorry! I must have tripped on the hem of my gown. Thank you, I'm quite all right now."

Belatedly, Richard had managed to stand up. "Are you sure? Come, I'll see you out." Before he could take her arm, Philip said, "My lord King, you must stay with your guests. I shall be happy to see Queen Joanna safely to the palace." He turned to Federico. "Fetch the queen's cloak. And see if Sir Alan or any of the palace knights are outside."

Sir Alan was indeed outside, having long ago finished his own more humble dinner. He was waiting with horses saddled and ready. But when Joanna, Philip and Federico emerged, she was still unsteady and unfit to mount a horse. It was agreed that since the distance was so short, they would walk to the palace. Joanna, embarrassed at needing help, was silent. So was Federico, remorseful at having been an over-zealous cupbearer.

Philip, as though reading her thoughts, spoke. "You mustn't think it was too much wine. You clearly haven't recovered yet from your fever, and no wonder you're feeling weak."

"Perhaps you're right."

He said goodbye when he'd seen her safely up the palace steps and in Lady Marian's charge.

"I shall hope to hear you're improved by tomorrow. Remember to send word if there's anything I can do."

"Thank you, thank you! How kind you've been." She held out her hand. He reached toward it, then seemed to think better of it, dropped his own hand, bowed and left.

Why didn't he kiss my hand the way he's done before? she wondered. But she was too dizzy to pursue the thought.

45

It was back to bed for Joanna. Her fever was even higher than during her first bout of sickness. Philip sent his personal physician, a courtly, soft-spoken Frenchman. He laid his cool, dry hand on her forehead—so soothing!—then asked her to cough while he applied an ear to her chest. He inquired about her appetite and her elimination, and scolded her gently for going out before she was completely recovered. She meekly agreed to mend her ways and to stay in bed until he pronounced her well enough to get up.

Philip didn't come, but sent fruit and flowers.

Richard came and commiserated.

"Sorry I couldn't come sooner. We've been busy taking Matagriffon down to see if we can load her into a galleon for the journey. I get these fevers often. Maybe it runs in the family. Have you heard from Philip?"

She was propped up on a mound of pillows, feeling just a bit better.

"No, not really. He sends things, including his doctor."

"I'm not surprised he stays away. He worries incessantly about his own health, and he's undoubtedly afraid he'll catch your ailment if he gets too close."

Aha, she thought. That must be why he wouldn't take my hand when he said goodbye after Richard's dinner.

"We had a curious conversation the other day," Richard went on. "He asked me if I thought you might ever consider marrying again. I said, why don't you ask her yourself, and he demurred, said it was just curiosity."

"Indeed!" She hoped the blush didn't show on her fevered cheeks.

"Either he has his eye on you for himself, or he's plotting something. He's a master plotter, you know. It may be he's thinking of arranging a marriage that would be advantageous to France—matching you up with some French prince. You'd be a prize, you know: a Plantagenet princess, widow of a king, sister of a king."

"I can't say I care to serve as the queen on his chessboard."

"Then the conversation got even stranger. He asked if I knew how many miscarriages you'd had and how many children who didn't live. I was glad to be able to tell him that I honestly didn't know."

"Now that's too much! Assessing the queen to see if she's fit to produce a lot of little pawns." She bowed her head into her hands, overcome with anger and grief. So many sorrows that she thought long-buried suddenly assailed her—the loss of William, the death of her baby, the failed pregnancy. "I'm sorry, Richard. I'm so sorry. I've been feeling depressed, and now this." She reached for a handkerchief and wiped her eyes. "I'm all right now." She sniffled and managed a little smile.

"Forgive me, sister. I shouldn't have told you all that." He patted her on the shoulder.

"No, I'm glad you did. It gives me a better idea of what Philip is like."

"He's devious, that's what he's like, and not always to be trusted. But I have to get along with him. We're in this Crusade together."

"And of course it will help if I get along with him too. I'll do my best." But from now on, she told herself, I won't be so taken in by his attentions and his fine manners. We shall see what we shall see.

The next visitor was a welcome surprise. Joanna hadn't seen Brother Jean-Pierre since long before she'd been sent to the monastery in Bagnara. Federico announced him gleefully; he knew this was one of Joanna's dearest friends. Not only that, if it weren't for Brother Jean-Pierre, Federico wouldn't be in this palace serving such a kind lady and learning to be a knight.

"I came the minute I heard of your illness. I've been in Palermo for weeks, just arrived here this morning. Have you been well taken care of? How do you feel?" He sat in the chair by her couch and got his breath—he'd been so anxious that he'd walked a good deal faster than his usual dignified pace.

"I feel much better, especially now that I see you. They told me you were in Palermo, but what kept you so long? Shall I send for wine? Do have some of Philip's excellent grapes."

"No wine, thank you." He looked around at tables laden with bowls and baskets of fruit, vases and pots of daffodils and lilies and ferns. "It looks more like a street market than a sickroom."

"Yes, everybody has been most attentive. Now do tell me about yourself. What were you doing in Palermo?"

"Tying up loose ends, mostly. I visited all the churches and abbeys that have been helping the needy with food and shelter. I wanted to make sure they had no problems, or at least no major problems. I commended them on the good work they do, and urged them to continue with generous hearts. Then, since I won't be able to supervise their efforts for the foreseeable future, I made sure there'd be somebody to take over."

"How wise of you. When you're back in England, you won't have to worry about all your hard work here going for nothing. Who will take over? Perhaps I could send a contribution, to encourage him to carry on as you've done."

"I'm not sure yet. I went to see old Archbishop Walter, thinking he might recommend somebody. But he, I fear, is very near death. I doubt if he took in much of what I was saying. I'll probably have to go back. I hope there'll be time."

"But Jean-Pierre, we haven't even heard yet from my mother about when we're to leave. Surely you'll be able to fit in one more trip."

"Ah. That's the next subject." He fidgeted with the tassel of his belt and looked at the ceiling, then down at his sturdy sandals.

What can be the matter? she wondered. He's usually so very collected.

He looked her in the face. "This was a very difficult decision. I won't be going back to England with you. I shall go with Richard to the Holy Land."

She fell back on her pillows with a little cry, "Oh no!"

"It pains me greatly to seem to desert you. But I've always dreamed of a pilgrimage to Jerusalem. I'm getting on, and I may never have another chance. Yet it can't be for long, Joanna. Surely our Crusaders will defeat the infidels quickly and take possession of Jerusalem, and we'll all come home."

She sat up, took his hand and said earnestly, "I understand. Of course you must go. But I shall miss you enormously. You've been part of my life for so long! But you may still do me a service, during this pilgrimage. Keep an eye on my brother. He can be foolish and impulsive at times. Remember poor Beatrice, whom he got with child?"

"I do remember. A most unfortunate affair. But I doubt if I can have much influence on King Richard. Of course I shall try. And I'll pray to our Lord to guide me." He stood up. "Now I must let you rest. I'll call again soon."

"Thank you, dear friend."

The mention of Beatrice set Joanna musing on those long-ago days, when she and her ladies had first arrived in Sicily, uncertain and apprehensive. Where were they now, Beatrice, Charmaine and Adelaide? She would ask her mother about Beatrice. Adelaide was probably still at Fontevraud Abbey. And Charmaine—hadn't she moved with her new husband to Messina? Perhaps I should make an effort to find her, thought Joanna. But that would mean finding that foolish, affected man she married, as well. No hurry. Plenty of time. And she drifted off to sleep.

Two weeks later in mid-March, when the first green was showing in the fields, the first pink buds had appeared on the almond trees and winter seemed finally on the wane, Joanna, thoroughly wrapped in shawls and cloaks, was permitted to go out for a stroll. Mary went with her.

"Shall we walk down to see what's left of Richard's castle?" Joanna asked.

The road was crowded with wayfarers, soldiers and sailors, peddlers, donkey trains and casual walkers out to enjoy the fine day. Still it took them only ten minutes to reach their goal. Aside from a few boards and timbers nothing was left. Where a magnificent banquet hall had been created there was only empty air. Joanna sighed. "*Sic transit gloria mundi.*"

Mary didn't know what that meant but nodded sagely.

They both looked up as a horseman approached, his galloping steed scattering everybody in his way. It was Richard. He dismounted hastily.

"What luck to find you here, I won't have go to the palace. I have news, Joanna. Come, sit by me on this pile of lumber. You too, Lady Mary."

He was so serious! Even somber. Joanna felt apprehensive.

"I have word from our mother."

"But that's wonderful! Does she say when I'm to leave and where I'm to go?"

"No, because you are to stay right here. She's on her way to Sicily from Spain. She says they're almost to Reggio and expect to be here in a week."

"From Spain? 'They'? Who's with her?"

"Princess Berengaria, daughter of the king of the Basques. Our mother went to Navarre to fetch her. She's bringing her here to be my bride."

No bridegroom could have looked less happy at the prospect.

"But what about Alice, Philip's sister? What about your promise to marry her?"

"That was just to keep Philip satisfied. I meant to get out of it somehow. But there'll be no getting out of marrying Berengaria. Once Queen Eleanor makes up her mind, nobody dares to say her nay."

"But King Richard, wait until you see the princess. Maybe you'll like her," said Mary.

"Humph. Maybe I will, maybe I won't. But even if I like her, why do I have to marry her? This is no time to tie myself down with a wife. Not with this stupendous task of a Crusade staring us in the face."

All three sat digesting the news. Richard was glum. Joanna was wondering what her future sister-in-law would be like. Mary was thinking that she for one would welcome a wedding and wishing that her suitor, the gallant Sir Stephen, would stop shilly-shallying and ask for her hand.

Richard emerged from his gloom with a start.

"Joanna, I'm sorry, I forgot the rest of the message. The queen says you're not to go back to France with her, you're to be Berengaria's companion. You and your ladies will be going with us on Crusade."

46

The prospect of going with the Crusaders to the Holy Land gave Joanna much to think about.

First there'd be the long sea voyage. What if she got seasick again? She'd never forgotten the extremely unpleasant journey from France to Italy.

Then they'd arrive in an unknown land. She thought of Palestine as one enormous battleground. Would they have to travel with the army? Would they live in tents? But surely Richard would lodge them somewhere safe, away from the fighting

Finally, there was the unknown quantity, Berengaria, her future sister-in-law. They'd be in constant, close contact. What if they didn't take to each other? What if they couldn't converse? What language did the Basques speak, anyway?

If only she could get Richard's attention and ask him some of these questions. But he was far too busy.

The more she thought about it, the less she wanted to go. She'd begun to look forward to returning to England and then to France, to the familiarity and comfort of her mother's palace in Poitiers where she'd spent so many happy childhood days. Everybody assumed she'd remarry. She knew better than to expect another William. That chapter was closed. Yet she might find someone she could respect and care for, with whom she could embark on a new life. If her mother presented a suitor who was such a man, who knows?

But her mother had decreed that she was to go to Palestine.

She asked Lady Marian if she thought it possible her mother could be talked out of the idea.

"Probably not," said Lady Marian, not looking up from her embroidery, which had reached a critical stage. "Probably a waste of time."

"I'm sure you're right." She sighed. "I suppose I shall just have to get used to the idea." But as she stood there brooding, she began to feel anger and resentment instead of resignation. She stamped her foot.

"She treats me as though I were still the obedient eleven-year-old she sent off to marry a stranger for the greater good of England. But I'm twenty-six now. Old enough to have some say about my own life!"

Lady Marian carefully snipped a thread with her tiny silver scissors and looked up at the fuming Joanna.

"If you feel so strongly, my dear, perhaps you had better take it up with Queen

Eleanor after all."

Joanna decided she would do just that.

Shortly word came that Eleanor had left Reggio, just across the strait in Italy. Joanna pushed aside her misgivings as she realized how keenly she looked forward to seeing her mother after fifteen years. She gave instructions to be informed the moment the queen's galley entered the harbor so she could be at the pier to meet her.

Word had spread throughout the city that the queen of England was coming. The citizens were almost as excited as Joanna.

Imagine—the renowned, the redoubtable Eleanor of Aquitaine coming to Sicily! The crowds who turned out to watch were nearly as numerous as those who had greeted her son King Richard, five months before. When the galley rounded the point of the hook where the lighthouse stood, they could see the same fluttering royal banners that had flown from Richard's vessels, and the populace broke into cheers. But there was no trumpet peal, no regal, gorgeously clad figure standing on the deck, no glitter of spears and shields. Neighbor turned to neighbor and said, "Maybe it isn't the queen's galley after all."

Only when the ship glided toward the long stone pier did the illustrious passenger appear from below. Those closest to the shore could see that this was a queen indeed: her crimson cloak, edged with white miniver, fell in stately folds to the deck. A dazzlingly white wimple covered her hair and was fastened at her throat with a ruby brooch. Her jewel-studded crown of state glowed and scintillated in the rays of the afternoon sun. She stood immobile as a statue, surveying the crowds and receiving their cheers in unsmiling dignity.

Joanna and Richard watched as the galley approached its mooring. Joanna was transported back to her childhood, when she and her baby brother John would be taken by their nurse to Winchester Cathedral on important holy days. She'd watched with awe while her parents in full royal regalia paced solemnly down the aisle after high mass, looking neither left nor right, their expressions magnanimous yet aloof, the personification of majesty.

"Just look at her, Richard! I may be a queen, but I shall never be able to act the part as Queen Eleanor does."

"I doubt if anybody ever will. Our mother has made it her life work." He stepped forward quickly to help Eleanor down from the galley. She embraced them both and presented her cheek, as cool and white as ivory, to be kissed. Eleanor had never been one for overt displays of affection, but these were her two best-loved children, and she was clearly pleased to see them. For a few minutes there was a flurry of claims and disclaimers.

Joanna to Eleanor, "You haven't changed a bit!"

Eleanor to Joanna, "Oh yes I have, look closer and you'll see the wrinkles. Whereas you, my dear, are now a fine-looking young woman, not the gawky child I sent off to Sicily."

Richard to Eleanor, "You seem to have withstood the voyage with no damage.

And have you noticed how the people love you?"

Eleanor to Richard, "In my experience, any head that wears a crown is sure to receive a certain amount of foolish adulation. But Richard, you appear a good deal more substantial than I remember you. Are you eating too many Sicilian puddings?"

In the midst of this banter Joanna noticed a silent figure in a hooded traveling cloak standing behind Queen Eleanor. She was listening intently to the give-and-take.

"Mother!" cried Joanna. "You haven't introduced us to your companion." She took the stranger's hand and drew her into the circle. "You are Princess Berengaria, of course. I'm Joanna, Richard's sister. Welcome to Sicily!"

"Thank you. You're very kind, and I'm glad to be here at last," said Berengaria. Her French was flawless. She let down her hood to reveal an abundance of softly waving hazel-brown hair. She looks about my age, thought Joanna. And what a nice face. Intelligent, alert, with a calm, steady gaze from her green eyes.

"And this is my brother Richard."

Berengaria smiled uncertainly up at him. Richard smiled back, the radiant smile that made whoever received it believe he was the most important person in Richard's life.

"I believe we've met before, Princess. But you may not remember. You were very young."

"Oh, but I do remember! I think I was about six. You came to Pamplona and you fought my brother Sancho in a tournament. And you knocked him right out of his saddle."

"Indeed I did, and you were cross. You scolded me for being so rough with him."

"Oh dear, did I? Well, it was the first tournament I'd ever seen. I didn't realize it was just a game." Joanna, who had been watching, was pleased to see them laughing like old friends.

"I didn't think you'd remember me," Berengaria went on. "You were so much older—you must have been fifteen—and you were so tall and handsome, and I was such a child. But you were kind to me, just the way my brother always was."

"And now," said Richard, "we meet again. Who would have thought that cross little six-year-old would grow up to be this beautiful woman?"

He tipped up her chin and regarded her quizzically. Suddenly he leaned down and kissed her lightly on the lips.

"I for one look forward to getting better acquainted," he murmured.

Joanna could read in Berengaria's face her amazement and joy. Later, she realized she'd been a witness to the exact moment when Berengaria fell in love.

But Joanna knew her brother very well, his faults as well as his virtues. She knew how ephemeral his affections could be and how he dreaded the thought of marriage. She remembered Beatrice. She felt uneasy for Berengaria. Was this Richard the seducer, or Richard the prospective bridegroom?

At that moment Eleanor seized Richard's elbow.

"Richard, don't keep us standing here. I suppose we're to lodge in the royal palace?"

She had finished assembling her three ladies, whom Sir Alan had gallantly helped down from the ship. The ladies and their maids were huddled on the pier with their bags and chests heaped nearby.

"Indeed you are, mother, and the horses are waiting. I will be happy to escort you." He looked dubiously at the mountain of baggage. "Though we may need to send for another half-dozen mules to carry all that gear! Come now lads, let's get the ladies aboard their steeds."

Several soldiers who had been waiting for orders sprang into action and shortly the whole party had been helped into their saddles. Off they moved up the avenue. Richard and Eleanor rode in the lead. The spectators cheered the queen, resplendent on her white horse, enveloped in her scarlet cloak and holding her crowned head high, and went home to their dinners. It had been a most satisfying spectacle.

Joanna and Berengaria rode side by side. At first, still shy with each other, they didn't speak. But Joanna wanted to make Berengaria feel welcome.

"When I first rode up this way and saw the palace, I was completely charmed. It was so different from any palace I'd ever seen. The Normans built the ones in Palermo as fortresses, then when they'd conquered the enemy and everything was peaceful, the kings did what they could to soften them. But here in Messina, there wasn't so much warfare. The Arabs didn't need battlements and defensive walls so they built themselves a monument to ease and comfort—and they do love their comforts! You must be very tired after that long trip. We'll be there soon; it's just beyond the next bend."

She realized she'd been chattering aimlessly and felt rather foolish. But Berengaria listened with interest.

"It sounds delightful, and different from the palaces I've been used to, too. I'm afraid the Basques take a dim view of too much comfort. And then, for the past year I've been living in a monastery, which was hardly the lap of luxury."

"A monastery! Really! Were you thinking of taking holy vows?"

Berengaria laughed, and Joanna noticed she had a dimple in the middle of her chin.

"No, not at all. I was studying the art of calligraphy with the scribes there, so I could learn how to copy manuscripts."

"But why did you want to copy manuscripts?"

"I had a good friend, a scribe, who used to visit my father in Estella. He told me that hundreds of rare manuscripts were languishing on the shelves of monasteries and abbeys, and that if anything happened like fire or flood, they'd be irretrievably lost. So I decided to do my bit to save them by making copies."

Before Joanna could pursue this novel idea, the sound of approaching hoofbeats behind them broke in on their conversation. A panting horseman reined in at

Richard's side.

"My lord King!" he gasped. "I think you should go back to the harbor. King Philip and all his officers and troops are gathering there and he has ordered his galleys in to the shore. Men are already beginning to board and to stow supplies."

Richard's face darkened with anger. Without a word, he wheeled his horse and spurred it to gallop back down the road. Sir Alan took Richard's place by Eleanor's side and the party proceeded soberly toward the palace.

"What a strange way for Philip to behave!" thought Joanna. "To leave so suddenly, without a word of explanation."

Berengaria thought it a most peculiar way for the co-leader of the Crusade to act, but she supposed it would all be explained in time.

"I never did trust that Philip," grumbled Eleanor to herself. "What could have set him off this time?"

When the weary travelers arrived at the palace, Lady Marian took over. Mary and Federico were waiting at her side. With their help, Lady Marian shepherded Queen Eleanor's ladies to their rooms. This took some time because of all the questions: When will dinner be served and where? Will someone order me a bath? Where is my little brass chest with my jewels?

Lady Marian sighed when the three of them were settled. "I'd quite forgotten what it's like to be in the household of a queen with so many privileged and demanding ladies! Thank you, Federico. It helped that they found you so adorable."

Federico was getting tired of being called adorable. After all, he was thirteen—practically a man. He decided he would stop smiling so much; that was what usually brought out the cooing and admiring whispers. "Will that be all, my lady?" he asked solemnly. At her nod he took his leave. She wondered why he looked so cross.

"Now Mary, I'll take you to Queen Eleanor's chamber and introduce you to her."

They found the queen at a window that looked out on the palace entry. She'd changed from her royal garments into a velvet robe. She turned at once, went up to Lady Marian and took both her hands. "Ah, old friend. I knew I could depend on you to sort them all out. You always were a good manager. Now let me look at you." Her searching gaze took in the sagging, deeply furrowed cheeks, the hair now completely gray. "Of course we've both grown older. But I see you're still the same kind, wise Marian I trusted my daughter to. I hope taking her in charge all this time hasn't been a burden to you."

"On the contrary. Every moment has been a joy. Of course I had a great deal of help, especially from this good lady. She's been with us from the start." She took Mary's hand and drew her forward. "May I present Queen Joanna's newest lady-in-waiting, Lady Mary."

"Lady Mary of...?"

Mary was confused and didn't answer.

"Your family name?"

"Oh. Broadshares, if you please."

"Broadshares? I'm not familiar with the name. It's surely not Norman?"

"Oh no, my lady, we're English through and through, all the way back to the Saxons, my father says. We've been farming the same land for hundreds of years."

Eleanor's nose wrinkled almost imperceptibly. "I see." She walked to the window again. Mary had flushed to the roots of her red hair. Eleanor's low opinion of her ancestry hadn't escaped her.

"Lady Mary's uncle is Sir Alan Broadshares, one of your son's most trusted and able knights," offered Lady Marian.

"Well, that helps." Eleanor turned and addressed Mary. "I'm glad to have made your acquaintance, my girl. Now perhaps you'd better go see if Queen Joanna needs you."

When Mary had left, Eleanor sank into a chair and sighed. "I suppose I hurt her feelings. But really, a farmer's daughter!"

"If I may say so, she's been of far more use and a better companion to Queen Joanna than those three highborn ladies who came out with us from England."

"Ah yes. They didn't last long, did they? But two of them to my knowledge have not turned out too badly. Lady Adelaide is still at Fontevraud Abbey and I see her whenever I'm there. She seems quite content with the cloistered life. And Beatrice married a Scottish lord and has produced several children for him. Bearing the king's bastard apparently didn't detract from her value in the marriage market."

"And what of that child? He must be nearly grown by now."

"Yes, Philip. He's fifteen. I see him sometimes. Richard did right by him; made him lord of Cognac, and has seen that he gets proper training in knighthood. He's in France now with his cousin arthur of Brittany."

"And that leaves only Lady Charmaine, the silliest of the trio, I thought. I believe I wrote you that she married an older man, a minor noble from Messina. But we've heard nothing of her for years."

"So she may still be here? I shall try to find her. It won't do for Joanna and Berengaria to go off to Palestine attended only by their maids and this 'Lady' Mary Broadshares." She grimaced as though biting into a lemon. "And you, of course."

"I fear I've decided not to go, to my great sorrow. With my lack of agility and my regrettable tendency to fall down, I'd be more of a hindrance than a help. I haven't told Joanna yet."

"I understand. But that means you will be able to come back to France with me. I shall be very glad of your company. It will be like old times to have you in my service once more."

She rose to look out the window again. The sun was low in the west and the glare almost blinded her, but she made out a horse approaching at a gallop, its rider bent over its neck urging it on. It was Richard at last. His hair streamed behind him like a banner. Within minutes he burst into the room, redfaced and fuming. Lady Marian, sensing this was a matter for mother and son only, departed.

"He's gone," rasped Richard. "I shouted and argued and did everything but raise my sword to him. Philip's gone."

"Now Richard, calm down. Come, sit here by me and tell me why he left so suddenly and where he's going."

He sat down heavily in the spindly gilded chair next to her, which creaked ominously. He took several deep breaths.

"As to where, he's bound for Palestine. I reminded him we'd agreed that all the Crusading forces should arrive together—the French, the English and the Germans—so we could make a concerted and powerful assault. He brushed that aside and said he'd have the advantage of surprise and might get to Jerusalem before we even left Sicily. Wouldn't listen."

He bowed his head in his hands and groaned. "And if by some miracle he succeeds, he'll get all the loot and all the glory."

It was getting dark. Eleanor went to the door and asked the page to send for wine, and to come in and light the candles.

"Foolhardy, if you ask me," she said, resuming her seat. "What possessed him?"

"His sister Alice, that's what. His obsession with getting her married to me. When you arrived with the Basque princess, he was furious. Apparently he had no idea that you were bringing me a bride. He's been more or less a recluse in his wing of the palace for the past week, nursing himself—afraid he was catching whatever it was that sickened Joanna."

"Joanna was sick? I didn't know. I have so much catching up to do. She seems very well now."

"Yes, she is. But for a few weeks she was quite ill. And Philip, to do him credit, was very solicitous. But he was clearly terrified that he might fall ill too, and secluded himself. Then when you appeared with Berengaria, he accused me of breaking my word."

"And did you?"

"I may have. That whole business with Alice has been back and forth so many times that one loses track. Hasn't she been engaged at one time or another to three of your sons? I suppose I may have told Philip that I'd marry her if he'd support me in my battles with Tancred over control of Messina. But he never brought it up again and I certainly didn't."

"So that's that," said Eleanor. "He's gone and there's nothing to be done about it now." She poured each of them some wine from the decanter by her side. After a small sip, she set down her glass, leaned her head against the chair back, sighed and closed her eyes.

Calmer now, Richard drank while looking at her over the rim of his wineglass. He noticed faint crowsfeet about her eyes and folds of flesh below her chin. He'd never seen his mother give in to weariness. But, he thought, she must be nearly seventy. She's earned the right to slow the pace. He touched her arm.

"Mother, you need your rest. You've had a long, difficult day. I'll leave you now." He finished his wine and stood.

She sat up as though to protest, but sighed again.

"You may be right. We sailed from Reggio at dawn. But come to me early to-morrow, and bring Joanna. I'd hoped to talk to her tonight, but it's grown too late. We have so much to settle."

"I will, mother." He bent to kiss her on the forehead. She watched him leave, marveling again at this godlike son of hers. But even the gods need prodding from time to time, she thought.

Weary as she was, before she retired she sent for a messenger.

"Early tomorrow morning, go to the archbishop of Messina and ask him to call on me tomorrow afternoon. I wish to consult with him about my son's wedding."

47

Joanna went to her mother's apartment at ten the next morning. She wanted to see her alone before Richard arrived. She found Eleanor dictating to her secretary, nibbling on a biscuit and sipping a spicy, sweet-smelling tea from a fine porcelain cup. Fennel? thought Joanna. Or anise? The queen's maid had just finished brushing her hair. Her beautiful golden hair—Joanna remembered it well. Now more silver than gold, it fell below her shoulders and lay like a gleaming scarf over her midnight-blue robe.

But as usual, after the brushing it was neatly pinned up to disappear beneath the white wimple that Eleanor always wore.

"Good morning, daughter. I'll soon be finished here. I'm a little late with my breakfast. Would you like anything? Where's Richard? Here, sit by me. What a pretty gown; that shade of green becomes you."

The secretary hastily vacated his chair, and Joanna seated herself. She looked around, admiring the way her mother had quickly made this room an outpost of Aquitaine, despite its probable past as an opulent nest for some potentate's favorite concubine. Eleanor seldom traveled without a few of her own belongings. A silver vase on the table by her side held three red roses. A small alabaster statue of the Virgin Mary, bearing a striking resemblance to Eleanor, stood in an arched recess on one wall. On the opposite wall, a very large white satin hanging that displayed the French fleur-de-lys almost concealed an exquisitely carved Arabic screen.

Joanna gathered her courage. "Mother, I must talk to you." She shook her head when the maid offered her a tray. "I don't want to go to Palestine and I don't think I need to. I'm sure we can find other companions for Berengaria. Brother Jean-Pierre knows several extremely worthy ladies connected to the abbey in Palermo, and…"

"Joanna! Not so fast. First tell me why you don't want to go. You're fortunate to have the opportunity. I shall never forget my own journey with the Crusaders when I was married to Louis of France, years and years ago." She paused, her teacup in midair, and seemed lost in memories. "I can see it now. It was glorious! My ladies and I rode right along with the army. Of course we got a lot of attention and I'm not sure King Louis totally approved…" Her voice trailed off and her lips curved in a little smile as she remembered the beautiful, headstrong young queen she'd been in 1147.

Joanna tried to imagine herself in such a procession and failed.

Eleanor came abruptly back to the present. She set her cup down and looked appraisingly at Joanna.

"Well, perhaps that kind of thing wouldn't suit you, and I'm sure it wouldn't suit Berengaria. She's quite retiring, I've found. I expect that both of you would prefer to ride separately from the Crusaders. Richard can see to that. Now, you ask why you must go. I have two particular reasons. First, to serve as a companion to Berengaria, somebody sympathetic and of her own status. She's led a sheltered life and it would be too bad to send her off into a strange new world without a confidante or a friend. We can't depend on the ladies-in-waiting for that kind of companionship, even if we add a few more from Jean-Pierre's abbey in Palermo. Don't you agree?"

"I suppose you're right. But why…"

Eleanor held up a hand to silence her. "Wait, there's an even more compelling reason. Your presence will help to insure the success of Richard's marriage. Now that he's king of England, he must produce an heir to insure the succession. We both know his propensity to stray from the path of righteousness. I want him to devote all his procreative powers to his lawful wife, and I want you to be vigilant in reminding him of his responsibility. You may feel I'm asking too much of you. But you're the only person I can turn to. Richard respects you and will take what you say seriously, especially when you impress on him that you're representing me."

Joanna felt totally deflated. What argument could she come up with when the good of the kingdom was at stake?

Eleanor patted her hand.

"Not so dejected, daughter. It won't be forever. With such a large army and with your brave brother in the lead, I shouldn't be surprised if you were in Jerusalem by Christmas. And then you'll come back to France and we'll see what can be done about finding you a nice new husband. I do wish I'd been able to see King Philip before he left. I don't suppose he gave you any idea of his intentions? Everybody's expecting him to marry again soon. He has only the one son and he'll need more."

"If you mean did he indicate he might ask me to share his throne and produce the requisite sons, no. But I believe he talked about such matters with Richard." She stood up and walked distractedly about the room. "You'd better ask Richard."

All her exasperation with Philip's inscrutability struck her anew. And she was increasingly ambivalent about whether she wanted him—or any man—as a suitor. It was true that she'd dreamed idly of a handsome admirer who would woo and win her. But realistically she knew she'd keep comparing other men with William. And she knew they'd never measure up.

She made a sudden turn and her skirt swirled about her like a whirlpool. She came to a halt before the chair where her mother sat calmly, as though waiting for a buzzing fly to settle.

"Why all this hurry about finding me a husband? William's been dead only a little over a year."

"Joanna, I must remind you that you have a duty, just as Richard does, to marry. Not only to insure that the royal line continues, but also to further our political aims. Perhaps Philip isn't your ideal. But an alliance with France could bring peace, a most welcome peace, instead of our eternal warring."

Joanna felt hot tears filling her eyes. Tears of anger.

"Duty! Didn't I do my duty in marrying William and cementing the alliance between Sicily and England? If I must marry again, why can't I have some say about who my husband is to be?"

Before Eleanor could reply there was a commotion at the door and Richard burst in before the page could announce him.

"Mother! I'm sorry I'm late. But I was looking for Joanna—oh, there you are. Why didn't you wait for me?"

"I wanted to talk to my mother about…never mind what about. Anyway, we're getting nowhere and I might as well leave." She escaped before either of them could remonstrate.

"By our Savior, what was that all about?" Richard asked, amazed.

"It seems your sister has developed a mind of her own at last. She doesn't want to go with you to Palestine. She doesn't want to get married. And I thought you were my problem child!"

He bent to kiss her lightly on the cheek and sat beside her.

"Nonsense, mother. How could I be a problem? I'm about to lead the Crusade that all Christendom has been longing for, and I've agreed to marry the bride you've chosen for me. I'm doing my duty by my God, my country and my mother. What more could you ask?" He looked at her with the smug, impish smile she remembered from his boyhood, when he'd been accused of some transgression of which for once he was innocent.

She laughed. Richard could always make her laugh.

"True. At the moment you're no problem. You're a dutiful son. And you may prove it by helping me to plan your wedding."

"Ah yes, my wedding. I was right, then, in thinking that was why you'd summoned me."

"Yes, and I'd hoped Joanna could help too. She knows from experience how they do these things in Sicily. But never mind, we must get at it. The sooner the better, so you and your Crusaders can take your leave. We'll have it in the cathedral, of course. And the banquet here in the palace. It will be quite suitable, from what I've seen of it. We'll have to move quickly, and I'll need your help in making a list of whom to invite. I'll talk to the archbishop this afternoon."

With his elbows on his knees, resting his chin on his folded hands, he watched and listened intently. At her last words he grinned.

"And when you talk to the archbishop, I'm sure he'll tell you it would be quite impossible to have the wedding now."

"What? Why so?"

"Because it's Lent. It would be unseemly to have such worldly festivities during the Lenten season. The wedding will just have to wait until we reach the Holy Land."

For once Eleanor had nothing to say. In her anxiety about Richard's single state, she'd forgotten it was Lent. But she had to admire him for finding an argument for postponement that was unassailable.

He stood up, bent to kiss her and left, with a cheery smile and a wave from the door.

Eleanor, never one to brood over a setback, began preparing the next morning for departure. With the wedding off there was nothing to keep her in Sicily. It was three months since she'd set forth from France to collect Berengaria and deliver her to Richard. She was tired of day after day on horseback and nights wherever they could find suitable lodging, in a nobleman's manor, an archbishop's palace or in a monastery where the beds were hard and the bread was usually harder. The familiar comforts of her palace in Poitiers beckoned.

But before she left she succeeded in tracking down Lady Charmaine, Joanna's former lady-in-waiting—recently and conveniently widowed—and enlisted her to accompany the royal ladies to the Holy Land.

Less than a week after her arrival she left, with far less public notice than when she had arrived. The Sicilians had other things on their minds than to turn out to watch her departure. The price of bread had risen again, by a shocking penny a loaf, and there was to be a demonstration in the cathedral square.

But the archbishop and a dozen or so of the local nobility came to wish her godspeed. What with these and the large party of the queen's own people— Lady Marian and her other ladies, servants and knights who would be sailing with her—quite a respectable little throng gathered at the pier. Respectable and colorful. Queen Eleanor set the tone in her crimson, fur-trimmed cloak. Richard too was royally clad in a crimson tunic, black leggings and black boots buckled in gold. He wore the state crown of his ancestors, with its jeweled fleurs-de-lys signifying the rule of England's kings over Aquitaine, Normandy and any other bits of France they'd been able to subtract from the clutches of the French kings.

Joanna, standing a little apart with Berengaria, Mary and Federico, watched as Eleanor gave Richard her final admonitions. He nodded his head repeatedly and cheerfully. Then she caught some of his words.

"Of course, mother. I'll send word at once, as soon as I have a clear notion of what King Philip's intentions are. And while I'm gone, you'd do well to find out what Count Raymond of Toulouse is up to. I've had reports he may be plotting another assault in Aquitaine. You might stop in Toulouse to see him on your return to France."

Eleanor looked taken aback. Joanna too was surprised. "Can this be?" she said to Berengaria. "Richard giving Eleanor advice? It's always been the other way around."

Berengaria had been observing the interchange. "Still, I've noticed the same thing in my family. My father is finding it hard to acknowledge that my brother Sancho has grown up enough to have his own ideas about governing the kingdom."

"Yes, and if they find that surprising, how much more shocked they'd be if you or I ventured to express an opinion about matters of state."

"I'm afraid you're right. So far at least, it's a man's world, except for the rare, extraordinary person like your mother. Shall we try to change it, Joanna?"

"Do you really think we could?"

Suddenly, she felt she could confide in Berengaria, tell her how during the early years of her marriage she'd wished she had more say in William's councils. He'd often ask her what she thought, but he was merely seeking reinforcement of his own views. Only later did he begin to realize she might have something useful and original to contribute. Following her train of thought, she said aloud, "I should have tried harder, I suppose, when I was William's queen."

She was interrupted by a shout from the pier. The queen's galley was approaching from the other side of the harbor. Everybody pressed forward. It was time for goodbyes.

Eleanor turned to Joanna. "Farewell, daughter. And remember what we spoke of. I'll be counting on you to represent me in watching over your brother Richard." Joanna nodded.

"And of course, you'll send me word of how you're getting along. I've seen to it that Brother Jean-Pierre will have an ample supply of your good Sicilian paper, and I'm sending along with you my two swiftest and most trusted messengers. So I shall expect regular reports from you." Joanna nodded again.

She managed to stay dry-eyed at the parting.

But she became tearful when she said goodbye to Lady Marian, her companion and friend for so long. They embraced and Lady Marian too wiped away a tear.

"Never mind," said Joanna. "I'll see you soon, maybe within a year if all goes as Richard expects. Meantime, take care of yourself."

"I'll do my best, but I'll worry about you. Thanks be, you'll have Lady Mary with you, and Lady Charmaine too. I've spoken to her seriously about her duties, now that she's to be the senior of your ladies."

"Did I hear my name?" The lady in question elbowed her way through the crowd, smiling brightly at those she jostled. Joanna had expected to see her changed, but not so much. She looked diminished, almost lost in her flowing plum-colored gown. Her blonde curls were streaked with gray and had lost their spring. But the chatter hadn't abated. She hurried to Joanna.

"My lady, how happy I am to see you again! And how well you look! Isn't it exciting that we're all to go on Crusade?" She fluttered her fan and her eyelashes. "But please introduce me to your companions. This must be Princess Berengaria, who is to marry our king."

Berengaria smiled. "So I am. And you are Lady Charmaine. Welcome to the Company of Lady Crusaders."

"Thank you! And who is this handsome lad?"

"May I present Federico," said Joanna, "my page, my knight, my right-hand man. And this is Lady Mary, who has served me since I came to Sicily."

Charmaine ignored Mary and cooed over Federico, who shortly managed to escape.

"Charmaine," said Joanna, "I was so sorry to hear of the death of your husband. I'm sure it was a great loss to you."

"Yes"—the fan in action again—"I shall miss my Mario greatly. But if truth be told, his time had come, as it must for all of us." She cast her eyes heavenward and sighed deeply.

Joanna, searching for an appropriate reply, was saved by a flurry of activity at the pier. The queen's galley had tied up. After one last hasty round of embraces and instructions, Eleanor stepped aboard, followed by her knights and ladies, and the oarsmen fell to their task.

Joanna and Berengaria mounted their horses and began the return to the palace. They rode for a few minutes in silence. Joanna turned in her saddle for one last look at the royal galley, now moving swiftly across the harbor toward the light-house on the point. She could see sunlight glancing off cascades of water from the flashing oars, the sail being raised to catch the wind, the helmsman standing aft, but no Eleanor. She was undoubtedly in her cabin, dictating a letter to the pope or the bishop of Winchester or the king of Castile.

"It seemed she hardly came and then she left," said Joanna. "Shall you miss her, Berengaria? You must have become good friends in all those weeks on the road from Navarre."

"I expect I shall miss the instruction I received along the way on my deport-ment, dress and duties as a queen of England. I became quite accustomed to daily tutoring. But I trust I paid enough attention so that I will not disgrace the posi-tion."

An ambiguous answer, Joanna thought.

Then she noticed Berengaria's suggestion of a smile and the mischievous look on her face.

Perhaps, Joanna thought, this Crusade won't be so dreadful after all if Beren-garia proves to be so compatible. She reached to take her companion's hand.

"I believe we shall get along very well. In fact, I already think of you as my sister."

Two days later the long-awaited galleys from England arrived and Richard ordered departure in four days. Joanna had never seen him so purposeful. He had no time for her, for Berengaria or for anybody or anything except getting the Crusaders to sea at last. The mountains of stores piled by the piers were loaded onto the vessels. With considerable prodding and imprecations, so were the horses and mules. Knights, grooms, oarsmen, sailors, cooks, and foot soldiers boarded their assigned ships. Finally, Richard personally saw the royal ladies and their retinues to their quarters on the capacious, if ungraceful, vessel that would follow his own flagship.

On April 10, 1191, the mighty fleet set sail.

It would be eighteen months before Joanna saw Sicily again.

48

J oanna to Eleanor
Cyprus, May 8, 1191
My dear mother,
 Although I promised to send you regular reports, it has been impossible up to now. We are at Limassol on the island of Cyprus, after a long and difficult voyage from Messina. A severe storm came up soon after our departure and scattered the ships, and only now has Richard been able to assemble the fleet here in the harbor.

 I was confined to my bed for nearly the whole voyage, suffering from the seasickness I am prone to. Berengaria did much better and tended me most faithfully. Ours was the first ship to arrive at Limassol but our relief at having found a safe harbor was soon shattered. The local ruler, Isaac Comnenus, sent a message promising to give Berengaria and me comfortable lodgings and fine food if we would come ashore. We might have gone, but our captain forbade it. He said Isaac was a conscienceless usurper and would hold us for ransom. Then I remembered that William too had told me that Isaac was not to be trusted.

 Richard was furious when he arrived and learned of Isaac's duplicitous offer. Now Richard has set out to capture him and punish him for terrorizing the people and falsely declaring himself emperor. He is confident that the villain will be taken in a matter of days.

 May 14. Yesterday we had a wedding, and how I wish you could have been here. Richard decided to have the ceremony now, because he says when we reach Palestine he will need to launch his Crusade against Saladin at once and will have no time for weddings. It was very hastily arranged but quite splendid nevertheless. It was held in the chapel of the royal palace and Bishop John of Evreux, who is accompanying the Crusaders, presided. Alas, the chest with the wedding gown and other finery you had provided for Berengaria was washed overboard during the storms, but we found a resourceful seamstress here in Limassol. The bride looked lovely, in a sleeveless blue silk coat over a white linen gown. Fortunately, her jewel chest with her gold-and-pearl coronet survived. I believe you would have approved. Richard too was handsomely clad, in his favorite scarlet and black, and seemed properly attentive to his bride.

 He asks me to tell you that he will send word as soon as he has captured Isaac and restored order to the island.

 I am happy to report that the precious supply of paper that you so thoughtfully provided survived the storms. Jean-Pierre wrapped it in three layers of oiled silk and sealed it well. Now I must hasten to give this to the messenger. One of the ships that were damaged is sailing tomorrow to Marseilles for repairs. By taking passage on it he can save weeks, since otherwise he would have to go overland through the Eastern Empire. So perhaps you will receive this by the Feast of St. John.

Your loving daughter, Joanna

Richard to Eleanor
Limassol, Cyprus, May 25, 1191
My lady mother,

    At last we are about to embark on the last leg of our voyage. I have captured the imposter Isaac, who is thoroughly detested by the people of Cyprus. He led us a merry chase, from the sea to the mountaintops, but he is now in chains and will be imprisoned at Markat Castle in Tripoli. His daughter Beatrix, who is blameless for his despotism, will go with us under my guardianship until I can send her to you. She is about fifteen and seems tractable. You might find her an advantageous marriage, if not royal, then at least among the nobility, even though her father was only a pseudo-emperor.

    As Joanna will have told you, Berengaria and I are now properly wed, which should ease your mind in that regard.

Your dutiful son, Richard

Joanna to Eleanor
Acre, June 24, 1191
My dear mother,

    The voyage from Cyprus to this port in the Holy Land took only three days and I came through it without any sickness. But after two weeks here I wish I were anywhere else, even back at sea. Although Philip has been besieging the city for a month, it seems unlikely to fall any time soon. Meantime, we are lodged outside the walls, not far from the unsightly, noisy, smelly army camp. I will say that Philip has been extremely helpful and arranged for us to live in as much comfort, even luxury, as tents can provide. He has even lent us the services of his cook. If you wonder if he has come any closer to declaring himself as my suitor, he has not. I suppose he still bears our family a grudge because Richard married Berengaria instead of Alice, Philip's sister.

    Richard has given me charge of Isaac's daughter Beatrix, who is as sweet and innocent as her father is evil and treacherous. All of us have become very fond of her.

    Berengaria and I are good friends by now, but not so close that she confides in me about her marriage. However, I sense some sadness on her part because Richard is almost invisible. He comes to our tents only to ask quickly if we are in need of anything, then goes off to see to his battles. He says the Turks who are inside the city walls have proved much harder to bring to their knees than he had expected. But he is sure the city will fall very shortly. Then I shall speak to him about his husbandly duties as you asked me to do.

Your loving daughter,
Joanna

Richard to Eleanor
Acre, July 20, 1191
My lady mother,

God be praised, six days ago the city of Acre fell to our forces. Will you please ask the archbishop of Canterbury to see that throughout England, Aquitaine and Normandy masses are said thanking God for giving us this victory over the infidels?

As soon as we finish treating with Saladin as to the exchange of prisoners, nothing will stop us as we advance to the Holy City.

During my absence, my sister, my wife and all their ladies and servants will be securely lodged in the Tour des Chevaliers, a well-fortified palace in the center of Acre.

You may expect your son to return victorious no later than next Lenten season.

Your dutiful
Richard

Joanna to Eleanor
Acre, August 1, 1191
My dear mother,

Sorry news: King Philip yesterday gathered his troops and left, claiming illness and the pressing need to return to France lest he lose Flanders. Richard is understandably angry. He and Philip had been quarreling ever since Acre fell. Philip left with only a few formal words of farewell to me. I believe you may remove him from your list of prospective husbands for your daughter. Duke Leopold of Austria has also departed, having been driven mad with jealousy of Richard and claiming, falsely or with reason I know not, to have been denied his share of the spoils. Richard is therefore now in sole charge of the Crusade.

He begs me to tell you he would write himself but he is far too busy rebuilding the city and planning the march south to Jaffa, whence he intends to launch the assault on Jerusalem. Berengaria, Beatrix and I and our people will remain here in Acre, which Richard says will be the safest place for us.

Brother Jean-Pierre sends you his respectful greetings. He is rejoicing that he will fulfill his dream of seeing Jerusalem. I shall miss his companionship, although in truth I have seen very little of him since we came here. Chaplains and priests are scarce and Jean-Pierre has been busy tending to the spiritual needs of the army and the hundreds of pilgrims who travel with it.

I shall also miss my page Federico, who is eager to begin service as a knight's squire. Sir Alan, Lady Mary's uncle, promises to take him in charge and watch over him. I trust Sir Alan, but I shall worry all the same.

Berengaria has now confided to me that Richard has been only twice to her bed since their wedding. To make matters worse, Beatrix has confessed to me that Richard sought her out and persuaded her to lie with him. Being so young and impressionable, she would have been easy for my brother to seduce. She is remorseful, to her credit, and has begged me to forgive her. Of course I confronted Richard with these shameful facts and implored *him to consider his responsibilities to the kingdom. He promises to do so.*

Your daughter, Joanna

Richard to Eleanor
Jaffa, October 1, 1191
My lady mother,

    I rejoice to tell you that we have won a fearsome battle with the armies of Saladin and we are now in possession of Jaffa. After you have read this message, please ask the chancellor to see that it is posted and read in all major cities in England and in our possessions in France.

    Richard, by the grace of God, King of England, Duke of Normandy and Aquitaine, Earl of Anjou, to his dearly beloved and faithful subjects, greetings!

    Know that after the taking of Acre and the departure of the King of France, who so basely abandoned the purpose of his pilgrimage and broke his vow, against the will of God to his eternal shame and the shame of his realm, we took the road to Jaffa. We were nearing Arsuf when Saladin swept down on us with a mighty host of Saracens. By the mercy of God we lost no knights on this day save one. Then through God's will we came to Jaffa, which we fortified because it was our purpose to defend the interests of Christianity to the utmost of our power. On the second day, Saladin lost an infinite number of great men, and being put to flight, he laid waste the whole land of Syria. On the third day before the defeat of Saladin, we were ourselves wounded on the left side with a javelin, but by the grace of God we have now recovered from the wound. We hope with God's grace, within twenty days after Christmas to recover the holy city of Jerusalem and the Sepulchre of our Lord, and after this we will return to our own land.

Richard

Eleanor to Richard
Winchester, November 20, 1191
My beloved son,

    Every day I hope for word that Berengaria is pregnant. If she is not, why not? You have been married six months. Have you been as dutiful in your attentions as you ought? Surely you have not forgotten my strictures about your responsibilities. Now that Acre and Jaffa are yours, for which God be thanked, you should be able to take some respite and devote yourself to being a husband instead of a warrior. If this reaches you by Christmas, what better way to celebrate the season than by insuring the continuity of the royal line?

    My concern in this matter grows as I observe your brother John insinuating his way into power and demonstrating his ineptitude for government. God help England if he were to be its king.

Eleanor
By the Grace of God, Queen of England

Joanna to Eleanor
Jaffa, December 19, 1191
My beloved mother,

 After many dreary months in Acre, we were summoned to Jaffa by Richard, where we have been treated most royally. He wishes us to celebrate Christmas with him, the last chance for any festivities for some time. He intends to begin the march to Jerusalem early in January. I learned that he had other reasons to invite us, as well.

 First, he has been unusually attentive, even affectionate, to Berengaria. Lady Mary, who has her ways of acquiring information, tells me that Richard visits Berengaria nearly every night. My dear sister-in-law is glowing with happiness. Why he has had such a change of heart I cannot imagine. But I welcome it.

 I was disturbed, however, when Lady Mary said that one of the pages told her he thought he saw Richard leaving the chamber of Beatrix, the Cypriot princess, late one night. I shall hope he was mistaken. I had thought her penitence for her first transgression would make it easier for her to refuse him.

 Richard's second reason for bringing us to Jaffa would be laughable if it were not so painful to relate. He has been making one last effort to treat with Saladin and agree on a truce, before they embark on any more bloody battles. Shortly after we arrived here he told me the following: He had entertained Saladin's brother and emissary el-Adel (also known as Saphadin) at a lavish feast and presented him with a fine warhorse. El-Adel gave Richard seven camels. Then el-Adel returned to his brother with Richard's audacious suggestion for the terms of the truce. Saladin was to give all of Palestine to el-Adel, and Richard would yield his conquests along the coast to me. Then el-Adel and I should marry and reign jointly over our new amalgamated kingdom. Christians and Muslims alike would be free to visit the holy sites in Jerusalem. I, of course, would have to convert to Islam.

 When Richard told me all this, I fear my scream of outrage was so loud that servants and maids came running. Richard belatedly realized he should have consulted me before making such an outlandish proposal. But he was not finished. He sent word to Saladin that though his sister was not desirous of converting to Islam, the marriage could still take place as suggested, but that el-Adel should convert to Christianity. Naturally, Saladin rejected this. It would seem he has a better understanding of what is possible and what is not than my brother. And the warring will resume.

 Soon after Christmas we will return to Acre to await news of Richard's advance toward the Holy City.

 I know you wish your daughter to make an advantageous marriage. But I am sure you agree that this would have been a disaster.

        Joanna

Eleanor to Richard
Rouen, April 1192
My son,

I have had no word from Palestine since Joanna wrote at Christmastide. I shall say nothing of what she told me of your scheme to marry her to the infidel el-Adel, beyond that I trust you have come to your senses and realize how misguided the proposal was.

I write about far more serious matters. Your chancellor, Longchamp, informs me that your brother John has been conniving with disaffected bishops and nobles to ally them with his cause, which is to gain control of England in your absence. Those who are loyal to you grow fewer. Worse, John and King Philip are hatching evil schemes to remove our lands in France from your suzerainty and divide the spoils between them. I am in France now doing what I can to prevent this.

Richard, if you would save your kingdom, come home, with or without Jerusalem as your trophy.

> *Eleanor*
> *By the Grace of God, Queen of England*

Joanna to Eleanor
Acre, May 1192
My dear mother,

I have very little to tell you except that alas, Berengaria is not yet pregnant. But, blessedly, neither is Beatrix. We receive only infrequent reports and rumors of the Crusaders' progress. It seems Richard has refortified Ascalon, far to the south, which Saladin destroyed to keep his enemies from using it as a base. We have not seen Richard since we returned to this dreary city. He sent a messenger last week informing me that you are in France where Philip is making trouble in our territories. Philip is not a man of his word because he and Richard solemnly swore not to interfere in each other's kingdoms while the Crusade continues. I am more convinced than ever that he would not have made a suitable husband.

Richard also said that as the weather improves, he will begin the pursuit of Saladin again.

> *Your loving daughter,*
> *Joanna*

Richard to Eleanor
Ascalon, June 2, 1192
My dear mother,

I have received your troubling message about the dangers threatening our kingdom of England. Others have also sent word of the nefarious plots of John and Philip. I agree that I should leave the Holy Land as soon as possible. However, my leading knights, indeed the whole army, urge me to make a speedy assault on Jerusalem. Their zeal has persuaded me and we shall set out in five days. I will take heart in knowing that God is on our side and that many who are dear to me are praying for our success—especially you,

my sister Joanna and my wife Berengaria.
Within a month victory should be ours. Then I shall return.

Richard

Joanna to Eleanor
Acre, August 29, 1192
My beloved mother,

After months of boredom, so much has happened lately that I hardly know where to begin. Some of what I tell you here is only rumor, but I do know that in late June the longed-for final march to Jerusalem began. Then to our dismay word came that Richard halted the advance when they were almost in sight of the Holy City and turned back to the coast. But he and Saladin's forces continued to skirmish all over the south. After one last fierce battle at Jaffa, where Richard distinguished himself for bravery and led the Crusaders to win the day, he collapsed, a victim of the fever he so often suffers from. Nevertheless he began negotiating with Saladin (through my erstwhile suitor, el-Adel) for a truce. They have now signed a treaty that will satisfy both sides. The Christians will keep control of the coast and the cities they have conquered, while Saladin keeps Jerusalem. But Christian pilgrims will be free to come and worship there at the Holy Sepulchre.

September 2

Two days after I wrote the above, Richard returned to Acre, gravely ill. He is subdued, with none of his usual cheer. Berengaria, Lady Mary and I have been nursing him as well as we can. Lady Charmaine has been surprisingly useful. It seems her late husband once had a fever like Richard's. Between her and Lady Mary, who knows so much about poultices and herbal infusions to reduce the fever, he is gradually improving. But his spirits are still low.

His army is already preparing to leave for home. We too should soon depart. I shall not be sorry to say goodbye to this benighted land which has dealt such cruel blows to the Crusaders and nearly destroyed my brother.

Richard asks me not to send this until he can add a page.

Your loving daughter,
Joanna

Richard to Eleanor
Acre, September 10, 1192
My dear mother,

Joanna tells me she has given you an account of much of what has happened here in the past month. I rejoice to add that, thanks to God's grace, I am nearly recovered from the fever. There is still much to do here. We must arrange for governors in the cities we have taken and strengthen their fortifications. We must disassemble our siege engines and stow them on the transport galleys. But I hope to leave by the end of next month. I shall dispatch Berengaria, Joanna, Princess Beatrix and their retinues well before then.

I beg a favor from you. Please try to counter the calumny sure to be heaped on me for my "abandonment" of the Crusade. I have already heard it here. I have not aban-

doned the Crusade. I shall return within three years to resume the good fight. But it was not God's will that I should risk the destruction of my army in an attack on the Holy City that would be assured of failure. Saladin had poisoned and polluted all the wells and burned the orchards and farmlands for two miles around the city. During the siege we would have had no food or water, no place to forage and our supply lines to the coast were impossibly long. Saladin's forces outnumbered ours three to one. It would have been suicidal to continue. And the truce we signed is a fair one and will preserve the status quo until we return.

Next time we shall prevail.

You doubtless wonder if I am remembering my responsibilities to create an heir. I am. Now that I am stronger, I shall resume my efforts in that regard. If Berengaria is not with child by the time she returns to France, it will not be from any lack of trying on my part.

God willing, I shall see you by Christmas.

Your son Richard

49

"Palermo," mused Joanna. "Do you suppose it will have changed much, Berengaria?" The sisters-in-law sat at their ease on the deck of the dromond, which was sailing slowly past Cefalù on the north coast of Sicily. Berengaria was admiring the proportions of the cathedral dome and the way the sheer gray cliff behind it provided such an austere, even intimidating, backdrop. After one last look—the city was rapidly disappearing from sight—she gave her companion's question her full attention.

"I shouldn't think so. It's barely two years since you left, isn't it? And from what you've told me Palermo's a durable city—full °of sturdy, stately stone buildings that have stood there for centuries." After a moment's thought she added, "Though from what you've also told me about ambitious Lord Tancred, whom we mustn't call *King* Tancred, I suppose he might have torn them all down and replaced them with dazzling new palaces for himself and his royal family."

Joanna laughed and then said thoughtfully, "Still, I mustn't be too hard on him. He did agree to give me my inheritance, after Richard threatened him with dire punishment if he didn't. But we left for Palestine and I still haven't seen a farthing of it. I shall just have to trust that in this at least he's a man of his word."

"Well, we'll soon know, won't we?"

They fell silent, each absorbed in her thoughts. During the months that they'd lived and traveled together they'd become the best of friends, comfortable with each other. Especially since leaving the Holy Land, they'd drawn even closer.

Each was, in her way, a woman bereft.

Joanna still grieved at the loss of her William. No matter what path her life now took—whether through her own choosing, her mother's machinations or God's mysterious decrees, she was sure Sicily would never again be her home. Therefore, she had decided on the detour to Palermo during the journey to France, for one last pilgrimage to William's tomb.

As for Berengaria, the two women had developed such a rapport that Joanna could tell her friend was confused and worried. Richard, so attentive while they were in Jaffa, had resumed his earlier neglect. Joanna had pled with him to offer Berengaria the affection she deserved as his wife. Again and again she'd reminded him of their mother's concerns about the succession. His only response was that he had done all he could. "I've sown the seed; now it's up to her to produce the child." It looked less and less likely that he would settle down as a dutiful husband when they were reunited.

But on this brilliant, sun-drenched day neither woman was giving in to gloom. It would have been impossible. The sea that stretched to the horizon on their right was a dazzling blue expanse. Along the shadowed cliff-lined shore to their left, the water was as green as polished jade. The wind had dropped and was little more than a breeze, fresh and cool on their faces but hardly enough to fill the sails. So it was up to the oarsmen, twelve on a side, to keep the vessel moving. Joanna watched, almost hypnotized by the perfect synchrony as they leaned forward, dipped their blades in the water, pulled hard, brought them up and smoothly returned them to the starting position. It looked effortless but she could see the rippling muscles of their bare arms and shoulders. As they rowed they sang, repetitively and rhythmically, in some language she didn't understand. Most of them were dark-skinned, from one of those mysterious lands in Africa, she supposed.

"What do you suppose they're singing?" asked Berengaria. "I expect it's something like 'Yo heave ho, over the waves we go.'"

"Perhaps. Or, let's see… how about 'The harder we row, the sooner to port, where the girls are waiting to give us some sport.' "

They heard a muffled snort of laughter and turned to see Federico, who had just come on deck and overheard the last interchange. He hastily rearranged his face in a more serious expression. "My lady, Beatrix asked me to ask you if there's anything worth seeing and should she come up."

Joanna sighed. At sixteen, Beatrix was going through what Joanna and Berengaria agreed was the "difficult" stage, though neither of them could remember ever being difficult themselves at that age. While they were all in the Holy Land she'd been docile and respectful, especially to Joanna who had known of her brief affair with Richard and had forgiven her. But now the girl tended toward moodiness, withdrawal from the company of her elders and an unspoken disdain for their counsel. Federico, a year younger, was the only person she seemed to communicate with freely.

"Tell her that before sundown we should be in sight of Palermo. You know it well, Federico, and you can point out the sights—Monte Pellegrino looming up out of the sea, then the harbor, with all the fishing boats coming and going, and then when you get near the shore you see the palm trees and the avenue leading up to the city…" she had to stop. She bowed her head, close to tears, remembering her first arrival and her first sight of William, waiting there at the pier to greet her.

Federico nodded. "I'll tell her just how it is, my lady," he said softly. She put her arm around him and rested her cheek for a moment on his curls. Dear Federico! He was always so quick to sense when she needed sympathy.

After a minute or so of silence, while both women gazed out to sea, Berengaria asked, "What will be the first thing you do when we reach Palermo, sister? Seek out the evil Tancred and demand your golden throne?" Joanna had told her how Tancred had refused to give up the ceremonial throne that William had given her at her coronation.

"I'm afraid that will have to wait. First we must settle in at La Zisa Palace, and then I'll announce our arrival to him. But since he's so clever and has so many spies and agents, maybe he knows we're coming and will meet us at the shore and forbid us to land!"

An hour later they entered the harbor.

Joanna had asked everybody to come on deck and a festive-looking group they were, except for Jean-Pierre in his customary brown habit. Lady Mary and Lady Charmaine had dressed in bright colors for maximum visibility. Sir Alan was not in battle dress but in leather doublet and leggings. His sword in its polished silver-embossed scabbard was buckled to his belt. Federico stood at his side as befitted a knight's squire, in sober gray but sporting a bright red velvet cap. Beatrix, caught up in the expectations of the group, had revived from her sulks. Her long black hair, adorned with a plain gold circlet, framed her lovely olive-skinned face. Her eyes were alive with the same excitement that animated the whole company.

The two queens stood in the bow, looking properly regal in their crowns and their velvet robes—Joanna's blue and embroidered with silver fleurs-de-lys, Berengaria's scarlet and bordered by the Plantagenet lions. High above their heads, more lions adorned the pennant that flew from the mast.

The oarsmen slowed the tempo and the ship slowly approached the pier. And that was when Joanna wished she hadn't made such a facetious conjecture about Tancred's refusal to let them land. A dozen horsemen were lined up in military order with their captain at the fore. With the sun in her eyes, she couldn't see whether they were armed, but each man had his right hand at his belt as though preparing to draw a sword. When the ship came to rest, Sir Alan stepped down first, then helped Joanna and Berengaria. The captain of the waiting troop dismounted and marched purposefully toward them. Joanna kept a tight hold on Sir Alan's arm. The captain spoke.

"My lady Joanna, King Tancred has sent me to greet you in his name and to conduct you and your party to your lodgings at the palace of La Zisa. He has ordered a full complement of servants to be on hand. He and Queen Sibylla will call on you and Queen Berengaria tomorrow at noontide to greet you in person."

The cordiality was welcome but suspect. "Why can he be acting so nice?" she wondered as she and Berengaria rode up to the city.

But she was so happy to be back in La Zisa that she forgot to worry about Tancred's motives. The next morning she ordered that the dining hall, still graced by its fountain, should be prepared for the meeting with Tancred and Sibylla. Bowls of raisins and almonds, plates of sweet biscuits, and flagons of wine were set out. A servant stood by, ready to serve. Joanna wanted to make it plain that she was the hostess here, not the supplicant.

When the couple walked in, they seemed to have reversed roles. Tancred was bent over and walked haltingly. He appeared even shorter than Joanna remembered, diminished in stature and bluster. Sibylla, whom Joanna had considered lacking in self-confidence, had assumed the position of dominance in this strange marriage.

Joanna introduced Berengaria and invited her guests to seat themselves and partake of some refreshment. Sibylla, who wore an elegantly simple blue silk gown instead of the unsuitable stiff garments Joanna remembered, placed a hand on her arm.

"My dear Joanna! We are so very glad to see you, and we'll do all we can to make your stay in Palermo pleasant." She accepted a glass of wine from the servant and plucked a raisin from a bowl.

"Thank you, thank you very much. But tell me, how did you know we'd be arriving last evening? It was most heartening to be greeted by the captain of the guard."

"Oh, King Tancred has his ways of finding out what's what, don't you my love?" Tancred responded with a nod and a wink.

"I'm sure he has," said Joanna. She turned to him. "Then you must know what Henry of Germany is up to in Italy. Before we left Acre we heard that he'd been crowned Holy Roman Emperor, his father having recently died. Do you think he has designs on the Kingdom of Sicily, thanks to the claims of his wife, Constance?"

"Of course he has! And haven't I..." he stopped to take a deep breath and hurried on as though trying to reach the end of the sentence before having to pause again. "And haven't I been fighting him all this past year to keep him from grabbing our possessions in Italy?" The words were what she'd expect from the belligerent Tancred she remembered but his speech was slurred and came in bursts. "And Sicily will be next." He took a gulp of wine and shook his head violently from side to side. He looked at Joanna with some of the old venom. "And this is all because your husband..."

Sibylla nudged him and gave him a warning look.

"Yes yes, I know, we mustn't offend her," he muttered to Sibylla, but everybody heard. "If your husband, God rest his soul, hadn't had bad advice, probably from that shortsighted Archbishop Walter, and named his Aunt Constance as his heir, and then encouraged her to go off to Germany and marry Henry..." He faltered, then fell silent and sat staring at his folded hands in his lap. He clutched them tightly to keep them from trembling. His lips moved but no words came out. Then he finished his sentence in one desperate spurt. "...then Henry wouldn't have the slightest reason to claim Sicily."

Sibylla stood and helped him to his feet. "Come my dear, it's time for your rest." He permitted himself to be led to the door, where she instructed the waiting servant to see that he got back to the royal palace safely.

She resumed her seat with a sigh. "As you see, he's not himself."

"I'm so sorry," said Joanna. "I suppose you've consulted physicians? What do they say?"

"They say this, they say that, but the truth is nobody knows what's wrong. I think it's the pressure of defending Sicily all by himself against Henry and his vastly superior armies. It's broken him. Where are our allies when we need them?"

She looked first at Joanna, then at Berengaria.

"Where indeed?" said Berengaria who, although somewhat confused by the conversation, thought somebody had to say something.

Joanna had seldom felt so conflicted. She still felt drawn to Sicily. It had been her home for so long and she had loved reigning over it at William's side. She hated the thought of this proud kingdom becoming an appendage of the soulless, ponderous Holy Roman Empire. Yet it was true that Constance—and she loved her too—Constance was William's rightful heir. Legally, Henry had every right to claim his wife's inheritance as his.

But then, there was Sibylla's question about allies. Hadn't her own father, Henry, made a pact with William, sealed by her marriage, that the two countries would be firmly allied against all enemies?

And finally, Tancred. She had never thought she could feel sympathy for him, yet the fact was that he had done his best to hold the kingdom together. Whether from love of the kingdom or love of power, the goal of his struggle with the threatening German army was the preservation of Sicily's independence. And clearly the struggle had broken him.

Sibylla spoke, almost apologetically.

"I—we—had hoped that we could ask you, both of you, to use what influence you can to enlist England on Sicily's side in this conflict."

Joanna had come to a decision. "Lady Sibylla, I'll do all I can. Richard's departure from Palestine was to be a little later than ours, but he'll undoubtedly arrive in France soon after we do. I'll talk to him and to my mother and remind them of the historic ties between our two countries."

Sibylla looked inquiringly at Berengaria.

"I've only recently become queen of England, and I have much to learn about the kingdom's governance. But your cause seems eminently just. I shall join my sister-in-law in seeking support for Sicily. And I suspect Richard may be persuaded. There's been no love lost between him and Henry."

Sibylla sighed—a deep sigh of gratitude. She rose. "I can assure you this promise of yours will raise Tancred's spirits. Thank you!"

Joanna signaled to the servant to fill their wineglasses. "Before you go, Sibylla, let's drink a toast to the three queens and their bold plan to save Sicily!"

They raised their glasses and drank with as much bravado as if they'd been three kings.

The next day Joanna made her visit to the cathedral at Monreale. She chose a gown that William had always admired, green velvet with a high round neck edged with white satin.

She went alone except for two of the palace guards, old acquaintances from days gone by.

When she entered the vast, echoing cathedral, a priest had just finished saying mass. He and the clergy were filing out, followed by the celebrants. A few people remained behind at prayer or, in one instance, napping. Nobody paid any attention to the well-dressed lady who strolled down the aisle, looking about her with interest. Tourists from Sicily and beyond came here all the time to see William's famous cathedral.

Everywhere Joanna looked she was reminded of William. This great edifice was his creation—he had seen to every detail, from the carvings on the columns to the beautifully crafted altar rail. As always, she was dazzled by the gleaming mosaics that covered the walls, telling the Bible story from the Creation to the Crucifixion. She walked slowly along, admiring them as though seeing them for the first time.

Next she approached the central apse to visit an old friend. Among the saints whose figures encircled the base of the enormous dome she sought out Thomas à Becket, whose mosaic portrait she herself had commissioned. His hand was still raised in benediction, and she imagined from his rather admonitory expression that he was saying, "So you've come back, have you? About time!" She smiled at him, then sat down and raised her eyes to the awesome figure of Christ Pantocrator that filled the dome. The compassionate face, the outstretched arms had never failed to move her. She sat there for ten minutes, lost in a reverie that was half prayer and half reliving her life with William.

Finally she knelt to pray at William's tomb in a side apse. The magnificent sarcophagus with its effigy had been moved, at Archbishop Walter's orders, to his cathedral in Palermo. Only a stone coffin-shaped tomb remained. Though she knew it contained William's remains, it seemed strangely impersonal, with no connection to the husband she had loved. After a few minutes she rose, smoothed down her skirt and walked slowly back down the nave. Here she was much closer to William, surrounded by the serene beauty he had created. Leaving the church, she felt consoled and at peace.

At the portico the waiting palace guards came to attention and watched the approach of the slim, graceful figure. Unconscious of their scrutiny, she turned for one last look inside, smiled and bowed her head in salute to William, to St. Thomas, to the Christ in the dome, to the whole magnificent temple. One guard whispered to the other, "Our queen was always a pretty one, but I think she's turned into a real beauty, eh?"

They helped her into the saddle and the little party began the descent down the green valley. From this height Palermo looked like a tiny fairytale city in the distance. As they drew closer, she could make out the familiar domes and towers. Still in pensive mood, she reflected that soon she would be saying goodbye to this beloved city, too. She would ask Jean-Pierre to take Berengaria, Beatrix, and anybody else who wanted to go to Monreale tomorrow. Then it would be time to resume their journey. Her thoughts moved ahead to the reunion with her mother and with Richard. But she felt none of the usual worry about her uncertain future.

I'm glad I made this little pilgrimage, she told herself. As to what comes next, what will be, will be.

Her newfound equanimity was tested as soon as she returned to La Zisa.

Sir Alan was waiting for her, pacing up and down in the entry hall. Before she could ask him what was the matter, he blurted his news.

"If you please, my lady queen, Lord Tancred has sent us a most disturbing message. He has just had word that your brother King Richard has been taken prisoner by Duke Leopold of Austria and is confined under lock and key in Durnstein Castle on the Danube River."

How very strange, Joanna thought. Strange, and frightening. How had Richard gotten himself in such a fix? Why had he left the Crusaders' ships, gone ashore and strayed into the territories of his enemies?

She went to the royal palace to see if Tancred and Sibylla could add anything. She was conducted at once to King Roger's throne room. Tancred was sitting in the tall, gilded royal throne, surrounded by so many pillows that he was almost invisible. Three courtiers whom Joanna didn't know stood behind him. Sibylla stood at his side, looking melancholy. But when Joanna came in, she became alert and quickly stepped forward to take her hand.

"Isn't this terrible news? You and Queen Berengaria must °be devastated!"

"Yes, we are. Have you had any further word?"

They had none. Tancred had sunk even deeper into depression with the disappearance of the ally he'd hoped to enlist.

"Berengaria and I must go to Rome," said Joanna to Sibylla. "We must ask the pope to intervene. Nobody else has any influence with Richard's captor, Duke Leopold. And Leopold's overlord, Henry of Germany, is Richard's sworn enemy too."

Sibylla thought this was a wise move. Tancred roused himself enough to agree and to wish them well. "Though from what I know of Pope Celestine," he growled, "he won't be much help. Flabby old man." He subsided into his pillows.

So back to sea everybody went except for Lady Charmaine, who decided to remain in Sicily.

"I was so happy here with my dear Mario," she said to Joanna. "Sicily is where my heart is"—she placed her hand on her bosom to indicate the exact spot—"and here I shall remain."

Later, Lady Mary told Joanna in private that she was sure Lady Charmaine had her eye on a suitable successor to Sir Mario, even older and richer.

"I shall miss her," said Joanna, and she meant it. Sometimes, she thought, old friends become more precious as time passes, and one forgives their foibles.

Joanna had sent word to Pope Celestine that they were coming. When they disembarked at Civitavecchia, a mounted papal escort welcomed them and conducted them on the two-hour ride to Rome. It was a bright April day and the promise of summer was everywhere—in the forests where trees were freshly leafed out in brilliant green, in the fields where the first shoots of grain were already a foot high, in the towns where housewives scrubbed the winter's mud off their doorsteps and exchanged assurances with their neighbors that it was a fine day indeed. In spite of the serious nature of their mission, the whole party was full of anticipation. None of them, not even Brother Jean-Pierre, had been to Rome.

Joanna, who had suffered from a spell of her old seasickness on the voyage, was listless and in no mood for conversation when they set out. But the countryside was so delightful that her spirits revived. She threw back the hood of her riding cloak and let the breeze play with her unbound hair. She basked in the warmth of the sun on her cheeks. She joined the others in laughing at the sight of a half-dozen frisky lambs that were gamboling in a green field and butting each other playfully while their mothers looked on indulgently.

"It takes me back to my girlhood days on the farm in Yorkshire," said Lady Mary.

Brother Jean-Pierre, after a minute's consideration, pronounced, "A lamb is a lamb, wherever it be, in Yorkshire or Devon or fair It-a-lee."

But the closer they got to Rome the more serious their mood became as they remembered why they were making this journey. All but Berengaria and Joanna were led to lodgings near the River Tiber. The two women, who had been bidden to proceed at once to the pope's audience chamber in his palace, were escorted through the crowded streets by a contingent of his personal guards. The city was thronged with pilgrims who had come to celebrate Easter and were staying on to roam about the famous ruins. But Joanna and Berengaria were thinking only of their forthcoming interview.

"What do you know of Pope Celestine?" Berengaria asked Joanna.

"Not much, except that he is very old, in his eighties I believe, and was elected only last year."

"I hope that Tancred was wrong, and that he'll make every effort to free Richard." She seldom betrayed her emotions, but the tremor in her voice told Joanna how deeply disturbed she was.

"Don't forget, sister, that my mother has considerable influence. She has probably already been in touch with the pope. Besides..." She stopped suddenly as they came out onto a large square with a regal palace, complete with tower, in its center. "Oh, that must be the pope's palace! Are we there already?" she asked the captain of their escorts. "And what is that beautiful building next to the palace? It looks so Roman with those graceful arches, and I think I see frescoes on the walls of the porticoes. We have nothing like that in Sicily."

"I'm sure you haven't," he said. "That, Madame, is indeed the papal palace, and has been for eight hundred years. And the church next to it is the Basilica of San Giovanni in Laterano, the cathedral of Rome, which was established by Emperor Constantine." He was clearly disdainful of anybody who didn't know these basic facts of Roman history.

Joanna reflected that if only she could have seen these wonders with William he would have taken great pleasure in pointing out to her their architectural virtues. But she had time for only a glance because the captain hurried them on.

"The pope is waiting," he said severely.

So they hastened after him into the palace and up the winding staircase to the audience chamber in the tower. Their escort nodded to the page at the door, opened it, announced, "Queen Joanna and Queen Berengaria," and left.

They'd feared they'd find an impatient pontiff, pacing the floor in his irritation at their tardiness. Instead they found a sleeping pontiff, or perhaps one in deep meditation. He sat perfectly upright on a huge gilded throne which was draped with red velvet. His head was slightly bowed and his hands were folded in his lap. His eyes were closed and the expression on the wrinkled old face was calm and peaceful. It was hard to tell if he were tall or short, fat or thin, because of his stiff white vestments, embroidered in silver and encasing him like a glittering cocoon.

On either side of the throne stood an attendant in the papal livery: black velvet from top to toe, and a short crimson cape that came just to the waist. Each had his hand on the jeweled hilt of the sword at his belt. They stood as stiff as statues, staring straight ahead.

Wondering whether to speak to awaken the pope, the two women looked at the attendants questioningly but received no guidance. Uneasy, they gazed about them at the magnificent chamber, dazzling in its display of riches—lustrous scarlet and purple velvet hangings, portraits of the saints in massive gold frames, silver flagons on polished ebony tables.

"This splendor makes me feel even dowdier," whispered Berengaria to Joanna. "I wish we'd had time to change." She tried to brush the dust off her cloak, the same one she'd worn since setting out from Civitavecchia that morning.

Pope Celestine gradually came to life. He raised his head. He opened his eyes. They might once have been blue but had faded to a dull gray. He reached up to straighten his mitre, which had drifted to the left. He sat up straighter. Finally, he held out his thin hand and beckoned to them to approach. His smile was restrained, as though at his advanced age he found it foolish to waste energy on displays of benevolence. The outstretched hand was unsteady, perhaps due to the weight of his heavy gold ring with its ruby as large as a pigeon's egg.

In turn they came forward, knelt and kissed the ring.

"Rise, my daughters," he said. His voice was high and faint but became stronger as he talked. "Welcome to Rome. We have arranged for you to be lodged here in the palace. I am sorry to have summoned you so quickly, before you had time to get settled. I had good reason. We have received further word about King Richard."

"Oh, I hope it's good news!" exclaimed Joanna.

"Alas, no. In fact, it could hardly be worse. Duke Leopold is treating King Richard like a chattel, and has sold him to his overlord, Emperor Henry. Henry will continue to keep him prisoner until a ransom is paid. I deplore in the name of all that is holy this reprehensible behavior by Christian monarchs, this disrespect to a noble king who has risked his life in service to his God." For a man of such restraint, the pope was getting quite worked up. His wispy eyebrows rose and fell and he twisted the papal ring on the papal finger.

"But surely, there is something you can do to free him!" cried Berengaria.

"How much ransom is Henry asking? Does my mother know of this?" asked Joanna, already assessing the practicalities of the situation.

Instead of answering, he spoke briefly to the attendant on his right, who quickly fetched two gilded, straight-backed, armless chairs and helped Joanna and Berengaria to seat themselves.

"Now, my daughters, know that I sympathize completely with your concern. We too are concerned. Let me tell you about the difficulties of this distressing situation."

They listened, leaning forward to catch every word. He explained that he had already excommunicated Duke Leopold as punishment. He assured Joanna that Queen Eleanor was abreast of developments and, he believed, had already begun trying to raise the ransom. He expressed his shock at the amount Henry was asking—100,000 silver marks—but said there was little he could do to persuade Henry to modify his demands.

"Whyever not?" asked Joanna, who forgot that she was addressing the supreme authority of the Christian world. "Why can't you excommunicate him too?"

"First of all," he said patiently, as though instructing a child, "because it was I who crowned King Henry of Germany as Holy Roman Emperor. For a pope to excommunicate one whom he himself has anointed would be a serious step. Furthermore, Henry has already demonstrated his scorn of papal authority and has even caused two of my papal nuncios to be murdered. I do not wish to put those loyal to me in such danger."

"But…" began Berengaria. Pope Celestine put up a hand to silence her and went on.

"And there are political considerations of which you may not be aware. Henry makes no secret of his desire to take possession of the Kingdom of the Two Sicilies, which he claims through the inheritance rights of his wife, Constance. I, as overlord of Sicily through agreement with the late King William, as well as one with the present king, Tancred, would vigorously dispute this, if the emperor did not have such a powerful army. I have none. He has already made one incursion into Italy and has caused grievous loss of life and suffering. Any public punishment on my part would, I am sure, only exacerbate his defiant and bloodthirsty aggression."

"So you are saying there's nothing to be done, that Richard must remain a prisoner of this cruel Henry until the exorbitant ransom is raised?" Berengaria asked, trying to contain her despair.

"I am afraid so. We shall of course pursue all avenues of diplomacy…" His voice was fading. His energy was failing him.

Joanna had stopped listening. At mention of Constance her mind raced: why shouldn't she write to her old friend and plead with her to persuade her husband to release Richard? But she wouldn't suggest this plan to the pope. He'd only think of a dozen reasons against it.

She squirmed on her uncomfortable chair, eager to be off. Celestine seemed to have said all he had strength to say, and made a vague gesture that may have been the sign of the cross.

"Bless you, my daughters," he whispered. The attendants stepped forward to assist the two women but they had already sprung to their feet. Just before they turned to go, Celestine spoke again, almost inaudibly.

"Come back tomorrow. We may have received more news." And his eyes closed.

Later that afternoon Joanna, Berengaria and Brother Jean-Pierre met to discuss the situation. They gathered in the elegant rooms the pope had provided. Elegant, but remarkably lacking in comfort. The women had already discovered that their beds, though tastefully draped in purple silk, were narrow and hard. In the reception room there was no place to sit but uncomfortable straight chairs like those in the papal audience chamber. It was cold. A fireplace was empty except for a few cobwebs. The elegant candelabrum on the marble mantel and others throughout the room held only stubs. Joanna thought regretfully of the cushioned benches and plump pillows of her warm apartments in Palermo.

But they weren't there for self-indulgence.

They told Jean-Pierre of their audience. He too was dismayed at the pope's reluctance to take action.

"Though I can't say I'm surprised. He was elevated to the papacy after a very long career of service to the church, more as a reward than in expectation that he'd accomplish very much."

Joanna reported that she had already written her letter to Constance. "I reminded her, of course, of our friendship and told her how much I'd missed her. If she's still the kind, intelligent woman I remember, I believe she'll do her best to persuade Henry to show mercy to Richard."

"Have you dispatched it yet?" asked Jean-Pierre.

"No. Why do you ask?"

"Because I have a suggestion. You might refer to your recent visit to Palermo and your talks with Tancred. You might hint that you could possibly influence him to abandon his resistance to Henry's claims to Sicily."

"But that's not true! I would never do such a thing, and Tancred would never give in to Henry!"

"You know that, and I know that. But Henry doesn't, nor does Constance. This, my dear Joanna, is what is known as devious diplomacy. It can do no harm and it might do some good."

She looked at him incredulously. Was he serious? Then she burst into laughter.

"Why not? It's certainly worth a try. Jean-Pierre, I wish you were the occupant of the papal throne. Then we'd see less temporizing and more action."

Berengaria had been watching and listening attentively.

"I agree! But also, I think we should have more than one string to our bow. It will be some time before the letter reaches Constance and possibly even more time before she can persuade her husband to be merciful. In the meantime I suggest that we return to France as fast as we possibly can. Queen Eleanor, to my mind, is our best hope. If she's working on raising that enormous ransom, maybe we can help. And if by some miracle or by Constance's influence Richard is freed, I for one would want to be in Aquitaine to welcome him when he arrives."

"Of course you're right," said Joanna.

Jean-Pierre concurred. "When you visit the pope again tomorrow I'd like to come with you. I suspect he'll try to persuade you to stay. He'll hold out the hope that he'll have good news any day now. I'll back you up in your decision to leave, and I'll ask his assistance in finding us an escort for the journey."

"How decisive we are!" exclaimed Joanna. "Thanks to you both for your good sense and advice. Now, what do you say, shall we try to rouse out some servants to bring in wood and make us a fire, and to provide us with some supper and wine?"

"Indeed we shall," said Jean-Pierre. "I saw several fellows in the papal black and red lounging in the hall when I came in. I'll remind them of their Christian duty to be hospitable to the pope's guests. But in the meantime, let me offer you, by way of celebrating our agreement on a course of action, a sip of the nectar produced by the Benedictine monks of Palermo." He reached into the deep pocket of his robe and produced a small flask and three tiny glasses. "I hope it has not suffered from the voyage."

It had not.

The next morning they called on the pope. They'd sent word that Brother Jean-Pierre would join them. He'd changed from his old brown habit with the rather tattered rope belt to a fine white linen robe that Joanna had not seen since her wedding. She and Berengaria had also taken pains with their attire, to make up for their travel-worn appearance the day before. Joanna's gown was one of her favorites, the sky-blue satin with silver fleurs-de-lys. Its neck was rather low. Smiling in recollection of what Lady Marian would have said, she added a silvery silk scarf. Berengaria chose a velvet gown of deep green. Both wore tiaras, not their many-jeweled crowns of state.

The three of them had to wait a few minutes before entering the audience chamber while a pair of self-important bishops and their entourage took their leave. Within, the scene was much the same as the day before. Pope Celestine sat erect with his hands folded in his lap but today his eyes were open. The two attendants stood motionless and expressionless as ever. However, three of the spindly chairs had already been placed before the papal throne. After the kissing of the ring, the visitors seated themselves.

"Welcome to Rome, my son," Celestine said to Jean-Pierre. And to the two queens, "I trust you have had a restful night and are recovered from your journey."

"Thank you, yes," said Joanna.

"And we're very appreciative of your hospitality," said Berengaria.

Neither thought this was quite the time or place to mention chilly rooms and hard beds.

"I had hoped that another messenger from Austria might have arrived last evening. Unfortunately, no. But a reply to my latest communication to Emperor Henry is sure to come soon. So I urge you to continue to be my guests here while we await developments."

"May I ask, Your Holiness, if you have also been in touch with Henry's wife, the Empress Constance?" Jean-Pierre asked respectfully.

Celestine's pale gray eyes widened and his eyebrows rose in his surprise. "No, why should I?"

"It's only that she is an old friend of Queen Joanna. They knew each other well in Sicily, before Constance went away to marry Henry. She might be persuaded to do what she can to encourage Henry to free her good friend's brother."

The pope looked at him, considering what he'd heard and drumming his thin fingers on the carved golden arms of his throne.

"Well. I'd forgotten that connection." He drooped a little and they could almost sense the energy draining out of him. His voice was weaker. "Still, I hardly see the benefit of asking her to become involved. What ruler listens to a woman to help him make up his mind?"

Joanna stiffened but held her tongue. Jean-Pierre hurried to change the subject.

"We are here to ask your aid on another matter, Your Holiness," he said. "We feel that we should continue our journey at once. Queen Joanna and Queen Berengaria wish to be reunited with Queen Eleanor as soon as possible and to assist her in raising Richard's ransom, should Henry persist in his outrageous demands. Eleanor will be fully informed of what is going on in Austria, thanks to her many agents who send timely dispatches."

The pope smiled grimly. There were those who said that Eleanor of Aquitaine had a better information-gathering network than the papacy.

"In brief, could you provide us with an escort for the journey from Rome to the borders of Aquitaine? We have only six knights in our party and in view of the brigandage that's rampant these days, we'd greatly appreciate an additional half-dozen."

"Of course," said Celestine. "Ask the captain of your knights to talk to Pietro Corleone, the chief officer of the papal guards. I shall instruct Captain Corleone to cooperate fully. I shall also instruct the household majordomo in the palace to see that you are well supplied with all you need." They could hardly hear the final words. He leaned back and closed his eyes. Not a word of farewell, much less urging them to stay. The attendants sprang to life and ushered them out of the room.

"Now," said Joanna, "we must get busy. I suggest that we invite Sir Alan, Lady Mary and the others to dine with us this afternoon so we can tell them what's afoot and make our plans."

The palace chef was surprised when Joanna outlined to him the simple meal she hoped to see on the dinner table: a soup of lentils or beans, some kind of roast fowl with onion sauce, fruit tarts. "And several flagons of your good red Italian wine."

He looked doubtful. "I shall try, my lady. But we aren't used to such fine cookery. The pope doesn't usually indulge in anything richer than chickpea soup and rice gruel. If he has guests who wish more he usually directs them to the nearby *taverna.*"

"Just do what you can." She smiled at him so sweetly that he resolved to do what he could and more.

Dinner was a great success. Thanks to Mary's resourcefulness in enlisting several palace servants, a fine fire blazed on the hearth and the room was brilliantly lit by candelabra fitted with new candles. She had even found cushions for the hard chairs. Everybody was pleased with the chef's achievements, especially the tarts. He'd created a variety—flaky little pastries filled with apples, figs, spiced pears or lemon pudding. These were served with sweet wine.

Joanna explained to the others that they would be leaving in a day or two, which suited everybody except Beatrix.

"But we've only begun to see the sights! Federico was going to take me to the Pantheon tomorrow and the Colosseum the next day, and he was going to tell me all about the gladiators and the lions and the poor Christians."

Joanna looked at Federico skeptically. Since when had he become an expert on ancient Rome?

Federico blushed and looked down.

Sir Alan assured Beatrix that they'd go through Arles when they were back in France, and Federico could show her its very fine Coliseum. "Though I'm not sure how many Christians perished there, if any."

They were interrupted by a knock and the entry of Captain Corleone, a stocky, soldierly figure, not in the papal livery but in leather jerkin, brown wool leggings and stout boots.

"I've been sent by His Holiness to offer our help for your journey."

Sir Alan stood and took his hand. "Welcome, and will you join us for a glass, while we tell you what kind of help we need and you tell us the route you recommend?" The two settled at one end of the table to confer. After twenty minutes and two glasses of wine, Captain Corleone stood, clapped Sir Alan on the shoulder, and said, "That's it then. We'll have six mounted knights, their squires and grooms ready the day after tomorrow, here in the square. And you should be in Saint-Gilles well before Pentecost."

He addressed Joanna. "My lady Queen, Pope Celestine has asked me to give you this further message. He is glad to provide this escort, which will be with you until you reach Saint-Gilles. But you will need protection as you continue your journey in France. He has sent word to Count Raymond of Toulouse, asking him to have his son, young Raymond, meet you with a small force at Saint-Gilles and accompany you to Poitiers."

After a moment's hesitation and a glance at Sir Alan, who nodded, she said, "Please extend our thanks to His Holiness. That is a generous act on his part, and we will be glad of the additional escort."

When Captain Corleone had taken his leave, Joanna and Sir Alan looked at each other uncertainly. They knew that Count Raymond of Toulouse was no friend of the Plantagenets. Eleanor as duchess of Aquitaine and later Richard as its duke had sparred often with Raymond, each side making incursions into the other's lands.

"Why would Raymond be willing to help us now? Does the pope know something we don't know?" wondered Joanna.

"What's troubling you about the offer?" asked Berengaria, who was still unfamiliar with European alliances and quarrels. "As far as I'm concerned, I'll welcome the aid of anyone who'll get us safely and quickly to Poitiers."

Federico tried to conceal a yawn. Beatrix was almost asleep in her chair. Even tireless Lady Mary was having trouble keeping her eyes open. The candles had nearly burned down.

"I propose we all go to bed," said Brother Jean-Pierre. "It's far too late and we're all too tired to make sense of it now." He rose to set the example.

"Right," said Joanna. "We'll find out what Count Raymond is up to in time, I expect."

51

"How charming!" exclaimed Joanna as she and her party entered the audience chamber of the counts of Toulouse in Saint-Gilles. Sunlight poured in through a row of arched windows that afforded an expansive view to the east. Lush green fields interspersed with clumps of forest stretched from the lazy river toward a hazy distant horizon.

Raymond, heir to the current count, rose from his chair where he'd been sitting in the shadows.

"I'm glad you think so."

As he stepped into the light he was the focus of everyone's eyes. Joanna was struck at once by his almost palpable air of controlled energy. He appeared to be in his mid-thirties and was tall, dark and lithe. If it weren't that his nose was just a trifle long, she thought, he could have been considered almost as handsome as William. He was beardless and wore his black hair cropped short, just covering the tips of his ears.

He moved quickly to welcome them, his short blue cloak swirling gracefully. As Jean-Pierre introduced the company, each received a smile and a word of welcome. The women were also favored with a slight pressure of the hand.

All her life Joanna had been taught to think of the counts of Toulouse as her family's sworn enemies, as ogres, as *les toulousains terribles*. But this man bore not the slightest resemblance to an ogre or the son of an ogre. He was affable and seemed anxious to please.

A semicircle of chairs had been arranged facing the view. While a servant guided the guests to their seats, Raymond seated himself at the center, stretched out his legs and studied his silver-buckled boots. Apparently satisfied with their brilliant polish, he looked up and spoke.

"We received the message from Pope Celestine two weeks ago, telling us of your departure from Rome and asking us to offer our services for the next stage of your journey. Unfortunately, my father had affairs in Toulouse that required him to leave Saint-Gilles yesterday. But I speak for him as well as myself when I say we are more than pleased to be of assistance. And I hope you will agree to stay a few days here to recover from what must have been an arduous journey." He glanced inquiringly at Joanna.

"Perhaps two or three days," she said, "though we're anxious to reach Poitiers as soon as possible. But I'll welcome the opportunity to revisit your wonderful church, which I saw for the first time when I was just a girl and on my way to Sicily."

"I too would like to revisit the town and the church," said Berengaria. "When I stopped here with Queen Eleanor I had only two hours to explore. But I've never forgotten those amazing carvings that told the whole Bible story."

"I'm happy to assure you that you'll find the church façade much as it was. True, the sculptors have found a few empty spots where they've managed to squeeze in two or three additional saint and sinners, but otherwise little has changed."

He turned next to Beatrix. She had let down the hood of her cloak. She'd tied her lustrous black hair back with a red ribbon.

"And Princess, how have you fared on this journey—if I'm not mistaken, your first venture into the world west of Cyprus? What wondrous sights have you seen that you'll never forget?"

She clasped her hands and her dark eyes sparkled. "Oh, so many! And the most wonderful was the bridge over the Rhone from Avignon. It was so exciting! I kept looking down at the river flowing along so swiftly, and trembling when I thought what it would be like to fall in."

"Federico would have jumped in at once to save you," said Sir Alan.

She blushed. Sir Raymond regarded her through half-closed eyelids.

"And who is this gallant Federico?"

"I suppose you might say he's my ward," said Joanna. "Brother Jean-Pierre rescued him from the slums of Palermo when he was only a child. Since then he's served as my page and my attendant. He's almost like a member of the family. But now he's on his way to becoming a knight, thanks to Sir Alan's tutelage."

"Most generous of you, Queen Joanna," he said. Did she detect a note of condescension? But he returned his attention to Beatrix.

"Tell me, Princess, what news you have of your father, King Isaac? I know he was imprisoned after King Richard defeated him on Cyprus. Where is he now?"

"As far as I know he's still in Tripoli. The last I heard, he was not well. I've had no word for six months." Her animation had left her and she looked stricken. Berengaria rose and went to put her arms around her. "Don't grieve, my dear. When we see Richard, we'll beg him to release your father. Surely at his advanced age he deserves some mercy."

"And if I have the opportunity, I shall add my pleas as well," said Raymond. There was an awkward pause while his listeners tried to imagine a situation when Raymond would have influence with Richard, who had frequently and publicly sworn to annihilate the entire House of Toulouse.

Beatrix rebounded from her depression. She had loosened the ties of her cloak and it fell from her shoulders to reveal her blue silk gown. It had such a low neckline that it hardly contained her nubile breasts. Joanna tried to catch her eye and show her disapproval but Beatrix had again fixed her eager gaze on Raymond.

"Sir Raymond, how far is it from here to Arles?"

"Only a half-day's journey. Why do you ask?"

"We didn't have time to see the Colosseum in Rome, but Sir Alan promised we'd stop at the one in Arles, and we didn't. And I'd so like to see where the Christians and the lions fought each other."

"I'm afraid you'd not see much of the original arena, where the gladiators fought and the lions roared and the chariot races took place. A number of indigent citizens of Arles have moved in and put up their shacks there. But later, when we get to Nimes, you'll see a much better-preserved Roman arena, which I believe hasn't yet been ruined by the rabble. I'll personally give you a tour."

He stood. "I mustn't keep you longer. I'm sure you're all eager to refresh yourselves. Your rooms have been prepared, and my servants are waiting to conduct you to them. We'll meet again at dinner."

Much later, sated with pigeon pie, roast whole hare, cherry tart, jellied quince confections and other local delicacies, Berengaria and Joanna met in the latter's chamber for a pre-bedtime tête-à-tête. They'd let down their hair, changed from their fine gowns into woolen robes and dismissed their maids. The room was a far cry from the pope's bleak apartments. Here there were plenty of couches and cushions, and thanks to candles in sconces all around the walls and an efficient fire on the hearth, the room was cheerful and warm.

Joanna half-reclined on a couch. Berengaria walked restlessly about, picking up various objects and setting them down.

"Have you noticed," she asked, "the refreshing absence of ostentation? The counts of Toulouse seem to appreciate the understated artistry of the region. Look at this—isn't it lovely?" She held out a pale-green ceramic vase with an embossed pattern of leaves in a darker green around the rim.

Joanna took it and ran her hands down its graceful, smooth curves. "It is." She handed it back and looked around the room, considering. "I expect poor Pope Celestine wouldn't sleep a wink here, where there's hardly any gold or silver or glitter."

Berengaria laughed and settled in a chair near Joanna. "Still, no matter how cultured the counts may be, there's something about this Raymond that makes me uneasy. It's as though he were playing a part to keep from revealing his true nature."

Joanna nodded. "I feel the same way. I'm not sure I trust him completely. But I admit I'm prejudiced by what I've heard about his father from my parents. Besides being deceitful and contentious, the elder Raymond has led a private life that's been far from edifying. It would be strange if the son hadn't been influenced by the example of the old count."

"Did you hear what he said at dinner when Jean-Pierre politely remarked that he was sorry Raymond's wife hadn't come with him to Saint-Gilles?"

"No, I missed that. Tell me."

"Raymond replied, with something between a grin and a leer, 'No matter, I doubt if she'll be my wife much longer.' I think he meant only Jean-Pierre to hear, maybe trying to shock him. But I was next to Jean-Pierre and I heard it all."

Joanna pursed her lips and frowned, trying to remember what she'd heard of Raymond's marriages. "I believe his first wife died some years ago so this would be his second. And I've heard that his father didn't hesitate to repudiate a wife if somebody else took his fancy."

At a rat-a-tat-tat on the door—Lady Mary's familiar signal—Joanna called "Come in."

Mary too was ready for relaxation. She sat down and took off the wimple that she usually wore these days, releasing a cloud of russet-red curls. She shook her head as though encouraging them to rejoice in their freedom.

"Why must you always wear a wimple?" asked Berengaria. "You're too young and pretty to cover your crowning glory."

"Ah, but I must try to look dignified and responsible, as my queen's senior—and at the moment, only—lady-in-waiting."

Joanna smiled affectionately and patted her hand. "Join us in a glass of wine. Our host maintains a superb cellar, I'm happy to find."

After a sip, Mary set her glass down. "Yes, it's excellent. Speaking of our host, he's something of an enigma, isn't he?"

They told her what Berengaria had overheard at dinner.

"I can add something almost as worrisome," said Mary. She paused for another sip. "One of Raymond's knights sat directly across from me at dinner. I heard him speak to the lady on his left, who may or may not have been his wife. 'No wonder,' said he, 'that Raymond is so willing to undertake this journey. He's always on the lookout for pretty ladies, and he'll have three of them—highborn, too—to keep him company.'" She paused while they considered this.

Mary went on. "At which, his companion looked a little miffed and he hurried to add, 'But none as pretty as you, my love.'"

"Was she pretty?" asked Berengaria.

"Not particularly."

Joanna set down her glass. "There's no point in worrying about Raymond's character now. We'll be vigilant but we'll have to trust him. I've no doubt that you and I, sister, can fend him off and so can Mary if she catches his eye. It's Beatrix I'd worry about."

"Yes," said Berengaria. "She's only sixteen, she's impressionable and she's unused to the ways of the world. I doubt if she's aware of how attractive men may find her. She's still so innocent. Maybe we should keep a closer watch on her."

She didn't see the quick glance that passed between Joanna and Mary. Neither had told her about Richard's seduction of Beatrix in the Holy Land. They were both sure that Beatrix had learned her lesson, and there was no point in distressing Berengaria with tales of her husband's infidelities.

"In any case," Berengaria went on, "I'm glad Raymond and his knights will be with us. We may need protection against worse perils than amorous young counts. I'll confess I was alarmed by some of the rough characters we saw on the road from Rome to Saint-Gilles."

The others nodded sleepily. Joanna stood up.

"Since we seem to have finished the wine, shall we retire and dream about our arrival in Poitiers in a few weeks' time, safe and sound, virtue intact?"

The next morning Berengaria and Joanna walked down to the abbey church.

They found the figures on the frieze were as realistic as ever—from the folds of the robes of the apostles to the patient expression of the ass bearing Christ into Jerusalem.

"It's like revisiting old friends," said Berengaria.

"Yes, and that must be one of the new ones Raymond spoke of—that cross-looking fellow tumbling down the steps to some horrible fate."

For some time they walked back and forth, admiring and commenting, until their thoughts turned again to their enigmatic host.

"Sir Raymond has been the soul of accommodation, hasn't he?" mused Joanna. "Why, do you suppose? Why would the count of Toulouse be so eager to be of service to the sister and the wife of his longtime enemy Richard?" She looked up at St. Peter as though seeking an answer. But he was otherwise engaged, watching David battle Goliath.

"I expect your mother can explain it. There may be some political reasons we aren't aware of." And they had to leave it at that.

It was a sizeable party that set out two days later. Those who had come from Rome numbered twenty-five: the ladies, their maids and servants, Brother Jean-Pierre, Sir Alan, Federico and six knights and as many grooms. Now Raymond provided ten more knights, five to ride ahead and five behind. Then there were the pack animals, laden with bags and boxes and some of the knights' excess armor, ambling along in the rear.

The procession was noisy. Armor clanked, muleteers loudly cursed their charges, hooves pounded out a drumbeat on the road. No wonder it got attention from other travelers and from villagers along the way.

Raymond was known to the local citizenry. He often rode about the county on his father's business. But who were his companions—the four elegantly clad ladies in their satins and furs, the monkish-looking man in the plain brown robe, the strikingly handsome black-haired youth in green velvet? And the brawny knight whose groom carried a banner with three golden lions on a field of scarlet—wasn't that the device of the English, who were no friends of the counts of Toulouse? And could one of those ladies be a prospective bride of the count-in-waiting? It was widely known that Sir Raymond was not getting on well with his present wife. He might be casting about for a successor. He might have already chosen one.

When Nimes came in sight it was late in the afternoon but there were still a few hours of daylight left. As promised, Raymond guided them to the arena. And as promised, Beatrix received his personal attention. First they admired the grand design from outside. The entire façade of the great oval consisted of tall stone arches, with another identical level above the lower.

"And to think that it's a thousand years old!" marveled Jean-Pierre. "I wonder if the Romans had any idea it would still be standing in this year of our Lord 1193. They truly built for the ages."

"Indeed they did," said Raymond. "But they also made sure their past was properly recognized." He took Beatrix by the arm and led her to a carving of a wolf suckling two little boys. "Do you know what that signifies, Princess?"

"I don't," she replied, "and I'm not sure I want to. Why should human children be nursing from a beast?"

"It goes back to the myths about the origins of Rome," he explained, and went on to tell her the legend of the she-wolf who took pity on two orphaned boys who grew up to be the founders of Rome. But she made a face and turned her back on the sculpture.

Not at all discomfited, he went on equably, "So, if that doesn't please you, shall we go inside?" He led the group through an arched entrance into the vast arena, with its dozens of tiers of seats rising to a graceful gallery that crowned the exterior wall. Joanna tried to imagine the arena filled with cheering spectators, while wild beasts fought each other, or a troop of fierce bulls was paraded around the ring, tossing their horns and snorting. And then there were the gladiators.

"I'd have liked to see it in those Roman days," Joanna said to Berengaria, "but I don't quite think I could have watched the gladiators, fighting each other to the death for the amusement of the citizenry." She shuddered.

Berengaria agreed. "War is so barbaric, it shouldn't be mimicked and presented as entertainment."

"But don't you see," said Raymond, "it wasn't just a show of men being killed; it was a demonstration of their skill, their bravery, even their nobility? Many of the best were viewed as heroes by the populace."

"And the more nobly they died, the more they were revered? Yet they did die, painfully." Berengaria seemed ready to embark on a philosophical discussion of life and death, but Beatrix interrupted.

"It's getting late. Please, Sir Raymond, show us where the lions and tigers were."

Most of the others preferred to sit on the stone benches, still warmed by the sun, while Raymond led Beatrix, Sir Alan and Federico down the ramps to the subterranean chambers where, long ago, gladiators and wild animals waited their turn to appear on the arena field.

To pass the time until the return of the explorers, three of Raymond's mounted knights raced each other around the oval, standing in their stirrups and shouting, pretending to be charioteers. This was mildly amusing for a time. But the sun was descending toward the western wall of the arena. The travelers, from queens to grooms, were hungry and tired, but they couldn't leave because only Raymond knew where they'd spend the night.

Suddenly Sir Alan and Federico popped out of a dark doorway, blinking in the daylight. Joanna hurried over to them.

"Where are Raymond and Beatrix? I hope they're on their way up too."

"We got separated. It's very confusing down there—little narrow passages going every which way." Alan wiped his forehead. "Federico and I had quite a time of it to find our way out."

"And we kept calling to the others, but they must not have heard us." Federico looked a little shaken by the experience. "And then our candle went out. But I saw a glimmer of light way up ahead and we aimed for that and here we are."

"Yes, here you are indeed, and that's a relief," said Joanna. "But where can Raymond and Beatrix be?"

Before she had time to get seriously worried the pair emerged from another doorway. Both Joanna and Berengaria studied them covertly, looking for signs of misbehavior. Was Raymond a trifle discomposed? Was his smile a little nervous? Was Beatrix's hair somewhat disheveled? Joanna looked at Berengaria and shrugged. Maybe, maybe not.

Raymond efficiently shepherded everybody out of the arena to the square. The royal ladies and their attendants were to be lodged in the bishop's palace.

Raymond, the soul of propriety, rode beside Joanna, pointing out other famous Roman ruins. When they reached the palace, with utmost courtesy he bowed over each lady's hand, just as he'd done when they'd arrived at the castle in Saint-Gilles. But this time there was no doubt about it: he held Beatrix's hand a fraction of a second longer, and a complicit look passed between them. Joanna watched him riding off, back straight, horsemanship impeccable.

Inside, the three ladies were conducted by a servant into a small reception room where they were drawn to the warmth of a blazing fire within an ornate marble fireplace. They'd all become chilled during the ride through the darkening city. But Beatrix was actually shivering.

"You'd better go up, my dear," said Berengaria. "Your maid will be there by now. You should really change into something warm and have her send for a hot drink."

"Yes, I think I will. It was so cold and damp down in those tunnels. Sir Raymond was kind and wrapped me in his cloak and kept his arm around me while we climbed the stairs. But I don't think I'll ever warm up!"

When she'd left, Berengaria brushed her hand across her forehead and sighed.

"It's still a long way to Poitiers. I think something should be said to Raymond about our young charge. She's a valuable property, whether she knows it or not, on the European marriage market. Your mother has probably already started talking to various royal and noble families about a suitable match."

"You're right, of course. He must be made to understand that we take very seriously our responsibility to protect her. But how can I bring this up without implying that I think he's trying to seduce her?"

"Joanna, maybe it should come from me. Nobody could accuse me of speaking out of self-interest, since I already have a husband. But you're a lovely royal widow who could well be casting about for an eligible new spouse. And there are few more eligible and sought-after than Raymond—if one can catch him between marriages! Raymond isn't stupid. He could well ascribe anything you said about Beatrix to jealousy."

"Jealousy? Me, jealous of *her*? Ridiculous!" She clamped her mouth shut to keep from making an angry reply. After a minute she regained her composure.

"If you can find an opportunity to speak to him, please do. You're very good to be willing to. Thank you, sister." She smiled tiredly.

"We'd better go up and change. I wonder what the bishop's serving for supper." And she started up the stairs.

Once alone, she walked to a mirror and stared at her reflection for a long time. She could find no fault with the face she saw. Her cheeks were smooth, her complexion was creamy, with a pleasing bronze tone from her years in sunny Sicily. Her lips were as rosy, her eyes were as brown, her hair as golden-brown as ever. But attractive as it was, it was the face of a twenty-seven-year- old woman. It had none of the bloom, the freshness, the eagerness to taste what life had to offer of a sixteen-year-old.

Could I be jealous? she wondered.

Maybe there was a grain of truth in what Berengaria had said.

52

Their first day out of Nimes, Berengaria watched for a chance to deliver her lecture to Raymond. It came before they'd been on the road an hour. A knight who had been riding next to Raymond moved up to join his companions in the advance guard. Berengaria glanced at Joanna, nudged her horse to a trot and took the knight's place. She was frowning slightly. She didn't look forward to the encounter.

Joanna, twenty paces back, could see but not hear the conversation. At first Raymond looked surprised when Berengaria reined in her horse beside him. She began speaking at once, earnestly and soberly. He listened intently. He nodded and then replied at some length. Again she spoke, again he replied. He looked inquiringly at Berengaria, who replied with only two words, which Joanna thought might be "Thank you" or "Very well." Raymond reached to take her hand as though assuring her of his sincerity. Berengaria rode back to take her place beside Joanna.

"I'm glad I talked to him. I think he took it well." She related how Raymond thought it strange that anyone could have found his attentions to Beatrix improper, when he was merely trying to show an eager, curious young person the sights along their way. "He denied any inappropriate behavior on his part or hers. But he admitted he found her attractive and had even entertained the thought of marriage some day."

"Did he indeed! Any mention of an existing wife?"

"Yes, he said, almost casually, that of course he couldn't remarry until his divorce was approved by the pope, but that he expected that soon."

"Hmmm."

"But this is the interesting part. When I emphasized to him that Queen Eleanor would be in charge of Beatrix's future, he said 'I understand. And I would never have spoken of marriage to Beatrix before talking to the queen. That is also true of any other ladies in whom I might take an interest in the queen's entourage or family.' I think he was referring to you, Joanna."

Joanna began to protest, but Berengaria hurried on.

"And this was interesting too. He volunteered that he'd probably do well to let up on his attentions to Beatrix, lest the poor girl get ideas that he was wooing her. I heartily agreed."

They rode in reflective silence for several minutes. Joanna let down her hood and raised her face to bask in the warmth of the morning sun.

282   A Reed in the Wind

"Well, we've done what we can," she said. "Now let's just enjoy this glorious June day!"

Still not far from Nimes, they rode through prosperous farmland and neat villages. Small yellow-green birds flocked and twittered in chestnut groves. In the orchards, cherries hung red and ripe from the branches.

Sir Alan smacked his lips. "Cherry tarts on the supper table tonight, eh?"

Soon, though, they departed from the comfortable lowlands and climbed forested slopes toward a high rocky plain, bleak and forbidding. It seemed to go on forever, but after two days the landscape became less stark. There were still many hills to climb, many streams to cross. Raymond had recommended this route as shorter, though more arduous, than the one that followed the Rhone River. Sometimes they had to ride until sundown before finding an abbey or some local lord's castle where they could spend the night.

As they approached Polignac, their objective for the evening of the seventh day, the road descended from a ridge into a deep valley. Joanna turned to Raymond, who was riding at her side. "I believe I detect the sound of swiftly running water. I hope this isn't another of your 'shallow little streams whose bridge has mysteriously disappeared but will take only a moment to ford.'" She meant to sound teasing but the words came out like criticism. To her relief, he smiled.

"I make no promises except to do my utmost to get you dry-shod to the other side."

And he very nearly did.

The stream, when they reached it, proved to be not very formidable—only a dozen yards across and it looked shallow. Joanna, with Raymond on her left, urged her horse forward. Midstream her steed stumbled over some hidden impediment—a root, a loose boulder—and sank to its knees. Joanna cried out as she began to slide down its neck. In an instant Raymond leaned down and clasped her about the waist, arresting her descent. For what seemed an eternity she hung in midair, saved from a plunge into the river by Raymond's tight hold. Then the horse with a gallant effort regained its footing. Raymond kept his arm around her until they reached the other side.

Joanna was trembling. Mary brought her a shawl. "Perhaps you'd like to dismount and walk about a bit and get your equilibrium back?" Raymond asked. "That wasn't the most pleasant of experiences."

"But without your help it could have been far less pleasant. No harm done—my shoes got a little splashed but that's all. I'm very, very grateful. And do let's go on to Polignac. We must be nearly there."

All the way up from the gloomy valley to the next ridge, she shivered intermittently, recovering from her narrow escape. But when they emerged into the bright afternoon sunlight she forgot everything in her amazement at what she saw.

A road branched off from theirs and wound down toward a town nestled in another deep valley. What captured Joanna's attention was an impossibly tall needle-like spire just coming into view. As their road dipped down a little she could see that it wasn't manmade but sprang heavenward from the rock of the valley floor. What was that at the top? A chapel! Then she saw the stairway that climbed the spire and tiny figures toiling up. She was full of questions and looked around. Raymond wasn't in evidence but Brother Jean-Pierre was. He smiled apologetically at her puzzled face.

"I'm sorry, Joanna, I can't explain it. I do know the town is Le Puy, a famous starting place for the pilgrimage to Santiago de Compostela in Spain. And I'd heard there were strange rock formations. See, there's another one, not quite so tall and closer to the town. I believe the one with the chapel is where the pilgrims officially begin their journey."

The whole party had reined in their horses and paused to gaze, awestruck. The rays of the descending sun bathed the valley in gauzy shafts of gold and reflected off the slender pinnacles so they seemed to glow from within. It was perfectly quiet except for the far-off cooing of doves.

Was this a fairyland? Or was this what heaven looked like?

The spell was broken by the sound of voices, some raised in song, some in shouted conversations so loud that they nearly drowned out the singers. A band of several dozen pilgrims appeared at the top of the steep road from the town.

They stepped along briskly, helping themselves up the slope with their staffs. They were as colorful as a flock of parrots. On this first day of their long journey they'd dressed in their finest. Farmers and tradesmen, millers and bakers, shepherds and drovers, soldiers at loose ends, spinners and weavers, butchers and publicans had dug into their chests and found scarlet waistcoats, purple sashes and caps as green as the new hay of the fields they were leaving behind.

"They don't look much like a band of devout Christians setting off on a holy pilgrimage," said Berengaria.

"It's as much a holiday for them as a serious pilgrimage," said Jean-Pierre. "I expect most of them have been dreaming of this journey for years and saving up for it."

Federico had been watching wide-eyed and open-mouthed as the pilgrims rounded the corner and set off down the road by which the Poitiers-bound travelers had come. "What a time they're going to have! Seeing all those strange lands, going all the way to the western ocean. If I weren't going to be a knight I'd like to be a pilgrim."

"They won't look quite so jolly when they come hobbling back in a couple of years," said Raymond. "I've seen plenty of returning pilgrims with their boots and shoes worn through, their clothes dirty and ragged and their money spent."

"But they'll be wearing the cockle shell on their caps." Brother Jean-Pierre spoke quietly, and he raised his hand to his own head as though in wistful hope that he might find a shell pinned to his hood.

"A cockle shell?" asked Joanna.

"Yes, you earn them only by completing the pilgrimage to Compostela. They're the emblem of Saint James's miracle when he came by sea to far-off Galicia. Any pilgrim who comes back with a cockle shell is envied and revered by his neighbors to the end of his life."

The pilgrims were disappearing around a bend in the road. The sound of a rousing marching song drifted back. Joanna watched the carefree throng until it was out of sight.

Beatrix had observed the pilgrims' procession without much interest. She was squirming in her saddle. "Please, can't we go on?" she asked Raymond. "I'm so tired of riding. How much farther is it to Polignac?"

"Not far. I've sent word to the count of Polignac that we'll be there before sundown. And the road is fairly flat and easy from now on."

"No more rivers to cross?" asked Joanna.

"Alas, no. So there'll be no more rescues of fair ladies." He was laughing at her and it sounded like a real laugh, not a false one produced for effect. She laughed back. How nice, she thought. We seem to be getting along more harmoniously after that little episode at the stream.

As the procession got underway again, Joanna paused and turned to look down the southbound road where the pilgrims had disappeared. She imagined she could still hear their joyful voices and their marching feet. Suddenly she felt a strange urge to ride after them. What would it be like to forget her responsibilities as a daughter of the Plantagenets, to devote herself to the blessed journey to pray at the saint's tomb in far-off Compostela? It would be a long and tiring trip. Could I perhaps have a little donkey to carry my effects, she wondered, and to ride when I got tired? Probably not. The whole purpose was to make the pilgrimage on foot. I'd have to get some sturdy boots.

Her musings were interrupted by the sound of a galloping horse. Federico appeared at her side. "My lady, the others are waiting for you." She didn't answer at once and seemed to be in a trance, her unfocused gaze directed southward. He was alarmed. "Are you all right, my lady?"

She came to herself with a start. "Oh yes, thank you. I was just thinking how I'd like to join that group of happy folk bound for Compostela. What a wonderful way to demonstrate one's faith! What do you think, Federico, shall we become pilgrims?"

"Maybe next year, when I'm a knight. Then as you trudge along I'll ride my big black horse beside you and guard you during the journey."

They both laughed at such a preposterous idea and rode quickly to rejoin their party.

But in the back of her mind a new thought hovered. She'd always considered herself as devout. She'd gone to mass regularly, confessed her sins and given to the poor. But what had she ever done beyond the minimum, what had she sacrificed? Those pilgrims were giving up years of their lives and probably their life savings to honor their God. What had she ever given up? What could she give up?

It was too much for her tired brain now. One of these days, she told herself, I'll give this some real thought. One of these days.

53

The road-weary travelers took heart when they caught sight of the castle of Polignac, an enormous sprawling structure with a tall donjon tower at its center. It stood on an eminence in the middle of the town and was highly visible from all directions, as would have been any assailants who approached it. Riding up the winding road that led to the imposing entrance, Joanna was enchanted by gardens in full flower and intersected by tiled walks. Here was a bed of crimson roses, there one of blue delphiniums, beyond were masses of yellow and white daisies. This promised to be the grandest lodging they'd encountered yet.

They were admitted to the reception hall where servants took their cloaks and brought ewers of water and towels so they could rinse the dust off faces and hands. After only a few minutes their host appeared. A portly man, he had a florid face and a mass of disorderly white hair that made his head resemble a dandelion gone to seed. Incongruously, his bushy eyebrows were as black as his hair was white. His tunic and leggings were deep maroon velvet, and his considerable paunch was encircled by a massive belt studded with jewels. Everything about him spoke of good humor, hospitality and wealth.

"Welcome, welcome," he cried as he approached them, smiling broadly and with arms widespread. "What an honor this is for the House of Polignac! Never in our history—which goes all the way back to Charlemagne, you know—have we sheltered two queens, a princess and a count all at once. I only hope our humble little abode will prove up to the honor." He looked at them solemnly, than broke into delighted laughter at his own drollery. He was so convulsed that the rest of them couldn't help laughing too. Raymond, obviously an old friend, turned to the others and said, "That's only the twentieth time I've heard Count Jules make that feeble joke about his humble abode," which set the count off on another fit of laughter, during which Raymond managed to make the introductions.

"Now," said Count Jules, more seriously, "I'm sure you're longing for a meal. Perhaps you've been thinking all day of a grand repast in my ancestral dining hall. Six or seven courses, maybe, from the stuffed quail to the flaming puddings? How does that sound?"

Joanna groaned inwardly and one of the knights groaned audibly. It had been a very long day and a meal like that would last till midnight. Count Jules, oblivious, offered his arm to Beatrix in a courtly gesture. "Princess, may I escort you to the dining chamber?" He led the way down a long corridor to a room that was clearly not anybody's ancestral dining hall. It was more like a royal salon, luxuriously furnished with divans and chairs. Costly Persian carpets were scattered on the marble floor. Candles in gilded candlesticks were everywhere, their light illuminating the glowing colors of the tapestries on the walls. Four large round tables were laid with silver cutlery, pewter bowls and crystal goblets.

"My dear count," said Raymond, "the humbleness of your abode continues to amaze me. I don't believe I've seen that really gorgeous tapestry"—he pointed—"which I believe depicts Jason and the Argonauts?"

"Correct," said Count Jules. "I've just received it from Constantinople. Yes, I rather like it too. Now my friends, may I suggest that the ladies seat themselves at this table closest to the hearth. Sir Alan, Federico and the knights may take the two tables at the other end of the room, and Count Raymond, Brother Jean-Pierre and I will be at this one, in the corner. Why this unorthodox seating? Because in my experience, ladies often have a great deal to discuss at the end of a day's journey. So do the brave knights. But the two groups may not wish to discuss the same matters. Meantime, I must inform Raymond and Jean-Pierre of certain items of news that have come to my attention and that concern us all. Satisfactory?" He peered at them, his black eyebrows moving rapidly up and down.

They found their places and at once a troop of servants entered. Instead of bringing intimidating platters of fowl and meats, each bore a steaming tureen of thick pea soup, in which garlic, rosemary and chunks of ham had not been spared, and ladled generous portions into the guests' bowls. Others placed big baskets of fresh-baked bread and crocks of butter on each table. Still others distributed plates of crisp, curly lettuce, dressed with oil, vinegar, and, Joanna decided, thyme. Finally the wine—ruby-red, fruity—was poured. When Raymond complimented him, "I send all the way to Bordeaux for it," Count Jules said off-handedly. As he seated himself he called out, "Save some room for cherry pies to come."

"Ahhh," said Lady Mary after her first spoonful of soup. "Just what we needed after this long day. I'm so relieved not to have to face a stuffed quail." There was general agreement as everybody fell to. For a few minutes there was no sound except discreet slurping and calls for seconds from the knights, accompanied by the dulcet melodies produced by a harpist in a corner.

When the first hunger pangs had been assuaged, when the wine was flowing freely and the pies had been brought in, the knights became garrulous, talking about whatever it is knights talk about. At Joanna's table the conversation veered from musings about the pilgrims—Berengaria admitted that she too had felt a pull to join them—to conjectures about what lay ahead.

Beatrix, who had been silent but had permitted her wineglass to be refilled several times, announced that she was weary of the journey and could hardly wait to get to Queen Eleanor's palace in Poitiers. "I'm sure there'll be plenty of handsome young noblemen there. Isn't Queen Eleanor famous for her brilliant court?" she asked Joanna.

"That's true, or at least it was when I was a child. My mother has a very wide acquaintance among French and English nobility."

Beatrix's smile was almost a smirk. She fluttered her eyelashes and remarked to nobody in particular, "Really, I'll be happy to see the last of Count Raymond. He was getting quite tiresome. I'm glad he's found someone else to devote himself to."

"Shhh," said Berengaria. "Do keep your voice down, my dear. I wonder if you may have had too much wine. Would you like me to accompany you to our rooms?"

Beatrix paid no attention and addressed Joanna again. "How gallant he was to rescue you from drowning!" Angrily, she gulped down the last of her wine and tossed her head. She jumped to her feet and stalked out of the room, holding up the skirt of her green silk gown as though keeping it out of the mud, though the marble floor was scrubbed and clean.

Count Jules, who had risen and was leading Raymond and Jean-Pierre to Joanna's table, looked at Beatrix in surprise but said nothing. He drew up chairs for himself and his two companions.

"May we interrupt you? It's time for a conference," he said.

"Of course," said Joanna. She beckoned to Sir Alan and Federico to join them. The rest of the knights were straggling out of the room, yawning and belching.

When everyone was seated, the count continued, no longer the jokester. "I've shared with Brother Jean-Pierre and Count Raymond the news I had from Germany last week. We've discussed the consequences and what action you might take." His audience looked increasingly worried.

"First, we learned that King Richard has been released from solitary confinement in the castle of Trifels and is now at Emperor Henry's court in Speyer."

"I had no idea they were keeping him in solitary confinement!" cried Berengaria.

"So is this good news, that he's with the emperor?" asked Joanna.

"Not very. He's still virtually a prisoner and prohibited from leaving Henry's palace."

"But as we're all well aware," said Jean-Pierre, "Richard is so eloquent, and his reputation for integrity and bravery is so well known, that he'll be far more influential in determining his fate at the royal court than he could have been in Trifels."

"What about the ransom?" asked Berengaria. "Is the emperor still demanding that impossible 100,000 marks?"

"I'm afraid he is. Emperor Henry, I regret, seems to care more about money than a reputation as a just ruler."

Joanna thought sadly about her friend Constance, married to a man so mercenary—and merciless.

Raymond picked up the account. "But this latest news the count has received is the most disturbing. King Philip of France would like nothing better than to have Richard in his clutches. Not for the ransom, but with Richard out of the picture, Philip would have free rein to take back some of the French lands that Richard controls. He's connived with Prince John and is offering to buy Richard from the emperor for a huge sum—well above the 100,000 marks." He'd been speaking dispassionately, like a legal expert outlining the facts of a case. Now he addressed Joanna directly, and she thought she heard real compassion in his voice. "It must be hard for you to learn that one brother is plotting treachery against another."

"Hard, yes. But not a surprise. John has always been crafty and unprincipled. But..."

Sir Alan interrupted, redfaced with anger, unable to control his outrage. "This is monstrous—to treat our king like a commodity, like a cow or a bale of hay to be bought and sold!"

Joanna looked sympathetically at Sir Alan. "It is monstrous. But Count Jules, you said you would advise us about steps we might take to prevent this calamity."

"Yes. My suggestion, which I think has a good chance of success, is to write to the pope. I understand you and Queen Berengaria have seen him recently and I'm sure he remembers your concern for Richard. Plead with him to use his influence with the emperor, to try to get the ransom reduced and above all to prevent the sale of Richard to Philip,which would only lead to more warfare between France and England. This pope is far more desirous of having soldiers go to rescue Jerusalem from the infidels than to shed blood here in Europe fighting each other."

"I'm sure," said Brother Jean-Pierre, "that Queen Eleanor has been assiduous in pleading with Pope Celestine. Your voices added to hers might spur him to do what he has resisted doing—threatening Henry with excommunication."

"He certainly resisted it when we saw him in Rome. But yes, if there's a slight chance that it might help, of course we'll write." Joanna looked at Berengaria, who was nervously plucking at the fabric of her skirt. She looked anguished, but nodded.

Count Jules rose.

"We'll meet again tomorrow. You all need your sleep." His eyebrows were in motion again and his infectious smile lit up his face. "And please, if there's any dissatisfaction with your rooms—as there well may be, I'm sure you're all accustomed to far more comfort than we can offer in our humble castle—but if you have the least wish for anything at all, ask the pages to fetch the majordomo."

When they stood up they realized how tired they were. "I hope there aren't too many stairs," sighed Lady Mary.

Joanna was near exhaustion too, but she still had questions. She caught up with Brother Jean-Pierre as he started up the steps—of which, fortunately, there were only six.

"I'd like to talk to you a little more about all this, if you could spare me just a few minutes before we all collapse?"

She saw that his drawn face showed lines of aging that she hadn't noticed before. He longed for his rest as much as she did. But "Of course," he said.

"Then when you're settled in your room, come back to mine."

The servant who was escorting them had bounded up the stairs and was holding open the first door along a long corridor.

"Your apartments, Queen Joanna, and as Count Jules said, you have only to ask if we can serve you further."

"Thank you. There's just one thing—could you bring some barley water with lemon and honey?" She turned to Jean-Pierre. "Or would you like more wine?"

"I would not. Count Jules was more than generous with his wine tonight. I've had enough to last me a week."

"Very well, my lady. Barley water it is." And the servant ran down the stairs.

A half-hour later, Joanna in her blue robe and Jean-Pierre minus his hooded cloak but still in his belted monk's gown, sat before the fire in Joanna's elegant outer chamber, sipping barley water.

"Most restorative," said Jean-Pierre. He leaned back in his chair, stretched out his legs toward the hearth and closed his eyes for a moment, then sat up straight. "Now, my dear, I think I know what's on your mind. Something to do with the motivations of our host, Count Jules, and our guide, Count Raymond?"

"Exactly! Much as I like him, I can't help wondering why Count Jules is taking such an interest in Richard's plight. And why is he being so kind to us?"

"As to your second question, I've learned already that Count Jules is inclined to take in, feed and lodge any who come to his door. He's proud of his 'humble abode,' out here in a region that's off the beaten path and where one least expects to find anybody with such elevated tastes. Some of his motivation is because he loves to play lord of the manor, especially to royalty. But most is because he is by his nature an open-hearted, generous man."

"And there are few enough such men in the world, in my experience."

"Ah Joanna, you're far too young to be a cynic. Leave that to men of my generation who've been observing humankind for decades."

"But you're not cynical, dear Jean-Pierre. I've never known anyone with more faith in the power of men to redeem themselves—with God's help of course. But let's go on. Why is the count so willing to help get Richard freed? I don't believe he's ever even met him."

"It may be as simple as this: Jules is deeply opposed to war and its devastation. There aren't many who feel as he does and he doesn't talk about it much. But he's seen its effects close up. He told us that he himself had to fight for King Philip in one of his wars with Richard's father, King Henry—a series of bloody affairs that didn't settle anything. Later, Count Jules lost his oldest son in a similar battle. And then, his remaining son died only two years ago in the Crusade. So he tries in his own way to prevent other parents from suffering what he's been through. In the present case, he sees conflict as more and more likely the longer Richard is a prisoner. Not only is England poised to take arms against the emperor. In addition, Richard has many potential allies right in the emperor's back yard. The restive German princes would need very little provocation to rise against their nominal ruler."

He paused for breath and to take a sip of his barley water. "As to the motivations of Count Raymond, that's a different matter. He's a close-mouthed man who doesn't volunteer much about what he thinks or believes in, if indeed he has any beliefs. But from what I've been able to pick up here and there"—he paused and peered into his goblet, as though seeking the right words—"it goes like this." He held up his hand and ticked off the items on his fingers as he recounted them.

"One. Queen Eleanor asked the pope to ensure your safe conduct to Poitiers. The pope agreed. Personages at that lofty level are happy to do favors for each other against the day when they'll need a favor in return.

"Two. The pope knew Count Raymond was eager to rid himself of his wife. He'd asked the pope to permit him to divorce her.

"Three. The pope agreed, but for a price: Raymond must deliver you and your party safely to Queen Eleanor in Poitiers.

"Four. Raymond agreed."

"But…but…" Joanna tried to interrupt. Jean-Pierre put up his hand to stop her.

"I know, this only raises new questions. Why was he so willing, in view of the long history of hostility between Toulouse and England? Can you guess?"

She frowned and shook her head.

He held up his fifth finger.

"Five, and this is only my surmise. It may be that Raymond's choice for his next countess isn't Bourgogne, the daughter of the king of Jerusalem, as everybody supposes, but Joanna Plantagenet. The resulting alliance would certainly make life easier for the counts of Toulouse."

She stared at him in alarm.

"I'm sure this is hard for you to accept. And I may be completely wrong. But it certainly explains why Raymond is happy to please the pope—to get his dispensation, and to do a favor for Eleanor to soften her up for his proposal of marriage to you."

Joanna hugged herself as though cold, and in fact the fire had nearly gone out. She looked soberly at Jean-Pierre. "You've given me so much to think about. Let's say goodnight, and maybe everything will make more sense tomorrow."

He stood and placed his hand on her head in a gesture of blessing and comfort.

"Yes, it's very late. Sleep well, my dear. And remember, much of what I've said is only conjecture."

To Joanna's relief, she didn't lie tossing and turning, worrying herself over Jean-Pierre's words. Sleep came almost at once. But later in the night she awoke after a vivid dream. Once more she'd panicked at the prospect of falling from her horse into the stream, and once more she'd felt the tremendous gratitude and sense of security when Raymond's protective arm encircled her waist and held her until she was safe. In her dream, she'd relaxed as she felt his strength and his gentleness.

Gratefully, she fell asleep again.

54

"What! Queen Eleanor is not here?"

Joanna, standing on the marble steps of the palace in Poitiers, stared in dismay at the man standing two steps above. It was her mother's seneschal, who was in charge during his mistress's absences. During all the long, tiresome journey she'd been sustained by the prospect of seeing her mother again in the palace where she'd spent much of her childhood.

"No, she has gone to England to raise the ransom for King Richard. A messenger was sent to inform you. Apparently he failed to find you." The tight smile on the seneschal's pudgy face expressed not so much sympathy as pleasure in imparting bad news. Joanna remembered how, as a very small child, she'd disliked him for being such a killjoy. He was fatter, balder and more wrinkled now but age had not mellowed him. He was still a killjoy. What was it her mother called him? Oh yes, Alphonse. Not Sir Alphonse or Lord Alphonse. Just Alphonse.

"However," Alphonse continued, "Queen Eleanor told me exactly what plans she has for you, Queen Berengaria and Princess Beatrix. If you will follow me to the audience chamber, I shall impart them to you. Servants are waiting to conduct the rest of your party to their rooms."

Joanna beckoned to Lady Mary to join her and the four women followed the seneschal. But Count Raymond, who had been just behind Joanna, ran up the steps to address him before he disappeared into the palace. As he passed Joanna, Raymond winked. He winked!

He placed his hand deferentially on the seneschal's arm. "May I detain you one moment? I'm Raymond of Toulouse, son of the fifth count."

"Of course I know who you are," harrumphed the seneschal.

"Of course you do," said Raymond, with his most ingratiating smile. "It has been my duty and my pleasure to conduct Queen Joanna and her party from Saint-Gilles to Poitiers. Will you please report to Queen Eleanor when you see her that I have delivered them all in excellent condition, no worse for the journey and unharmed by mischief-makers or wild beasts? Furthermore, will you tell her that I am desolated not to have the opportunity to see her in person, since we have some important matters to discuss? But I will hope that after the rescue of King Richard, which I'm sure she'll conclude successfully, I'll have the pleasure of meeting with her." He looked doubtfully at the seneschal. "Do you think you can remember all that?"

Alphonse sputtered, "Indeed I can. I've delivered much more complicated messages to my lady."

"Good. Then I'll say my adieux." Raymond turned to Joanna, bowed over her hand and fixed his black eyes on her brown ones. She felt mesmerized. "I mean it—it has been a pleasure. I hope we shall encounter each other again soon." Before she could think of an answer he was gone, with a smile and a little bow to Berengaria, Beatrix and Lady Mary.

They walked toward the great hall and Joanna heard the clatter of hoofbeats as Raymond and his knights galloped down the hill from the palace precincts.

She remembered the great hall well. It was a magnificently proportioned room that served as Queen Eleanor's audience chamber as well as a banqueting hall and setting for entertainments and civic events. But today it was desolate. A few servants were replenishing the fires and sweeping the floor, but absent were the crowds that used to come here when Eleanor was in residence, holding court as the countess of Poitou.

"It's so different when my mother is here," she said to Berengaria. "You'll see, when she returns. When I was little I used to come in to watch the fine ladies and gentlemen strolling about, seeing and being seen. Some of them came to ask my mother to settle disputes. Some had favors to ask. She always sat on her throne on that dais at the end. And people came from all over to admire the frescoes." She pointed to the brilliantly colored paintings of Biblical scenes on the walls. "They're amazing!" said Berengaria. She walked over to examine Daniel facing a very fierce lion in its den. Lady Mary and Beatrix joined her.

"Ahem!" said Alphonse. "May I have your attention?"

He was sitting on the queen's ornate gilded throne. Several chairs were drawn up before him. Joanna was shocked at his effrontery. She could remember vividly how regal, how beautiful, her mother had looked when seated there. How dare this little turnip of a man dishonor the throne so? Then she saw how ridiculous he looked, his short legs dangling half a foot from the floor. His red velvet tunic did its best to contain his bulging stomach. His hands clutched the arms of the throne as though he expected it to rise into the air at any moment.

Joanna caught Lady Mary's eye and they exchanged surreptitious smiles.

The women mounted the steps and seated themselves. They had dressed with great care that morning in anticipation of meeting Queen Eleanor, arbiter of taste, fashion and much more. Joanna wore an emerald-green gown with white lace at the neckline, a close-fitting bodice, and a full skirt. Her mother had often told her that green was her best color. The others were equally dazzling. Berengaria was in dark blue silk shot with threads of silver. She and Joanna wore jeweled tiaras. Lady Mary had chosen plum-colored velvet. Only Beatrix strayed from the elegant conventionality of her companions. She wore a gown of rose silk, not quite diaphanous, that revealed more than it concealed of her full-bosomed, slender-waisted figure. She'd thrown a filmy scarf of the same hue about her shoulders, perhaps for modesty, perhaps to suggest the illusion of a blooming rose. It succeeded better at the latter than the former.

Joanna was reminded of her onetime friend Yasmin and how they used to comment on the gowns of the ladies of the court in Palermo. She'd have had much to say about Beatrix! But I'm being unkind, she decided. The poor girl thought she was going to find herself in the midst of a throng of elegant ladies and gentlemen gathered by Queen Eleanor and she had dressed to impress them. And now there was no one to admire her except Alphonse. But he hardly glanced at her as he unrolled a long parchment and peered at it nearsightedly. He read without inflection and without looking up.

"These are the wishes of Eleanor, Queen of England, Duchess of Aquitaine and Countess of Poitou.

"In my absence from Poitiers, I desire that my daughter, Queen Joanna, remain in the palace and represent me in dealing with my subjects and their petitions. She will also provide hospitality to visitors, preside at meetings of my council and in all matters act in my place. She will have the guidance and assistance of Alphonse, my seneschal, and Lord LeBrun, my chancellor." Joanna had never met or heard of Lord LeBrun, but resolved that he would be the main source of her guidance and assistance. "As to her personal affairs, she is to have the services and companionship of two of my ladies in waiting, who reside in the palace: Lady Nicole Duvalier and Lady Mireille de Montfort. Also, Lady Adelaide Bourneville will arrive shortly from Fontevraud Abbey to attend Queen Joanna. Next, …"

"Lady Adelaide!" cried Joanna. "My Lady Adelaide, who was with me in Sicily?"

Alphonse looked up from his parchment, placing a finger on the spot where he'd stopped reading. He looked at Joanna severely. "I don't know whose Lady Adelaide she is or whether she's ever been to Sicily. All I know is that she'll arrive the day after tomorrow."

Joanna was touched. Her mother had rightly guessed she'd welcome an old friend in this demanding new life that faced her. Though she and Adelaide had never been really close or had much in common, she'd been fond of her. And they shared many memories of those long-ago days when they'd journeyed to the unknown realm of Sicily. Joanna smiled when she remembered how the blandishments of her uncle Earl Hamelin had seduced naïve Adelaide into believing he meant to marry her. Though it was funny now, it hadn't been then.

Alphonse was again bent over his document, droning on. Something about Beatrix.

"…the princess, being the ward of King Richard, is to remain in Poitiers under the care of Queen Joanna until my return with Richard, when we will begin negotiations for a suitable marriage. In the meantime, I ask my daughter to provide opportunities for Beatrix to meet and mingle with the local nobility and to become accustomed to the ways of the court."

All eyes were on Beatrix to see how she reacted to this news. She'd been looking glum and uninterested until her name was mentioned. Now she brightened. In fact, she was sparkling with anticipation. "Oh Joanna," she exclaimed, "Does this mean we'll have dancing and music? Minstrels? How soon will it begin?"

Joanna laughed but in truth she was dismayed. It seemed her mother was asking a great deal of her. She could manage the council meetings and entertaining distinguished visitors. She'd had plenty of experience with that as queen of Sicily. But serving as nursemaid and duenna to a flighty, quick-tempered and extraordinarily attractive young woman—was she up to it? She'd have to discuss the charge with Berengaria. Between them they should be able to keep Beatrix out of harm's way. And there were all those ladies in waiting. They'd need something to keep them occupied, wouldn't they? Let them play chaperone!

Alphonse was reading what Eleanor had to say about Richard.

"As you know, the price that the emperor is exacting for Richard's freedom is enormous. During the next few months I shall be traveling throughout England as well as our domains in France to raise it. The loyal people of Poitiers have been generous, but if there is any opportunity to encourage further contributions, it should be acted on. This will fall mostly on Joanna's shoulders, for I have arranged for a castle in Beaufort, three days' journey to the north in Anjou, to be prepared for Berengaria. It is time Berengaria had her own residence and her own court. The castle has belonged to our family for centuries and, though small, should prove satisfactory when repairs are completed. I am sending Lady Héloise de Mainteville to serve as Berengaria's lady-in-waiting. At Beaufort, Berengaria will await Richard's release and there, God willing, she will welcome him to a resumption of their married life."

Joanna and Berengaria looked at each other in alarm. They'd both assumed they'd take up residence in Poitiers. They didn't wish to be separated, much less by a three days' journey.

Before they could protest, Jean-Pierre wandered in, looking meek and harmless in his brown monk's robe. Alphonse regarded him suspiciously.

"May we assist you, brother?"

"I came in only for nostalgia's sake, to take a look at Queen Eleanor's audience chamber. I haven't seen it for thirty years. But I see you're busy. I'll come back later."

Joanna hurried to intervene. "This is Brother Jean-Pierre," she told Alphonse. "My mother appointed him to serve me when I left England and he's been with me ever since. I suggest you ask him to join our group."

"Ah yes. Jean-Pierre, Jean-Pierre..." The seneschal was running his fingers down the parchment, peering at it. "I know Queen Eleanor mentioned him. Yes, here he is."

"And what does my queen propose for me?"

"Finally, to my loyal friend and onetime diligent tutor to my children, Brother Jean-Pierre, I send greetings and request him to join me in England as soon as possible. His tact and his wide acquaintance with the religious community will prove valuable when we appeal to the monasteries and abbeys for contributions to Richard's ransom."

Another shock. It seemed the whole group of those Joanna held most dear was to be scattered. She looked with dislike at the bearer of these ill tidings. He had rolled up the parchment and was sitting smugly, as though waiting for commendation. She felt more like berating him. But it wasn't his doing—it was her mother who had rearranged her life so drastically.

There was to be even more scattering.

She left the great hall and, discouraged and drooping, walked along the path that led to her tower apartment. Dusk was coming on. She was startled by a large figure that loomed before her. It was Sir Alan with Federico behind him.

"My lady!" said Alan, "I'm glad to have caught you. We've come to say good-bye."

"No! I won't have it! Not you as well!"

By now she was near tears. But she collected herself.

"I'm sorry, it's just that everybody seems to be deserting me." She managed a smile and took Federico's arm. How he'd grown—taller now than she was. She had to look up to him.

"Now walk along with me and explain yourselves."

"I beg your forgiveness. I shouldn't have spoken so hastily," said Alan. "But we're rather in a hurry. We must leave this evening if we're to make connections with a boat that leaves next week for Dover."

"Dover! So you're returning to England? Why now?"

"Partly because of family affairs. I've had word that my old father is near death and I wish to see him once more. Then I'll need to help my brothers in settling the estate. And then…"

"And then," said Federico, breaking away from Joanna and looking at her with more excitement and pride than she'd seen since he first toppled the straw man when he was learning jousting, "then I'm to be made a knight by King Richard! Sir Alan says he can arrange it. But we must be there when the king disembarks, because he'll be so busy right away with his coronation."

"His coronation? I've heard nothing about any coronation. He's already been crowned king of England. Why a repeat?"

"It's only a rumor, my lady," said Sir Alan, "but we've heard that as soon as Queen Eleanor pays the ransom and Richard is freed they'll leave for England. Then they'll have the coronation so that King Richard can appear before his subjects and thank them for their generosity in contributing so much to the price of his freedom. We heard about it from a German merchant whom Brother Jean-Pierre met yesterday. He said it was all the talk of Vienna."

"I see. It does make sense. A grand, spectacular coronation would be just the thing. The people will feel they've gotten something for their money."

They walked on for a few moments in silence. Joanna took some comfort in observing that though her life was changing radically, the palace grounds were much as she remembered. Here was the rose garden, her mother's pride. Here were the three apricot trees espaliered against a sun-warmed wall, three times as tall as she remembered. They'd finished blooming and she could see tiny green fruit hanging from the branches. And here were the shiny-leaved laurel hedges where she'd played hide-and-seek with her little brother John. Even then he'd shown signs of the mean man he would become. He'd hide, than jump out at her with a terrible screech, a face contorted with menace and as often as not a painful squeeze of her arm.

The thought of John brought her back to the present. John was still making as much trouble for Richard as he could, in France as well as England. Of course Richard should have a great show of a coronation to demonstrate to one and all that he was their king and that he was back.

"Yes, I understand why you must go. It's time for all of Richard's loyal soldiers to rally around him and show their support."

She took Sir Alan's hand. "I'll miss you, though. You've been such a stalwart friend for so many years, my mainstay through all kinds of trials." Tears welled in her eyes. She wished she could keep from crying at times like this.

Now she had to say goodbye to Federico, to the boy she'd known and loved so well, so long. He was about to become someone else, someone whose life she couldn't share. How long ago it seemed that Jean-Pierre brought the bright-eyed, black-haired little gamin to the palace to be her page! He was still bright-eyed and still had his curly black hair. But now she wouldn't think of tousling it as she used to do. He'd be terribly embarrassed. At sixteen, on the verge of manhood, he'd reached the age of self-consciousness.

But she could hug him and she did. He hugged her back. He too was moved. She distinctly heard a sniff.

"I've so much to thank you for, my lady," he said huskily. "And when I'm a knight in King Richard's service my first aim will be to make you proud of me."

She held him at arms' length, looking up at him, smiling in spite of the tears coursing down her cheeks.

"Yes, you'll be my knight in shining armor…Armor!" She turned to Sir Alan. "He'll need armor, won't he? And a fine steel sword from Damascus, and a jeweled scabbard, and a strapping big horse… Oh, why didn't I think of this sooner? Sir Alan, let me know how much all this will cost and it will be my pleasure to supply it."

Sir Alan, who had been fidgeting, eager to be off, looked at her in doubt, then relief. "Do you mean it? Then I thank you. I'll admit I've been worrying a wee bit about outfitting the lad properly. I promise when you see him in a month or two in England, he'll be the knight in the shiniest armor in the realm. But now we must go."

She waved farewell, wiped her tears away and walked slowly up to her room where Jeanette, the maid her mother had designated for her, would be waiting to help her out of her finery. She was tired, so tired. She wanted only to lie down and try to get used to the new state of affairs.

The freeing of Richard took far longer than anyone expected. Eleanor pled with the pope, who temporized and did nothing. Nor did he reply to the letters

Joanna and Berengaria sent him. Even Constance, Joanna's old friend, was silent. Joanna supposed that when one is married to the Holy Roman Emperor one may lose the freedom to take independent action.

Meantime Eleanor concentrated on raising the ransom. She journeyed up and down England, sent emissaries to Anjou and Aquitaine. She taxed the barons a fourth of their annual income and lesser subjects on a descending scale. No one was spared. She persuaded churches and monasteries to give up their gold and silver vessels, their precious reliquaries and altar crosses, their treasure accumulated over the centuries. When at last the tireless queen had amassed the 100,000 marks, it was December 1193. She hastened to Germany, but even then Emperor Henry's parleys and negotiations delayed the freeing of the prisoner.

Finally in February 1194 Richard was at liberty. Mother and son set off for England, not stopping in Poitiers for Joanna nor in Beaufort for Berengaria. When the coronation took place during the Easter season of 1194 in Winchester Cathedral, neither Richard's wife nor his sister was there to witness it.

The news didn't reach Poitiers until the end of April. By then Berengaria was long gone, settled in the castle at Beaufort. Joanna wrote to her:

My dear sister,

I have had a letter from my mother with an account of Richard's triumphant arrival in England and of his coronation. It seems to have been as magnificent as everyone had hoped. My brother wore a sumptuous red cloak with a train, all embroidered with gold and trimmed in ermine. I can imagine him striding down the aisle, while a pair of little pages charged with bearing the train scurried to keep up with him! He loves to dress himself in the royal regalia and show himself to his subjects. The archbishop of Canterbury placed the crown on his head and he then ascended his throne and sat there during the mass. My mother saw it all from a special dais.

I'm sure you'll wonder why we weren't there. Queen Eleanor wrote that she still depended on me to take her place here in Poitiers, implying that I was more useful to her in France than in England. So be it. As for you, she said only that she and Richard would be returning in a few weeks and, though she had no doubt that he would join you as soon as possible, his first concern will be to recover the lands Philip has seized.

Since you left, we have managed to hold two banquets and to enjoy performances by a group of jugglers and any number of itinerant musicians. I am fortunate that Eleanor's chancellor, Lord LeBrun, is a very social person and enjoys organizing things. So do the two resident ladies in waiting, Nicole and Mireille. So Beatrix has had her fill of gaiety and admiration. Two young noblemen are acting very much like serious suitors, but anything along those lines will have to wait until my mother returns. My old friend Lady Adelaide has taken on the role of duenna and is doing her best to teach Beatrix the finer points of adult behavior. I do believe I observe a little less pouting and temper and a little more consideration for others.

I was very sad for some weeks after saying goodbye to Federico, Jean-Pierre and Alan and then to you. I felt quite deserted! But thanks to the passage of time and to Lady

Mary's good sense and understanding, now I am more myself. All it would take to complete my contentment would be a visit from you. Please send word that you are coming.
Joanna

Below the letter Joanna added a hastily written postscript.

Just as the messenger was about to leave with this, we had astonishing news. Raymond of Toulouse finally received the pope's permission to dissolve his marriage. He immediately married Bourgogne de Lusignan, daughter of the king of Jerusalem! I think I am relieved—it removes many uncertainties about my future—but I long to discuss this and so much more with you. J.

55

In due time Queen Eleanor returned to Poitiers, after a triumphal progression through England and its dominions with Richard. By now mother and son performed as a smoothly operating team, showing themselves to their subjects, thanking them for their support in freeing Richard and demonstrating as publicly as possible who was in charge: King Richard, not the would-be usurper John.

When they arrived at the palace, Richard took his mother directly to her own chambers in the south tower. Here, rather than in the intimidating great hall, was Eleanor's favorite place in the whole palace, her elegant little reception room. Here she was surrounded by beauty and comfort and all the precious objects that meant so much to her. Here was her gilded, jeweled Bible on its polished ebony stand. Here were four ornate silver candelabra, each bearing twelve creamy beeswax candles that cast a soft golden glow over the room. The candelabra had been a present from her husband, King Henry, when they'd been young and in love. And here was her favorite chair, almost a throne in its generous dimensions but far more comfortable, with its goosedown-stuffed pillows covered in smoothest scarlet silk. Eleanor relinquished Richard's arm and sank into the welcoming softness.

Joanna had meant to be in the room waiting for them but Alphonse stopped her on the way with some inconsequential question. She hurried on and entered almost at a run but caught herself before her mother could look down her nose at such unseemly haste.

Why can't I remember that I'm a twenty-nine-year-old woman? she chided herself. Maybe I'm reverting to my childhood when I tried so desperately not to displease my mother by being late.

She embraced Eleanor. She observed few signs of aging, though in the four years since they'd said farewell at the harbor in Messina, Eleanor's seventy-two years had begun to catch up with her. There were tiny wrinkles radiating from the corners of her eyes. But the finely chiseled features of her face and the ivory-white complexion with just a hint of a rosy blush on the cheeks were those of a woman half her age. The blue eyes flashed as piercingly as ever.

"My dear daughter," said the queen, pressing Joanna's hand in both of hers and looking up at her with affection, "at last we meet again. How well you look! Sit here beside me. You must tell me all the news of the court and the city. I'm particularly interested in Beatrix. How has she taken to life here in the palace? Is she behaving herself?" Joanna wondered if her mother had received some hint from Richard about his escapade with Beatrix in the Holy Land. But she felt it wise not to bring it up.

"She seems to thrive on the busy social life we lead, for which we have your chancellor, Lord LeBrun, and your ladies to thank. They've made it their mission to show her the best of the local society. She's had an opportunity to meet most of the eligible young men in Poitou, and two young nobles appear to be seriously interested. I believe her current favorite is Raoul de Roqueville. He's quite devoted to her."

"Never heard of him. I hope her life isn't one long round of frivolity. Is she learning anything?"

"Well, Lady Mary is teaching her embroidery, and Lady Adelaide does her best to instruct the princess in decorum. In fact they're even now spending a week in Fontevraud Abbey, which Lady Adelaide felt would be a beneficial respite from all the music and dancing and banqueting. They'll be back the day after tomorrow. I think I can assure you that her virtue has not been imperiled."

Eleanor nodded. "Thank you, daughter. You've done well. Before long I hope we'll be able to choose a suitable husband and get the girl securely wed."

"Mother, I've been wondering why you take such an interest in Beatrix? You've never even met her. And her father was really an imposter. He called himself emperor of Cyprus but Richard defeated him and stripped him of the title."

"True, true. But as daughter and heir of an emperor, no matter how dead or deposed he is, she has an attraction for ambitious men. Can't you imagine it? An unscrupulous noble or minor royal takes her to wife and then lays claim to the island of Cyprus in her name. This could cause all kinds of trouble for us. We must maintain our hegemony there because it's vital to our interests in Palestine. So we take no chances. We choose for the girl's husband some influential count or duke here in France who doesn't give a fig for Cyprus and who will support us in our wars with King Philip."

"I suppose that makes sense. I hope Raoul de Roqueville will meet your specifications."

"Whether he does or doesn't, I don't anticipate much trouble from her. She's young, she's impressionable and she owes her freedom and her position to us. I expect her to be quite amenable to our choice. Richard and I have discussed this and we already have several names on our list. Which reminds me—where is Richard? I must have a few words with him. He insists he must leave tomorrow morning to assemble the troops he'll need to keep Philip from besieging Rouen. Richard! Now where can he have gone?"

Her tall son rose from a bench in a shadowy corner and loomed over them, yawning mightily and rubbing his eyes. "Just getting caught up on my sleep, mother. You've kept me going at such a merry pace these past few weeks, I'm quite worn out." Richard, like many a soldier and sailor, had developed the ability to snatch a few minutes of sleep whenever the occasion permitted.

Joanna jumped up to greet him. Just as he'd always done since she was a little girl, he picked her up and gave her a bear hug. She giggled, then gasped. "Richard! You're squeezing all the air out of me!" He set her down as gently as though she were a delicate crystal goblet.

"Sorry, little sister. But I'm so glad to see you! You seem to have survived your trip home from the Holy Land very well—I wish I could say the same."

"But Richard, you look to be in excellent health, though—how shall I put it— you seem somewhat…"

"Somewhat bulky, not to say fat," broke in Queen Eleanor drily. "Your captors must have fed you very well."

"Never mind," said Richard. "I'll soon be back in the saddle, rounding up my troops and chasing Philip from pillar to post. You'll see, in no time I'll be as lean as a willow sapling."

"Yes, we'll see. But we have more immediate concerns. Sit down, both of you." She indicated the chairs on either side of her own, facing the fire. A servant came in and adjusted the logs. "Thank you, Henri," said Eleanor. "And will you bring us some *hypocras*?"

"If you don't mind, mother, I'd rather have good red claret instead of that sweetened wine you favor. And Henri"— he turned his persuasive smile on the lad—"you're a clever fellow, I can tell. Would you see if you could find some of those little jellied quince candies the cook used to make? *Cotignac*, I think we called them."

Henri, who'd never before seen the far-famed Richard the Lionheart, nodded, blurted "Of course, my lord King," and scurried out, captivated and befuddled by the Plantagenet charm.

Richard and Joanna, waiting for their mother to speak, thought she'd fallen asleep. Her eyes were closed and she leaned her head against the cushioned chair-back. After half a minute she sat up straight and turned to Richard.

"The first thing you must do, Richard, even before you march to Rouen, is to see Count Raymond of Toulouse. The new Count Raymond, that is."

"New?" asked Joanna. "What do you mean, new?"

"Oh, haven't you heard? Raymond the Fifth died two weeks ago. Finally. It took the old fox long enough." Her lips curved slightly and she uttered a barely audible "huh, huh." It was as close as Queen Eleanor ever came to a chuckle.

Henri came in with a silver tray laden with a bowl of *cotignac*, a tall flagon of red wine and a crystal pitcher of *hypocras*. He placed them carefully on the ebony table in front of Eleanor.

"Good work, Henri," said Richard. He picked up one of the glistening little cubes and licked off its dusting of sugar. "I knew you'd find them."

"We were in luck, my lord King. The cook made a fresh batch only yesterday." He was beaming with pride of accomplishment and basking in the royal approval. What a tale he'd have to tell his wife tonight! After a poke or two at the fire he left as unobtrusively as he could.

"So." Eleanor poured the wine. "Now we have Count Raymond the Sixth to deal with, and deal with him we must, Richard, if you're to have any security on your southern borders while you do battle with Philip in the north. I believe the new count will be more receptive to an offer of alliance than his father ever was." She looked at Joanna speculatively. "In fact, I'd hoped, not long ago, that an alliance could be cemented by a marriage. But that hope didn't last long. Young Raymond lost his head over that feather-brained little Bourgogne de Lusignan and couldn't wait to marry her."

"However," said Richard, yawning again and stretching out his legs to the fire, "They've been married several years by now, I believe. If Raymond's past performance is any guide, he'll soon tire of her and start petitioning the pope to dissolve the marriage. In the meantime we can keep in touch with him and make him aware of the advantages of marrying into the royal house of England. I'll leave tomorrow for Toulouse and feel him out."

Joanna could hardly believe what she was hearing. It was as though they'd forgotten she was still in the room. Richard began to rise from his chair. She jumped to her feet and gave him a push in the midriff. He returned to a sitting position with a thud and looked at her in astonishment.

Joanna stood facing them, her brown eyes almost black as they darted from her mother to her brother. Her lips were quivering with outrage.

"Have I no say in this? Am I nothing but a pawn in your marriage games? Richard, have you forgotten your foolish attempt to marry me to that heathen prince in Palestine? What makes you think I'd be more likely to accept a fickle, womanizing count in Toulouse? You're treating me exactly as you plan to treat Beatrix. Why must women always agree meekly to what their elders decide is best for them? Why are their own preferences of no account?"

Afraid that her anger would lead to tears, she brushed her hand across her eyes and ran from the room. Eleanor and Richard looked at each other. Eleanor was the first to speak.

"Spoken like a true Plantagenet. If I'd been in her place, I might have made the same response."

"Hmph," said Richard, rubbing his stomach. "If you'd been in my place, you might wonder where that delicate little person found the strength for such a blow." He chewed slowly on a quince jelly. "Nevertheless, when I see Count Raymond I'll broach the subject of an alliance and do my best to learn his views."

Later, Joanna told Lady Mary about the incident. As they often did, they were having a chat in Joanna's chamber before retiring. Joanna had propped her legs on a footstool. Both had changed to their loose-flowing nightrobes. They were sipping spiced wine, considerably diluted with hot water. The fire, recently replenished, crackled companionably on the hearth, a third party to the conversation.

"Maybe I was too headstrong," said Joanna. "And maybe I was too hard on Raymond. It's true he rather led me on about his intentions and then went chasing after that Bourgogne. But as Lady Marian used to tell me, that's the way men are and we might as well accept it. What I can't accept, though, is not being consulted by my mother and my brother about something that affects me so deeply,"

She walked to the fire, gazed at the flames for a minute and returned to her chair. Sipping her wine, she looked at her friend's face, so familiar, so concerned.

"Forgive me, Mary, for running on like this. You have your own worries. Is there any more word from Sir Stephen?"

Mary's suitor, the knight whom she'd met in Sicily, hadn't been heard from since he'd sent a message that he'd finally arrived home from the Crusades and would come to Poitiers soon. That message came six months ago. "I had many adventures and misadventures on the way home," he'd written. "But what kept me going, my dear Mary, was the prospect of seeing you and setting a date for our marriage, if you'll still have me."

Mary shook her head.

"No, nothing since that one message."

There was a knock but before they could answer, Richard came in. Typically, he made no reference to the recent confrontation. His active mind had moved far ahead to other matters.

He nodded to Mary and sat down besides Joanna. "I'm sorry to intrude so late, but I probably won't see you in the morning before I leave. When I head north I'll make a detour to Beaufort to call on Berengaria. Can you tell me how she is?"

"I was wondering when you'd ask. As far as I know she's well. I visited her in Beaufort this summer and she was here for two weeks in September. But when I asked her to come again she replied that she thought she should stay there, in case you came looking for her. I'm glad you plan to do so. She seems contented enough but I know she worries when she doesn't hear from you."

"Well yes, I've been remiss on that score. Our mother says so too, and practically ordered me to go see her. So I shall."

"Please give her my best love when you do, and tell her she's always welcome at Poitiers."

"Certainly. I'll do it. Goodbye and be well, little sister. And you too, Lady Mary." And he was off.

Joanna sighed. "He hasn't been much of a husband for Berengaria. I'm not surprised my mother insisted he go to Beaufort. She's been after him ever since they married to take his conjugal duties more seriously and see that an heir is produced. "

"It's strange, isn't it? She's such a lovely woman, and he's so—may I say lusty?"

"You may. And it is strange. I suppose the lesson is that my mother should have talked it over with him before she decided who his bride should be."

She looked up to see Mary trying to hide a smile.

"Now what do you find so amusing?"

"It's just that two minutes ago you were complaining about how women have no say when others choose their husbands. Now you explain away Richard's behavior for the same reason: he wasn't allowed to choose his wife. So do men whose marriages are arranged deserve sympathy as well?"

Joanna thought a minute. "Clever argument. I see what you mean. But it's not quite the same. A man like Richard can go blithely along, sort of pretending that he isn't married and nobody thinks the worse of him. A woman can't do that; I certainly couldn't do that. I'd be frowned on and ostracized."

"I suppose so. But it's late and we aren't going to solve any of these problems tonight. Shall I brush your hair, my lady? You might find it restful."

"Oh, please do. Maybe you'll untangle some of the snarls inside my head, too."

The rhythmic strokes of the brush and the tune Mary was humming made her drowsy. When she climbed into bed, Mary pulled up the warm woolen coverlet and they exchanged "Good nights."

Just before Mary closed the door she heard Joanna say sleepily, "Just the same, Mary, sometimes it's enough to make me wish I'd been born a man."

56

December 20, 1195. One of those rare days when Nature shows how benign she can be despite the season. The temperature was below freezing but no wintry wind blew, not even a breath of a breeze. The sun beamed as cheerfully as in midsummer. A light snow had fallen the night before and the whole city of Poitiers wore a dusting of glittering white. The townspeople seized the opportunity to wrap themselves in woolen coats and scarves, pull scarlet caps over their ears and go out to stroll and enjoy the scene.

Joanna heard the crunch of the snow under their boots and their cheery greetings as an annoying distraction. She was sitting at a small table near the window of her tower room, frowning as she pored over a sheet of parchment. She wasn't in the least charmed by Nature's benignity. She was, in fact, quite cross.

"Oh dear, why am I so stupid? Why can't I make it out?"

Her maid Jeanette, new to her service, got up from where she was working on her embroidery and looked over her mistress's shoulder.

"Don't call yourself stupid, my lady. Who could make sense of all those strange squiggles?"

"It's Arabic. A few years ago I could have read it easily. But I've forgotten so much! How I miss William!"

She'd been feeling depressed and at loose ends and thought getting out her Arabic lessons would prove a distraction. But they only reminded her of happier days long gone. The palace was quiet—too quiet. Queen Eleanor was in Tours, dealing with a recalcitrant bishop who refused to pay the church's fair share of taxes. Adelaide and Mary had gone to Fontevraud Abbey for a few days. They'd asked Joanna to go too but Richard had sent word he intended to come to Poitiers for Christmas and host a banquet. He'd said he'd arrive today and she wanted to be there to greet him. She was eager to see him, after nearly a year. He could always find a way to cheer her up when she was downhearted.

She put the parchment away and walked restlessly up and down the room. Like her mother, she had made her quarters in the palace a reflection of her individual taste in furnishings and décor. But where Eleanor valued elegance more than comfort, Joanna clung to the Arabic notion that comfort is paramount and even better when combined with brilliant color and furnishings to give the discriminating eye something to feast on. She'd commissioned a skilled craftsman to create a screen like the wonderfully worked Arabic ones she'd so admired in Sicily. With this she partitioned off half of her spacious reception room and here, in miniature, was a re-creation of her apartment in the royal palace in Palermo. Well-cushioned benches lined the walls. Large puffy pillows were scattered on the pale-blue carpet in lieu of chairs. She changed the color scheme sometimes. Today the pillows were indigo blue, magenta and deep purple. Out of consideration for those who might not care to sit on the floor, she'd added a pair of ottomans, covered in dove-gray wool.

She settled herself on a purple pillow because, though there was nobody but herself to admire the effect, it went so well with her violet gown.

She heard a knock at the door. Richard at last!

But instead of the roar of the Lionheart, "Ho there! Where's my little sister?" she heard only Jeanette's "Yes, in here," then the rustle of skirts. A dear, familiar face peeped around the screen and Joanna sprang to her feet, overcome with joy.

"Berengaria! But what... why... where...?"

There was a confused flurry while Jeanette helped Berengaria out of her cloak and gloves, Joanna kept asking questions and Berengaria tried to reply through the wool shawl that she was pulling over her head. Finally the two friends were seated side by side, each on her pillow, crosslegged, with skirts spread decorously. Jeanette brought two pewter mugs and a pitcher of mulled wine and placed them on a low table between them.

"How lovely and warm it is in here!" said Berengaria. She squirmed a little, getting comfortable, and looked around appreciatively. "Braziers everywhere. We've had such a cold ride today, but this is heavenly." She sipped her wine. "Mmmm. Now I take it from your surprise that Richard didn't tell you I was coming?"

"Not a word. He said only that he planned to celebrate Christmas at Poitiers. I supposed he was still being the neglectful husband and I determined to scold him again. But here you are! Can you tell me how things are with you two these days?"

"I can, gladly." Her face, already glowing from the warmth, turned even pinker. "Joanna, I've never been so happy!"

She poured out her story while Joanna listened in amazement.

Three weeks ago Richard had appeared at Beaufort, completely unannounced. He'd said he intended to spend some time there shoring up the castle walls, which he said had been disgracefully neglected. "And so have you, my queen." His whole attitude toward her had changed. Gone were the impersonal politeness, the perfunctory attention. He was loving and thoughtful.

"For the first time, I feel Richard really cares for me. He's a different person. He's the husband I'd dreamed of but never knew."

"What could have caused such a change?" marveled Joanna.

"I don't know and I don't care. I'm just going to be happy with this new Richard."

Joanna had misgivings. This was so unlike her brother. But she pushed them aside.

"And I shall be happy for you." She stood up, stretched and pulled Berengaria to her feet. "I can see you're not comfortable with my exotic eastern seating arrangements. Let's move to the windowseat and you'll tell me more."

"No, first you must tell me about your own affairs." When they were seated she took her friend's hand and looked at her searchingly. "You're looking pale and strained, it seems to me. Are you worried about something? Are you unwell?"

Joanna sighed. "I'm perfectly well. But lately I've been feeling rather lost, almost friendless. Much as I love Mary and Adelaide I can't confide in them as I can with you. But you're so far away! My mother is always traveling hither and yon and even when she's in Poitiers she hasn't much time for me. I need someone to be close to. And there's no one."

"You don't need another woman friend. You need a man." Berengaria spoke with the assurance of one who has her man. "In my opinion, you've been comparing everyone you met with your William and nobody ever measured up. Am I right?"

"I suppose you are. My mother, when she thinks of it, tries to interest me in some prince or duke who she says would make a valuable ally for our royal house. But he's usually twenty years older than I am, or has a harelip, or talks about nothing but battles, or doesn't talk at all. She had a much easier time getting Beatrix married off."

"So that's happened at last, has it? Is the princess content with her new husband?"

"More than content. She's been smitten with him and he with her ever since they met six months ago. It was a miracle that Eleanor agreed that he'd do."

"And what are his qualifications for this desirable alliance?"

"He's wealthy, for one thing, which Beatrix, in spite of being a princess, definitely isn't. He has enormous land holdings, including some very profitable vineyards near Bordeaux. He fought in the Crusade, which pleases Richard. And since Beatrix is Richard's ward, Richard must be pleased. Finally, he's only five years older than his bride, and reasonably handsome."

"You almost sound as though you wish he were *your* husband."

"Mother in Heaven, no! His idea of a conversation is a monologue about how he couldn't decide between a gold belt buckle or a silver one when he was dressing; or how much trouble he's having training his new horse to be a good hunter. Beatrix, bless her, hangs on his every word and contributes the occasional 'Really!' or 'Oh dear!' or 'How clever of you!' They're meant for each other."

"Well then, we'll have to look elsewhere for the man meant for you. Richard dropped a few hints that he has some ideas about that."

"He did, did he? His record at trying to marry me off isn't too good. By the way, where is Richard? Why didn't he come here with you?"

"He wanted to walk about outside to make sure the palace walls were in good shape. He said he'd join us here in time for supper."

At that very moment Richard had entered the palace and stood unobserved in the doorway of Queen Eleanor's great hall. He watched as Jacques Blom hung the last of one hundred pine boughs from its peg in the wall.

Jacques, the poulteror's son, had been charged with decorating the hall for the Christmas festivities. He was pleased because he'd finished well ahead of schedule. He stretched to get the kinks out of his neck and arms and stood back to admire the effect. The spicy scent of pine filled the air.

"Not like that, you numbskull!"

He jumped and turned around to see the seneschal Alphonse looking even more disapproving than usual.

"You'll have to do them all over again. They're supposed to be right side up like trees in a forest, not hanging down droopily like so many wet nightshirts on a clothesline. What will King Richard think?"

"What will King Richard think of what?"

There he stood, the Lionheart himself, his hand placed jauntily on his hip and his blue eyes glinting with amusement.

"Oh my lord King, I beg your pardon. I didn't know you were here." Alphonse spoke respectfully. Richard was the only person besides Queen Eleanor to whom he showed deference.

"Well, of course not. I've only just come in. Now as I see it, you're trying to create the illusion that we're in a forest. Excellent concept. I suggest we bring in some live pine trees and place them in big tubs along the walls. We'll leave the pine boughs as they are—they'll make a nice green woodsy background." He turned to Jacques. "What's your name, my lad?"

"Jacques Blom." He was almost tongue-tied with awe at the royal presence but he managed to keep his voice from trembling.

"Very well, Jacques. You seem a knowledgeable lad. Do you know the Forest of Vouillé?"

"Oh yes—my father used to take me hunting there when I was a boy..." He suddenly remembered that the Forest of Vouillé was a royal preserve. Was the king going to accuse him of poaching, all those years ago?

But Richard was imbued with the seasonal spirit of peace and goodwill as well as the lingering euphoria produced by an excellent wine at his dinner. He contented himself with a dry "Oh he did, did he?" and went on. "Then you may recall a fine stand of pines at the eastern edge of the forest. Tomorrow you can lead a work party out there and dig up a few score of the smaller trees. But not too small—they should reach at least halfway to the ceiling. I'll send a crew of my knights to do the digging. It'll do them good to get some fresh air and exercise instead of carousing in the wineshops. Can you handle that, do you think, Jacques?"

"I'm sure I can." His self-confidence shot up. "And we'll need a good many carts and mules to get the trees here."

"So you will. Good thinking. Alphonse my friend, you can arrange that, can't you?"

"Yes, of course." Not my usual line of work, he thought. But I'll turn it over to the drayman.

Richard looked around, envisioning the pine forest that would soon transform the room. But something was missing.

"Birds!" he exclaimed. "Any self-respecting forest has birds, flocks of the little rascals, flitting about and twittering. How could we manage that?"

Alphonse looked appalled. Birds were definitely not his line of work.

"But maybe not," said Richard. "They might fly over the guests during dinner and, um...." He sought a euphemism.

"Crap on them," said Jacques helpfully.

"Exactly. So, no birds. Thanks, my friends. I'll expect to see what you've accomplished in a couple of days. And Alphonse, please arrange for supper to be served in half an hour in Queen Joanna's apartments for myself, my wife and my sister. After supper I'll go over the guest list for my banquet with you. You must tell me who has accepted the invitations I asked you to send."

Having successfully launched the Forest of Vouillé project, he was already engaged in planning the next campaign. There was one name in particular he wanted to make sure was on the list of acceptances: Count Raymond of Toulouse.

57

King Richard's Christmas banquet was beginning very merrily. The roast suckling pig had been borne in and consumed down to the trotters. The pork custard had been indifferently received, but its accompanying saffron rice, golden and studded with raisins, met universal approval. Everybody was waiting eagerly for the next course, having heard rumors that Richard and the chef had devised something quite out of the ordinary.

Meantime the noise level in the great hall rose steadily. Half a hundred knights, nobles and their ladies, ranged along the two long tables that formed the arms of the U-shaped seating, found more and more to say or shout to each other as the servants kept their wine goblets full.

Yet it could have been worse, Joanna reflected from the head table on the dais. She was impressed with Richard's pine forest, which muffled the sound that would otherwise have been bouncing off the stone walls. She could actually hear the musicians, a trio of flute, vielle and drum who perched on stools in the open area between the long tables. Their costumes were as cheery as their tunes: the flautist in a green tunic with chestnut-colored leggings, the drummer in red festooned with gold braid, and the viellist in red and green stripes. The flautist played with concentration, seldom raising his eyes. The viellist swayed back and forth as he drew the bow across the strings, looking dreamy and carried away by the sweet tones. The man with the tabor was the liveliest. He beat on his little drum energetically and bounced up and down on his stool, grinning infectiously at the audience. Joanna felt a little like bouncing too. She'd been looking forward to this festive event, such a contrast to what had become for her a rather dull existence.

She was on Richard's left and Berengaria sat on his right. Queen Eleanor, pleading the need for rest, had stayed in Fontevraud. This was just as well, since the presence of three queens would have made for a knotty seating problem.

The chair on Joanna's other side was still empty. When she asked Richard why, he said mysteriously, "You'll find out soon enough," which was no help. He turned back to Berengaria, whom he was plying with toasted walnuts and plump red grapes. Observing him, Joanna had to admit that he was transformed. When he filled Berengaria's wineglass and urged her, "Drink up, my love. We have the whole evening and the whole night ahead of us," Joanna wondered: was there something false in his tone? Was he play-acting? But when she leaned forward and saw Berengaria's face, so full of love and trust, she hoped she was mistaken and persuaded herself that she was. It was Christmastime, the season for good cheer and optimism, not for suspicion.

A clamor behind the door to the kitchens got everybody's attention.

"Go! Go now!" somebody cried. It sounded like a very nervous Alphonse. The door was flung open and Alphonse pushed in a page holding the Plantagenet pennant with its three rampant lions. Behind the page marched a trumpeter in the red-and-gold Plantagenet livery. His bold military tune was so loud that it drowned out the conversation, which shortly ceased altogether and gave way to gasps as eighteen knights in armor emerged from the pine forest and marched around the tables in single file, each bearing a spear held upright. Impaled on each spear was a roasted pheasant, still feathered in luminous gold and green, its wings outstretched as though in flight. Big plump birds, they'd probably never gotten this far off the ground while alive. Servingmen followed and distributed silver platters along the tables. The knights carefully transferred the birds to the platters and the servingmen began to carve. The rich aroma of roasted fowl and of sage-and-sausage stuffing filled the air. The company, delighted, cheered and raised their glasses to Richard. His grin was the broadest in the room. The spectacle had gone exactly as he'd planned.

Joanna, like everybody else, was entranced. She turned to Richard and hugged him. "Congratulations, big brother! That was amazing." He laughed and said, "I thought so too," with no pretense of modesty. "But Joanna, I believe you're going to have another surprise. Look who's arrived."

Raymond of Toulouse was sliding into the empty chair on her left. He was a little breathless and disheveled, and drops of water—melted snowflakes, she supposed—spangled his black hair. He sent her a quick smile and gave her hand a squeeze. "I'm so glad to see you again. It's been too long." Before she could respond, he leaned forward to address Richard as well.

"Good evening, and my deepest apologies to you both for turning up so late. I should have given myself more time for the journey in weather like this. We ran into quite a snowstorm just as we approached Poitiers. But here I am, and I'm honored to be included at your Christmas feast."

Very proper, as always, Joanna thought. She'd already suspected that Richard the matchmaker was at it again and that Raymond might prove to be the absent guest. She was surprised at how glad she was to see him after two years. But she decided she would not be too welcoming until she learned the facts about his marital state. She'd heard rumors that Bourgogne had, like past wives, been displaced.

"We too are honored to greet you as our guest," said Richard, raising his glass in salute. "I'm sorry my mother isn't here to welcome you as well, but my sister has become very skilled at taking her place as resident queen. I'm sure she'll see that you're comfortable and entertained during your stay, as shall I. We're hunting for boar tomorrow and I hope you'll join the party."

"With pleasure," said Raymond. "Your hunting here is so much better than ours. There are few forests around Toulouse and very little game."

A servant filled his goblet and placed on his plate a generous serving of roast pheasant with a couple of glossy green feathers still attached as decoration. It was accompanied by a mound of gravy-laden dressing. After several bites, he put down his knife and looked at Joanna appreciatively.

"I've never seen you look more charming. Green is definitely your color. And what splendid emeralds! Do you mind?" Without waiting for her reply he reached to raise one of the lustrous green stones of her necklace and examine it. His fingers, warm and dry, brushed briefly across her neck. "Extraordinary—I hadn't noticed these tiny pearls in the settings. The gold chain too is of such fine workmanship." He turned back to his plate and she gave her attention to her own.

She congratulated herself for taking so much care with her attire, a sea-green gown with a low but not too low neckline, a fitted bodice and a full skirt. She reflected that few men of her acquaintance would have even noticed, or at least wouldn't have known how to articulate their appreciation. She glanced at Raymond, who was still valiantly attacking his pheasant. He put down the drumstick he'd been gnawing on and wiped his mouth with a handkerchief pulled from his pocket.

"It's a fine bird," he said, "but I suspect there's more to come and I must regretfully desist. Tell me, would you care to join us on the hunt tomorrow? If we should come upon any raging torrents I'll be happy to assist you in the crossing, but this time I'll do my best to keep your feet dry."

She hadn't thought of that incident for months but at his words the memory came back vividly. She felt again the reassurance of his strong arm around her waist as he saw her safely across the stream. It was the only time he'd ever touched her except for taking her hand at meeting or parting.

She tried to reply in a tone as light as his. "Ah, but I trust this time I'd keep better control of my horse."

"It wasn't your fault that the horse stumbled. Nobody could have foreseen that. No, you're an excellent horsewoman. So why not come along on the hunt?"

"I think not, but thank you."

Where is this conversation going? she thought. Then she remembered her resolve. Time to change the subject.

"And what a pity you didn't bring your wife. She and I could sit by the fire tomorrow feeling smug because we're so warm and cozy, unlike hunters and other foolhardy folk."

That put an end to the badinage. His face darkened and he pinched his lips together as though trying to hold back an angry reply.

"I'm sorry. Have I said something to upset you?"

"No, it's not you who's upset me. It's my worthless wife. She's decided we're incompatible. She's left me. To which I say, good riddance!"

She looked at him in surprise and concern. He was staring straight ahead, his eyes glaring as though focusing on the unfortunate Bourgogne. She'd never seen him angry. "And were you a party to the decision?"

"Indeed I was. I'd had enough of our quarrels and her nagging and fault-find-ing." With an effort he regained his composure. He smiled at her. "But this needn't concern you, except very indirectly."

How could it concern her at all, she wanted to ask.

But Richard was on his feet and bellowing. "My friends, your attention, I beg of you." After a couple of repetitions, even louder, the roar of raised voices died down and all eyes were on Richard. The musicians, after one last major chord to support his exhortations, put their instruments aside.

Joanna looked up at her brother, who was not entirely steady on his feet but grinning broadly. When in his cups he could be even more charming and eloquent than when sober.

"Thank you and welcome to our Christmas celebration. I salute the many good friends I see here. Come, drink a toast with me." Beaming, he looked up and down the tables, raised his goblet and took a healthy gulp. "I hope it has been as good a year for you as it has for myself and my kingdom. We have successfully thwarted King Philip at almost every turn, and after the Christmas truce we shall resume the good fight. We are at peace, at least for the time being, with Aquitaine's neighbors to the south, Navarre and"—he raised the goblet in Raymond's direc-tion—"Toulouse. Count Raymond, your health. We rejoice in the company of our dearly beloved queen, Berengaria"—another salute, another quaff from the goblet. Berengaria raised her own and smiled up at him, blushing.

"And we salute our dear sister Queen Joanna, whose companionship has sustained us since we were children together. We also give a special welcome to Bishop Etienne, who has guided us toward the path of righteousness and who has not become discouraged despite our occasional backsliding." He nodded to the bishop and sat down.

The bishop, a jolly man who looked as though he'd dined well at many a ban-quet, raised his goblet to Richard and sipped, then rose. "My lord King, I'm sure I speak for the entire company when I say, first of all, we thank God in His goodness for giving us the opportunity to come together and wish our king and our friends well at this holy season. And we thank you, King Richard, for this magnificent re-past in such a delightful setting! How original of you to entertain us in a veritable forest of greenery, without our having to undergo cold or wind or snow!"

Joanna was hardly listening. He seemed primed to go on interminably. She looked down to see that that the plate with the remnants of pheasant had disap-peared and been replaced by a serving of fish of some sort, glistening in its coat of aspic. She was pleased to see that the cook had given free rein to his esthetic sense. He'd decorated the fish with a swirl of bright yellow mustard sauce and ringed it with an assortment of colorful vegetables: tiny roast beets, slices of carrot, turnips carved into little balls, and over it all a sprinkling of chopped green leaves which proved to be spinach. She tasted a beet and marveled—it was sweet as a summer's day.

She saw that the bishop had subsided and was happily savoring his fish, but

Richard surveyed his plate uncertainly. After one mouthful of fish he smacked his lips and took a chance on a beet. He smacked his lips again. Scattered cheers came from the diners as they made their way through the novel display.

"Congratulations, Richard!" she said. "What did you tell them in the kitchen to encourage such creativity?"

"Simple. I told the cook that for every dish that raised a cheer I'd give him a gold piece and another to divide among the rest of the kitchen crew."

"How brilliant, Richard!" She turned to Raymond, "Did you hear that? The cook is going to be a rich man."

He'd been talking to the bishop. He looked at her absently but said only "Indeed," and resumed his conversation.

Still more dishes came, some quite interesting, but there was just too much. Too much food, too much noise, too many guests who'd drunk too much of Richard's good wine. Raymond was paying no attention to her. He and the bishop continued to converse earnestly but Joanna couldn't hear what they were talking about though twice she heard a reference to the pope. Richard was exchanging loud remarks with one of the knights at the lower table. Joanna was sated and bored and wanted to escape. Why not? she thought. She rose. Raymond was instantly on his feet.

"Joanna! Are you leaving us?"

"Yes, I've had far too much to eat and drink and the din makes my head ache. I want only the quiet and peace of my room.

"Then I shall accompany you. Let me first make my excuses to the king."

After exchanging a few words with Richard, he took her arm and they made their way to the door. She noticed that some of the other ladies, several with their reluctant husbands, followed her example. But Berengaria stayed loyally by Richard's side though he paid no attention to her. He was engaged in a loud argument with the knight below him about the details of the battle of Acre in the Holy Land.

Joanna and Raymond walked in silence along the dimly lit corridor leading to her tower. A page materialized and led the way with a candelabrum. At the top of the stairs to her apartments she asked Raymond, "Would you like to come in for a bit? You can see how I live." The page opened the heavy oak door and left, after assuring himself that she required no further services. Jeanette, who had been waiting for her mistress, tactfully left as well.

Joanna led Raymond to her private Arabic-style chamber. He looked around in amazement. Joanna seated herself demurely on a cushion. Raymond hesitated and sat on an ottoman nearby. The room was warm and softly lit by firelight and a few candles. Finally he spoke.

"I had no notion of this side of you. I'd always thought of you as calm and proper, keenly aware of what's fitting, thoughtful of others, and..."

"Dull?" she asked.

"Certainly not! I was going to say, as embodying the best traits of the English.

Yet here we are in what could be a sultan's private chamber. And it suits you very well. I'm charmed, I'm delighted."

"I'm glad you like it. My mother thinks it's outlandish but she tolerates me."

"Well, it's already given me ideas, and I hope that someday... but I'm getting ahead of myself. I'd like to apologize to you for neglecting you at dinner and talking so long to the bishop. But it was very important to me. May I tell you what we were discussing?"

"Of course. I admit I was wondering."

He looked up at the ceiling as though uncertain as to how to begin, then plunged in.

"I asked him what he thought my chances were of getting the pope to agree to a dissolution of my marriage to Bourgogne. When I told him the whole story, he thought a long time, then said he believed the chances were very good. He said the pope would undoubtedly urge me to try to mend matters, but he'd have to agree that since my wife had clearly left me of her own will and declined to live with me anymore, I was blameless."

Joanna wasn't too sure of that, but she listened attentively.

He went on to explain why his first two marriages hadn't worked either. The first, when he was sixteen, had been arranged by his father, the fifth count. It had been tragically cut short when the young bride died after only a year. As for his second, it had been entered into for political reasons, though he admitted he'd been attracted by the beauteous Beatrice of Beziers. But before long they had a serious disagreement, so serious that they became irreconcilable.

"What did you disagree on?"

"I'm sorry to say it was about religion. The Cathar heresy, to be precise. I'm sure you've heard of it? Some call the heretics Cathars, some say Albigensians because the city of Albi was their first major center."

"I've heard of the Cathars but I confess I know very little about them. I believe they refuse to recognize the church hierarchy, all the way up to the pope, because they claim they don't need an intermediary between man and God?"

"Yes, that's part of it. They also have very strict rules about daily life. For example, they abstain from killing animals and eating meat. They don't believe in hell or purgatory. Obviously the Catholic church can't condone such unorthodox beliefs."

"They do seem very extreme." But she wanted to get back to Beatrice of Beziers, the beautiful but repudiated wife.

"So I take it that Beatrice was sympathetic to this heresy but you weren't, so you parted?"

"Not only was she sympathetic, she joined them and went to their services. I couldn't tolerate that. My father detested the Cathars and he taught me to do the same. She finally left me when I absolutely refused to join the sect."

"Dear me," said Joanna. "Truly, an impossible situation."

"Yes. She was immovable and so was I. But now...now, I'm beginning to believe that maybe they needn't be persecuted as the pope directs us. The more I observe them, the more I admire them. They're industrious, they're peaceable, they make no trouble and their only fault is in believing that they and not the traditional churchmen have found the way to salvation. Which is not to say that I'd ever change my own beliefs. But I don't see why we can't just leave them alone."

"So you could tolerate Beatrice, but still didn't want her as your wife. I see."

He sighed and stood up.

"Enough of this. I wanted you to try to understand what may look like a dubious marital record. God knows I'm not perfect but I've truly tried to be a kind and patient husband. I hope you can agree that not all the fault was on my side. Because now…"

She'd never seen him at a loss for words. She was beginning to guess what he might be leading up to and her heart beat a little faster. He paced from his chair to the window and back. He stood looking down at her while she gazed up at him, trying to read his eyes—dark as night, scrutinizing her face. He took her hands and raised her to her feet. Her skirt billowed, then settled with a sigh.

"Joanna, my dear Joanna. I find myself at last in a position to say what is in my heart and has been for two years, ever since the end of that long journey we took together. I've always admired you for your beauty, your active mind, your good sense, your kindness—so many things! But now I've come well beyond admiration. Joanna, I love you and I want you to be my wife."

He drew her to him. He rested his cheek on her hair for a moment. In the silence she became aware of a candle guttering in a corner and the crackle of the fire. She nestled in his encircling arms.

He tipped her head up and his lips brushed hers as lightly as a butterfly's wing. He tightened his embrace, and the butterfly became a ravenous wolf. The passion of his long, lingering kiss was almost frightening. She was pressed so tightly against his woolen tunic that she felt suffocated. Yet she wasn't sure she wanted this to end.

Reluctantly he let his arms drop. They drew apart and looked at each other—Raymond half smiling, Joanna in confusion. He'd aroused in her a desire she hadn't felt for years—not since William. But was that enough reason to marry him?

Raymond spoke first. His voice was husky and his words tumbled out as though they'd been pent up. "I've wanted that for so long! You're what I've been searching for all these years. For the first time in my life I know what true love is. My dear Joanna, I know your life hasn't been easy since you left Sicily and you've had to face it on your own. I only hope you can find it in your heart to accept my offer of a loving refuge. And that soon you'll come to care for me as I care for you." He took both her hands in his and drew her to him.

While she hesitated, fumbling for a reply, they heard the clatter of boots on the stone floor in the corridor below. The banquet had finally broken up and the diehards were making their adieux. Raymond kissed her on the forehead.

"My dear, I must leave you. I promised your brother that I'd confer with him tonight about various matters that concern Toulouse and Aquitaine. I don't ask you to say anything now. Shall I come to you after we return from the hunt and learn your answer?"

Half of her wanted to say, "Raymond, you need not wait until tomorrow. I'll happily become your wife!"

But her more sensible, realistic self prevailed.

"Yes, please do come. You've given me a great deal to think about. But I'll try to have an answer."

58

"Thank you, Joanna, for an excellent breakfast." Berengaria took half of the last slice of bread, added a dab of cherry jam and chewed it appreciatively. The friends were in Joanna's private chamber, snug and warm.

"Now how shall we amuse ourselves today?" Berengaria asked. Joanna was sipping her barley water and looking pensive. "Shall we go walking in the town? I haven't been in a real city for so long, it will be good for me to see a larger world than little Beaufort-en-Vallée."

"Yes, of course." Joanna was suddenly energized. "It would do me a world of good to get out. Ever since Lady Mary left I've had nobody to go walking with. Adelaide spends most of her time at Fontevraud. My mother would disapprove if I went alone, even with attendants. So I feel as though I've been cooped up forever. You're a godsend, for many reasons."

"Thank you. But I didn't know Mary had left—when, why?"

"Oh dear, it's been only two weeks, and how I miss her. She's been my companion for twenty years. Remember that nice English knight, Sir Stephen, one of the Crusaders? He and Mary had an understanding that they'd marry when everybody was home again. But although he sent numerous messages that he was on his way to claim his bride, she almost gave up on him. Then at last he turned up with tall tales of his adventures on the way home—pirates, bandits, I don't know what all. And off they went. They were to be married in England, and I suppose they'll stay there."

Berengaria stood up. "That's a blow for you. I know how fond you were of her. But let's be happy for her and go on with our walk. A bit of exercise will help us work off the effects of that enormous meal last night. Shall we visit the cathedral? I've never seen it."

"Yes, let's. It always soothes me. It's so calm and quiet, almost unbelievable in the heart of this noisy city."

When they emerged from the palace, well bundled up, they were pleased to see that all the snow had melted and the sun still shone. They walked briskly along, followed and preceded by palace servants. Though the streets were crowded, the townspeople made way when they saw the royal livery of the servants and recognized the two fine ladies in their fur-lined cloaks and elegant boots. But there were many puddles along the way and conversation ceased while they gave all their attention to where they stepped.

At the cathedral square they paused so Berengaria could admire the huge structure. Joanna acted as guide and instructor.

"It was built by my mother and father, you know. In fact it's *still* being built. There's talk of two side towers, but I don't see any sign of serious construction. Shall we go in?"

Inside, Berengaria gasped at the sheer size of the long nave with its two rows of monumental pillars. "Why, you can hardly see the altar from here. It's magnificent! And so bright, I suppose that's from all the stained glass."

"Yes, especially when there's sunshine. See how it streams in and makes this window glow. Do you see anybody you recognize?"

Berengaria dutifully studied the large east window. "Well, you've given me a hint so I suppose that rather angular lady in blue, looking woebegone, is Eleanor. But I must say, it doesn't do her justice. And the man next to her, wearing a crown, must be your father, Henry."

"Right." Joanna pulled her fur collar tighter about her neck. "Brrr. It's so chilly in here. Let's go out to the garden. I know a sheltered nook where we can catch whatever sunbeams there are."

When they reached the secluded bench they sat down and Berengaria put her hand on her friend's arm. "Now my dear, you've been fidgeting and looking distracted all morning. Won't you tell me what's on your mind?" Before Joanna could answer a cloud covered the sun. They looked up to see an advancing bank of gray taking over the sky.

"Dear me," said Joanna. "If we don't hurry we may get drenched before we get back."

They stood and the two servants, pleased at the prospect of getting out of the cold, promptly took their places before and behind. By the time they reached the palace a few snowflakes were drifting down. Shivering, Joanna and Berengaria ran up to Joanna's chamber, where their maids, clucking and murmuring their sympathy, helped them out of capes, boots, scarves and gloves. They sat by the fire, grateful for the warmth.

"Now, you're right, I do have something on my mind." Joanna stretched out her hands toward the hearth. "I need to know what you think." She glanced at Berengaria and hesitated before she spoke. "As you must have guessed, it has to do with Count Raymond."

"Aha! And when you two left the banquet last night, I wasn't the only one to notice. Richard said to me, 'I hope that's the good sign I think it is.'"

"He did, did he? At least he's stopped pestering me to think of Raymond as a suitor."

"And is he a suitor?"

Joanna blushed. "He is. In fact, he asked me to marry him."

"Just like that? No preamble?"

Joanna's blush deepened as she remembered the embraces and words of the night before. "Oh yes, he professed his love most convincingly and said he'd been thinking only of me for two years. And I believe he meant it."

"But what about his reputation? Did he say anything about those marriages that didn't last?"

"Yes. I told him I had to know how he could justify them before I could even consider his suit. He was very frank." She related Raymond's explanations of his complicated marital history.

"Hmm." Berengaria laced her fingers together and stared thoughtfully into the flames. "It sounds plausible, despite the fact that apparently he lays all the blame on his wives and keeps none for himself. Do you accept his version of events?"

"I do. I know we've commented on how smooth and persuasive he can be and we've wondered how much to believe. But I think in this case he was completely sincere."

Neither spoke for a few minutes. Outside, Joanna noticed, the snow was falling more seriously.

"One more question," said Berengaria. "And dear Joanna, forgive me if I pry too deeply."

"No, no, of course we must be frank. I have nobody but you to advise me, and I value your opinion."

"Very well. You seem sure that Raymond cares for you. What are your feelings for him?"

Joanna chose her words carefully. "That's exactly what I've been asking myself. I need to get to know him better. Now, all I know is that I'm very attracted to him and I find it exciting to be with him."

"And are you at all influenced by the political advantages of the marriage?"

"I know my mother and my brother would congratulate me on making such a wise decision. But though I welcome the prospect of peace between our two houses, that hasn't influenced me one way or the other. Actually I'm thinking only of myself."

She leaned forward toward Berengaria and spoke more earnestly. "What's most important to me is Raymond's promise to shelter me, to protect me. He wants to give me a loving refuge—those were his exact words. All these years since William died I've had no one. That's all I ask, someone to take care of me and to care for me. Someone to give my life purpose again." She looked down at her hands folded in her lap and said, so low that Berengaria could hardly hear, "I'm not equipped to live alone."

"Few women are." Joanna guessed she was thinking of her own years of living alone while Richard ignored her.

Berengaria quickly moved on. "I did say I'd asked my last question, but I have one more, even more personal. Did you and Raymond talk at all about the possibility, the hope, of having children?"

"We didn't. I'm sure we will. He must want a son badly—he's had no children by any of his marriages. And my dearest wish is to be a mother. I came so close with William but God didn't will it. But I'm only thirty-one, it's not too late.

Maybe now…"

"My prayers will join yours for such a happy outcome. But how did you leave things with Raymond?"

"I didn't encourage him. I was far too flustered to know what to say. I asked him to come back this evening when they return from hunting, and I'd have an answer."

Berengaria got up and gave her a hug. "And by now I know what your answer will be. My dear, dear friend, let me be the first to wish you joy."

Joanna hugged her back, laughing but with a few tears welling in her eyes. "Thank you, thank you, for listening and for not telling me I was making a terrible mistake."

"Of course not. And may the palace at Toulouse be filled with calm and serenity."

As she spoke, the calm and serenity in the palace of Poitiers were abruptly shattered. They heard a familiar voice, loud and imperious, outside the door. Queen Eleanor was back from Fontevraud.

"You don't need to announce me. I'll go right in." And so she did. She nodded to Berengaria, kissed Joanna on the cheek and sat down by the fire, looking uncharacteristically weary.

"A terrible journey, terrible. Thank God I'm here at last." She threw back the hood of her damp cloak. Some hair had escaped from her wimple and was pasted on her pale cheeks. Her face was wan. She bowed her head and supported it with her hands for a moment. This was not the invincible Eleanor the world was accustomed to.

"I must go lie down but first you must tell me your news. I saw Richard below, just back from hunting, but he and his boisterous friends were so busy congratulating themselves on bringing back three fine boars that we were hardly able to talk. However, he managed to tell me that you, Joanna, would have something interesting to tell me."

Joanna spoke firmly. "Maybe later, at supper. Not now. Here, have some of this spiced wine we've been warming by the fire. And let's get you out of that wet cloak. Then you must go get some rest. Jeanette," she called to her maid, "will you send for the queen's ladies to conduct her to her chambers?" She was surprised to hear herself ordering her mother about.

Eleanor didn't argue. "Yes, perhaps you're right." She accepted a goblet of wine and sipped it while she sat quietly for a few minutes. Then she pulled herself together and sat up with her back as straight as usual. "I shall see you in my chambers at supper, then."

Before she reached the door a page entered and addressed Joanna.

"My lady, Count Raymond asks when it will be convenient for him to call on you."

"Please tell him in half an hour."

Eleanor sent her a sharp look of inquiry but went on her way. Berengaria, tactfully, withdrew as well.

Alone, Joanna considered the gown she was wearing. It was dark blue, a supple silk, and fell straight from her shoulders in soft pleats. She decided it would do, perhaps with a sash. I don't want him to think I'm trying to dazzle him with frippery and jewels, she told herself.

Raymond arrived punctually. When she saw his darkly handsome face, the smile playing about his lips, the intense gaze of his eyes, she felt the same wave of excitement that had swept through her body when he'd kissed her. He held out his arms and she moved into his embrace. He looked down at her and they kissed, not passionately but gently, as though sealing a pact.

"I can read in your face that your answer is what I hoped. All day I've been waiting for this moment. Thank you, dear Joanna." He led her to an ottoman. She was glad to sit down. She felt almost dizzy with tremulous happiness and amazement.

"Was it a hard decision?" he asked, holding both her hands in his.

"In some ways, yes. I needed to think things through. But I do believe, Raymond, I knew last night, deep down, what my answer would be."

"And I promise you will never regret it. Have you told your mother?"

"Not yet, but I'm to see her at supper in her chamber and I'll do so then. She'll expect me very soon."

"So we haven't much time now—but before long we'll have all the time in the world to be together." He took her hand and kissed it on the palm. "But I must leave tomorrow, so I fear we must get practical."

They discussed the wedding date. "The sooner the better, of course," said Raymond, "but I have various matters to settle over the next month. Perhaps the end of February?"

"Certainly, as far as I'm concerned. We'll see what my mother has to say. She loves to organize weddings and such. She may well demand more time."

"It may be," said Raymond, "that Queen Eleanor will have to accept the fact that she's no longer in charge of your life."

Joanna laughed, but she saw that he was quite serious. She changed the subject. "What about Toulouse, Raymond? I've never been there. What's your palace like?"

"It's not nearly as big and comfortable as this one in Poitiers. We do, however, have a very fine cathedral, one of the largest in France, just the place for a state wedding. I can see you now, walking down the aisle while the lords and ladies exclaim at your beauty. And I join you at the altar, hoping against hope that you haven't changed your mind."

She envisioned the picture he had called up and smiled. "That's not likely. I'm a woman of my word."

Jeanette came in, apologetic at interrupting. "My lady, Queen Eleanor sends word that you're late to supper."

Reluctantly, they parted. "We'll say goodbye before I leave tomorrow, and then it won't be long before we start our new life together." One last quick kiss, and he was gone.

Joanna found her mother, Richard and Berengaria already seated at table. In less than an hour Eleanor had changed her gown, put on a fresh wimple, ordered up a respectable supper and regained her usual energy. A servant was ladling thick soup with a tantalizing odor into big bowls. Peas, ham and—rosemary? Joanna guessed. She sat down. All eyes were on her.

"I'm sorry to be so late. I hope you haven't been waiting long."

"No, we've been here only five minutes," said Richard. "Just time to compare opinions on what you and Raymond were up to. And my close-mouthed queen refused to divulge what she knew." He winked at Berengaria but Joanna could see how curious he was. He hadn't even lifted his spoon.

"I'll be glad to tell you." She paused, and blurted it out. "Raymond has asked me to marry him. And I've accepted."

Eleanor looked at her with a restrained but approving smile. "So you've shown some sense at last."

"Good girl," said Richard, diving into his soup.

Not a word of surprise or congratulation, thought Joanna. Am I so predictable?

Berengaria sent Joanna a look that said, "I know what you're thinking." She raised her wineglass. "Wonderful news! We're very happy for you. This calls for a toast."

"So it does," said Richard. "I'll send for a bottle of the best Bordeaux."

Eleanor was already thinking ahead. "We'll have the wedding in the spring, late April or May."

"I'd thought perhaps sooner," said Joanna. "Why wait?"

"Nonsense. It takes time to prepare for a state wedding, especially one of this importance. I'm sure Raymond would agree. Marrying into the royal family of England is a great achievement for a count of Toulouse. We'll need time to make it as grand as possible. You'll need a whole new wardrobe, what with the wedding ceremony, the receptions, the banquets, as well as cloaks and furs for traveling. And there'll be hundreds of guests we'll have to invite. We must start on that at once. It will take time for us to get the word to them and for them to arrange their journeys. And we'll have to provide suitable lodgings for them in Rouen."

"Rouen?" asked Joanna. "In Normandy? So far? Raymond and I thought Toulouse."

Before Eleanor could answer Richard entered the conversation. "Of course, mother. Rouen is just the place. That will show King Philip that we're serious about keeping Normandy for the English."

The celebratory wine arrived and Richard filled their glasses. Eleanor took a sip and said, "Yes, and it will please our loyal Norman subjects that we consider their capital city the proper place for a wedding of this significance."

"What's more," said Richard, "with the count of Toulouse as my brother-in-law I won't have to worry about quarrels between his lords and mine squabbling here in the south while I'm in the north. Sister, you have done a great service to England this day. I salute you." He raised his glass.

It wasn't quite the toast Joanna had imagined, with no congratulations to the happy couple or wish for their wedded bliss. But she smiled in acknowledgement and drank.

Soon enough, she told herself, I'll be able to lead my own life without needing advice or approval from my family. And I'll have Raymond's help.

59

"Your mother is a formidable woman." Raymond lowered himself into a chair and wiped his hand across his forehead. Joanna had never seen him so discomposed.

It was the next morning. He'd come to say goodbye to her and to report on his meeting with Eleanor and Richard, during which they'd discussed the upcoming wedding and their new alliance.

"She is indeed. I take it you had a difference of opinion. I think I can tell by your face who won." She was standing by his chair and looked down at him with amusement and affection.

"It wasn't that important, really. We were talking about when and where to have the wedding. I could see her point in putting it off until later in the spring. We all want it to be a magnificent affair and if we give Queen Eleanor the time and support she requires she's the one who can make it so."

"That's true. And I for one could do with a little magnificence. There hasn't been much in my life lately, unless you can count Richard's Christmas spectacle."

He looked up at her. "Or unless you count that elegant gown you're wearing. It's very becoming."

"I'm glad you think so." She knew this would be their last meeting for some time and she wanted him to remember her at her best. Her gown was the color of Burgundy wine, close-fitting from neck to hips, with a full skirt and long puffy sleeves caught in at the wrists. Her only adornment was a single string of pearls.

"Do go on. You yielded to my mother on the wedding date."

"Yes, and with a very good grace, I might say. But I really did want it to take place in Toulouse. The *toulousains* would have been so proud. Your mother, however, explained most cogently that the relations of the English monarchs with their subjects in Normandy needed constant reinforcement and that to entertain them with a royal wedding in Rouen would strengthen the ties. I didn't think it was worth arguing about. At which your mother was agreeably surprised. She's used to dealing with my father, who automatically opposed anything your family suggested."

"Yes. I remember hearing about some of those encounters. But what about you and Richard? Are you really on good terms, still allies?"

"Yes. Circumstances require it. He's obsessed with building his ambitious castle up north to put the fear of God into King Philip. Or the fear of God's ally,

King Richard! He won't want to worry about what's going on down here. As for me, I'm happy to prolong our truce. War is an expensive, distracting business."

He stood and took her into his arms, "I must go. So this is goodbye for now, dear Joanna. You've made me a much happier, more hopeful man than when I came. You won't regret it, I promise." She was learning to feel safe and cherished when he held her like this. She raised her face to look into his eyes. She felt absolutely certain by now that he was speaking sincerely. Their lips met in one last kiss.

She stared at the big oak door after it thudded behind him. She imagined his lithe, lean figure walking down the stairs, along the corridor and out of the palace. She saw him gracefully mount his waiting horse and urge it to a trot. She saw his knights and retainers take their places. Just before he was out of sight, did he turn with one last look at the palace where he'd said goodbye to his bride-to-be?

Richard and Berengaria had left that morning for Beaufort. She missed Berengaria already. She missed Lady Mary, far off in England.

I need someone to talk to and get some perspective, she thought. She'd just made a hasty decision that would determine the course of the rest of her life. Had it been too hasty? She decided to take some air and clear her head. A walk in the garden, that's it. But when she looked out she saw that the skies had opened and released a torrent of rain.

For four days the rain continued. She got out her Arabic manuscripts but couldn't concentrate. She took up a long-discarded tapestry project but had no interest in resuming it. This was more than boredom. It became close to panic as she recognized how quickly and heedlessly she'd taken such a major step. She thought back to her first marriage which, as a child, she'd entered into unquestioningly at her parents' bidding. But how fortunate she'd been! She found herself remembering her years of happiness with William and wondering if Raymond could be so kind, so considerate, so unfailingly loving.

Maybe she should open her heart to her mother. Eleanor had lived through two marriages—the first, with the king of France, unsatisfactory; the second, with the king of England, begun with passion on both sides, then deteriorating into conflict, not always civil. But in all those years, surely she'd learned something of how to how to judge a man. Though she'd never found the time to be a real confidante for Joanna, and though she undoubtedly thought of this marriage as her own doing and a brilliant solution to strained relationships with Toulouse—surely she'd listen to her daughter's doubts and offer reassurance.

That's all I need, thought Joanna. Someone I trust to tell me I'm doing the right thing.

She went down to the great hall to see if her mother was there. She was, but conferring with her council.

She broke off and asked, "Yes, Joanna, did you need to talk to me? Can it wait?"

"It's not important." She went into the small chapel beyond the hall and sat staring at the statue of mother and child near the altar. She tried to pray. "Help me find peace of mind," she pled. Mary continued to smile serenely but offered no guidance.

She wandered out to the palace entry to assess the weather, unheeding of the buzz of palace activity—footsteps of hurrying servants in the corridor, chattering of visitors on their way to or from the great hall, distant clangs and shouts from the kitchens. The rain had stopped but the courtyard was muddy and strewn with puddles. A weak sun peered hazily down through the overcast.

She saw a lone horseman riding into the courtyard. He wore a long dark mantle and his hood hid his face. He dismounted and trudged slowly toward the palace steps, nodding to the groom who came to tend to his horse. He looked up to see her standing there and only then did she realize that this stooping man was her old friend Brother Jean-Pierre.

She ran down the steps and took his hands in hers.

"What a wonderful surprise! And here you are, just when I need a friend. It's been years. I was beginning to think you'd taken up permanent residence in England. I suppose you've come to report to my mother? But you must find time for me. I have so much to tell you!" She kept talking to hide her dismay at how he'd aged. He'd never been plump but now she could see, in spite of his enveloping cloak, that he was quite thin. When he threw back his hood she saw that his sparse fringe of hair had turned iron-gray. Deep furrows ran from his nose down to the corners of his mouth.

But when he smiled, it was the same warm, unfeigned smile she remembered. It told her he was as glad to see her as she was to see him.

"All the time in the world, my dear—after I see your mother, that is." As they walked up the steps, Adelaide appeared and stopped short when she saw the visitor. She greeted him warmly.

"Queen Eleanor will be very glad to see you as well. Only this morning she said she'd sent for you ages ago and she wondered why you hadn't come. She's just gone to her chamber. Shall I run up and tell her you're here?"

"Yes, that would be a kindness. Tell her I'll come to her as soon as I've cleaned off the grime of the road."

"And I'll see you at dinner," said Joanna. Her spirits had risen immeasurably. Their reunion would take her mind off the concerns that had been tormenting her. Already they seemed less consequential.

It wasn't complicated, she thought. Raymond had proposed marriage. She'd wholeheartedly accepted. What could be simpler or more satisfactory than that?

Dinner was served in the small reception chamber rather than the cavernous great hall. Only a dozen were present. Besides Eleanor, Joanna and Brother Jean-Pierre, there were Lady Adelaide and two other ladies in waiting, two members of the royal council and a bishop from Limoges who had mistaken the night Queen Eleanor had invited him to dinner and was there a week early. Eleanor, who had no patience with such carelessness, placed him far down the table. He was next to Lady Adelaide, who kept up a running one-sided conversation throughout the meal so he had little to do but nod, murmur a few words occasionally and enjoy his meal.

Queen Eleanor was less profligate than Richard and had ordered only four courses whereas the Christmas banquet had offered ten. Joanna preferred this evening's menu. The flying peacocks had been spectacular but no better eating than a well-roasted capon.

She was seated between her mother and Jean-Pierre. As usual, Eleanor ate rather slowly, chewing carefully. Joanna had never known whether this habit was in order to detect any bones, or to avoid undue strain on the muscles of her face and thus prevent wrinkling. Or it may simply have been the way she was reared as a daughter of French nobility. In any case she wasn't given to conversation during the meal. This left Joanna free to talk to Jean-Pierre.

"Now you must tell me what you've been doing all this time and give me news of my dear friends, Sir Alan, Federico and
Lady Mary."

"Gladly." In between spoonfuls of a thick, spicy chickpea soup, he began his account. "It happens I saw both Sir Alan and Lady Mary just six months ago during a journey up to York. Sir Alan is officially retired and has settled down at his estate near Nottingham. He's still hale and hearty though he moves a little more slowly. But he's not comfortable being a country gentleman and itches to be serving his king as a soldier. He knows there's little chance he could go back to France, but whenever the forces King Richard keeps on active duty in England are within fifty miles he hies there and joins them. And from what I hear they're glad to have him, with his experience and good sense. Even the younger ones know his reputation."

"As well they should. Dear Sir Alan. I'm glad he's doing so well. Now tell me…"

She stopped because servants had just carefully set a heavy silver platter on the table before them. It was laden (thanks to Richard's hunting expedition) with thin slices of roast boar, served with a pepper sauce and roasted chestnuts.

Jean-Pierre watched appreciatively as he was served.

"I take it you didn't eat this well in England," Joanna teased him.

"I'm afraid not. There was always too much, and most of it was tasteless. They don't give much attention to subtle seasonings. They've hardly heard of pepper, much less cinnamon and such."

Conversation flagged for some time. Finally, Jean-Pierre looked uncertainly at the few morsels left on his plate, decided to leave them, leaned back in his chair and sighed with contentment. "Now, my dear, I think you were about to ask me what I knew of Lady Mary. She and Sir Stephen live between Nottingham and York, so I was able to pay them a visit on my way north. She's not far from her father's farm, so she sees the rest of the family often. And I can report that she's healthy, contented and expecting a child."

"That's wonderful news. How I miss her. I'd been hoping I might persuade my mother to send me on some kind of mission to England, but that will have to wait now."

"Aha. You haven't said a word about your own situation, but news travels fast. You'll not be journeying to England soon because you're about to become the countess of Toulouse, right?"

"Yes. I'm glad you'd heard. I've been wondering how to tell you. Please, Jean-Pierre, tell me you approve?"

"It's not for me to approve or not. But I know you well enough to be sure that this was your own decision, not dictated by your mother, and that's enough for me. You obviously hold Count Raymond in high enough regard to agree to become his wife. I pray you'll find peace and contentment with him."

She looked at him gratefully. She'd been afraid he'd object on the grounds of Raymond's history of failed marriages.

He raised his goblet and toasted her: "To your happiness, my dear."

As they finished their almond flan, Joanna looked around and saw that the other diners were drifting out of the room. She just glimpsed Eleanor's blue skirt as the queen swept out the door. Adelaide had risen and Joanna heard, "And if I find myself in Limoges, you must show me the famous abbey where blessed Saint Martial is buried."

"Of course, with pleasure," the bishop replied genially. When she'd departed, he leaned back, gazed at the ceiling and patted his stomach. He didn't demur when a servant refilled his wineglass. He picked up a candied orange peel from a silver salver before him.

Jean-Pierre had been watching too, and caught Joanna's eye and smiled. She whispered, "I can imagine he's thinking, 'For a dinner like that, I could listen to twenty talkative ladies.'"

She rose. "Why don't we sit over there by the fire? And you must tell me what you know about my dear Federico, and what you've been doing all this time."

Jean-Pierre settled into a high-backed chair with a plump velvet cushion. Joanna fetched another cushion for his back—she feared he'd become so bony that the unyielding wood might cause him discomfort.

"Thank you, that's welcome. I'm more weary from the journey than I thought. But it's wonderfully reviving to be back in this familiar palace. Do you remember, Joanna, that it was in this very room that I taught you your alphabet and gave you your first reading lessons?"

"Barely. I must have been only five or six. I do remember resenting your insistence that I spend time indoors instead of playing in the garden."

He chuckled. "So you did. And more than once you simply ran away."

"But I've long since forgiven you for being such a strict teacher. Now tell me, have you seen Federico?"

"Not for years. But Sir Alan told me he's rising in the ranks of Richard's army. He may be a captain before he's twenty-five. "

"I'm not surprised. I wonder if he's found a lady-love? With his looks he should be surrounded by eager girls."

"He may well be. But Alan thinks that for now, he's much more interested in the footloose life and serving his king, even at a distance."

She thought a minute. "I wonder if I couldn't persuade Richard to bring Federico over to France to join the army here."

"Richard is going to need to strengthen his forces now that he's launching a major assault against Philip This would be a good time to approach him."

"I wonder if he's still at Beaufort." She signaled to a servant who was clearing the tables to bring more spiced wine. They sipped slowly and stared into the fire. Jean-Pierre fidgeted. At last he spoke.

"No, he isn't at Beaufort. I stopped there before coming here. I'd hoped to see him but he'd left the day before. I must now tell you something that will pain you. I'll try to be brief."

She listened in growing dismay as he told how he'd found Richard gone and Berengaria distraught. He described how her face had shown signs of tears and her voice trembled as she welcomed him. He persuaded her to explain what had happened.

"Richard left yesterday morning to go back to his castle-building," she'd told Jean-Pierre. "I asked him when I would see him again. 'When you send word that you are with child,' he said without looking at me while he buckled on his sword. 'I've stayed a month and my work here is done. If I haven't fathered a child in all this time it won't be my fault.' And he was gone, without an embrace or affectionate word. Oh Jean-Pierre, all this time I've been so happy, thinking at last our marriage was working. And it was all a pretense."

"Poor Berengaria!" exclaimed Joanna. "I must go to her. She doesn't deserve this." She wrung her hands. "How could Richard be so cruel and thoughtless?"

She had a sudden qualm. What if Raymond proved as fickle as Richard? She was quite sure that he genuinely cared for her now. But what if in time he too lost interest and rejected her? He'd done it to other wives before.

She collected herself. Jean-Pierre was speaking.

"And yet, it may not have been all a pretense. We know that Richard's emotions are volatile. It may well be that, having decided to give their marriage a chance of being productive, he discovered at last what a treasure he had in Berengaria, and for that month he truly loved her. But then his other priorities took over and he left her."

"That may explain, but it doesn't excuse," said Joanna.

"Certainly not. And as you can imagine, there was very little I could say to make her feel better. I couldn't justify Richard's behavior, nor could I criticize my king. I think it would do her worlds of good if you went to Beaufort."

"I'll send word to her at once." They'd finished the wine and the fire was dying. "It's late—shall we say good night until tomorrow?"

The next day she began making her plans for the journey to Beaufort. But Queen Eleanor demanded her attention to her bridal gown and her trousseau, which had to be commissioned immediately, so she sent word to Berengaria to expect her in ten days.

But everybody's plans were disrupted when word came two days later that several of Raymond's barons in the east had suddenly risen in defiance of his truce with Richard and begun taking over territories claimed by Aquitaine. Richard was not pleased. Raymond sent Joanna a brief message, saying he'd almost succeeded in reining in the rebels and he would keep her informed.

A few days later he sent another message arrived, even more alarming.

"My dear Joanna, you may have already heard of this or you soon will. Pope Celestine has excommunicated me. The clerics of the Abbey of Saint-Gilles maintain that I'm claiming more than my share of the benefices. But it's exactly the same proportion the counts of Toulouse have been receiving for decades. They put their case to the pope and he agreed to issue a decree excommunicating me. I must go to Rome.

"I'll do all I can to persuade him to relax his decree so our wedding can take place as planned—or perhaps just a bit later. I embrace you. Raymond."

Shocked, she put down the parchment, then picked it up and read the brief message again. Excommunication! It meant the church would have nothing to do with Raymond and certainly wouldn't officiate at his marriage.

All her doubts about the wisdom of her decision to marry had been replaced by anxiety and concern for Raymond. She realized now that she deeply, truly wished for their union.

But in the face of all this, how could the wedding possibly take place as planned?

60

Joanna wondered what good it would do for Raymond to go to Rome but hoped for the best. Pope Celestine had already been old and vague when she and Berengaria had seen him five years ago in 1191. By now he must be well into his nineties and even less decisive.

"Still," said Eleanor, "a pope's a pope."

In mid-March Raymond came to Poitiers to report to Queen Eleanor and Joanna. He arrived about noon, well before the dinner hour. He was directed to Eleanor's chambers where she and Joanna waited. They were partaking of barley water with honey and lemon. Eleanor's goblets, engraved with lions and fleur-de-lys, gave even such a modest drink authority.

Raymond, offered barley water but requesting wine, delivered his account succinctly. He was pleased to tell them that he'd been successful. The pope tended to be influenced by the last person he talked to. So though he'd originally been easily persuaded by the urgent pleas of the administrators of Saint-Gilles to issue the excommunication, he now listened carefully to Raymond.

"By the time I saw him," Raymond said, "he really didn't seem to care one way or the other. It wasn't hard to get him to agree not to enforce the decree."

"I see," said Joanna. "The excommunication has been officially issued. And that takes care of the pope's obligation. But since he's not going to order anyone to enforce it, it won't really have any effect? Then there's nothing to stand in the way of our marriage."

"Well…" he hesitated. Eleanor looked him with calm expectancy, Joanna with worry. "Yes, there is something, Affairs in the County of Toulouse will require my presence there for a time."

"It's something to do with that trouble around Beziers, isn't it?" Eleanor took a sip and peered at him over the rim of her goblet. "When your local lords took matters into their own hands and led forays into our Aquitaine?"

"I'm afraid so, or at least that's part of it. Richard wants me to demand that they swear a solemn oath to respect the borders he and I have agreed on. That means I must go in person to deal with four powerful lords who think of themselves as supreme in their domains. It may take some time."

"You said that was part of it. What else?" Joanna couldn't keep a hint of annoyance out of her voice. When she'd accepted Raymond, she'd blithely assumed they'd be married soon and her totally new life would begin. But it had been delay after delay.

"Richard and I must agree on the terms of the marriage settlement before we can with confidence set the date."

"But I thought we agreed on all that at Christmas," said Eleanor tartly. "What do you have to discuss now?"

Raymond's usual aplomb was cracking. He looked uncomfortable.

My mother often has that effect on people, Joanna thought.

Raymond took a sip of wine, hesitated and plunged ahead.

"The situation has changed somewhat since Christmas. Forgive me but I must be blunt. By now Richard's totally obsessed with finishing his "Chateau Gaillard" before the present truce with Philip runs out and they go at each other again. This means that he depends on me, his future brother-in-law, to maintain the peace on his southern borders so he can keep all his forces in the north. This places me in a much better bargaining position than before. So I shall ask Richard for a slight revision in our agreement."

"How slight?" asked Eleanor. "Surely you aren't going to go back on your promise to give Joanna the Agenais and Quercy?"

"No indeed. But as count of Toulouse, I have the responsibility of maintaining the integrity and independence of my domain of Languedoc. This independence has often been threatened by England, even by your husband King Henry, as well as by Richard when he was duke of Aquitaine before he became king. Now is my opportunity to ask Richard to give me a solemn pledge to renounce any present or future claims to our lands on the part of England."

Joanna was fascinated. This was a new side of Raymond, as clever negotiator if a bit pompous. It suddenly occurred to her that as countess of Toulouse she too would have the responsibility to maintain the borders and insure the peace. Where did her loyalties lie? To the interests of England? She could see that Eleanor was already fuming and about to denounce such a ridiculous proposal. Joanna knew where she must stand. She plucked up her courage and spoke before her mother could.

"That strikes me as a very sensible settlement. For years and years England and Toulouse have been quarreling about who has a right to what along their borders. But have the borders changed? I suspect very little. Mother, think of all that will be saved by this agreement—the lives of brave soldiers, the enormous expense of maintaining armies in the field. When it's put to Richard, I'm sure he'll see the logic of it."

"So you intend to support Raymond in this?" Eleanor's tone was frosty.

"I do."

Raymond looked at her in astonished approval, But instead of arguing, Eleanor sighed, leaned back and closed her eyes. It was dismissal.

"I think you had better leave me now." Her voice was flat and toneless.

"Will we see you at dinner, mother?"

"I doubt it."

Once outside and in the corridor, Raymond threw his arms around Joanna and hugged her.

"Bravo!" He stood back and surveyed her in admiration. "You were clearly the winner in that encounter."

"I suppose I was. But I've never seen my mother accept a setback so passively. Maybe she was in a state of shock to see me so assertive. I even surprised myself."

"And maybe she's finally tired. She's been battling her whole life for what she believes in. I respect her for that. How old is she, by the way?"

"She'll soon be seventy-five. But I doubt if she's giving up. She may not fight this but there'll be other causes."

Neither Joanna nor Eleanor spoke to each other about the subject again. And when Raymond approached Richard the latter saw the merits of the cease-fire and readily agreed. Anything to keep the peace in the south while he fought in Normandy.

With the wedding postponed again, Joanna now had time to make the long-planned visit to Berengaria in Beaufort.

She was always surprised at the modest scale of Beaufort, after the grandeur of the imposing palace in Poitiers. It was quite a small castle, though from its location atop a small hill it dominated the little town. As her party wound its way up the hill she looked around her at the countryside and reflected on what Richard had told her. The Romans chose this spot for a fortress and her ancestors built their own castle on the Romans' ruins, recognizing how well it commanded a view of all approaches. "There'd be no way for an invading force to creep up unseen," he'd said. In fact, she thought with amusement, Berengaria is probably observing our invading force from Poitiers right now.

As the travelers reached the top of the hill, a horse and rider burst through the gate and galloped across the bridge.

At the last minute the man saw them and reined in his horse just in time to avoid a collision, eliciting a scream from Adelaide. The steed swerved and came to a full stop. He must have been used to his impetuous master.

The horseman was an extraordinary sight. He was immensely tall and dressed in leather jerkin and leggings. Over these unremarkable garments he wore a black velvet cape embroidered with a coat-of-arms that looked familiar to Joanna—a coal-black eagle, wings outstretched on a field of gold. A heavy gold chain and cross hung around his neck. A jaunty crimson feather sprouted from his black velvet cap. Joanna guessed that he might be close to forty—a very hale and hearty forty. Beneath the massive man his sizeable horse looked like a pony. He surveyed the party and fixed his eyes on Joanna.

"You must be Queen Joanna," he said. "My sister is eagerly awaiting your arrival."

"Of course—you're Berengaria's brother Sancho. You're king of Navarre. I've heard so much about you. She looks up to you tremendously."

"In more ways than one," he grinned. Joanna liked him at once.

"But you're leaving just as we get here. What a pity."

"I'd gladly stay but I must be in Angoulême by nightfall. I'm on my way to see your brother Richard in Normandy. We have urgent matters to discuss. I expect my sister will tell you about them." He doffed his hat, spurred his horse and was off. His squire, a normal-sized man on a normal-sized horse, trotted after him.

"Brusque, isn't he?" commented Adelaide.

"Yes. He speaks plainly and doesn't waste time on meaningless pleasantries. I find that refreshing."

"But what a fine-looking man! Too bad you're engaged to Raymond. You could marry a king instead of a count."

"Not a chance! Besides, Berengaria told me he'd recently been married."

They rode on into the bailey, and Joanna was pleased to see that it had been considerably spruced up since her first visit. Decrepit outbuildings had been razed or repaired and a garden flourished in the middle of the extensive courtyard. A vine-covered pergola overlooked the rose garden. The castle itself, little more than a U-shaped array of low buildings, with a tower at either end and one in the center, also looked in better repair.

Their approach must indeed have been observed because servants were waiting to see to their horses and show them to their lodgings. They'd barely dismounted when Berengaria appeared at the door of the central tower and hurried to greet them.

An hour later the two friends were settled in Berengaria's reception room, one tenth the size of Queen Eleanor's great hall and ten times as inviting. Joanna looked around admiringly.

"Such a pleasant room! You've acquired several fine pieces of furniture. And those lovely tapestries! I've seen nothing like that anywhere else in France.

"I had most of the furnishings and the tapestries sent from Navarre. Though my brother Sancho is king now, he's seldom in the palace, too busy fending off Castile and Aragon. So we agreed I might as well be using some of our parents' things rather than have them just gather dust. I'm glad they please you."

She took Joanna's hand and led her to a divan where they sat side by side.

"Now you must tell me why the wedding was postponed and how things are with you and Raymond."

"I'll get to that. We have so much to talk about, haven't we? But first, I'm dying of curiosity. We ran into your brother Sancho just outside the wall, or rather, he almost ran into us! He was in such a hurry that he couldn't stop to talk, but he did say he was on his way to see Richard about something important and that you could explain it. Can you tell me more?"

"I can, though it will be hard for me." She chose her words carefully and spoke in a low voice, not looking at her friend.

"As I think you know, when Richard left me after Christmas he told me he would not be back unless I sent word I was pregnant."

"Yes, Jean-Pierre told me about it. My heart went out to you. It was cruel."

"By now I'm over the shock and simply trying not to think about it. But not only has Richard rejected me, so has your mother. She avoided me when we were in Poitou. She's decided, I'm sure, that since I haven't provided the heir they expected, there's no need to pretend I'm still important." She bowed her head. The tears she'd been holding back ran down her cheeks.

"My dear, I can't defend Richard and Eleanor. I wish they hadn't hurt you so." She put her arm around her friend's shaking shoulder. "When I can, I'll urge them to show more Christian love and charity." But I don't know what good that will do, she thought.

Berengaria gulped, took a deep breath, and went on.

"Sancho stopped to see me on his way to see Richard about another matter—renewing the treaty between Navarre and England that your father and my father signed when I was affianced to Richard. But when I told him how Richard had treated me, he was furious. After he'd calmed down he gave me his brotherly advice. He thinks I should accost both Queen Eleanor and Richard and tell them that by denying me my rightful place at his side, Richard will be seen by the church as in violation of his wedding vows. He also urged me to write to the pope and enlist his support." She was calmer now.

Joanna was fairly sure that neither her mother nor her brother would be persuaded by such a plea. But she merely said, "And will you take his advice?"

"No. At least not all of it, not yet. I'm simply not brave enough or strong enough to confront either Richard or Eleanor. And even if I were, I have my pride. I'd feel like a beggar."

"You shouldn't feel that way. You're only asking for what's rightfully yours."

"I suppose so. Sancho told me I need more backbone. But for now I shall write to the pope, though I don't know what he can do."

Joanna unexpectedly laughed and Berengaria looked at her suspiciously. This wasn't a laughing matter.

"I know what he can do. He can threaten to excommunicate Richard. This pope is remarkably good at issuing decrees of excommunication. If he weren't, Raymond and I might be married by now."

"What are you talking about? Was Raymond excommunicated? And that's why you put the wedding date off?"

Joanna was glad to change the painful subject. She told about Raymond's dispute with the clerics of Saint-Gilles, Pope Celestine's decree excommunicating him, Raymond's trip to Rome and the pope's agreement not to enforce the decree. And then began the problems with his troublesome vassals and the matters he had to take up with Richard.

"So of course the wedding had to be postponed while all that was straightened out. But everybody seems confident that we'll be well and truly married by October. So that gives you plenty of time to have a grand gown made to wear to my wedding."

"And what will *you* be wearing? I wouldn't want my grand gown to clash with yours."

"My mother recommends a purple brocade with gold embroidery. But I'm thinking of a straight, sheath-like gown, maybe green, with a sleeveless redingote of white lace over it."

"I can see it now! But I predict some serious negotiations ahead. Have you asked Raymond's opinion?"

"No, I've had no chance. But I'm quite sure he'd be on my side. One of the things I like about him is that he comments on what I wear."

"Which brings me to my next question. So much time has passed since you agreed to marry him—are you still convinced it was the right decision?"

"More than ever. The more I see of him the better I like him. I may never feel I know him as well as I knew William. But I believe he'll do as he promised. He'll take care of me and help me give my life some direction. I'll be my own person again instead of the widow who had to go home to mother."

For a few minutes each thought her own thoughts. Joanna wasn't sure if they'd settled anything, but at least they were caught up on each other's news.

At a knock on the door, Berengaria said, "Oh, that must be Lady Héloise, my lady-in-waiting. I told her to come in before dinner so she could meet you. She's become a real friend."

In came a tall, angular woman with a kind, cheerful face.

"Here's my dear Joanna, Héloise. Isn't she as pretty as I told you?"

"Indeed, even more so. I'm very pleased to meet you, my lady."

She turned to Berengaria. "Since it's such a nice day I took the liberty of asking that our dinner be served outside in the pergola by your rose garden."

"What a good idea! Let's go to table at once. I'm suddenly very hungry."

Out they went to dine companionably on roast chicken, bread warm from the oven, mushroom tarts and ripe red cherries, while the June sun beamed and the scent of roses sweetened the air.

When the last glass of wine had been drained and the last sparrow had found a crumb in the grass, Joanna leaned back contentedly. Sunlight that made its way through the leafy vines warmed her face. She leaned back, closed her eyes and heard Berengaria and Héloise talking about whether the gardener was dealing properly with rose blight.

How glad I am to be here, she thought, and to see Berengaria again. It's good to be able to confide in each other. I hope I gave her some comfort. We'll talk some more before I leave. And then…and then…it's only three months until I marry Raymond. Surely nothing can stop that now.

She dozed.

61

"Everybody said it was a beautiful wedding," said Joanna dreamily. It was the morning after the ceremony and they were guests of the bishop in his palace in Rouen.

Joanna was lying on her back in a huge bed between lilac-colored silk sheets and with her head resting on a lilac pillow. If Raymond had been looking he would have observed that she lay wide-eyed, with a little smile on her face and with her tousled brown hair spread like a fan on the pillow. But Raymond, lying next to her, wasn't looking. He was still asleep, though twitching a little.

"Didn't you think it was a beautiful wedding?" She tickled his ear. He moaned, not unhappily, and opened his eyes.

"Yes, it was beautiful. So was the dream you awakened me from. Do let me go back to sleep, if only for a few minutes!"

"Why? What was happening in your dream?"

"We'd just come from the banquet," he said, "which went on far too long, didn't it? But here we were, alone at last, and we undressed and it was the first time I'd seen you like that and you were so lovely and just a little shy so you got into bed and so did I and I just looked at you and you smiled at me like an angel and—and then you woke me up!" He pled with her. "Please, Joanna, let me finish my dream."

"But Raymond, I can remember everything that happened after that. Surely you can too."

"Yes, I think so. But I want to dream it again to make sure."

"Then let me help. I'll show you. First you put your arms around me." She lifted her head and he slid an arm under it and pressed her close to his chest.

"Like this?"

"Yes, just so." Her voice was muffled. "Then we kissed. Like this."

"And then...I caressed you here..."

"Oh yes! And then..."

And then, the next thing they knew they woke again to find themselves entwined and the sheets in a tangle. A strange light flooded the room.

Joanna pulled the bed curtain aside and peeped out.

"Raymond! We're in the middle of a rainbow!"

She pulled the curtain all the way open and slid out of bed. Two tall stained-glass windows dominated the facing wall. In vibrant shades of blue, gold, red and green, they depicted the Annunciation and the Resurrection. They captured the rays of the sun and transmuted them into shafts of brilliantly colored light that played about the room.

He looked at the spectacle and blinked. "I suppose those windows were there last night but I didn't notice them."

"Neither did I." She giggled. "Maybe it's just as well. We might have felt we were misbehaving in church."

She put on a robe, got back in bed and propped herself up against the pillows. William yawned, stretched and sat up beside her.

"Why so serious all of a sudden, my countess? Why do you frown? Have I displeased you already?"

"No, I'm thinking about Toulouse."

"But you'll love Toulouse. It's a beautiful city and our palace is extremely comfortable, if not quite as luxurious as this one. I wonder how Bishop Nicolas manages."

"My mother has hinted that he receives generous contributions from both England and France. Both sides hope to buy his support in their territorial quarrels."

"How clever of him." He paused and she could imagine his agile brain trying to figure out a way he too could play one side against another to add to his revenue. She'd learned that Raymond had a calculating side to him, always on the alert for ways to stay ahead of the game. She rather liked that about him.

He took her hand and gently rubbed her palm with his fingers. She liked that too.

"But back to Toulouse. What do you find so alarming about it?"

"Oh, I know I'll like it. The bishop was telling me at the banquet about the beautiful churches and how they call it the Rosy City because of the color of the bricks they build with. He lived there several years when he was a young priest. But he said they also call it the City of Towers because so many of the houses are fortified with tall brick towers. He said your subjects are a quarrelsome lot, always finding new things to fight each other about. Raymond, am I going to live in a battleground? Will I have to dodge arrows when I go out on the streets?" She was trying to make light of it but she was half serious.

"No, my love. The bishop exaggerated. It may have been true when he lived there but those days are gone. To be sure, some of my subjects get restive and even rebellious once in a while but not to the point of armed conflict. It's different in Béziers and Montpellier, where the local lords like to take matters into their own hands. But Toulouse is far more civilized and urbane. I promise you'll be perfectly safe." He put his arm around her. She remembered how secure and cherished she'd felt the first time he did that, all those months ago in the palace in Poitiers. It was the same now. She rested her head against his shoulder.

At a gentle knock on the door, he reached for a robe and hastily put it on.

"Yes?" called Joanna.

It was Queen Eleanor's lady-in-waiting Mireille, the one with the sweet face and the curly brown hair. She spoke quickly, plainly embarrassed at intruding on the honeymoon couple.

"If you please, Queen Eleanor says that since everybody is leaving tomorrow, will you come to her chamber so she can bid you a proper farewell?"

"Of course," said Joanna. "Tell her we'll be there shortly."

Forty minutes later, they entered Eleanor's apartment, the rooms reserved for the bishop's most honored visitors. Joanna wore a gown of ivory wool, caught at the waist with a sash of green lace. Her hair was pinned up high on her head. Raymond, svelte and self-possessed, was in black velvet, as he'd been for the wedding, but today without the silver cross and silver-embroidered cape he'd worn the day before.

Eleanor peered at them appraisingly.

"That hair style becomes you, Joanna. Now Count Raymond, I believe you intend to leave for Toulouse tomorrow?"

"We do. So I'm glad to have this opportunity to see you before we part company."

"Yes. Well, perhaps I'll find time to come visit you in the south some day."

"We shall hope that day comes soon."

"So we say goodbye for now. I wish you Godspeed and a safe journey. Now if you don't mind I wish to speak to my daughter alone. Remember, I shall depend on you to take good care of her."

Joanna saw the flicker of annoyance on his face at the abrupt dismissal. He spoke quickly, not quite as smoothly and circumspectly as usual.

"You may be sure I shall." He put an arm around Joanna. "And I'll expect her to take good care of me."

Joanna laughed and Raymond bent to whisper in her ear, "Don't be long. I'll be waiting in our chamber. I'll order supper and then we'll practice taking care of each other."

Eleanor watched this exchange with a mixture of indulgence and impatience. When Raymond had left, she took Joanna's arm and led her to the fireplace. They sat opposite each other, the mother in a high-backed thronelike chair, the daughter in one quite clearly subordinate but still elegant. The room was warm and dimly lit and Joanna, catching a whiff of a sweet floral scent, saw a bowl of rose petals on the table at her side.

She prepared herself for a lecture. Was she to be instructed in wifely obedience? Or warned against Raymond's inconstancy? Or merely congratulated on making such a politically desirable marriage?

Uncharacteristically, Eleanor reached to take Joanna's hand. Looking into her mother's eyes, Joanna noticed the first time how the brilliant blue had dulled.

"I shall miss you, Joanna. Your being with me in Poitiers these past few years has been a comfort to me. I know I often seem to ignore you, but blame it on my preoccupation with the never-ending details of administering Aquitaine. Not to mention substituting for Richard in managing English affairs."

"Yes, don't you wish sometimes he'd spend less time building castles and more in ruling his kingdom?"

"I do. But we both know he's unlikely to change his ways."

"And there's John for you to worry about as well." Joanna was perfectly happy to keep the conversation on other topics than herself.

"Yes, but that's another story. Though I do tremble to think of poor England if Richard should die without an heir. It looks more and more likely that Berengaria will continues to be childless. And if John should succeed, I won't be here forever to keep an eye on him." She bent her head and looked meditatively at her folded hands, then pulled herself together and sat straight again.

"But we're here to talk about you, not your brothers. I have high hopes for this marriage. You seem genuinely fond of each other. I believe Raymond has finally found the right partner, who can share with him in the duties of governing. You were a successful queen, surely you'll shine as a countess. However, there's one aspect of your new situation that may not have occurred to you."

Joanna steeled herself. Here it comes, she thought.

"You feel loyalty, of course, to Raymond and the House of Toulouse. But you're still a member of the English royal family. If both Richard and John should die leaving no male heir, a son of yours would be in line to inherit the throne. And Raymond will be eager for a son to inherit Toulouse. I urge you to guard your health when you become pregnant. I intend to send one of my best physicians to Toulouse against the day when you may need him."

"Thank you. Though I don't know what I can do beyond what I did when I was William's wife. But of course I'll be careful."

"I'm sure you will." Eleanor leaned forward and spoke even more earnestly than before, her eyes fixed on Joanna's.

"The crucial matter, of course, is becoming pregnant in the first place. Here you can indeed affect your fate. I have an idea that you and William were so attached to each other that he came to your bed without being cajoled into it. Raymond may be another matter."

Joanna felt an intense distaste for the subject. Somewhere in the back of her mind still lingered the foreboding that Raymond might prove unfaithful to her, as he had been to her predecessors. But she'd managed to keep it at bay. Now her mother had raised the possibility. And was she being urged to act like a flirtatious seductress? To pretend to be someone she wasn't?

But suddenly she remembered a long-ago time when she had found it necessary to seduce William—there was no other word for it. It was after the tragic death of their baby son. As after her miscarriage, she'd been deeply depressed. But soon she'd come to her senses and saw that the future still held hope for her and William. Unfortunately, as she recalled, by then William had become so fearful of causing her to undergo another disastrous pregnancy that he had given up his conjugal duties—or pleasures. So there was nothing else for it. She fell back on feminine wiles she didn't know she had. She dressed in a revealing gown, had

Mary arrange her hair in the style that William liked best, applied a little discreet color to her cheeks and invited her husband to an intimate romantic dinner in her apartment. And it worked. He was easily lured back to her bed.

She smiled at the memory. Eleanor peered at her suspiciously. She'd been expecting an outburst. Joanna rose and bent to kiss her mother on the cheek.

"I see what you mean, mother. I'll do my best. And we'll hope to see you soon in Toulouse."

62

Joanna to Berengaria
16 March, 1197
My dear friend, it has been far too long since you heard from me, and even lon-
ger since we saw each other—not since my wedding, over a year ago! I pray you are well
and content. I'm glad to say that I have little to complain of and much to make me happy.
I shall tell you more of what my life is like when I see you, which I hope will be soon.

But now for my news: I am with child! Will you consider coming to see me in
Beaucaire? The Counts of Toulouse have a castle there, overlooking the Rhone. At present
it's inhabited only by Raymond's Aunt Mathilde, whom I understand to be a lady of
advanced years. Raymond says it will be a quiet, comfortable place for me to spend the
last few months before the birth, which we expect to be in August. I plan to leave for
Beaucaire in a few weeks. I am feeling very well and I am full of hope. It would make
me even happier if I could look forward to seeing you.

You may wonder why I don't stay in Toulouse for the lying-in. The situation in Tou-
louse is unstable right now. I'll explain that when I see you. Please make plans to come.
Joanna

Berengaria to Joanna
4 April, 1197
Dear Sister Joanna,

I rejoice with you about the baby you are expecting. Of course I will come to Beau-
caire. A journey would be a pleasant change from my very quiet life. I could come in mid-
June and stay for the birth if that suits you. I'll bring my maid Cristina, her husband,
and Lady Héloise, whom you met when you were here. She has proved a good companion.

I wonder if your mother will come to Beaucaire. I've heard nothing from her in
months though I regularly receive the stipend that her majordomo Alphonse sends for
maintenance of Beaufort Castle. Nor have I heard from Richard, though that doesn't
surprise me.

I shall think of some news to report when I see you, even if only of my herb garden.
Berengaria

On a fine day in mid-May Count Raymond of Toulouse, with the captain of
his knights at his side, headed a long train of riders traveling northward from Toulouse to Beaucaire. Their route led them along a poplar-lined road that ran beside

the river Rhone. Joanna was near the forefront, just behind Raymond. After her came Henri de Jarnac, one of Raymond's counselors, and his wife, Lady Elaine.

Joanna felt at peace, enjoying the warmth of the sun, the gentle breeze that caressed her face, and a general sense of well-being. Her horse, a large, broad-backed, easy-gaited gray, trotted placidly along, needing no direction from her and content to follow Raymond's steed. The reins lay loosely in Joanna's hands and her thoughts strayed. *How good it will be to see Berengaria! We have so much catching up to do. She'll want to know more about why I'm not staying in Toulouse for my child's birth. I'll explain that some of Raymond's vassals in nearby regions were making demands he didn't agree with and that he felt I'd be safer elsewhere in the very unlikely event of violence. Then I'll ask her how life is in Beaufort and the subject of Richard will come up. That might not be pleasant. But then we'll talk about the baby boy I pray for.*

She was imagining holding the newborn baby in her arms and looking into his wrinkled little face, when Lady Elaine drew up beside her.

"Henri says we're almost to Beaucaire and you might appreciate it if I told you something about it, since we've been here before and you haven't."

She had a high, whiny voice and Joanna resented being jolted so abruptly out of her reverie. She'd found Lady Elaine hard to get to know, often withdrawn, almost sullen. She was a small woman with a face that once may have been pretty but looked as though it had been soured by years of unhappiness, perhaps by an inharmonious marriage.

Before Joanna could assure her that Raymond had already told her a good deal about Beaucaire, Elaine rattled on as though reciting a lesson. "Now, that's the town just coming into sight and you can see all the boats moored along the shore. It's quite a fishing town, and some of the bigger boats go all the way to the Mediterranean Sea, can you imagine!"

Joanna wanted to tell her she was far less interested in the fishermen than in the castle —how well it was furnished, the condition and number of the latrines— when Raymond reined in his horse, turned in the saddle and announced, "There it is! Beaucaire Castle." Startled, she followed his gaze up to where two lofty stone towers on a hill lorded it over the town. A high wall connected the towers, hiding whatever constituted the rest of the castle.

"But it looks so big! Why did you tell me it was just a modest little castle?"

"I didn't want you to expect too much. It's neither as roomy nor as elegantly furnished as our palace in Toulouse. When we get up there you'll see how modest it is."

The captain of the troop of knights approached Raymond. "I'll leave you now and get the men settled here below in the town, shall I?"

"Yes, their lodgings have been arranged. See that the horses are well stabled and then come report to me in the castle and we'll discuss tomorrow's trip to Paris."

Joanna knew that Raymond would go on to Paris but, aside from the fact that

King Philip had urgently summoned him, she wasn't sure why. He wasn't always forthcoming about his plans and motives. She believed that it wasn't so much that he didn't want her to know about his governance and political activities, he merely forgot to tell her. Maybe he wasn't used to a wife who cared about such thing.

And maybe she'd be able to tease some information out of him later.

The depleted party, still sizeable, started up the narrow road that wound its way to the castle. Joanna patted her horse to encourage it to make the last climb. "It won't be long now, Grisette. We're almost at the end of this long journey." As though sensing that rest and oats were almost at hand, Grisette quickened her pace. Joanna turned in her saddle to see how the rest of the party were faring. It looked like a small army straggling up the hill. Besides Joanna's and Raymond's personal servants, there were Sir Henri de Jarnac and Lady Elaine; Lady Adelaide and two other ladies-in-waiting; cooks and grooms; potboys and pages; manservants and ladies' maids; messengers; a physician, and a chaplain.

"Aunt Mathilde doesn't require many servants," Raymond had explained when Joanna asked why they were taking so many people. "But with you and all your party, there'll be many more demands. And of course I'll be coming as often as I can to see you and make sure all's well with you. And I'll need to confer with my vassals here and to convene my council. So for a time Beaucaire will be like a small Toulouse, with its own court and court activities. Very different from the quiet way you see it now, when Aunt Mathilde is here alone." Joanna was beginning to see this aunt as a silent, reclusive old lady who would keep to her rooms and appear only for meals, if then. I'll be glad, Joanna thought, to have Berengaria's companionship. In the meantime, there's Lady Adelaide.

As she passed over the drawbridge, Joanna looked up at the formidable towers. They would intimidate and repel the most stout-hearted enemy. They were pierced with dozens of slits through which flights of arrows could be launched simultaneously. Embrasures all along the high wall provided for still more bowmen.

Once they were through the stout gate and in the bailey, everyone dismounted, glad of a chance to get the kinks out after so many hours in the saddle. Surveying what stood before her, Joanna saw what Raymond meant. The two towers were the most impressive features, dwarfing the row of undistinguished low stone buildings that ran along the wall between them. The one in the center was the largest, three stories high, with glazing in the windows and a high arched double door.

"Aunt Mathilde lives on the top level," said Raymond. "You and your ladies will have the other two." While Joanna was wondering how poor old Aunt Mathilde managed all the stairs, the doors opened and a tall woman in a purple gown appeared and walked briskly down the steps. She had iron-gray hair, cut short so it barely reached her earlobes, and a face dominated by a classically dimensioned Roman nose. Her expression was open and welcoming, and her eyes were as blue as cornflowers. She had a wide mouth, and her lips were raised at the corners as though ready to smile. Joanna was to learn that Aunt Mathilde generally found life amusing.

"So you are Joanna." She took both of Joanna's hands in hers and stood look-ing at her, her head cocked to one side. "I like you already. My nephew chose well."

"And you are Aunt Mathilde—may I call you Aunt? I'm so happy to meet you and to find that you're not…" She paused in her confusion.

"Not decrepit? Yes, many people think that only a bedridden recluse would live in this solitary spot. I'll hope to show you how one can occupy oneself without a crowd around. We'll have plenty of time for that—about four months, I'd guess." She looked appraisingly at the slight bulge of Joanna's midsection. "That's when the little one is due? Ah, here's Raymond. Greetings, nephew."

Raymond permitted Mathilde to plant kisses on both cheeks, responded in kind and gave her a squeeze of the shoulder and a smile. Joanna could see he felt real affection. She looked forward to knowing Aunt Mathilde better.

It took several hours to get settled and stow the mountains of baggage they'd brought. But by evening, all was in order. Supper was served in the dining hall of the count's palace, as the large central building was called. It was a quick, subdued meal. Most of the travelers were tired and eager for bed. They'd run out of things to talk about to each other long ago. The exception was Lady Adelaide. Seated next to Lady Elaine, she delivered a commentary on what she thought of the castle, how glad she was they could rest at last, and what she expected life in Beaucaire would be like. Elaine listened stoically and murmured an occasional "Ah!" or "I expect so."

Joanna looked across the table, caught Elaine's eye and smiled. She made a mental note to assure her that despite Adelaide's talkativeness she was loyal, gener-ous and unfailingly good-humored.

Henri de Jarnac, seated to Joanna's right and who up to then had paid more attention to his rabbit stew than to her, happened to look up and caught the smile.

He was a large, broad man with a beefy face and full red lips that were mostly concealed by his bushy blond beard. His cap of tightly curled hair was the same washed-out-looking blond. His pale eyes constantly darted about as though on the alert for anything suspicious. Now they were fixed on her, as though challenging her.

"Now what do you find so amusing, my lady? I must say I find this a rather dour company, except for that talkative magpie over there next to my wife."

These were almost the first words Joanna had heard from him. He'd ridden in the rear with the knights for most of the journey. Neither the words nor the tone were as ingratiating as he obviously hoped.

"I smiled because I've known Lady Adelaide so long, and she's never let up on the conversation, one-sided as it is. I must tell your wife that she really is a good soul and she'll get used to it."

"I see. That leads me to thank you for befriending my wife. I was pleased to see the two of you chatting earlier as we approached Beaucaire. Frankly, Elaine will need a friend while we're here. It was hard enough for her to be uprooted from Béziers for Toulouse, and now this. What a primitive pigsty!"

She looked at him in surprise, then examined the room more attentively. The tables were scrubbed and polished, the chairs reasonably comfortable. The floors had been swept clean. There were no mice darting into holes or hungry hounds skulking in corners on filthy rushes.

"If I were a pig, I'd be perfectly happy here. Especially if my meals were served as expeditiously as ours are today."

He ignored that. "It's just that it's nothing like what she's used to." He sighed like a solicitous husband. But Joanna had her doubts. There was something false and devious about this man. She felt he would bear watching.

"It won't be easy for any of us to adapt to new circumstances. But of course I'll do my best to make things pleasant for Lady Elaine. Tell me, if you were so happy in Béziers, why did you leave?"

He shot a wary glance at her. She could almost guess what he was thinking: I've said enough. "Perhaps you'd better ask your husband about that. It was his wish." And he turned back to his plate, picked a dripping thighbone out of his stew and began to gnaw on it. It struck her that he looked rather like a pig.

Very well, thought Joanna. I will indeed ask Raymond.

By the time she and Raymond were alone that night in their bedchamber, she had quite a list of things to ask him. But first they made love—gently, tenderly, carefully, so as not to disturb the new life within her. Afterwards, reclining on a pile of pillows, Joanna absently stroked Raymond's hand that rested lightly on her breast. She looked around the room with its stone walls softened by tapestries, the cream-colored damask curtains for their bed, and gilded candelabra in sconces on the walls. A fire was cheerily aglow and a-crackle, with two chairs drawn up before it.

"Why is this so much nicer than the other rooms in the palace?"

"It was my father's doing. He found himself spending a good deal of time in Beaucaire, and he got tired of the drab, comfortless old castle and set out to do something about it. But he didn't get any farther than Aunt Mathilde's rooms and this apartment before he died."

"Bad luck for Sir Henri. He compared the castle to a pigsty."

"Ha. He would." Raymond snorted. "He takes a morose view of the world in general."

"So I decided. If he's that kind of a man, why did you appoint him to come along? Some of your other counselors seem much more congenial."

Raymond pulled himself up to a sitting position. "So they are. I've been meaning to tell you about Henri de Jarnac. I strongly suspect him of being the instigator of the troubles we've been having in Toulouse. I brought him to Toulouse from Béziers when I first had information that he planned to lead a rebellion against me. I thought if I could keep an eye on him he'd be less able to make trouble. But he's a wily sort and I finally decided my best course was to remove him from his fellow conspirators altogether. When I'm not here, you'll need to watch him carefully."

"But what if he appears to be up to something while you're off in Paris? It would take days and days to get word to you."

"I've thought of that. The captain of the knights will stay here in the castle.

I trust him completely. He's a resourceful man. If you suspect anything, tell him
at once. He'll take action if he sees fit and he'll send a swift messenger to me."
He leaned over to kiss her on the cheek and smoothed her hair. "Now don't look
so alarmed. I'm sorry to place this responsibility on you, but very likely nothing
will happen. Besides, you're pretty resourceful yourself. From what you've told me
you've been through a few palace intrigues in Sicily."

"I suppose that's true." She thought of her disputes with William's underhand-
ed chancellor, Matthew of Ajello, and with William's unspeakable mother, who'd
tried to kill her. She'd been a young, untried queen yet somehow she'd managed to
circumvent their scheming. "But now…" She didn't go on. She wanted to say, what
about the safety and security you promised me if I'd marry you? But this wasn't the
time. She still had questions. Raymond had lain down again and was yawning. She
snuggled next to him.

"I wish I were going to Paris with you. I've never been there. And I'll miss you."

"I promise I'll take you one day, but you must take care of yourself now.
No more jolting horseback travel until after the child is born. Besides, this is no
pleasure trip. King Philip has summoned me, but I know it isn't an invitation to a
garden party at his grand Parisian palace."

"What is it then?"

"Very likely a command to stamp out the Cathar heresy that defies the church
and the pope and insists on seeking salvation in its own way. He'll order me to turn
all suspects over to the church for questioning."

"And what will you say to that? I know you have some sympathy for the Cathars."

I'll say yes sir, and that will be that."

"But will you do as he asks?"

"I shall procrastinate. As long as they're law-abiding citizens I see no reason to
deprive them of their place in society. Some day I suppose I'll have to take a stand.
But I hope that day's long in coming."

After Raymond fell asleep, Joanna lay awake, worrying. She thought Raymond
was more apprehensive than he let on about the interview with King Philip. It's
no light matter to disregard an order from one's king. But more than that, she
felt uneasy about being responsible for what amounted to spying on Sir Henri.
Whom could she turn to? She didn't think Aunt Mathilde would be much help.
Her talents lay in household management and crafting a fulfilling life for herself in
her chosen solitude. When Berengaria came at least they could talk freely but she
wasn't sure what they could really do if some crisis arose. It was reassuring to know
she could call on the captain, but Raymond had placed the primary responsibility
on her shoulders.

What she really needed was her old friend Brother Jean-Pierre with his calm,
wise counsel. But as far as she knew he was in England on some mission for Queen
Eleanor. But if he were here, what then?

She closed her eyes, not so much inviting sleep as summoning up his brown, lined face with the little smile that said, "I'm on your side and always will be."

And his words?

"Joanna my dear, you've reached a point in your life when all your past can be drawn on to support and guide you. You've risen to new situations and found the way to navigate new paths. You've been a princess, a queen, a widow, a countess, and soon you'll be a mother. Now you may be called on to act on your own. Don't be fearful. Ask God for strength and wisdom and he will hear you."

She opened her eyes to darkness, except for the flickering light of the dying fire. Beside her Raymond snored almost inaudibly.

She closed her eyes again. She murmured, "Thank you for your advice, Jean-Pierre. I'll sleep on it."

63

"And what do you think of Henri de Jarnac? Have any of you had time to form an opinion?" Joanna asked. "How about you, Aunt Mathilde?"

The ladies had sought refuge from the July sun in Mathilde's grape arbor. She'd just led a tour of her garden. It wasn't large, but presented a nice balance of floral display (roses, columbines, daisies) and utilitarian plantings (lettuce, beets, onions, herbs). Berengaria and her companion, Héloise, who had their own garden at Beaufort, made intelligent comments. Joanna, never much of a gardener, confined herself to admiring exclamations. But she liked the way the expanse of vibrant colors, where all was vigorously alive and in order, offered such a cheerful contrast to the gray, forbidding Beaucaire castle.

In only a few weeks the foursome had established an easy-going rapport. Joanna had taken to Héloise at once, partly because she knew Berengaria was so fond of her. In appearance she was almost a caricature of Mathilde—tall, long-legged and so thin as to resemble a stork. But she'd come to terms with her ungainly body, wore loose flowing gowns and walked without hurry and with surprising grace. She had a calm, unruffled demeanor and none of Mathilde's brusque outspokenness.

At Joanna's question, Mathilde exploded with a derisive "Henri de Jarnac? Ha! Indeed I have an opinion and it's not favorable." She folded her arms and glared at the others as though accusing them of Henri's shortcomings. "I can't imagine why Raymond keeps him on his council, such a crude example of humanity."

Joanna was about to explain Raymond's reasoning (keep the potential trouble-maker in plain view) but caught herself. It would be a breach of her husband's trust to divulge their private conversations. She merely said, "I agree. And I deplore the way he treats his wife, poor woman."

"Only yesterday," said Berengaria, "when she said at dinner that she particularly liked the peas with onions and saffron, he growled, 'What are you babbling about? There wasn't any saffron. Turmeric, more likely. You wouldn't know saffron from sausage.' And poor Elaine was as deflated as a pricked bladder. She didn't say another word for the rest of the meal."

But the Elaine now approaching through the garden with Adelaide looked far from deflated. For once, Adelaide was doing the listening as Elaine enthusiastically pointed out the herbs and their names and uses. Joanna had never seen her look so animated. She resolved to try harder to befriend her.

The newcomers found room on the benches in the arbor and sat down with sighs of relief. "So hot!" said Adelaide. "So much hotter than Poitiers."

"Well, of course. We're considerably to the south of Poitiers," said Mathilde.

Joanna was feeling the heat too, and longed for a nap. She'd found carrying her unborn child around increasingly fatiguing. And she was disinclined to spend time discussing the weather. She rose.

"I believe I'll go in now and have a rest."

"I'll come with you," said Mathilde. "I must make sure the cook got the message that we'll be ten at dinner. And bless me, I forgot to make sure he ordered up enough partridges. We'll need at least fifteen. I fear I may have told him a dozen." She muttered to herself, counting on her fingers, while Joanna, fascinated, observed her. Besides admiration for Mathilde's attention to detail, she felt profound gratitude that she herself didn't have to worry lest, should the worst befall, she'd have to divide twelve partridges among ten diners.

Fanning themselves, they made their way slowly back to the palace. They'd barely set their feet on the first step when they heard the rapid clop-clop of hooves on the drawbridge. A horseman rode into the bailey at a near gallop but, when he saw Joanna and Mathilde, approached more sedately.

Dismounting, he mopped his red and perspiring face with his sleeve, drew several deep breaths and addressed Joanna.

"I bring you a message from Count Raymond, my lady."

"Then you are very welcome. We haven't heard from him for three weeks. Come in out of the sun and we'll send for cool water."

Inside, Mathilde sent the page on duty for water and wine. The messenger gratefully accepted a mug of water and dispatched it in three gulps. He came to attention and delivered his message.

"Count Raymond sends greetings and informs you that he is on his way to Beaucaire from Toulouse with three of his counselors. He plans to hold a meeting of his council tomorrow and hopes that the countess will feel well enough to attend."

"I see," said Joanna, but she didn't. She'd seen Raymond only once since coming to Beaucaire in May. He'd stopped on his way back from Paris to tell her that he'd correctly guessed why Philip had summoned him. Raymond was directed to show more zeal in apprehending the heretics. Beyond that, King Philip told him that the church, under instructions from the pope, planned to send several more inquisitors to speed the subjugation of the Cathars.

"It might be quite unwise for me to delay and try to avoid strict obedience," Raymond had told her. "I'll need to hurry back to Toulouse and get a better idea of what the situation is." So, after conferring with the physician and assuring himself that Joanna's health was all it should be, he'd left again. But why was he coming now, she wondered, and planning a council meeting? And why had she been bidden to attend? He'd never asked her to do so in Toulouse. But the messenger, now appreciatively drinking his wine, wouldn't have the answers.

Mathilde too had questions, but she could voice hers. "When will they arrive?

Surely not in time for dinner?"

"No, Madame, they are still half a day away. They should arrive tomorrow in time for a late breakfast."

Relieved, Mathilde went on to the kitchen. Breakfast needn't involve partridges.

Joanna thanked the messenger and retired for her nap.

Raymond arrived the next morning at nine and breakfasted privately with Joanna. Though he'd taken time to wash and change from his travel-worn clothes, he still looked tired. When he greeted her and kissed her she saw with concern that his face showed lines of worry on his forehead and around his eyes.

He sighed with relief as he sat down opposite her at the small table by the window, just right for two. A servant brought a plate of cold meats and fresh bread. A flagon of ale was already on the table. Raymond poured himself a mug and surveyed Joanna.

"Are you really my very pregnant wife? It's hard to tell what's concealed by that voluminous gown. Are you feeling as well as you look?"

"I feel very well, thanks be. The physician can find nothing to be concerned about. I do tire very quickly. I need a lot of sleep, but he says that's to be expected and good for me."

"I wish he'd prescribe more sleep for me. I've been on the road for ten days, all the way from Montpellier."

"I suppose you were there because of this matter of the heretic Cathars? And is that what the council meeting this morning is all about?"

"You're right." He drew a deep breath and let it out before going on. "I've decided to make a show of complying with the king's orders. I've enlisted a few of my most influential vassals to help me carry out my scheme. There'll be Arnaud Cabot from Montpellier, François Compagne from Toulouse, Jacques de Fauchet from Carcassone and of course Henri de Jarnac from Béziers. You may remember the other three from seeing them in the palace at Toulouse from time to time."

"I certainly remember Arnaud Cabot—a big, noisy, black-haired man. He always seemed to be shouting at his companions or laughing immoderately at some *bon mot* he'd loosed."

"That's Arnaud all right. But he's always been loyal and willing to help when I need his services. In fact I think I can count on all of them, except possibly Henri de Jarnac. I gather he's shown no signs of plotting or collusion or I'd have heard from you or Captain Floret."

"I can't point to any signs of misbehavior on his part, but that's because we see so little of him. Captain Floret says he seems to spend most of his time in the town, drinking with his cronies among the knights. We see him only at dinner, if then."

"What about his wife? Have you been able to learn anything from her?"

"Not really. I've tried to get to know her better. I do feel sorry for her; Henri is so unkind. But when I try, as tactfully as I can, to feel her out about him she becomes close-mouthed or tries to turn the conversation to me, and what I hear from you. I have the idea by now that Henri has instructed her to dig up what she can about you and your intentions. Of course she learns nothing from me. So we actually cancel each other out. She's not a very good secret agent."

After a pause she added ruefully, "But then neither am I."

He laughed and placed his hand on hers where it lay on the table. "Ah, but you have other attributes, my dear."

"Such as?" She loved it when he relaxed enough for this kind of intimate raillery.

"Such as…motherhood. It seems to make you even more beautiful. Do you have any idea how your face just glows with some private happiness?"

"I don't know how I look but I know how I feel, and I am happy, eager for the birth but content to wait until God says the time has come." They smiled at each other in quiet, shared anticipation. He drew her to her feet and embraced her.

"Much as I'd like to stay here, we must be off to the council meeting. Are you going to be warm enough? It gets a bit chilly in that room."

"I'll put on a wool shawl, and that will also help conceal my ungainly figure. But Raymond, you haven't really told me why you want me at the meeting."

"No, I suppose I haven't. I'll explain quickly, while we walk along. I'd like you there because I'm afraid you're going to be called on to get more involved in my affairs. When I was growing up I used to wonder why my father was gone so much. Now that I've been count of Toulouse for two years I understand. The count must oversee all of Languedoc, from Gascony in the west to the Rhone in the east, and from the Mediterranean to the borders of Queen Eleanor's Aquitaine. He must stay ahead of events, and that means constantly calling on his vassals, allaying their concerns, rewarding them for their services, deciding whether they're about to foment some mischief and asking them if they know of others who might do so."

"I never thought of it just like that. It's a tremendous responsibility. How can I help? How can we smooth out those wrinkles?" She reached up to brush her hand across his forehead. He took her hand and pressed it between both of his while fixing his eyes on her face.

"I need a surrogate in Toulouse when I'm away, and you're the only one I can trust absolutely. You'll need to meet with the Toulouse counselors and hear what they have to report on local affairs and anything else they think important. You'll need to get word to me if you think it's necessary. We'll have time later to talk about this. I don't plan to travel much until after the child is born."

They were at the door to the dining hall, which would serve as council chamber today.

She had a dozen questions but she had time for only one.

"Are you sure these four members of your council share your tolerance for the Cathars?"

"No, not at all. But I'm absolutely sure that they share my aversion to being ordered about by King Philip."

They went in and found the four councilors seated around the table, at ease with each other and chatting. An attendant stood by, watchful for wine goblets in need of refills. The men rose when Raymond and Joanna entered.

At this hour the dining hall was bleak and cheerless. Joanna shivered and pulled her shawl up to her chin. Why wasn't the fire lit? Just because it was nearly August didn't mean the interior of the thick-walled old castle became appreciably warmer. Raymond saw her discomfort and instructed the attendant to tend to the fire immediately.

He gestured to his vassals to be seated and saw to it that Joanna was settled in the chair beside his at the head of the table. He himself remained standing.

"Good morning, gentlemen. We all know each other well and I think you all know the countess. I expect you have a good idea of why I've asked you here."

"I hope you're finally going to do something about those accursed heretics." That was Henri de Jarnac, truculent as usual. Joanna noticed an unsightly wine stain on his wrinkled linen tunic.

"Yes, in a way I am, as I'll explain. But first, you may have heard that the pope has sent several new representatives to help in discovering and interrogating the leaders of the Cathar heresy. King Philip has ordered me to cooperate with them. Much as I resent his imperious ways—and I know you do as well--I suggest we make a show of obeying. I propose that each of you give one name to the inquisitor in your region, implying that more will be provided as you discover them. Ideally, you would name a person already known for criminal activity and also suspected of heresy, but not necessarily a leader in the sect. I'll do the same in Toulouse. After this initial demonstration of our obedience we'll sit back and see what happens."

In silence they took this in. Raymond continued.

"This approach should sound reasonable to the papal delegates and to the king. You're the logical ones to identify a likely suspect. Who has better knowledge of your own fellow-citizens? Certainly it will be more efficient than if the churchmen went about trying to dig up information from strangers."

"Right," boomed Arnaud Cabot, tossing a shock of black hair out of his eyes. "I can think of half a dozen likely miscreants right now." He held up his thumb. "There's Richard Goncourt, the farmer on the road to Saint-Denis. Everybody knows he's stolen cattle from his neighbors. He held up his forefinger. "And the butcher in …"

"That's all very well," Raymond interrupted, "but for now all I want from you is one name each. That should give the inquisitors something to chew on for quite a while. They tend to be extremely thorough and deliberative in their interrogations."

"Even so," said François Compagne, "this is at best a delaying tactic." Younger than the others, he had a fine head of red-gold hair that reminded Joanna of her brother Richard. But François was shorter and a good deal slimmer than Richard. "What next, when they want new names?"

"That concerns me as well. I hope by the time that happens the whole thing will have blown over. Maybe the pope will find some other target. Maybe he'll urge another Crusade to Jerusalem."

"But if not, we'll have to provide new names, won't we?" François was persistent.

"We will." Raymond said shortly. He didn't need to be reminded that sooner or later he was going to have show more support for the inquisitors.

"Meantime," said Henri, "it's a fine short-term plan. Anything to keep Philip and those black-robed Roman vultures from meddling in our affairs. Besides, it's a chance to get rid of a few troublemakers at the same time."

Joanna had been listening with growing uneasiness. Somebody should ask this question and it seemed to be up to her.

"I wonder..." she began tentatively, but stopped when she saw the surprise on the councilors' faces. It angered her. Why did they think she was there, if not to take part in the deliberations? She went on, more firmly. "What would happen if one of you made a mistake and named an innocent person, one who perhaps isn't even sympathetic to the heresy? And what if they imprisoned or even executed him? Wouldn't you be sorry, if it came to that?" She looked at each of the four men in turn, finally at Raymond. His face was in the shadows but she thought she detected the slight pressing together of his lips that showed his annoyance.

"I agree there is that risk," he said. "But I've concluded that it's better to sacrifice one who may be guiltless than to let the inquisitor pull in a dozen suspects, equally likely to be innocent."

"It's a fine point," said Jacques de Fauchet, hitherto silent. "But I'm inclined to agree with Count Raymond."

"Nevertheless," said Joanna, "I can't believe a just God would condone it."

"Dear countess, the ways of a just God are sometimes difficult for us mortals to comprehend," Jacques said, twirling between his fingers his small unimpressive mustache. Joanna felt an instant distaste for his condescension but knew better than to start an argument.

"Indeed, I'm sure you're right," she said, smiling as sweetly as she could.

Raymond sent her a quick look of approval. She thought perhaps she was acquiring some skill at guile.

The others went on to discuss more mundane matters—the difficulty of collecting taxes from some of the more wealthy landowners and whether the bridge across the Rhone, in need of repair to its buttresses, was the responsibility of Beaucaire or Tarascon. Joanna was hardly listening. So this is a council meeting, she thought. I remember being present at William's meetings sometimes, but they were nothing like this. William didn't have to be so cautious and on his guard with his council. He knew them and trusted them. Then she remembered Matthew of Ajello and Archbishop Walter. Wily, loyal only to themselves, totally untrustworthy. Would any of these four men prove equally despicable? She considered them. The only one she'd remotely trust was François Compagne, who had openly and without bombast questioned Raymond's plan. He seemed honest and without self-interest.

She was beginning to feel a strange physical uneasiness as though something were churning about in her stomach. With no warning she was struck by an agonizing pain. She kept herself from crying out but when it had passed she rose to her feet.

"I'm sorry, but I'm feeling unwell. I think I had better get some rest."

Raymond saw how stricken she looked.

"Just sit a moment and I'll call Jeanette to see you to your room. I'll send for the physician and we'll come up in a few minutes."

She looked at him in tremulous gratitude. They both knew what was happening. Though it was three weeks too soon, the child was ready to be born.

64

All during her pregnancy Joanna had never doubted that this birth would go well. In spite of previous miscarriages and the untimely death of the infant Bohemund, she was serenely confident. One night she had a vivid dream. The Virgin Mary appeared and told her, "Your prayers will be answered, my daughter. You will bear a healthy child who will live long." Joanna tried to ask her if it would be a boy or a girl, but the apparition vanished into a golden haze.

Mary spoke truth. After a short labor a perfect, healthy baby boy came into the world. When, washed and well swaddled, he was brought for the parents' inspection, Joanna wept tears of joy. Raymond beamed with pride and consented to hold the child gingerly for a minute.

"What a very red face he has. He looks angry."

"Newborns usually look like that," said Nurse Marie. "Everything's so strange to them and they have so much to take in all at once, poor babes."

When in ten days the bishop of Toulouse came for the christening, there was no question of the name: Raymond, future Count Raymond VII of Toulouse.

Joanna was a nervous mother. She resisted turning the baby's care over to others, but she was just as hesitant in trusting herself to tend to him properly. To her dismay, she didn't have enough milk so she had to depend on a wet nurse. She worried and fussed about the baby constantly. Raymond offered sympathy but very little practical help. Once the child was christened, his duties beckoned and he became abstracted, receiving and dispatching messengers and writing instructions for the governing council in Toulouse. Often he was gone for days at a time with little or no explanation to Joanna. But she was too taken up with motherhood to notice. She forgot to eat properly and became alarmingly thin.

Finally Berengaria decided she had to speak. She and Joanna had finished breakfast and Joanna rose, saying she'd go up to see if the baby had been nursed and put back in his cradle.

Berengaria put a hand on her arm. "Do sit down a minute, my dear. There's no hurry. The nurses know what they're doing and they're devoted to your son. And goodness knows they've had experience in caring for babies—Marie's the mother of five and Jeanne even more, seven I think she told me."

"Six," said Joanna. She felt like putting her hands over her ears. She didn't want a lecture.

"Very well, six. But the point is that you're wearing yourself out needlessly.

And it's affecting your health, to say nothing of your looks. Excuse me for saying so, but you've taken to putting on any old garment instead of paying attention to your clothes as you used to. Look at that brown shapeless bag you're wearing. You're getting thin and you always have a worried frown. You hide your beautiful hair under a cap. Do you want Raymond to see his wife grow careless and unattractive?"

Joanna's cheeks flamed with anger. If it had been anyone but Berengaria she would have jumped up and flounced out of the room. But this was her best friend, the one she always listened to. She bent her head and, shoulders hunched, waited for calm to return. At last she straightened and looked up.

"You may be right. It's just that now, after so many losses, I have a healthy, gloriously alive child and I'm terrified something will go wrong."

Berengaria got up and put her arms around Joanna. "I understand, truly I do. And I'm sorry if I was too blunt."

"No, no. Thank you for speaking so frankly. Of course the nurses are competent. I must try to let them handle things and not feel I have to do it all myself. So I'm always too tired to spend more time with Raymond. I'll try to mend my ways." She looked with distaste at her brown sack of a gown. "I'll go up and look in at the nursery, and then I'll have my maid transform me into a new person."

"Not too new. All we want is the Joanna we've always known."

In another week Berengaria left for Beaufort, encouraged by Joanna's improved attitude as well as her appearance. Shortly Raymond told Joanna he too would have to leave, though they'd planned to make the journey back to Toulouse together when the baby was a few weeks older.

"I wish I could stay," he told her, "but I must see to matters in Albi. There's a sizeable colony of Cathars there, and Jacques de Fauchet and some of his vassals have practically declared war on them. I must try to douse the fire before it gets out of control. To tell you the truth, Joanna, I'm getting just a little tired of those bothersome heretics and how hard it is to keep matters from getting explosive."

Another parting, thought Joanna. If this keeps up I might get tired of the heretics too. But I must get used to it.

On Raymond's last morning at Beaucaire she walked with him to the courtyard where his groom was holding his horse's bridle. They stood side by side near the palace steps. Nurse Jeanne had brought the baby out, but he slept soundly in her arms, oblivious of the activity. Half a dozen knights, already mounted, waited while their steeds whinnied and snorted and stamped their hooves on the hard ground. Henri de Jarnac had just eased himself into his saddle, looking grumpy at having to be up and about so early in the morning. His wife, Elaine, would go later with Joanna. She didn't come out to tell Henri goodbye.

Joanna looked up to the sky, clear except for a long bank of clouds hugging the western horizon. If she hadn't known better she'd have thought it was a snow-clad mountain range. There was definitely a cool autumnal tang to the air. She saw with surprise that the leaves of the poplars beyond the rose garden were beginning to turn.

"It feels like the end of summer," she said. "Perhaps you'll be spared from a hot journey."

"I believe I shall. And it should be quite comfortable by the time you set out." He tickled the baby under his chin. "Take care of your mother, my son." The nurse looked disapproving of the tickle, but the infant only made a few suckling movements with his rosebud of a mouth and slept on.

Raymond turned to Joanna and held her close for a moment, resting his cheek on hers. "Goodbye, my love. You'll be in good hands. Captain Floret and the knights are still here and they'll see you safely back to Toulouse. If something comes up once you're there that you need advice on, you can call the council together. I'll surely be home by the end of September. And I'll expect to find you even more blooming and beautiful when I join you."

As Raymond led his knights out of the courtyard, Joanna smiled to herself. So he'd noticed how she'd regained her good disposition and paid proper attention to her looks. She was glad she'd put on the green velvet gown and that her figure now filled it nicely, as it used to.

In three weeks Joanna was on the road as well. The party took the journey in short stages, and Captain Floret kept watch to make sure the horses maintained a slow, steady gait. Joanna, Elaine and the two nurses took turns carrying the baby. Adelaide demurred, on the grounds that she might hold him the wrong way or drop him. She'd never had a child.

Back in Toulouse Joanna settled into the familiar surroundings. How different from the cold, cramped quarters at Beaucaire! As always, she felt grateful to the counts of Toulouse who had over the years made improvements to the venerable palace. Raymond's father, the fifth count, perhaps at the prodding of his several wives and mistresses, had ordered major interior remodeling. He'd created large rooms by combining several small ones, added glazing to all the windows, installed wood paneling here and there and thick carpets imported from the East. Now the count and countess could spread out in their commodious apartments, which included a reception room, an audience chamber, two bedchambers and a private sitting room with a fine view of the River Garonne. They even had an enclosed latrine instead of having to resort to a hole-in-the-wall along a cold stone corridor. Baby Raymond and his nurses had their own quarters next to Joanna's bedroom.

Joanna had been home only a week, with Raymond still away, when François Compagne, the red-haired councilor, sent word that he had something of import to tell her. She received him in the reception room, which was smaller and less intimidating than the austere audience chamber downstairs.

He came quickly to the point. She recalled how she'd liked his directness and good sense when she met him in Beaucaire.

"I've just learned that two of the *capitouls* have declared their adherence to the Cathar heresy. It's the first public admission by anybody of such prominence. I believe we should inform Count Raymond, but in the meantime you might want to call the council together and get their advice."

For a moment she felt at a loss. *Capitouls?* Then she remembered that Raymond had once explained to her, in a rather offhand way, that these were the twelve men who governed the city of Toulouse, while he and his council were concerned with the entire Languedoc region. Though their interests converged or differed sometimes, the two bodies generally maintained their independence, each with its own jurisdiction.

"But isn't this a matter for the *capitouls* themselves to deal with?" she asked, perplexed. "If it's a threat to their ability to govern, shouldn't they decide what to do? Why should it affect Raymond and his council?"

"You're right, it shouldn't. But it might. We should always be looking ahead, calculating the effects of events like this. To my view, this is a sign that the Cathars are growing even more influential. Up to now they've been mostly laborers and farmers and merchants. But they seem to be popping up in the higher ranks. It puts the whole movement in a different light."

He paused and looked at her to make sure she understood. She noticed for the first time how blue his eyes were, an intense blue with no hint of gray or green.

"I see. And I suppose you suspect that if it's true in Toulouse, it's likely to be true elsewhere in the Languedoc."

"Exactly." He was silent, as though waiting for her to make another comment. She was silent as well, trying to remember something Raymond had once said.

"I remember now that Raymond said that if, God forbid, the heresy should spread beyond the common, ignorant folk, he'd be suspicious of motivation. He said if someone in the nobility declared himself a Cathar it could be for one of two reasons: true belief, or as a gesture of defiance to King Philip and his ally the pope."

"And did he say which he thought would be more likely?"

"Yes, the latter. And it worried him. He said anyone who made such a rebellious gesture could also be delivering a threat to his own authority if he continues to appear as a supporter of the king and the pope's inquisitors." She sighed. "It's complicated, isn't it? Such uncertainty, so many ways to go."

His smile was kind, understanding. She felt reassured. "Yes, it's complicated indeed. You're getting a useful introduction to the art of governing the county of Toulouse. And I compliment you on how quickly you grasp the situation."

"I'm not sure about that, but thank you. Now, I must send word to Raymond and urge him to hurry back. And you're right, we should convene the council. How soon do you think we can meet?"

"I'd suggest in two days' time. If you like, I can inform them. We won't find all of them here and available, but I know Henri de Jarnac and Arnaud Cabot are in the city, and several others whom you may not know."

"I'd be most grateful. You've been enormously helpful. Won't you stay a bit longer and let me send for refreshments?"

He stood up. "I'd like to, Countess, but I should start rounding up the councilors. But ask me another time. Perhaps after the council meeting, when we may feel we've accomplished something."

She held out her hand in farewell. He pressed it and walked out while she looked after him. How fortunate I am, she thought, to have the help of the one man in Raymond's council who seems disinterested and truly loyal. She felt relieved, but at the same time apprehensive about the upcoming meeting and whether she could deal with the councilors if there was dissension.

She decided to go up to the nursery and visit Baby Raymond to take her mind off these new concerns. She found him in his cradle, gurgling, and Nurse Jeanne buttoning up her blouse.

"He's just had his dinner, and what a hungry little boy he was! Oh, look how glad he is to see his mother." The baby smiled his angelic smile that always made Joanna's heart nearly stop in her breast. She knew they said babies smiled that way at anyone and everyone and it didn't mean a thing. But she was sure he was beginning to recognize her and do his best to greet her. She leaned over the cradle and picked him up.

"I'll just sit here by the window with him for a few minutes." She carefully lowered herself into a chair. Solemn now, he looked up at her as though trying to memorize her face. She rocked him a little, hummed a tune and thought, the only thing I need to be completely happy is to have Raymond here too.

"Your father will soon be back, my sweet," she assured the baby. "And then we'll all be together again."

When she met with the council two days later, she still doubted her ability to take charge. But she'd given the matter a great deal of thought. She'd observed that Raymond, when presiding, would state the subject to be considered and then ask his councilors what they thought should be done. Almost always one or more would recommend the action Raymond had already decided on, and agreement came quickly. On rare occasions he had to assert his authority and overrule someone. But he was far more interested in harmony than dissension and was often willing to compromise.

She took special care with her appearance. She recalled her mother when she presided over a gathering in her great hall in Poitiers. She always dressed for the occasion in regal gowns and always wore the crown of the queen of England. To the child Joanna, the golden crown with its profusion of brilliant emeralds and rubies epitomized majesty.

She'd realized long ago that she could never be another Eleanor—who could? But she could certainly apply to her own life what she'd learned from her mother's example.

"I'll wear the black velvet with ermine trim," she told Jeanette. "And see if you can find the crown I wore as queen of Sicily. I haven't had it on since I married Raymond, but I think this is the time."

"And I know just where it is, my lady. In the locked chest that we keep behind the screen. I'll fetch it at once and see if it needs a polish."

When Joanna entered the audience chamber she found six men seated at one end of the long oval table: François Compagne, Henri de Jarnac, Arnaud Cabot the black-haired blusterer, and three she knew only vaguely. They all stood quickly while she took her place at the head of the table. They looked at her with unconcealed admiration. They'd never seen their countess in such fine feathers.

The meeting went as she'd hoped. She told them of the development among the *capitouls* of Toulouse and the possible implications. She assured them that Raymond would soon return, and asked if they had any suggestions for immediate action.

"Can't say I'm surprised," snorted Arnaud. "I suspect three of my highborn vassals of supporting the heretics, though I've no idea if they're ready to switch to the Cathar faith. And there may be others for all I know."

"It's the same around Béziers," mumbled Henri, who was slouching in his chair and looked ready for a nap. Maybe too much wine at dinner, thought Joanna. But he sat up and became more animated. "We hear rumors all the time of this lord or that going over to the Cathars. And when it comes right down to it, I'm not sure I wouldn't do the same if I had to choose between that and inviting King Philip to send his army down here to squash our little rebellion."

"And to lay claim to our rightful lands while he's at it," growled Arnaud.

Several others chimed in noisily with their own tales of defections, mostly hearsay, Joanna noted. The gathering was threatening to get out of control.

"Well and good," said François. "But what we need now are facts, not rumors. How far has this gone? How many men and of what rank are taking sides with the Cathars? I'm sure that's what Count Raymond will want to know. We can help him by going back at once to our *demesnes* and asking around. Then he, and we his council, can decide whether to let it ride or to take some kind of punitive action."

"Good idea, but we must keep this to ourselves," said Arnaud. "We managed to put those nosy inquisitors off, back when they wanted names of suspected heretics. We mustn't let them get wind of what we're up to now. We'll have to be discreet." Joanna couldn't imagine loud-mouthed Arnaud being discreet, but hoped for the best.

"Right," said Henri. "This is our problem, not the king's and not the pope's."

"Excellent. We seem to be agreed," said Joanna. "It's something we can start to do now that will be really constructive. And I'll send a messenger at once to let Raymond know how things stand."

She looked around the table. She could tell they were surprised at her decisiveness, but nobody could find a reason to demur. So it was settled. The meeting broke up much sooner than anyone had expected. She thanked them for their counsel and signaled to the servant at the door to bring in the wine and bowls of almonds and sweetmeats that she'd ordered to be ready. She had no chance to speak to François privately, but he raised his goblet to her and they exchanged looks of satisfaction.

When Raymond arrived a week later, she gave him a full account of the meeting.

"I ran into Arnaud Chabot at an inn two nights ago," he said. "All he could talk about was how beautiful you were and how royal you looked. 'It's like we have our own queen of Toulouse,' he said. 'And I give you credit for finding her and marrying her.' Which credit I modestly accepted. But he said very little about what went on at the council meeting. It sounds as though you handled it very well."

"I merely tried to do exactly what you'd do. And I had excellent guidance from François Compagne, both ahead of time and at the meeting. It might have gotten chaotic without him."

"Yes, he's a sound man. I should see more of him. I might ask him and his wife to join us at dinner sometime soon." He stood and stretched. "But now I'm more interested in getting reacquainted with my wife and son. Shall we go up?" He helped her to rise and, arm in arm, they mounted the steps to their private quarters.

When in due time the councilors reported on conditions in their areas, there was little real evidence of alarming support of the Cathar cause from the upper classes. For several months calm reigned from Auch to Avignon. The inquisitors investigated and interrogated as usual, but King Philip seemed to have his mind on other matters than sending troops to put down the unrest. There was no unrest to speak of. Raymond decided it was prudent to lie low and stay alert.

Early in the new year of 1198 on a sunny but cold morning, a messenger was admitted to Joanna's chamber and presented her with a rolled-up parchment. When she saw the familiar Plantagenet seal with the three leaping golden lions she felt a pang of nostalgia. It was a long time since she'd heard from her mother. She unrolled the parchment eagerly—but it was from Richard. He planned to hold his Easter court in LeMans and hoped that his dear sister and brother-in-law could be present.

"The time is right for a celebration. I have nearly completed my new castle at Les Andelys on the Seine. King Philip and I have agreed on an Easter truce. So we can gather together in peace and harmony. Queen Eleanor will be there and we hope we will see my brother John as well, with whom we are for the present on better terms. It has been too long since our family met together. I promise you a festive Easter season."

No mention of Berengaria.

Nevertheless, Joanna keenly looked forward to the gathering. She missed her mother and Richard. She couldn't honestly say she missed John, but he was her brother. She anticipated introducing them all to her son Raymond, the most beautiful and remarkable baby in the centuries-old history of the Plantagenet dynasty.

65

The party from Toulouse arrived in Le Mans on Good Friday of 1198. It was an unpleasant, blustery day. The wind whipped showers of cold rain around corners and into the travelers' faces as their tired horses toiled up the last hill. Neither Joanna nor Raymond had been in the city before. It was formidable: completely encircled by high walls bristling with towers. As they got closer they peered out from their dripping hoods to see that in spite of the gray day the walls glowed with tawny and rosy stonework arranged in a variety of patterns—squares, crosses, arrows, circles.

"The Romans built these walls, I've heard," said Raymond. "I'm amazed that they took such pains to make them decorative as well as defensive. Nobody bothers with such niceties nowadays."

"So they've stood here since the Romans? That's a thousand years!" She stopped her horse to gaze, awestruck, but hurried on. It was too wet for sightseeing.

Sentries must have been keeping a lookout from the towers because no sooner had they reached the city gate than two knights appeared, in the familiar livery of the Plantagenets. One of them addressed Raymond and Joanna.

"I bring you greetings from King Richard. We will escort you to the palace of the counts of Maine, where he is lodged and where you will be as well."

Within ten minutes they'd reached the square in front of the palace, which was tall and massive with a tower on either side. The ten-foot-high door stood open and there, framed by the arched doorway, stood Richard. His broad smile, the gleam of his red-gold hair and the scarlet of his tunic made the rain and gloom seem inconsequential.

He sprang down the steps as agilely as ever, Joanna noted, in spite of his increasing girth. He strode toward her, reaching out his arms to help her dismount, and she stretched out hers to embrace him while he gently lowered her to the ground.

"My little sister! Here you are, as pretty as ever, and here is my brother and ally Raymond. But where is my nephew? Surely you didn't carelessly leave him behind in Toulouse?"

At that moment Nurse Marie appeared, carrying young Raymond. Richard poked aside the blankets that enveloped the baby and they regarded each other.

"So, young Count Raymond. Welcome to Le Mans, capital city of Maine. Remember what you see. You might be the king of England who maintains his continental residence here some day."

The baby blinked and gurgled. He reached up to explore Richard's beard. "Richard!" expostulated Joanna. "Don't be ridiculous."

"It's not so ridiculous. If I don't have an heir, which I fear will be the case, and if John doesn't have an heir either, your son will be next in line, won't he?" He tickled the baby under the chin and they grinned at each other. "But I mustn't keep you out here in this foul weather. In we go and I'll meet you in the dining hall after you're dried off and changed. I hope you'll be comfortable in your lodgings."

They were not only comfortable, but extremely well served by the palace staff. Joanna hadn't realized how tired she was until she entered her chamber and found it warmed by a fireplace and braziers and brightly lit by candles in sconces on the walls. She saw a bed with fine white sheets, a mound of pillows, a gray silk coverlet and curtains of pale gray velvet.

She flung her sopping cloak on a chair. "I'll lie down for just a few minutes," she told herself. But before she could move two maids came in with basins of warm water, sponges and soft towels. One helped her shed her wet clothes and bathe while the other unpacked her chests and bags. Cleansed and dry, Joanna asked Jeanette to bring a gown she'd often worn and felt at ease in, rose-colored with bands of white ermine at wrists and neck. As the gown settled over her shoulders the fur and silk gently caressed her bare skin. So warm, so reassuring.

When Raymond entered to escort her to dinner he looked at her in pleased admiration. "Can this be the same damp and bedraggled lady who entered Le Mans not two hours ago?"

"So it is, and thanks to your obvious approval I feel confident enough to go down and confront my family."

"Let us hope," said Raymond, placing her hand on his arm, "that it won't be a confrontation."

"One can always hope. But you have never been present at one of our family gatherings."

With which sobering thought they walked down the stairs and paused at the entrance to the dining hall.

It wasn't a large chamber and the presence of three highly volatile, argumentative people made it seem even smaller. Eleanor was already seated at the table, listening morosely to John and Richard who stood in front of the fireplace with raised voices and, occasionally, fists.

Joanna caught Richard's curt "Certainly not. Not now. Are you mad? Do you have the faintest notion of what kind of unrest that would stir up here in Maine? To say nothing of Anjou?"

"But you promised!" John voice rose to a whiney treble. "You've acknowledged to me and to our mother that you intend to make me your heir. Why not make a public declaration?"

Richard was trying to contain his disdain. "Because, you idiot, that would give a clear signal to the barons of Maine and Anjou that I've gone back on my vow to them that I'd make Arthur of Brittany my heir, if the children of King Henry don't produce a son. Arthur, as you may remember if your brain hasn't gone completely soft, is the son of our late elder brother Geoffrey. His claim to the throne is as direct as yours. He may be little more than a child but he's become a rallying point for those local lords who are already teetering between France and England. Do you see, do you see, you dolt? We can't antagonize them now or they'd go straight to Philip."

"But you promised!" bleated John. He glared at Richard and his expression changed from a pout to a sneer. "And if you think you can shunt me aside from my rightful place you'll have another thing coming one of these days! King Philip would be happy to accept my allegiance and make my battles his battles."

Richard's face turned a fiery red and he was temporarily speechless. In the moment of silence Eleanor spoke, not loudly but with perfect clarity.

"John, come sit by me and let your brother calm down enough to eat his dinner, which will be brought in shortly. I'll explain to you a lesson that apparently you've yet to learn: a monarch cannot always follow his first inclination."

John, sulky, walked slowly to the table. Joanna recognized the same sullen obedience he showed when as a boy he was reprimanded by his parents.

She and Raymond were still standing, unnoticed, at the door. Joanna had been watching with weary familiarity, Raymond with incredulity. His councilors didn't always agree with each other or with him but their disagreements were more like bickering than the naked antagonism he saw here.

Richard, still fuming, snatched the goblet that a timorous servant offered him and downed the wine in two gulps. He saw Joanna and Raymond and walked to greet them.

"Come in, and welcome, Raymond, to the happy Plantagenet family at home." He led them to the table. "I think I hear them bringing our dinner now. We'll see how the cooks here compare with that fine fellow in Poitiers." Joanna could tell that he was making a tremendous effort to regain his composure. "I'm glad to say they agreed to observe the modern dispensation, that we may break the Lenten fast any time after Maundy Thursday. If my nose doesn't deceive me there's roast pork on its way."

Several invited guests from Le Mans were shown in—the bishop, another churchman and two local magnates with their wives. Sensing the tense atmosphere, they confined themselves to polite greetings to Eleanor and nods to the others. They took their seats at table and conversed quietly among themselves. The brothers still smoldered. Echoes of their dispute hung in the air and made it difficult for Joanna or Raymond to think of a harmless topic of conversation. Eleanor ate methodically and deliberately and had hardly finished the first course, poached fish with leek sauce, when John polished off the last of his apple tart and without a word or look to anyone stamped out.

Richard brightened as soon as the corner of John's black cloak disappeared through the door. Joanna was always surprised at how quickly he could switch from fury to affability. He made an expansive gesture that took in the guests as well as the family.

"Now, good people, let us remember this is the Easter season, a time for rejoicing and coming together by men of good will. I'm sure my brother John will remember that and by tomorrow he'll become his usual jovial self." He looked around, straight-faced, daring anyone to laugh. He caught the bishop's eye.

"Shall we pray for that happy eventuality, my lord bishop?"

"We shall. For truly, the age of miracles has not passed."

At that, good humor was restored. Even Eleanor produced a thin smile. Richard and the bishop raised their goblets in salute to each other.

Replete, the diners moved to armchairs by the hearth for nightcaps of mulled wine. The bishop settled into a commodious chair and sighed the contented sigh of a man who has enjoyed a fine free meal and is ready for a nap. The other guests from Le Mans, after a few minutes of polite conversation with Queen Eleanor and words of gratitude to Richard for his hospitality, took their leave. Joanna sat by the bishop, content to relax in an atmosphere free of discord.

Raymond, seated next to Richard, asked, "Can you tell me more about this Arthur? I know nothing about him except that his father, your older brother, died when the boy was very young. Is he actually a serious contender for the throne of England?"

"I think it's unlikely that most Englishmen would accept him. It's his ambitious mother, Constance of Brittany, who's so serious. She's drilled into him since he was a babe that he's the true heir. He's been brought up in Brittany and in Paris under King Philip's wing. He's become, willynilly, the one whom all Frenchmen who oppose the English presence in France look to as their leader. Though the lad's only eleven."

"And," said Eleanor, "he has some support in England too from those who do not wish for a King John on the throne."

"Hmm," said Raymond. "It seems to be open season for would-be kings of England to enter the fray." Joanna had been listening with growing uneasiness. She thought it unseemly to be discussing events that would take place after Richard's death. But Raymond seemed impervious to any such sensitivity. He went on. "And in fact..."

Joanna interrupted without taking time to choose her words. "I suggest we leave off talking about any future kings of England. My brother is in the prime of his life and not anywhere near giving up the throne. And besides, he himself might still..." she stopped in confusion. Eleanor came to her rescue.

"He might still have a son who would be the undisputed heir. Which leads me to ask, Richard, why is Berengaria not here?"

All eyes were on Richard. Even the bishop, who had been nodding, sat up and paid attention. Richard's desertion of his queen had become common knowledge and a subject for gossip.

His face, already flushed from wine and the heat of the fire, reddened even more.

"She was invited. I sent a message telling her we would be holding our Easter court in Le Mans. And I told her I would understand if she feared she would feel unwelcome and would prefer to stay in Beaufort. She replied that was her wish."

"Of course she did," said Eleanor. "After such an ungracious invitation, how could she do otherwise?"

Richard looked ready to explode. Joanna hastily intervened.

"Well, what's done is done. If you will permit me to change the subject, I have a question for Bishop Robert."

The bishop turned his bland face to her, all attention.

"Will you tell me how far it is to your great Cathedral of St. Julien? I am eager to see it. But can one walk, or must one ride?"

"It's but a fifteen-minute walk, up a very gentle incline, from the palace square to the cathedral. When do you think of coming?"

"I'd thought tomorrow around midday. We'll be there the next day for Easter Mass, but I'd like to see it more informally first."

"Tomorrow at noon it is, then. I would be honored to show you around." He turned to Eleanor, seated on his other side. "Would you care to join us, Queen Eleanor?"

"I think not. I saw St. Julien some years ago, and I doubt if it's changed much." She rose. "Now if you'll all excuse me I shall retire." Without waiting to see if she was excused or not, she left.

The bishop and Joanna fell to discussing cathedrals they had seen and admired—or not. Joanna was acquainted with six: Winchester in England; three in Sicily—Monreale, Cefalù and the Messina Duomo—and three in France: Poitiers; Rouen, and St. Sernin in Toulouse. When she closed her eyes she could see each one clearly. They were like milestones marking the course of her life from childhood to motherhood.

The bishop's list, though shorter, included two that eclipsed hers in fame and magnificence: Notre Dame in Paris and Chartres. Both, he said, were far from complete but promised to become the most glorious temples in Christendom. He described them to her with more animation than he'd shown all evening.

"How I'd love to see them!" she said wistfully. "Raymond says we'll go to Paris some day. But I wonder when the day will come."

"If you do get to Paris you must come back and report to me on one matter in particular. We've heard that King Philip intends to support the walls of the towers of Notre Dame with what they call *arcs boutants*—flying buttresses. It's quite a new idea and we hope to use them at St. Julien. We also hope to complete ours before King Philip has finished his. So I ask anybody who's going to Paris to take note— have they begun building their *arcs boutants* yet?"

She promised to do so.

Meantime Raymond and Richard, the latter all amiability again, were discussing hunting opportunities in the area. Richard wanted to form a party and go out the next day in search of deer or boar or whatever could be found. "I'm sure the two men from Le Mans who were here tonight will want to join us. They're keen huntsmen. I'll send word at once." They raised their goblets in a toast to good hunting on the morrow. Richard called to Joanna, "I suppose you won't care to join us?"

"No, thank you. You remember my feelings on the subject, I'm sure."

Richard came to her side and rested a hand on her shoulder.

"Pardon me, bishop, for interrupting but I must tell my sister something."

Bishop Robert nodded. He rather thought they'd exhausted the subject of cathedrals anyway. Joanna looked up at Richard.

"Since I'll be gone tomorrow, I hope you'll welcome a visitor I'm expecting. I may not be back from the hunt when he arrives."

"Gladly. And who is it I'm to welcome?

"I'm not going to tell you. But it's someone you'll be happy to see." And she could get no more information out of him.

Joanna pondered this as she and Raymond went up to their chambers.

"Who do you suppose it is, Raymond? Maybe Jean-Pierre, I'm always happy to see him. But why make such a mystery of it?"

"I can't imagine. Maybe Jean-Pierre wants to surprise you." He yawned. "Anyway, you'll soon know. As for me, I must get some sleep if I'm to be off at dawn in pursuit of the timid deer and the pugnacious boar." He was already pulling off his tunic as he headed for the bed. "Good night, my love."

"Good night. I'll join you soon but first I'll go see that all's well with the baby. Maybe if he's awake he'll say 'maman.' I'm sure he tried to yesterday."

The tour of the cathedral the next day was a great success. The bishop made sure they didn't overlook any of its remarkable features—the lofty vaulted ceilings, the locations of the anticipated *arcs boutants*, the likenesses of the apostles and the Virgin Mary at the portal. Finally he led her to the Ascension window. While she stood there the afternoon sun came from behind a cloud and suddenly the whole window sprang into life, a rich display of a thousand bits of brilliant color—blue, green, gold and crimson. Joanna was transfixed by the detail the artists had achieved with their tiny pieces of glass. She felt she could read compassion and benevolence in the face of Christ as he rose toward heaven while the apostles watched in awed devotion from below.

"It's one of the oldest windows anywhere," Bishop Robert told her. "People come from all over the world to see it. It was created soon after the pope consecrated the cathedral. That was in 1096."

"More than a hundred years ago," she mused. "Thank you so much for this wonderful afternoon. If you don't mind, I'd like to just sit here for a few minutes and meditate, and maybe say a prayer to St. Julien."

"The pleasure has been mine. We don't often have a visitor so knowledgeable and so appreciative."

After he left Joanna sat on her bench and thought about sin. She studied the ascending Christ, remembering what she'd been taught. Having lived on earth as a man, he had a special affinity for mankind and would intercede with his heavenly father on behalf of all sinners. But who were these sinners? She counted up the out-and-out sinners she had known. She could think of only two: Matthew of Ajello, who had tried desperately and criminally to prevent her marriage to William, and William's crafty old mother, Queen Margaret, who had tried to poison her. But of course there were plenty of murderers and thieves she'd never run into, as well as other, less deadly sinners: merchants who cheated their customers, men who coveted their neighbors' wives, promiscuous women, pickpockets, heads of families who ran off and left them. Yes, there was no lack of sinners whose souls a merciful Jesus would try to save. But would he have to intercede for her? She'd tried to be a good Christian and avoid sin. She'd gone to mass, gone to confession, tried to do unto others as she'd have them do unto her. Looking back, she believed she'd lived her life as God would wish. And though there'd been tragedies along the way—the loss of her baby Bohemund, the death of her William—she'd been rewarded with many blessings. She'd had years of happiness as William's queen, while becoming a good helpmeet to him. She'd had the companionship of fast friends like Jean-Pierre and Berengaria and the joy of seeing her surrogate son, Federico, grow from a ragged urchin to a fine young man, serving her beloved brother Richard. Then just when she'd become mired in self-pity and insecurity, she'd found renewed happiness in marriage to Raymond. And now the final, incredible gift: motherhood.

She looked up at the Ascension window again and said a prayer of thanks to Jesus for the many blessings she'd been granted. She sat on, captivated by the dazzling colors and caught up in a strange feeling of closeness to the risen Christ. She didn't know how long she sat there, transfixed, but suddenly it seemed that he was looking straight at her, calmly and reprovingly, and he spoke.

"Beware of pride, Joanna. While you congratulate yourself on the rewards of a sin-free life, have you forgotten that there are sins of omission as well as sins of commission? What have you done for others outside of your small circle of friends and family? Have you kept in mind my teaching that true Christians are to do God's work on earth? To what strangers have you given food or drink or care, as I bade men to do if they would be truly blessed? Beware of pride, Joanna."

Stunned, she struggled to understand how those words applied to her. The church darkened and she looked up to see that clouds had again obscured the sun and the window lost its brilliance. She rose slowly, stiff from sitting so long. The cathedral was gloomy and empty. The manservant who had accompanied her was dozing outside on the steps.

On the way back to the palace she was almost in a panic at the thought of the opportunities for Christian charity she'd ignored. She saw now how smug, self-satisfied and selfish she'd been. Only once, years ago in Palermo, had she made more than a token effort to help the poor and downtrodden, when she joined Jean-Pierre in his work. Then, after rescuing just two people, her beloved Federico and the waif Emilia, from a dismal life, she'd thought no more about it. Was it too late?

Her thoughts were still tumbling about in her head when, as they neared the palace, she heard shouts and hoofbeats. They arrived at the crowded palace square just as the hunters were dismounting and accepting the congratulations of the spectators on their trophies. A small mule was laden with a magnificent buck with an impressive set of antlers. Its feet were trussed together under the mule's belly. Its sightless eyes stared into the crowd. Joanna thought it looked as though it had made a great leap and to its surprise landed on the mule in that ignominious position. Another mule bore a smaller deer, and a third had two large lumpy sacks that probably contained pheasants and pigeons.

She was about to walk over to greet Raymond and Richard when another mounted party trotted into the square from the opposite side. Four knights, all with the golden Plantagenet lions on their scarlet tunics, approached the palace entry, halted and dismounted. The tallest, who seemed to be the leader, was black-haired with a small, neat black beard. She stared in dawning recognition. She gathered up her skirts and ran, pushing her way through the crowd, to throw her arms around him.

"Federico! Is it really you?"

They stood there a minute, holding each other close. She drew back and looked up into his face. She could tell he was as glad to see her as she was to see him, and not at all embarrassed to show it. With years he'd gained assurance.

"Yes, here I am, and I gather nobody told you I was coming."

"No, Richard told me only that he was expecting a visitor today and that I should welcome him if the hunters were still out in the forest. But I never guessed it might be you. And here you are! And if you'll forgive my maternal pride, you're even more handsome, if that's possible. Oh dear, I'm not making sense. But I'm so very glad to see you!"

"And I you." He surveyed her with the merry black eyes she remembered so well. "But if you'll pardon me, you're the one who's even more handsome. Marriage and motherhood must agree with you."

"Thank you, my dear. I believe they do. Now tell me, why are you here?"

"King Richard has appointed us"—he gestured to the other three, who were conferring with grooms about the horses—"to serve as his honor guard in the procession to the cathedral tomorrow. Ah, here he comes. I must report to him."

The crowd's fascinated attention had been divided between the hunters and their prizes and this mysterious black-haired soldier who seemed to be on such good terms with the countess. Now they made way as Richard, Raymond and the others approached. Federico bowed his head and bent his knee to Richard.

"Your Majesty," he said. "We report for duty."

"Very good. Your duties will start tomorrow but tonight we feast. I trust you've been properly welcomed by my sister."

"Yes, we've had a most joyful reunion." And to Raymond, "And this is my first opportunity to congratulate you on your marriage to Queen Joanna."

Joanna was startled to hear herself referred to as Queen Joanna. But that was who she'd always been to Federico.

Raymond darted a sharp look at him. "Or, as she's known nowadays, the Countess Joanna."

Richard announced that he was going to confer with the cook and impressed on all that they must not be late to dinner. The group dispersed. Raymond took Joanna's arm and without a word propelled her up to their chamber. He closed the door and with no warning struck her on the face.

She was more astonished than hurt. She put a hand to her cheek and looked at him in amazement.

"How could you disgrace me so?" His face was contorted with anger.

"What are you talking about? Disgrace you how?"

"You know perfectly well what I mean. Before half of Le Mans, to throw your arms about another man and make such a public display of affection. What will people think of me when my wife has so little regard for appearances?"

"But Raymond, it wasn't 'another man,' it was Federico whom I brought up like my son since he was nine. I still think of him as my son and love him as a son. Nothing will change that. Certainly not blows."

It was as though she hadn't spoken.

"Furthermore, how do I know what went on between you two during that journey from Saint-Gilles to Poitiers? When I thought I saw signs that you could care for me? Was that just to divert me from where your real affections lay?"

His face was contorted with scorn and he was shouting. She had never seen him so out of control. It was frightening. But she was calmer now. She struggled to sound reasonable, to contain her outrage.

"Raymond, listen." There was a catch in her voice and she had to stop and take a deep breath. "I've been a true and faithful wife to you. I've come to love you as I hoped I would when we were married. Your suspicions are completely unfounded. Before you say something that you will regret even more I think you'd better leave."

Without looking at him she turned, walked into her dressing room and closed the door. She sank onto a chair and buried her face in her hands, letting the tears flow over her clenched fingers. Presently she heard him slam her chamber door.

What had happened to the marriage she'd thought so secure? Was this simply a temporary aberration? Should she look on it as a sign of his regard for her that he hated to see her show affection for another man? Yet to be jealous of Federico, of all people!

Or was this madman the real Raymond and had she been deceived all along?

66

Joanna sent word that she wouldn't attend the Easter feast that evening. She wanted a quiet time alone in her chamber so she could recover from the horror of the ugly encounter with Raymond. She longed to recapture the sense of communion and purpose she'd felt in the cathedral.

She sat by a window and looked toward the west where the sun was sinking below the city walls. She closed her eyes and imagined herself again in the dim quiet of St. Julien, surrounded by a magical luminescence from dozens of windows. She recalled her first view of the Ascension, her fascination with its message of hope and redemption, the way that Christ's eyes seemed to meet hers before he spoke. Once more she heard his words, the gentle chiding.

She opened her eyes. She knew at once what she must do.

She walked up and down the room, arms folded and mind busy. As soon as I get back to Toulouse, she told herself, I shall go see Bishop Garnier at St. Sernin. He'll know if anyone is doing what needs to be done to help the poor and hungry folk. Oh, how I wish Jean-Pierre were here to guide me! But I remember what he said—that every big city has its share of people in need, and that because we don't see them we pay no attention. Well, I shall pay attention.

She wished she could start this minute, she was so full of energy. She'd succeeded in pushing Raymond's unpardonable behavior to the back of her mind.

Her maid Jeanette came with a message. "Nurse Marie says if you want to see the baby before he goes to sleep, you'd better come now."

She found Marie holding Raymond le Jeune, as they'd taken to calling the younger Raymond. He squealed when he saw her, pounded the air with his tiny fists and kicked vigorously.

"Oh my lady, I'm so glad you came. We want to show *maman* what we can do, don't we, my cherub?" She gently set him down on the carpet. He immediately flopped over onto all fours and started crawling industriously toward Joanna. She laughed in her delight and when he reached her she scooped him up. She ran her hand lightly over his hair, remembering how it was a golden fuzz when he was newly born. Now it was smooth as a kitten's fur, darkening to a reddish brown. He's growing up before my eyes, she thought. Yet he's still so vulnerable, so innocent, so trusting. I must do all in my power to keep him from harm. She kissed him on the cheek and held him close for a moment.

"So you've learned to crawl, have you? *Maman* is very proud." He gazed at her intently as though trying to take in her words and said, perfectly clearly, "*Maman.*" She laughed again and cradled him in her arms.

"Marie, isn't this amazing? Imagine, his learning to crawl and to speak real words, so young!"

"Oh no, he's nearly eight months and many children begin to do both by then."

"But he's so assured, as though he'd been practicing for weeks." She refused to believe her son was anything but unique.

Marie smiled indulgently. She'd known many proud mothers.

"Now I'd better take him. See, he's closed his eyes."

Reluctantly, Joanna surrendered the baby and watched while Marie laid him in the cradle, tucked in his blankets and began to sing a soft lullaby. Joanna walked back to her room, feeling soothed and comforted by the brief time with her son. She smiled again when she remembered how he'd called her "*Maman.*"

When she opened her door she saw a supper tray on a table by the fire. She grimaced. She wasn't in the least hungry. Then she saw a figure standing by the window. It was Raymond.

Before she could react he walked swiftly to where she still stood by the door.

"I know I've come uninvited. But please listen to me."

Her hurt and anger returned twofold. "What can you possibly say that I'd want to hear?" She tried to move past him, but he took her hand and spoke quickly. "Please, give me two minutes." She snatched her hand away.

"I suppose I must." She sat down at the table, lifted a spoon and regarded her soup, as though ready to start on it as soon as his two minutes were up.

"I was wrong to suspect you and very wrong to strike you. I can't ask you to forgive me yet, but I do hope you will let me prove to you how sorry I am, by my actions and words from now on." She put down her spoon and looked up at him. He hurried on.

"It's just that now that I've found you and made you mine, I can't bear the thought of any other man in your life. It drives me mad."

"Yes, I witnessed that. I don't want to see you so out of control ever again. Can't you understand, Raymond, that my wedding vows are sacred to me, as I believe yours are to you? That I would never leave you for anyone else? Can you promise not to yield again to this senseless, needless jealousy?"

"I do promise." He spoke as solemnly as if repeating the wedding vows.

But she remembered that when she first met him and they were traveling from Saint-Gilles to Poitiers and getting to know each other, she'd sometimes felt his words weren't sincere; that he was saying what he felt she wanted to hear. Was he doing that now? She looked at him searchingly, wanting to believe him. Belief would be so much easier than doubt.

"And I shall believe you mean it." He took her hand again and she let him continue to hold it.

Their life resumed, almost as before. The assault, the accusation, the harsh words were never mentioned. But sometimes Joanna would awake, feeling the sting of Raymond's slap on her cheek, and gasp with her unbelief. Then she would see him lying peacefully sleeping at her side, turned toward her with his arm around her waist.

At the end of April Raymond left for Toulouse. The others followed in a few days. But when Joanna and the sizeable retinue of nurses, guards, manservants and maidservants, muleteers and baggage handlers arrived, he was no longer in Toulouse.

François Compagne came to report to Joanna. As always, he was well groomed and his bushy red hair had been subdued by vigorous brushing. She was glad to see him. She thought he was the most open and dependable man on Raymond's council. She liked his intelligent, observant face and the blue eyes that missed nothing. He stood before her respectfully until she asked him to sit down.

"The count asked me to tell you he's sorry not to be here to greet you but he had to go to Béziers."

"Not again! What's the matter there now?"

"The same old thing, but worsening. The area is like a tinderbox waiting for the match. Men like Henri de Jarnac are itching for a fight. They're getting a lot of support, not just from the Cathars. Most of the people, upper and lower classes alike, resent the bullying by the church and King Philip's meddling. I don't know how long Raymond can avoid getting involved in the dispute. It's a slippery road he's traveling. He has to persuade the bellicose nobles that he's on their side, but urge them to pursue a wait-and-see course. Not easy."

"And if he doesn't succeed?"

"If the leaders aren't convinced Raymond supports their cause, they're likely to turn on him."

"So he's in danger?" This was more serious than she'd thought.

"Not yet. But he may be."

"Oh, how I wish I knew some way to help!"

"And so do I."

They were both silent for half a minute. "Well, I fear," said Joanna, "that we can't solve these problems today. Let me change the subject. Are you acquainted with Bishop Garnier at the cathedral?"

"Slightly. My wife knows him much better."

"Then she's the one I need to talk to. I've heard that the bishop has taken the lead in charitable assistance to the poor. I've barely met him, and I'd like to know more about what he does before I approach him to see if I could help."

"In that case, Marie-Louise is just the one you need. She's been involved in that work, though I don't know exactly how. I'll ask her to call on you. I'm sure she'll be delighted to hear of your interest." He rose and she accompanied him to the door.

"Better yet, could you both come to dine here tomorrow? I've been wanting to get to know your wife better anyway. It won't be a large party, just Lady Adelaide and perhaps Sir Florian and his wife."

"We'd be very pleased. And why not ask the bishop too? If you're really interested, you might as well take the first step now."

"Thank you, what a sensible suggestion. You are always a source of wisdom, Sir François!"

The dinner party was a great success, Joanna felt. She'd given much thought to the menu: not too elaborate but not too ordinary. She sat at the head of the table with the bishop on her right, Marie-Louise on her left, so they could converse easily. The bishop, a square-jawed and smooth-shaven man, wore a purple cassock under his white surplice, no cope and no mitre; he was bareheaded and had a fine crop of black hair. Joanna knew that for a bishop this costume was the height of informality and she was pleased that he obviously saw this as a friendly, nonofficial visit.

Marie-Louise greeted him with the ease of an old friend. Before the venison stew had been consumed he'd satisfied himself that Joanna's interest in the charitable endeavor was genuine and had explained to her its nature.

"The core of the effort is the order called the Sisters of Charity. These women have taken sacred vows but are not cloistered. They go out into the world to help the helpless. Here in Toulouse they've learned where the greatest need is, mostly in the northern outskirts of the city where poverty is extreme. They bring the solace of the Word of God but just as important are the food, clean water and healing they offer. We learned some time ago that these dedicated women have a huge task and need assistance."

He paused as his bowl was removed and a platter of roast partridges was placed on the table. "Ah, partridges. We'll see how your cook prepares them. Marie-Louise, perhaps you could explain to the countess how you fit in this picture." He expertly speared a partridge for each of the three of them and began to dissect his bird.

"Gladly." Marie-Louise, a plump little woman with a round face and a ready smile, put down the partridge leg she'd been nibbling and addressed Joanna. "There are about ten of us. Among ourselves we call our group "The sisters of the Sisters of Charity." One of us accompanies each Sister of Charity on her weekly visit. Many of those we visit, young and old, have some kind of ailment. Most are undernourished. We don't pretend to be physicians but the Sisters know a great deal about care of the sick. We do what we can to make them more comfortable. We wash them if they can't do it for themselves. And we always bring food. Not much, not enough to last them a week, but enough for at least one good meal per person. We try to get them to eat while we're there, otherwise it might go down the gullet of some greedy family member or neighbor. Then we pray with them if they want it. We don't insist."

Joanna listened attentively. "I think I could do that. It doesn't sound too demanding."

"Physically it isn't but it takes a lot out of you emotionally. It's devastating to witness the deplorable living conditions, the misery, the despair. But there are compensations. Their gratitude is touching, and every once in a while we come across a mother who in spite of everything manages to keep her humble home clean and her children washed. Or a man who's found some kind of work and brings his pittance home without spending it in a tavern on the way."

"One question for both of you. I know my husband will ask this. Are you safe? Aren't you venturing into a lawless area where robbers and worse roam freely?"

The bishop put down his knife and looked regretfully at the bones on his plate, all that remained of his partridge. "Yes, many people think we're foolhardy, though it's not nearly as lawless as they paint it. But we take precautions. Besides the servant who carries the supplies and is trained to be alert, you'll always be accompanied by a stout guardsman, fully armed."

Joanna nodded. "I think Raymond will accept that. You're doing a wonderful service, and I'd like to join you."

"Excellent! You might go along with Marie-Louise the first time so she can help you get accustomed to the duties. Now may I ask you to compliment your cook on the stuffing in the birds? I've often had the onion and apple combination, but never with both cloves and cinnamon, if I'm not mistaken."

"You're quite right, and Michel will be glad to hear you approve."

That night in her chamber she reflected on what she had committed to. She felt that she was now fulfilling the charge she'd received in the cathedral of Le Mans. Before going to bed she knelt to pray. She tried to summon the vision of Christ in the Ascension window, but it was a blur of color with no discernible meaning. Nevertheless she prayed. "Thank you, Lord, for setting my feet on this path. Thank you for showing me where my duty lay. I beseech you to intercede on my behalf with our heavenly father, and I pray my good works will help to atone for my sins of omission heretofore. Amen." Did that sound as though she was bargaining? But she thought she did deserve a little credit for finding this opportunity to do the Lord's work.

She climbed into bed and pulled the covers up to her chin. Almost asleep, she heard a ghostly voice, faint but distinct. "Beware of pride, Joanna." She was shocked but then she laughed to herself. Once more, Christ was deflating her when she yielded to self-congratulation.

Finally at the end of October Raymond came home and Joanna told him about her new involvement with the Sisters of Charity. He listened absently and to her surprise he made no objection, after she explained about the guards. Neither did he applaud her for her concern for the downtrodden. He seemed even more preoccupied than usual.

To take his mind off his worries, she persuaded him to come to the nursery to witness his son's new accomplishments. From Joanna's chair Raymond le Jeune walked purposefully and with just a few wobbles to Raymond and stood, holding on to his father's knees. He looked up and said gleefully, "Papa, look at me!" Raymond had emerged from his abstraction. "Remarkable!" he exclaimed, picking the child up and hugging him. "Well done, my son. It won't be long before you can learn to sit a horse and go out hunting with me."

The count and countess walked back along the corridor to their chamber with their arms around each other's waists. Raymond said, "How lucky I am, to have such a beautiful wife and such an accomplished son to come home to."

"And how lucky I am that you do come home."

For two months harmony and calm prevailed in palace and city. Raymond, though still much occupied with conferences with the city government and his council, didn't undertake any long trips. Joanna found the weekly duty with the Sisters of Charity to be unexpectedly rewarding when she could see at first hand that their efforts bore fruit: a persistent cough that had gone away, a child whose emaciated body began to fill out, a look of hope rather than despair on an old man's face.

Another reward was her new friendship with Marie-Louise. Besides her seemingly unquenchable good humor, she had a plentiful supply of good sense. She and her husband became frequent guests at the palace dinner table.

One frosty December day a message came from Richard. "My dear sister: this is for your eyes only. I shall be passing through Aquitaine on my way to Perpignan next week and I shall make a side trip to Toulouse to see you."

She was puzzled. What could be so secret and so urgent that Richard would go far out of his way to see her? Toulouse was a long way from the route to Perpignan. And why was he going to Perpignan anyway, almost in Spain?

But she didn't share the message with Raymond. Clearly, Richard didn't want her to. It would all be explained in time.

Besides, she had some much more momentous and joyful news for Raymond. She had just discovered that she was pregnant again.

67

"I can't believe this," Joanna said. "I don't want to believe this." She ran her fingers through her hair and shook her head violently, in denial of Richard's unwelcome words. "I know this is hard for you," said Richard. "But I thought you should know. I'd have told you sooner but I haven't been able to come before now, and it's not the kind of news to send in writing."

"No, of course not. And all this time I thought that Raymond…" She couldn't hold back the angry, despairing tears any longer. Richard patted her on the shoulder and walked to look out the window and give her time to recover.

"What a pleasant prospect you have from your chamber! I've never been in the counts' palace. That must be the River Garonne. And to think, that modest little stream becomes the great wide river that flows into the sea at Bordeaux."

Joanna gulped, wiped her eyes and let out a shuddering sigh.

"I'm sorry, Richard. I'm better now. But this has been so sudden, and I'm confused. Tell me again, please, how you knew Raymond had struck me and shouted at me. From my maid, did you say? How did she know?"

"She was sitting on a bench in the corridor that afternoon, sewing, and she heard everything. She saw Raymond when he stormed out but he didn't see her. But she heard him mutter, 'She hasn't heard the end of this!' before he went into his room and slammed the door. Those words scared her and she tracked me down in the kitchen where I was talking to the cooks about the game we'd brought back from the hunt. She's a good, quick-thinking girl, your Jeanette."

"Yes, and considerate. She didn't tell me she'd reported the quarrel to you. I suppose when she saw that Raymond and I were reconciled later that evening, she didn't want to remind me of how abusive he'd been. So then what, Richard? You talked to Raymond?"

"Yes, I went immediately to his chamber and confronted him."

"And did he admit he'd done anything wrong?"

"Not he. He was truculent and wouldn't listen to me. So I reminded him of the agreement he and I made at the time of your marriage, that the English and the toulousains would no longer encroach on each other's lands. I told him that unless he apologized to you and promised to behave himself in future I'd consider our treaty void. Whereupon he fumed and tried to shout me down. 'The two things have nothing to do with each other! Joanna is my wife and you have no say in how I treat her.' So I reminded him that she was also the sister of King Richard of England and that his treatment of her would greatly affect future relations between us."

Richard, still standing, seemed to become even taller and more assertive as he spoke the words "King Richard of England." Not for the first time, she thought how lucky she was to have him as her champion and protector. Calmer now, she took a deep breath and smoothed her disheveled hair. Richard continued.

"That persuaded him. He's always shrewd about seeing what's in his best interests. He knew that if the peace treaty were broken I'd waste no time in invading Languedoc. He'd have far more trouble on his hands than he has now with the Cathars and Philip. He was still surly but he agreed to apologize. Did he do so?"

"He did, that very evening. God help me, I believed in his sincerity. He asked me to forgive him, and I did." Her smile was bitter as she remembered Raymond's words, "I was wrong." How trusting she'd been!

Richard sat beside her. "I was dreading telling you all this. I'm sorry you couldn't know of it sooner, but I didn't dare trust it to a messenger. You've taken it very well, as I knew my level-headed little sister would. Now tell me, how have the two of you gotten along since then? I've heard nothing."

"Almost as usual. After I accepted his apology he became quite the model husband. In fact, I'm now bearing his child. But I don't know what to think about that now. Am I glad or sorry?"

"I think in time you'll be glad. You mustn't blame the child for the father's iniquities."

"I suppose not. I hope it will be a girl, so I can warn her not to put too much trust in what men say!"

Richard laughed. "How cynical you've become! Now shall we put this painful subject aside for now and talk about something more pleasant? Since I must be off in the morning, what entertainment have you to offer me this evening? And did I understand correctly that Raymond is unquestionably out of the city and I won't run into him lurking in a corner?"

"Never fear. He left yesterday for Albi. He won't be back for a week. As to this evening, I'd already asked François Compagne and his wife to join us at dinner. Even though Raymond won't be here I saw no reason to put them off. We're old friends and you'll like them. François is on Raymond's council and Raymond considers him his most valuable adviser. And there'll be a musician to entertain us during dinner. Maybe you can persuade him to accompany you while you favor us with one of your ditties."

"Ditties! I'll thank you to have more respect for my songs. They're often performed by Bernard de Ventadorn and many other troubadours, as you well know."

"I do know. I salute my brother, King of the Troubadours!" She kissed him on the cheek and they smiled at each other, happy to be together again.

Joanna was surprised that she could be so lighthearted. She'd expected it would take her days or weeks to recover from her shock at Raymond's deceitfulness during the past few months. Maybe in some twisted way it was a relief, she thought. She'd had doubts about his sincerity that she'd managed to repress. Now she knew, and it was as though the burden of so much agony and uncertainty had been lifted. She'd worry later about how to deal with her new situation.

More immediate was the question of what to wear to dinner. She decided on the green silk and the emerald necklace. She asked Jeanette to coil her hair in a chignon and fetch her silver tiara with the single emerald.

When she entered the dining chamber she saw that the room was thronged. No one, including the cook, had foreseen that when word got out that King Richard would be present and might give them a song or two, the small circle of courtiers who usually came would be multiplied threefold. Servants dashed into the kitchen, crying out for three more roast fowl, another loaf, a tureen of fish soup, another platter of pickled salmon. The wine servers were extraordinarily busy.

An hour later Joanna was having an animated conversation about the care of young children with Marie-Louise. The latter, mother of three, had much useful advice to share. On the other side of the table, Richard and François were engrossed in a discussion of the proper design of castles. It was a subject about which Richard knew a great deal and François very little. But he was always willing to learn something new.

Finally, when the guests were attacking their plum tarts and ginger cakes, the musician, who had been strumming his vielle to universal inattention, picked up his tabor and produced a drumroll so loud and sudden that silence fell like a blanket over the hubbub. The man stood, doffed his cap and addressed Richard.

"My lord King, we would all be honored if you would give us a song. I will do my humble best to accompany you."

Richard strode down the hall and greeted the musician. "Good cheer, Jacques. We met at my mother's court in Poitiers, many years ago. You play as skillfully as ever."

Jacques blushed at this notice from the mighty Lionheart.

"A fine figure of a man, your brother," murmured François to Joanna. Richard stood tall and assured, waiting for his audience to become quiet. His hair fell smoothly to his shoulders, as golden as his royal crown. He wore black leggings and a doublet the color of ripe cherries, held in with a jewel-encrusted belt. True, the belt had a little more to hold in these days, but on the whole Joanna agreed with François. Richard bent to confer with Jacques, then announced, "First I will sing you a song by my friend and onetime teacher, Bernard de Ventadorn. He dedicated it to my mother, Queen Eleanor." He looked around the room to make sure everybody was listening. His pure tenor voice rang out while Jacques produced a subdued accompaniment on the vielle.

> *Lady, I am yours and shall be*
> *Vowed to your service constantly.*
> *This is the oath of fealty*
> *I pledged to you this long time past.*
> *As my first joy was all in you,*

So shall my last be found there too,
So long as in me life shall last.

A hush, then cheers, stamping on the floor and cries of "Now one of your own songs, King Richard!"

He borrowed the vielle from Jacques and plucked a few notes, bending his head to make sure the instrument was in tune. He stood a minute in thought, as though deciding what to sing, and then smiled, pleased with his decision. He ran his fingers rapidly up and down the strings in an attention-getting arpeggio and broke into song to his own accompaniment while Jacques contributed an occasional soft tap-tap on the tabor.

Brightly beam my true love's eyes,
Like twin stars sparkling in the skies.
When on me her glance doth dart,
I swear it pierceth to the heart.
Yet, pleasuring in cruelty,
She turns her lovely face from me.
Oh lady, lady, hear my prayer
And I'll be your true knight for e'er.
But life is short and time is fleeting
And other ladies wait my greeting.
So lady fair, do not delay
And hear my plea, or I'll away.

He ended on a crescendo, holding the last note, bowed to Joanna and to his listeners and resumed his place at table to noisy approbation. Jacques played a few notes on the vielle, ready for an encore.

Joanna, applauding with the rest, caught sight of movement at the door.

Raymond had just entered. At first he smiled as broadly as Raymond ever smiled, believing this to be an unusually vociferous welcome to himself. Then he took in the number and merry mood of the guests around the tables, and his smile gave way to a look of incomprehension. When he saw Richard seated between Joanna and François with an arm around each, his face darkened with fury. He approached Joanna, and without a word or glance to anyone else, bent and spoke in her ear. His voice was cold and controlled.

"I shall be waiting for you in my chamber."

68

Within five minutes the banquet hall was empty. The guests filed out, whispering to each other, nonplussed by Raymond's behavior and feeling vaguely guilty for having such a delightful evening in his absence. François Compagne and Marie-Louise also departed, after thanking Joanna for her hospitality. They made no reference to Raymond but the pressure of their hands on hers and their looks of sympathy and understanding told her what they were thinking.

Alone except for the servants who hurried to clear the tables and sweep the floor, Joanna and Richard looked at each other.

"I'll have to see him," she said. "I want to get whatever's enraging him out in the open so we can deal with it. But you'll come with me?"

"Of course. He won't like it but I'll not leave you alone with him." He took off his heavy crown, placed it on the table, scratched his head and paced back and forth. "We must give this some thought. I'm sure he's so angry because he guesses I've come to tell you about the pact he and I made—that he'd stop abusing you and I'd not invade his lands. He'll become even angrier if he realizes I've told you it wasn't penitence but self-interest that made him suddenly start playing the role of the loving husband."

"So we must be prepared for a very angry Raymond."

"We must. Let's try to get the first word, before he starts accusing you of whatever's upset him."

When they entered Raymond's chamber Richard saw that it was far less comfortable and charming than Joanna's, though there were indications of an expensive if austere taste: mother-of-pearl-inlaid carvings on the bedposts, chests embossed in silver with the crest of the counts of Toulouse. The sixth count was sitting in an elegant, highbacked chair before a polished table on which lay a single sheet of parchment that he was studying. Every black hair was in place. His tunic and leggings were supple fawn-colored velvet. Joanna thought he looked as though he were posing for a portrait of patrician elegance.

When he saw Richard he scowled and gestured toward the door.

"Please leave us, Richard. I asked to see Joanna, not her meddlesome brother. What are you doing in Toulouse anyway?"

Richard ignored him and calmly took a seat. Joanna remained standing, her gaze fixed on Raymond.

"Raymond, whatever you have to say to me you may say in front of Richard."

He scowled even more fiercely. Joanna had thought her husband one of the most handsome men in the world. Now looking at his angry, twisted face, she saw him transformed into one of the ugliest.

"Richard is here because he is my brother and he's welcome to call on me whenever he likes. He brought me some information, an old story to you, that he wished to tell me in person. I think you can guess what it is."

Raymond glared. Joanna had never stood up to him like this before. Her brown eyes blazed like embers. There were no tears, only a steely calm.

"Telling tales, is he, of that night in Le Mans? Well, it's his word against mine. Nobody else knows what passed between us."

"True. But I prefer to take the word of a man I know to be unfailingly honest than one who's a past master at guile."

"Guile, is it? Who are you two to accuse me of guile, when the minute my back is turned you begin conniving with that two-faced François Compagne? I've suspected him for some time. And now he's cozying up to Richard, no doubt telling him everything he wants to know about my affairs. If I hadn't had to return sooner than I intended I'd never have known what you were up to until it was too late, would I?"

He moved threateningly toward Joanna. Richard quickly stepped between them. Joanna knew Richard as a man of action rather than one of diplomacy, but now he was both. She had to admire the way he adroitly reduced the tension.

"Nobody was conniving. We were gathered tonight for a pleasant evening of dining and music, and I heard more than one say what a pity you'd been called away and weren't present to enjoy it. Joanna had engaged one of your favorite minstrels." Raymond was still glowering but he sighed heavily as though humoring a bothersome child and sat down. Richard continued.

"As to your question about what I'm doing here, I'm on my way to Perpignan to confer with my brother-in-law, Sancho of Navarre. King Sancho and I have a firm agreement to protect each other's borders. It goes back to long before I went on Crusade, and it's time we met to bring each other up to date. I hope I may tell King Sancho that my similar pact with you, to refrain from invading each other's territories, will give him the same assurance it does me—that he has nothing to fear from an aggressive count of Toulouse. What do you say, Raymond? Surely you see the wisdom of affirming our agreement and surely you'll give me your word—again—that you won't mistreat my sister."

Raymond looked at Richard coolly as though considering his options. Then, "Very well," he said sullenly. "You have my word." His voice had lost most of its menace. As if to demonstrate that he was still master of the encounter, he turned his back and picked up the parchment he had been studying when they came in. They were dismissed.

"Well done, Richard," Joanna said as they walked along the corridor to her room. "You got his compliance, yet you let him save face."

Richard left the next morning after an inspection of Raymond le Jeune at Joanna's urging. She never missed a chance to show off her son.

"You're the one who said he could be king of England some day," she teased. "Don't you want to see if he still looks like royal material?"

Richard hefted the child and jiggled him up and down. "He's put on a bit of weight, that's good. A king needs to be solid and strong." Nurse Marie stood by, looking anxious. Richard stared down at his nephew, who stared back as though memorizing his face. "And I believe he's developing the Plantagenet nose. That's good too." The baby grinned and said "Nose!" He pointed at his own nose, then at Richard's. Marie giggled but with relief took the child when Richard handed him over.

Before he left Richard impressed on Joanna that she must send him word at once if Raymond became threatening again. "I'm leaving two of my knights here to keep an eye on you, and they'll always know how to reach me. I hope you'll have no more trouble, but I've ceased to trust Raymond."

"So have I," she admitted sadly, "at last. This insane jealousy and suspicion have finally killed any respect I had for him."

After Richard's departure she and Raymond made no reference to their recent clash. To Joanna's relief, they saw very little of each other. He made no pretense of seeking her bed, for which she was thankful. They met sometimes at dinner, always in the company of others. Any conversation they had was about their son and her health, about which he dutifully inquired. But she could tell he was far less concerned about this unborn child than he had been about Raymond le Jeune. Now that he had his heir, another child was less relevant.

He was away a great deal, seldom telling her where he was going or when. He didn't include her in council meetings anymore. Occasionally François knew something of his affairs and told her. "He's off to Albi again," which meant the trip had to do with the Cathars. Or "He's going to Bordeaux, though I don't know why." She didn't either, but supposed he might have some commercial ventures there. Bordeaux was a major trading port.

She refused to give in to melancholy, to sit around brooding. She threw herself into her work with the Sisters of Charity, taking food to the hungry and tending to their needs. Sometimes she went out with the Sisters twice a week. She spent as much time as she could with Raymond le Jeune, who at a year and a half had become a very active child. She delighted in his growing awareness of the world and the people around him. He was full of curiosity and had a sunny disposition. How fortunate I am, she thought, and wondered if her husband could have been such a happy, loving child at this age. She doubted it.

One morning in the third month of her pregnancy she sat down to write to Berengaria and ask if she could come for a visit. Ever since Richard had come and gone, she'd scolded herself for not asking him how things stood between the two of them. I was so full of my own concerns, she sorrowed, that I didn't bring up the subject. If he's continuing to ignore her I could have at least tried to persuade him to go back to her. My poor friend, she must be suffering as much as ever. Just getting away from her lonely castle at Beaufort would do her good.

She smoothed the sheet of parchment, picked up her pen and dipped it in the inkwell. Before she'd written a word there was a knock on the door.

"Sir François Compagne and his lady wife," announced the page. Joanna, all smiles, rose to greet them.

"Such a pleasant surprise! What brings you here on this dull, gray March morning?"

"We're sorry to burst in without warning," said Marie-Louise. Her round, rosy-cheeked face, ordinarily so bright and smiling, was far from cheerful. François too looked unusually serious. Joanna urged them to sit down. She seated herself opposite them. She felt unease, then dread.

"You must have bad news. Has something happened to Raymond?" In spite of everything, he was still her husband, the father of her children, a central figure in her life.

"No, well, not exactly, but yes, in a way. And we thought you should be told…" He stopped and looked at Marie-Louise for help. Joanna had never seen him unable to express himself clearly and succinctly.

"He's trying to say that it's something Raymond has done that affects you directly," said Marie-Louise.

Joanna forced herself to speak calmly. "And what has he done?"

François, now more in control of himself, took a deep breath.

"This is hard for me to tell you and even harder for you to hear. We've learned that Raymond plans to repudiate you and take a new wife."

Involuntarily, Joanna pressed her hands against her stomach as though to protect the child. Her face was ashen and she felt frozen, unable to get out more than "Are you sure?"

"Alas yes, we're sure. Raymond has made no secret of his pursuit—and conquest—of the woman. It was only a matter of time before you heard the gossip."

"And we felt it was far better for you to hear it from friends," said Marie-Louise. "But, dear Joanna, there's more. Raymond's inamorata is known to you."

Joanna stared at her, bewildered. "I know this person? Who is she?"

They looked at each other, both unwilling to deliver the final blow. François said, as gently as he could, "She is Beatrix, the Cypriot princess who was with you in the Holy Land and who returned with you to Poitiers. She and Raymond became acquainted during that journey."

The memories rushed back. Joanna saw Beatrix and Raymond emerging from the subterranean chambers of the arena at Nimes, looking disheveled and self-conscious. She remembered her worries that he might be trying to seduce the young and impressionable Beatrix, and Berengaria's warning to Raymond that his attentions might be misconstrued. Whereupon Raymond had assured them that he saw himself as Beatrix's guide and friend, not as a suitor. And from then on he had almost ignored Beatrix and had become more attentive to Joanna.

"But I don't understand," she faltered. "Beatrix married that conceited rich man from Bordeaux, I forget his name. She seemed to adore him. What happened—did he die?"

"I don't know," said François. "Either he did, or they found themselves so incompatible that they agreed to live separately. We do know that she has been spending most of her time without him, at one of his estates in Bordeaux.

Joanna sat motionless, looking down at her hands clasped in her lap. She was not weeping nor was she moaning or crying out. Her anger was too deep for tears. Her lips were closed tightly over clenched teeth as she struggled to maintain control. She took several deep breaths, trying to calm herself.

Marie-Louise sat beside her and put her arms round her. "My poor dear friend, we're so very sorry to be the ones to bring you this pain. I wish we could offer you something beyond sympathy."

"I think we can," said François. "Advice. If I were you, Joanna, I would leave Toulouse as soon as possible. Take the initiative before Raymond comes to drive you out. Marie-Louise and I must do the same. Raymond makes no secret of his suspicions that our friendship with you masks some evil plot to undermine his authority."

"It will be hard for you to leave," said Joanna. "And I feel responsible. If it hadn't been for your kindness to me…" François broke in. "No, you mustn't think that. I've seen Raymond turn against his best friends in the past."

"And more than one wife," said Marie-Louise.

"And now I join the list. But you're right. I must go. I don't think I could stand another confrontation with Raymond."

"Then you had better leave tomorrow, before he gets back from Albi," said François. "You'll go to Richard, I suppose?"

"Yes. I'll send at once for the knights he left to guard me and tell them my plans. They'll be able to find out where he is now."

"Then we'll leave you to your preparations," said Marie-Louise. "But I'll stop on the way out to ask Lady Adelaide to come to you."

"And we'll be here in the morning to see you off." François took her hand to wish her farewell, and the steady gaze of his eyes, the kindness and understanding that shone from his face, gave her heart. Marie-Louise enfolded her in an encompassing motherly hug. As she told them goodbye, tears came into her eyes for the first time in this painful meeting—tears of gratitude.

When they'd left, Joanna suddenly felt full of energy. She couldn't give in to her anguish. There was too much to do. She wanted only to escape. Much as she'd come to love the city of Toulouse and the counts' palace, she now saw it as a place of menace, not welcome.

She sent a page to find Richard's knights. They promised to send messengers at once to track Richard down. Then she sent for Captain Floret, the knight who'd been her guardian whenever Raymond had had to leave her alone in Beaucaire. Since then he'd often been on duty at the palace in Toulouse and they'd developed a solid, trusting relationship. He'd told her more than once to call on him if she ever needed his help. Sure enough, he willingly agreed not only to join her but to enlist three others whom he knew to be disaffected with Raymond's highhanded, imperious ways.

Finally, her son. He'd been in the forefront of her mind ever since she decided to leave. Raymond would be furious when he returned to Toulouse and found them gone. What would he do? He'd pursue them, of course. Not because he wanted to get back his discarded wife, but to retrieve his only son and heir. All the more reason for haste, to gain as much of a headstart as possible. She was just leaving to tell Nurse Marie about the plans when Adelaide arrived.

Adelaide, like others close to Joanna, had sensed the strained relationship with Raymond, but they hadn't discussed it. Now Joanna filled her in quickly on what was happening.

"You know you need not come with me if you don't wish to," she said.

"Ha! And stay here to dance attendance on that foolish, deceitful little Beatrix if she's the next countess of Toulouse? No indeed. I can't imagine leaving you, my lady. Now what can I do?"

Joanna asked her to tell Nurse Marie to get herself and the baby ready to leave by nine the next morning. "Tell her I'm very sorry about the suddenness of all this. Tell her I'll come in to see her as soon as I can."

"She won't like it," said Adelaide. "You know how she hates any disruption of routine. But I'll try to soothe her." She set off at once. Aha, thought Joanna. She sees the urgency. How fortunate that I have such good people near me when I need them.

She called Jeanette to help her assemble her clothes and effects for the journey. Jeanette was a sensible, no-nonsense young woman, calm and trustworthy in any emergency. She had a very good idea of how things stood with Joanna and Raymond and needed no explanation, for which Joanna was glad.

"I'll just take warm traveling clothes," Joanna said. "Only two fine gowns and a few jewels and my queen's crown. And let's not forget the pouch of gold pieces I've had ever since I left Sicily."

Finally Joanna went to the kitchen. She spoke confidentially to Michel the cook, and told him she was called away suddenly to see her brother Richard. Could he pack up several hampers of food? And could he spare one of his assistants and two or three servingmen for a week or so? She promised to send them back as soon as they reached their journey's end.

Joanna knew from experience that there came times when a party of wayfarers sought refuge at the end of the day at a baronial hall or a monastery that was taken by surprise, unprepared for these hungry, tired visitors. She knew how they'd welcome additions to the larder and extra hands to help.

Michel, ruddy-faced and stocky, respected Joanna. She always came to thank him for a particularly good meal. They'd had many friendly arguments about roast beef, which Joanna remembered fondly from her youth in England but which Michel scorned. "Dried-out, loses all its flavor from the juices that drip into the fire," he complained. No arguments now. He was immediately cooperative and promised to provide what she asked and more, and to have mules laden with supplies by nine the next morning. She thanked him sincerely and was on her way to the door when he called after her, "Excuse me, but would you perhaps consider permitting me to accompany you?" She turned back.

"I can be spared here—we have very few big banquets these days and my staff can easily fill in for me. It would be an honor and a pleasure for me to serve you during what may be a difficult, uncomfortable journey." With every sentence he became more eager. "Also, I have relatives in Agen and Fumel whom I've not seen for years. If we pass through those cities they might be able to help us in some way. Maybe they'll give us a few rounds of cheese or some of their famous sausages!" His smile at the thought of these delicacies was so broad that it seemed to split his jolly face in two. Joanna laughed and patted him on the arm.

"Thank you, Michel. I accept your offer with great pleasure. I'll be delighted to have the company and the skills of the finest cook in Toulouse."

Back in her room, she loosened her sash and sat down to take stock. Jeanette and a servant were tying a cord around a wicker chest. A half-dozen other chests and bags, securely trussed, were lined up on the floor. Joanna rested her elbows on the table before her and supported her head with her clasped hands. She sighed and closed her eyes. In a minute she'd go to the nursery. But first she had to face the question that she'd been trying all day not to think about.

It wasn't the question of what she'd do if Raymond arrived and prevented them from going. There was no point in worrying about that. It was in God's hands.

No—it was whether this arduous journey would endanger the child she was bearing. She was beginning the fourth month of her pregnancy and felt perfectly well. But she remembered vividly her miscarriage in the past and still feared another. Yet did she have an alternative? She couldn't stay to be reviled and probably driven out by Raymond.

She sighed again and raised her head. The packing was finished, the servant had left and Jeanette was looking at Joanna with concern. She approached and put her hand gently on her mistress's shoulder.

"I'm so very sorry for you, my lady. You shouldn't have to suffer like this. But you're doing the right thing. And we'll all make the journey as easy for you as we can."

The next morning the party of fifteen gathered in the courtyard. In spite of leaden skies and the seriousness of the situation, there was an air of subdued excitement and anticipation. This was an adventure, a daring escapade to thwart the forces of evil. Even Raymond le Jeune was caught up in the spirit, bouncing up and down and squealing with glee. He and Marie had been carefully positioned on a substantial, dependable horse. Everyone admired the special saddle that one of the grooms had devised, with its child-sized leather seat affixed to the front of Marie's saddle and a miniature pommel to hold onto.

As they rode out of the palace square and through the city, Joanna wondered when she would see Toulouse again. She'd miss its narrow cobbled streets that threaded their way between the familiar buildings with their elaborate towers. She watched as the bell tower of the Basilica of St. Sernin disappeared from view, then set her face resolutely forward. It was time to look ahead, not back. Ahead to the day, not far off now, when Richard would rescue her from the tattered remains of her marriage and help her find a road to the future.

69

"What's that—thunder?" asked Adelaide, who was riding at Joanna's left. She pulled her cloak up around her neck and looked anxiously at the sky.

Immediately ahead of them were Marie and Raymond le Jeune. He'd fallen asleep and the nurse had an arm around him. On the fourth day of their journey everybody had begun to feel safe from pursuit by Raymond from the rear. But danger might still lurk ahead. Captain Floret and the knights led the way, on the lookout for trouble. Since at the moment there was no large-scale war or Crusade, many unemployed soldiers roamed the countryside in search of vulnerable travelers.

"I don't hear anything," said Joanna. But then she did. She realized it was the pounding of many hooves on the roadway behind them. The noise grew louder, closer. Before she knew it a dozen men were upon them, brandishing swords. One huge fellow rode at a gallop past her and snatched the reins from Marie's hands. He yanked until the nurse's terrified horse reversed course and was swept along with the abductors' steeds while Marie clasped the wailing baby to her breast. The whole troop rushed off in the direction they'd come. Captain Floret and his men wheeled their horses and galloped after them.

"Don't stop!" he shouted to Joanna as he tore by. "We'll catch up with you."

All this had taken less than a minute.

Joanna felt that she was going to faint but managed to stay upright in her saddle. The urge to turn back, to join the search, was almost overpowering, but Captain Floret was right. There was no way she could help. They must keep going, and hope against hope that he and his men would return with her son and Marie. Tears coursed down her cheeks and she stared straight ahead. Adelaide and Jeanette rode close to her, one on either side.

Joanna looked around at the others. She saw that everybody appeared stunned, unable to comprehend what had just happened. It was up to her, Joanna, to give them hope and direction. She beckoned to Michel the cook. He was the only one in the party who knew this area. Though his jolly face was far from jolly, he tried to smile encouragingly as he rode up. In return she tried to sound confident and in control.

"Where are we, Michel? I know we're on the road to Agen, but do you know what our goal for tonight is?"

"We're not far from the abbey at Moissac. Captain Floret had already sent them word that we hoped to be there this evening. We'll be safe with the monks. They'll welcome us and give us dinner. And they'll offer compassion and comfort to you about this grievous abduction. In fact, they may well have some word on your brother's whereabouts."

The worried servants and muleteers had crowded around to hear this. They took some comfort from the prospect of a good meal and a warm dry bed. Even the tired horses sensed that rest and oats might lie ahead and the pace quickened. Presently, sure enough, the tower of the abbey church came into view across the fields. In the fading afternoon light the tower caught the last few rays of the sun and glowed like a welcoming beacon.

Captain Floret and his men overtook them as they entered the abbey enclosure. They did not have Raymond le Jeune and Marie. They were dirty and damp and looked completely worn out from hours of hard riding. The captain, still catching his breath, reported to Joanna.

"We never even laid eyes on them. They must have turned off the main road on one of the little lanes, or simply melted into the trees. We searched and searched. They were Count Raymond's men, of course. I recognized the fellow who seized the horse, and one other." He stopped to wipe his sweaty face and to gulp down some water from the flask Michel handed him. "Once we thought we heard a baby crying, but when we followed the sound it turned out to be a bird. I'm so very sorry."

"You did your best and I'm grateful. I suppose we'll have to accept this as God's inscrutable will and keep on." But she thought wearily that God was being far more inscrutable than necessary, sending so many misfortunes her way in quick succession. First Raymond's unforgivable behavior, then the sudden disruption of what she'd thought was a safe and settled life in Toulouse, and now this snatching away of her only, her beloved child. She agonized over what lay ahead for him, but she persuaded herself that almost certainly he was in no danger. The abductors' instructions would have been to deliver him, safe and unharmed, to his father. And it was a tremendous comfort to know that Marie would be there to care for him. So while she grieved and worried, she held onto the hope that soon, somehow, with Richard's help she'd be reunited with him.

Bodies and spirits were much revived by the stay at the abbey. An important way stop on the Pilgrimage Road to Compostelle, it was a sprawling enclave of church, cloister, dormitory, refectory and gardens. Outside its walls stretched cultivated fields and orchards, where even now at dusk monks could be seen at work.

Abbot Bernard greeted them as they entered the reception hall. A tall, substantial man, he was dazzling in vestments of heavy white silk embroidered in gold. His voice was low-pitched, mellow and resonant. He seemed easy in his role as God's ambassador on earth. "You are welcome to the Abbey of Saint-Pierre. Most of our guests are hungry, dusty, road-weary pilgrims so it's an unexpected pleasure to entertain a countess—or should I say a queen who is also a countess—and her retinue. We've heard of the day's grievous events and we will pray that your son may be restored to you. Meantime, please make yourselves at home, and I shall look forward to seeing you at dinner."

Joanna, however, was not looking forward to dinner. She had no appetite for an uninspired meal in a drab refectory, where the monks would eat quickly and in silence. She'd have to converse with the abbot, who seemed a rather pompous sort. All she wanted was to be left alone in her room which, though small, was snug and well furnished, with a comfortable chair and a cheerful fire. She decided to ask Jeanette to send word that she needed to rest, and would be glad of a tray sent to her room. "Tell them just a small bowl of soup."

"I beg your pardon, my lady, but I believe you'd do much better to go in to dinner with the others."

Joanna liked Jeanette for her thoughtfulness and level-headedness, but this was a new side of her. She'd never given her mistress advice before.

"And why is that?"

"Because nothing will be served if you stay here alone, brooding and worrying. It won't get your baby back to you any sooner, and it won't get us to King Richard any sooner. It will only make you more unhappy." She spoke with complete seriousness, but with compassion. "What you need is some distraction, to take your mind off your troubles."

"Well…" said Joanna, half convinced.

"And besides, you heard the abbot say what a pleasure it was to entertain a queen instead of a scruffy batch of pilgrims. Why deprive him of that? Let's show him Queen Joanna, in all her regal splendor!" She was not at all serious now and her enthusiasm was contagious. Joanna couldn't maintain her glum mood. She smiled.

"How right you are. I've been forgetting who I am. I'm Joanna Plantagenet, Princess of England, sister of King Richard and Queen of Sicily. Far more than the discarded wife of the count of Toulouse! I shall go to dinner dressed like a queen. Abbot Bernard deserves no less."

She'd brought only two suitable gowns and chose the crimson satin with its sash embroidered with miniature Plantagenet lions.

"And why don't you wear your diamond tiara, the one you told me you've had ever since you left England for Sicily?" Jeanette asked.

"Why not indeed?"

When she stepped into the refectory for dinner she was astonished at the unmonastic luxury. The room could easily be taken as the great hall of a wealthy secular lord. The table was set with silver platters and crystal goblets on a white cloth. The room was brightly lit by a dozen candelabra and was pleasantly warm, thanks to logs burning cheerily in a huge fireplace.

The abbot led her to a seat at his right at the head table. To his left were three local lords and their wives, all looking plump and prosperous. Farther down the table were Captain Floret and his knights and a dozen of the more senior monks. The latters' habits were of white linen instead of the dull brown or black Joanna was used to. They were conversing freely—apparently there was no rule of silence here. At the second table she saw a clump of pilgrims, looking out of place in their motley costumes but uninhibitedly garrulous and merry.

"I wonder what our friend Jean-Pierre would think of all this," Joanna whispered to Adelaide on her right.

To the abbot she said, "This is like no abbey or monastery I've ever seen. How well you live!"

"We do, and we see no reason to hide the fact. Much of what you see is due to our own industry. This oak table and the armchairs on which we sit, for example, were crafted by our monks who specialize in fine woodworking. We follow the rule of the mother abbey at Cluny. We're encouraged to live off of what we can produce. So we raise livestock, grow wheat, cultivate our gardens and vineyards, make our wine and bake our bread—we're quite proud of our self-sufficiency."

Not a word about giving thanks to God for all these blessings, thought Joanna.

The abbot continued, explaining that because of the monks' industry, they always produced more than they could use. So they sold the surplus, adding thereby to the abbey's coffers.

"Besides which, many generous and devout friends contribute to our endowment." He nodded graciously to the three complacent dignitaries on his left. "In fact, your own mother, Queen Eleanor, has been quite liberal in her donations." He paused and she guessed he was giving her an opportunity to say she would follow her mother's example. She'd think about it.

A servant had placed a platter of roast meat before him and was carving it into succulent slices. "Aha, kid with saffron sauce," Abbot Bernard said. When he and his neighbors had been served, he speared a chunk with his knife, chewed judiciously and nodded. He turned back to Joanna. "Our cooks do this quite well, don't you think?"

She'd thought she wouldn't be able to eat a morsel but the smell of the roast meat was tantalizing. She took one bite and then another. "I've never had roast kid so I have nothing to compare it with. But I agree, it's delicious."

"I agree as well," said Adelaide. "In fact, I must tell you I'm astonished at how different your abbey is from the only other one I'm familiar with, Fontevraud. I've always thought Fontevraud very welcoming, with all the comforts one could wish in a peaceful refuge from the distractions of the world. They too have farms and produce much of what they need. And the nuns who do the cooking are excellent. But I'm sure roast kid with saffron sauce has never been on the menu there, nor do they serve their meals on linen cloths or from silver plates. Compared with your Saint-Pierre, Fontevraud is positively austere! I'm quite overwhelmed with what you've accomplished here."

During Adelaide's monologue Joanna, half listening, had been looking around the room and saw in a niche in a far corner, almost out of view, a statue of Christ on the cross. Dimly lit by a few votive candles, Christ seemed to be gazing reproachfully at the worldly diners. He looks lonely, she thought—unnoticed, unworshipped. After dinner I'll go pray for his help in getting my baby back.

She brought her attention back to her neighbors. Abbot Bernard was responding to Adelaide.

"I must try to visit your Fontevraud some day. From what I hear it's an admirably administered abbey, considering that it's run by women." Before Adelaide could make an indignant reply the abbot adroitly changed the subject. "And I thank you for your kind words about our Saint-Pierre. Indeed, we manage, we manage. And we're happy to share our good fortune with anyone in need of rest and refreshment. We ask nothing in return although, if they have a few coins to spare, we gladly accept them for the furtherance of our charitable work. But all are welcome, rich or poor, pilgrims, soldiers, troubadours, merchants, nobles, kings and queens." He turned to Joanna. "I believe you have come from Toulouse? And where are you bound?"

Joanna was momentarily at a loss. Should she tell him the real purpose of her journey—to escape from an abusive and deceitful husband, to find Richard and enlist his help? She thought not. Or perhaps he already knew.

"I have some matters to take up with my brother Richard, but he's hard to track down. Our last word was that a message would be waiting for us at Limoges, so that's our next goal."

"That's a good two weeks' journey from here. Why don't you plan to spend two nights with us? That will give me time to see what we might learn about King Richard's whereabouts. Some of our monks are adept at keeping up with what's going on in the world, and besides we know townsfolk who often talk to wayfarers. They're very likely to provide useful bits of information they've learned in their travels."

She accepted with gratitude this generous offer of assistance and resolved to donate more than a few coins to the abbey's charitable work.

To her relief the rest of the meal was relatively modest. A salad of chickpeas accompanied by thick slices of the monks' excellent, crusty bread followed the kid, and the meal concluded with almond blancmange. The wine didn't flow freely. One glass per guest seemed the rule, except for a few convivial pilgrims who wheedled the servers into bending the rule.

After bidding the abbot and her table companions goodnight, Joanna went to the tiny chapel and knelt before the crucified Christ. First she gave him thanks for bringing her this far on her journey, for the abbey's hospitality, for her good health and the well-being of the child she was carrying and for that of her fellow travelers.

Then, "I beg you, O Lord, to grant me three things. First, that my son may arrive safely in Toulouse and that he may in time be restored to me. Second, that we may speedily learn where Richard is and go to him. And third, that you will set me on the course that my life will take from now on."

She wondered briefly if she should pray for a reconciliation with Raymond and rejected the thought. It was an unrealistic request—Raymond was clearly determined to carry out his evil schemes. Besides, she couldn't bear the thought of living with him ever again.

She rose. Her fate was in God's hands now. But as she walked back to her room, despair at the loss of her baby assailed her again.. No matter how firmly she told herself there was nothing she could do about it, she relived the violent, clamorous scene of his abduction over and over.

She pinned her hopes now on receiving word of Richard. Maybe tomorrow. The abbot was right—they'd do well to pause and see what news the monks could discover.

Meantime she might as well take advantage of this unexpected day of respite and build up her strength for the hard riding yet to come. As she prepared for bed, she thought she'd visit the abbey church first thing in the morning. It would fill the waiting time and take her mind off her troubles for a while. Abbot Bernard had told her at dinner that the sculptures at the portal and around the cloister were exceptional and that experts in these matters claimed they were the finest in all Europe. Joanna had protested that she'd been told that honor should go to Saint-Gilles.

"Yes, I've seen those, and they're certainly splendid examples of the sculptor's art. Undoubtedly worthy of being rated second-best in Europe."

Joanna didn't argue. She'd learned it wasn't worth it to try to crack the abbot's confidence in his own infallibility. Besides, it would gratify him if she seconded his claim that his sculptures were Europe's finest. Agreeing with him would keep him well disposed toward her. And she needed all the help she could get to further her efforts to find Richard.

The next day dawned bright, cloudless and warm for April. Joanna sent for Adelaide, who'd said she too wanted to see the sculptures. At the church they stood before the huge arched portal, divided by a substantial stone column. There was so much to see that they hardly knew where to begin.

"Abbot Bernard said to pay particular attention to the central column, but I forget why." They saw that it was almost covered with sculpted figures, two of them human and the rest a host of mythical beasts and fishes.

"Perhaps I can help." A monk appeared at their side. Joanna remembered seeing him at the dinner table the night before. She'd noticed that, unlike his brother monks, he managed to look disheveled though his white habit was identical to theirs. She'd decided it was his bushy head of gray hair. Every time he nodded or shook his head a few more hairs sprang up to join the disarray.

"Good morning, and let me introduce myself. I'm Brother Anselmo, and the abbot asked me to be on the lookout for you. I've been studying these sculptures for years so he thought I might be able to answer any questions you might have. That column you mention, for example, includes a fine depiction of the prophet Jeremiah. See, up at the top on this side?" He led them to a good viewpoint. Obediently, they craned their necks and saw, at the very top of the tall column, the prophet. He stood slightly stooped as though discouraged and his face spoke of sorrow with resignation.

"One can only admire the sculptor who was able to capture that expression," said Joanna after an awed inspection. "And those magnificent mustaches!" exclaimed Adelaide.

The monk smiled. "Between you, you have hit on the features that I myself consider most remarkable about the Jeremiah. Though I would add to the magnificent mustaches the graceful flow of the long beard. Now, shall we move on to the tympanum?"

The first thing to catch their eyes was the row of a dozen or so seated figures looking up at God, who stood in his majesty at the apex of the arch. After a minute of studying them Joanna caught Adelaide's eye. She too was trying to repress a giggle.

Brother Anselmo noticed. "You're quite right to find it amusing. I believe the sculptor meant us to laugh." His eyes ran along the row. "Each one is unlike all the others, isn't he? A collection of individuals!"

"Yes, how different their expressions are! Some of them look incredulous, some look beatific, some are obviously skeptical, that one near the end seems to be falling asleep, and there's a man who looks as though he's just been playing his lute."

"And several of them are holding wine goblets," said Adelaide. "On the whole, a jolly gathering. And they're so realistic! They look like men one might see every day, in the market, or in a shop, or walking down the street. I wonder if the sculptor found his models here in Moissac?"

Before Anselmo could answer they saw Abbot Bernard hurrying across the courtyard, looking serious and untypically flustered.

"I apologize for interrupting, but I've just received some news that I must pass on to you at once, Queen Joanna. Shall we step inside?"

"Is it about my baby? Have they found Richard?" Breathless in her anxiety, she followed him into the church. But she remembered her manners and turned to Brother Anselmo. "Thank you so much, and I'll hope to continue the tour some day."

"I'll hope for that as well." With a nod in their direction and another to Jeremiah, he departed. His hair, now completely out of control, hovered in a ring around his pate like a halo.

The abbot sat on a bench toward the rear of church and Joanna and Adelaide sat on another, facing him. He began speaking at once. His voice was gentle, too gentle, as though he were trying to soften a blow.

"This isn't good news and I can't make it easy for you. King Richard was in Châlus--"

"I've never heard of Châlus. Where is it and why was he there?" She was trying to put off hearing the dire tidings that she sensed were coming.

"It's a small town on the road to Limoges. The news was brought to us by a monk who arrived this morning from St. Martial's Abbey in Limoges. He said his information was that Richard had gone to Châlus to punish one of his vassals who had traitorously declared his allegiance to King Philip instead of to Richard. He said others maintain that Richard was seeking a treasure of golden coins the man had discovered buried near his castle, which Richard claimed as rightfully his. But our informant didn't believe that."

"Nor do I. Richard isn't a greedy man."

"No. At any rate, while Richard and his men were besieging the castle, an arrow launched by the defenders pierced his upper breast. The wound festered and there was nothing the physicians could do. Your brother died on April seventh. Queen Eleanor had been sent for and arrived just before the end."

As the shocking words sank in, she moaned and bent over, burying her face in her hands. Her shoulders trembled and she began to sob loud, wrenching sobs. Adelaide put her arms around her. The abbot watched compassionately, and Joanna raised her tear-stained face to ask, "Do you know when and where he'll be buried?"

"Our monk said he'd heard that Queen Eleanor was taking him to Fontevraud and that the services would be held as soon as you and Queen Berengaria arrive."

"Then I'll leave at once. I must be there, I must!"

70

When the travelers reached Solignac, ten days from Moissac, they sheltered again in a hospitable abbey. Here they were heartened by the arrival of an armed escort and fresh horses, sent by Eleanor. She also sent her personal physician to see to Joanna's health and a message:

My dear daughter:
I pray that with these reinforcements you will be able to reach Fontevraud well before Palm Sunday, when Richard's memorial will take place. The bishops of Agen, Angers and Poitiers will attend, and our old friend Hugh of Lincoln. The pope is sending his personal representative, Cardinal Pierre de Capua. I have invited King Philip, in hopes that for this event he will lay aside his enmity for the English and join us in mourning the loss of a great warrior. Your brother John will be here. I understand he is already wearing the crown of the king of England, though his coronation is yet to take place.

Joanna read the message carefully, marveling at the distinguished roster of guests Eleanor was assembling. She wondered what it would be like to see King Philip of France again. But the whole Crusade adventure and his brief role as her possible suitor now seemed like a chapter in someone else's life.

She disliked Dr. Basilio, Eleanor's physician, the instant she met him. He was a wizened little man who may have known all about medicine but had no notion of how to conduct a civil conversation. He examined her in her room at Solignac Abbey.

When he was satisfied, he pronounced, in a voice as scratchy as his personality, "You seem to be in surprisingly good health, in spite of the chances you have taken. But I make no promises that that will continue. Have you any idea how foolhardy you were to undertake this long, difficult journey in your condition? You have needlessly endangered not only your life but also that of your child. You would have done much better to stay in Toulouse until after the birth."

She was speechless with anger and wanted to cry out that it wasn't her choice to leave Toulouse, that she was fleeing from a vindictive husband. But the doctor was gone.

From Solignac the trip proceeded uneventfully until they were only two days from Fontevraud. Joanna was riding between Adelaide on her left and the physician on her right. The latter sat hunched over, looking not at the purling river at their side nor at the tender green leaves of the poplars, but down at the dusty road and the plodding hooves of his horse. She thought grudgingly that he was undoubtedly carrying out Queen Eleanor's orders to the best of his ability, staying close to his charge, ready for any sudden need of his services.

Her horse, an easy-gaited, even-tempered sorrel, stepped along smoothly. She held the reins loosely and gave the steed its head. It was a mild spring day when everything conspired to make a traveler smile. The noontime sun beamed with equal benevolence on riders, villagers and farmers plowing their fields. Under any other circumstances Joanna would have been gladdened by the promise of the greening countryside. But she was sunk in grief at the loss of Richard and discouragement about the future. She wondered what Raymond le Jeune was doing, whether Nurse Marie was taking proper care of him, whether he even remembered his mother. She was gradually accepting the likelihood that she could not be reunited with him. His father would never give him up. Without Richard, she was helpless.

Added to this was a new fear—that Raymond would snatch the new baby from her when it was born, especially if it was a boy.

Absorbed in her melancholy and with head bowed, she came to with a start to see they'd left the open fields and were making their way, single-file, along the dark, narrow main street of a town. Houses leaned precariously toward each other and blotted out the sunlight. The townspeople had come out to speculate loudly on this curious procession. If it hadn't been for the knights and the banners flaunting the Plantagenet coat of arms, it might have been taken for a band of tired, disconsolate pilgrims returning from Compostelle.

Joanna, still trying to get her bearings, was riding just behind Adelaide. Suddenly Joanna's horse shied sideways, perhaps at a dog in its way or a bystander who made a sudden move. Taken unawares, she tumbled from her saddle to the ground. The breath was knocked out of her and for a moment she lost consciousness. When she opened her eyes she saw Dr. Basilio on his knees, leaning over her. Captain Floret was standing behind him. The other travelers had dismounted and were crowding around.

"Move away!" the doctor snapped. "Give us some room here. Captain, ask that woman standing in the doorway if this is her house and if there's a bed on this level." Then he gave his attention to Joanna.

"Do you feel any pain, any pain at all? As far as I can tell you've broken no bones. Try to move your legs. That's right. Does it hurt?"

"No. And I can move my arms. The only place it hurts is my lower back and hips. I landed awfully hard."

"You did. We're lucky you didn't land on your head, as I recall your late husband did. Your discomfort should be only temporary. Our main concern now is the baby. You must rest." He looked up. "So, Captain?"

Captain Floret reported, "Yes, this is her house and she said she'd give us a bed in the room just inside the door. It looks clean and tidy and it's warm, with a good fire on the hearth. She's getting some blankets and fixing the bed now. Her name is Berthe and she lives here alone. She said she'd expect payment, in advance if possible. I can take care of that."

"Well done." The captain nodded and went off to look for lodging in the town for the rest of the party.

Under the doctor's supervision, three knights carefully lifted Joanna, carried her into the house and laid her on the bed. She groaned at the pain and looked around. The room was certainly clean, as promised. It was also decidedly bare. She saw a table near the fireplace with two straight-backed wooden chairs drawn up to it, a small table and another chair by her bed, a pine armoire against one wall and a small narrow cot against another. It would do for one night. She drew the blankets up to her chin and closed her eyes. But she opened them when the doctor pulled aside her coverings and bent to put his ear to her stomach.

"What, doctor? Is the baby all right?" He didn't answer right away and she looked up at him, wide-eyed, frightened.

"It's very hard to tell at this stage. But I believe the baby is stable. The important thing is for you to avoid any more shocks or sudden movements. Complete rest, right here, for at least a week."

"A week! Oh no, I must be in Fontevraud by Sunday."

Since her fall he'd been attentive and professional, almost likeable. Now he reverted to the short-tempered scold she'd first met.

"When will you stop thinking of yourself first and your baby second? This helpless child depends on you and no one else for its safe delivery. Yet you insist on rushing about for your own selfish reasons. If it were up to me I'd be tempted to leave you to deal with the consequences. But my duty is to Queen Eleanor and her wish is that you and your unborn child arrive in good health in Fontevraud. Now I must talk to your maid and to the woman of the house about your care. I shall call in and check up on you often, whether you like it or not."

He turned brusquely and went in search of Jeanette.

Joanna felt chastened. She'd risked the life of her baby through a moment of carelessness, of inattention. She lay there a long time, immobile under her blankets. Suffused in guilt and despair, she sighed deeply. It came out as a moan.

"So you're awake? But not in pain, I hope?"

She looked up and saw that a tall, thin woman with gray hair pulled back into a knot stood by her bedside. This must be Berthe. Joanna's first impression was that her face showed the ravages of a hard life. Her second was that she'd accepted the buffetings of fate with humor and acceptance.

"No, I feel no pain except from the fall. But it's my fault that this happened. I should have paid more attention to where I was going. I shouldn't have let my horse follow Adelaide's so closely. And now I can hardly bear to think I may lose the baby."

"You mustn't rush to conclusions. The longer you go without any discomfort, the likelier it is that everything's going to be all right. Don't let the doctor scare

you. We'll be very careful and watchful." Her matter-of-fact manner gave Joanna
more confidence than Dr. Basilio had done.

"Thank you. I'm so glad you could make room for me. Is Jeanette here too?"

"Yes, we've already gotten acquainted. Between us we'll manage very well.
We'll take turns sleeping on the cot over there in the corner, so someone will
always be here."

She sat in the chair by the bed and smoothed Joanna's tousled hair off her
forehead. Her touch, despite her work-roughened hands, was gentle and soothing.

"And since you'll be here a while, we might as well get to know each other better. As to my making room for you, taking in travelers happens to be my business.
Our town of Mellon is on the route to Compostelle, and this is really a hostel for
pilgrims. I can put up a dozen or more in the small rooms on the upper floors. I
keep this room for travelers who want a bit more space and privacy. I don't normally provide meals; there are several inns nearby that do. But for you I'll make an
exception, though I'm not much of a cook."

"Never mind, my cook, Michel, is with us. He hasn't had to do much cooking
lately and I'm sure he'd be happy to get back in a kitchen. With your approval, of
course."

Berthe's smile transformed her face from impersonal politeness to glad relief.

"I shall welcome Michel, indeed I shall. I've been worrying about taking in a
lady of your rank. Not so much about keeping you warm and quiet and comfortable, we'll manage that all right, but about what you'll want on your plate. I kept
my late husband satisfied with porridge in the morning and soup in the evening.
But that won't do for the countess of Toulouse."

"Good, that's settled. Perhaps you could ask Jeanette to find Michel so you can
put him to work right away. I seem to be very hungry."

"Well, you should be. You're eating for two, as they say. Now why don't you
have a little nap while we get things organized."

After she left, Joanna smiled to herself, snug and warm in her bed. She liked
Berthe already. She wasn't nearly as stern as she'd first appeared. She was kind, she
seemed alert and intelligent and altogether unlike the greedy crone she'd expected
from Captain Floret's description. With her sensible counsel she reminded Joanna
of Lady Marian, who had been far more than a lady-in-waiting, but a friend and
confidante for so many years.

During succeeding days Berthe often settled by her bedside to keep her company. When they knew each other better, Berthe asked diffidently, "Do you mind
if I get inquisitive? I know so little about you. Of course I know that the late King
Richard was your brother, and your mother is Queen Eleanor, and that you were
queen of Sicily and now you're countess of Toulouse. And you're in a great hurry
to get to Fontevraud Abbey. Beyond that, only rumors. But I can tell you're deeply
troubled. Would you like to talk about it? Sometimes that helps."

"What kind of rumors?"

"For one thing, they say that when you began this journey your little son was with you. But he was seized by kidnappers. That must have been a terrible blow."

Joanna found herself pouring out her story, finding relief in telling it to a stranger who had no preconceived notions of blame or sympathy. She held nothing back, not even her displacement by a younger woman. Berthe listened carefully, asking few questions. When Joanna reached the final episode—finding a refuge here in Mellon—she laid her hand on Berthe's arm. "And how lucky I was that I took my tumble right in front of your house!"

"Lucky, yes. But I'd rather believe that God led you to me, just when I had no other guests and would be able to give you the attention you need."

"You're very kind. And I hope I haven't bored you with my tale of woe."

"Not at all. It's an absorbing story. It's not over yet, to be sure. When you get to Fontevraud and your baby is safely born, you'll see where life will take you next. But don't worry about that now. If I've learned one thing in my fifty years, it's to take one thing at a time. God will let us know soon enough what he has in mind for us."

"Maybe so."

She was getting drowsy, nestling in her cocoon of woolen blankets. "Thank you for listening to me. I think I'll rest now until suppertime."

She'd hardly closed her eyes when there was a knock on her door. "A messenger for you, my lady," said Jeanette. In he came, damp and travel-worn. Mud had splashed onto his leggings and water dripped from his cloak. Jeanette looked shocked and ran for a mop. He handed Joanna a rolled-up parchment.

"I've been a long time looking for you, my lady, and I'm right glad to have found you at last. I was told I needn't wait for an answer."

Jeanette returned, mopped up the puddle that had formed around his boots, and took him off to get dry and have a meal in front of the kitchen hearth. Joanna, oblivious, unrolled the parchment.

It was from Brother Jean-Pierre and the message had been written three weeks ago. It was brief:

"My dear Joanna: I send sorry news. Our young friend Federico has died as a result of wounds in battle. After Richard's death, Federico and six others of Richard's knights went back to Châlus to seek revenge. They tried to storm the castle but Federico took an arrow that went straight to his heart. He was dead in a matter of minutes. I join you in grieving and we will pray for his soul.

"I write this from Poitiers. I plan to be in Fontevraud for the services for your brother. I shall look forward to seeing you there."

She read it again and again, trying to comprehend the dreadful news. She pulled the covers up over her head and wept. Finally, exhausted, she sat up. Jeanette had brought a basin of warm water and soft cloths. Gently, she washed and dried her mistress's face.

"Thank you. I've lost someone who was very dear to me."

"I know. The messenger said that your friend Jean-Pierre told him the young man was like your son. I am so very sorry, my lady."

Joanna couldn't even take comfort in the hope of seeing Jean-Pierre at Fontevraud. The doctor had decreed that she must make the rest of the journey in a litter. They wouldn't reach the abbey until a week and more after the service. Jean-Pierre would certainly have left.

She lay awake for what seemed hours that night, helpless under the onslaught of so many misfortunes coming at once. She mourned Federico and she was depressed because she wouldn't be in Fontevraud for Richard's service. She tried to pray but nobody seemed to be listening. Just before dawn she fell asleep, exhausted.

The next day when Berthe had come to take her breakfast tray, the manservant entered to announce that three travelers were on the doorstep, desirous of lodging. He asked Berthe what he should tell them. It was raining and they were drenched and forlorn.

"Do they look respectable?" asked Berthe.

"Very much so. They're monastics of some sort—their cloaks were so wet that I couldn't tell which order they belong to."

"Well then, let's welcome them. They can use the two rooms upstairs. Tell them that after they've dried off I'll come up and discuss terms." Berthe the businesswoman had taken over. She turned to Joanna. "I'll see you at dinnertime. Michel is busy in the kitchen already. He seems to be doing something quite interesting with a pork roast and apples and onions."

Lonely and downcast, Joanna was left to her own devices for the rest of the day. She thought wistfully of Berthe's unquestioning trust in an all-seeing God's wisdom. She longed to find the same consoling certainty. She asked Jeanette to find her psalter. Surely in the psalms she'd find words of comfort and reassurance.

She opened the soft leather binder and studied the first manuscript page. It was elaborately ornamented with a brilliant red inscription, the first words of the first psalm. She knew it by heart from the days when studying the psalms was part of her education: "Blessed is the man that walketh not in the counsel of the ungodly." She hadn't been walking in the counsel of the ungodly but she hadn't been walking in the counsel of the godly, either. She sighed, feeling more lost than ever.

Yet she could remember a time when her life was quite the opposite, filled with companionship, warmth and love. Why had everything changed?

She closed her eyes and imagined a sunny day in Palermo. She and Lady Marian were walking in the park. They were surrounded by cascades of purple bougainvillea and beds of fiery red poppies. Their path led them through a grove of palms where birds were calling to each other. Federico— still a black-haired, incredibly handsome fourteen-year-old in her memory—walked to meet them and to tell her that King William was asking for her. She went into the cool palace courtyard and she and her husband embraced as though they'd been apart for days though it had been only a few hours.

She turned to her psalter again, opened it at random and leafed her way through the vellum pages. But she found no consolation, only proof that the psalmists, too, had their moments of doubt and despair.

My soul waiteth for the Lord more than they that watch for the morning.
I watch, and am as a sparrow alone upon the housetop.
Lord, why castest thou off my soul? Why hidest thou thy face from me?

Discouraged, she leaned back and closed her eyes. She tried in vain to summon up the dream of Palermo again. She was roused from a fitful sleep by footsteps and saw that Jeanette was standing by her bed.

"I'm sorry to disturb you, my lady, but one of the monks who came this morning asked if he could see you briefly. I don't know why. Shall I tell him you aren't well enough?"

"No, have him come in. Maybe he'll help me to deal with Federico's death. Maybe he can make me understand why things like this happen."

Brother Sylvester was tall and robust, square-jawed and self-possessed. Though he wore the black habit of the Benedictines, he looked as though he'd be more at home in full battle garb, riding a warhorse. But he spoke in a surprisingly calming, modulated voice, not the stentorian tones she'd have expected. He told Joanna that he was en route from Paris to Moissac, and had recently stopped at Fontevraud.

"It was the day after the service in honor of your late brother, King Richard, which I understand you had hoped to attend. I extend my sympathy that you weren't able to be present. Most of the guests who had come for the ceremony had left when we arrived, but your friend Brother Jean-Pierre was still there. We fell into conversation and when he learned what route we would take south, he asked us most particularly to inquire along the way as to your whereabouts. If we should come across you, we were to deliver this message: 'Brother Jean-Pierre will remain at Fontevraud until you come.' And in his infinite wisdom God led us to you straightaway."

She felt like jumping out of bed and hugging him. "Oh, that's good news—the first I've had in months!"

"Then I'm glad to be the bearer. Your friend Jean-Pierre gave me to understand that you've had your share of misfortunes lately, besides the loss of your brother. May I say that I hope the welcome message I've brought will remind you that God sends us joys as well as woes? Sometimes, when we are oppressed with sorrow and despair, we need to reflect on our blessings. As we add them up we may be surprised to find they quite outweigh the misfortunes. I'll wish you good day now, and may God grant you a safe journey." He was off before she could thank him.

She felt comforted. She hadn't been foolish after all to hope for a useful conversation with a wise man of the church—though this had hardly been a conversation. It was more like an abbreviated sermon. Yet in so few words he'd given her much to think about.

The baby chose that moment to produce a vigorous kick. Joanna laughed. "What are you trying to tell me, little one? To stop this introspection and get us to Fontevraud so you can escape from your confinement? Very well, I'll try to persuade the doctor."

To her surprise persuasion wasn't necessary. Dr. Basilio decreed the next day that it would be safe for her to travel. She bade farewell to Berthe, both of them promising to see each other again, both knowing it was highly unlikely. She said goodbye to Captain Floret and his knights, who were no longer needed thanks to the escort Eleanor had sent. The party was further depleted when Michel and his kitchen helpers decided to return to Toulouse.

"Count Raymond was away from Toulouse so much that I doubt if he knew who his cook was," he told Joanna, "so I doubt if he'll notice if I come back."

"I'll miss you, Michel. You've spoiled me for anybody else's cooking."

"Ah, but you'll still eat well. I hear there are excellent cooks at Fontevraud."

Borne along in her litter, with little to look at except sky and treetops, Joanna had plenty of time to dream and to conjecture. She dreamed of the baby to come in little more than a month. What should she name her? Eleanor would be the easy, tactful choice. But there were already three Eleanors in the family. What about Mary? Yes, she liked the name. And if by chance it was a boy, she was ready. Richard, of course.

She mused on the past week. Though she'd fretted at the delay in the journey, it had had its rewards. First of all, of course, she hadn't lost the baby. She had to admit she had Dr. Basilio to thank for that. Then there had been the supportive, wise presence of Berthe. And now, the assurance that soon she'd see Jean-Pierre, the dear friend and mentor who had instructed her since she was ten in matters spiritual and temporal, from interpretation of the Scriptures to Latin declensions, from the power of prayer to the geography of the Mediterranean world. They'd have so much to talk about!

He'd undoubtedly have news of her friends in England—Lady Marian, who'd helped her through many a hard time during the Sicilian years and who could be a grandmother by now. Mary, who'd started as her flighty, red-haired little chambermaid and had grown up to be a responsible lady-in-waiting and a true friend. Loyal Sir Alan, who'd been her faithful guardian and who'd helped Federico achieve knighthood. Where were they now?

Then there were the questions that had been troubling her. Why did she feel God wasn't listening when she prayed for guidance? Why did she feel so lost, so rudderless, when she tried to imagine what lay ahead? Jean-Pierre would surely have some answers.

Her mother would have some answers too, if to different questions. Joanna already guessed that Queen Eleanor would have decided on a new marriage as the best solution to her situation. She might have the bridegroom already selected. Well, this time she wouldn't find her daughter so compliant. I might even bring up my mother's championship of Count Raymond's suit, Joanna thought. And look how that turned out.

But there was no point in worrying about all that now. Unbidden, Berthe's words came back to her. "Take one day at a time. The Lord will let you know soon enough what lies ahead." Maybe I'm finally learning to do that, she reflected.

After five days of slow travel, Joanna and her party reached the lane that led from the main road to Fontevraud Abbey. She persuaded Dr. Basilio to let her leave the litter and walk the rest of the way. At the end of the lane there it was, the massive church with its tall square tower, the centerpiece of the whole extensive complex. A cluster of smaller buildings surrounded it like chicks around the mother hen. She marveled at how the afternoon sun transformed the drab, dun, stone walls and lent them a tawny glow. The sunlight glancing off the brilliant colors of the stained glass windows was almost blinding.

Joanna stood there silently for several moments, remembering the carefree days of her early childhood when she'd stayed here so often with her mother. She'd visited only twice while she was in Poitiers after returning from the Crusade. Her last visit had been five years ago. She hoped nothing had changed.

It hadn't. To prove it, here came Abbess Mathilde, a short, rotund figure enveloped in a gray cloak and with a lofty white headdress. Her face was just as Joanna remembered it, as wrinkled as an overwintered apple. She was perhaps a little plumper and certainly walked more slowly and carefully, but she still demonstrated by her demeanor who was in charge here. And she still delivered her remarks in a steady monologue with no pauses for interruptions or questions or comments.

"Good afternoon, my lady, and to you as well, Lady Adelaide. I'm sorry to say Queen Eleanor is not here. She has gone to Rouen where your brother John is holding court. I suppose we must call him King John now. She wishes you to be lodged in the apartment next to hers, where you have stayed before."

She paused to get her breath and Joanna managed to interject, "Is Brother Jean-Pierre still here?"

"He is, and he asked me to tell you that he looks forward to seeing you as soon as you feel rested. Your mother has requested that he accompany you to Rouen, where she will expect you to join her after you have recovered your strength. I was to tell you that she wishes to discuss your financial situation with your brother John."

Oh no, thought Joanna with dismay. Not another tiresome journey, when I was looking forward to staying quietly here at Fontevraud until the baby comes. But when Queen Eleanor issues an edict, one does not dispute. And on reflection she decided the meeting with John was a good idea. Now that she was estranged from Raymond she had no income whatsoever.

The abbess pursued her toilsome way along a lane that led past dormitories, gardens, the nuns' and monks' convents, the refuge for fallen women and, well away from the others, the lepers' shelter. Joanna, Adelaide and Jeanette followed, and bringing up the rear of the procession were several servants carrying chests and bags.

They met three nuns in black robes and white wimples who nodded and smiled as they passed. One was carrying a basket of herbs and lettuce from the kitchen garden. Joanna guessed she was on her way to the communal kitchen. The other two bore between them, each holding a handle, a large basket piled high with neatly folded linens. How comfortable they look with their tasks, Joanna thought, performing them with grace and efficiency. Far down the lane she saw a half-dozen brown-robed monks returning from the fields outside the walls, shouldering their pitchforks and hoes.

Everything Joanna saw was ordered, peaceful, serene. If I lived here, she thought, I believe I could be as content with my lot as those nuns. If only I could be one of those nuns! Safe from the world and its perils. She felt the stirring of a new idea but pushed it aside to think about later.

Finally they reached the substantial structure reserved for important visitors. And none was more important than Eleanor, who had donated generously to the abbey over the years.

Abbess Mathilde conducted Joanna to her door and left to show Adelaide to her room. Joanna and Jeanette walked into a cozy welcoming chamber. A modest fire dispelled the chill that, even in July, was trapped by thick stone walls. Late-afternoon sun poured through the mullioned windows to make graceful patterns on the polished wood floor. Joanna flung off her cloak, sank into a chair and looked appreciatively around at the familiar furnishings. It wasn't as elegant as Eleanor's quarters but it suited her very well.

"I spent a good deal of my youth here," she told Jeanette. "I'm glad to be back. But I'm so tired!"

"Of course you are," said Jeanette, who was unpacking and arranging Joanna's effects. "That's more walking than you've done in weeks. Here's a cushion to rest your feet. And I'll see about getting you some supper. You've hardly had a morsel today."

"I suppose I should eat something. Maybe later. All I want to do now is lie down." She looked affectionately at the high bed with its rose-colored hangings. They looked somewhat faded. Could they be the same ones she remembered from her childhood? And there was the squat little stool she'd had to use to reach the bed when she was five, still there as though awaiting the day when she'd come back in need of it again.

Yet even with the stool and with Jeanette's help, climbing up onto the bed was a chore. Lying there with the covers pulled up to her chin, she looked at Jeanette and smiled apologetically.

"What's the matter with me? Why am I suddenly such a weakling?"

"It's to be expected when you're so close to giving birth. And you've had a very active day. Don't worry, tomorrow you'll wake up feeling quite yourself again."

"I hope so." She closed her eyes and was instantly asleep.

71

J oanna spent the next day in her room: dozing, reflecting, doing her best with the tidbits and meals Jeanette brought to tempt her appetite, walking from her fireside seat to the window and back again. She welcomed the quiet respite, the time to gaze into the flames and take stock of where she was and what lay ahead. By the end of the day she felt stronger in body and spirit. She'd examined her doubts and worries of the past several weeks and had arrived at what looked like a perfect solution. She was eager to discuss it with Jean-Pierre before she broached it to her mother in Rouen.

She sent word to ask if he could meet her the next morning in the secluded cloister of the convent of St. Lazarus, well away from the comings and goings of the abbey inhabitants. Joanna arrived first. It was a still, warm day but Jeanette had urged her to wear a woolen cloak over her gown. She'd also given her a cushion because the stone bench would be cold.

She settled herself and surveyed with pleasure the herb garden in front of her: green, flourishing, tidy. The sage bushes had been properly trimmed, the walks that crisscrossed the square were swept, the scent of sun-warmed thyme filled the air. She let down her hood, closed her eyes and raised her face to the sun, luxuriating in the warmth.

She felt a tap on her shoulder.

"Pardon me for interrupting your nap, Joanna. Shall I go away for a bit until you're ready to greet an old friend?"

She laughed and made room for him on the bench. "Oh, Jean-Pierre, I'm so glad to see you! And how can it be? In spite of the strenuous life you lead, you've hardly changed from when I saw you in Poitiers three years ago." But he had, a little. Though he hadn't grown any thinner and his face was still brown and weathered from miles of travel in wind, sun and rain, his scanty fringe of gray hair had shrunk so he was almost completely bald. But the benevolence that shone from the familiar face was the same.

"Thank you for staying here until I came," she continued, now very serious. "You're the only one who will understand what I feel I must do, and why."

"I shall do my best. Now tell me all."

She told him about her flight from Toulouse, the abduction of Raymond le Jeune and her growing fear that Raymond would try to steal her newborn child. She had to find a place of safety, not only for the infant but also for herself.

"I believe he cares more about vengeance than he does for the child. But he may feel emboldened by his first abduction. If he can steal one child, why not two? And if he attacked me physically once, why not twice?"

"I see your point," said Jean-Pierre. "It sounds like the kind of thing he'd do."

"Well, I think I've found a refuge he couldn't possibly broach. At the same time, the refuge would give me a way to carry out a plan that's only recently occurred to me." She glanced at him. He was listening attentively, waiting to hear more. She plunged ahead.

"Here is my plan. For some time I've been searching for a way to serve others, instead of being absorbed in what I see now are my own self-centered concerns. I don't want to get married again. I've had a wonderful husband and another who was far from wonderful. That's enough. If my mother presents me with a ready-made bridegroom I shall resist. I want only to find peace away from the world and to find a refuge for myself and my child."

"So far, that seems reasonable." Jean-Pierre squirmed on the hard bench, trying to make his bony frame more comfortable. Joanna wished she'd brought him a cushion too.

She resumed, looking straight ahead. This was the hard part. "And I've thought of a way to achieve both those goals. I shall take the veil and become a nun in the convent here. Not even Raymond would dare to break into such a sanctified place. It would scandalize all Christendom. He's in enough trouble with the church as it is."

After a shocked silence Jean-Pierre spoke. She'd never heard him sound so severe.

"Joanna, that is impossible. Face reality. It's absolutely forbidden for a married woman—and technically you're still married—to become a nun. And a pregnant woman to boot. I know you're desperate, but this is not the answer. It's against the laws of God and man."

"Surely, though, God would have pity on me and bend the rules in these very unusual circumstances."

"God might, but Abbess Mathilde wouldn't, and it would be her decision. She's adamant about strict observance of the Rule of St. Benedict."

"But couldn't you speak to her? You can be so persuasive!"

"I could speak to her but I won't. In all the years Mathilde and I have known each other I've never once interfered in the abbey's affairs. She rules over Fontevraud, and I respect that. No, Joanna, I wouldn't even suggest such a radical step to her, much less insist on it."

"Then I shall just have to persuade her myself."

"I wish you well but I don't think you'll succeed."

Dejected, she slumped and bent her head. She felt that for the first time in her life Jean-Pierre had let her down.

Suddenly she sat up. She wouldn't give up so easily. She'd only begun to fight.

She launched her campaign against Abbess Mathilde the next day. Strangely enough, she'd never been in the abbess's quarters, which were in a small, unobtrusive building next to the nuns' convent. The room Joanna entered was plain but comfortable enough. She saw a few fine objects that seemed out of place, given the abbess's starchy demeanor, unsoftened by any esthetic sense. A copper vase held sprays of lavender to sweeten the air. A lovely little ivory statue of the Virgin Mary occupied a niche in the wall. The prie-dieu before the statue had a cushion embroidered with a floral pattern in indigo and lavender. Gifts from my mother, I suppose, Joanna decided.

The abbess was seated at a table near the window that had a good view of the entrance to the nuns' convent. She was studying a parchment. Joanna had never seen her without her white mitre-like headdress that made her look like a lady bishop, if there were such a thing. Her gray hair was surprisingly curly, incongruously youthful with the deeply lined face. Without the headdress she looked diminished. But her authoritarian ways were not.

When Joanna had made her case, much as she had done to Jean-Pierre, the response was even more negative.

"That's out of the question." The abbess shook her head energetically and her curls bounced. "In spite of my gratitude for the many benefactions of your family to the abbey, rules are rules. To be sure I'm very sorry for the hardships you've suffered. But you ask this for selfish reasons." Joanna, insulted, was about to protest, but the abbess could not be interrupted.

"Have you discussed this with your mother? I can't believe she'd condone it."

"I have not, but I shall when I go to Rouen."

"I'll be very surprised if she doesn't agree with me. But there's one more thing. Do you truly have a vocation for the religious life? If you did, you'd have demonstrated it by good works, by self-sacrifice, by piety. Have you done so?"

"In Toulouse I helped the Sisters of Charity…" Before she could go on the abbess continued. Joanna could no more stem the flow of words than she could keep the sun from rising.

"A few random acts of charity aren't enough. One must devote all one's time and energy to the Lord's work. Are you capable of that? I doubt it, Joanna." She held up her hand to discourage Joanna's response. "But if you really wish to reside at Fontevraud, there's another way. You must be aware that we provide very comfortable lodgings here in La Madeleine for noble women who wish a quiet place of retirement and who can afford it. That would be much more suitable."

"But that's not the kind of life I want to lead!" protested Joanna. "Selfish, idle, self-indulgent."

The abbess ignored her. "Furthermore, you say you are asking this in order to keep your child with you rather than risk his or her being kidnapped by your husband. Are you aware that even if you succeeded in gaining refuge in the convent, after the birth your child would be removed to be reared in the shelter for orphans and would be trained to become either an oblate, a monk or a nun, as the case may be?" She waited for an answer, fixing Joanna with an accusatory stare.

"No, I didn't know that. Why?"

"Because of the rule, of course. Any nun who gives birth is presumed to be a sinner and therefore an unfit mother."

"But I'm not…" She stopped. Arguing was getting her nowhere. She felt completely deflated. To lose the child no matter what she did—the child she had hoped to rear and to love—was an outcome she hadn't imagined. She brushed tears from her eyes and looked at the abbess with such a woebegone expression that at last Mathilde showed a grain of pity. "I'm sorry, my dear. I've spoken to you very bluntly, but as you see you haven't thought this through. Your mother may be able to suggest a less drastic course than the unrealistic one you've set your heart on."

"Perhaps. So the sooner I go to Rouen the better. I'm grateful for this talk." She really was. Now she knew exactly what she was up against.

And perhaps, she thought as she made her way down the lane to her apartment, my mother will agree with me for once. Perhaps she'll persuade Mathilde to change her mind about me and the baby. Her hopes rose again.

The journey to Rouen wasn't nearly as long or difficult as getting to Fontevraud had been. The weather was better and so were the roads. Still, they progressed very slowly because Dr. Basilio said they must. The party included Joanna, Adelaide, Brother Jean-Pierre, Jeanette, the doctor, two servingmen, one of Michel's kitchen assistants who had decided to stay with Joanna, and four of Queen Eleanor's armed guardsmen. The last rode with their swords at hand and their sharp eyes on the alert for brigands or robbers. Joanna, still fearful of Raymond, took comfort from their presence.

They arrived in Rouen on September 10, a little after noon. They went straight to the royal palace. Joanna had never felt comfortable in Rouen. She thought it a cold, austere city, flaunting its importance as seat of her family's power in France ever since her great-grandfather, the Norman William I, conquered England in 1066. Though Toulouse held bitter memories, she found herself comparing its lighthearted, lively ambience with this chill, straitlaced northern city.

When she dismounted, she staggered and almost collapsed onto the flagstones. Jeanette and Adelaide caught her and helped her up the steps, with Dr. Basilio just behind. She stopped and caught her breath when they reached the top.

"I'm sorry—thank you—I don't know when I've been so tired. I feel like a wet rag that's been wrung out and tossed aside. I suppose I look like it too." But when they reached her room, and Jeanette was helping her out of the dusty, wrinkled traveling gown and into a robe, she lectured herself: I mustn't give in to this. I must gather my strength for the coming encounter with my mother. She sent Adelaide to tell her mother she would come to her chamber in two hours.

Two hours later, feeling somewhat stronger after a nap and in a fresh gown, she entered Eleanor's apartment. She was amazed at how Eleanor could make any place she inhabited uniquely her own. The room was almost interchangeable with those in Fontevraud and Poitiers, crowded with the same evidence of her refined and expensive taste. Some things Joanna remembered from previous visits—a jeweled Bible on an ornate stand, a thick Persian carpet, glazed windows. The queen always insisted on that.

Eleanor was seated on a throne-like chair, wearing a robe of wine-colored velvet. Her white wimple had slipped to one side. She was asleep.

At the sound of Joanna's footsteps her eyes opened, she adjusted her wimple, sat up straight and turned her head to receive her daughter's kiss on her cheek. She peered up at her.

"My dear child! How very pregnant you appear! Dr. Basilio has been here and said that we may expect the birth within the month. Now sit down, you look quite worn out with the journey. Are you?"

"In truth, I am. I don't want to climb on a horse ever again." She sat down heavily and groaned. "I think the birth may be sooner because the baby's getting very active. I'd hoped to have it in Fontevraud, but I see now that the journey back, in the state I'm in, would be a very bad idea."

"Yes, much better to stay here. Have some of this spiced wine. Maybe it will put some color in your cheeks."

They both sipped. Joanna put down her goblet. "Now mother, I need to ask..." She was interrupted by a knock and the entrance of Jean-Pierre and the queen's secretary, Henri.

Eleanor held out her hand to Jean-Pierre. "Ah, there you are, my friend. I'm glad you could come. You'll need to witness the agreements we'll be signing. I'm expecting John at any minute. But while we wait I'll explain what he and I have discussed. You may take notes, Henri."

The secretary had arranged a parchment, a quill pen and an inkwell on the small table before him. He assumed an attentive, respectful expression.

Joanna, at first confused, remembered that Abbess Mathilde had said something about John being in Rouen and her mother's plan to talk to him about Joanna's need for money, because Raymond had stopped supporting her. Though she fervently hoped that soon, as a cloistered nun, she'd have no such worldly concerns, it was gratifying that her family cared. Eleanor continued.

"But before I forget, Joanna, I've asked your former lady-in-waiting, Mary, to come here for your lying-in. She sent word that she would and I assume she's on her way. Jean-Pierre, can you find out how far she's come?" He nodded as though locating an English lady somewhere between Yorkshire and Rouen were the kind of task he undertook every day.

"That's good news!" exclaimed Joanna. "I'll be happy to see her after all this time."

"Now, to business. John has agreed to grant you one hundred marks now, and an additional three thousand marks to be paid in installments so that you will be well endowed when you make your will. I suppose you haven't done so?"

It took a minute for Joanna to take this in. Henri's pen could be heard scratching on the parchment.

"No, I've never thought of making a will. I've never had much money to dispose of. But now I suppose I should." Why this sudden concern about my will?

She wondered. Then it came to her. They think I may not survive the birth. I'll show them! I've got to live—for my child, and somehow, somehow to find a way to live away from the world and to serve God.

"No time like the present, daughter. It took some persuasion for John to agree and he isn't likely to be this generous in future. I advise you to give it some thought. After we've signed the documents and the money is legally yours, send for Henri when you're ready. He'll record your wishes."

"I'll start thinking about it at once. I'm grateful to you for arranging this with John. Now may we talk about something else, before he comes?"

"Certainly." Eleanor took another sip of wine and waited for Joanna to begin.

At which moment John strode in, preceded by two young pages. If clothes make the king, John was totally regal, bedecked in so much gold that Joanna wondered he didn't stoop under the weight. The massive crown of his Angevin forefathers rested atop his cap of black hair. A heavy gold cross on a chain hung around his neck, glittering all the more brilliantly against the ink-black background of his velvet tunic. His waistline was kept firmly under control by a broad gold-mesh belt, studded with rubies. His black cape, fastened at the neck by a clasp in the shape of a golden lion, was flung back over his shoulders to display the scarlet lining. If his expression were not so sour and if he were just a little taller she might have admired the result.

"So, sister. Here you are, and looking somewhat better than I expected."

She almost laughed—did he think that was a compliment?

He seated himself in the chair on Eleanor's other side. "I expect my mother has told you what we've agreed on to insure your welfare. If the terms meet with your approval, we might as well sign the documents now."

"Of course, John. You're very generous."

"It might have been more but Richard left the royal exchequer in a sadly depleted state."

Eleanor signaled to Henri, who brought the table and set it in front of John. The secretary carefully placed the parchment—a single sheet inscribed in flowing letters—the inkwell and the pen on the table. John signed with a flourish. Henri repeated the process with Eleanor, then Joanna. Finally Jean-Pierre, who had been seated near the fireside, stepped over and signed as witness.

So quickly and simply done, thought Joanna. But what a difference it will make. She was already thinking of bequests to make in her will. She was anxious to have Jean-Pierre's advice.

John stood up. The pageboys, who had been whispering in a corner, came to attention and resumed their places. John adjusted his crown.

"So that's that. Now I must go back to the cathedral. I still have several vassals to receive this afternoon. Normandy seems to be overflowing with lords and nobles who want to see their new king for themselves."

He left with as much pomp as he'd entered. Henri slipped out after him.

After the door closed, Eleanor rose, plumped up her cushions and sat down again. "Jean-Pierre, join us in a final glass of wine before I ask you to leave so I can have my nap."

"Certainly," said Jean-Pierre, taking the chair John had vacated. The three of them sat in contemplative silence for several minutes.

"I'm surprised John didn't have a trumpeter to blow a fanfare on his arrival," said Eleanor. "He's certainly relishing being king of England and duke of Normandy."

"To be charitable," said Jean-Pierre, "he's been waiting a long time. He probably never believed that he'd outlive all his brothers and this day would come."

"Nor did I," said Eleanor. Joanna knew she was thinking how different things would have been if Richard had lived.

Jean-Pierre finished his wine and rose. "I'll be off now. Queen Eleanor needs her rest and so do you, Joanna. And if I'm to track Lady Mary down, I'll need to find some sleuths and hounds for the hunt."

"But I hope you yourself aren't going sleuthing," said Joanna. "I'd like to talk to you tomorrow. Perhaps you could come to my chamber in midafternoon?"

He agreed and took his leave.

"I want his advice on any charitable bequests I make in my will," Joanna told her mother.

"Very wise. Jean-Pierre will know where the needs are greatest. I'm sure you won't forget Fontevraud Abbey, and the kitchen in particular. With the abbey growing so, six hearths simply aren't enough. More than once my dinner has been late because my cook had to wait in line for a free hearth."

Joanna smiled at the memory of the communal kitchen, one of her favorite places at Fontevraud. She'd loved, as a child, watching in awe as each cook at her hearth prepared meals for her house, whether Queen Eleanor's and the noble ladies' domicile, the nuns' or monks' convent, the refuge for the old and decrepit, the infirmary, the lepers' dormitory, the school, or the house of retirement for dissolute women who were repentant. Joanna had studied that cook in particular, wondering if she might be one of the scandalous former sinners. But she wore the same sober, workaday garb as the other cooks and seemed as righteous and as skilled at cookery as the rest.

Eleanor recalled her from her reverie.

"But you said there was something in particular you wanted to talk to me about. I don't think we'll be interrupted now."

So Joanna poured out her story again, leaving nothing out and ending with a plea for Eleanor's support of her wish to enter the convent and take the veil now, before the birth of her child. She steeled herself for another firm rejection.

"Have you discussed this with anyone else?"

"First I talked to Brother Jean-Pierre. He said he was sure the abbess would not agree, that such a thing was against the rules of the order. He urged me to give it up. But I approached Abbess Mathilde anyway. She doubts if I have a vocation for the cloistered life. I tried to tell her how truly and sincerely I want to retire from the world and devote myself to the Lord's service. But she wouldn't listen. She thinks I'm being selfish, and only thought of doing this to protect my child. And she says that anyway, the Benedictine rules wouldn't permit me to keep the child."

"And I take it you refuse to give up your plan in spite of all the opposition? You always did have a stubborn streak, Joanna."

"You're my last resort, mother. Surely you can see how I feel. Won't you speak to the abbess?"

Eleanor was silent, looking at the anguished face of her daughter. She sighed deeply. "In all my years, my family has presented me with more problems than I can remember and asked me for help, a decision, advice. This is, I believe, the first time that I could imagine myself so vividly in the same predicament as the one pleading for help. I'm well aware, daughter, of the trials and disappointments you've suffered ever since you left Sicily. I'm sorry I haven't often told you of my sympathy. Now perhaps I can help. Because in your place I might also have set myself such an impossible goal and refused to give it up. So yes, I do understand."

"And you'll talk to the abbess?"

"First we must have an abbess to talk to. I'll send for her at once. And meantime, I suggest—no, I order, just as though I were Dr. Basilio—I order you to go to bed and stay there. Frankly, my dear, you look worn out. You still haven't begun to recover from all your traveling. And these last few weeks are your only chance to regain some of your strength. I'll send for Jeanette to see you back to your room." She signaled to a page, who scurried out.

Joanna would have liked to jump up and hug her mother in her gratitude. But Eleanor had never been one for hugging. Besides, Joanna was in no condition for jumping. Instead she rose as carefully as she could, pushing herself up by gripping the arms of her chair.

"I thank you from the bottom of my heart. You've given me new hope. Now you must have that nap and I'll seek my bed." How weak she felt! She looked at the door and wondered if she had the strength to walk that far. But before she took a step Jeanette appeared with Adelaide close behind. Each took an arm and supported Joanna as she slowly took her leave.

Eleanor called after her. "It has occurred to me that there's another person who could be sympathetic to your cause. I'll come to see how you are tomorrow. By then I should know more."

72

Joanna obediently went straight to bed but her sleep was fitful, interrupted by wakeful periods when she lay wondering what potential savior Eleanor had in mind.

The next day, true to her word, Eleanor came at midmorning. Joanna was still in bed and tried to sit up, but Eleanor gently pushed her back onto the pillows. She sat on the edge of the bed and came to the point at once.

"I can tell you now that Hubert Walter, the archbishop of Canterbury, will be here within the week. He's the one I referred to as a possible ally in your wish to enter the convent. You probably remember him as bishop of Salisbury."

"Yes, I do remember him. He went with us on the Crusade, though I saw very little of him. He stayed with the army, while we were always far behind the battle lines. But I remember that he was so handsome that I thought he couldn't possibly have a brain in his head. In time, though, I learned how clever he was. I know Richard thought very highly of him. But how can he help me?"

"He's become one of the most powerful men in England. Richard made Hubert his justiciar and if John has any sense he'll reappoint him. However, all that's neither here nor there at the moment. The main thing is, in his capacity as archbishop of Canterbury, he's coming to Rouen to consult with John about ecclesiastical appointments. While he's here I shall tell him about your wishes. And then we'll see."

"This is good of you, mother, but why should he be more willing to listen than Abbess Mathilde? Surely he too will uphold the rules of the order."

"For one thing, he's always been a friend of our family. He was particularly devoted to Richard and is likely to transfer some of that regard to you, knowing of the deep bond between brother and sister. Aside from that, though, he's compassionate, probably more so than Abbess Mathilde. She tends to see things in black and white with no room for compromise."

Joanna was listening intently, watching her mother's face. She felt encouraged, but she needed to know so much more.

"And then there's this, or there may be. Hubert, like many churchmen in high places, disapproves of the autonomy of religious houses like Fontervraud that claim to be responsible only to God, not to the ecclesiastical hierarchy. He may welcome this as a chance to overrule Mathilde."

Joanna's thin, worried face came alight. "Thank you, mother. You've given me new reason to hope." She gave a start. "Oh!" Then she laughed and patted her stomach. "And the little one must feel the same way. That was quite a kick!"

"Good, I'll leave you two to discuss it. And I'll keep you informed of when we may expect Hubert Walter to arrive. Now who is this knocking? You mustn't let your visitors tire you."

In came Jean-Pierre, who had overheard her last words.

"I'll leave the minute she finds me tiresome."

"In that case," said Joanna, "you may never leave! Goodbye, mother, and thank you, thank you."

Jean-Pierre settled himself in the chair by her bed.

"I assume we're to discuss your will. But first may I be unpardonably inquisitive and ask why you're thanking your mother so fervently?"

She told him about the coming visit of the archbishop of Canterbury. "And my mother thinks he may support my wish to take holy orders."

"Hmm," he said noncommittally. She knew better than to open that subject again and hurried on.

"As to my will, I've been thinking of it, and I've decided to give most of the money away. First, though, I'll reserve enough to pay for the care and education of my child, just in case..." She stopped and blinked, then stumbled on, "in case it's needed. Abbess Mathilde said I wouldn't be able to keep my baby." She couldn't keep the quaver out of her voice. Jean-Pierre was looking at her with concern, but before he could speak she forced herself to continue.

"Then I'd like to give 500 marks to the Sisters of Charity to aid the poor in Toulouse. And something to improve the kitchen at Fontevraud. They need room for more cooks, and I hear the roof is leaking."

"I wouldn't be surprised, with all those chimneys poking up through the roof. No wonder the rain finds crevices to drip through. And the last time I was there, it was still smoky inside."

"Yes, it does need work. So I'll do what I can. Besides that, Jean-Pierre, I thought I might divide two thousand marks among worthy and needful religious houses. But I wouldn't know where to start. That's where I'll need your guidance. And I'd like to leave a small legacy to my maid Jeanette. She's turned out to be a tremendous help."

"This is all very well, Joanna, and you may count on me to give you what advice I can. But you must not worry too much about the future yet, especially about the future of your child." He spoke with great seriousness. "Trust in God and concentrate on the present, on resting and recuperating. I'm afraid you tend to undertake too much. Just stay in bed, don't go walking about, and let others wait on you."

"Yes, Dr. Basilio," she said with mock humility. "I'll try to behave."

"See that you do," he said in a good imitation of the doctor's gruff, peremptory manner. "And eat your breakfast," pointing to the untouched tray, "before your dinner arrives."

She nodded solemnly, picked up a piece of bread, by now quite dry and brittle, and took a small bite. It crackled loudly as she chewed, but she got it down and looked at him triumphantly. He laughed and stood up.

"Well done! I'll leave you now, and I'll think about your bequests and where they'll do the most good. You're being most generous. We'll talk again soon."

At the door he turned, the fierce doctor again. "And remember, stay in bed!"

She was glad to do so. She felt utterly fatigued and couldn't imagine getting up and walking. To this lassitude were presently added a slight fever and headaches, which Dr. Basilio said were to be expected in view of the stress she'd been under. She had visitors but lacked the energy to match their cheer.

Adelaide came often, passing on what bits of gossip she'd gathered. The ladies of Rouen were agog over the arrival of a merchant from Venice with a collection of gorgeous silks from far Cathay. Jean-Pierre had ascertained that Lady Mary had reached the coast of France. And—most sensational—King John was said to be enamored of a fourteen-year-old girl, the daughter of the count of Angoulême, and wanted to marry her.

The cook came in concern, wondering if there were something he could do to make her food more appetizing.

The archbishop of Rouen, in whose palace they were staying, sent word that he would visit soon. Joanna asked her mother to put him off. There was only one archbishop she wanted to see.

As the arrival of Archbishop Hubert Walter approached, Joanna was no better. In fact, she was worse. The fever and fatigue persisted. Her headaches became agonizing. Under the doctor's direction Jeanette applied poultices of fenugreek, brewed tea with leaves of lemon balm and kept the room darkened and very warm. Nothing helped. Joanna lay motionless in bed or moved about restlessly, trying to find a more comfortable position. Sometimes she moaned, sometimes she dozed.

One afternoon her mother came in and, seeing that Joanna's eyes were closed, went to the window where Adelaide sat sewing, taking advantage of a sliver of light that made its way past the heavy draperies. Joanna, half dozing, caught a few words of their conversation.

"Richard often had fevers, and they laid him low for weeks," mused Eleanor. "It's just unfortunate this has come when the birth is so close."

"It is indeed. But you know…" Adelaide put down her sewing, trying to think what that reminded her of. "Yes! Now I remember. When we were in Naples on our way to Sicily, and Joanna had been so dreadfully seasick, she fell into a fever just like this one. We were all worried that King William's ambassadors would go back to Palermo and report that this scrawny English princess wasn't fit to be his bride. We'd tried everything." Eleanor, well acquainted with Adelaide's talkativeness, waited patiently for her to get to the point. So did Joanna, now fully awake and with the glimmer of a memory of what Adelaide was recalling.

"But I remembered—and so did Mary, Joanna's maid who later became Lady Mary—we both remembered an old remedy from our families. It was simple. Just an infusion of hyssop in hot water with honey and anise seeds."

"Yes!" came a voice from the bed. "And you and Earl Hamelin went out into the city to find some hyssop. And you got lost."

"Oh, we woke you! Sorry! But do you remember? We found the hyssop and brought it back."

"And did it help?" asked Eleanor.

"I think so," said Joanna. "I remember it was the first medicine they'd given me that tasted good, so I drank all they brought."

Eleanor approached her bed.

"Why, I believe the very mention of it has helped. You do look brighter," she said. "Adelaide, I commend you on your memory, and I commission you to repeat your triumph of twenty years ago. Now please go call on the cook and see how soon he can send up this magic potion."

At midmorning the next day after a dose of the hyssop drink, Joanna lay drowsing but trying not to sleep, in case a message came from the archbishop. She came to with a start at a knock on the door. To her astonishment it was Berengaria, still in her traveling cloak and looking somewhat rumpled.

"I can hardly believe it!" said Joanna, holding up her arms to embrace her friend. Berengaria bent over to hug her back, trying to hide her shock at how Joanna had changed. Her arms were so thin, her face was flushed and her eyes were unnaturally bright.

Berengaria pulled up a chair. "I left Beaufort as soon as word came from your mother. I'm eager to hear all your news. I see I'm still in time for the birth." She looked appreciatively at the bulge under the covers that was the baby-to-be.

"Yes, and the sooner the better from my point of view. Except that first…" Joanna hesitated. But Berengaria, of all people, would understand and sympathize with her wish to take holy orders. She might as well just blurt it out. "First I plan, or rather hope, to be admitted as a nun in the convent at Fontevraud."

Berengaria was about to protest and argue when she saw the set of Joanna's chin. She knew that look. When Joanna had fixed her mind on a course of action she could be as stubborn as an ox.

"I see, or rather I don't see yet, but you'll explain this strange decision."

Joanna told her how she'd decided that she wanted to spend the rest of her life in service to others. She'd determined this could best be accomplished as a nun at Fontevraud, the abbey she'd known and loved since childhood. "But Abbess Mathilde refused. I'm pregnant and I'm still married according to the church, though my husband has repudiated me. She wouldn't listen to my arguments. Now I'm hoping that the archbishop of Canterbury will be more understanding. We're expecting him any day now."

"What does your mother say?"

"She supports me."

Berengaria's eyes widened. "She *supports* you? I'd have thought she'd want to marry you off to somebody suitable so you could produce more Plantagenets."

"I was surprised too. But grateful." She hesitated again. But this was her dearest, oldest friend and she could confide anything to her. "Sometimes I think she's humoring me because she fears I may not survive the birth."

Berengaria took her hand and spoke as firmly and reassuringly as she could. "My dear, of course you will. The most important thing is to believe that you will. You have great reserves of strength and many loving friends, and all of us will be praying for you."

Joanna smiled up at her. "I'm so glad you're here. You've already done me a world of good."

Jeanette approached with a tray holding a pitcher and a mug.

"I'm sorry, my lady Berengaria, but it's time for her potion and then her nap."

"Of course." Berengaria rose and peered into the pitcher. "That smells delicious. I don't suppose I could have some too?"

"Certainly not," said Joanna. "They've measured it to the last drop and I'm supposed to drain the mug."

Berengaria rose. "Then I'll leave you to your selfish pleasures." She looked with distaste at her wrinkled, dusty cape. "Now I must try to become presentable enough to pay my respects to your mother. I'll see you again tomorrow."

"Thank you for coming, dear friend."

Several days later a message came from Archbishop Hubert Walter saying he would arrive at midafternoon the next day. Joanna was feeling somewhat better, whether from the hyssop tea or her faith in the hyssop tea. Her headaches had abated, and the fever came and went. She was determined to receive the archbishop in as much state as she could muster. He'd find her sitting up, not recumbent in bed, and becomingly but not extravagantly dressed, as befitted a future nun. "No airs, no crown, no jewels," she told Berengaria and Jeanette.

Jeanette arranged her hair in what she assured Joanna was a mature, dignified style: parted in the middle and swooping back, to be knotted loosely on her nape. As to her dress, they all agreed on a pale-blue cape over a white gown. After Jeanette settled Joanna in an amply cushioned chair with a stool for her feet, she and Berengaria stood back to admire the effect.

"Just right," said Berengaria. "The archbishop will see at once that you're modest, virtuous, and in need of protection."

"And about to give birth at any moment," said Joanna. Despite the artful draping of a fur lap robe that Jeanette brought at the last minute, the mound of her stomach was impossible to disguise.

She'd expected the archbishop to appear in full arch-episcopal garb, wearing a two-pointed white mitre and a scarlet cloak. But he walked in looking somewhat as she remembered seeing him in Palestine, when he rode at Richard's side clad in a reasonably clean white surplice over a worsted cassock of indeterminate color. Today, however, she could see that under his white linen surplice he wore a cassock of fine English wool, purple as a ripe plum. She noted streaks of gray in his chestnut-brown hair. He was still as handsome, friendly and outgoing as in her memory.

He went straight to her and took her hand. "It's a pleasure to meet you again after all these years, Queen Joanna. I'm delighted to see you sitting up. I hope this means you're on the mend."

"I hope so too. The doctor gave me special permission to get up, since I'd be receiving such a distinguished visitor." She didn't want to waste time on discussions of her health. "It's very kind of you to consider my request and to come, when I'm sure you're so busy."

"Few things are more important to me than my friendship with and duty to the family of Queen Eleanor. She has told me all she knew of your situation and your hopes. I'm aware of your rift with Count Raymond. Though I deplore the breaking up of a marriage, I can fully understand your need to extricate yourself. May I ask, is there any possible way I could persuade you to reconsider?"

"None." She closed her mouth firmly on the word, leaving no doubt that she had nothing more to say on the subject.

He smiled faintly. "I expected that. And I understand the count has remarried—illegally of course, and outside the church—so he is no more likely than you to seek a reunion."

"That's true."

"I'm also aware of your desire to enter the convent at Fontevraud and that Abbess Mathilde has flatly forbidden it. I need to ask you to answer me as honestly and in as much detail as you can: what led you to this?"

She'd been asked this question before but had not fully explained, even to Jean-Pierre, the long months of doubt when she felt her prayers were not being heard and when she was uncertain of what God required of her. The archbishop listened attentively while she told how at last she admitted to herself that she was asking the wrong question.

"I'd been demanding of God, 'What can you do for me?' when I should have been asking, 'What can I do for you?'" She paused, trying to remember just when she'd reached that point. As though guessing her thoughts he asked, "Can you recall under what circumstances you realized this?"

"I think the first time it began to dawn on me was at the cathedral of St. Julien in Le Mans. I was studying the Ascension window, and it seemed that Christ, as he rose into heaven, was looking right at me. I was in a trance and I thought—I *knew*—that he spoke. He warned me about the sin of pride. He chastised me for ignoring God's stricture that to be truly blessed one must do God's work on earth. I thought about that for a long time, how it affected me. But nothing really crystallized until I was at Fontevraud and saw how contented, even happy, the nuns there were in their tasks of serving others. And I thought, that's what I should be doing."

He put his hands together, fingertips to fingertips, and studied her for a minute. "And was that what you had in mind when you tried to convince the abbess that you had a vocation for the religious life?"

"It was. And she pooh-poohed it and said I wanted to enter the convent for selfish reasons, to protect my baby from being abducted by Raymond."

"Did that indeed have anything to do with your decision?"

"Back then it may have. But by now I'm not so fearful of Raymond's vengeance. Perhaps I was unduly alarmed. And of course I feel much safer in Rouen. He'd never venture into this stronghold of the English. So I'm glad the birth will be here."

He closed his eyes in thought. Joanna watched him, wondering what was going on in his head. She'd been leaning forward in the intensity of her wish to persuade him. Now she rested her head on the back of her chair. Suddenly she felt hot all over. The fever had come back. She was consumed and weakened by its fiery assault. She felt a sharp pain in her abdomen—different, more alarming than the minor pains she'd been having.

Jeanette, who had been quietly watching her mistress from her seat by the fireside, quickly brought a basin of water and a cloth to sponge her forehead.

Hubert Walter rose.

"I'm sorry. This hasn't been easy for you. I've kept you out of your bed too long. I'll leave you with my blessing and my wish for your improved health, and with this assurance: when the abbess comes I'll do my utmost to persuade her to admit you to the order as soon as possible."

The fevers didn't abate and were interspersed by chills when Joanna shivered in her bed under a mountain of blankets. Dr. Basilio could only prescribe a continuation of the potions, compresses and complete bed rest.

Meantime the abbess didn't come and didn't come, though they kept getting bulletins about her progress and sent messengers to urge her to hurry.

"Mathilde doesn't like to be pressured," said Eleanor. She, Archbishop Hubert Walter and Jean-Pierre were conferring in Eleanor's chamber. "And in truth, her joints are stiff and it pains her to ride more than two hours a day. I wonder, Archbishop, if you couldn't perform the ceremony, or the ritual, or whatever it is, yourself. You're second only to the pope in stature and authority in the church. Frankly, I begin to doubt if Joanna will survive many more days of this grievous illness. To make her a nun might be the last gift we could give her."

"It would be highly irregular," said the archbishop. "Such admissions to a convent are always made by the abbess and senior residents."

"But it may be time for us to do something irregular," said Eleanor.

"I agree," said Jean-Pierre. His previous opposition to Joanna's plan had melted, as she grew steadily weaker while her determination to retreat to the convent grew stronger. "The very fact that the abbess has agreed to come indicates her readiness to accept Joanna. If she were still opposed she could have simply stayed home and sent us a 'No.' Besides, you wouldn't have to act all on your own, Archbishop."

He was warming to his argument. "We could convene an appropriate group to lend the proper legality to the procedure. There's a monastery here in Rouen, St. Etienne, that observes the Rule of St. Benedict, just as Fontevraud does. I imagine the abbot and abbess there would be flattered if the archbishop of Canterbury asked them to be present at the induction of a nun into a sister convent."

"And we must invite the archbishop of Rouen, since it's here in his palace that the ceremony will be held. And a few clerics from the cathedral as well," said Eleanor. "They too would be flattered." She and Jean-Pierre watched as Hubert Walter, sunk in thought, drummed his fingers on his knees.

"Very well," he said. "You're extraordinarily persuasive, both of you. I do believe this is what we must do, out of Christian charity to a suffering soul."

When they told Joanna that the ceremony was scheduled for three days later she was overjoyed. Though each day found her weaker, she determined that she would find the strength to get up when the day came. She insisted in spite of Dr. Basilio's strenuous objections.

"It won't be hard on me. They can simply prop me up in a chair and carry the chair in."

About a dozen people crowded into the palace's reception chamber on the morning of September 20, 1199. The abbot and abbess of the Rouen monastery, St. Etienne, had accepted. The archbishop of Rouen had brought three priests from the cathedral. Those present were talking quietly to each other while they waited. Most knew the bare outline of Joanna's tragic story but few details.

She entered at last, seated in a chair that was borne by four serving men. They gently set it down on the dais next to Archbishop Hubert Walter. All eyes were on Joanna. She was wearing a plain white gown, completely unadorned and with a lap robe of white wool. Her hair was confined by a white wimple. Her face was almost as white except for two bright spots of red on her cheeks. She looked calm, but Eleanor, sitting next to her, noted that her hands were trembling slightly.

"It won't take long, daughter. The archbishop has promised to be brief. Then you can go back to your bed and wait for the birth."

"I feel it's going to be very soon. I only hope my child will have the courtesy to refrain from arriving until after the ceremony." Her voice was faint and Eleanor on one side and Berengaria on the other had to bend toward her to hear. But Joanna, with a major effort, got hold of herself, sat up straighter and smiled and nodded to Hubert Walter to show him she was ready.

He rose. He spoke briefly, though eloquently, welcoming the assembled company who had come to bear witness to Queen Joanna's petition to join the company of nuns in the Convent of St. Mary at Fontevraud Abbey. "I speak in the absence of our dear and respected colleague, Abbess Mathilde, who wished to be here but unfortunately has been delayed." He went on to commend Joanna on her determination to forsake the world and devote herself to a life of service, piety and prayer. "It is clear to me that she truly has a vocation for the religious life."

He turned to address her directly. "Finally, my daughter, I must ask you to confirm that you recognize the seriousness of the step you are taking, that it is solely your decision and that you vow to uphold the rules and customs of the Fonteyrists and to serve the Lord to the end of your days."

"I so confirm and I so vow." Her voice was stronger now and she felt strength coursing through her whole body with the realization that she'd achieved her goal.

"Now who will welcome Joanna into the sisterhood at Fontevraud?" He knew who; they'd arranged it ahead of time. The abbess of St. Etienne rose to reply. She was much younger than Abbess Mathilde and not nearly so forbidding. Her mitre was only half as high and her manner bespoke twice as much goodwill.

"My lord Archbishop, I speak as proxy for Abbess Mathilde in accepting Queen Joanna as a sister in the Convent of St. Mary's at Fontevraud." She sat down but the nun next to her nudged her and thrust something into her hands. She got up again, looking flustered. "And we've brought a white habit suitable for novices, which we thought she might like to start wearing now, since she's entitled to it." She walked forward and gave it to Joanna, whispering, "It's quite roomy. I'm sure it will fit you, even in your present condition."

Joanna, deeply moved, thanked her. How good people are, she thought.

The ceremony was over. The archbishop of Rouen was thanking everybody for coming and inviting them to his dining hall where a light collation had been set out. Most went, but Joanna asked to be taken back to her chamber. Berengaria accompanied her.

Jeanette was waiting. The four serving men carefully lifted Joanna from the chair and laid her on the bed. "That's better," she sighed. She stretched and then snuggled under the blankets. Berengaria perched on the bed and took Joanna's hands, rubbing them. "Now you're cold and a few minutes ago you were burning with fever."

"It comes and goes. Nobody knows why."

She lay quietly with her eyes closed. Just when Berengaria thought she was asleep, she opened her eyes and asked, "I did quite well at the ceremony, didn't I? I quite surprised myself. I didn't tumble out of my chair, or cough, or fall asleep."

"You surprised me too. I'm proud of you. And how relieved you must feel, knowing you've taken your vows."

"I can still scarcely believe it."

"May I ask you something, Joanna? I've noticed that you don't talk about what will happen to your child. You told me that Abbess Mathilde said you wouldn't be allowed to keep him."

"Keep *her*. I'm sure it will be a girl. I don't talk about what will happen to her because I don't know what to think. I'm hoping that the abbess will change her mind. If she doesn't, I suppose I'll just have to accept that she'll be cared for in the shelter for orphans at Fontevraud. But to have no contact with her at all, never to see her—that would be very, very hard."

"I take it you aren't so afraid now that Raymond will try another abduction."

"Everybody assures me that the abbey is well guarded. And I can't believe Raymond would be so rash as to violate such a holy place. He's already in trouble with the church and any new offense could mean excommunication."

She paused, looking doubtfully at her friend. "Now that we're talking about this, I've thought of a service you could do for me. I know this is asking a great deal, but if by chance I should die during the birth or after, will you take the baby and rear her as your own?"

"Joanna, don't even think such a thing! Of course you'll live."

"It does happen, all the time. It would give me such peace of mind to know you'd agreed."

"I do agree, naturally. I'm honored that you trust me so. Now let's not talk about it any more."

Joanna shivered and pulled the blankets closer about her.

"Oh dear, I'm still so cold. Where's Jeanette?" The maid appeared at once. "Jeanette, could you ask them to build up the fire? And bring me something hot to drink? Then I might be able to sleep."

"I hope you do." Berengaria kissed her friend on the forehead. "Good night, my dear. I'll see you in the morning."

That very night Joanna's labor pains began.

73

Joanna lay on her bed motionless, eyes closed. The room was dim, lit only by a few candles. Beside her in a cradle, a tiny, wrinkled face was visible. The rest of the baby was enveloped in layers of blankets. He was asleep. The baby's nurse sat by, knitting.

Lady Mary, seated next to the bed, was gently applying cool, damp cloths to Joanna's fevered forehead. She was frowning with concern, willing her dear lady to wake up and recognize her.

The eyelids fluttered and the brown eyes opened wide.

"Mary!" she exclaimed. "How did you get here?"

Mary laughed. "By the speediest horses and fastest ships we could find. The minute I heard from your mother that you were about to give birth and that I might be needed, Stephen and I were on our way."

"I'm so glad, so glad. You must tell me all about it, and your home in England." She was talking very fast, as though she had more to say than time to say it. "It will be good to see Sir Stephen again. And how is your child?" She stopped, looking stricken. "Oh Mary—where is my child? They said I had a son but I haven't even seen him. Where is he? How long have I been sleeping?" She tried to sit up but fell back, groaning.

"Now now, my lady, don't you exert yourself," said the nurse reassuringly. "He's right here, and we'll lift him and settle him by your side where you can get a good look."

"No, put him in my arms. I want to hold him."

The nurse carefully placed the small bundle in Joanna's arms. Joanna's face as she looked down at him was suffused with silent love. She caressed his fuzzy, almost invisible eyebrows, touched her finger gently to his nose. He slept on. But—"He's so light! He hardly weighs more than a kitten. Mary, do you know if °anybody has called for a priest to baptize him? His name will be Richard, of course."

"I understand Archbishop Hubert Walter is still here and plans to baptize him tomorrow. He'll be here to see you later this evening."

"Thank you, Mary. You're always such a comfort to me. Maybe you'd better take the baby now. He's getting heavy. I'm so tired! And so thirsty! Do you think you could find me something to drink?"

"Dr. Basilio said you could have a little of this sweetened wine. He said it would help you sleep."

"Yes, I must get more sleep. Everybody says so." She clutched the goblet with both hands and drank. "I must be fresh and fit for the baptism ceremony tomorrow. I think I should wear the habit of the sisters of Fontevraud that they gave me the other day. You'd better ask Jeanette to find it."

Her voice became fainter. She fell back against the pillows and slept.

The nurse came and took the baby. She whispered to Mary, "The doctor says he shouldn't sleep in the same room as his mother. He might be exposed to the same ill humors that are troubling her."

When the archbishop came toward evening, he found the room crowded. Eleanor and Dr. Basilio sat by Joanna's bed, one on either side. The others—Lady Mary and Sir Stephen, Jean-Pierre, Berengaria and Adelaide—stood and paced, sat down, got up, occasionally murmuring to one another. Jeanette stood at the foot of Joanna's bed, alert to her needs.

Joanna was turning from one side to the other, as though trying to escape from some peril. Her eyes were wide open and she was mumbling, but the words were unintelligible.

"I'm afraid she's taken a turn for the worse," the doctor told the archbishop. "The fever is burning her up and she's delirious."

"I'll wait a bit and see if she becomes coherent. If she does, I believe we should baptize the child now. I'll keep it very brief."

A serving man came in as quietly as he could and added a log to the fire. The dry wood caught at once and the fire flared up and crackled with unseemly cheer.

Another man came and asked Eleanor if she required anything in the way of refreshments.

"I think not. Well, perhaps you could bring some wine and a pitcher of warm *hypocras*." He hurried out. "That will give us something to occupy us while we wait," she said to the archbishop.

Dr. Basilio put a hand on Joanna's forehead. "I think the fever may have gone down slightly."

Joanna looked at him with recognition and said in a normal voice, "I think so too, though I'm still very warm. And thirsty. My mouth is terribly dry. Jeanette, maybe you could turn down this top coverlet."

"Try some of this wine. It's just come up from the cellar," said Eleanor, filling a mug. Joanna tried to raise her head but fell back. Jeanette held her head up, and Lady Mary held the mug while she sipped.

"Thank you. That does help." She saw the archbishop behind her mother and could vaguely see that there were others present. "Why are all these people here?"

"I thought we might have the baptism this evening instead of waiting until tomorrow," said the archbishop. "If you feel up to it, that is. I really should be getting back to my duties in England."

That sounded plausible, but Joanna had a good idea what the real reason for the haste was.

"Yes, by all means, let's do it now. Has anybody asked the guest of honor if he's agreeable?"

The archbishop looked confused. Eleanor smiled—it was so long since Joanna had made any attempt at humor. "He's in the next room. We'll have the nurse bring him in." Eleanor the queen, welcoming the need for action, was taking charge. "And Adelaide, could you go to my chamber and look for my long white lace scarf? It would do very well as his baptismal garb."

She asked the archbishop, "I expect you brought the holy water, just in case?"

"I did. I'll go tell the assisting priest that we're almost ready. He's been waiting outside."

There was a flurry of activity.

The nurse brought the baby, clad in a trailing robe of deep blue with gold embroidery. His eyes were open. They were the same warm brown as Joanna's. He looked around as though wondering what all the activity was about. Apparently it wasn't worth the trouble. He closed his eyes. "You may hand him to Joanna when I tell you," said the archbishop.

The priest came in with a silver bowl of holy water and with the archbishop's mitre. He placed the former on a table by the bed and the latter on the archbishop's head, just so.

Eleanor held up the scarf Adelaide had brought. "It's beautiful," said Mary. "I wonder—wouldn't it look lovely draped over Joanna's hair during the ceremony?"

"Excellent idea," said Eleanor. "I expect Joanna will be glad to have something pretty to wear, and the baby won't know the difference."

Jeanette brought the nun's habit, a large, tentlike white garment with a hood. Adelaide and Berengaria held it up. Standing by Joanna's bed, they looked at her, considering how and whether to put it on her. Dr. Basilio overheard them. "Certainly not! Getting the garment on her would be far too disruptive. Just that much exertion could finish her."

They're talking about me as though I weren't here, thought Joanna. Just because I'm lying so quietly, not adding to the fuss.

She spoke up. "Nothing is going to finish me until Richard is properly baptized. I'm ready, the baby's ready and the archbishop appears to be ready. Why don't we proceed?"

The ceremony took less than five minutes. At Archbishop Hubert Walter's signal, the nurse handed Baby Richard to his mother, who cradled him to her breast.

The archbishop knew he'd have to shorten the normal ritual quite drastically for Joanna's sake. He was forced to improvise, but his listeners weren't aware of it.

"Do you, Joanna, wish to entrust your child to God's loving care and do you promise to rear him in the faith of the Holy Catholic church, ever mindful of his Christian duty to honor his parents and love his neighbor?"

"I do."

"Will you teach him to resist temptation and to obey the commandments of our Lord Jesus Christ?"

"I shall."

"By what name will he be known?"

"His name is Richard."

"Please hand Richard to me."

He took the infant from Joanna and held him in the crook of his arm. He dipped his other hand in the basin of holy water that the priest was holding. He allowed water to fall in drops over the baby's head. The baby let out a surprisingly loud squawk and looked indignantly up at him.

"I hereby baptize thee, Richard, in the name of the Father, the Son and the Holy Spirit." Richard frowned and closed his eyes.

The archbishop turned to the assembled listeners.

"Remember the words of our Lord Jesus Christ. 'Let the children come to me, for to such belongs the Kingdom of God.' To Queen Joanna and to all of you, I entrust you with the spiritual welfare of Richard, on this twenty-fourth day of September, the Year of our Lord 1199. Now go in peace."

Richard was returned to his mother, who held him close for a minute, then addressed him. "So now, my son, you're well and truly Richard. See that you live up to the heritage of your namesake." She kissed him on the top of his head and sank back on her pillow. The nurse took the baby. "Please, let him stay in the cradle by my bed for a little while. I want him here when I say goodbye. It won't be long now."

Her voice was so weak that nobody overheard those words except the nurse and Berengaria. Not the archbishop, who was taking his leave from Eleanor and Jean-Pierre. Not Adelaide or Lady Mary, who were remarking to each other on how well behaved the baby had been. Not Dr. Basilio or Sir Stephen, who were looking out the window and wondering if it would rain. Not Jeanette, who had gone to get fresh compresses for Joanna's forehead.

But in a moment of silence, everybody heard Berengaria. She took her friend's hand. "My dearest Joanna, don't say goodbye, don't leave us yet." Her voice broke. The others hurried to gather around the bed.

Joanna was now very pale, but composed.

"Yes, it's time to say goodbye. God has granted me the two things I'd begged of him—the child I prayed for, and my acceptance as a nun at Fontevraud. In his wisdom he calls me to him before I can enter the convent, but I'm at peace at last." She gasped and had trouble catching her breath, then fell silent, staring into the distance as though at something only she could see. Dr. Basilio bent to listen, looked up and shook his head. He gently closed her eyes.

74

When Abbess Mathilde finally arrived, she went at once to Eleanor's chamber. Eleanor told the story of the past few weeks, including the last heartbreaking event—the death of Baby Richard, two days after his mother died.

The abbess listened with hardly an interruption.

"I deeply, deeply regret that I wasn't here."

"If you had been, would you have changed your mind and permitted her to take holy orders?"

"After what you've told me, I believe I would. I've always loved Joanna. Perhaps it was because of that love that I didn't want her to take such a wrongful step. Now I see that my opposition was misguided. I was more preoccupied with observing the rules than with helping a tortured soul serve God in her own way. May the Lord forgive me."

"Don't accuse yourself. She died as she lived, surmounting each blow of fate as it came, going on to meet the next."

Mathilde's wrinkled old face broke into a smile. "I'm just remembering when Joanna was born. She lay there in her cradle and I asked you what you would name her. You said, 'Joanna, after John, who was a voice crying in the wilderness to prepare the way for Christ. Then if she is buffeted by the winds of the wilderness, God will give her the strength to go on.'"

"Yes, I remember. And then I think I said, 'And when those winds assail her, she will not break, but bend like a reed and hold her head high.'"

EPILOGUE

Eleanor of Aquitaine died in 1204, outliving Joanna by five years. In fact, she outlived all her children except King John of England and her daughter Queen Eleanor of Castile. At the very end of her life she wearied of governing and the constant travel throughout the English possessions. She retired to her ancestral Aquitaine, first to Poitiers and then to Fontevraud Abbey. Here she found peace and, according to some chroniclers, took the veil just before she died. It would be tempting to think that Joanna's example influenced her to do so, but probably not. Eleanor was always one to influence others rather than be influenced.

She was buried in the abbey church. Her tomb is between those of her husband Henry and her son Richard. Joanna's tomb is nearby.

Count Raymond VI of Toulouse embarked on one more marriage after Joanna's death and the collapse of his relationship, perhaps marriage, with Beatrix. His final wife was Leonor, daughter of King Alfonso of Aragon.

He continued to maintain cordial relations with the heretic Cathars, many of whom were his important supportive vassals. He became a master at temporizing when pushed by the pope, the church and the king of France to pursue and punish them. He refused to join what became known as the Albigensian Crusade, so named for Albi, where many Cathars lived.

Presently the dispute became deadly. Raymond had always been a reluctant warrior. Nevertheless, along with other powerful magnates, he joined the battle against the Crusaders—who by now were as motivated by greed for territorial gains as they were by holy zeal. His major enemy was Simon de Montfort, ruthless and fearless in battle. To Simon, Raymond lost Toulouse, then Béziers, Carcassonne and Beaucaire. After Simon de Montfort was killed in battle in 1218, Raymond, aided by his son Raymond VII, eventually prevailed and won back the lost cities. He died, once more count of Toulouse, in 1222.

History has judged Raymond to be, in his maturity, an able and fair ruler who promoted the welfare of the middle classes under his governance, reducing taxes and confirming freedoms.

He was just not a very good husband.

Raymond and Joanna's son, Raymond VII, never knew his mother, but there is evidence that he revered her memory. He named his daughter Joanna and, possibly at his own request, was buried next to his mother in the Fontevraud Abbey church.

From the age of nineteen he fought against the Albigensian Crusaders at his father's side. After the latter's death in 1222, his son continued the battle and, victorious, made peace with France. Peace was short-lived. Louis VIII resumed the war and eventually Raymond yielded. As a provision of the peace treaty, he had to agree to the marriage of his daughter and heir, Joanna, to the new king's brother, Alphonse. After Raymond died in 1249, Alphonse became the last count of Toulouse. Thus did Louis IX gain the long-sought control of Languedoc, which was annexed to France after Alphonse's death.

The seventh count's marital record was less mind-boggling than his father's— only two wives. His first marriage, to Sancha of Aragon, lasted thirty years. His heir Joanna was their daughter.

King John of England, Richard's successor, is better known for his faults than his virtues. Though he paid close attention to government, far more so than Richard ever did, his reign was marked by cruelty, deviousness and the loss of most of the English lands in France that his predecessors had struggled to acquire and to hold. He is perhaps most noted for presiding over the signing of the Magna Carta in 1215, which guaranteed the rights of England's feudal barons. John signed under pressure and renounced it as soon as the barons left. After his death in 1216 it was resuscitated, amended and lived on to become the basis for English law.

After Constance said goodbye to Joanna and left Sicily in 1185 to marry King Henry of Germany, she dutifully tried to be good German queen, but it was a loveless and childless marriage. In 1194 she went with Henry when he set out to claim Sicily in her name as the legitimate successor to King William. During the journey, to the amazement of all who'd ceased to hope that she'd produce an heir, she gave birth to a son at the age of forty. Tancred died, Henry claimed Sicily's throne, and he too died in 1197. That left Constance as co-regent of Sicily with Frederick, her four-year-old son. She fought to assure his succession to the throne and succeeded. But she died in 1198, and never saw Frederick become a brilliant and learned ruler, eventually Holy Roman Emperor, known as "Stupor Mundi"— Wonder of the World.

If Constance and Joanna had had a reunion, they'd have had much to talk about—memories of Sicily, difficult husbands, and the joys of late motherhood.

Berengaria, Joanna's dear friend, went through a few hard years.

Her brother-in-law, King John, promised repeatedly to give her the inheritance due her as Richard's widow, but repeatedly failed to deliver. With no income, she went to live with her sister Blanche, the countess of Champagne. Berengaria kept after John and enlisted the aid of the pope, who threatened John with excommunication. Nevertheless, John never kept his promise. After his death in 1216 his son, Henry III, sent Berengaria all that was due her.

Meantime, help had come from an unlikely source. King Philip of France named Berengaria as Dame of Le Mans in 1204. The city was her fief for her lifetime. Until her death in 1230 she was a wise, skillful administrator, beloved by the citizens. Her legacy is visible at the Abbey of Epau, which she founded in Le Mans.

BIBLIOGRAPHY

Déjean, Jean-Luc, *Quand Chevauchaient les Comtes de Toulouse*. Fayard, Paris, 1979

Hallam, Elizabeth, ed., *The Plantagenet Chronicles*. Weidenfeld and Nicolson, New York, 1986

Hallam, Elizabeth, ed., *The Plantagenet Encyclopedia*. Viking Penguin, London, 1990

Kelly, Amy, *Eleanor of Aquitaine and the Four Kings*.
Harvard University Press, 1950

Norwich, John Julius, *The Normans in Sicily*. Penguin, 1991

Strickland, Agnes, *Lives of the Queens of England. Vol. I*,
London, 1857

Vic, C.D. and Vaissette, J.J., *Histoire Générale de Languedoc*. 1736

23294913R00276

Made in the USA
Middletown, DE
22 August 2015